THE DRAGONRIDER CHRONICLES

COMPLETE SERIES

BROADFEATHER BOOKS
www.AuthorNicoleConway.com

LUN

LAPILOQUE'S TREE

CLARAX

CERNHEIST

BARROWTON

BOWFIN

AUSTLEN

Brine's

WESTWATCH

Brinto

FARCHASE

CANRACK
ISLANDS

MARSH

Blybrig
Academy

IVANGOL

SALTM

...RDA

LUNSURAI

AVLAR

NORTHWATCH

HIGHLAND COUNTRY

DAYRISE

OSBRAN

Port Murlowe

Breaker's Cliffs

LDOBAR

EASTWATCH

Solhelm

FARROW ESTATE

N
W E
S

HALFAX

PRISON CAMP RUINS

TWO RIVERS

...ATCH

...ILSPOT

THE DRAGONRIDER CHRONICLES BOX SET BOOKS 1-4

NICOLE CONWAY

This book is a work of fiction. Names, characters, places, and incidents are either products of the author's imagination or used fictitiously. Any resemblance to actual persons, living or dead, business establishments, events, or locales is coincidental. The author makes no claims to, but instead acknowledges the trademarked status and trademark owners of the word marks mentioned in this world of fiction.

Copyright © 2020 by Nicole Conway

All rights reserved.

No part of this book may be reproduced in any form or by any electronic or mechanical means, including information storage and retrieval systems, without written permission from the author, except for the use of brief quotations in a book review.

Title and cover design by COVERED BY NICOLE

For Carrie

THE PANTHEON OF MALDOBAR

THE FOREGODS

God of Was: Itanus
God of Is: Enais
God of Still to Come: Milontos

THE OLD GODS

God of Earth: Giaus
Goddess of the Sky: Astaris
The Fates: Viepol

THE LESSER GODS

God of Life & Nature: Paligno
Goddess of Death & Decay: Clysiros
Goddess of the Sea: Undae
Goddess of the Moon: Adiana
Goddess of Mischief: Iskoli
God of War: Proleus
Goddess of Love: Eno
God of Luck: Tykeron
God of Mercy: Ishaleon

DAWN OF FLAME PREQUEL

Long before the Chronicles...

I

CHAPTER ONE

"Look there, Porter. See them?"

I whirled around and squinted, my heart pounding in my throat as my gaze slowly tracked the far horizon. Twenty miles from our outpost, the flat, windblown prairie abruptly ended with steep cliffs that plummeted straight down into a dark, deep, and bitter cold ocean. Breaker's Cliffs—that's what they called it. A dangerous place for many reasons.

Even this far away, the faint smell of sea salt on the evening breeze made my insides twist. A dull ache deep in my chest took my mind back to days spent in the sun on my father's creaky fishing boat, dragging and baiting nets until my back ached and my skin was sticky with sweat and sea-spray. All five of my brothers heckling one another as they lugged bait buckets. My two eldest sisters sitting on the porch on either side of our mother, weaving new nets and repairing old ones with purple flowers in their hair. The musical clinking of the long strings of sea glass hanging from the eaves.

I swallowed hard. I hadn't seen my home or any of my family members in—gods, months? Four years? Maybe longer. Honestly, I'd lost count. My last memory of the place, sitting in the back of a recruiting wagon with two of my older brothers, stuck in my brain like a thorn. My last glimpse of home had been of my mother standing there, tall and thin as a reed, with the sea wind wild in her hair and tears in her eyes.

I'd never seen her cry before that.

Suddenly, my stomach dropped to the soles of my ragged boots. Several miles away, two dark shapes moved just above the ground, flapping broad wings and soaring like a pair of eagles.

Only ... these were not birds.

"Dragons," I breathed shakily.

"Two of 'em. Hunting, I bet." My shift-mate, Errol Stallmark, gave an unconcerned grunt and scratched at his bearded chin. I didn't know for sure, but he must've been nearly as old as my grandfather. He'd been serving in the cavalry long before I'd ever even thought of enlisting and had seen more than his fair share of combat. The years had left him wrinkled, scarred, and sour—but smarter than most when it came to the ways of war. Well, in my opinion, anyway.

Errol had taken me under his wing almost immediately after I'd graduated my basic infantry training and passed the rigorous testing to join the cavalry division. I'd always been decent on a horse, but Errol had spent long hours teaching me how to ride in combat and perfect my fighting skills. He wouldn't admit it, but I had a suspicion he was the reason I'd been granted a position in the cavalry in the first place. Maybe I'd impressed him during my testing. Or maybe I'd just done a good job of not looking stupid. Who knew?

Now, almost two years later, we'd wound up at the edge of the abyss together—cavalrymen on what remained of the northern frontlines. Errol and I had fought in three battles already, struggling to hold against the onslaught of the Obsidian Army. They came like a never-ending storm. Wave after wave of their black-sailed ships struck our shores and emptied more of their soldiers, war machines, and monstrous beasts into Maldobar. They'd ravaged every corner of our kingdom, driven people from their homes, enslaved and murdered them, burned fields, poisoned wells, and executed any nobles they found. Their demands? Well, there hadn't been any. No emissaries offering terms for surrender or peace. Only slaughter.

It didn't take long to pinpoint their leader. The man the Obsidian Army called "God Bane" was more than just some bloodthirsty tyrant on a conquering spree. He was a dark sorcerer, or so people claimed. He could call on the spirits of the dead and rip the soul right out of your chest. I'd never seen him in battle, but others told stories of the horrors he brought with him, monsters straight from the darkest pits of the underworld. They said he carried a staff tipped with a black crystal—the source of all his wicked power. It was why everyone called them the Obsidian Army. Without that crystal, some believed he could be defeated.

But no one had ever been able to get close enough to him to find out for sure.

We weren't the first kingdom God Bane's armies had ravaged this way. We probably wouldn't be the last. And tonight, well, tonight would probably be our last on earth. Word had already spread through the all ranks of Maldobarian soldiers camped around the city of Dayrise—the Obsidian Army had overrun Osbran. They were headed straight for us.

We were the last of the king's forces, about two-thousand infantry and cavalrymen. Many of us were wounded from earlier battles. Our weaponry was dulled and battered. Our supplies were gone. We didn't stand a chance.

But Maldobarians did not surrender.

Beside me, Errol gave a dry, hacking chuckle. "Hey, don't look so pasty, boy. They're a long way off. Besides, with the ranks camped nearby, you can bet they won't come close. Dragons hate the smell of humans."

"How do you know they won't get curious and come closer?" I cast him a nervous glance. "I heard they attack legions sometimes."

He shrugged. "Maybe. If they go too close when they're nesting, they might get territorial. Some fools even try to swipe eggs. Got crazy ideas about trying to tame one of them. Can you imagine that! Taming a dragon? Fools and nannies, all of 'em." He cracked a smirk that made the heavy wrinkles around his mouth deepen. "Dragons came straight from the gods, they say. You can't take something that's god-touched and make it your pet."

I watched the two dark shapes soar higher, veering and wheeling gracefully until at last, they disappeared into the distance. "Have you ever seen one up close?" I asked.

Errol chuckled again. "Alive? Fates, no. Saw a dead one once, though. Group of trappers down near Solhelm managed to net one that'd been getting too near the village and making all the common folk nervous. Probably the smell of the horses and cattle, you know."

"And they killed it?"

He gave a nod, his cold eyes as sharp as steel as he flicked me a meaningful look. "Took sixteen men to do it—and nine of 'em died in the fight. That venom dragons spit, you know, it burns like nothing else. It can melt through armor and steel. Sticky like sap. And the second it touches air it catches flame and burns as hot as oil."

Thankfully he couldn't see me shiver beneath all my armor and outfitting. He might've teased me otherwise. "What, uh, what did they do with it? The dead dragon, I mean."

"Cut off the head and brought it to the village square. That's where I saw it, you see. Couldn't do much else with it, I suppose. The hide can be sold. Makes the finest armor you've ever seen. No arrow, blade, or flame can damage it. The bones, claws, and teeth make fine trophies, too. But you can't eat dragon meat and no one would dare mount the head as a trophy. Good way to get yourself cursed—defiling a god-touched creature like that."

I sank back on my heels, staring at the place where the two dragons had vanished on the horizon. "Why do people think they're god-touched? What does that mean?"

"So many questions." Errol smacked my back hard enough to make me stumble as he ambled back over to his post on the far side of the rickety wooden platform. "They don't have dragons down in Tailspot?"

I shook my head. "They don't come that far south."

"Ah. Well, the old songs say the dragons are the agents of destiny, that they came straight from the underworld long ago when the gods walked the earth. That's why they're smarter than common animals, and why they despise humans and elves—they can sense the wickedness in a man's heart." Errol's tone grew softer and he crossed his arms, staring with me out across the scarlet sunset as he explained, "It's also why no mortal hand can tame them. You can't break a spirit that wasn't made for this world."

"And you really believe all that?" I couldn't help but sound dubious. Coming from a family of fishermen, I was no stranger to superstitions and old legends. But Errol had never struck me as that sort before. Hearing him talk about gods and the underworld left me fighting back a grin.

"I don't know, boy," he admitted with a heavy sigh. "Before this war, I never put much stock in stories like that. But these are strange times. A dark sorcerer is about to crush this kingdom under his heel like a chicken's egg with monsters he brought back from the dead and stitched together with foul magic. I suppose after seeing all that, anyone would start believing ridiculous things."

OUR SHIFT ENDED AT SUNDOWN. WHEN THE NEXT PAIR OF INFANTRY LINEMEN appeared to relieve us of duty, Errol and I buckled our shields to our backs and climbed down from the rickety wooden tower at the eastern edge of the encampment. We untied our horses, saddled up, and set off for the encampment at a canter.

I tried not to let my mind settle on anything—thoughts of home, the fact that this was probably my last night alive, or that somewhere out there in the dark, an army made up of tens of thousands of men and monsters marched under black banners directly for us. By dawn they'd be here. And we'd begin the fight for our lives and the fate of our entire kingdom.

A fight we would lose.

The atmosphere in our military camp, where all that remained of Maldobar's once large and powerful army, practically reeked of fear. Men huddled around small fires in groups, talking quietly while the dancing flames illuminated their haunted faces. They didn't even look up as we rode past on the way to our tent.

Normally, the cavalry and general infantry would've been camped separately. But there were so few of us left now that it didn't make sense to spread out. Of the roughly two-thousand men still able to lift a blade against the Obsidian Army, only about five hundred were mounted cavalry like Errol and me. King Arran had called upon anyone and everyone left in Maldobar's armed forces to come and fight.

In the end, however, it wouldn't matter.

"I heard there's a company of elven warriors coming to fight with us." One of the other cavalry riders in our regiment had already struck up a debate before I even took off my helmet to sit down. He was one of about ten others sitting around our campfire, nibbling on stale rations while they talked quietly.

"What good'll that do? They don't wear metal armor. The Obsidians will plow right through them," someone else scoffed.

A younger soldier piped up, his tone hopeful. "What if they brought those flying creatures? Shrikes, isn't it? They're fast devils. I bet they could—"

"You think Obsidian archers can't shoot down a shrike? Sure, they're fast, but their hides aren't very thick. Any decent archer could still hit them."

"Have you ever even seen a shrike fly? Show me an archer that can hit a tongue of lightning, and then maybe I'll believe he *might* be able to shoot a shrike down."

They rolled into an argument, debating the speed and ability of the Gray elven mounts while Errol and I settled in around the campfire. Hearing them squabble over stupid things like the speed of a shrike made me smile as I unbuckled my shield from across my back. I'd never seen a shrike myself. The elves rarely brought them out of the jungle, and by all accounts, they were vicious, ruthless beasts that didn't like the scent of humans any more than dragons did.

"Any word on the ranks at Osbran? Did any of them make it here?" Errol asked.

A haunted silence fell over the group gathered around our campfire.

"A few from the frontlines, too wounded to be any good to us now," someone murmured at last. "And a handful of city folk, soaked in blood. That was all."

I bit down hard, using unbuckling my sword belt as an excuse to look away. Osbran was the largest settlement on this side of the kingdom. Not that it had been any great military fortress—it was a trading center for merchants coming to and from the elven woodlands to the north—but it represented the last true city still controlled by Maldobar.

Gods and Fates, this really was the end.

The fireside chatter resumed after a few minutes, but I couldn't join in. Sitting beside my mentor, I picked at what was left of my rations. A few scraps of dried pork, a piece of bread so stale it was more or less a cracker now, and some hard cheese I'd been saving back for a special occasion. My last meal seemed like as good a reason to finally eat it as any.

I looked up as another hush fell over our group. Everyone sat straight and stiff, looking in the same direction. I looked, too.

Through the other canvas tents and crackling campfires, a glimmer of silver fur made my heartbeat stammer. My jaw dropped. Was that ... ?

It was.

A woman sat on the back of a massive stag with fur as white as snow and sweeping horns of gold, passing through our encampment like a vengeful goddess. The beast was bigger than any horse we'd brought along, but it didn't make a single sound as it walked along, flanked on all sides by a company of Gray elven warriors in full battle dress. Their colorful silk robes and gold-leafed leather armor caught in the light of the campfires. Their long white hair hung in braids interwoven with metal beads, and the portions of their exposed skin on their faces, necks, and arms were painted with swirling designs.

The woman riding the animal at their forefront seemed every bit as ethereal, beautiful, and powerful as her mount. Her silvery hair hung down her back in hundreds of intricate braids that brushed her waistline, and her deep bronze skin had been painted in swirling designs of gold. Just the sight of her strong features focused ahead with all the quiet ferocity of an eagle made my throat go dry. She carried an ornate long bow in one hand, the weapon much larger and more intricate than any I'd ever seen before. The quiver of arrows strapped across her back matched, and the colorful fletching practically sparkled in the light.

Wow.

"The queen of the elves?" someone guessed in a whisper after she'd passed by.

"No," another timid voice whispered. "Their royals wear battle headdresses with horns."

"Then who—?"

"It's the lapiloque," I replied, my pulse still racing with a mixture of terror and wonder.

"Aye," Errol confirmed. "Their most powerful sorceress. They believe she speaks for the god of life."

"Is she ... is she here to fight with us?" I asked, flicking him a sideways glance.

Errol sat eerily still, staring in the direction she'd gone. He didn't even seem to be breathing. "I don't know. Pray she is, boy. Pray she is. We could use a little divine magic on our side."

I swallowed hard. I'd never done much praying in my life. Tonight, I might have to give it a try.

Hours passed and the tension left in her wake lingered. The men fidgeted, muttered, but didn't seem too eager to start back into any of their petty arguments. Errol didn't say another word, and I could hardly force myself to eat. One by one, the rest of our company broke off to retire for the night. There were only a handful of us left at the fireside when an infantry soldier dressed out in his battle armor marched up and gave a salute.

We glanced at one another, and only a couple of us remembered to awkwardly salute him back. What was this about? Orders for tomorrow, maybe?

"Is Lineman Levran Porter present?" the soldier asked as he looked at each of us one by one.

Oh gods. What now?

I sucked in a breath and got to my feet. "I am."

"His Majesty King Arran will speak with you immediately. Come with me," he commanded. Then he spun on a heel and marched away, not even bothering to wait and see if I followed.

What? The king wanted an audience with me? But why? I-I was no one! A common cavalry lineman not even three years into my service since graduating my basic training. What could he possibly want with me? Unless ... gods, unless one of the survivors who'd come back from Osbran happened to be someone I knew.

Or one of my brothers.

My breath caught and my face went numb at the thought. I hadn't seen a single one of them since I'd joined the cavalry. They'd all stayed with the infantry. After all this time, with no letters or knowledge of where everyone had ended up, I'd just assumed ... well, I'd assumed I might be the only one left alive. Especially since Tailspot had been overrun by the Obsidian Army almost a year ago. Everyone said it was nothing but cinders now. My father, mother, and sisters ... all of them were likely dead now.

My heart sat like a knot of solid ice in my chest as I grabbed my helmet and sword belt. I fumbled with buckling them back in place as I jogged to catch up with the soldier, leaving Errol and the rest of my comrades behind.

2

CHAPTER TWO

"Gods and Fates, Nesryn! I told you not to come here. Why now? Why like this? There's nothing I can do to ensure that you won't be slaughtered!" A young man's angry voice carried from inside the large blue and gold tent erected in the center of our encampment. "And what then? It is bad enough to have the blood of my entire kingdom upon my hands. But to have yours as well? Go back to Luntharda. If you depart now, you can be well across the border before—"

"Stop it, Arran," a woman's voice snapped back. "You send me a letter like *that* and expect me not to come? I won't let you ride into this alone. My queen knows as well as I do that my allegiance lies with Paligno, god of all living things, not Luntharda. I am free to do as I please. She will not fault Maldobar for my death, should it come to that."

Arran? The king? Oh boy. I shouldn't be listening to this. Not that I had much choice, really. Standing just outside the tent's door, I could hear every word they shouted as I stood waiting. Sweat rolled down the sides of my face under my helmet. What did the king want with me? I'd never met him in person before. I … I hadn't broken any rules, had I? Committed some crime on accident?

Suddenly, the voices went silent. I gulped. A few seconds later, the soldier who'd brought me here reappeared and gestured for me to come. Oh, gods, please have mercy. Whatever I'd done, it hadn't been on purpose—hopefully.

With my hands clenched at my sides, I followed.

Gathered in the warm light of several glass oil lamps, a group of older, much more finely dressed men glowered in my direction as I stepped inside. Two I recognized right away because of their armor, which marked them as the Cavalry

General and one of the Command Sergeants in charge of leading all of the king's mounted forces. The others must have been infantry officials because their splendidly polished armor certainly marked them as upper-ranking officers, but not in the cavalry.

The only woman in their midst happened to be the same one I'd seen only a short time ago riding through our camp. The lapiloque stood by, her arms crossed and her hips cocked in a defiant stance. The elves had much different ideas about clothing styles, which made it nearly impossible not to stare. Her fitted corset top left most of her midriff bare and her intricately engraved leather loincloth-like skirt exposed most of her long, shapely legs. Strings of raw gems hung around her neck and were pierced through her long, pointed ears. One necklace in particular caught my eye—an odd piece on resin string with a bone-carved pendant about the size of my thumb. It'd been cut in a teardrop shape and etched all over with little swirling runes, but it was a good bit plainer than the rest of her clothes. Interesting.

She arched a brow when she caught me staring. Her strange, multicolored eyes studied me. All Gray elves had eyes like that. Bizarre and beautiful, they weren't one color like humans. Rather, their irises sparkled like fiery opals in dozens of hues, almost seeming to change depending on the light or surroundings.

I flushed and quickly looked down at the toes of my boots.

"You all have your orders," the only man not dressed in armor spoke up suddenly. He stood, bent over a broad table where a ragged map had been spread out upon it. "Do what you can. I'll see you at dawn. Gods and Fates be with us all."

The officers saluted and, one by one, filed out of the tent without saying a single word.

"Your Majesty, I've brought Cavalry Lineman Levran Porter as you requested," the soldier announced.

The man—King Arran—didn't even look up. He waved a hand and went on staring at the map before him. "Good. You're dismissed."

The soldier saluted and quickly departed, too.

Left alone in the tent with King Arran and the lapiloque, I couldn't decide what to do. Should I bow? Introduce myself? No, that would've been stupid after that soldier had already told them who I was.

"Arran?" The beautiful Gray elf woman cleared her throat, shifting her weight as she tipped her head in a gesture to me.

He sighed and pushed away from the table. "Yes, yes. I know."

Every muscle in my body locked up with a jolt when he finally looked up to meet my gaze. I didn't know what I'd expected our king to look like, but this ... well, this certainly wasn't it. Not that I hadn't heard what had happened to the previous three royals before him. His father, King Vallan, had died in an earlier battle right after the Obsidian Army landed. Then his mother, Queen Lysandra, had fallen while leading forces along the southern coast. His older brother, Prince Ian, had suffered the same fate at a small city called Barrowton.

Now Arran, formerly a second-prince and now our king, had no choice but to pick up the crown and sword. Not the ideal way to come to power—losing your entire family and suddenly ruling a kingdom under siege. But this was the first time I'd ever seen him up close. He seemed to be only a little older than I was, although he stood a good bit taller. His golden hair hung to the shoulders of his fine leather doublet in a disheveled mess, and dark circles ringed his bloodshot eyes.

"Levran, is it?" he asked as he walked around the table to stand before me.

"Y-Yes, Sir—er—Your Majesty," I stammered like a total fool. Too late, I remembered I wasn't supposed to look him in the eye and snapped my gaze back down. Gods. Somewhere in the afterlife, my brothers were probably cackling like hyenas watching me right now.

"At ease, soldier. There's hardly any point in formalities now, is there? Take off that helmet and let's talk."

"O-Oh, um, all right." My hands shook as I unbuckled the chinstrap and slid my helmet off again.

King Arran watched, rubbing at the stubble on his squared jaw as he seemed to study me closely. "How old are you?"

"Twenty-three, Your Majesty."

His brows rose. "I see. And how long have you been with my cavalry?"

"I graduated my infantry basic training three years ago. I've not been with the cavalry two years yet," I answered.

"Interesting. And yet I've been told that you ride as well as any First Sergeant Maldobar has ever had. Better, even. Where did you come from?"

"It's a—er, well, it *was* a small village on the southern coast called Tailspot. My, um, my father was a fisherman. I worked his boat with my brothers." I shifted, glancing quickly between him and the elven woman. I was half-hoping she would give me some clue as to why I'd been summoned here.

Nope. She seemed to be studying me with the same appraising curiosity. Why? What was happening?

"Do you have a wife? Children?" he asked.

"No." I'd never been good with women. Apparently, I lacked the confidence that seemed to come so naturally to the rest of my brothers. My mother had tried to console me, saying that it was perfectly fine that I was a man of few words—shy, like my father. She'd believed eventually I would find someone.

I suppose now it didn't matter.

King Arran gave a brief, humorless chuckle as though he couldn't believe his bad luck. "A young man from a fishing village? Then how is it you can ride so well? I don't imagine they do much horseback riding on fishing boats, do they?"

"Well, that is, um," I panicked aloud. How had I learned to ride? For a few terrifying seconds I couldn't even remember. Who was I, again?

The Gray elf sorceress gave a small, bemused grin. It sent a bolt of embarrassment through me like I'd been struck by a runaway fruit cart. I suddenly remembered how to breathe again.

"There are a few herds of wild horses on the flatlands between Tailspot and Two Rivers," I replied, trying not to choke. "My family couldn't afford to buy proper work horses to pull our carts to market, so my brothers and I set out to catch a pair of the wild ones. It took us several weeks. I was the one who, um, who would jump on their backs and get the rope around their necks after we'd snared them."

"Sounds dangerous," the elven woman purred in a strange accent. It flowed from her lips like silk and made me stare again.

I rubbed the back of my neck. "Ah, yes, it was. I got bucked a lot. But I had a good hand with them—the horses, that is. After a few months, I was able to break them to the saddle and cart. I suppose I've never been all that afraid of falling."

"Or being trampled to death, apparently," King Arran added. He and his mysterious Gray elf guest exchanged a weird little knowing glance. Then he sighed deeply and nodded. "Very well, then, Levran Porter. I've got a job for you."

"A job, Your Majesty?" What did that mean? In addition to the one I already had?

"Indeed." He went to a corner of his tent and pulled out a polished silver shield with a gleaming golden eagle inlaid into the front and a royal blue tabard. "Today all but one of my corporals and sergeants threw down their weapons and defected. They've fled for their lives, along with many of the men under their command."

Shock stole all the breath from my lungs as I gaped at him. Our senior cavalry officers had ... *abandoned* us? On the eve of battle? Gods and Fates, how many of us were left now? Who would lead us tomorrow morning when the Obsidian Army arrived and—

"I'd like for you to accept a promotion straight to Sergeant. You'd be leading two regiments, about two hundred riders in all, at dawn. Normally, there would be a lot more men behind you, but I'm sure you can appreciate why the numbers are so low." He dropped the shield and tabard onto the table, his eyes narrowed as he watched my reaction. "It's not a command, though. Merely an offer. If you feel you're unequal to the task, you may refuse."

My heart stalled and started wildly as I stared at the lamplight shimmering off the front of the shield. He wanted *me* to lead *two* regiments? As Sergeant?

"But, Your Majesty," I managed to wheeze. "I'm honored to have my name mentioned, but surely there are other men with far more experience and skill."

"More experience, yes," he agreed. "But more skill? Apparently not."

"I-I ... " My voice died in my throat. "I've never led a charge before."

He crossed his arms and made a thoughtful noise in his throat. "Well, it's not all that hard. You know the commands, don't you?"

"Yes." Of course I did.

"And you know the proper way to call reformations for additional charges?"

"Yes." My voice came out squeaky and breathless as I struggled to think of any legitimate reason to refuse.

I couldn't. Not a single one came to mind.

"Listen, Levran, we're all doing things now we aren't qualified for. These are mad times. End times, honestly." He gave me a grim, empty smile that never reached his eyes. I suppose he knew what was coming as well as we did. Defeat. Death. After all, he was our king now. Out of everyone left fighting for Maldobar, he was sure to be the enemy's number one target. They'd be looking to kill him first and foremost. "If nothing else, take comfort in the fact that if you do happen to make a mistake out there tomorrow, there likely won't be a soul left to remember it at the end. They'll only remember that you tried—if they remember any of us at all."

I gulped hard against the bile that burned at the back of my throat. My hand trembled as I reached out to take the shield and tabard. "Very well, then. If this is what Maldobar requires of me, then I am honored to serve."

I nearly jumped straight out of my boots in a panic as he clapped a hand onto my shoulder gruffly. Gods, were royals normally this casual with commoners? Surely not.

"Good man. Consider me in your debt," he said as he walked with me to the door of the tent. "If, by some madness or divine mercy, we happen to survive tomorrow, come to me with any favor you like and I'll see that it's done."

I WAS RELIEVED WHEN NONE OF MY COMRADES DROPPED THEIR WEAPONS AND deserted on the spot after I told them what had happened. A few of them laughed, yes, but mostly they seemed pleased. Some ruffled my hair and punched my shoulder in passing. Others teased me about how I couldn't possibly screw this up because, as long as we all wound up dead, I'd have done a good job. Great. Well, at least they were in better spirits than when I left.

Even Errol grinned in approval as I pulled the long, royal blue tabard over my armor. "Ah, well, it'll be good to know the one calling the commands has at least half a brain. Puts you ahead of most riding in the sergeant's seat."

I ran my hands across the golden eagle—Maldobar's royal symbol—that had been embroidered on the chest. "I hope I can do this," I sighed. "I've never led a charge or called a command."

"You'll do fine. I've got every confidence in you, boy." Errol grunted as he stood and shuffled by on his way to the tent. "Get some sleep if you can. Gonna be quite a day tomorrow."

My throat closed up so that I couldn't reply. Quite a day? Yeah. It would likely be our last. Somehow, spending my last few peaceful hours on earth sleeping didn't seem quite right, so I sat by the fire with a whetstone, sharpening my sword by the light of the smoldering embers while my thoughts ran in circles.

Growing up next to youngest in our family meant I'd never been in charge of or led anything in my entire life. On our boat, Father called all the shots. My elder brothers and sisters always went first. My one and only baby sister had been too young to help out much beyond feeding chickens or folding laundry. Mother coddled her some, too. Or maybe that was just a little former-youngest jealousy rearing its ugly head.

At any rate, I'd have given anything—my very last breath—to see any one of them again. The idea that my life might be over in a few hours sent pangs of white-hot panic through my belly. I hadn't even done anything with my life, yet. I'd never married. Never even courted anyone. Never owned anything besides the clothes on my back.

Was this really it? This was all of life I'd ever get to experience? Just a few years on a grimy fishing boat and a few more in the war trenches and then ... nothing?

I clenched my teeth, staring at my reflection in the polished blade of my sword. My black hair hung wild around my face, almost covering my dark brown eyes. A fresh scar sliced over one side of my chin, almost hidden by my lengthy stubble. That was where I'd nicked myself taking off my helmet with an arrow stuck part of the way through it. A close one. If that archer had been standing even a few feet closer, his arrow would have hit the mark and killed me. My journey would have ended then. At the time, I'd thought I was lucky to have walked away from that with only a scar.

Now, I wasn't so sure.

A sudden *WHOOSH—BOOM—WHOOSH—BOOM* as loud as the crack and growl of thunder shook the ground under my boots.

I jumped up, sword in hand, and searched the horizon all around. Other soldiers ran out of their tents, groggy and terrified. What, by all the gods, was that?

I spun in a circle, staring around with my heart thrashing in my ears. Trebuchet fire? Or some new Obsidian weapon? Where was it?

WHOOSH—BOOM—WHOOSH—BOOM!

The earth shook again. From somewhere overhead, a piercing roar boomed so loud it rattled my bones all the way down to the marrow. A monstrous dark shape zoomed by, flying low and blotting out the stars like a living shadow.

Gods and Fates. I-It was ... It was a—

"DRAGON!" Errol yelled as he surged toward me, grabbing my shoulder and wrenching me to the ground. "Stay low! Don't move!"

A dragon? Here? But why? "I-I thought you said they hated the smell of humans?" I rasped, lifting my head enough to search the sky again.

"They do," Errol insisted. "Maybe it can smell the blood from the battlefield at Osbran. Or the Obsidians getting too close to their nesting grounds."

WHOOSH—BOOM—WHOOSH—BOOM!

A chorus of screams and terrified yells went up through the encampment. Men scrambled for their weapons and fired arrows up into the dark night sky.

"Stop it, you idiots!" Errol barked. "You'll provoke it! What are you even shooting at? You can't pierce dragon hide with a bow!"

No one listened. They went on yelling and running around like scared chickens. More archers fired up into the moonless night sky.

A blur caught my eye from off to the right—the sweeping motion of two enormous black wings that eclipsed the silver wash of starlight. My pulse went quiet. My breath froze in my lungs. The beast flew low, as big as a nightmare, and passed right over us.

My mouth hung open as I lay on my stomach, completely paralyzed, staring up into a pair of glowing yellow eyes as they passed over.

Wind from the dragon's wingbeats ripped past us, throwing up dirt and snuffing out our campfires. It let out another shattering roar that made my body flail out of control. I dropped my sword and clapped my hands over my ears.

Then, just as quickly as it appeared, the monster vanished. The booming of its wingbeats faded. Silence fell over the camp.

I lay on my back, hands still over my ears, as I struggled to wheeze for breath. What, by all the gods, had just happened? Why had that creature come here? Just to size us up? To see if we would make for easy prey? It hadn't even breathed fire. It kept on making low passes while those enormous eyes searched our camp —almost as though it were looking for something.

But ... what?

CHAPTER THREE

We were mobilizing by dawn. As the swollen, red sun rose over the cliffs to the east, the distant thrum of war drums from the Obsidian Army beckoned. The final stand was calling. And we had no choice but to answer.

No one bothered breaking down the tents or packing up our bedrolls as we gathered our gear, strapped on our armor and weaponry, and brought the horses around to check our saddles. Odds were, we wouldn't be returning to camp at all, let alone need to move it.

My hands shook until I could hardly get my sword belt buckled. Cold sweat made my whole body shiver as I pulled my helmet on and slung my new shield over my back. Beside me, Errol's face stayed locked into a stony look of focus as he tightened his saddle's girth strap. One look around at the heavy-lidded, grim expressions of my comrades, and it seemed like I wasn't the only one who hadn't been able to sleep. Especially not after that dragon had made its appearance. Most of the men had sat up frantically discussing the creature. They'd decided that it hadn't been a dragon at all—not really. They agreed it was an omen straight from the goddess of death. A taunt to all of us who dared to stand against her sorcerer.

I didn't join in their speculation. Gods and goddesses, omens and curses—none of that mattered now. I only had a few choices left that I could make before the end. I chose not to listen.

All speculating had ended now, though. We hardly spoke at all as we pulled our halberd pikes off the racks and mounted up. A few of the younger recruits, boys hardly big enough to hold up a shield properly, sobbed as the older soldiers helped them onto their horses. They wouldn't last long. Not in a fight like this. I tried not to look at them for more than a second—I didn't want to remember their faces.

I already had enough faces like that haunting my nightmares.

"Form up," I shouted as I brought my horse around at a trot, encircling the tents where my two regiments were camped. "I want a double-line! Nose to flank!"

With so few of us left, it didn't take long to get everyone in order. There were only two other sergeants like myself mustering their forces. One was another heavy cavalry unit like mine. The other was a light cavalry unit of men armed with bows. The rest of our forces were either infantry foot-soldiers or artillery teams charged with moving the three trebuchets we had left. That was it. Roughly two thousand men and boys to stand against the tens of thousands of Obsidian soldiers, war machines, battle monsters, and wicked magic.

I galloped my buckskin stallion down the length of my line and back again, checking every rider's gear. At least they all had a halberd or spear in hand and a shield on their backs. That was something. At least we *looked* competent.

When I came around to the front, I tipped my chin and lifted my halberd to the other two sergeants. They'd just checked their lines, as well. We were ready to move at the king's command.

The mournful wail of a horn echoed over the grassy plain an instant before he appeared—King Arran—sitting astride a swift gray mare. Riding beside him, the Gray elven woman held onto the horns of her magnificent white stag as he loped casually along. Those beasts, faundra, could supposedly run faster than any horse. Watching him go, his long strides impossibly smooth, certainly made that seem true.

With all the remaining generals and higher-ranking officers speeding along right at their heels, the king and elven sorceress thundered by on their way to the front of our forces. Maldobarian kings always led from the front—even in battles they were doomed to lose.

After a few more minutes of forming up and calling the rest of our meager forces to assemble, another wail of horns went up. Time to move.

In the pale light of dawn, we rode the short distance into the city of Dayrise at a trot. Bells in the tall towers around every square rang out, almost drowned out by the clattering of hooves over the cobblestones as we passed. The city was mostly deserted. King Arran had called for an evacuation days ago, sending what remained of his people to Luntharda for shelter. The Gray elves weren't keen on getting involved with other kingdoms' wars, but they were more than willing to take in the refugees and give them safe harbor.

For now, anyway. After what I'd seen, I doubted anywhere in the world would be safe from the Obsidian Army's reach.

The few people still lingering in the city gathered along the sides of the streets. Normally, a war march like this would have been cause for spirited cheering, chanting, and war cries from the citizens who believed we could only be victorious. But no one said a single word as we went by. They tossed down flowers before us, gazing along our lines with anguished, tear-streaked faces. They knew as well as we did.

We were marching to our doom.

As I passed through a narrow avenue, leading all my men in formation, a young woman in a blacksmithing apron with soot and ash smeared on her cheeks rushed out toward me. Her dark golden hair blew around her face as she stood on her toes and quickly passed a handkerchief up to me with an earnest expression. Our gazes locked. My heartbeat skipped. I'd never been given a token before. Any other time, I might've thanked her for it. Or asked her name.

But there wasn't time. I couldn't stop. All I managed was a brief nod in thanks. She turned and retreated back to the side of the street with the rest of the city folk without a word.

I quickly tucked the handkerchief under my breastplate, over my heart. That was the tradition, or so I'd been told. Maybe I'd see her later, somewhere in the afterlife. Then I could thank her properly.

Beyond the city, the wide grasslands that stretched all the way to the feet of the western mountains opened up before us. The land rose and fell with hills like wrinkles in a quilt, but there wasn't a tree to be found in any direction. Well—unless you looked north. There, like a living wall over five hundred feet tall, was the boundary to the Gray elven kingdom of Luntharda. The monstrous trees loomed, literal giants compared to any other creature, plant or animal, found in our world. I'd never crossed that barrier or seen what lay hidden in that wild jungle. Few from Maldobar dared to even go close to it. The merchant caravans that came and went were always heavily guarded. Supposedly, there were creatures lurking in there that could devour you whole.

King Arran called the final order, sending out another eerie echo of horns over our forces. We moved quickly, assembling into our battle lines. I unclipped the horn from the back of my saddle and brought it to my lips to give a sequence of three blasts.

Before me, all my riders moved in unison. They divided into their regiments, blocking off into lines fifty across. Behind them, the other mounted regiments aligned with the heavy cavalry in the front and the light in back. They'd be firing arrows from horseback, trying to break the first few enemy lines for us on the charge.

I galloped down my lines, checking them one more time. At the far end, I spotted Errol. He nodded and I gestured to him, calling him forward. Then I pointed at the man next to him and motioned for him to come, too.

"I want you both on my flank. We are punching through first and marking the nearest enemy commanding officer. Our goal is to eliminate him. Obsidian soldiers scatter without their commanders," I ordered.

"On your orders, Sergeant," Errol agreed with a nod. I could hear the smile in his voice without being able to see it beneath his helmet.

Next to him, the other man I'd pulled from the ranks gave a salute.

I glanced him over, barely able to make out any of his features because of his own helmet and armor. "What's your name, rider?"

"Dennick Cromwell, Sir," he replied.

"Very well, Dennick. When we find the commander, do not hesitate. Don't try to reserve the kill for me. There will be no honor in this fight. We will only have a short time to do as much damage as possible. Every Obsidian soldier we kill is one less that will ravage and burn the rest of our kingdom. So there will be no mercy. Not today. Understood?"

He gave a brisk nod. "Understood."

The front lines of the Obsidian Army appeared over the hilltops line like a rising black tide. The ground shook under the thundering of their footsteps. The echo of their war drums hit me like a rhythmic punch in the chest. The air rushed out of me. My body went cold. Staring over the endless storm of approaching enemy soldiers, terror stopped my heart and turned my blood to ice in my veins. Tears welled in my eyes as I counted the blocks. Ten. God Bane had brought ten full regiments of foot soldiers to fight us. Ten thousand men.

Behind them, monstrous beasts like overgrown bears dragged trebuchets into place. At the front, a line of cavalry in lightly armored chariots formed up. Each one was pulled by two horses and manned by two soldiers—one to drive and one with a bow.

The booming bellows and roars of war beasts made my horse spook and stir beneath me, his nostrils puffing at their strange scent. I'd never seen anything like them, either. Each one must have been thirty feet tall with leathery, bald hides, huge forearms, and heads shaped sort of like the business end of a hammer. They lumbered along with a gait like giant apes, dragging heavy chains fixed to wagons on each side.

Suddenly, a glimmer of white caught my eye. I looked, still hardly able to draw a full breath, as a single figure strode away from the front of our battle lines out into the open prairie ahead of us.

The lapiloque.

She stood alone with the wind stirring in her long white hair and lengths of her ornate loincloth. What, by all the gods, was she doing? She couldn't stand out there alone. Soon, she'd be within range of the Obsidian archers and then—

The elven woman crouched, placing her hands on the ground on either side of her. Her head bowed to her chest.

No one moved a muscle or made a sound until a blinding flash of green light burst out from her, spreading over the prairie and stretching out like a ripple on a pond. When it hit me, my horse pitched and I bore down hard on the reins to keep him steady. Every tiny hair on my body prickled with a warm shiver. My heart tingled wildly in my chest.

Was that ... magic?

The earth groaned and shook, giving me my answer.

Four monstrous creatures tore free of the ground, wrenching and climbing straight out of the dirt as though they'd been buried there a thousand years. Each one stood every bit as large as the enemy's war beasts, with hides made of solid rock, root, and clay. Their bottomless green eyes glowed like bog fires as their gnarled bodies lumbered away, leading the way into battle. Gods and Fates—what were they?

Then the lapiloque stood. Her own eyes glowed like two fiery emeralds and her shoulders flexed as two magnificent white feathered wings stretched from her back. Horns of gold grew from her head and a sheen like pearly white scales dotted patches of her skin. All around her, an aura popped and sizzled in the air like rippling green heat. She snarled, baring pointed fangs, and gave one gesture of her hand. The ground before her cracked open as though the earth itself were being torn open.

Out of the depths, another monster rose. It slithered from the ground like an enormous serpent. Its body glowed red, formed entirely of molten rock apart from its shining green eyes.

A chorus of shouts and cheers went up through the ranks behind me as all of the lapiloque's earthen beasts surged forward, leading the charge. And when her white stag emerged, galloping as fast as a silver arrow, she simply grabbed hold of its horns as it passed and swung herself onto its back.

Our battle horns blared, making an ominous harmony. King Arran on his gray mare thundered ahead at a full gallop, his sword drawn and his golden armor flashing in the light of the rising sun.

Putting my horn to my lips one last time, I blew a final command, sank my heels into my horse's flanks, and charged forward into the teeth of combat.

4

CHAPTER FOUR

We hit the Obsidian lines like waves upon a black rocky shore.

Arrows flew, blotting out the sun passing storm clouds. Swords clashed. Shields buckled. Horses shrieked and battle monsters bellowed in fury. Every breath tasted of blood, sweat, and ash. Everywhere I looked, there was carnage. Death. Fire. Madness and slaughter.

Blood ran down the shaft of my halberd and dripped from the tri-edged spear point at the end, making my grip slip whenever I went to drive it forward again. But I didn't stop. Forward—right into the oncoming forces—was the only direction. On either side, Errol and Dennick hung close and held firm. We cut a charging path through the first dozen lines that had already been broken by the lapiloque's monsters. Soldiers ran and clashed like ants scrambling in the smoke.

My body burned with every motion, muscles screaming in protest. Raw adrenaline hummed in my veins like fire. Arrows pinged off my breastplate and helmet, but none punched through. I cursed and brought my shield up. There must have been a few enemy archers that had managed to regroup.

With a hard pull on the reins, I brought my horse hard to the right to try and shield him from the assault. Where were they? If I could find those archers, then I might be able to charge them.

My horse staggered. His hind legs buckled and he let out a shrill cry of pain.

Next to me, Dennick cried out my name somewhere in the fray.

I barely managed to slip free of the stirrups before my horse went down, kicking and pitching. His rump and legs bristled with arrows. That was it. Obsidian archers dipped their arrows in poison. There was nothing I could do for him now.

Still gripping my weapon, I staggered to my feet and ducked behind my shield. A massive boulder launched from the trebuchets hit the ground nearby with a bone-rattling *BOOM*. I couldn't tell if it was one of ours or the enemy's. It didn't matter. I had to move—*now*.

Keeping low, I threw down my halberd and drew my sword. Two Obsidian soldiers, decked out in their black armor from head to foot, rushed me immediately. I met them head-on, swinging wide and surging forward with my shield up like a battering ram. We'd learned early on in the war that when it came to foot soldiers, God Bane preferred quantity to quality. These men had nowhere near the training of a Maldobarian infantryman.

I hit them hard. The first soldier staggered under the impact from my shield, buying me a few seconds to deal with the second. I whipped around and dropped to a knee. One fast strike upward locked us in a parry. I bared my teeth, letting out a primal shout as I twisted my hilt and tore his blade from his hand. A kick to the chest and downward thrust of my blade ended the fight—just in time for the first soldier to collect himself and rush me again.

He didn't make it two steps.

A cavalryman sitting astride a sturdy chestnut mare ran him over—literally. One swift punch with the point of his halberd finished it, and the rider wheeled around to face me.

Gods and Fates, it was Errol!

I looked around for Dennick, but there was no sign of him anywhere in the chaos. Had he fallen? Or simply gotten snagged up by a fight, as well?

"Lost your legs already, boy?" Errol shouted over the roar of the battle. He stuck his halberd down in my direction.

I smirked and ran to him, ready to grab ahold of the halberd's long shaft and haul myself up onto the back of his saddle. I reached out, fingers barely brushing the wood before the world around me exploded. Dirt and bits of rock flew in every direction and I flew backward, landing yards away flat on my back.

For a few seconds, all I could do was lie there. Was I dead? Dying? How badly was I injured? Could I move?

And what, by all the gods, had happened?

Shakily, I lifted my head and tried to sit up. My ears rang and my vision tunneled in and out, threatening to leave me in the dark.

Less than fifteen yards away, a large rock sat where it had smashed into the earth—another boulder fired from a trebuchet.

I gaped in shock, groggily looking down at all the chunks of rock now embedded into the front of my breastplate. As far as I could tell, none of them had made it through. But I might not be able to feel it regardless. I'd bleed out without realizing it.

No way I was about to take it off to check, though.

I coughed and wheezed as I scrambled back to my feet. "E-Errol?" Where was he? Had he been thrown by the impact, too, or ... ?

I spotted the legs of his horse sticking out from *underneath* the rock.

Oh, gods. *NO!*

A primal noise tore past my lips as I ran forward. I leaned against the massive rock, pushing with all my strength. My feet slid over the ground. The boulder didn't move an inch.

"Y-You can't move mountains, boy ... " a weak voice called out to me.

I whirled around, searching the battlefield nearby until I saw him. I gasped out a few, garbled breaths of relief, stumbling as I ran to where Errol lay not far away. He must've been thrown from his horse when the rock hit.

But the way his body lay, his legs bent in different directions, like that. Fates, no. He ... couldn't. Not like this. He was the closest thing to family I had left.

"D-Don't look ... so afraid ... b-boy." He gave a weak, broken chuckle as I dropped to my knees next to him. Blood oozed from the corners of his mouth. "I-It's just ... my t-turn ... t-that's all."

My hands shook as I unbuckled his helmet and slid it off, tossing it away. I took his hand and squeezed it hard. "I'm, gods, I'm so sorry."

A smile ghosted over his face. "F-For what? It's ... j-just death, boy. I-It's the one thing ... w-we all do the s-same." He squeezed my hand back weakly, his eyes seemed to grow distant even as he stared back at me. "P-Proud ... of y-you," he managed weakly, his breath catching.

Then his head dropped back. His hand went limp in mine.

I screamed. On my knees in the mud, blood, and filth of the battlefield, I yelled his name until my throat burned.

All around me, the dark symphony of war raged on. The shouts grew closer. More soldiers were coming, pressing in on all sides. They'd overtake my location soon and try to cut me down like chaff.

Just like they'd done to everything and everyone else I'd ever loved.

Something inside me snapped. My eyes flew open. Rage like hellfire rose in my chest. Fury so strong it sent strength blooming through my body.

I threw down my shield and snatched up Errol's sword, still gripping my own in the other. Spinning them over my hands, I turned to face the nearest group of Obsidian soldiers coming my way.

No. They wouldn't take me down. I'd die today. I'd reunite with my family and Errol on the silver shores—but not yet.

And not before I'd taken a few dozen of these miserable wretches down with me.

MY BLADES HUMMED A DARK MELODY IN THE AIR AS I DUELED, BLURRING through parries, strikes, and complex maneuvers one after another. Everything had gone numb in the wake of that internal fire that still blazed through my body. Time seemed to drag, the world around me nothing but a dark haze as I rammed my weapons to the hilt into my enemies.

Standing over Errol's fallen body, I refused to let any of the Obsidian soldiers get close. They would not touch him. Not unless they killed me first. But strike by strike, I knew my strength had already begun to fizzle. How long had I been at this? How many had I killed? How much longer would I last? Which of these men would be the one to bring me down? Would they let me die there in the mud, next to Errol?

Gods, I hoped so.

A sharp bite of pain through my gut suddenly made everything snap back into focus. The fire in my veins snuffed out instantly. I looked down, my body shaking and the flavor of warm copper filling my mouth, at the shaft of a spear sticking out of my middle. It'd pierced my armor like a toothpick through butter.

This ... this was it.

Setting my jaw, I raised my blade and hacked downward with all my strength, cutting the shaft of the spear off so that only about six inches stuck out of me. Then I looked around for the person who'd thrown it.

Through the smoke and swirling dust, he approached like a demon straight from the pits of the abyss. I knew him immediately. The black armor studded in silver spines, the symbol of a silver serpent emblazoned on his breast plate, and the long, wicked staff in his hand tipped with a jagged obsidian crystal—there was no mistaking him.

God Bane.

He sneered down at me from the back of a huge, wolf-like creature. Its shaggy fur hung as dark as pitch and its white eyes glowed with ancient power as it eyed me and snapped its toothy jaws. It perked tall, pointed ears as God Bane dismounted, running a hand along the beast's side. It ... it almost seemed like the whole creature's body flickered and wavered—as though it were made of shadow or dark flame.

"Look what we've found, Noh." God Bane's voice laughed from beneath his helmet. "Such a mess this little mongrel has made of our ranks. We can't let this go unpunished, can we?"

The dark, wolf-like creature gave a snarl in response. Its lips curled back and snout wrinkled to show me all of its long, jagged teeth.

"I agree. But I've work yet to do. I must find that wretched little king and end this." God Bane gave a bemused snort and turned away, taking his vile staff with him. "Have your way with him, Noh. But see that you don't take too long. That savage forest witch is somewhere out here, as well. I will have her for my prize."

God Bane's towering, dark shape disappeared into the battle, leaving me before his foul demon pet. My heartbeat slowed, thudding hard as though every beat were a fight. The feeling in my hands and feet began to ebb away and I could hardly keep a grip on my blades. Blood dripped from under my breastplate and filled my mouth until I had to spit it at my feet.

The huge wolf growled low as it prowled closer, head down and hackles raised. It paced back and forth, leaving a wake in the air like a trail of curling smoke. Something about it—the bottomless white pits of its eyes or maybe the licking, flickering outline of its body—sent a cold pang of fear up my spine. Whatever this monster was, it hadn't come from our world.

The wolf snapped its jaws and slicked its tall ears back as it coiled to lunge.

I narrowed my eyes, staggering as I tried to widen my stance. My head was swimming so badly from the loss of blood that I could barely stay on my feet. I wouldn't last. This was it.

I stole one quick, final glance down at where Errol lay at my feet. Then I squeezed the hilts of the swords in my hands tighter. I set my jaw and leveled my glare upon the wolf just as it sprang for me, mouth open to crush my head like an egg.

Out of nowhere, fire exploded into the air with such force that it blew me back on my rear and knocked the swords out of my hands. Pain from the spearhead still lodged in my gut ripped through me. My vision went dark for a moment, and I struggled to breathe. Dying—I was dying.

Slowly, everything came back into focus.

I blinked hard. Hot air filled my lungs as I sucked in deep breaths. It reeked of something acrid and strange. What was that smell? Oil or some sort of fuel from another Obsidian-made weapon?

I looked up, through the licking, crackling flames ...

... right into the face of an enormous dragon.

CHAPTER FIVE

I stood, completely paralyzed with horror, practically nose-to-nose with a huge black and blue dragon.

Crouched before me, the beast's lean, muscular body rippled as it swished its long tail back and forth. I could see my reflection in its large yellow eyes as it studied me. Scales as black as the night sky were adorned in a pattern of light, teal-blue that ran like a blaze from the end of its short snout all the way to the end of its spiked tail. More blue markings striped its legs and great horns like black spines ridged its back. Overall, it must've been twelve feet to the head—big enough to take my head off with one bite.

But instead of doing that, or burning me alive with its scorching breath, the dragon perked its small, scaly ears and titled its head to the side. It made a series of low, popping and clicking sounds.

W-What? What was it doing? Why had it come here? Had it just saved me from—

My gaze snapped to where the huge wolf monster had already gotten back up. It snarled in dismay, hide shivering as it hunkered to lunge again.

The dragon hissed. All those spines along its back bristled as it moved with an awkward, lumbering gait like an enormous bat between me and the wolf and curled its huge tail around where I stood. Rearing onto its muscular hind legs, the dragon spread its black wings wide and let out a challenging, booming roar.

I clamped my hands over my ears and hunkered back. Gods and Fates, what was happening?

The wolf didn't back down. It sprang again—only to meet a sudden blast of burning dragon venom that filled the air with another explosion of fire and that acrid smell.

The wolf flew back, thrown end over end until it smacked the ground with a yelp and crunch. Immediately, it scrambled up and ran, only to take a couple of strides before it vanished in a wisp of black smoke like a phantom.

The dragon fell back on its winged forelegs beside me, fangs the length of my fingers bared and nostrils puffing furiously. Its deep growl rumbled like thunder as some of that burning venom dripped from its jaws, forming puddles of liquid flame.

"Y-You," I managed to rasp hoarsely. "You saved me."

The dragon swung its huge, horned head around to stare at me again. It made more of those musical, chirping sounds.

This couldn't be real. It wasn't possible. It ... It made no sense! Why?

I reached out a shaking hand toward the beast's snout.

A bad idea, I knew. But I was already dying. What would it matter if I was missing an arm when I did? Or maybe it would just burn me on the spot and end my suffering now.

I stared back into the dragon's eyes, my heart thumping in my throat as I inched my hand closer. The heat of its breath wafted against my palm. A bit more. Just a few inches and then ...

My fingertips touched the dragon's scaly snout. Its eyes rolled closed and it went on making low, chittering sounds as it pushed its head against my hand.

A gasp slipped past my lips.

Every one of those black and blue scales flowed together, locked like plated mail, but as smooth and warm as sun-tanned leather. Its horns were thick and solid, and its small ears soft with tiny, much more flexible scales. Running my hand along its neck, I could feel the steady *THUMP ... THUMP ... THUMP* of its heartbeat against my palm.

"Thank you," I said as I pulled back. I didn't know if the creature could understand me or not.

Suddenly, it didn't matter.

In the distance, a concussive *CRACK* and *BOOM* made that tingle of fear climb my spine again. A piercing, eerie howl turned my insides to ice. It must be that wolf-creature again. Something was happening. Maybe they'd found King Arran or the lapiloque.

I couldn't leave either of them to fight alone. As long as I was alive, I'd keep my oath to defend Maldobar.

"I-I have to help them," I stammered, more to myself than anyone else, as I staggered away to pick up one of my swords. Every movement made my vision dim. I stumbled, nearly falling.

A big, scaly head appeared in my path again.

The dragon crawled in front of me, flattening out with its belly on the ground.

What was this?

I eyed the creature in bewilderment. Maybe it was only trying to stop me from returning to the fight. A valid point, honestly. I was in no shape to fight.

But I had to.

"I can't leave them to die. Someone has to help. Someone has to stop God Bane. If King Arran falls, then so does Maldobar."

The dragon swept its tail around, smacking against my back and forcing me forward until I stood right next to it. It gave an annoyed snort, intelligent yellow eyes watching me carefully. When it stretched out its wings, lying them flat on the ground on either side, an odd and potentially deadly idea popped into my head.

Was it ... asking me to ride it?

No. Absolutely not. I'd lost too much blood and now I was losing my mind, too. The dragon had saved me, yes, but there was no way it meant for me to—

It gave another impatient huff and scooted sideways, closer to me.

I dropped my sword again. Gods and Fates.

My whole body trembled as I edged closer. I put my hands on its side, struggling to get a grip or even move at all. My injury made it impossible to pull myself up onto the dragon's back. I couldn't do this, even if it wanted me to.

Swinging its head around, the black and blue dragon shoved its nose under my rear and gave me a boost. It lifted me up so I could climb over onto a spot at the base of its neck, right between its powerful wing arms. I grabbed on to some of those thick black spines and clung for dear life as the beast made a satisfied grunt and rose up.

I yelped and cursed, trying in vain to keep balance with my legs like I did on horseback. It didn't work very well. Those scales were dangerously smooth. In a moment of pure panic, I unbuckled the sword belt from around my waist and quickly bound it between two of the spines as tightly as I could. It gave me something more solid to hold onto as the beast reared up onto its hide legs.

Spreading those powerful wing arms wide, the dragon let out a booming roar and kicked off the ground. It pumped those wings in graceful sweeps and took off into the sky—with me still clinging to its back.

THE DRAGON CARRIED ME LOW OVER THE BATTLEFIELD. IT WHEELED LIKE AN enormous eagle, occasionally blasting a line of Obsidian soldiers with another spray of burning venom. It belted out more thundering cries and below, I watched the enemy scatter in terror. My stomach dropped and flipped with every movement of its powerful form, but not from fear. The raw, untamable power of the monster that carried me sent energy buzzing through my body with every second. Seated on the back of a dragon, I felt—no, I *was*—invincible.

Then, through the rising smoke, I spotted them.

God Bane and the lapiloque stood only feet apart, locked in battle. Their magic sent wave after wave of power that rippled outward through the air, hitting my senses like a blast from a furnace.

The Gray elf sorceress held fast, her stance wide and hands outstretched as she stood beneath a shimmering, dome-shaped shield of brilliant emerald light. At her feet, a figure in golden armor lay. Gods, was that King Arran? Was he dead? No—surely not. She wouldn't still be protecting him if he'd fallen, right?

Flashes of green sparked like fireworks every time God Bane struck her barrier. Streaks and ribbons of his foul, inky black energy tangled and wavered through the air all around her, as though probing for some way in. The dark wolf that'd attacked me paced around it, too. She was cornered, outnumbered, and I could have sworn I saw streaks of crimson dribbling down her chest and legs. Blood. She'd been injured.

She wouldn't be able to keep that shield up forever.

"H-Hey!" It took all my strength to yell up to the dragon.

No response.

I patted its neck and tapped its sides with my heels. "Hey! Down there! I need to get down there! She needs my help!"

The dragon flicked a look back at me and I quickly pointed down to the ground where the lapiloque and God Bane still dueled.

"I need to help her!" I yelled again.

Not that I could do much to help her. I'd lost my weapons and my injury made it nearly impossible to breathe now. Every second my head swam more. My arms and legs were so heavy it was a fight just to move them. I wouldn't last much longer.

But I might last long enough to distract God Bane so she and King Arran could make a clean escape.

"J-Just put me down as close as you can." My voice cracked and halted. I didn't expect the dragon to stick around for the fight, after all. Did it even understand me?

With a thundering growl, the dragon snapped its wings in close and dove straight for them. I hung on, willing every bit of strength I had left into gripping the belt between its horns. As we dove, the beast's scaly sides swelled against my legs as it took in a deep breath. That mighty maw opened wide and it sprayed another blast of explosive venom around God Bane.

A triumphant cry tore from my throat when I saw the dark tyrant falter. He stumbled back, shocked as his helmeted head whipped up to see us still coming in full speed.

I couldn't help it. I thrust a finger directly at him. I wanted God Bane to know we were coming for him.

At the last second, the dragon flared its mighty wings and landed between God Bane and the lapiloque with a *BOOM*. It threw back its horned head and unleashed a shattering battle cry and shot a column of flame into the air.

"You dare to challenge me? You are nothing to me, Maldobarian dog!" The dark sorcerer's eyes narrowed through the slit in his helmet. He raised his staff, summoning a mass of those flickering dark shadows around the black crystal at the tip.

I set my jaw. Not this time.

"Levran!" a female voice shouted at my back. "Hand out!"

I didn't even look. I knew who it was. And I trusted her.

I thrust my arm out to the side and held my hand open and almost screamed in surprise when the gnarled wooden staff of a long halberd appeared in my grip. Both ends sparkled with curved blades of white crystal like raw quartz. A half-delirious smirk spread over my mouth. Perfect.

Releasing my hold on the leather belt, I slid off the dragon's back and hit the ground. Pain like white-hot fire shot through me from the spearhead still buried in my gut. I crumpled, leaning against the halberd as I struggled to breathe. Blood soaked my tabard, armor, and squished in my boots. I-I ... I didn't have long. I had to make this count.

Hauling to my feet, I staggered forward with my jaw set and my eyes locked upon my enemy. Beside me, the black dragon hissed and gaped, threatening another fiery breath.

"Look at you," God Bane laughed as his monstrous black wolf materialized at his side. "One nearly-dead soldier and a dragon? Pathetic. I hold the power of death itself. And you alone *dare* to defy my will?"

"He is not alone!" the Gray elf sorceress snapped, suddenly appearing on my other side with her eyes blazing like green flame.

Next to her, King Arran shambled forward. He seemed to be about as well off as I was. He favored one arm that hung limp at his side, probably broken. But he gripped his sword with the other. Flashing me a meaningful look, King Arran gave me a confirming nod. "No soldier of Maldobar ever stands alone."

The dragon roared again, as though in agreement.

My grin widened. Well, at least now I would have a grand story to tell Errol in the afterlife. He might not believe it, though. Riding a dragon? Fighting God Bane alongside our king? Hah!

A sudden chorus of booming cries filled the air from somewhere overhead. It made everyone look up.

My mouth dropped open. Through the haze of smoke rising from the battle-field, more monstrous dark shapes dove in. Dragons—hundreds of them! They swept in on powerful wings, scales gleaming in the sunlight, and bathed the Obsidian ranks with blast after blast of flame. They tackled those giant war beasts head-on. They landed on the enemy trebuchets and tore them apart like eagles shredding a freshly killed fish.

The dragons were fighting with us.

And they were turning the tide.

The lapiloque let out a gasping string of Gray elf words I couldn't understand. Then she looked at me, her eyes rimmed with tears that poured down her cheeks. A trembling smile on her lips, she fitted an arrow to her bow.

The dragon bristled his spines and flared his wings over us. Two more, smaller dragons—one of bright yellow with black stripes and another of deep green—dropped from the sky and landed on either side.

King Arran hefted his sword with a shout, pointing the tip right at God Bane.

And together, we charged straight for the dark sorcerer.

6

CHAPTER SIX

I awoke to the strong smell of herbs and the soft murmur of hushed conversation. My eyelids fluttered as I struggled to focus. Everything—my arms, legs, head, and especially my chest—felt heavy and sore. I was ... alive. But how? Everything about the battle, our final stand against God Bane, was a hazy blur. What had happened? Had we won? Was God Bane dead?

I groaned, swallowing against the raw agony in my throat. Water. I needed water.

"Shhh," a woman's voice cooed over me. "Try to stay still, Levran. Your injuries were severe, but I was able to repair them. Your body may feel weak and strange for a bit, though. You lost quite a lot of blood. For a moment there, I wasn't sure I would be able to bring you back."

I clenched my teeth as I concentrated on forcing my eyes to open. At first, everything appeared as a mashed-up blur of colors and vague shapes. Little by little, every blink brought the world back into focus.

I stared groggily up into the familiar, beautiful face of a Gray elven woman with braided white hair and eyes that shone like opals. She smiled from where she sat at my bedside, holding a small cup of a pungent green goo. Herbal medicine?

"There you are," she said approvingly. "How do you feel?"

"T-Thirsty," I croaked.

Her smile brightened. She set her cup of medical paste aside and held my head while she brought a waterskin to my lips. Every sip brought cool relief to my throat. When I relaxed into the bed again, my head even seemed clearer. I glanced around the room, at the other narrow beds set up on opposite walls.

More injured men lay stretched out while they slept, or sat propped up so they could eat from bowls. Whatever they had, soup or stew, it smelled rich and delicious. My stomach growled loudly.

It made the lapiloque laugh as she sat back. "Well, that's a good sign. Would you like some?"

I blushed and nodded.

"I'll see to it, then." She combed a few of her braids behind one of her pointed ears. "But first, I think we should talk about what happened."

Right. I still couldn't remember much. Everything was a tangled mess of smoke, flame, steel, and blood. "Is ... is it over? Did we kill God Bane?"

Her expression dimmed. "Physically, yes. God Bane is dead. But I'm afraid it's not as simple as that. So long as the crystal that links him to his goddess remains, so does his essence. King Arran believes guarding it here in Maldobar will deter anyone from trying to wield it again. But that goddess ... she is clever. I fear we haven't seen the last of her." Her brow furrowed as she lowered her gaze. One of her hands drifted up to wrap around that teardrop-shaped, bone pendant around her neck. "For now, we are charged with driving the remainder of God Bane's forces from our land. It won't be easy. But your new *friends* seem eager to help."

The way she said that word—friends—made me wonder. I'd only ever really had one friend, Errol, and he was gone. "What do you mean?"

Her strange eyes glistened secretively and she tipped her head toward the window on the far wall. "Why don't you see for yourself, hm?"

My stomach flipped as I struggled to sit up. Was I ready for this? I'd only just woken up, and that spear had—

I ran a hand over the place on my abdomen where it had pierced me. My heartbeat skipped. Jerking up the clean white tunic I wore, I ran my fingers over the smooth, unbroken skin along my stomach. Gone! The spear—the wound—it was all gone! Only a faint scar suggested I'd ever been injured at all.

I gaped at her, too shocked to even speak. How long had I been out? Months? It must've at least taken that long for a wound like that to heal.

"My healing abilities come from Paligno, the god of all living things," she explained with that wistful smile still making her lovely face glow.

"You *healed* me?" I guessed.

"Yes. And many others. King Arran included. He wishes to speak with you when you've gotten your strength back," she said. Then she stood and offered her arm to help me to my feet. "Come. You should see what it is you've done, Levran Porter."

It took a few steps to feel steady and sure again. By the time I reached the window, I could stand on my own without her help. But nothing could have prepared me for what lay beyond it.

From the second story of what seemed to be a rural farmhouse, the silhouette of Dayrise's buildings and steeples stood out against the sunset. We weren't far, maybe only five miles away. Between the farm and the city, however, many dark shapes clustered on the rolling grassland. Some lay in groups, preening one another. Others stretched out to bask in the last few rays of sunlight. More tussled and growled, wrestling like oversized puppies. But one particular lay right beside the house, its black scaly hide mottled with brilliant teal blue markings.

Dragons—Gods and Fates, there were dragons everywhere!

More dark specks walked among them, keeping a distance. Were those ... *men*? I leaned in and squinted just to be sure. They were Maldobarian soldiers!

"I-I don't understand," I gasped. "The dragons stayed? Why? What made them help us in the first place?"

The Gray elf woman stood beside me, her arms crossed and her expression thoughtful. "I wish I could tell you, Levran. As Paligno's chosen, I am able to communicate with all the creatures created by his will. I hear their thoughts as my own. But dragons are more complex. They can refuse to speak to me, if they wish. Many of them still do. And the one who chose you doesn't answer my questions. He only repeats the same phrase over and over."

I stared down at the black creature, watching in awe as he yawned and went on preening his wing arms like an enormous scaly cat. "What does he say?"

She met my gaze with a worried sort of smile. "*The brave one is good. He is mine,*" she replied.

For a moment, I forgot how to breathe. What did that mean?

She must've been able to read my thoughts easily because she puffed a small sigh and shook her head. "I don't know what's happened, but something about you drew him in. He's chosen you, Levran. There's no talking him out of it."

"Chosen me for what?"

She put a hand on my arm. "To fight with him again. To fly together and drive what remains of the Obsidian Army out of our lands. Levran, I think he wants you to be his rider—his partner."

Every single thought in my mind went silent as I tried to rationalize what that meant. This dragon wanted *me* to be his rider? For how long? And ... why?

The Gray elf sorceress didn't offer any more suggestions. Instead, she reached into her flowing, silken robes and took out a small, blood-stained piece of cloth. She placed it into my hand. "I believe this is yours."

I blinked down at the handkerchief. It was the one that young woman had given me in the street before the battle. I'd stuffed it into my breastplate. Somehow, it'd survived the battle.

"That is a woman's token, isn't it?" she asked. "You said before you did not have a lover who might come asking what had happened to you."

"I-I don't. It's not, um, I mean, I don't know who she was. She gave it to me when we marched through the city on our way into battle." I blushed again and carefully tucked the handkerchief into the pocket of my light linen pants. "Thank you."

"You should return to her," the sorceress suggested, grinning knowingly as she stared back out the window. "Whoever she was, I'm sure she would like to know you survived."

"Oh, um, yes," I agreed, my voice suddenly weak and shaky. I'd never imagined I might live. The lapiloque was right, though. I should find that young woman and give it back. Maybe even thank her for it, if I could manage to put together some intelligent sentences. Speaking with lovely women had never been one of my finer skills. "I will."

I WASN'T THE ONLY ONE CHOSEN BY A DRAGON. AS THE DAYS PASSED AND OUR forces struggled to recover, some of the dragons departed back to their nests on the eastern cliffs.

But many others stayed behind. They paired themselves with other soldiers, seeming to take great pride and care in the one's they selected. The dragons stayed close, and at first, it made a lot of people anxious. Understandable, of course. As the time dragged on, though, the atmosphere steadily relaxed. The dragons didn't cause any significant problems. They didn't light fire to anything or eat anyone. They listened to the men they'd chosen, obeying their requests ... most of the time, anyway. Bizarre didn't even begin to describe it.

Standing before the king drake who'd chosen me, I ran my hand along his snout and smiled. He didn't like for anyone else to touch him, which suited me fine. It was a reminder that while he might agree to carry me in flight and remain at my side, he wasn't a dumb animal. He wasn't a horse or a pet. He was an ally. A friend.

And I'd named him Arius.

Standing beside his head, I scratched at the scales behind his small ears. A deep purr rumbled from his throat and he closed his eyes as he pushed his head harder into my hand. Now that we'd had some time to get to know one another, I'd found he had a personality that reminded me a lot of the fat tomcat my sisters lugged around and dressed in their doll clothes. He tolerated me looking him over and even peering in his mouth with only mild complaining. Offering him bites of fresh fish usually worked miracles toward getting him to do whatever I asked.

I ran my hands experimentally over the place on his back where I hoped I could put a saddle—that crucially stable spot between the base of his neck and his wing arm shoulders. After all, I couldn't very well go on riding into battles clinging to his spines and praying I didn't slip off and fall. I had to come up with something better for myself and everyone else who now had a dragon sniffing after them like a curious puppy. There was a lot to consider, and somehow, I'd become the person everyone else came to with questions about the dragons. I wasn't sure why since I'd only been partnered with one for about two days longer than they had. How did that make me an expert?

Luckily, I wasn't completely alone. Although he'd been gravely wounded in the battle, Dennick Cromwell was one of the many soldiers that the lapiloque managed to heal before he succumbed to his injuries. I'd gone to meet him as soon as I found out, if only to thank him for standing with me as long as he did. That's when I'd discovered he'd been chosen by a dragon, as well. His was a female, muscular and a brilliant yellow striped in black. With Dennick now stuck in the same situation, it didn't feel quite as overwhelming. At least I had someone I knew I could count on to help figure all this out.

"We're almost ready to move on Barrowton. You and your new friends will be quite a game-changer. I daresay we stand a chance of cleaning every last Obsidian soldier out of Maldobar before the year is up," King Arran announced as he walked up behind me. He still kept a cautious distance from most of the dragons. With his decorative golden breastplate polished to perfection and a regal blue cloak trimmed in white fox fur fastened over his shoulders, he regarded me from a safe distance with a broad grin. "If you're still willing to continue the fight, that is."

I smiled. "We are."

"Good." He crossed his arms and studied my monstrous ally. "I've been told there's nearly a hundred of you now. Soldiers with dragons, that is."

Turning to face him, I rubbed at the back of my neck. There was something else—something I needed to ask him. I'd rehearsed it over and over in my head, but looking at him now, I couldn't remember a thing I'd wanted to say. "Your Majesty, I … uh, that is, when you promoted me before the battle … " I started, stumbling all over my words.

"I promised you a favor if we survived," he guessed.

I sank back on my heels in relief. "Yes, well, I'd like to make that request now, if that's all right."

"Go ahead, then."

"It's, um, it's two things actually."

His brows rose and his expression became curious.

"First, I … I'd like to ask for a bit of personal leave. Just a day. Two at the most." Embarrassed heat crept up my neck and spread over my face.

"Dare I ask what for?"

I swallowed hard. "A woman in Dayrise gave me a token the day we left for battle. I'd like to find her and give it back."

One corner of his mouth quirked up into a roguish smile. "Ah. Well, that explains why you're beginning to resemble a radish, then. Very well. Take as long as you need. We likely won't be mobilizing for another week." He glanced me up and down as though appraising my casual uniform. "I might suggest dressing for it, though. If you're going to be the knight returning from a glorious victory in battle, do yourself a favor and put on your armor. And here, wear this." He took off his long royal blue cloak and handed it to me.

I took the cloak carefully, running my fingers over the white fox fur collar. I'd never owned anything that fine before. "Thank you, Your Majesty."

He waved a hand dismissively. "Don't mention it. Call it one soldier's favor to another. Now, what else was it you wanted?"

I stiffened. This bit would be harder, but necessary. "Your Majesty, I—"

"Please, just call me Arran. You've no idea how exhausting it is to hear people call me that a thousand times a day."

I gulped. "Arran, sir, I was thinking that given the situation and that there's so many of us partnered with dragons now, it might be a good idea for us to have a place to train and practice for battle. Some of the soldiers chosen weren't in the cavalry. They don't even ride a horse well in combat, let alone a dragon. We need to teach them and learn ourselves. We need to learn to coordinate our movements and attacks so that we don't wind up setting fire to our own ranks by accident. We need to experiment with gear and find some sort of saddle that will work but won't interfere with the dragons' flight."

King Arran rubbed his jaw thoughtfully. "I see."

"I was hoping it could be somewhere fairly isolated. The less risk there is of accidentally setting fire to someone's fields or home, the better."

He stood silent for a moment, still rubbing at his chin. At last, he snapped his fingers and pointed at me. "I think I know just the place. It's abandoned at the moment, so it may need some repair. It was an old keep built back when my family first settled here ages ago. It's so deep in the mountains, getting to it by horse is difficult, so no one's bothered to do anything with it in quite some time."

I couldn't disguise the hope in my voice. "That sounds perfect."

"Good. Then it's yours, General."

I choked out loud. "General?"

He pursed his lips and shrugged. "Indeed. If you're mounting efforts to train an entire group of dragons and riders to fight in Maldobar's name, then you'll need a leader. Seems appropriate that it should be the first one of you deemed worthy of a dragon's loyalty. I'm sure you'll need to delegate, form up a ranking system of your own. But we can work on that later, once you've had some time to establish yourselves and who among you has the most skill." King Arran stretched a hand toward me, offering to shake. "What do you say?"

I could hardly breathe let alone answer. After a few seconds of awkward hyperventilating, I finally managed to take his hand and shake it back. "Thank you, sir. I will ... do my very best to be worthy of this honor."

"I'm sure you will," he replied, and turned to swagger away. "I'll have the information on Blybrig Fortress drawn up for you. Expect it before the week is out. And see that you comb your hair a bit before you find that lady friend of yours. I won't have my generals presenting themselves in a mess."

IT TOOK THREE DAYS TO VISIT EVERY BLACKSMITH'S SHOP IN DAYRISE. I might have made better time if not for the occasional *visits* from my enormous, scaly companion who didn't seem to understand that landing in the street and terrifying the townsfolk created a constellation of problems every time he did it. It took some convincing to get him to wait outside the city limits. I guess he didn't like having me out of his sight. We'd have to work on that later.

Now, however, I'd almost given up. The young woman who'd given me the token had been wearing a leather smithing apron that day, so apart from starting in the same area where I'd seen her, I didn't have much else to go on. But after the tenth shop, my spirits sank. I couldn't find any sign of her and no one seemed to know who I was talking about.

How else could I find her?

The handkerchief itself was fairly plain. A small cluster of pale purple blossoms that resembled the blossoms that grew along the shore where my father used to spread our nets, had been stitched into a corner, but there weren't any initials or seals. I'd reached a dead end.

Sitting on the edge of a stone watering trough in one of the smaller city squares, I stared down at it. If I focused hard enough, I could picture her face. She'd had long, light-colored hair. Blond, I think. Her face had been pretty, even smudged with soot. She'd looked about my age, maybe somewhere in her early twenties. That was all I could remember, though.

Part of me wondered if she might not be from Dayrise at all. Maybe she'd only been passing through on her way to Luntharda with other refugees. She could be long gone, on the other side of the kingdom by now. If that was the case, then I'd likely never find her.

I sighed and folded the handkerchief up, prepared to stuff it back into my pocket. A shrill cry, like the excited squeal of a small child, came from the other side of the square. I looked up—just in time to see a little girl with ginger hair toddle out into the street. She couldn't have been any older than two. And right behind her, a very flustered-looking woman called after her and ran, lugging a heavy burlap sack over one shoulder.

My breath caught.

The young woman had long golden hair the color of honey woven into a messy braid down her back. She wore a blacksmithing apron tied up around her neck and waist.

It was her!

My heart leapt as I got to my feet. Before I could think about it, I jogged across the square to intercept the little girl before she got too far into the street. She stumbled to a halt right in front of me, big green eyes blinking up in surprise for a quick second. Then she ducked between my legs and hid under the lengths of my long blue cloak.

"Elara! Come back here right this sec—" The woman halted, nearly crashing into me, bag and all. She stumbled back, her face going pasty white with surprise. "I-I'm so sorry, sir. My daughter is … " Her voice trailed off as her brow crinkled slightly, her own deep, olive-green eyes searching my face as though she recognized me. Her mouth opened again, but she didn't speak again.

So I tried. "I, um, it's fine. Honestly. I've got, er, well, I had a lot of siblings. A little sister, too. I'm used to it."

She still didn't say a word.

Oh, gods. This was even more awkward than I'd feared. In a desperate attempt to salvage my dignity, I dug into my pocket and took out her handkerchief. "I … forgive me, but I believe this is yours, isn't it?" I held it out.

Her eyes widened as she stared at it. Rosy color flushed her cheeks as she took it. "Yes."

"I wanted to return it. And to thank you. I, um, I'm very grateful." I stammered and sputtered, making an even bigger idiot out of myself. "My name is Levran Porter."

"I'm Maristella. Maristella Watford." Her brows shot up suddenly. "A mouthful, I know. My mother named me for a—"

"A flower," I finished before I could stop myself. *Oops.* I chuckled and dipped my head apologetically. "I'm sorry. It's just that I grew up in Tailspot, much further south. My family were fishermen by trade. We, uh, we saw maristella flowers blooming along the water's edge all the time. My sisters liked to wade in the shallows to pick them."

She blinked up at me, apparently shocked that I'd known that. "Oh. Well, that's … quite a coincidence, isn't it? Most people just call me Mari, though." She hesitated. "Wait, did you say *Porter*? From the cavalry?"

"Yes, that's right."

"You're the one they're calling a dragonrider." Her voice was hushed with awe.

"Ah, well, that's actually—"

The little girl hiding in my cloak popped her head out to peer up at me, her freckled cheeks as rosy as apples as she grinned. Quick as a cat, Mari snatched her up with her free hand and balanced her on her hip.

"My husband, gods rest him, was in the infantry that tried to hold Solhelm. He fell there a year ago," she explained, huffing as she tried to steady the lumpy sack on her other shoulder. "It's just the two of us now. But we get along."

I reached out and quickly took the bag from her. The hard lumps inside must have been potatoes. "I'm sorry to hear that."

"Oh, please, you don't have to do that. I can manage," she protested.

"I'm sure you can. But you shouldn't have to. Please, allow me. I can carry them the rest of the way for you." I gestured for her to lead on. "It's the least I can do."

She did, although her face flushed pinker than ever and she walked quickly back along the side of the square. "Thank you, sir."

"What made you settle here?" I asked as I followed her through the twisting city streets. "We're a long way from Solhelm."

"After the city fell, many of us managed to escape over the mountains and camp in the hills. We were in Port Marlowe for a bit. But my father-in law lived here alone after his wife passed years ago. He offered to give us shelter. But when the war reached us here, he volunteered to join the ranks and fight to hold the city." Her features fell, becoming dejected, and the light in her eyes seemed to dim. "He didn't return."

"I see." Stealing a glance at her, I wondered at how she'd managed on her own with a child like this. To be widowed so young and then be left to fend for herself and her daughter in the middle of a war? I couldn't imagine attempting that myself. She must have been strong—stronger than anyone I'd ever known—to have endured all of that. "I'm sorry for your loss. For both of them, I mean."

Mari's gaze caught mine with a hint of something like desperation, as though she were struggling to keep her emotions in check. "They both died honorably, fighting for Maldobar. The least I can do now is go on living and helping to rebuild. My husband worked as a swordsmith, and I tried taking over the trade after he passed. He trained me quite well and I used to help him fill orders, but it's not been easy trying to start over. I'd hoped to make weapons and armor to help restock the infantry. The blacksmiths don't like a woman in their workshops, but I found a farrier nearby who doesn't mind lending me his small forge at night, so long as I clean up when I'm finished. It's filthy work. Hard work. And a small forge for shaping horseshoes doesn't come close to the way I worked before. But I've managed to turn out a few acceptable pieces and even some things I can sell to buy food for us." She paused before a skinny little house on the corner of two narrow roads. It was tiny, and the thatched roof looked slumped and in dire need of repair.

Someone should fix that. But who?

Hmm.

Mari opened the door and set her little girl back on her feet. The child immediately took off inside with another delighted squeal, leaving us standing on the front steps. "She's ... Gods, I'm sorry. She's wild as a buck, that one."

I laughed and sat the bag of potatoes down at my feet. "It's fine. Really, don't worry about it."

"Right, well, I suppose to a man who wrangles dragons, it mustn't seem so bad." Mari flicked me a tentative smile. "Do you like potato stew, Mr. Porter?"

My pulse quickened and skipped. I barely managed a panicked, "Yes!"

Her smile widened beautifully, spreading over her features and dimpling her cheeks the same way it had her daughter's.

My throat constricted and all of a sudden, the collar of my uniform and cloak felt unbearably tight. Gods and Fates. Was she really inviting me to stay for dinner? I mean, that's what it sounded like, right? I tried not to hope.

"Good," she hedged a bit closer, nibbling on the inside of her cheek as she ran her fingers experimentally over my polished breastplate, almost as though she were inspecting the quality. Then her eyes went wide and she quickly backed away and avoided my gaze. "You should come in and join us, then. For dinner, I mean. What do you say, dragonrider?"

I forced myself to take in a few deep breaths and cleared my throat. "Yes. I ... I would be honored, Miss Mari."

FLEDGLING

The Dragonrider Chronicles Book One

CHAPTER ONE

I had never seen my father before my twelfth birthday. Not even once. Up until then, my mother had raised me all by herself in the royal city of Halfax. We lived like all the other gray elves in Maldobar—separated from the rest of society in the heavily guarded wartime ghettos. We had to follow a strict set of rules about where we could go, what we could do, when we got food, and what we could own. If you broke any of the rules, it was an immediate sentence to the prison camps, which I always heard was a fate worse than death. We were supposed to be grateful. After all, we were war refugees. Maldobar didn't have to take us in, much less provide us somewhere to live. This was their act of charity toward us.

Our house was not much more than a tiny shack made of old recycled wood, and it only had one room. You'd expect a place like that to smell terrible, but my mother was a genius when it came to making anywhere feel like home. She could grow absolutely anything, and that was how she made our living. She grew vegetables, flowers, tiny fruit trees, and strange vines that climbed all over the walls and windows. It made the inside of our house feel like a jungle, and it smelled earthy like fresh soil and the fragrance of flowers. We couldn't legally sell anything she grew since gray elves weren't allowed to have any money, but we could still trade. So early in the mornings, my mother packed a sack full of peppers, fruit, vegetables, and anything else ready for harvest, and sent me out to the shops to trade for things we needed.

It was a lot harder than it sounds. Not the trading itself, that part was easy, but I had to be very sneaky about it. I was always on the watch for city guards or any of the common folk that might notice me. Gray elf children were rare, even in the ghettos. Any elf living in the kingdom of Maldobar as a refugee was absolutely not allowed to have children. It was forbidden. Having children was a great way to get thrown into a prison camp, or worse.

But I didn't just have to worry about that. It was bad enough to be a gray elf kid, hiding until you were old enough to be overlooked. But I was a halfbreed. My father was a human from Maldobar. So instead of looking at me with anger, everyone looked at me like I was a cockroach. The humans didn't like me touching their stuff because I was mixed with the filthy, wild blood of a gray elf. If they hadn't liked my mother's produce so much, they probably would have turned me in to the guards. The gray elves didn't like me, either. But there was a very strict code amongst them: you didn't betray your own kind no matter what. So they ignored me rather than ratting me out to the city guards.

I really didn't fit anywhere, except with my mother. She loved me unconditionally. She was the most beautiful person in the world. Her hair was long and silvery white, and her eyes were like stars. All gray elves had eyes like that. When she smiled at me, her eyes would shine like gemstones in the light, as white and pale as diamonds with faint flecks of blue, yellow, and green in them.

When she died, I had just turned twelve. I got the feeling right away that no one really knew what to do with me. I didn't fit into anyone's plans. If I were a pure-blooded elf, they would have taken me straight to a prison camp. If I were a human, someone would have adopted me. I wasn't either, and yet I was both at the same time. I think the guards were just baffled that my mother had done such a good job of hiding me for so long, or that she'd somehow managed to have an affair with a human man.

Ulric Broadfeather was the only one who would take me in, and I'm pretty sure he only did it because my mother had left a letter behind naming him as my biological father. If it weren't for the public shame of disowning a child, he probably would have just let me go to a prison camp anyway.

From the very beginning, my father was the most frightening man I had ever known. He was hugely tall, like a knight, and stronger than anyone else I had ever seen. Once, I saw him pick up and pull the family wagon while it was loaded with bags of grain all by himself. He could have crushed my neck with one hand if he wanted to. His hair was jet-black like mine, except it was cut short. My mom always insisted I wear my hair long, like gray elves traditionally did. I also had his cold blue eyes that were the same color as glacier water. There definitely wasn't any doubt he was my father. I looked too much like him for anyone to deny it.

I wish I could say that he welcomed me with open arms into his home; eager to make up for lost time he hadn't gotten to spend with me. But he already had a family, living on the outskirts of a small city called Mithangol, and he wasn't interested in adding me to it. I was an unwanted guest right away.

He had a human wife named Serah who made it perfectly clear she didn't want me in her house. Serah absolutely hated me. She glared whenever she looked at me, accused me of being responsible for anything that went wrong, and refused to let me sleep in her house because I gave her a "bad feeling."

So I slept on a cot in the loftroom of Ulric's workshop, instead. As bad as it sounds, I actually preferred it. It was quiet there, and even though it was cold in the winter, I liked the smell of the old hay and the leather that was stored up there.

Ulric also had another son, Roland, who was four years older than me. Roland chose to ignore my existence completely. I got the feeling that he was in survival mode, trying to be as aloof and uninvolved with the family as he possibly could until he was old enough to move out. I couldn't really blame him for that. Like me, he favored our father. He was really tall, muscular, and had the same ice-blue eyes that looked like they belonged to a powerful bird of prey. I was a little afraid of him, even though he never said more than two words to me at a time. I could sense a lot of anger coming from him, and I was always paranoid I'd be standing too close when he finally snapped.

Ulric had two more children, a pair of twin daughters named Emry and Lin. They were six years younger than me, but they were meaner than a pair of hungry jackals. Every day, they tried to get me in as much trouble as possible. Of course, Serah believed every word they said. They would break things, let the chickens and goats out, or steal jewelry from their mother's room. Once, Emry got ahold of the sewing scissors and chopped up Lin's hair. When Serah found out, Emry blamed it all on me and told her I had done it. Serah believed it, and I got a beating from Ulric as soon as he came in the house. Inventing new ways to get me into trouble was their favorite pastime, and there was nothing I could do about it. They were sneaky and smart, a lot smarter than me I guess, because they never got caught.

The only good thing about living with my father was watching him work. Ulric was a tackmaster—he made saddles for the dragonriders from Blybrig Academy. But he didn't just make saddles; he made the very best saddles in Maldobar. I watched him through the slats and gaps in the floor of the loft room, shaping leather and stitching intricate pieces together. He did it all by hand, and it took him several weeks to craft one saddle. But when it was finished, each one was the most beautiful thing I'd ever seen. It made me envy him, even if he probably wished I had never been born.

That's why I almost keeled over when Ulric growled my name, calling me down from my room into his shop. He'd been working for two weeks solid on a new saddle, one more beautiful than ever, and it was finally finished.

"Wrap it up," he barked at me in his gruff, gravely tone, and threw a few old quilts at me.

I was stunned. Ulric had never asked me to do anything before, especially nothing to do with his work. This was my chance, I thought. If I could be useful, maybe he wouldn't hate me so much. He might even teach me to make saddles someday.

Ulric left me alone in his shop, and I walked over to the saddle that was set up on one of the big sawhorses. I ran my fingers over the freshly oiled leather. It was as red as blood, engraved with intricate designs and images of mountains and vines. All the buckles were made of silver-plated iron. I couldn't even imagine what it would look like when the dragon it had been made for would finally put it on. A powerful beast, bound for the skies with a snarl and a flash of fire. It made my skin prickle and every hair stand on end.

I was small for my age. Ulric's stature apparently hadn't been passed on to me. To make matters worse, I was so skinny that I pretty much looked like a scarecrow. Emry and Lin like to call me "stick boy" because they knew it bothered me. If I were as big as Roland, no one would have tried to push me around.

It took all my strength to wrap the saddle up in the quilts so it wouldn't get scratched or damaged, and then lug it outside. The weight of it made my arms and lungs ache. I could feel myself wobble dangerously if I leaned too far in any direction. I didn't want to imagine what Ulric would do to me if I dropped this saddle.

The knights who rode on dragons just about never came to pick up their saddles personally. Most of them came from rich, powerful noble families, and had plenty of servants to do those kinds of errands for them. So when I saw Ulric standing outside talking to a man in formal battle armor with a sweeping cape of royal blue brushing at his heels, I stopped dead in my tracks. The saddle weighed more than I did, and I almost dropped it in surprise.

It was a muggy, overcast day. The clouds were so low and thick you couldn't see the mountains that hunched over our small city. Even so, the knight's armor still managed to gleam like liquid silver. He had his helmet under one arm, the white-feathered crest on it tipped in black, and the king's eagle engraved upon his breastplate.

They both turned to look at me as I stood there, my arms shaking under the weight of the saddle, staring at the dragonrider. Ulric scowled darkly, and stomped over to take it from me. He slung it over his shoulder like it weighed nothing at all, growling curses under his breath at me as he went to tie it down to the knight's horse.

The knight, however, was still staring right at me. He gave me a strange look, narrowing his eyes some and tilting his head to the side slightly like he was sizing me up. It made me blush from head to toe, the tips of my pointed ears burning like torches under my long hair. This was a warrior who had probably fought against gray elves for years, and I knew what I looked like.

He curled a finger at me, calling me toward him. It made me cringe as I obeyed. I hedged toward him, my shoulders hunched up because I half-expected him to hit me just out of pure resentment for what I was. But he didn't.

When I got close enough, he grabbed my chin in one of his gloved hands, cranking my head around so I had to look up at him. I was shaking all over, wondering if this was it for me. Maybe he'd crush my head like a grape in his hand. Or maybe he'd throttle me to death. Either way, I was pretty sure Ulric wouldn't go out of his way to save me. He might have even thanked the knight afterwards for saving him the trouble.

"What's your name, boy?" the knight asked. His voice was deep, but not angry or resentful. He was turning my head this way and that, pulling back my hair to see my pointed ears, and looking me over like he was inspecting livestock.

"J-Jaevid," I told him through chattering teeth.

He frowned, looking back into my eyes before he finally let me go. His own eyes seemed dead to me. Dead—like someone who had seen many years in battle and knew what it meant to kill without mercy.

"How old are you?" he asked again.

"Fifteen, sir." I took a few steps back away from him. If he came after me suddenly, at least I had some hope of outrunning him. I was small, but I was fast.

Ulric was finished tying the saddle down, and came over with a growl meant to shoo me away. I took the hint and retreated back into the workshop, up to my loft room where I had a wooden cot piled with old, holey quilts. I went to the small window along the far wall. It was a good place to peek at them through the cracks in the boards that had been nailed over it. I could hear them talking, and it made my heart jump into my throat.

"You didn't tell me you had a halfbreed son," the knight chuckled, like it was a bad joke. "Looks just like a half-starved, miniature version of you, except for the ears."

Ulric just shook his head and kept growling rumbling words, glaring at the ground. "Serah wants him gone," I heard him say.

"Can't blame her for that." The knight seemed to sympathize. "You thinking of taking him on as an apprentice?"

Ulric just snorted like it was a ridiculous idea.

"Ah, my mistake then. I figured since your older boy had chosen to join the infantry you'd pass your skill set onto someone else in your family. I doubt your girls would be interested." The knight rambled on, beginning to stroll back to where his horse was waiting. The new saddle was bundled up and ready for transport. "A shame he's such a small, sickly-looking thing."

That stung me. Yes, I was small for my age. But I hadn't thought I looked sickly. It made me angry at myself, and at my inability to grow even a few inches taller. What a difference even two inches and a few pounds of muscle would have made.

"Where's his dragon?" a whispering voice suddenly asked from right beside me.

It scared me out of my wits, making me scramble away. I was half-afraid it was one of my sisters. But it wasn't.

Katalina Crookin was probably the only friend I had in the world. Her father was a very good blacksmith who worked with Ulric sometimes, helping him craft unique pieces that required a more skilled metalworker. They only lived about a mile away, so Katty and I had found each other inevitably. She was small and skinny, like I was, with a head full of wild gold curls. She had big dark blue eyes, and just about every inch of her face was covered in freckles. The other kids in town teased her and called her ugly. I knew it must have hurt her feelings, but she never let it show. And when the other kids would come after me, trying to cut my hair or throw rocks at me, she was always there to defend me ... and no one could throw a rock harder or more accurately than Katty. She had blacksmith's hands.

I shook my head at her, moving back to the window to peek outside again. The knight was getting on his horse, dropping a purse of coins into Ulric's hand before he rode out of sight.

"I don't know. I don't think he brought it," I whispered back. Neither of us had ever seen a dragon before.

Katty puffed a sigh of disappointment while shaking her head. It made her gold curls swish back and forth. "I saw him coming up the road. I knew he had to be a dragonrider. Normal soldiers don't wear armor like *that*," she told me. "Can you come over today?"

I didn't know. Normally, I could've easily slipped away to visit the Crookins without Ulric or Serah noticing I was gone because usually they didn't care where I was. But Ulric had actually asked me to do something for him today. Not to mention, he and the knight had been discussing my future—or lack thereof. I wasn't so sure I could get away with leaving without getting caught.

Katty was watching me waffle between my desire to go to her house, and the inevitable beating I would get if Ulric ever caught me over there. She smiled. "Momma's making sweetbread," she baited me. "With wild honey."

That decided it for me. I grinned back at her, nodding because we both knew what goodies were sure to go along with sweetbread. Thoughts of whipped butter with cinnamon and sugar, and warm milk with a hint of honey, were already swimming happily through my brain as we climbed down from my loft room. We darted out the back of Ulric's shop before anyone noticed, and took the narrow footpath we'd made ourselves through the prickly briars. It was our secret path, so no one would see us.

The Crookin's house was not as big as ours, but it felt more like a home instead of the prison I lived in. Smoke came out of the chimney in the house, and out of the stack for the bellows in Mr. Crookin's forge. Mr. Crookin didn't really like me. That's not to say he hated me as much as Serah did, but he didn't like me coming around his house too often. He hadn't minded it so much when I was younger, but now that I was fifteen, I could tell he was on the verge of telling me not to come back anymore. He didn't talk much, and he had a face that was mostly hidden behind a thick, wiry beard. He wore his long smithing apron every day, and his face and arms were almost always smeared with soot.

Mrs. Crookin, on the other hand, was one of the few people who didn't make me feel unwanted. She smiled at me when we came inside, wiping her hands on her apron before she pulled me in immediately to kiss my forehead and ruffle my hair. She always hugged me until I couldn't breathe and asked me if I was getting enough to eat.

"What a good boy," she said, patting my cheeks until it stung a little. "But still so skinny. Doesn't Serah feed you at all? Sit down, Jae. I'm making your favorite."

Katty plopped down in a chair across from me at their kitchen table, grinning as she slid a plate and spoon in my direction. "There was a dragonrider at his house today, Momma." Her eyes were still sparkling with excitement about it.

"Yeah, but he didn't bring his dragon." I added, sighing and twirling the spoon through my fingers.

Mrs. Crookin brought over a platter of steaming hot sweetbread, fresh out of the oven. The smell made me dizzy with hunger, and it was hard to sit and wait while she put out jams, that delicious cinnamon butter, and mugs of warm milk for us on the table. "Not surprising, is it dear? It's nearly springtime."

I knew what she meant. Every spring, Ulric packed up his tools and materials onto a wagon and left for Blybrig Academy. The new riders started their training just as the weather was getting hot, and Ulric had to take molds and build brand new saddles for them. It was when he made most of his money, but it also meant that he'd be gone for a while. He was always completely exhausted when he came back. In a month, the snows would melt in the Stonegap Pass, and Ulric would start packing his tools again. If any other knights wanted a saddle from him, they'd have to get it before he left, or wait until after spring.

"I wish Papa would let me go with him," Katty whined while she was smearing a spoonful of jam onto a large piece of bread. "It's not fair. Other apprentices get to go."

"Soon, dear." Mrs. Crookin smiled fondly at her daughter. They had the same gold colored hair, but Mrs. Crookin's was flecked with silver. She was a much older woman than my stepmother.

Katty was eager to go to Blybrig, not that I could blame her. She wanted to see dragons just like I did. Her father had been teaching her his craft for a long time, and she was already strong enough to do most of the little tedious jobs for him, even if she was small and fragile looking. Mr. Crookin went to Blybrig for spring training, just like Ulric. But he went to make armor, not saddles.

"You'll have to tell me what they look like," I told her. I wasn't able to keep myself from sounding sad about it. When she started working with her father full time, I wasn't sure where that would leave me. I'd be on the brink of adulthood with no idea where I should go, or what I should do. I wouldn't have a skill to sell, or even a place to live.

Katty smiled at me hopefully from across the table, leaning forward and grabbing my hand at the wrist. "You'll see them, too, Jae. Maybe Papa would let you be his apprentice with me."

Mrs. Crookin smiled at us, but I could see it in her eyes; she didn't think her husband would ever allow that. They were all right with me coming to visit, and with me being friends with their daughter, but they had to draw the line somewhere. I was still a halfbreed.

I didn't let Katty see how that hurt me. It wasn't their fault, really. And it wasn't my place to try to weasel my way into their family business like that. "Nah." I shrugged and gave her as confident a grin as I could muster. "I'm going to the coast. I want to work on one of the ships going out of the harbor. I'll get to see the ocean, and eat fish every night."

Katty looked deflated. I guess she'd wanted us to work together. Or, she'd at least hoped I would want the same thing as her. "You'll smell like a fish, after all that," she grumbled, wrinkling her nose.

We ate until there were only a few scraps of the bread left, and Mrs. Crookin wrapped those up for me to take. It was dark outside when I started for home. Katty always walked with me as far as the property line, and she had a blanket wrapped around her so that only her face and some of her curls peeked out.

"Jae," she started. I could tell by the tone of her voice she was about to ask me something serious. "Do you really want to go to the coast?"

I've never been a very good liar. When it came to Katty, well, she could smell deception on me like a hound. I couldn't lie to her if I wanted to. I quirked my mouth while I thought about the ocean, about ships, and about eating fish.

"Not really," I confessed.

"We'd never see each other if you left." She reached a hand out from under her blanket to grasp mine, squeezing my fingers. "After Papa retires and I take over the business, I'll make you an apprentice myself. Then we can work together and no one will be able to say anything about it."

I tried to smile for her. I tried to show her some optimism. But we'd be in our twenties before her father let her take on any authority in his smithing business, and even then, I wasn't sure blacksmithing was my calling. It required physical strength, which I clearly didn't have.

"Thanks, Katty." I squeezed her hand back.

We talked about dragons and knights all the way to the property line. Then I gave her a hug, and she kissed my cheek like her mom did, and we parted ways. I walked a few feet into the darkness before I stopped and looked back, watching her disappear into the gloom and thorny shrubs. She was the best friend I had—my only friend really, and sooner or later, she'd have to leave me behind. She'd outgrow me. She'd get tired of having to stick up for me all the time.

With the bundle of leftover bread still under my arm, I walked back to my room in the loft. Ulric's shop was quiet and dark, like it always was once he'd finished for the day. He was probably already inside, having dinner with his real family, and talking about how soon he could get rid of me. Roland was probably just sitting there at the table, glaring down into his plate without a word. The twins were probably throwing food at each other like savages. I didn't expect any of them to even notice I was gone.

But I was wrong.

2

CHAPTER TWO

Ulric was waiting for me in the dark. I didn't see him until I had already shut the shop door and turned around to go up the rickety ladder to the loft. I smacked right into him, bouncing off his chest like a rubber ball, and landing squarely on my rump at his feet. I dropped the package of bread scraps, and they scattered out all over the ground.

"Where have you been?" Ulric's voice boomed in the dark like thunder.

Before I could even think about answering, much less running, he had me by the hair. He yanked me to my feet and pushed me up against the wall, kicking the scraps of bread across the floor all the while.

"Stealing from the neighbors?" He reared back a hand to smack me across the face so hard it felt like my eyeballs might pop out of their sockets. "Or squeezing on their daughter?"

I hadn't been stealing or squeezing, but I knew better than to try to tell him that. My cheek was burning like it was on fire when he smacked me again on the other side of my face even harder. As much as I tried not to cry, I couldn't keep my eyes from watering up. I was terrified of him already, and now I was afraid he might just solve his own problem and kill me. No one would ask questions about where I had gone, except for maybe Katty and her mother.

"If I ever catch you running off this property again, I'll beat your skull inside out," he promised, yanking me away from the wall and flinging me toward the ladder. I hit it before I could catch myself. My head cracked off the edge of the ladder, making me see bright spots of light in my vision.

"Get up there," he snarled at my back. It made a cold pang of fear shoot through me like a lightning bolt. "And you better have yourself down here ready to work as soon as the sun is up tomorrow. Understood?"

I scrambled up the ladder with my ears ringing and my vision swerving. I didn't stop to ask any questions. I didn't even realize what he'd said until I was curled up underneath my cot, shaking with fear, and anticipating hearing Ulric scaling the ladder to come after me. Instead, I heard the shop door slam, lock, and the crunch of his footsteps storming back toward the house.

I was bewildered. It wasn't the first time Ulric had come after me swinging, but he'd caught me completely off guard this time. My heart was still drumming in my ears when I finally dared to crawl out from under my bed. I touched my cheeks, wincing at how they still stung. I probably had handprints on both sides of my face.

Ulric had never wanted me anywhere near his work until today. Now he was ordering me to help him? I couldn't even begin to guess why, and it made my head spin with the possibilities and hopes that seemed too stupid to say out loud. I wanted to believe that maybe, just maybe, he was going to let me be his apprentice. If he taught me his trade—heck, if he taught me anything at all—I was prepared to learn as much as I could. I needed this if I was ever going to get out from under his roof.

I didn't sleep at all. I lay awake until the sun started to rise, thinking about what I'd be in for the next day, and whether or not I would able to do whatever Ulric asked of me. Being willing was one thing, but being physically capable was another. My heart could be in it all day long, but I couldn't will myself into greater strength.

When I heard Ulric unlocking his shop, I was on my feet and in my shoes, waiting for him down the ladder before he could even swing the door open. He glared down at me like he'd found a dead mouse in his shoe, brushing past me without a word.

I stood awkwardly by the door with my hands clenched into fists, and my feet ready to run in case he turned on me again. He started into a routine I knew all too well. I'd seen him pack up his tools before, and it made my stomach twist into those painful, hopeful knots all over again.

"Sweep out the mess you made," he mumbled with his back to me. "Then hitch up the wagon, and bring it around."

"Yes, sir," I answered quickly, and went to get the broom. I swept away the dried-up leftovers of Mrs. Crookin's bread that were still scattered on the floor. I swept the whole shop out, working so quickly that it had me sweating before I went outside into the cold morning air.

The fog was thick and heavy, making the steep countryside look ominous and grim as I went to the barn and brought out the old draft horse Ulric used to pull his wagon. The giant horse could've kicked my head off if he'd had the mind to, but the sad old thing didn't act like he had enough energy to trot, much less kick anyone. I hitched him to the small cart Ulric used every spring to carry his tools and materials to Blybrig.

When I led the horse and wagon around to the workshop, Ulric was already stacking crates outside to load onto it. He commanded me to help him, and I tried my best. My arms weren't strong enough to lift the heavy wooden crates full of tools, but I could carry the sawhorses, and I helped pile the rolls of uncut leather onto the wagon. We covered everything with blankets to offer some protection from the elements, and tied ropes tautly over the load to keep anything from falling out during the trip.

By that time, my clothes and hair were absolutely drenched with sweat. I stood back, not looking for any gratitude from my father, but hoping for at least some acknowledgement that I'd done a good job. He didn't even look at me on his way to climb up into the driving seat of the wagon, grumbling under his breath the whole way.

Serah came out of the house carrying a big bag I knew would be packed with plenty of food and changes of clothes to last him the journey. I knew better than to think there'd be anything for me in that bag. She handed it up to him, and the two just exchanged a stiff, stern-faced stare before she backed away and crossed her arms. Her cold eyes flicked to me, her face looking sharper and angrier than usual. Sometimes I got the feeling she blamed me for my own existence, or that she was jealous of any attention Ulric gave me that didn't involve punishing me for something.

"Just going to stand there like an idiot?" Ulric barked at me suddenly.

My mouth opened, and no sound came out. I didn't know what to say, or what he expected me to do.

He jerked his head, gesturing to the driver's seat beside him.

My heart jumped. I still couldn't move, much less speak. I was terrified of making the mistake of assuming he actually wanted me to go with him. I took a few steps, and Serah's venomous glare stopped me dead in my tracks.

"Get over here, you dumb kid," Ulric growled in a dangerous tone. "You're wasting daylight."

It was a leap of faith, to think I was invited on this trip. But I took it. I walked quickly past Serah with my head bowed low, avoiding meeting her eyes, and climbed up to sit on the driver's seat beside my father. He didn't wait until I was settled or even balanced to snap the reins. The wagon lurched into motion, and I almost fell over the seat.

We took off at as fast a trot as the old horse could manage, leaving Serah and the house in a swirling cloud of dust behind us. It started to sink in, then. I was going to Blybrig Academy. I was going to learn to make dragon saddles. Either that, or Ulric was going to drop me off at a prison camp on the way there.

My father waited until we were out of sight of the house to pull a wad of chewing tobacco from his pocket and cram it into his mouth. Serah hated it when he chewed that stuff, and even more when he spit it into her gardens. He didn't say a word to me as we rattled down the road, and I couldn't think of a good reason to try to talk to him, either.

When we passed the Crookin's house, I leaned to look up the twisting dirt path that led to their house. I craned my neck, hoping to catch a glimpse of Katty helping her mother hang laundry, or feeding their chickens, so I could wave goodbye to her. She'd know just as soon as she saw me sitting in the wagon with my father that I was going to Blybrig. She'd be so happy, knowing we'd see each other there eventually. But I didn't see her or her mother, and it made me slump back into my seat with disappointment. Maybe she'd figure it out, or maybe I could write her a letter once I got to Blybrig.

It took a long, exhausting, miserable week to get from Mithangol to Blybrig Academy. The only thing worse than being at home with my father was being alone with him. We didn't talk. He didn't say anything to me at all. There was always tension in the air, and it made it hard for me to feel safe. I was afraid to turn my back to him while we were out here, alone in the wild.

The road wound away from our little city, twisting through the high cliffs, and carving a steep path upward through the Stonegap Mountains. The higher we went, the thinner the air got. It got dryer, too, and made my throat feel raw. My lips were chapped and peeling, but Ulric wouldn't let me have any more than the small ration of water he'd planned out for us every day.

At night, we ate a little bit of dinner that consisted of flatbread and some dried meat, and then went straight to bed. Ulric had a bedroll, and he slept by the fire on the ground. I curled up with a blanket on the seat of the wagon, looking up at the stars in the cold night sky. Some nights, it was too cold to sleep at all, and I sat up by the fire on the ground, my teeth chattering and my toes numb, until morning.

That's when I thought about my mom. When I was alone like that at night, when it was quiet, I always thought about her. I took out the necklace she'd given me when I was little. I kept it hidden under my tunic. I didn't want anyone to see it, and no one except for Katty even knew that I had it. It was carved from white bone, engraved with designs and words in elven that I didn't understand. It hung around my neck on an old leather cord, exactly where she'd put it the day she gave it to me. I rubbed it with my fingers while I remembered her. The memories I had of her voice, her face, and her smell were all beginning to fade. I was afraid that eventually I'd forget her completely.

I felt like I'd been dragged behind the wagon, rather than riding in it, all week when we finally reached Blybrig. I was tired, sore, hungry, and thirsty. Even Ulric was beginning to look pretty road-weary and miserable. We didn't have much left in the way of supplies, and I was beginning to worry we might run out before we got to the academy.

Then all of a sudden, none of that mattered. As we crested one final, steep rise in the road through Stonegap Pass, I got my first look down into the valley hidden below.

They called it the Devil's Cup because the land in the valley was so arid and dry. It was a small desert nestled into a crescent of mountains, cut off from the rest of the world except for Stonegap Pass—unless you could fly. The only small portion of the valley that wasn't guarded by white-peaked mountains bordered the coastline and looked out to nothing but blue ocean. I could see the water, sparkling in the distance, and stretching out across the horizon beyond.

I saw it all, spread out before me so suddenly that it took my breath away. I couldn't help but stand up to get a better look, able to see exactly how the road wound down the mountainside into the valley. It twisted across the parched earth, past thorny shrubs and cacti, until it stopped before the only standing structure in the whole valley: Blybrig Academy.

Then I saw them. What I'd mistaken for a flock of birds circling far overhead weren't birds at all. The nearer they came, the more aware I became of their size. They were huge, bigger than any animal I'd ever seen, with powerful wings stretched to the morning sun. Dragons were everywhere I looked, flying in V-shaped formations overhead in groups of two or more. The light danced off the gleaming armor of the knights riding on their backs. They soared like eagles, majestic and graceful, riding the wind that blew in from the ocean. They were perched on the high circular ramparts that enclosed the academy complex, and even from a distance, I could hear their bellowing calls.

We rattled down the road that led up to the only gate in and out of Blybrig. The walls were enormous, at least five stories tall, and made of stacked gray stones that looked like they had been mined right out of the mountains surrounding the valley. The enormous iron gates stood wide open, letting us into the world of the dragonriders—a place only a select few actually got to see.

As I understood it, its location was secret. Only dragonriders and the craftsmen who worked for them actually knew where this place was. That had seemed ridiculous to me before, but now that I'd been through that grueling, narrow, and dangerous path that was the only way through the mountains, I understood. If you didn't already know where this place was, odds were you weren't going to find it just wandering around in the mountains.

Ulric drove the wagon through the gate and into the complex, passing students and knights on the way. All the buildings seemed to be set up around one central, massive circular structure. It had a covered domed roof, and the entire thing looked like one large cave carved right out of the rock.

"The breaking dome," Ulric explained when he saw me staring at it. I was surprised he'd actually cared enough about my interest to say anything at all, but maybe this was part of the job. I needed to know where everything was so I could run errands for him.

"What's it for?" I dared to try my luck to see how much he was willing to tell me.

Ulric just shrugged and made a grunting sound at first, leaning to spit some of his tobacco juice onto the ground. He'd been chewing it nearly nonstop since we'd left home. "Training."

I stared at the massive structure as we passed it. It was hard not to feel intimidated by it. It looked like a giant stone turtle shell, with a rounded opening like a gaping maw. As our wagon rolled by, I was almost certain I heard it growl.

Ulric pointed out the buildings the further we went into the complex. There were two dormitories, one meant for instructors and high-ranking riders, and another for students. They both looked the same on the outside, the same height and shape, with narrow windows. There was a separate place for academics, and a gymnasium for combat training.

One very long, especially strange-looking building was set at the back, directly behind the central dome. It looked like a dollhouse with one wall missing so that you could see all the rooms inside it. Extending from each of the ten levels were platforms made from iron beams laid out like latticework. I watched the dragons come in close to the building, flaring their wings to slow their speed, and stretching out their strong back legs to grip the platform with curled talons as they landed. It was like a stable for dragons, with each room being a separate stall for a dragon to nest in. Ulric said they called it the Roost.

We stopped at last outside of one of the two armory houses. One was set up especially for blacksmiths, with already established forges and plenty of room for the smiths to work fashioning and repairing armor. Its tall chimneys belched black smoke into the air, and I could smell the familiar scent of scorched metal. It reminded me of Katty's house.

As soon as we found our workstation in the armory house meant for tackmasters, Ulric backed the wagon up to it, and we started to unload all the crates and rolls of leather. He put me to work opening the crates with a pry bar, telling me to set out his tools while he went to stable the horse.

Even here, in the desert valley of Devil's Cup, it was still cool this early in the spring. But the air was so dry, and I was so tired already, it didn't take me ten minutes to be drenched with sweat again. I tied my hair back to get it away from my face, not thinking about it until I heard someone say the word *"halfbreed."*

Then I remembered. Tying my hair back like that exposed my pointed ears. They weren't elongated and slender like a full-blooded Gray elf's would have been, but their subtle points were definitely noticeable. And people were definitely beginning to notice.

There was a group of four older boys standing just outside Ulric's workstation, and they were staring right at me. I didn't know any of them, but I could tell they were new students right away. They weren't wearing uniforms or armor yet, and they all looked seventeen. Naturally, they were all a good foot taller than

I was, and I knew they were laughing at me even without looking up to make sure.

I tried to ignore them. Nothing good would happen if I said anything back, and I didn't have much of an ego left to defend anyway. They could say what they wanted; I'd come here to work.

I was stacking the empty crates outside our workstation, making room for dragons to be brought inside like Ulric had told me to, when I felt someone pull my hair. Someone grabbed my ponytail, and yanked it hard enough to make me fall backward. The empty crate landed squarely on my chest.

It knocked the breath right out of me, and I laid there for a few seconds looking up into the sky and the glare of the sun in a daze. I thought maybe I'd imagined it. Maybe I'd just tripped. But then a menacing face appeared over me. One of the guys who had been laughing at me earlier was leaning over, smirking and looking back to his friends for approval. For some reason bullies always needed validation that they were doing a good job. Or at least, it seemed that way to me.

"What are you doing here, scum?" He sneered down at me. "We don't like traitors, you know." I watched him disappear, and then a few seconds later, there was a boot in my face. He put the heel of his shoe on my forehead and started to grind it back and forth.

I hadn't even thought about fighting back yet. I was just trying to figure out how to get the boot off my face and the crate off my chest. But suddenly both were gone, and I heard the group of older boys cursing and yelling.

Rolling over to cough and blink the dirt out of my eyes, I lifted my head to see a much larger, fully armored man holding the boy who'd been using me as his doormat by the ear. The knight was pinching the boy's ear in his gauntlet-covered hand, making him scream in pain, before finally letting him go. Something about the knight was familiar. I couldn't figure out what it was until he was standing over me, grabbing me by the arm and hauling me back to my feet.

"You attract a lot of attention, boy." The knight's voice was immediately familiar. It was the same one who had come to pick up his saddle from our house.

I opened my mouth to say something, and immediately forgot what it was. I hadn't expected anyone to come to my rescue, least of all a knight. I remembered to at least be grateful. "Thank you, sir."

He made an annoyed sound as he removed his white-crested helmet. Now I was certain it was the same knight from before. He looked down at me with his sea green eyes narrowed and scrutinizing. His dark hair was cut very short and beginning to turn gray around his temples. Even though his skin was weathered, there was still something wild and unpredictable in his eyes, which made it hard to place his age. Still, I couldn't imagine him being any older than Ulric.

"You should keep a low profile," he warned me. "Unless you intend on growing a spine in the near future."

Couldn't he see me? Sure, standing up to bullies and the other kids who gave me a hard time sounded good in theory, but I knew better. I had no chance of ever winning a fight like that. Better to let them kick me around some, use me as a doormat, and get away with no broken bones, than get my arms cracked off just to prove a point.

"Save it, Sile. The kid's a coward. Better that way. He'll live longer if he keeps his mouth shut," Ulric's voice growled, surprising me as he strolled up behind us. Immediately, I went back to work moving crates.

The knight frowned at me, looking disappointed, and I tried not to notice. It made an urgent feeling twist in the pit of my stomach, so I turned my back to him while I worked and tried not to listen to anything else they said.

"Who is that?" I asked when the knight finally left to go back about his business.

Ulric was setting up sawhorses, and scowling at all the work I'd done like none of it was up to his standard. But I never saw him fix anything. He made another annoyed grunting sound in response to my question. "Sile Derrick," he answered, and spat another mouthful of putrid tobacco juice on the ground. "Stay away from him. He should mind his own business, instead of telling me how to mind mine."

We got the workshop ready just after sundown. It took a long time for me to drag out base molds and fill them with packed wax shavings from huge sacks I had to drag out of a storeroom. My arms were sore, and my stomach was growling so loudly I knew everyone could hear it. I'd never been so tired in all my life, but when Ulric glanced at me, I tried to look as composed and ready to work as I'd ever been.

"We start at dawn," he told me, finally spitting out the wad of tobacco he'd been gnawing on into a trash barrel. "You sleep in here, and mind our stuff. Have the molds ready when I get here."

Ulric left me standing in the workshop, wondering what I was supposed to eat or where I could sleep, as he disappeared into the complex. I was immediately afraid. After the sun had set, the air had gotten very cold, and the wind howled through the valley making an eerie, screaming sound.

I couldn't find anything to eat, but there were a few good swallows of water left in one of the canteens we'd used on our journey here. I found Ulric's sleeping pallet and unrolled it in a corner of the shop behind a few stacked up crates of materials where no one would be able to see me. I didn't want to run the risk of those older boys finding me again.

Hours passed. It was bitter cold. Even under the two quilts I had, I was still freezing. More than anything, though, I was starving. I hadn't had a good meal since Mrs. Crookin's bread, and thoughts of those wasted crumbs were making my stomach tie up in knots. It hurt so much it put tears in my eyes. I didn't know how I was going to find the strength to work the next day if I didn't get something to eat before then.

Sometime after midnight, I just couldn't take it anymore. I got to my feet in pitch black, and snuck out of the workshop. The complex was quiet in the dead of night. Almost all the students and riders were asleep, and their dragons were snug in the Roost. Only a few were still out flying low patrol patterns around the walls. I couldn't see them, but I could hear the hum of the wind off their wings and long scaled tails whenever they swooped in close.

I was looking for anything edible I could get my hands on without being caught. I walked past the two armories, spotting the smoldering fires from the forge that still glowed. I wondered if I could sneak in there to sleep. At least it would be warmer closer to the forge.

On my way past the breaking dome, my steps got slower, until finally I was standing before the gaping doorway, staring into it with my skin shivering. It felt deep and monstrously dark in there, as though it were the bottomless abyss of some dark cave.

That's when I heard it. Before, I thought I was only imagining that building growling at me. This time I was sure.

A deep, rumbling growl echoed from within, and I tripped over my feet backing away from it. I looked back over my shoulder. There was no one else there. No one was watching, or playing some kind of trick on me. But I didn't feel like I was alone. There was definitely something in that deep, dark cavern of a building, and it felt like it was calling out to me.

CHAPTER THREE

I knew I should have just gone back to the workstation and tried sleeping again. Ulric might remember to bring me something to eat in the morning, if I was lucky. After all, nothing good could possibly come from nosing around in the secret places of the academy. Going into the breaking dome alone so late at night was a terrible idea. Probably the worst idea I'd had yet.

I had almost talked myself out of it. I was scared of what I'd find in there, or worse, of getting caught red-handed by my father. Whenever I got caught somewhere I wasn't supposed to be, people tended to suspect the worst right away. I'd probably get accused of being a traitor again, or a spy, or something ridiculous like that. If the Gray elves were going to try to spy on Blybrig, I was pretty sure I'd be the last person in the world they'd ever want to send to do it. Too bad no one else was ever going to agree with me about that. This couldn't end any way but bad for me.

But I just couldn't help myself.

Like an idiot, I started to walk toward the gaping mouth of the building, staring up at the cavernous entryway that towered over me. It was so dark inside I couldn't see my hand in front of my face. I smacked right into a wall. Stumbling around with my arms out, I followed that wall and realized it was actually rounded to follow the circular external shape of the dome. It was like an enclosed arena made of solid rock. A structure like this wouldn't be fazed by a dragon's snapping jaws or flashing flames.

A sudden sharp hiss off to my left made me flinch and gasp, spinning around to see there was a faint, golden light trickling from around the corner. It felt far away, and as I walked toward it, I couldn't tell if I was getting any closer or if it was actually moving away from me. A few more steps brought me around the curved inner wall, and there was a sudden thundering roar. It was so loud it rattled the floor, and made me clamp my hands over my ears. I could feel the pulsing under my boots coming from some kind of impact, like when Ulric was working with his hammer and I could feel the ground vibrating under my feet.

The gold light was coming through a half-cracked set of massive iron doors. They towered over me, so big a giant could have used them without having to worry about bumping his head. One of them was open just enough that bright light poured out from within. My heart was hammering in my ears. Something smelled like smoke, and I could still hear the sound of that rumbling growl like thunder.

I'd come too far not to see whatever was making such a racket inside. Inch by inch, I hedged toward the crack in the door, and finally peered in. The light was bright at first, so I had to squint to see. All I saw was a flash of blue scales, and another trumpeting roar made me run for cover behind the heavy door. I was shaking so badly I could barely stand up, and I still wasn't sure what I'd seen in there.

"Get a good look?" an angry voice snapped at me suddenly.

I almost fainted from terror. A big man-shaped shadow was looming over me, standing right behind me. I couldn't think, I couldn't even breathe, and didn't know how to even begin explaining myself.

Then he stepped into the light, and I knew right away who it was. Sile Derrick was frowning down at me with his big, muscular arms crossed over his chest. He wasn't wearing his armor this time, instead he had on a tunic and pants that stank like sweat, and were a little scorched around the corners. He glared down at me like I'd done something terrible, still waiting for an explanation.

"I-I thought I heard ... " I started to speak, but lost my nerve. None of the excuses I could think of sounded even slightly convincing.

He shook his head, frowning harder down at me with his dead eyes narrowed. "Go on, then. Get a good, long look, boy."

I opened my mouth to protest. I didn't really want to see what was in there anymore. I'd seen enough.

He wasn't going to let me off that easy, though. With one of his big hands planted on my shoulder, he steered me around and back toward the crack in the door. Again, the bright light blinded me, and I had to squint to see what was inside. But as I blinked away the glare, I saw the arena.

It was a huge, circular room with a dirt floor and a domed ceiling made out of solid steel with big iron cross beams. It had to be at least thirty—maybe even forty—feet tall, lit by torches that filled the room with golden light. I'd never seen a room so big before, and my mouth was hanging open long before I even saw the dragon.

He saw me at the same time, and our eyes locked from across the wide arena floor. At first, all I could do was stare at him while he glared back at me. I stopped, terror making my legs go completely stiff even with the powerful knight's hand still gripping my shoulder. I didn't want to go any closer than was absolutely necessary. Part of me was beginning to wonder if my punishment for nosing around would be becoming a late-night dragon snack.

I'd never seen a dragon up close before, but now I was standing only a few yards away from one. He was tied down to the floor with heavy iron chains. His head, neck, wings, legs, and tail were all clamped down to the ground so that he couldn't do much more than snarl at us. And that's exactly what he did.

His big yellow eyes stared right at me, pupils narrowed into slits, and he curled his lips up to snarl. Then I heard that growl again, that thunderous rumble, and all my hair stood on end. I must have gone a few minutes without taking a breath, because I started to feel faint.

"It isn't very often we are able to catch a wild dragon." Sile Derrick was looking at the creature, but he wasn't frowning anymore. He looked almost sad, watching the dragon that was still showing us his rows of pointed teeth. "In the old days, all dragons were born wild. When they chose a rider, they were brought here to be broken to a saddle. It was like a sacred bonding ritual that paired the two forever as allies. That's why they call this place the breaking dome. But now, dragons are bred like horses. They don't have a choice about who will become their rider, like they did in the old days. That is—unless we come across a wild one like this."

I'd stopped trembling, and started breathing again. It didn't look like the dragon could move, otherwise we probably would have already been his midnight meal. "Who did he choose?" I wanted to know.

Sile shook his head. "No one. We've tried about twenty different candidates, but he won't even let us put a saddle on him. He's sent a few of them home on crutches, in fact. They were lucky to get away without losing a limb."

I swallowed hard. The dragon blinked at me, giving a loud snort out his nostrils that sent a puff of hot air blasting at my face.

"The Academy Commander has decided he's too dangerous to let anyone else try. He's too old to be ridden. If he were younger, maybe then we could break his spirit enough to let someone ride him. But we can't risk anyone else getting hurt. It's bad enough to have riders die in battle, let alone in training." Sile let his hand slide off my shoulder, and he gave a loud sigh. "I've been trying to reason with him. It's a shame. He'll have his wing tendons cut, most likely, and be used for breeding."

That didn't sit too well with me. He refused to conform, to be broken to the will of a rider, and so they were just going to take away his freedom altogether? Why did they have the right to do that? Hadn't he been born free? The more I looked at the dragon, tied down to the ground and glowering at us with wild fury, the more I understood his anger. He'd never fly again, if these knights got their way.

"If he had a rider," I started to ask, "if someone could ride him, I mean. If it were possible, would he still have to have his wing tendons cut?"

Sile met my gaze as I glanced back up at him. There was a strange twinkle in his dark eyes when he answered. "I'd like to think that if he was willing to take a rider, then there's no reason he couldn't fly forever with the other dragonriders."

I stared back at the dragon again. His yellow eyes were glaring right back at me, but he'd stopped snarling and growling. I saw the end of his tail twitching back and forth, and the way his sides rose and fell under his blue scales as he breathed. "Can I ... can I try?" I didn't even realize I'd asked that out loud.

Sile was very quiet. It made me terrified of what the answer was going to be. I thought he'd probably just laugh at me, call me stupid, and send me on my way. After all, the idea that I would ever be allowed to be a dragonrider was totally ridiculous. Dragonriders came from rich noble families. I was the nobody of nobodies. I was just a halfbreed.

"Move slowly," Sile answered quietly. "And keep looking in his eyes."

I nodded shakily. My legs felt like jelly as I took a step toward the dragon. One step, then another, and the creature looked bigger and bigger the nearer I got to him. His scales were a sapphire color mottled in darker, slate blue. Three sets of horns as black as onyx crowned his head, matching his black claws on his wing arms and hind legs.

When I was only three yards away, his ears perked up in my direction. He had two small, almost feline looking ears that swiveled in my direction for a moment before flattening back against his skull. His snout wrinkled up again, and he let out a low growl of warning. I was too close for his liking.

I couldn't imagine I looked nearly as intimidating as Sile did, or even as any of the other new riders who'd already tried to get on him. I was a scrawny little kid. I'd make a good toothpick for him. But now, I was praying that would work in my favor. If I didn't look like a threat, maybe he wouldn't treat me like one.

"Please," I spoke to him. I didn't think he could understand me. It just made me feel better to talk to him. "I know what it feels like, believe me. They don't know what to do with you. And now they want to keep you here like some kind of prisoner. It's not fair. It's not right."

The dragon kept growling at me, but he didn't move again. I just locked my eyes on his and tried not to think about how close I was to the end of his snout as I kept moving forward. His head was large, much bigger than a horse's, and I could see his nostrils flaring as he breathed in my scent. His scales were larger than some of the other dragons I'd seen already. They shone under the golden torchlight like polished blue steel.

The more I looked at him, the more I noticed his features were sort of feline in shape. He was like a cross between a lizard, housecat, and a bat. His snout was short, and his eyes were large like a cat. The undersides of his hind legs and the thumbs on his wing arms had pads on them, too. His body shape was almost like a bat's, except for the long lizard-like tail and lean muscles rippling under his scales. He had two powerful back legs, but his front ones were connected to his wings. All dragons had that same kind of basic physique, though I hadn't noticed any of the others looking as cat-like in their faces, and I certainly hadn't seen any other blue ones.

"I think we can agree that things are pretty lousy for both of us," I went on talking to him, closing the distance between us. My voice was shaking because I was scared out of my mind, but at least he hadn't made a lunge for me yet. "Let's make a deal, all right? I don't want to keep living with my father for the rest of my life, and I definitely don't want to go to a prison camp. I want my life to mean something. And I'm pretty sure you don't want them to cut your wings so you can't fly anymore. You want them to let you go, but they'll force you to stay here one way or another. Alone, neither of us can do anything to change the way things are going for us. But together, we could change both our destinies."

I was standing so close to him, I could smell the musk of his breath. I could feel it, too, hot and humid against my face. Reaching out, I could see my own hand trembling as I crept toward him. Just a few more feet. Then a few more inches.

"Let me be your rider," I pleaded with him. "I swear I won't make you do anything you don't want to do. And when we're finished, when the war is over, you'll be free to go back to the wild. I won't treat you like a dumb animal. You'll be my partner. We'll get through this together. We'll be a team."

My hand touched his head. My heart felt like it had stopped beating. I could feel his scales under my palm. They were smooth like polished marble, but warm and alive.

The dragon perked his ears again, his snarl finally fading away. He made strange popping, clicking noises like the chattering sparrows did when they squabbled with each other. His yellow eyes stared at me, and his nostrils puffed as I moved my hand down toward his nose, letting him sniff me.

"I swear," I told him, and my voice wasn't shaking anymore. I didn't feel afraid. "You have my word."

Something went skidding across the floor and stopped just beside me. It was a set of iron keys. I looked back at Sile, who was watching with his eyes wide. He looked completely stunned, like he was in awe. He didn't have to explain to me what the keys were for.

I bent to pick them up, moving to the huge black padlock that bound the dragon to hooks in the floor with the heavy chains. I unlocked the one that kept his head flattened against the ground. As soon as it clicked and the chain went slack, the dragon began to flail.

I was too close to get away. The dragon's lashing tail hit me and swept my legs right out from under me, sending me sliding across the floor on my back. I heard the chains groaning and snapping, hitting the ground as the dragon let out a surging bellow of victory. I'd had some near-death experiences before, but this was definitely way worse than any of the others.

Sile was shouting, and I glimpsed him brandishing what looked like a long spear, running toward me like he was going to try to rescue me again. The dragon wasn't going to allow that, though. With a vicious snarl, he tore off the rest of the chains, and reared back onto his hind legs to open his wings.

He was as fast as he was big, and snapped his head forward when Sile tried to stick him with the spear, grabbing it in his jaws, and snapping it like a twig. The dragon spat out the pieces of the spear, taking a threatening snap at Sile, who was already beginning to retreat.

"Stop! Don't hurt him!" I cried. I didn't expect that to make a spit's worth of difference ... but it did.

The dragon stopped, hunkered on all four of his feet, and shot me a glare of pure frustration with those huge cat-like eyes. His tail kept swishing as he sat there, the leathery skin of his wings folded up along his forelegs like a bat, and gave me an angry snort. He made those popping, chattering noises again as he swung his head back around to look at Sile, who looked just as stupefied and shocked as I was.

The dragon was *listening* to me.

"Unbelievable," Sile whispered. I could see his expression twitching, like thoughts were racing across his brain, until at last his gaze panned slowly over to me. He didn't have much color left in his face. "Do it again."

I swallowed hard; I didn't want to try it again. Any time now, my luck was bound to run out. Then I'd be torched with dragon fire, or gobbled up like a kid-shaped biscuit. Gathering my feet under me, I stood back up. The dragon was watching me again, studying my every move.

"If you're really going to make this deal with me, you have to show me," I spoke to the creature again. "Show me that I can trust you."

The dragon turned and started walking toward me. His large, curled black claws dug into the dirt floor of the arena, and I couldn't help but stagger back a few feet as he crept toward me, chattering loudly all the way. His gait was strange to watch, oddly smooth and feline for the way his body was built.

He stopped right before me, craning his neck to sniff at me again. Then he started to crouch down. The dragon lowered himself until his belly was flat on the ground. His huge horned head was low, too, and he looked at me expectantly.

Before I could figure out what I was supposed to do, Sile was right there beside me. "He wants to seal the bond," the knight explained as he grabbed me by the waist and pretty much tossed me up onto the dragon's back. "Don't be afraid."

Easy for him to say; Sile wasn't the one straddling the neck of a wild dragon who'd already proven he had a nasty temper. With my legs slung around the base of the creature's neck, sitting between the shoulders of his wing arms, I clung to anything I could when I felt him start to move. There wasn't much to grab, though. His scales were slick, and the little knobby black horns that ran down his spine to the tip of his tail were cone-shaped and hard to grip. I just had to lay flat against his neck, my arms as far around him as I could reach, and hang on for dear life as the dragon stood.

Sile was laughing loudly. I saw him smiling up at me as the dragon gave a wide yawn that showed me just how many of those teeth he had. My heartbeat was skipping and pounding erratically. My head spun like a top. I was sitting on a dragon. Not just any dragon, though. This one was *mine*.

4

CHAPTER FOUR

"You'll be stacking stones over my grave before I allow that repulsive little wretch into this academy! Have you absolutely lost your mind?" The Academy Commander was yelling so loudly I could hear him from outside his office. So could my father, and all the other instructors who had come to gather outside the door. They all wanted to see what the verdict would be, too. If the commander allowed me to join in the training program and become a dragonrider, it would be the first time in history a drop of elven blood had ever been in a dragon's saddle.

Normally, I would have been humiliated. But I was so tired and hungry, I just wanted it to be over. I stood beside Ulric, staring down at the tops of my boots while I listened to Sile Derrick argue my case. For whatever reason, he was still insisting that I should be allowed to join. I didn't understand why. No one else had ever fought for me like this before.

"You'd spit in the faces of our ancestors? On our most sacred tradition?" Sile yelled back. I heard what sounded like someone smacking a fist down onto a tabletop. "This is how we began, Commander Rayken. It is our creed; the very foundation of what this brotherhood was built upon. Any rider chosen by a dragon must be allowed to join us—that is our first law!"

"And what about all our glorious dead who have fallen in battle to those silver-headed heathens? Are you willing to spit in their faces, instead?" The commander started yelling again. It made my throat begin to feel tight. "By letting that boy in here, you are acknowledging that there is nothing wrong with what he is. He would be a stain on the reputation of our brotherhood. I don't care if it was a king drake that chose him. That does not forgive his bloodline!"

There was silence for a moment. I thought it was over. I didn't know whether to be relieved that a decision had finally been reached, happy that I wasn't going to have to endure being bullied by knights who were supposed to be training me, or sad because I wasn't going to get to fulfill what might have been my destiny.

I flicked a glance up to the dozen or so instructors, all ranking officers, who were standing around waiting to hear a decision as well. I was afraid of them. They were all strong, powerful-looking men with the same cold eyes that Sile had. Did I really want to become one of them?

"If you don't let him in, you are sending the message that our old ways really are dead. You'll be suggesting that the spirit of the dragon no longer matters at all, that we've bred them down to stupid beasts no better than winged pedigree dogs!" Sile countered, but his voice was somewhat calmer. It carried more emotion than anger now. "I know you've heard those accusations whispered at our backs, just as I have. They say we've fallen from our glorious past, and become nothing but power-hungry relics without souls. That is not the legacy I want to leave here for the world to remember. That boy can help us change it. We can prove that our heritage is not dead, that we still honor the creed of our forefathers."

"Have you even seen that boy? He couldn't possibly weigh a hundred pounds soaking wet. He won't last two weeks. The other fledglings would be three years his senior. They'll eat him alive." The commander's tone wasn't any less hostile. "You'll be scraping what's left of him off the dormitory walls."

"I'll watch over him," Sile interrupted. "I'll be his sponsor."

"You're a fool, lieutenant. What's come over you? Why does this halfbreed mean so much to you?" The commander sounded suspicious, but he didn't wait for Sile to give him an answer. "What has his father said? Even as a tackmaster, I doubt he has the income to pay for the equipment needed."

"I'll take care of that, too. If these are your only real objections, then give me your blessing so I can begin my work. I only have two days to get him fully outfitted and ready to begin," Sile snapped sharply.

I heard the commander sigh. It was the sound of defeat. My heart jumped with hope, making my eyes water.

"Very well," he relented. "But you are going to get that boy killed. His blood is on your hands, Lieutenant Derrick. Remember that. You wanted this."

There was a brief silence before the door opened, and Lieutenant Sile Derrick came out of the commander's office. His expression was steely and focused. He didn't give my father a second look as he stormed past the crowd of other knights who were still gathered around. He grabbed my shoulder on his way down the stairs, and started to drag me along with him.

"What are you doing with him?" Ulric barked, lunging forward like he might try to stop us.

Sile stopped at the top of the stairs long enough to look back, casting my father a look that I'd seen Ulric give me many times; that look of superiority and disgust. "He's no longer your concern, tackmaster. Remember your place."

Ulric's eyes were burning like torches. His fists clenched in rage as Sile pushed me on ahead of him down the stairs. It was surreal, and I wasn't even sure if it was really happening. Just like that, Ulric couldn't put his hands on me anymore. Just like that, I was free.

Or maybe I'd just traded in one horror for another.

I should have been exploding with gratitude for Sile. He'd just fought fiercely so I could stay here and be trained as a dragonrider. But as we paused outside the officer's dormitory, I couldn't help questioning his motives. No one had ever helped me do anything before, and generosity of this magnitude was a foreign concept to me. It was frightening. I barely knew this man, and already I owed him my life.

He seemed to pick up on my hesitance as we walked in silence toward the breaking dome. "Commander Rayken is right, you know. The other students will be at least eighteen. They are probably going to give you a hard time."

I rolled my eyes. "Everyone gives me a hard time, sir. I'm used to that already. That's not what I'm worried about."

"Well, all right then." He laughed under his breath. "What are you worried about?"

It was hard to pick just one thing. I was worried about my own physical ability. I was worried about owing a stranger my life. And more than anything, I was worried I wouldn't be able to keep my promise to my dragon. If I couldn't make it through this training, then I'd be failing more than just myself. I'd made a deal with that creature, and I wanted to keep my word. Both our lives depended on it now.

"I haven't eaten in about two days," I told him instead. I didn't want to look weak. Well, weak-*er*. "I guess I'm just worried about food, right now."

Sile laughed again, clapping a hand on my back that made me stumble some as I walked beside him. "That we can fix. You look like a scrawny stray cat, boy. Maybe some decent food'll put more meat on your bones."

I blushed. It was embarrassing to have my stature pointed out more than once in a day. "Yeah," I mumbled back. "Maybe."

The dining hall was on the ground level of the student dormitory, and that's where Sile sat me down in front of a tray stacked with roasted meat, freshly baked bread, boiled eggs, and cold milk. My mouth was hanging open. The smells were fantastic, and I seized my fork like a weapon, preparing to go to war with the first thing I could get my hands on.

"Eat up," he commanded. I noticed he wasn't sitting down to join me for this incredible breakfast. "I've got to go get your paperwork filed and put in orders at the armories for your gear. You know where that is, don't you?"

I nodded.

"Good, come straight over when you're finished. We've got some catching up to do." Sile smirked, going on about his business, and leaving me with a fork in my hand and a mountain of food to tackle.

I was too busy stuffing as much into my mouth as I could to realize I was being watched. I gulped down three boiled eggs, shoveled in several big bites of the roasted meat, and drained my glass of milk before I even stopped to breathe.

The food was so good I didn't even notice it when someone came over and sat down across the table from me. There were lots of empty seats in the dining hall. The four long tables stretched from one end of the room all the way to the other, with wooden benches on either side. A few hundred people could have easily sat in the dining hall to eat without being too crowded. So there was really no reason anyone would have sat by me ... unless they just wanted to.

I looked across the table into the grinning face of a boy I didn't recognize. He was a lot older than me, maybe eighteen or nineteen, with shaggy dark blond hair and light brown eyes the color of amber. I got the feeling right away that he was probably going to make fun of me. That's generally how things went. So I braced for the inevitable.

"You keep eating like that and you'll make yourself puke," he said. I watched him reach out to tear a hunk off my loaf of bread and pop it into his mouth. "You must be the new kid."

I sat back away from the table some, still armed with my fork, but not willing to fight him for my food. I could part with a few pieces of bread as long as no one was wiping their boots on my face. "Yeah," I answered hesitantly. "H-how did you know that?"

He just laughed. "It's a small place. Word travels fast here. Especially when it concerns a halfbreed and a wild dragon. And in case you hadn't noticed, you're the only halfbreed here," he pointed out matter-of-factly. "Word is you'll be joining us in the fledgling class in a few days. Guess that means we'll be classmates."

I wasn't sure if I should be talking to him or not. I didn't get the feeling he was going to hurt me, not like I had from the boys who'd beat me up the day before. He looked at me like I was an interesting insect he wanted to mess with, not squash under his heel. Even so, I wasn't sure who I could trust.

"We're both new kids, then." I tried to sound confident, like I wasn't afraid of him.

It made him laugh again, and he stole another piece of bread off my plate. "Right, right. I guess so, huh?" He was chewing loudly, looking at me with a thoughtful expression for an uncomfortable minute before he spoke again. "So what happened to your face?"

I blushed so hard the tips of my ears were burning. Whenever Ulric hit me, it tended to leave hand-shaped bruises on my skin. I bruised easily anyway, and he never held back just because I was a kid. Of course, I'd also cracked my head off the ladder pretty hard. I probably had a nice black eye to show for that, too. And then there was the whole mess with the other older boys. After all that, I probably did look like a walking corpse.

"I fell," I told him guardedly.

He arched a brow at me like he wasn't buying that for a second. "Into a giant foot, apparently. You've got a boot print on your face, you know."

My ears were on fire, and I couldn't stand to look at him much less answer that. I sat with my shoulders hunched and tense, staring down into my lap while he kept picking at my plate. Finally, he stood up and left without saying another word. He sauntered out of the dining hall with a confident swagger in his step. I didn't even know his name.

Stuffing down a few more bites of food, I cleaned up my tray quickly and set out for the armory. The dragons were taking flight from the tops of the high outer wall, already grouping together in patterns as they soared overhead. I could glimpse their riders for a few seconds whenever they swooped past, and see that they were using hand signals to communicate to one another. It was unfathomable to think I'd ever be like that. Dragon or not, I couldn't see myself as one of those powerful armored men. I couldn't see myself as anything.

A familiar thundering growl made me look back over my shoulder just in time to scramble out of the way as my dragon swooped in low to land. He cupped his leathery wings, and only missed crushing me by a few feet as he touched down. He let out a deep bellowing roar. Under the shining light of the morning sun, he was even more fierce and beautiful than he had been the night before. His blue scales gleamed, and his black horns shone like volcanic glass.

"Try not to kill me before we even get started," I grumbled, turning away to continue on toward the armories. I wasn't feeling confident about this at all, anymore. I was beginning to think I'd made a huge mistake by agreeing to this.

The dragon followed me, looming close and making those chattering, birdlike noises as we made our way toward the armory buildings. I was hoping I wouldn't see my father, but I caught a glimpse of him as I searched the workshops for Sile. All the craftsmen were very busy taking orders or measuring riders for saddles and armor. My father was casting molds for saddles, which I'd never actually seen him do before. Thankfully, he didn't look up when I walked past.

Sile was talking to a blacksmith when I finally found him. They were haggling over the cost of vambraces, and I stood by quietly until my dragon finally made an impatient barking noise. That got their attention, and it made me smile a little.

"Hurry up. Stand there," the blacksmith grumbled in a raspy voice. I knew his type well, thanks to Mr. Crookin. Blacksmiths liked to get down to work, no nonsense, and get their money as quickly as possible so they could move on to their next order.

Sile gave me a nod of encouragement, gesturing for me to come close enough for the blacksmith to start working. "Come on, we've got a lot to get done today."

The blacksmith measured me from head to foot, handling me roughly like someone feathering a chicken, and occasionally squeezing an old bruise hidden by my clothes that made me wince. Occasionally, he stopped and wrote down numbers, noting the length of my arms and legs, the circumference of my chest, and the span of my shoulders. It didn't take him long to get all my measurements taken, and then he started handing me pieces of roughly-made test armor to determine how they felt for size.

It took a few tries of different sizes of helmets to find one that didn't fit me like I was just wearing an empty bucket over my head. It had a big number three painted on the front of it, and the blacksmith made a gruff noise of disapproval. "Been a long time since I made a three. You sure you're big enough for this? War is a man's game."

"No," I answered truthfully.

Sile sent me a scolding glare. "He'll be fine. Size and strength are not all that make a good soldier."

Once I'd been fitted for armor, and the smith had been paid, we moved on to a workstation in the second building—the one where the tackmasters were making saddles. Sile, in all his wisdom, had decided not to hire my father to make mine. Judging by the last look my father had given me, I wouldn't have been surprised if Ulric intentionally compromised my saddle on the off chance that it might kill me.

My dragon followed us to the open-sided workspace, plopping down onto his haunches outside and beginning to preen his scales. The tackmaster was a man much older than my father, with snowy white hair, and knobby withered hands that were covered in protruding veins. He took one look at me, at my dragon, and his bushy brows shot up for a moment. But he didn't say anything.

"Are you ready for us yet?" Sile talked to the man like he'd already struck a bargain with him.

The old tackmaster nodded. "Have the dragon lie down."

All eyes were suddenly on me, expecting me to get my dragon to perform like a trained show pony. I swallowed hard. I wasn't sure just how much of what I said the dragon actually understood, or how smart he was. It was time to find out.

As I walked up to his head, my dragon was watching me with large yellow eyes bright with what I hoped was intelligence. I raised a hand to him, showing him my palm, and then gesturing in a downward motion. "Lie down, will you?" I asked him nicely. It was strange to give something that huge, and that potentially deadly, orders.

The dragon watched my gesture, and made a few soft clicking noises as he tilted his head to one side. His ears perked and swiveled.

"Down," I repeated. "Lie down."

He was already sitting back on his haunches, and little by little, he started to lower himself until he was lying flat on his scaly belly. He watched me carefully the whole time, looking for indication that he was doing the right thing.

"Yes, that's right." I couldn't keep myself from grinning. Even if he didn't understand me word for word, my dragon was smart. He could figure out what I wanted. "Good."

Sile was impressed again. He watched us with his arms folded, and I saw a glimmer of envy in his eyes when I turned back to face him. "You think of a name for him yet?"

I glanced back at my dragon, who was still watching me intently as he lay still. Naming him hadn't even crossed my mind. "No. How do other riders usually choose names?"

"Well, these days young dragons are named after their sires, or mothers, whichever was the more impressive specimen." Sile grabbed the back of my shirt while he talked, pulling me out of the blacksmith's way as he began dragging one of the large molds toward my dragon.

The old blacksmith worked slowly, but he was strong like my father, and he didn't act like he wanted us to help him. He, like all tackmasters, had his own way of doing things. For these men, I knew making saddles was a sacred ritual. He wouldn't want us to interfere.

Standing back with Sile, we watched the old smith work at pressing the wax-filled mold against the space between my dragon's neck and his wing arms, where the saddle would sit. The mold would become the base that the rest of the saddle would be built to fit onto, so that it was snug against the dragon's body and didn't slide around. It also had to fit over the little horns growing down his spine.

"You know, the other instructors had started calling him a maverick. For a wild-born dragon who refused all but a halfbreed rider, that name might suit him," Sile muttered.

"Maverick?" I wasn't sure what that meant.

Sile was smirking to himself while he studied my dragon with his dark eyes. "A rebel. That's what it means. That's what he is. A stubborn mongrel, albeit a smart one."

I liked the way that named sounded. It rang well, and when I looked at the blue-scaled dragon lying on his belly, yawning widely to show us his white teeth and black gums, it just seemed to fit him. I took up a stick and squatted down to scribble the letters into the dirt at my feet.

M-A-V-R-I-K.

"You didn't spell it right." Sile was grinning at me, and shaking his head.

I looked up at him, then back down at the name. Spelling had never been my strong suit. My mother had taught me to read pretty well, but I'd never had much need for writing.

"It's fine, boy." Sile squatted down next to me to get a closer look at the name

I'd scribbled in the dirt. "Mavrik. I like it spelled that way. What do you think, dragonrider? Is that the name for him?"

I couldn't keep from smiling back at the older knight who had quickly become my closest friend. Well, besides Katty, anyway. A little glowing bit of warmth started to rise up in my chest, and it made me want to smile even wider. When I looked at my dragon, at Mavrik, I started to feel that sensation bloom out all over my body. It was like a rush of energy and hope.

"Yeah, I think so."

CHAPTER FIVE

It'd been a long day. After getting all my armor and my saddle ordered, my admission paperwork signed and submitted, and making sure Mavrik was settled in at the Roost, all I wanted to do was sleep. I didn't even care where anymore.

Sile left me standing outside the student dormitory with a stack of books and uniforms in my arms. "Your room is on the second floor," he told me as he turned away. "Students have to share a room with one other person their first year. He'll be your partner in training for the duration. It supposedly promotes comradery, though in your case, I'd advise you to keep a low profile. Room four."

My spirits fell. I was going to have a roommate. A partner. Sile had explained a lot about how the first year of training was going to work. There were nine students starting, including me. All were boys. Girls weren't allowed to become dragonriders. So, odds were, I was going to end up in a room with someone that hated my guts. There was only one boy from my new class that had even been remotely nice to me—while he was stealing food off my plate. I knew chances were slim that he would end up being my roommate, but I would have happily roomed with a food thief than someone else who might want to beat me within an inch of my life.

I dragged my feet up the stairs to the second floor of the student dormitory. The hallways were narrow, with rows of doors on either side. I stopped outside door number four, staring up at the engraved lettering hanging on a placard in the very middle of it. It read:

Sn. Lt. Derrick

The other doors had signs on them, too, and from what I could tell each one had the name of a Lieutenant on it. That must have been what Sile meant by being my "sponsor." Even if I wasn't sure what a sponsor was, I was glad that I'd at least be in some proximity to the knight who'd vouched for me.

I had just reached out to touch the doorknob, when I heard a familiar voice snarl behind me, "You've got to be kidding me."

I recognized the older boy right away. It was the same one who'd wiped his boots on my face. He was glaring at me like he'd found a diseased rodent in his food, and immediately I froze up. He was bigger than me, and I knew I wouldn't stand much of a chance if he came after me again. I could run, but I wouldn't get far.

"There's no way!" He yelled like it was my fault. Apparently Sile was his sponsor, too. "I'll cut my own ears off before I share a room with you!" He was practically screaming, and I started to worry about what he was going to do to me.

He started to move in closer, backing me up against the door while he snapped angry words just inches from my nose. I couldn't escape, and I couldn't think of anything to say to defend myself. The more furious he got, the louder he became, and it made me wince as I tried to hide behind the stack of supplies in my arms.

Some of the other new students were starting poke their heads out of their rooms down the hall, staring. I could sense their anticipation as they started to flock toward us. They were hoping for a fight. It would be a free-for-all, and I would definitely be on the losing end of it. Every single one of them was at least half a foot taller than I was, and much more muscular. I was a sheep surrounded by a pack of hungry wolves, ready to make a meal of me.

"Hey," another, strangely familiar voice spoke up from within the crowd. I watched the other students step aside, making way for the boy who'd stolen bites of my lunch earlier. He was coming straight for us with a canvas bag slung over his shoulder.

"I'll switch with you," he said "I'll room with the halfbreed."

My mouth fell open.

"Well if it isn't the local celebrity, Felix Farrow. Come to see how the other half lives?" The boy was still snarling in my direction with his eyes narrowed, bowing up defensively at the one who'd interrupted his fit of rage. "What does the son of a duke want with a halfbreed, anyway?"

"The way I see it, that's not really any of your business, is it?" Felix shot him a threatening look. "You want to switch or not? This offer's going to last for about thirty more seconds."

It didn't take that long for him to make up his mind. The boy who had used my face as a doormat agreed to switch rooms without any more yelling, and he sent me a mocking sneer over his shoulder as he walked away.

The crowd started to disperse, as everyone went back into their rooms, seeming unhappy that things hadn't come to blows. I was left standing alone in the hallway with Felix Farrow, wondering what had just happened. How had I gotten out of that situation with all my limbs and teeth intact?

Felix gave me a look from top to bottom like he was sizing me up, and then he just rolled his eyes. "You've got a knack for getting in trouble. Let's hope that doesn't apply to the battlefield, too."

I didn't know what to say to him except, "Thank you."

He just shrugged and opened the dorm room door, holding it so I could go in first.

"Is Sile going to be all right with this?" I wasn't sure switching like this was allowed.

He gave me a strange look. "You mean Lieutenant Derrick?"

I nodded. "Yeah. Will he be your sponsor now, too?"

"First off, you can't call him that anymore, kid," Felix corrected me as he shut the door behind us. He wandered over to one of the two single beds set up on opposite sides of the room. He plopped his canvas bag there, claiming it as his own. "He's Lieutenant Derrick to us. We're not on a first name basis with our superior officers. Understand? That'll get you smacked upside the head. Whatever relationship with him you had before, it ends the minute you put on your uniform. He's your sponsor; he's responsible for making sure you survive this training. That's his job. Private training, individualized attention, and providing you with anything you need that your parents didn't already give you."

"Oh, right." I nodded again.

Felix unbuttoned his bag and started taking out his own books and uniforms, putting them away into a small bedside table with a few drawers in it. "And to answer your question, yes. I'll have to talk to him about it to make sure it's all right, but I'm pretty sure they won't care. In fact, I'm willing to bet Lieutenant Derrick will be glad that you're not rooming with Lyon. I heard he was the one who bruised your face up."

I sank down to sit on my own bed, watching him unpack from across the room. I'd never had a bed like this before. It was just a single-sized, hard mattress covered in a stiff white sheet and wool blanket, but it was still nicer than anything I'd ever had before.

"Is that his name? Lyon?" I asked while I unfolded one of my uniform shirts to look at it. It was just a plain, dark blue tunic with a golden eagle stitched on the breast. It was made of a coarse, rugged fabric, and the sleeves were long enough to be tucked into my vambraces, whenever I got them.

"Lyon Cromwell," Felix confirmed. "Son of Viscount Cromwell, and a third generation rider in his family."

Hearing that made my spirits sink some. I hadn't even had my first day of training yet, and I was already making powerful enemies. I looked up at Felix, who was still busy putting his things away. "Why did you do that?" I dared to ask. "Why did you agree to switch? No one else wants anything to do with me."

He stopped long enough to give me another strange look, arching one of his eyebrows. I knew he was a noble, too. I'd heard Lyon call him the son of a duke, and that was just a step below a prince. He definitely had that rich kid look about him. His dark blond hair was cut feathery around his face, and his clothes were clean and expensive-looking. He even had a gold signet ring on his hand with his family crest on it.

"You think I should be worried about my reputation?" he asked.

"Well." I was hesitant to answer that. "I think anyone else would be."

Felix gave a noisy sigh and came around to sit on the edge of his bed, too, staring at me while he sat across the room. "I don't know," he admitted. "I'm sure my dad's not going to like it, but he doesn't like a lot of things I do. Besides, you're interesting. A halfbreed paired with a wild-caught dragon? Maybe I'm just waiting to see what amazing, unexpected thing you do next."

I was able to smile at him some, glancing back down at the uniform tunic in my hands. "Like what? Surviving a year of dragonrider training at Blybrig Academy?"

Felix laughed loudly, grinning at me in that same mischievous way he had when I first met him. "Yeah, exactly like that."

The dormitory was dark and quiet once we were all settled in. Felix was already snoring in his bed when I got back from the washroom down the hall. I hadn't had an opportunity to bathe in almost a week, and probably stank to high heaven. I finally got a chance to look at myself in the mirror behind the washstand before I left. Now I understood why Felix had asked about my bruises. Some were green and healing, but others were still deep purple. I could trace the outline of Ulric's hand on one of my cheeks, and a boot print on my forehead.

I hated seeing my reflection. It reminded me just how different I looked from everyone else. If I combed my hair just right, no one could see my slightly pointed ears. But you could still tell I was a halfbreed. My features were a little sharper, and my cheekbones were high. Katty always told me I had a pretty face, and somehow that never made me feel any better about it.

Crawling under the stiff sheets of my bed, I curled up and tried to sleep. It didn't come easy, though, even if I was exhausted. Felix snored loudly, and sometimes mumbled in his sleep. I couldn't get over the sinking, swirling panic that made me sick at my stomach whenever I thought about what I was about to do. I still wasn't sure I was cut out to be a dragonrider. Lieutenant Derrick had faith in me, obviously. He was paying for all my gear, after all, and had agreed to be my sponsor. Mavrik had faith in me, too, or he wouldn't have agreed to pair up with me. I didn't want to disappoint either of them.

The night passed slowly, and I stayed awake rubbing the necklace my mother had given me while I stared at the shadows on the walls from the moonlight outside. It was hard not to miss her. I wondered if she'd be proud of me.

Early in the morning, I heard the trumpet sound that signaled it was time to get up. It wasn't even sunrise yet. I hadn't slept much, so I was still tired. I moved sluggishly to get up and start dressing.

Felix, on the other hand, popped out of bed like he'd been bucked off a horse. I couldn't figure out how he'd even heard the trumpet over his own snoring. He started scrambling to get dressed, putting on the same dark blue tunic and black pants that matched my uniform. Neither of us had vambraces yet, but he had a belt that he buckled around his waist before he sat down to put on his boots.

"Don't you have a sword belt?" he asked me.

I shook my head, wondering if Lieutenant Derrick had forgotten to get me one. He probably hadn't expected he'd have to provide me an entire wardrobe.

"Here." Felix rummaged around through his belongings, tossing me a spare.

I'd never worn a sword belt before. It was way too big, and I had a hard time getting it to fit like I thought it should have. Finally, Felix came over with a sigh to help me.

"Looks like puberty forgot all about you, huh?" He chuckled as he punched a new hole through the belt so it would fit me without falling off. "How old are you anyway?"

I told him, and he stared at me like I'd grown a third eyeball.

"Geez." He made a sympathetic whistling noise. "You really are just a kid."

"My name is Jaevid," I told him with a frown. I was getting tired of being referred to as just a halfbreed or a kid. I was both, yes, but I had a name.

Felix smirked. "Jaevid, huh?"

"Or just Jae," I added.

He laughed as he stood back, eying the belt like he was trying to make sure it looked good. "You've got boots, right?"

"Yeah." I nodded, and sat down on the edge of my bed to start putting them on.

"Good, 'cause I don't think my spares would fit you anyway." Felix started talking while he cleaned up his side of the room, advising me to do the same once I was dressed. "They do random room inspections, so you better have all your stuff put away. Uniforms have to be folded neatly, boots by the bedside if you aren't wearing them. Your bed has to be made, books stacked up, and no trash on the floor. Pretty standard stuff."

I started cleaning my side while he talked, not that there was much to clean. I put my clothes and books away, and followed him down toward the dining hall on the first floor. He grabbed a large piece of bread, breaking it in half and shoving some in my direction. He ate while he rushed me out into the cold morning air, talking around the food in his mouth.

Felix explained that official training wouldn't start for a few more days, when everyone finally had all the gear that was being made for us. But this was our chance to get a leg up on the others and start getting some preliminary training from our sponsor.

Lieutenant Derrick was outside the Roost, fitting a saddle to his own dragon. I recognized it was the saddle my father had made for him. The gleaming white creature flared the fins on the side of her head when she saw us coming close, hissing and snapping her jaws. It made Sile look back, arching a brow questioningly at us as we approached. For once, I wasn't the one he narrowed his eyes at, like he was expecting some kind of explanation.

"Felix Farrow, sir." My new roommate introduced himself, clasping a fist over his chest and bowing at the waist. "There was some trouble with room arrangements, and I volunteered to switch ... with your permission, of course."

Sile did look at me then. It made me flinch. I didn't know what to say.

"I suppose," Lieutenant Derrick answered hesitantly. "If that's what you want."

Felix nodded. "Yes, sir, I'm sure. With all due respect, I'm probably the only one who isn't going to try to snap his skinny neck during the night." He laughed tensely.

Sile gave a snort, but didn't answer. He went back to fixing the saddle onto his dragon. The beautiful, sleek female had scales like polished pearl. Her eyes were a pale, glacier blue and she looked at us like we were something to eat. She wasn't as big as Mavrik, and her build was more lithe. She hissed at me again, her wild eyes turning away when Sile gave her neck a slap.

"Well, I'm glad you've both come," he announced, turning back to face us. "Every morning, I expect you to meet me here before sunup. You'll be doing drill rides, once you get your saddles. You'll be running in full armor, four laps around the outer wall. There is a reason dragonriders are the preferred soldier of his majesty, the king. We are an elite breed. We are held to a higher standard of performance—one you have only just begun to appreciate. I expect the very best from you at all times. It isn't lineage or bloodlines that make men good soldiers, it is sweat and blood. I can assure you, you'll be drenched in both before your time at this academy is over."

Felix wasn't smiling or laughing anymore. I was horrified.

"For today, I'll be taking you up one at a time for a demonstrational ride, then you can get to running those laps. It'd be in your best interest to get over your air sickness now, so you aren't throwing up on your first day of formal aerial maneuvers," Sile went on, curling a finger at me to call me forward. "You're up first, Jaevid."

I didn't want to go anywhere near him, the saddle, or the snarling white dragon that was swishing her long tail. But I had no choice now. I staggered forward, watching as Sile gave the seat of the saddle a pat. It looked intimidating, and much too small for two people.

He gave his dragon a hand signal and she put her belly on the ground, lowering so we could climb onto her back. I was practically sitting in Sile's lap, which was awkward and uncomfortable. Clearly this saddle wasn't made for two people. It felt like I might fall off as soon as we got moving.

Sile was a little more secure in his seat, with his legs put down into two sheath-like leather sleeves built into the saddle. They came up to his knees, fitting like boots. I saw what they were meant for; those leg-holsters were what would keep him in the saddle when his dragon turned at awkward angles in the sky. I was shaking all over as Sile showed me the handles on either side of the saddle.

"I won't let you fall," he assured me as he belted a leather harness around my shoulders that literally strapped us together. It was like he was wearing me as a backpack in the front. "Valla will go easy on you, at first."

Valla didn't seem to like me being on her back one bit. When she stood, she shifted and shook herself, flexing her shoulders and snapping her jaws like my added weight was uncomfortable for her. She growled and hissed, making flustered chirps as she turned her head to the side to glare at me with one big, blue eye.

Sile gave her neck a pat again, gave a sharp whistle, and she reared back onto her hind legs, spreading her forearms wide to flare her wings. I saw Felix stumbled back a few feet as she let out a shrill roar and leapt skyward. The earth fell away from beneath us, and the sudden force of gravity on my body smashed me back against Sile's chest.

I'd experienced fear a few times, but this was my first encounter with sheer terror. I didn't handle it very well. It took everything I had not to throw up as we rocketed up into the sky. The initial ride was so rough I was afraid something was wrong. Valla took in forceful sweeps with her wings. It felt clumsy and chaotic, like we weren't making any progress, until I caught a glimpse of the ground far below.

She leveled off once we were several hundred feet above the academy, circling at a gentle speed. Looking down made me dizzy, and I was gripping the handles so tightly my hands felt numb. The air was cold, and the sky above was pink as the sun began to rise. I could still see stars peeking through the twilight.

That's when I realized how beautiful it was, and I forgot all my fears.

To the right, I could see where the mountains sloped down, opening to let in a view of the ocean far away in the distance. The rest of the way around us, the peaks of the mountains were still covered in snow. Sile pointed over my shoulder, showing me a few dark spots in the distance. There were other dragons already flying with their riders.

My feelings of awe and exhilaration lasted for about three minutes. Once I had finally gotten comfortable, maybe even decided this was kind of fun, Sile turned up the speed again. He gave Valla another nudge, and with a few forceful wing beats, we went lurching forward.

We did spins. We did spirals. We went up so fast all I could see was blue sky and blurs of clouds. We went down so suddenly I lost my breath and couldn't catch it again until we'd slowed down. All the while, Sile was trying to shout directions at me, and I couldn't understand anything he said with the wind in my face.

Swooping back down toward the earth, Valla cupped her wings and hovered for a moment while she stretched out her strong hind legs and landed. We came to a sudden lurching halt, and immediately I felt like I was going to throw up.

I barely made it out of the saddle in time. Sile must have heard me gagging, because he frantically started unbuckling the harness that tethered us together. He all but dropped me out of the saddle, and as soon as I hit the ground, I started throwing up. When I finally pulled myself together and looked up, Felix as standing over me with a look of horror on his face; now it was his turn.

I sat in the shade while Felix had his demonstrational ride. It still felt like the world was spinning around me. Sile had given me a canteen of water, and told me to keep drinking until I felt better. When they landed again, my head had finally started to clear, but I was still really embarrassed that I'd actually gotten motion sick.

Until Felix threw up, too.

He seemed all right, at first. He unbuckled, got down, and staggered a few feet. He was even grinning, and giving me a thumbs up. Then I saw his face get really pale, his eyes went wide, and he hunched over to puke in the grass just like I had.

Sile was laughing when he got out of the saddle, shaking his head at us and wrinkling his nose at the smell. "Looks like you boys have a lot to get used to." He chuckled, giving me a nod. "Let him drink some, too. Take a few minutes, then you both have laps to run. Meet me again in the dining hall for lunch after you've cleaned yourselves up."

6

CHAPTER SIX

Four laps around the outer wall of the academy was about the equivalent of four miles. It probably doesn't sound like much, but for someone who'd never run that far just for exercise, it was pure torture. My legs ached, my lungs felt like someone with big fists was squeezing them shut, and I was soaked with sweat.

Felix seemed to handle it much better. He ran behind me the whole time, and gave me a shove if I slowed down too much. I knew if I stopped, he'd drag me by the ears if he had to. I couldn't imagine what it was going to be like to run those laps in full armor.

As we rounded the last corner on our final lap, I was limping because my calves felt like they were about to pop off the back of my legs. I was starving, dripping sweat, and ready to lie back down and sleep the whole afternoon away. But Sile had a full day planned for us.

We hurried through bathing, changing into clean uniforms, and getting back down to the dining hall. It was a little after noon, so there were a lot of other students and instructors eating while we sat and waited for Sile.

Felix plopped down across from me at one of the long tables, bringing a tray he'd piled high with food for us to share. "Eat while you can," he said as he grabbed a leg of roasted chicken for himself from one of the plates. "I bet we're about to get a jump start on some academics."

I groaned, hesitantly taking a loaf of bread and piece of fruit for myself. "I guess if my brain is hurting, too, it'll take some of the focus off my legs."

He laughed with his mouth full. "Get used to it. We've got two whole years of this ahead of us now."

Even after everything I'd been through so far: the aches, the pain, even the throwing up—hearing that still made me smile somehow. This was going to be the most difficult thing I'd ever done, but it was the first time in my life I'd ever felt like I was doing something worthwhile. It was the first thing that ever promised any kind of future for me.

Sile finally joined us after we'd eaten, sitting down and dumping a pile of maps onto the table between us. They smelled musty, and were made of thick parchment that had been crinkled and weathered from use. He started to spread some out on the table, using cups and plates to hold them out flat.

"Meet your new best friend," Sile announced, sitting back so we could lean in and get a good look. "You're only useful if you know where you are, and where you need to be. In and out of the saddle, knowing your maps is vital. You'll spend more time with your nose pressed against this paper than doing anything else. In a week, I expect you both to be able to duplicate this purely out of memory."

My jaw dropped. The map was so detailed, I had no idea how we'd ever be able to memorize it all. It wasn't just a map of the valley; it was a map of the entire kingdom of Maldobar. I'd never actually seen a map of it before, and my eyes were immediately drawn across the paper at all the details written with black ink.

Maldobar was a very large peninsula, bordering the sea on the east, west, and south sides. There were forests, rivers, streams, mountains, cities, roads, islands, and even the small desert in the bottom. Every feature had a name, and was labeled in curled writing. There were also different elevations noted in various places, mostly in the mountain regions.

To the north was the forbidding wall of forest labeled with only one word: Luntharda. I stared at it. It was just a solid mass of forest that covered the whole top part of Maldobar, cutting it off from the rest of the continent. The Wild Forest. The kingdom of the Gray elves. That was where my mother had come from, and it was the same kingdom Maldobar had been at war with for so many years.

Sile explained to us about the various markings on the map key, letting us ask questions while he ate his lunch. We discussed the features of the mountains, flying at the different elevations, and the four watch posts where we might get deployed when we finished training. Northwatch was by far the most dangerous, since it was only a few miles from the border of Luntharda. Sile said that was where all new riders had to go if they wanted to earn their stripes.

Felix sat back and let out a noisy sigh. "So what starts first? I mean, as far as training goes. Where do we even begin?"

Sile sat back in his seat some, glancing between us as he folded his arms across his chest. "Boys, this is as much a mind game as it is a test of physical strength and stamina. You'll be stretched beyond your limits every single day. You're going to feel like you're drowning, but just don't let yourself give up. I expect you to get up before the call to arms in the morning." He paused, and glanced at me with a meaningful prick of his brow. "That's the morning horn blast. You run the drills I told you about, in the air and on the ground. I'll show you the flight pattern on your first official day—you probably won't have your saddles by then, so you'll have to piggy back for a while. You need to be back at the breaking dome for your morning brief right after the call to arms. Then you'll head to the gymnasium after the brief for your first lessons in ground combat training. That will take up the first half of your day, so be prepared."

Felix snorted. "Yeah. I've heard about that. They're going to beat the basics into us, right?"

"We all start at the bottom as fledglings. In this brotherhood, respect must be earned." Sile shrugged. It made me wonder what kind of respect he'd won for himself. I didn't know what he'd been through, or what battles he'd fought. I didn't really know much about him at all, except that he had a strange interest in my future.

"You'll be allowed to break for lunch, and then you'll report to the Roost for basic flight patterns and maneuvers. Although, on your first few days, you'll probably be learning how to actually put a saddle on your dragon." Sile smirked like that was funny to him. I could understand why the idea of watching me try to wrestle a big saddle that weighed more than I did onto the back of a wild, ornery dragon might be amusing to someone else. It made me sick to my stomach, though. "Your afternoons will be spent in classes learning the language of hand signals we use in the air, and of course, studying your maps."

"Can't wait." Felix was grinning. He actually looked happy about all this, like he couldn't wait to get started.

Sile just rolled his eyes. "We'll see how you feel about it after your first week. Unless you're psychotic, you'll be writing your mother begging her to let you come back home to your soft, warm bed."

As we settled back into our room for the night, Felix was especially chatty. I could tell he was really excited from our talk with Sile. He went on about his own dragon, a female he'd named Novalla. He called her Nova for short, and told me she was bigger than most females he'd ever seen bred.

"You'll like her," he promised with a wide grin. "She's like a lazy housecat, once you get to know her. I bet she'll get along with yours. What's his name?"

"Mavrik," I answered as I shucked off my boots.

Felix couldn't sit still for a second. He was sitting, then he was up and laying out his gear, then he was looking for his maps, and then he was back sitting on the bed again. I couldn't believe he still had any energy left after what we'd been through all day.

"So, tell me about yourself," he demanded. "I don't know anything about you, well, except that you've somehow landed in the last place in the world I'd ever expect to see a halfbreed. We're going to be roommates for the next two years, so we might as well get to know one another."

"What is it you want to know?" I looked at him from across the room.

He'd gotten up again, and was obsessively adjusting the laces on his boots. "Well," he spoke without looking up, "your dad is Ulric Broadfeather, right? The tackmaster?"

I frowned. Already I could tell this was going to be an uncomfortable conversation for me. "Yeah, that's him."

"What about siblings? Or is it just you?"

I told him about Roland and the twins, who were my half-siblings. There wasn't much to tell, really. Roland was rarely around, and I'd made a point to avoid Emry and Lin at all costs.

"I never had any brothers or sisters," Felix said as he put one boot down and started working on the other. "My dad popped off a son right away, which is all he wanted, and that was it for kids. He's not exactly a family man. He comes around to tell me when I'm doing something wrong, or when I've embarrassed the family name somehow, but beyond that ... we don't really know each other."

Felix and I had more in common than I'd anticipated. Or at least, it was starting to sound that way. "Yeah, Ulric doesn't really like me." I couldn't keep from laughing some at that. It was a huge understatement. "Actually, I'm pretty sure he hates me."

"What about your mom? I mean your real one, not your stepmom," he asked. "What's she like?"

I hesitated. No one had ever asked me about her before. She was obviously where the elven half of my blood had come from, so generally people avoided acknowledging she'd ever existed. I looked up at him warily, and wondered if this was going to end with me having to defend her honor.

Felix met my gaze, waiting for my reply with a curious arch to his brow. "What?"

I looked away quickly, and shrugged. "She's dead." I decided to be vague.

"Did she have a name?" He wasn't going to let me off with that pitiful answer.

"Alowin," I answered reluctantly.

"Well, I'm sorry to hear she's gone." He actually sounded sincere. "You must miss her."

I just bobbed my head. It hurt to talk about her. My memories of her were precious, and I didn't want to share them with anyone I thought might smear her name or accuse her of something she'd never done. People had called her a witch before and worse.

"So," Felix started to speak again, and I could tell by his voice that he was changing the subject. "On to the important stuff. Girls. You have one in the pocket back at home?"

"What?" I gawked at him. That was ridiculous, but for some reason, it made my face started to burn with embarrassment. "No, of course not."

"You sly pup." He grinned at me cunningly. "You do! Look at you, blushing like an idiot. What's she like, eh?"

I tried to glare at him, to look convincingly resentful of his accusations. But it was no use. "She's just my friend. It's not like that at all."

"Oh sure." He rolled his eyes. Putting his shoes aside, he leaned forward where he sat on the edge of his bed. He looked very interested in what he thought was my love life. "A name, Jae. She's got one, doesn't she?"

"Katalina," I grumbled back. "Really, she's just a friend. I didn't even get to say goodbye to her before I left to come here. She probably thinks I'm dead."

"Dead? *Pfft*, yeah right." Felix finally started to settle in for the night, kicking back onto his bed, and getting comfortable. "Just write her a letter. Tell her what happened, that you're staying here for a while to be a dragonrider. I bet she'll be after you like flies on flop, then. It just kills the girls, you know."

"What does?" I wasn't sure what he meant by all that, or if I even wanted Katalina to be after me.

"The dragonrider bit," he answered like I should have known that already. "You don't get it do you?"

No, I definitely didn't.

"The ladies love us, Jae. We're the heroes. We're the ones all the other foot soldiers, knights, and cavalrymen *wish* they were. We're masters of the sky, the best of the best, and believe me ... the ladies know it. They can't get enough of us."

He jumped out of his bed again, looking at me with a huge grin on his face, and that light of mischief wild in his eyes. "Picture this: the annual officer's ball, and all the big names are there. We're talking generals, colonels, knights, and everyone who's anyone. Of course, all the nobles come to pay their respects, and they bring their dainty little daughters with them to go husband shopping. They're all dolled up and looking for a hero's arm to hang on. Sure, the ground men and cavalry boys can show them a few scars, talk up a few stories, but as soon as *we* hit the doorway—everything changes."

I wasn't convinced. At least, not for my own sake. Sure, I could see rich noble girls going after someone like Felix. He was a dragonrider, and he was also a duke's son. Dragon or not, I was still just a halfbreed. I couldn't imagine noble girls flocking to dance with a bruised up, scrawny halfbreed who was three years younger than all the other students in my class. Girls, even the ones my age, were pretty much always taller than me, anyway.

Felix seemed to be able to tell that I wasn't buying it. He just kept grinning as he lay back down onto his bed, putting his hands behind his head, and chuckling under his breath. "Write a letter to your little sweetheart, and you'll see that I'm right."

7

CHAPTER SEVEN

The days all started to blur together. We started every morning the same way. We were up before the call to arms, on our feet, and flying drill patterns with Sile. Then we were running laps, and studying our maps. I wish I could say that the longer I kept up that routine, the easier it got. But that wasn't the case. Being in Sile's saddle still made me airsick. The way his dragon flew felt so chaotic to me. Things always started out all right, and then before I knew it, the ground was swirling in my vision and I was back on my hands and knees throwing up. Running was still difficult. Felix kept after me, though, and wouldn't let me fall behind too far. Studying came easier once Sile showed us a strategy of dividing the map up into quadrants to memorize in smaller chunks.

One night Felix caught me trying to write a letter to Katty. After some teasing, he actually helped me with it. My spelling was horrible, or so he said, and he started showing me the mistakes and format for writing a letter. He told me he'd had tutors and scholars teaching him all his life. Actually, he was a pretty good teacher himself.

We kept up that schedule right up until our gear and armor was finally finished. It was the day before training was supposed to start, and Sile told us to meet him at the smithing armory first. A different blacksmith had made Felix's armor, so we weren't together when we got fitted.

I stood on the dressing block while the old blacksmith from before put the different pieces of armor on me over the layer of black thermals I'd been given. Sile stood by, watching, and making comments about the fit being too loose.

"Not my fault," the blacksmith rasped in his raspy voice. "It's like dressing a scarecrow."

The chestplate fit against the top part of my torso, and it was as simple as the light colored steel it was made of. It didn't have any of the ornate designs and engravings I'd seen on Sile's armor before. In fact, none of my armor did. It even felt like I was missing some pieces. I only had the chestplate, gauntlets, vambraces, greaves on my legs, and a helmet. They were all very plain, and felt clunky when I moved.

The helmet was the most interesting to me. It had one long slit across the front where my eyes were so I could see, and there was a thin pane of cut clear glass fitted into it. It was like a miniature window built into the helmet.

"So the wind doesn't mess with your vision," Sile explained when he saw me looking at it.

"Are there pieces missing?" I finally had the nerve to ask.

Sile shook his head, taking the helmet from me to look it over before he crammed it back down on top of my head again. "For now, this is all you need. You're just a fledgling, so there's no need for full battle dress. Don't worry, no one else will have a full set of armor yet, either."

"Oh," I answered. My voice echoed inside the steel helmet.

"Besides, I'm hoping puberty remembers you at some point in the next year. Then we'll have to order a whole new set to be made," he added.

He wasn't the only one hoping that. I wasn't even worried so much about getting taller anymore, even though that would have certainly helped. Now, I just wished for a little more muscle mass. Anything at all, even a pound, would have made me look less like a joke.

On our way out of the armory, I caught a glimpse of a familiar face out of the corner of my eye. There were a lot of blacksmiths working with riders, and I hadn't even thought about the fact that Mr. Crookin would be there until I saw him talking with an older student. Without thinking, I broke away from Sile and bolted toward him. I didn't have Katty's letter with me, but now I had the perfect way to make sure it got to her.

"Mr. Crookin!" I called out to him, my voice still echoing under my helmet.

He looked down at me, seeming confused by the sight of me until I took the helmet off. Then his eyes got wide, and he put down the hammer he'd been using. "What are you doing, boy? Does Ulric know where you are?"

"Not exactly." I gave him a strained smile. It was a lot to explain. "I'm staying here. I'm going to be a dragonrider."

His eyebrows shot up, and then furrowed down like two bushy storm clouds over his eyes. He glared at me like he was silently accusing me of lying, but one look over my armor was testament that either I was telling the truth, or someone was funding a very elaborate hoax. He just shook his head, and there was a look of restrained sympathy on his face. "Jaevid, I don't think you understand what you're getting yourself into."

I didn't really. But I wasn't ready to admit that just yet. "I wrote a letter to Katty. Would you please take it to her when you go back home? I never got to tell her what happened, or where I went. I didn't get a chance to tell her goodbye, and I don't want her to think I'm dead."

He eyed me again, seeming skeptical, but finally rolled his eyes and nodded. "Put it in my saddle bag before I go. She'll find it."

I smiled and thanked him, preparing to go back to where Sile was waiting, watching me with his arms crossed in disapproval.

As I turned to go, Mr. Crookin barked out another word. "Jaevid."

I stopped and glanced back.

Mr. Crookin's eyes flicked past me, seeing Sile standing there waiting. When he looked back at me, it was like I was as good as dead. "Watch yourself. No need for anyone else to die."

His warning left a lump in my throat, and I clunked back to stand beside Sile again without answering. He was frowning at me like he was waiting for an explanation. "A family friend," I told him as vaguely as I knew how.

Sile didn't ask anything about it. He just grabbed my shoulder to keep me from running off again, and steered me directly toward the second armory building. I had a new saddle waiting for me there.

Getting Mavrik into the saddle was a spectacle. We even had an audience. A few other riders and students started to gather around to watch me trying to put a saddle on my wild dragon.

It wasn't a very big saddle, because I wasn't a very big person, and I could carry it fairly easily. But when Mavrik saw it, he hissed at me where he was crouched on his belly. He made angry chattering noises, swishing his long tail, and tracking my movements with his bright yellow eyes as I lugged the saddle over toward him.

"Come on, it's not that bad," I grumbled.

He snorted, sending a blast of hot air into my face. A few of the spectators laughed.

"I don't like it any more than you do. Let's just get it over with." I slung the saddle over my shoulder, lifting it up as high as I could to sling it over his neck. Mavrik growled lowly, snorted again, and narrowed his eyes angrily.

Sile stepped in to help me get the hard, shaped bottom of the saddle fitted onto the grooves and horns of Mavrik's back. It fit like a glove, and he quickly walked me through a blurred lesson in strapping the saddle into place. A pair of very thick leather belts went around his neck and under his wing arms. Lesser straps stabilized it, running under his belly to keep the saddle from sliding around.

Once we'd finished, Sile pulled me back quickly as Mavrik rose up and shook himself. The saddle stayed put, fixed to his back between his neck and wing arms. He snarled at it, twisting around like he didn't approve, and finally cutting an accusing glare right at me.

I threw my hands up in surrender. "It's not my fault! I can't just cling to you and hope you don't drop me."

The dragon licked his chops, and slicked his ears back like an angry cat as he hunkered down again.

"Time for a test drive." Sile was smirking from ear to ear.

My stomach fell, and as he helped me up into the saddle, I was already feeling sick. He showed me how to fit my legs down into the pair of deep, boot-like sheaths crafted into the sides of the saddle. They came up to my knees, and were so snug it was like wearing a second pair of extra tall boots.

"How's the fit? Can you move your feet?" Sile asked.

I shook my head. "No, not much."

"Good." He started rattling off instructions, making me queasy as I tried not to think about what I was about to do. "This is primarily what anchors you into the saddle. Here, you see these handles are like the ones on my saddle. During takeoff and high-intensity maneuvers, you're going to have to lean into his speed and hold on. The gauntlets you're wearing are meant to help you keep a grip. That's why the palms are coated with resin. Don't fight against his speed. Move with it. If you resist, you're going to get slung all over the place. It's like any relationship, if you go into it unwilling to move and think as one, it can only end in disaster."

"How do I steer?" I was beginning to panic. I could tell my brief lesson in the basics of flying was almost over. Mavrik was beginning to shift around anxiously again.

Sile grabbed my hand, showing me how to grip the polished bone handles. They were positioned on what looked like a circular pieces of metal, about the size of a dinner plate, built into the sides of the saddle. I'd assumed they were just to keep the handle from coming unstitched, but Sile twisted my hand and showed me that the round metal pieces actually rotated if you pushed hard enough.

"Left and right." he told me in a hurried voice. "When you twist them, it puts a small amount of pressure against his side. He can feel it, and knows which way you want him to go. You'll have to work with him to get used to it. Remember, he's never flown with anyone, either. You have to teach each other. You'll come up with your own signals and body language to communicate in the air."

I was about to ask how to tell him to land, but Sile was gone in a flash. He jogged backward away from us as Mavrik began to stand, making me bob around in the saddle as I gripped the handles for dear life. I squinted my eyes shut, clinging with all my might as I felt the dragon shake himself again. He was still writhing around, snarling about the strange feeling of the saddle on his back. All I could do was hang on and pray he wasn't going to kill me.

Right away, the feel of Mavrik's flight was completely different from anything I'd experienced with Sile. When he leapt into the sky, I could feel the force and power of his body working around me as he pumped his wings. I heard him roar, felt his sides swelling and shrinking against my legs as he breathed, and watched the earth fall away. The crowd of spectators became like little dark spots far below.

When Mavrik took off, it wasn't chaos. I didn't feel like I was going to get flung off his back. I felt anchored, and almost as though I was a part of him. It felt right, and it gave me such a rush of excitement that I couldn't help but scream out. He stretched his wings wide, leveling off and letting out another belting cry of his own. He flicked a look back at me, as though making sure I was still attached to him. I was grinning like an idiot, laughing as I held on for dear life.

Suddenly there was another trumpeting roar directly to my right. It was so loud, and seemingly out of nowhere, that it startled me. I looked over, and couldn't believe it. Felix and Nova were flying upside down right next to me, so close I could have reached out and grabbed his helmet if I wanted. He waved at me. I could hear him laughing, too, even over the rush of the wind.

Just as quickly as he'd appeared, I watched him dive away. Nova spun into a tight roll, swirling down toward the ground. Before I could think about the intensity of a move like that Mavrik decided to take up the chase. He snapped his wings in tight against his sides, and immediately we plummeted downward. I screamed because there was nothing else I could do other than hang on.

We chased Nova like two eagles playing tag, darting through the sky. We did dives, we rolled, we flew up until we breached the clouds and saw nothing but endless sky above.

Nova really was a big female. She was way bigger than Mavrik, with golden and brown markings on her scales like a jungle snake. She was bigger, but Mavrik was faster. When he switched on the speed, there was no catching us, and we dove through the clouds like a charge of blue lightning.

It was indescribable, and right away I knew it was the greatest rush I'd ever experience. I also knew I'd never get enough of it. If being a dragonrider meant I got to do this every day, I'd jog as many laps and memorize as many maps as I had to. I wasn't going to give this up—not ever.

8

CHAPTER EIGHT

"We're going to be the best," Felix declared as we lay awake in our beds. After a day like that, neither of us could sleep. My heart was still racing, and I couldn't stop grinning. All I could think about was flying again, and how soon I'd be allowed back in the saddle.

"Trust me, I know. I can feel it. We're going to be the best riders this academy has ever seen," he went on.

I laughed. "We haven't even had our first real lesson yet, Felix," I reminded him.

He didn't seem to think that was a problem. He went on and on, talking about our bright future, until he finally fell asleep. As soon as I heard him start to snore, I got up and put my boots back on as quietly as I could.

The craftsmen were going to be leaving tomorrow. All the saddles and armor had been finished, and so they would go back to their homes and private workshops. Mr. Crookin would go with them, and I had to get Katty's letter into his saddlebag before he left.

I crept out of the dormitory and into the night. The academy was quiet, and every building was dark except for a few rooms in the instructors' dormitory. I slipped through the shadows, and was out of breath by the time I reached the smithing armory. All of Mr. Crookin's gear was still there, packed up and ready to move out in the morning.

I took Katty's letter, folded it up the way Felix had shown me, and tucked it carefully into one of his saddlebags. With a big sigh of relief, I stood up and started back for my room. Thousands of stars twinkled overhead, and the moonlight made long, ghostly shadows on the ground.

I'd just reached the edge of the tackmasters' armory, keeping out of sight as much as possible in case there were any instructors still awake, when the sound of two voices made me freeze in place.

A cold shiver of fear ran down my spine. The voices were coming closer. I sucked in a sharp breath, and ducked into the nearest workstation that was still crowded with equipment. Hiding behind a big wooden crate, I waited.

The voices kept coming closer, and I could hear the crunch of footsteps. I recognized one of the voices right away; it was Lyon Cromwell. But I didn't recognize the other one. It sounded like a much older man, maybe even an instructor.

"You're absolutely sure about that? Every morning?" the man's voice asked in a snapping tone.

"Oh yeah, we've all seen them," Lyon was quick to answer. "Trust me. He's up there before the call to arms, running drills with both of them like clockwork. He's giving them all the lessons a week ahead of time, so tomorrow they should start aerial maneuvers."

The unknown man made a thoughtful, growling noise. "We hadn't anticipated on the halfbreed, but I suppose it won't be a problem. Fledglings wouldn't know how to respond to such an ... unforeseen accident."

"Oh, I wouldn't worry about that little rat," Lyon scoffed. "He won't last a week in real training. It's a joke they've even let him stay here this long."

The man didn't sound so sure. "Lieutenant Derrick is not an idiot. If you had half a brain yourself, you'd realize that. He's up to something. Our best chance is to act now, before any plan he's cooking up has had time to be fully realized."

"Right." Lyon didn't sound too happy about being called dumb, but he didn't argue. "Well, I held up my end, so I expect you to hold up yours."

It was the older man's turn to scoff. "Watch your mouth, boy, and remember your place. You will be compensated, as long as everything goes according to plan."

I ducked down, and tried to make myself into the smallest ball I possibly could when their footsteps went past. Their voices started to get faint then, and they moved away toward the Roost. After a few minutes, I couldn't hear them at all anymore.

At first, I was too afraid to even think of moving. I couldn't believe what I'd heard. Lyon was planning something bad, and it sounded like it was going to be aimed at Sile. I was so terrified of being caught out here alone, where no one would hear me scream for help, but I couldn't stay in the armory all night. So I waited a few more minutes, until I was absolutely sure they weren't coming back, and started for the student dormitory in a sprint.

I didn't stop or look back until I'd slammed the bedroom door shut behind me. There wasn't a lock on it, so I just stood with my back against it, gasping for breath. My heart was pumping like mad, and I was numb from head to toe.

Felix bolted upright as soon as the door slammed, and he glared at me sleepily with his hair ruffled up like a messy haystack. "What's the big idea? You scared me to death!" He growled as he grabbed his blanket and rolled back over.

"F-Felix!" I could barely get the words out because of how hard I was breathing. "Outside, I heard someone talking to Lyon! Tomorrow morning, when we fly, Sile is—!"

"—probably gonna kick your butt for staying up too late," he interrupted angrily. "Would you go to sleep already? And quit slamming the door. You scared me to death."

"But I heard—!" I tried to spit the words out before I ran out of breath.

"Right now all I can hear is you keeping me awake!" Felix growled again, grabbing his pillow and covering his head with it. That was the end of the conversation.

I sat down on the edge of my bed and tried to think. There had to be some logical explanation for what I'd heard; something that wasn't as bad as how it had sounded. But no matter what I came up with, I was still left with a swirling sense of doom in the pit of my stomach.

Something bad was going to happen, and I was the only one who knew.

9

CHAPTER NINE

It was hard to get excited about my first day of training when I had a big black cloud of worry hanging over my head. I got up before Felix did, got dressed, and waited on him to catch up so we could meet Sile before the call to arms. We had patterns to learn and laps to run before our day officially began.

"What's with you?" Felix asked me on the way to the Roost. "You look like you've seen a ghost."

I shot him a glare. "I tried to tell you last night. I heard Lyon talking to someone. He's plotting against Sile."

"*Pfft!*" Felix slapped my shoulder teasingly. "You're just paranoid. Sile is one of the most decorated instructors here. Why would anyone want to plot against him?"

I didn't know. All I knew is what I'd heard, and it hadn't sounded like they were planning a surprise party for him.

Sile was waiting for us. He was already saddled up and ready to fly, standing in his full armor like he had been the first day I saw him at Ulric's house. He coached us hurriedly through putting on our own saddles again, and then we were off.

The sun was just beginning to rise over the eastern mountains, making the sky a deep purplish red. The air was cold, and my teeth chattered under my helmet as I watched Sile and Felix surge forward into the sky on either side of me. We gained speed and altitude, leaving the dark ground behind and charging toward the sunrise.

Mavrik seemed to be able to sense my apprehension. He kept flicking his big yellow eyes back at me, making curious chittering noises as he chased Valla and

Nova through the air. I kept my eyes on Sile, watching as he took the lead and began to give us signals to follow him in a V-shaped pattern.

I could see him clearly off my left wing, and he started to guide us through a long sweeping pattern that took us around the outermost perimeter of the valley. We did steep climbs, steeper dives, and sharp banking turns.

I was beginning to think Felix was right. Maybe I was just being paranoid, and I'd just misunderstood what I'd heard last night. There really was nothing to be worried about at all.

Then Sile gave the signal to do a barrel roll.

I watched him veer to the right, toward me, and begin another steep descent. Valla drew her wings in, and they began to roll downward into a layer of clouds. Out of the corner of my eye, I saw Felix start to follow, mimicking Sile's movements.

Suddenly, something snapped.

It made such a loud crack I could hear it even over the rush of the wind that hummed past my helmet. I ducked just in time as a piece of metal went flying past my head so fast it probably would have knocked me out cold. I looked back over my shoulder, trying to figure out what it was. I was almost sure it looked like a buckle.

Valla let out a high-pitched shriek that sounded like pure panic. Mavrik answered her with a thrumming roar, and before I could think, he snapped his wings in tight and started to dive after her. All I could do was hang on, searching frantically for some sign of Valla, or even Felix, as we dove through the clouds. We streaked downward, and I couldn't see anything except the occasional blur of ground through the haze.

Then I saw her. Valla flared her white wings right below us, catching the air and coming to a sudden halt. I yelled at the top of my lungs. We were going to hit her!

Mavrik put on more speed, making a sharp twist so that we just barely missed her as we blitzed down through the air. A second later, and we would have struck her head-on. I caught a glimpse of Valla as we blurred past; she wasn't wearing a saddle anymore. My heart stopped, I looked frantically through the clouds below, searching for Sile.

He was in freefall, lost somewhere in the haze.

We hadn't been trained to handle something like this yet. I couldn't hear anything but the rush of wind, couldn't see anything but the clouds all around us, but I could sense the ground was growing closer and closer with each passing second. If I couldn't find him in time, if he hit the ground from this high up ...

Then I saw him.

Sile was falling through the air like a stone. His helmet was missing, and I could see his mouth was open like he was screaming as he flailed through the air.

He saw me in that same instant. Our eyes met, and I knew I was about to watch him die unless I did something.

I leaned down against Mavrik's back, squeezing the saddle handles and giving the signal for him to fly faster. The ground was getting closer. I could see it rushing up to meet us. Mavrik rolled to avoid cliffs as we glanced near the sides of the mountains.

Just a few feet away from Sile, I reached my hand out toward him. He was clawing at the air, trying to grab onto me. I couldn't reach him. My arms were just a few inches too short. I tried to lean out further, and still keep a grip on my own saddle. My fingertips brushed his. I saw the panic, the sheer terror in his eyes.

Something came over me like a flood of eerie calm. Everything got quiet in my mind. Fear melted away. I let go of the saddle completely, anchored to it only with my feet in the sheaths, and lunged out toward him. I grabbed Sile by the front of his breastplate, and he clung to me as I dragged him in toward the saddle.

Sile just barely got his fingers hooked onto my saddle before we were jerked violently backward. Mavrik flared his wings to put on the breaks, stretching out his hind legs and kicking off the ground just in time. He leapt back into the air, and I felt my heart jump into the back of my throat as the ground fell away again.

When we landed safely back at the academy, I was shaking so badly I couldn't even get out of the saddle at first. Felix landed nearby, and he was yelling and waving his arms as he ran toward us. Sile climbed down from where he'd been piggybacking on my saddle, and he looked shaken, too. He was cradling one of his arms against his body like he'd been hurt.

I pulled off my helmet, taking a few deep breaths and trying to calm down. But I was still trembling all over, and feeling lightheaded like I might pass out. When I tried climbing down from the saddle, I got my foot stuck and I fell flat onto my back, looking up into the early morning sky. Mavrik's big head appeared over me, sniffing and pressing his scaled nose against my chest.

"Good job," I told him breathlessly, patting his snout.

Felix was frantic as he rushed over to haul me back up to my feet. "What happened?"

I shook my head. "I'm not sure. I think something happened to his saddle."

When I looked up to find Sile and ask him, he was walking away. An audience of other students and instructors was gathering around us. Someone had sounded the alarm when Valla had landed without a saddle or rider on her back.

Sile was staggering away from us, and his face looked pasty. He leaned on one of the other instructors and hobbled away through the crowd. He didn't even look back.

Felix was looking me over like he was searching for damage. "How is that possible? I've never heard of that happening before. Someone would have to intentionally compromise it for it to just break like tha—" He stopped short, and gave me a wide-eyed look.

I glared at him darkly. "Still think I'm just paranoid?"

Felix didn't answer. He didn't have to. I could see on his face that this was bad. Someone had just tried to kill Sile Derrick by breaking his saddle on purpose. They'd tried to do it and make it look like a terrible accident.

The instructors still standing around began shouting at us to move along, to get back to our routine. Gradually, everyone began to disperse. Felix gave me a little shove with his elbow, and I knew we had to get back to our own schedule. Sile wouldn't want us slacking off, even if he was hurt.

It took us longer to run our laps while dressed in full armor, but since our flight had been cut short, we still made it to the breaking dome before the call to arms sounded. All the other students in the academy flooded in, almost a hundred total. The older classes looked more distinguished, more like men or proud warriors, and they glared at me like there was a diseased mouse in their midst when we came inside.

I stayed close to Felix, following him to stand at the front of the group with the other first-year fledglings. Academy Commander Rayken was talking with a few of the other high-ranking instructors in full battle armor, whispering to each other in low voices before they finally turned to the crowd of waiting students. The dome became silent, and we all watched as Rayken stepped forward to address us.

"I'm sure you've all heard about Lieutenant Derrick's unfortunate accident this morning," the commander spoke loudly. "You'll be relieved to hear that his injuries were minor, and he will be back in service tomorrow. Let this be a lesson to all of you. Check your gear each and every time you ride. Never assume anything, and be prepared for everything."

I swallowed stiffly, and was glad he hadn't said anything about my involvement. I had a pretty good idea that people would look at me more as a culprit than a hero.

The commander waved a hand then, dismissing that topic with no more ceremony. "Back to business. Allow me to welcome you to Blybrig Academy. For some of you, this is your first time to stand in our midst. For others, you are already a part of our brotherhood."

He went on, talking about the proud history of the dragonriders and our place as the pride of the king's forces. It was inspiring to look around and see the other, older young men standing around me. We all wore the same style of uniform, tunics and black pants. But we fledglings all wore navy blue tunics with the golden eagle, while the second year students wore black tunics with blue stripes down the arms and sides. They also wore long navy blue cloaks pinned around their shoulders by a golden clasp shaped like the king's eagle. It made them look more professional and polished than we did.

The older students also had a hardened ferocity in their eyes, and they stood stiffly at attention with their hands clasped behind their backs. I still didn't see how I would ever fit in with these guys. I felt like a fox that'd been lined up with the hunting hounds. Sooner or later, someone was going to sound the horn and I would have to run for my life.

The Academy Commander dismissed us with a salute, clasping a fist over his breastplate that all the older students returned with a shout. Then we started to break up into our respective classes. The older students left first, dispersing outside to go about their schedules, and the rest of us in the fledgling class started to flock to the gymnasium for our first round of combat training.

The gymnasium was just a big, open building with a dirt floor. It was lit with bulky iron chandeliers that had thick candles burning, making the place feel like some kind of dungeon. There were practice dummies made out of straw lined up against the far walls, and several large chalk circles drawn out on the floor for sparring.

The instructor in charge of teaching us combat was another lieutenant named Morrig. He wasn't an especially large or burly man, but he had that same coldness in his eyes that made me immediately afraid of him. He gave us all blunt practice swords, and broke us up into groups of two. I made sure to partner with Felix. There were thirteen of us in all, so he pulled one student aside to be his partner while he showed us how to move through each maneuver.

We started with simple parries and strikes, and ran through drills taking turns being offensive and defensive until everyone was exhausted. Then we moved on to hand-to-hand sparring.

I had been dreading this from the beginning. I was so much smaller than everyone else; I knew I didn't stand a chance in a wrestling match. Thankfully, today was just for instruction, for learning the different ways to pin someone, or disable an enemy that was armed with a sword.

Felix was really good at it. He was one of the tallest of the boys, and he was incredibly strong. So naturally, he pinned me every time, and I wound up with a face full of dirt. He wasn't going easy on me just because of my size.

Morrig ran us through drill after drill, move after move, and ended the first day of combat training by having us do pushups, sit-ups, and spend nearly an hour lifting big iron weights. When we finished, everyone was absolutely filthy and none of us even had the energy to look one another in the eye.

By the time we got to the dining hall, I'd forgotten all about Sile's accident that morning. All I could think about was lunch. Felix brought us a tray of food to share, and I started stuffing my face before he even sat down.

"So, you're sure it was Lyon you heard last night?" Felix asked suddenly. I couldn't help but notice how nervous he looked.

I nodded. "I'm sure."

"The instructors are writing this off as an accident. But I've been thinking about it, and there's just no way it could have been. You've seen our saddles. You'd have to intentionally cut the straps for one to fall off like that." Felix leaned in to whisper. "Tonight, when we're done with academics, we're going to go looking for his saddle. It's got to be just lying in the dirt out there. I want to see if the straps really were cut."

I swallowed my mouthful of food. "What if we get caught? That's a long way to walk."

Felix shook his head. "I'm not saying we walk. We fly out there, check it out, and come back. It's the only way to be sure."

I wasn't sold on the idea. But then, I'd heard Lyon plotting first hand. I knew what I'd heard, and there was no question in my mind that someone had done something to Sile's saddle to make him fall like that. But once Felix got an idea in his head, there was no way to talk him out of it. I was beginning to realize that was a trend with him.

After lunch, we had our first official lesson in flying. We were taught how to properly put on our saddles, piece by piece, which buckle went where, and how the fit should be. After going to so much trouble, I started to realize why Felix was so baffled at the way Sile's saddle had fallen off. Someone really would have to intentionally damage a saddle in a big way to make it come off like that.

The instructor checked all our saddles twice over, making doubly sure they were put on properly before we took to the air and began learning basic patterns. Felix and I had already gone over this basic stuff a few times with Sile, so we knew what to do. For the first time, I felt a little bit confident.

After flight training, we began our studies in academics and cartography. That lasted the rest of the afternoon, and we were dismissed for the day as the sun started to set. Of course, we were expected to study and practice everything we'd learned that day, but all I wanted was a bath and something to eat.

When I finally flopped down onto my bed, I tried not to think about how every muscle in my body ached. I thought it was safe to steal a few minutes of sleep before I tried studying my maps again. Then the door opened, and a shoe hit me in the face.

"Hey, what're you doing?" Felix laughed, armed with his second shoe in case the first one didn't wake me up. "We've still got to study, you know."

I groaned, and rolled onto my back. I was prepared to take his other boot to the head if it meant I could sleep for even fifteen minutes. "I'm exhausted. I can't feel my legs."

"Oh come on, don't be a baby," he teased. "We need to at least look busy. As soon as evening roll call is over, and everything gets really quiet, we're going to find that saddle."

He had gone over his plan with me about thirty times already. I still wasn't sure this was going to work. I hadn't paid much attention to where we were exactly when I'd caught Sile in the air, much less where his saddle had landed. However, I did have a pretty good idea of what would happen if we got caught.

"It was incredible. You know, the way you caught him like that," he said suddenly.

I rolled my head over to see if he was making fun of me or not. He wasn't. His face looked serious, if not a little proud. "I couldn't just let him fall like that. Besides, I'm pretty sure none of the other instructors would want to take me on as a student. If he dies, that's the end of my career."

Felix laughed a little. "Yeah, good point."

I only snoozed for a half hour or so before guilt forced me to study. Felix and I sat up by candlelight, studying our maps, and going through the complex language of hand-signals we'd only just begun to learn. Right after the evening horn blew, we started hearing the sounds of talking and footsteps outside as the various sponsors checked their student's rooms to be sure everyone was accounted for.

Sile knocked on our door, and I got a hard lump in the back of my throat when I saw him standing in the doorway. He had one arm in a sling, and a bandage on one side of his neck. He looked between us as we sat on our individual beds, our maps spread out in front of us.

"How was it?" Sile asked. I noticed he was making an effort not to look me in the eye.

"Not bad," Felix piped up. "I've got some questions about a few of the parry moves, but I figured I would just wait and see if we could go through them tomorrow morning before combat training. How's the arm?"

Sile sighed and shook his head a little. "It's just a precaution. The infirmary insisted I wear it for at least one day. Knocked out of socket, they said. No real harm done." He looked at me then, and I felt like I'd been nailed to a wall. "Jae, I need to talk to you."

I swallowed hard. "Yes, sir."

Felix cast me a haunted look as I got off my bed, stepped into my boots, and followed Sile out into the hallway.

We were alone outside the closed door of my dorm room, and Sile stood with his side to me for a moment as though he were collecting his thoughts. I had no idea what he was going to say, but before he got a word out, my mouth ran away with me.

"Lieutenant Derrick, I think someone is trying to kill you," I blurted.

He turned a perplexed expression down at me. "Because of what happened today?"

"Well, yes, but there's something else." My face got hot, and I dropped my gaze down to the tops of my boots. "I was out at the armories last night, I wanted to send a letter back home with one of the craftsmen, and I heard someone else out there. They were talking about us, and it sounded like they were going to do something bad."

His expression became intensely serious. "Who? Did you see them? Did you recognize who it was?"

I choked. I had recognized Lyon's voice, of course. But I hadn't seen him. I hadn't actually seen anyone. I didn't want to run the risk of pointing a finger at the wrong person, so I just shook my head. "No, it was really dark. I couldn't see who it was. I mentioned it to Felix, and he said I was just being paranoid. I really thought maybe he was right. I didn't want to assume anything. I'm sorry, sir. I should have said something."

Sile let out a loud, noisy sigh. I wasn't sure what he'd do or say to that. I almost expected to get struck for not speaking up sooner. Instead, I felt a heavy hand fall on my shoulder.

He was smiling down at me, and I could have sworn his eyes seemed almost sad. "Jae, you saved my life today. What you did was stupid, but incredibly brave. Thank you."

I hesitated. "Sir, is someone trying to kill you?"

His expression twitched. I saw darkness in his eyes, and that sense of doom burrowed into the pit of my gut. It made me nauseated.

"Apparently so," he answered. He didn't sound surprised at all.

10

CHAPTER TEN

Felix was eager to get out and find the remains of Sile's broken saddle. He still wanted hard evidence. As soon as the academy was silent, and anyone with any sense was resting up for the next day, he dragged me out of bed and out the door. I was nervous about it; we weren't allowed to be out of our rooms like this, much less flying without an instructor's permission. If something went wrong, no one would even realize we were gone until tomorrow morning.

But Felix wasn't backing down. He had decided we would take his dragon and ride together. She was big enough to carry both of us without any problems, and it would be easier to sneak one dragon out instead of two. I was just anxious to get this over with. The sooner he got his proof, the sooner I could sleep.

Standing outside the Roost, I kept a lookout while he went inside to saddle her up. I didn't like standing out there alone in the open. Somehow, I had the feeling that if we did get caught, I'd be the one who got blamed for this regardless of anything Felix said. I was the bad influence, after all. I was the halfbreed.

The night air was quiet and the wind was still. Looking up, the stars were so bright they made the whole horizon glitter. There was plenty of light to see by, so I started to hope that maybe we would actually find the lost remains of Sile's saddle.

I heard a rustling behind me, and let out a sigh of relief. I just assumed it was Felix coming back with his dragon.

But it wasn't. Not even close.

I turned around right into an oncoming fist. Someone hit me so hard across my face that it sent me stumbling backward. My vision blurred. My nose stung. I could taste blood coming from my nose and mouth.

"You just keep getting in my way." I couldn't see who hit me, but I heard Lyon's voice laughing over me. I knew it was him. "You really should've just taken the hint and quit while you were ahead. Now you're in my way again."

There was more laughter coming from some other guys standing behind him. My vision cleared enough that I could see them under the starlight. Four older boys, including Lyon, were circling me. They were all fledglings from my class—Lyon's friends.

I scrambled to get back up, but Lyon was quicker. Just as soon as I'd gotten my feet under me, he hit me again in the stomach so hard I fell forward. I was gasping and wheezing for breath, crawling across the ground to get away.

"No one wants you here. You'll never be one of us. Don't you get that?" He snarled over me, and grabbed a fistful of my hair to jerk my head back so I had to look him in the eye. "You will never be worth anything to anyone. You think Felix cares about you? He doesn't. No one cares anything about halfbreeds. You're nothing but filth, and that's all you'll ever be."

The other three boys circled me again, and one reared back to kick me in the ribs. I couldn't catch my breath to even cry out for help. It might take half an hour for Felix to get his saddle ready, if he did it the way he was supposed to, and by then I wasn't sure how much of me would be left.

They were kicking me, hitting me as hard as they could. One of them had come armed with his riding gauntlets, and when he hit me, it was like being smacked with solid iron. I curled into a ball, covering my head with my arms, and prayed for it to end.

Suddenly, it stopped.

I was afraid to look up and see why. I was afraid maybe one of them had come with a sword, or gone to get some other weapon to finish me off. But what I heard was the sound of fighting, of frantic shouting, and punches being swung.

When I finally looked up, I saw Felix standing over me with his hands balled into fists. He had a crazed look of rage on his face, and his lips were curled up into a snarl. One of the other boys was already lying unconscious nearby.

"Get up, Jae," Felix growled down at me. "I can't take them all by myself."

I was in pain from the hits I'd already taken. But at that moment, it didn't matter. I got up. Felix was fighting for me, and I wasn't going to let him do it alone. I put up my fists, facing the three boys left standing. Lyon was one of them, and he looked like he wanted to kill me. He dove at me first.

And then it was a brawl.

Even if I wasn't a good fighter, I could at least watch Felix's back. He hit them so hard it made me cringe. He was a pretty big guy already, bigger than Lyon, and twice as strong. I saw so much pent up anger in the way he fought them, and even when he took hits, he never quit. At least, not until he had his boot on Lyon's face and was grinding it into the dust.

"Come after him again, and I'll break both your arms," Felix promised with a snarl. "Not even your parents will be able to recognize what's left of you."

When Lyon managed to worm his way out from under Felix's heel, he immediately started to run, and the rest of the boys went with him. They disappeared into the night, and left their unconscious friend just lying there.

I couldn't believe it was over. I was afraid to relax, expecting another attack to come out of nowhere. But they didn't come back. The night was just as quiet as it had been before.

I stood beside Felix, blood dripping from my nose down the front of my nightshirt, and didn't dare let my guard down until I saw him drop his arms. We were both breathing hard, spattered with blood, and looking at each other with no idea what to say.

At last, Felix's shoulders sagged and he came over to grab my chin, jerking my face up to poke at my bloody nose.

I winced and tried to squirm away. "Stop it! I'm fine!" I didn't like the way he hovered over me like some kind of worried parent. It was humiliating to be treated like a little kid, and I was already embarrassed that he'd had to save me in the first place.

"You're lucky it's not broken," he reminded me as he let me go.

I staggered back, still panting as I glared defiantly up at him. "Why do you keep doing that? Why do you care what happens to me? No one else does!"

Lyon's venomous words were still ringing in my ears, reminding me of the cold truths I feared the most. I didn't know why Felix was being so nice to me. I didn't want to suspect that he was just toying with me. But I couldn't help it. No one else wanted to be a friend to me, especially none of the other fledglings.

"You think I should just let them kill you?" he yelled back. "Just because of who your mother was?"

I fought to choke back the tears that stung in my eyes. "Anyone else would! So why? Why do you keep doing this? I deserve to know!"

He looked at me like it was the stupidest question in the world. I heard him curse under his breath. "You'd do the same for me, wouldn't you?"

I stared at him. He'd answered my dumb question with another dumb question. "Yes."

He pointed at me accusingly. "That's why. You understand that this isn't just a contest to see who can be better between you and me, who can outrank the other, or screw the other over behind their back. Just because your mother is a Gray elf doesn't make your life any less valuable than mine. I know you'd sacrifice just as much if it were my face being kicked into the dirt. Am I right? So you tell me, why would I stick my neck out for someone like that? Why would I want someone like that as my friend?"

I couldn't answer him. I just stared at him, unable to keep tears from streaming down my face. He stomped toward me, grabbing the back of my shirt and giving me a shove back toward the dormitory.

"Come on, we've gotta get back inside before someone sees us. Forget about the stupid saddle." He growled through clenched teeth as he kept me moving onward.

I knew he was angry. Even if I wasn't sure why, I still felt like it was my fault. After cleaning my face up, pinching my nose to stop the bleeding, and assessing the damage to the rest of my body, I curled into my bed. Except for some bad bruises, I'd gotten away without any serious injuries.

Felix was awake, still looking like he was fuming with rage where he sat in his own bed. As soon as I was settled, lying with my back to him, he doused the candle and the room went dark.

"Felix?" I asked, not really expecting him to answer.

"What?"

I squeezed my eyes shut. "Thank you."

He was quiet for a moment, and then I heard him make a loud, exasperated sigh. "You're welcome."

CHAPTER ELEVEN

As the weeks passed, every morning started early with us flying drills as usual. Then we ran our laps, and Felix always ended up practically pushing me like a wheelbarrow so I didn't collapse. Then combat training lasted the rest of the morning, and I was essentially Felix's practice dummy. He never slacked off, never went easy on me, but always apologized whenever he nearly choked me unconscious or gave me a new horrific-looking bruise. I knew he was trying to help me. No one else was going to go easy on me, and he wouldn't be doing me any favors if he did.

I had been hoping I'd get tougher, or stronger, but it felt like I was actually getting worse. My parries weren't right. My strikes were too slow and weak. Watching me try to wrestle and pin Felix, who was twice my size, probably looked like a chicken trying to pin an angry bull. The instructors yelled until it bored into my ears, telling me to be faster, to work harder, and to quit being an embarrassment to the academy.

In the air, however, I wasn't an embarrassment. Even the instructors had to give me some credit for that. Maybe I couldn't pin Felix on the ground, but in the air it was a whole different story. Mavrik was fast, aggressive, and he could outmaneuver anyone. It was like he wasn't even aware I was on his back. Sile was right; we did form our own little language of body signals and touches to communicate while we flew. Mavrik was smart, and he seemed to understand me better and better each day. We became two parts of the same powerful entity.

I was also good at memorizing the maps. I had mine down like the back of my hand in two weeks flat. I never missed a mark or a single detail, and I even coached Felix some because he struggled with it a lot more than I did.

Things weren't going great, but they weren't going as badly as they could have been. After our showdown that night at the Roost, Lyon stayed away from me. He shot us poisonous looks from afar, but pretty much kept his distance. Felix had hit him hard enough to make an impression, apparently.

The days were so blurred together, with every hour either filled with some kind of training, studying, or sleeping, that I totally lost track of time. I didn't hear anything else about a plot against Sile. There were no more malfunctioning saddles, or aerial rescues. Things fell into a predictable, constant routine that gave me a sense of comfort and stability I'd never had before. For the first time, I had a plan. I had something to do, somewhere I had to be, and responsibilities.

Our combat training became more intense, and more specific to weapons we were better suited to use. Lieutenant Morrig wasn't sure what to do with me. My arm wasn't long enough for a short sword. I wasn't tall enough for a spear. I wasn't strong enough for an axe or a mace. He was puzzled, and so I just kept switching weapons, hoping one would eventually be the right fit.

We also learned archery, and the academics shifted from memorizing maps and hand signs, to learning about the native plants and animals of Luntharda. They made it sound horrifying, and described huge bloodthirsty beasts, poisonous streams, and even carnivorous trees. Secretly, I found it all really interesting. My mother had always told me stories about the forest, but never in such detail.

We also learned about how to treat wounds in the field. We learned to set broken bones, to make poultices and salves from various plants to stave off infection, and how to stitch up gashes and cuts. I was pretty good at it because my fingers were smaller, and I'd seen so much of my own blood that being around wounds didn't make me queasy like it did some of the others.

Summer made the valley incredibly hot during the day. It baked the earth like clay in a kiln, and made all the plants and grass shrivel up. At night it was pretty cool, so we usually stayed inside and studied. None of us had the energy left at the end of the day to risk getting caught out on the grounds anyway.

I wasn't aware how much time had passed, or even what month it was, until Felix started jabbering about the officer's ball. Apparently, once a year, every officer of note was invited to a grand ball held at a certain noble's home. The rich families of Maldobar argued over who should host it since it was, according to Felix, the best place to go shopping for a potential spouse. It was a status symbol because sometimes the king attended. There'd be wine, dancing, music, food, and pretty girls as far as the eye could see. Felix was absolutely giddy about it.

"We aren't officers yet," I reminded him as we sat at the dinner table. I had my face in a dusty old book, reading about the carnivorous trees that grew in Luntharda. "What makes you think we'll get to have any fun?"

"We will, we just won't be allowed to dance or talk with any of the girls," Felix countered. "We can look, but we aren't supposed to approach."

A few of the other fledgling students sitting around us nodded in agreement.

Since our confrontation with Lyon, little by little, I'd started to earn the tiniest amount of acceptance from my peers. I wasn't dumb enough to think they liked me, but they were willing to tolerate me now. I guess they'd figured out that if they couldn't get rid of me, they might as well get used to me being around.

"So, what you mean by that is you're going to do it anyway?" I peered over the top of my book at him.

Felix was grinning from ear to ear. "Of course. It's only punishable if you get caught."

I rolled my eyes. "I don't see what the big deal is. It's just a bunch of silly, giggling girls. What's so interesting about them?"

Felix smacked my book out of my hands down onto the table. "Are you crazy? Don't you have a girl back home?"

I glared at him. I'd made the mistake of telling him about Katty when this all started. I'd even let him talk me into sending her a letter. But I hadn't received any reply at all from her. I didn't know if she'd even gotten my letter in the first place.

"No," I grumbled, crossing my arms over my chest. "I told you, she's just my friend."

"It starts with friends." Felix was grinning cattishly again, and a few of the other students around him had joined in. "Then you go in for the kiss."

"You sound like an idiot, you know." I arched a brow at him. "Even if you did find some way to sneak off and talk to a girl, you're not an officer yet. None of us are. We're just students. And aren't we supposed to be serving food and manning the doors and carriages? What girl is going to want to talk to a glorified butler?"

Felix wasn't listening anymore. He'd started snickering and talking to someone else who appreciated the topic of girls more than I did. I wasn't going to let myself get caught up in any kind of grand vision of how the ball would be. It would be interesting to be in a noble's home, watch the couples dance, and see how the rich and glamorous got to live. But I was sure I'd get stared at worse than usual. What noble wanted a dirty halfbreed in their house?

We finished dinner and dispersed to our rooms. I took my time bathing. When I came back our room, Felix was stretched out on his bed studying.

"You got something today," he said, pointing to my bed on the other side of the room.

There was a small square envelope sitting on my bed with my name, Jaevid Broadfeather, written on the outside. I was bewildered. We were more than halfway through the training year, and no one had sent me anything before. I went over and picked it up, tearing it open carefully to unfold the paper tucked inside.

"It's from your girl, isn't it?" Felix was standing right over me, breathing down my neck. "I want to see. C'mon you owe me, especially after I helped you write the first one."

I didn't want to share it. I tried to turn so he couldn't see it, holding it down and away. Before I could read a single word, he snatched it out of my hands and darted away. I chased him, trying to grab it back while he laughed. He held it high over his head and started reading it out loud.

"Stop it, Felix!" I yelled, jumping to try and grab it. "Give it back!"

"Ooh look, she says she misses you. She even drew a little heart there for you at the bottom of the page." He teased, finally let me have the letter back. I gave him a good punch in the arm before I retreated back to my bed and started reading it.

I didn't interpret anything in Katty's letter as even remotely out of the ordinary, much less romantic. And there definitely wasn't a heart drawn at the bottom of the page. She wrote that she was glad I was doing well, and proud that I'd made it into the dragonrider's academy. She was looking forward to seeing me when I got to come home between training years, and said that she missed me. Her father had started teaching her blacksmithing full time now, and had even given her the official title of his apprentice. I knew that must have made her really happy. She asked about the academy, about what I was learning, and if I'd made any friends. I read the letter over three or four times before I folded it back up, tucking into the envelope, and slipped it under the corner of my mattress. I couldn't keep a smile off my face.

"So, everything's good with her?" Felix asked as he looked up from where he was studying again.

I sighed. "Yeah. Seems like it."

He nodded, smirking to himself like he thought it was funny. "Just look at that grin on your face. You should just tell her you like her, you know. Go ahead and get it out of the way before some other guy snaps her up."

I glared at him tiredly. "I told you, we're not like that. She doesn't—" I paused to think. "What do you mean snaps her up?"

Felix shrugged some. "You know, if she's pretty, you're probably not the only one who's going to notice her. It's all about timing, my friend."

That didn't sit too well with me, not that there was a single thing I could do about it. I sat up, pretending to study while I mulled it over. I didn't really know if I liked her or not. She'd been a friend, my only friend, up until recently. She was one of the few people I knew I could really trust. To tell her that I liked her would change everything, and not necessarily for the better.

When Felix went to sleep, I took out a clean piece of parchment and wrote a letter back to her. Since I'd come here, there had been plenty of time to practice writing. My spelling was still a little wonky sometimes, but it was much better than before.

I told her everything I could think of about the academy. I told her about Sile, and all the rigorous morning drills he made us do. I told her about Mavrik, and how together we'd saved Sile from being killed when his saddle malfunctioned. I told her about Felix, who was becoming more like an annoying older brother than a classmate. I told her about how he'd rescued me from being bullied a few times, and how he liked to tease me about everything. Finally, I told her that I liked it here. It was hard. Every day was tougher than the one before it, but I really did like it. I liked feeling like I had a purpose, and a future to look forward to. Even if only a few of these dragonriders liked me, I could deal with that. I could be happy anyway.

I paused to think about what else I should say. Felix thought I needed to tell her that I liked her, but I still wasn't sure about that. Leaving the letter unfinished, I folded the paper up and tucked it under the bed with the one she'd sent me. I would just have to think about it some more.

When it came to Katty, things had always been clear to me before. She was my very best friend, and definitely someone I cared about. But asking myself if I liked her the way Felix was talking about meant I'd be putting all that on the line if she didn't feel the same way. I just wasn't sure I was ready to risk that yet.

CHAPTER TWELVE

The day before the annual officer's ball, all our training was suspended for preparations. There were no morning drills, no pushups, and definitely no academics for us. The older students and officers had to have their formal armor refitted, polished, and perfected, so the hallways of the dorm were filled with the smell of shoe polish and clean laundry.

As fledglings, we didn't have anything like that yet. Instead, Sile came into our dorm room with a bag filled with new navy blue tunics that had the king's golden eagle stitched on the shoulders and breast, long black capes with a gold-colored chain around the neck, knee-high black boots, and black pants. There was a set for each of us, and Sile told us to go ahead and try everything on to make sure it fit.

"Can't have you two looking like bums at Duke Brinton's estate," Sile grumbled. He came over and started adjusting the collar of my tunic, then did the same to Felix's.

"Is that who's hosting it? Brinton? Well, at least there'll be a lot of wine." Felix snorted. "Duke Brinton loves his vineyards more than his own children. He talks about them like they were people instead of a bunch of plants. You should hear him at dinner. Just on and on—there's no stop to it. About the leaves, and the grapes, and how he's perfected the aging process. And his son, there's a real piece of work. You may have been born a halfbreed, Jae, but be glad you never had to endure a play date with Fredrick Brinton."

I snickered, and Sile cast us both a dangerous look. "Just keep your thoughts to yourself when you're at his estate, am I understood? No talking with the distinguished guests. No drinking. No dancing. You're there to help ladies from carriages into the ballroom, not flirt with them. You're there to serve wine, not drink any. This is a night for men, so remember your place, boys."

I was actually getting excited about it now. There would be food there unlike anything I'd ever tasted before. Even if most of the people there looked at me as if I were a cockroach, I was still going to enjoy it. I was still a fledgling dragonrider—so they couldn't exactly kick me out.

When we had packed our new uniforms up, with Sile standing over us, watching to make sure we didn't leave anything behind, we went to bed early. Everyone else did, too. For once, it was Felix who was too restless to sleep. He kept me up with his excited whispering, going on about Brinton's obnoxious fat son, Fredrick, and how his wife had a hooked nose and nasally laugh. I was relieved when he finally drifted off and I heard him start to snore. It didn't take me any time at all to fall asleep, too.

The call to arms sounded, and purely out of habit, I was already awake. Felix had no trouble sleeping in the extra few hours, though. He was still snoring and drooling, so I just finished my letter to Katty.

I promised her I'd come to visit as soon as I could, told her how I hoped to get another letter from her soon, and ended it at that. No emotional gushes or confessions of liking anyone. I just wasn't willing to risk it. In the whole world, I could count the number of people I could call friends on one hand, and one of them was a dragon. I didn't want to do anything to jeopardize the relationship I had with her. At least, not yet.

When Felix woke up, we started to get ready to go. We put on our fledgling's armor, grabbed our bags, and started down toward the Roost. It didn't take much time to get ready to leave, but it was really crowded. Every other rider in the academy was in the process of leaving, too. All around us, riders were fixing their saddles, tying down their bags, and taking off into the sky. Some of them had already left and were on their way to the east.

Sile was waiting for us. We hurried through fitting on our own saddles, tying down all our bags, and taking off. With the ocean to our backs, and the sun rising over the mountains before us, we started for Duke Brinton's estate.

A few twilight stars were still glittering in the west when Blybrig Academy emptied of all its dragonriders into the morning sky. It was an incredible thing to see. All around me in the sky were magnificent dragons and proud knights in gleaming armor. There were more than a hundred in total, all heading toward the break of day. And the best part was, I was one of them.

It was almost a full day of riding over mountains frosted with snow, steep desert canyons, lush green valleys, and rolling grasslands to get to Brinton's estate. We didn't even stop to rest, and by the time we could see the city below, my rear end was sore from sitting in the saddle for so long. We circled in a pattern, following Sile as he signaled to us that we were landing in waves, five at a time. I guessed that was to keep from overwhelming the Duke's front door with a flock of dragons.

Duke Brinton was opening his enormous home and all its rooms to us. All the dragonriders from Blybrig were staying with him until tomorrow morning. It was an honor to spend the night in a noble's house. Even if they made me sleep in the stable with the horses, it would probably still be the nicest place I had ever stayed in.

We kept circling in a tight pattern until it was our turn to land and quickly unpack our bags before sending our dragons back into the air. They'd hang around in the area, waiting for us, but there was nowhere to stable them here. Besides, keeping dragons around livestock was generally a bad idea. Even tame dragons got hungry.

I stood back, watching Mavrik take to the air and soar skyward like a huge, blue-scaled eagle. He was so powerful and majestic, and seeing him join the flock of dragons in the air, swirling in a giant circular column like buzzards over a kill, was amazing. I still wasn't used to it, and it still took my breath away.

"Come on, we've gotta get ready!" Felix gave me a nudge and nodded toward the door.

Brinton's estate looked like a massive castle made of stacked white stone. There must have been a thousand rooms with gleaming windows on every side. The front lawn was like a front field, and in the center was a huge lake with white swans paddling around on it. In the back, there were acres upon acres of vineyards, stretching as far as I could see across the rolling landscape.

Two maids in matching blue and white dresses were holding the front doors open for all the dragonriders to come inside. As soon as we were inside, I forgot to look anywhere but up. The ceilings were incredibly tall, and painted with images of clouds, angels, and the old gods from the old fables doing battle with mythical beasts. I noticed that one of the demonic monsters looked a lot like a Gray elf, only with pointy teeth and glowing yellow eyes.

The windows stretched up the walls, and chandeliers made of glittering crystal looked big enough to kill a few people if they happened to fall. Porcelain pots squatted on the floor, so big I could have climbed inside one to hide, but instead they were filled with blossoming fruit trees that made the air smell sweet. I felt totally out of place as I stood with my bag in one hand, and my helmet under my other arm.

Felix kept nudging me to keep me moving, and we followed Sile into the house, through the long hallways, up a grand staircase, to the east wing where we dragonriders were staying for the night. Maids dressed in that same blue and white dress went back and forth past us, and one paused to let us into a large suite that was for the three of us.

Sile waved us off as soon as he sat his bags down. "I've got to run a few errands before I dress. Go ahead and clean yourselves up. Try not to get into any trouble. In fact, just don't leave this room until I get back," he commanded before he went back outside.

The room was as big as Ulric's whole house, and then some. It had four bedrooms and a washroom attached to a big sitting room. One whole wall of the main room was entirely covered by a window that looked out onto a beautiful garden three stories down. There was a big silver platter of fruit, cheese, a whole table of desserts set out for us to eat, and a fully stocked wine bar. Felix was eyeing that as I went from room to room, checking things out.

I couldn't believe I'd actually have a room all to myself. Not just a cot, or a shared room; I'd have my own bedroom with a double bed, soft sheets, and fluffy pillows. It was surreal, and I was afraid to touch anything for fear I'd get it dirty.

"He's gone to get his family, you know. The wives always come to this kind of thing. They love the show." Felix was leaning in the doorway, looking around at the glamorous bedroom. "So what do you think?"

I turned to look back at him. "About what?"

He waved a finger in a circle, gesturing the suite we'd be staying in for the next day.

"It's incredible." I couldn't hide my amazement. "Do you live in a house like this? Your father is a duke, too, isn't he?"

Felix shrugged like it wasn't a big deal. "Bigger, actually. But not nearly as gaudy. Brinton's family manages a much smaller area, so I guess he feels like he has something to prove. My family line is much older. You know, there's a slim chance I could even be heir to the throne someday. King Felix. Sounds good, eh?"

I smirked and rolled my eyes at him, setting my bag down and beginning to take out the pieces of my uniform for the night. "No wonder you were excited about this. I'm actually kind of looking forward to it, now."

"Told you so." He smiled back at me, giving me a mischievous wink before he went to his own room to get ready. "And the real party hasn't even started yet."

I washed up, scrubbing dirt from my face and hands and neck, and combing my hair to make sure it covered my pointed ears before I got dressed. I checked in the big floor mirror in my room to make sure my collar was straight, and there wasn't a wrinkle out of place.

Sile came back in a hurry. He was alone, and didn't look very happy. He started rushing through his own preparations, cursing and muttering under his breath as he fought to get his cape buckled onto the pauldrons of his shoulder armor. As I finished getting ready, I wandered out into the parlor to watch him fighting to get his cape situated.

"Is everything all right, sir?" I dared to ask.

He didn't stop to look at me, finally getting the cape on right, and going on to hurriedly buckle up his beautifully engraved vambraces onto his forearms. "My wife has decided to stay at home. She's late on in her pregnancy, and just can't stomach to travel this far. But she sent our oldest child here with a nanny, and now the nanny's come down with some kind of stomach bug. She's emptying her guts, and it doesn't look like she'll be able to take care of herself for the rest of the night, let alone anyone else. So I'm left with an unchaperoned kid to worry with when I'm already supposed to be babysitting you two. I tried to find Brinton to ask him about using one of his own girls as a nanny, but of course he's nowhere to be found. Not that I blame him. There'll be about five hundred officers in attendance tonight, total. The whole house is in an uproar. He's got his hands full."

Sile had never mentioned his family to us before. I didn't even know he had a wife or any children. He was still growling and muttering under his breath while he finished getting dressed. "I can't just haul a kid around all night. I don't know why she'd even bother to send Beck at all," he grumbled. "She knows young kids aren't welcomed at events like this. It's not a play date."

"I could do it, sir." I offered before I could even think it through.

Sile stopped in the middle of fastening his last buckle to frown at me. "Do what?"

"Watch after your son. Beck, right?" I clarified. "I've got two younger siblings, so I'm used to taking care of kids." That wasn't exactly true. Whenever I'd been forced to watch Emry and Lin, it always ended badly. They did everything they could to get me into trouble, and I was helpless to stop them because I was outnumbered. But one kid? Surely I could handle just one.

He narrowed his eyes, and opened his mouth like he was going to protest, but the door to our suite opened. One of the other instructors stuck his head into the room long enough to tell Sile we were ten minutes away from needing to report for presentation. We were out of time.

Growling more angry words under his breath, Sile shot me a quick glare. I could already tell, just by the look on his face, that I'd just blown my chance at seeing the officer's ball. I was going to be on babysitting duty for the night.

"Fine, you'll have to do. I'm out of time and out of options. You have to stay in the room, am I understood? No roaming the halls. I'll make sure there's a servant on call, in case you need anything," Sile told me as he ran out the door again.

All the air rushed out of me as soon as he shut the door. I deflated. I'd come all this way for nothing. I tried to tell myself it was for the best. I would probably cause more problems than I'd solve. Me working around nobles was the perfect recipe for disaster. I could just see some dainty noble girl screaming in horror when I tried to help her down out of her carriage.

Felix came out of his room already dressed and ready to go. He noticed my gloomy appearance right away. "What's wrong?"

"I'm not going," I told him bluntly. "I'm staying here in the room to babysit Sile's son."

"What?" Felix's expression was pure horror. "That's what nannies are for!

Don't tell me he didn't bring someone to look after his brat? Wait—did you say son?"

"He did bring a nanny, but she's sick. There's no one else to watch him. It's fine, Felix. Don't make a big show. I offered to stay behind and do it." I shook my head, wishing I'd just let Sile handle the problem himself.

He stared at me like I was dumber than he'd originally thought, and rolled his eyes. "You need to learn when to pocket that conscience of yours, you know. Or at least keep your mouth shut."

"Yeah, well there's nothing I can do about it now. It's fine—I'll be fine." I tried to sound confident. I knew I could babysit. That wasn't a problem. This kid couldn't possibly be worse than Emry and Lin were. "Besides, at least it's a boy, right? I'll just teach him to sword fight or something."

The suite door opened. Sile came back into the room holding the hand of a girl who looked only a little younger than I was. She was wearing a simple sky blue dress, and her dark hair was tied into a braid down her back. She had her father's dark green eyes, and there were a lot of freckles across her nose and cheeks. My heart sank to the bottom of my stomach. Suddenly I was having horrible flashbacks to all the times Emry and Lin had gotten me into huge trouble.

"B-Beck?" I looked at Sile for an explanation. Beck sounded like a boy's name, but Beck was obviously anything but a boy.

He just smirked like he'd fooled me good. It was as though he were daring me to withdraw my offer to babysit her. "Beckah. We call her Beck for short. Is there a problem?"

My mouth was hanging open. I was totally stunned as I stood there, looking between him and the girl. She still didn't say a word. I was shocked, but I wasn't stupid enough to take back my offer just because it was a girl instead of a boy. I figured trying something like that would probably make me look like a hypocrite ... and Sile would just make me do it anyway.

"N-no sir, no problem," I finally managed to answer.

Felix snickered. I saw him grinning at me out of the corner of my eye. Somehow, I got the feeling he'd known Beck was a girl all along and just didn't want to ruin the surprise. He wasn't even doing a good job of stifling his laughter as he ducked out of the room, giving me an exaggerated little wave on his way. I guess he thought this was hilarious. He'd never let me live it down.

13

CHAPTER THIRTEEN

I was officially on my own.

Felix and Sile both left right after another maid came in with two trunks full of Beckah's stuff. Sile only gave me a few instructions before he rushed out the door: no leaving the room, no breaking anything, and Beckah had to be in bed in three hours. Now I was standing before a girl who still didn't look convinced that I could be trusted, even though Sile had assured her I was harmless. She looked at me warily, like she might run if I made one wrong move.

I wasn't sure what to say. She was definitely older than my sisters, but still younger than I was. I had no idea what girls her age liked to do. Well, other than torture me occasionally.

"Um, so your name is Beckah?" I asked her. Since I was small for my age, I was just about looking at her eye-to-eye.

She just blinked and didn't say anything. I could see traces of Sile in her expressions, especially when she frowned at me. He definitely had to claim her as his child.

"I'm Jae," I told her.

She was beginning to hedge a few steps closer. I noticed how her eyes were quick, and darted over me curiously. You could just tell by the way she was examining me that she was smart, probably a lot smarter than I was.

"Daddy won't let me go to the party with him," she said at last. "He says it's for adults only, but you were going to get to go."

"Well, not really," I explained. "I was going to have to work. You know, serve food and open doors. Not exactly much fun. Maybe it'll be more fun to just stay here, after all. They left plenty of food in here."

I saw her smile for a moment, just a little bit. It was like watching a star shine out from behind a veil of clouds. I knew Sile would beat me within an inch of my life for thinking it, but I couldn't help but notice that she was really pretty. There was something earthy about the mixture of her green eyes, dark hair, and the freckles sprinkled over her nose. Something about her, for whatever reason, reminded me of my mother. Maybe it was that curious twinkle in her eyes.

"You're half elf, aren't you?" she asked me suddenly.

I felt my heart twist in my chest so hard it hurt. This was the moment I'd been dreading, because pretty much everyone felt the same way about halfbreeds like me. I just nodded and braced myself, fully expecting her to give me a look of disgust.

Suddenly her smile came back, spreading over her face and making her cheeks get rosy. "That's what daddy told me. He said your momma was a gray elf." She sounded curious. She started coming closer to me, and I was immediately on red alert. I stiffened, staring at her uncomfortably as she looked me over from head to toe. "What was she like? I've never met a gray elf before."

"Not like what you've heard, I'm sure." I was quick to defend my mother's honor. "She was the kindest person I've ever known. And she could grow anything."

Beckah was nibbling on her bottom lip as she reached out to touch my hair. I couldn't help myself; I flinched away. Her expression was as surprised by my reaction as I was that she'd actually wanted to touch me. And then, for whatever reason, she looked sad.

"Okay, then. We'll just have our own party here," she announced. "Since daddy won't let us join his. What's for dessert?"

I wasn't so sure about this anymore. Beckah was the strangest girl I'd ever met, which was saying something since I'd grown up with two goblins for sisters. But Beckah wasn't like them. She wasn't mean to me, and she didn't seem to be disgusted by me, either. Just like her father, she seemed to think I was interesting.

There was a big tray of desserts already set up and waiting for us, and she breezed right past the rest of the food and headed straight for it. I watched her eat three big bowls of fruit drizzled in chocolate, honey, candied nuts, and whipped cream. I just nibbled on a peach. I had a good idea what rich food like that would do to my stomach, and that wasn't how I wanted to spend the evening.

She kept me distracted, anyway. She asked dozens of questions about my mother, my father, and the academy. It was a little strange. I assumed Sile would have told her most of this stuff already, but she seemed really interested to learn anything she could about dragons and the academy.

"Daddy doesn't come home much, anymore. He's busy with training all the time," she said with a mouthful of food. "It makes momma really angry. That's why she said I had to come, even if daddy doesn't want me here. She said he doesn't spend enough time with me. I wish I could go with him, just once. I'd like to see the dragons."

"Maybe he'll bring you when you're older." I couldn't keep from smiling at her. She just said whatever crossed her mind. I'd never met anyone like that before. "What about you? Do you wish he was home more?"

She shrugged and looked down into her third bowl of dessert. "I guess. But even when he is home, it's like his mind is far away. He doesn't really see us. We just make him frustrated and upset when he's home. It's always been like that. He and momma fight a lot. I don't think she's very happy about the new baby. I've heard her crying at night. I think she wishes daddy would just quit being a dragonrider and come back home."

I could see the pain on her face, even if she didn't realize she was showing it. I knew how she felt. Wanting her dad's approval, or just a little of his time, was something I understood completely. "It's not your fault, Beckah. It's nobody's fault. He's got a lot to think about. His job is stressful, and dangerous. I'm sure he loves you."

"Are you going to be like that, when you're grown up?" she pointed an accusing gaze at me suddenly.

I wasn't sure how to answer that. I just sat there staring at her, and tried to think of a good reply, with my mouth hanging open. I couldn't get any sound to come out.

"Don't be that way, okay? You're really nice, I can tell. So don't be like that. Don't forget about everyone else—especially the ones who need you the most." She stood up to refill her bowl, and it seemed like she just wanted to get away from me for a minute. She was upset. I wasn't very perceptive, and I knew nothing about girls, but even I could tell she wasn't happy. Talking about her family made her upset. She wanted to go to the ball, but not for the same reason everyone else did. She just wanted to be near Sile.

"So what else do the adults do at parties? Other than eat too much dessert?" I gave her a hopeful smile, and tried to change the subject.

Beckah sighed loudly. "There's always dancing, and they stand around and gossip about each other." She came back to sit on the floor next to me, a little too close for my comfort. "Sometimes the men fight, but only when they've had too much wine and decide to act stupid."

I smirked; that reminded me of Felix for some reason. "I don't know any gossip, or how to dance."

Her eyes popped open wide, and she grinned at me like she had a brilliant idea. Grabbing my wrist, she bounded to her feet and started pulling me toward the door eagerly. "Come on! I know where we can go and see the real party! I'll teach you how to dance."

Suddenly Sile's warning that we should stay in this room was ringing in my ears. I dug my heels in. "We can't go out. Your dad said—"

"My daddy just doesn't want me to bother him. That's how it always is. But we won't get caught. He won't ever know we're there. I promise! Please?" She begged, and puckered her bottom lip out some. "Don't you want to at least see the party?"

Of course I did. I also didn't want to imagine what Sile would do to me if I broke any rules—especially ones about his daughter. I started to shake my head.

Then Beckah gave me the best begging face I'd ever seen. Her big, round green eyes blinked up at me sadly, and I folded like a wet napkin. I was helpless against that kind of manipulation, especially when her chin started to tremble.

"Fine, fine. Just a quick look, but then we come straight back." I surrendered.

She started pulling me toward the door, opening it to lean out and peer left and right before we went outside. I got a sick feeling in the pit of my stomach that this wasn't going to end well. Even though the hallways were empty, I could still hear the sounds of laughter and music echoing faintly like whispers over the marble floors.

Beckah led the way through rooms decorated with expensive rugs and furniture. The further we went, the louder the music became, although it seemed to be coming from everywhere. We went through doors, down stairs, up stairs, and I was beginning to worry we'd never find our way back again. Reaching to grasp her hand tightly, I reeled myself in closer to her. I couldn't get my bearings in this place at all, and if I lost her, I'd never find my way back to our room alone.

"How do you know where we're going?" I whispered. We'd come up several narrow flights of stairs, and I was out of breath.

Beckah stopped on a landing where a single door was hidden in the shadows. She started opening it, and peeking through the crack. Light spilled in from the other side, and suddenly the sound of the music was much louder. It seemed to be coming from below us.

"Haven't you ever been in an estate like this before? All rich people's houses are basically the same, you know. Big, fancy, and with lots of hidden passages for servants," she whispered back. She opened the door just enough for us to slip through, and quickly shut it again.

A broad open space stretched out before us. Overhead, the wooden rafters were visible going up into the gloom. Brilliant golden light bled up through the cracks in the floorboards, shining from the ballroom below. There were ghostly pieces of furniture standing along the walls, covered up with white sheets. I started to realize this was a storage room.

I could hear the music, the sounds of laughter and conversation, and even smell the food coming from party under our feet. It filled me with excitement, even if I was still worried about being caught up here. Neither one of us could resist the urge to squat down and peer through one of the cracks.

The ballroom was massive, sparkling with the light from big crystal chandeliers, and filled with beautiful people that stood around talking, drinking wine, or were twirling on the dance floor. There were officers with all kinds of uniforms. Ladies wore fancy ball gowns encrusted with jewels, and white gloves up to their elbows. I saw the other fledgling dragonriders carrying silver platters with wine glasses on them.

"Look, there's daddy!" Beckah whispered, pointing toward a corner where there was a large group of high-ranking dragonriders gathered. They were laughing and drinking, probably telling war stories.

For some reason, seeing everyone like that made me sad. I sat back on my knees and sighed. I couldn't help but wonder if this was as close as I'd ever get to a party like that. Granted, this was a lot closer than I'd ever been before. But was I really just kidding myself? Did I really have a place with people like that?

"Jae?" Beckah was looking at me with an unhappy quirk to her mouth. "I'm sorry you got stuck with me, instead of going to the party."

It wasn't hard to smile at her. "No, it's not that. I just always end up wondering how I'll ever fit in with people like that. It was . . . kind of a fluke that I even ended up being a dragonrider at all."

"Well, do you like it?" she asked me frankly.

"Like what?"

"Being a dragonrider?" she asked again.

I nodded. Just thinking about it made my heart beat faster. "Yeah. I love it."

She shrugged a little. "Then nothing else matters. Who cares about fitting in with them? If it's something you really care about, then it shouldn't matter what anyone else thinks."

She sat back on her heels right across from me, looking me up and down with her intelligent green eyes. She was pretty sharp, for a kid. I had to give her credit for that. She really was a lot smarter than me, which was kind of scary.

"I guess you're right." I looked back down at the floor and the dancing couples far below. Maybe I'd never be one of them, but Beckah was right. Compared to the other places I could have ended up, this was a pretty great one to be in.

14

CHAPTER FOURTEEN

"Let's dance," Beckah demanded as she stood, dusting off the front of her blue dress.

I stared up at her, and started trying to think of a good excuse not to. "I already told you I don't know how."

"And I said I would teach you, so come on!" She was relentless, and grabbed my arm to pull me back up. She took my hands and showed me how to stand so I was holding her. I did my best not to touch her any more than was absolutely necessary, but my face started to get hot right away. I wanted to pull away. I could just imagine Sile walking in just in time to see me dancing with his daughter.

"Daddy showed me how. Look, like this." She coached me through a few wobbly dance steps with a big grin on her face.

After a few minutes of stepping on her feet, shuffling around, and feeling like an idiot, I was beginning to realize that I was a terrible dancer. But she didn't seem to mind, and so neither did I. She laughed, twirled, and refused to let me give up, even when I stepped on her toes. As long as she was having fun, that was all that mattered to me.

"You have to practice, Jae," she told me. I could tell she was teasing me a little. "You can't step on anyone's shoes next year. What if you squash some princess's toes?"

I smirked, and just rolled my eyes at her. "Right, because all the noble ladies will be lining up to dance with a halfbreed."

She flashed me a punishing look, and got a thoughtful twinkle in her eyes. "I'll dance with you. I'll be fifteen next year, so I can come to the party, too. Daddy won't be able to just dump me on some nanny—no offense."

"None taken. But for what it's worth, this is a lot more fun than serving drinks." I twirled her again. I could tell that was her favorite, and I liked it because it meant I didn't have to move around much.

Beckah's cheeks got a little red, and she stuck her tongue out at me. When she stopped twirling, she let go of my hand and stood there for a moment. It got really awkward. She was just looking at me with this weird expression, nibbling on her bottom lip. It made me nervous.

"We should go back, huh?" she mumbled.

I was starting to think that was good idea. "Yeah, probably."

She led the way back out of the storage room, down the stairs, and into the hallways of Duke Brinton's estate. I still couldn't figure out where we were, or which way we were supposed to be going, but I trusted her. She held my hand tightly, her small fingers laced through mine. It made me feel strange, no matter how hard I tried to ignore it. I wasn't sure if I liked it, or if it just made me really nervous.

We were as fast as shadows as we crept through the house. We slipped from room to room, taking the shortcuts through empty servant tunnels. We hid from passing maids and butlers by ducking into dark corners whenever we heard footsteps or voices coming too close.

It felt like we were getting close when we came to a dimly lit hallway that was very close to the ballroom where the party was still going strong. I could hear the music clearly, even feel it vibrating the floor under my feet. I could smell the food, the perfume of the flowers, and see the bright golden light gleaming far away down the hall. Voices echoed toward us, but it wasn't the sounds of laughter and excited conversation I'd expected to hear.

Beckah stopped so suddenly I crashed into her back. Her eyes got wide.

Then I heard it, too. It was Sile's voice. He was shouting at the top of his lungs, and it sounded like he was arguing with someone.

Beckah just stood there frozen with her eyes as big as saucers. I reacted in an instant, and grabbed her by the back of her dress to pull her into the shadows to hide. We stood stock still as the voices came closer. I held my breath, keeping a firm grip on Beckah with an arm around her waist to keep her from slipping into view.

Five people passed us. Four men all dressed in black, their faces covered with masks painted white with two red lines over the eyes. Sile was in the middle of them, and they were shoving him along with his hands tied behind his back. One of them was holding the point of a long black dagger against his side.

"You cowards," Sile was growling at them. "You really think killing me is going to make any difference? What that madman has done won't be absolved with my death! It will tear this kingdom apart!"

The masked men didn't answer. They just kept shoving him onward, jabbing at him threateningly with that dagger.

"You can take me all the way to Halfax and it will make no difference!" He continued to fight against them, struggling to get free. "Don't you get it? This is what happens to those who tamper with gods!"

Beckah flinched against me. I could feel her shaking with panic. I slapped a hand over her mouth to hold her back before she could move or make any noise. If they found us, then they might kill us, too. She let out a faint, muffled whimper against my palm.

The five men disappeared into the dark, never stopping once. They didn't see us. Once I was sure they were out of earshot, I let Beckah go. She jerked away from me violently, and started to sprint after them. I ran after her.

"What are you doing?" I whispered as I snatched her by the wrist, forcing her to stop.

"They're going to kill my daddy! Didn't you hear? We have to do something!" She looked back at me with a furious, pleading expression. There were tears running down her cheeks. "Help me, Jae. Please!"

"We can't just go after them, not by ourselves! Look at us, Beckah, we can't fight men like that! We have to find some of the other officers. Come on!" I started to pull her in the opposite direction, back toward the party. She didn't fight me, but I could hear her sobbing. If we could find another officer—someone trained to handle this kind of thing—then maybe we could stop those men before they did something terrible to Sile.

"W-who were they, Jae? Who were those men?" Beckah cried as I pulled her along after me, sprinting for the ballroom.

I didn't know. I'd never seen anyone wear masks like that before. My head was swirling with confusion and terror as we ran toward burning light that poured into the hallway. It felt like we were running toward the gates of heaven in some kind of nightmare. No matter how hard I pumped my legs, it still felt like I was moving in slow motion.

When we finally got to the doorway of the ballroom, the roar of the crowd and the surge of the music stopped me dead. I was dazed, panicked, and searching for someone I knew. But I didn't see a single familiar face in the crowd. There were hundreds of people all around, and none of them even looked my way.

"Jae, we have to hurry!" Beckah pleaded.

I clenched my teeth and nodded. There wasn't time to stand here and wait for someone to notice us. I went up to the first officer I could find, and started tugging on his sleeve. "Sir, excuse me! I have an emergency!"

The officer glared down at me, brushing me away angrily. "My wine cup is fine, boy. Move along." He didn't look back down at me again.

I tried other officers, and one after another, they all ignored me in pretty much the same way. Not one would even give me a second look. They couldn't be bothered to step away from their conversations with the ladies, or their cups filled with Brinton's precious wine. Beckah was sobbing hysterically, and I was beginning to get frustrated.

In a moment of desperation and pure stupidity, I spotted Academy Commander Rayken standing with his wife and a few other noblemen, and marched right up to him. I pulled on his sleeve like I had the others, but this time I shouted at the top of my lungs. "Commander Rayken! Someone has kidnapped Lieutenant Derrick!"

The people around us went silent for a moment, turning stare down at me. It must have scared Beckah, because she pressed herself up against my back, and squeezed my hand even harder. I could feel her trembling.

Academy Commander Rayken looked at me like he'd just found a stain on his shirt. He scowled, and didn't say a word. He didn't have to; I could tell he was waiting for me to explain myself.

"I saw it myself, sir. Four men in white masks took him just a moment ago. He was yelling, but no one else could hear." I started to get nervous. Maybe going up to Commander Rayken like that had been a huge mistake. He could still kick me out of the academy if he wanted to, and he was probably the last person in the world who would believe a word I said.

He just scowled at me even harder, like I was wasting his time, and rolled his eyes. "What you're describing is the king's private guard, and as you can see, there are none of them present because they *only* accompany the king himself when he travels. You're mistaken. Lieutenant Derrick is here, somewhere in the ballroom. I saw him not an hour ago." He growled down at me, making me back up a few feet. "Go back to your duties, fledgling, before I lose my patience."

My heart sank to the soles of my boots. I wasn't going to get any help from these people. They didn't believe me, just like before when Sile's saddle had been tampered with. Once again, it was up to me to do something to save Lieutenant Derrick.

So I made another desperate, stupid decision that was probably going to end up costing me more than I wanted to lose.

CHAPTER FIFTEEN

"Beckah, you have to take me up to the roof. You know how to get there, don't you?" I turned to face her as soon as we got out of the ballroom.

She hesitated, looking at me with wide eyes filled with tears. I could see the fear on her face. Her chin was trembling when she finally nodded. "I-I think so. But why?"

I wasn't sure exactly what was going on with Sile, but it just had to be something bad for these guys to come after him twice. After what happened with the saddle, I couldn't afford to take this lightly. Lives were at stake. And just like last time, no one else believed me. So if *I* didn't do something, Sile might die.

I was just one fledgling with no real training, so it was going to take something pretty radical to make any difference at all. Fortunately, radical was my middle name. Or at least, it was about to be.

"I'm going to save your dad, Beckah. Don't worry," I tried to reassure her. "So let's go, and hurry!"

Beckah led the way through the duke's mansion at a sprint, and I actually had a hard time keeping up with her this time. She was faster than she looked, and I was out of breath as we went up staircase after staircase, climbing the levels of the estate toward the roof. We dashed past maids and servants, who stopped to stare or yell at us to slow down.

A few things started to look familiar as we came close to the suite we were supposed to be staying in for the night. I recognized a big oil painting and a small orange tree growing out of a big porcelain pot right outside the door of our room as we ran past. It gave me a sick feeling to think of what was going to happen when the other officers, especially Commander Rayken, figured out Sile and I were missing. I could probably kiss the academy goodbye. So much for my bright new future.

"Jae?" Someone shouted my name and I screeched to a halt to see who it was. My heart was hammering in my chest, and I half hoped it would be Sile. Even if he was furious with me for leaving the room with his daughter, I'd just be so relieved that he was okay.

But it wasn't Sile.

Felix was leaning out of a doorway back down the hall, and his face was smeared with something red. I couldn't tell what it was until he started walking toward me. It looked like lipstick. His hair was all messed up, too.

"What're you doing?" He frowned at me suspiciously. "I thought Sile said you weren't supposed to be out here? He's gonna chew your head off if he catches you." He was one to be talking. Out of the corner of my eye, I saw a noble girl in a party dress run out of the room he'd been in.

"Jae!" Beckah whimpered impatiently. We really didn't have time for this.

"I can't explain it to you now. Sile is in trouble again, and I have to go," I told him.

"Wait, what?" Felix looked stunned. "Go where? What's going on, Jae?"

"I can't, Felix. I'm sorry. There's no time." I shook my head, and turned to start running again.

I got about three feet away before I suddenly came to a jerking, choking stop. Felix had me by the back of my cape so that the chain drew up tight around my neck. He started dragging me back toward him, and when I saw his face again, he looked furious.

"Let me go!" I shouted at the top of my lungs. "Sile is going to die if you don't let me go!"

That definitely got his attention. Felix let me go right away, and just stood there, staring at me like I was out of my mind. "What are you talking about?"

I stumbled when he released my cape, and started taking steps back away from him. "I saw it, Felix. Four men in white masks kidnapped him from the ball. She saw it, too. This isn't a joke." I glared at him, and tried to look as confident as I could despite the fact that I was terrified about what I was about to do. "I tried telling Commander Rayken and the others, but they don't believe me—just like *you* didn't believe me last time. So it's up to me again. I'm going to save him, even if I have to do it alone."

I regretted bringing up the saddle incident, especially since Felix was my friend. I knew it'd probably make him angry, but I wanted him to take me seriously. I didn't stick around after that, just in case he tried to stop me. I ran back toward Beckah, who stood there waiting for me before she started sprinting down the hall again.

We took off into the duke's estate, and it wasn't until we were climbing another steep, spiraling staircase that I realized we weren't alone. Felix was right behind me. He wouldn't look at me, even when I almost tripped over my own feet in surprise.

"What are you doing?" I gasped, trying to talk as I panted for breath.

Felix shot me a punishing glare, like I should have known better than to think he wouldn't believe me this time. "You really think I'm going to let you do something this stupid by yourself?"

I was about to say yes. Actually, I'd expected him to laugh at me as I ran off to ruin my career and probably get myself killed in the process. But I couldn't catch my breath long enough to say anything else. Good thing Sile had been making us run all those laps, or I would have passed out.

Beckah led the way through the mansion, up to the top of one of the towering spires that had a cone-shaped roof. It was a watchtower with a huge lantern in the top to light the grounds below, like some kind of really tall, skinny lighthouse. But there weren't any guards watching it tonight because of the party. In fact, when we finally made it to the landing at the top of the stairs, the door was locked with a big iron padlock. Beckah pulled on it, clawed at it, and finally let out a little scream of panic when it wouldn't budge.

"Oh would you just move?" Felix grumbled, shoving her out of the way so hard she bounced off my chest and almost fell down the stairs. Lucky for her, I was quick to catch her by the shoulders.

Felix pulled what looked like a small metal hairpin out of his pocket, and started poking it into the keyhole. It only took him a few minutes to pick the lock. When it sprang free, he pushed the wooden door open for us to go up into the chamber above.

The room at the top of the tower was round with open stone windows all the way around. We had an excellent view of how high up we were—which was really, really high. So high that it made my head swim at first, even though I had gotten pretty used to flying with Mavrik. The night air blew through the open arched windows, and since the lantern in the center wasn't lit, you could see thousands of stars glittering overhead.

"What now?" Felix came to stand beside me with his arms folded.

I started walking toward one of the windows. "Just a crazy idea," I told him as I leaned out, looking at the ten-story drop below.

It was pretty crazy to think that Mavrik would ever hear me, even way up here. I didn't even know where he was. And yet it had always seemed like he could understand it when I spoke to him, so it was worth a try. I had a strange feeling in my chest, like a hard knot of heat that tingled and made me shiver. I guessed it was just fear, or just a wild sense of desperation.

I took a deep breath, and climbed out onto the ledge. The wind whipped in my hair, and tugged at my cape. Every time my boots slipped a little, my heart jumped into my throat.

"Jaevid!" Felix was yelling at me. "Are you nuts? Get down from there!"

Beckah was yelling at me too, but I tuned them both out. I closed my eyes, and let my mind go quiet for a moment. I felt a strange sensation in my chest, like pressure, and a tingling of heat in the back of my mind. Then it was my turn to yell, and I screamed as loudly as I could. *"Mavrik! I need you!"*

At first, nothing happened. I started to feel like a real idiot, standing out there on that ledge, yelling for a dragon that couldn't hear me. Minutes went by, and I started to give up.

Then I heard him roar.

I opened my eyes, and saw two black shapes flapping toward us like shadows on the wind. Mavrik and Nova wheeled in circles around the tower, their wing beats like thunder in the air, as they tried to figure out how to get to us. The tower's cone-shaped roof was too small for them to land. It was time to earn that radical middle name.

I reached toward Beckah, offering her my hand. "Come on. You have to trust me!"

She looked absolutely terrified. Her eyes were as big as saucers, and she trembled as she took a few small steps toward me. Even Felix looked like he thought I'd totally lost it as he stood there with his mouth hanging open.

I caught Beckah by the hand and started to bring her in closer, helping her climb out onto the ledge with me. That's when Felix finally woke up from his trance of shock and awe. Suddenly, he grabbed Beckah by the back of the dress before she could climb out the window.

"She's not coming with us," he declared. "It's too dangerous."

"What if those masked men come back for her? We can't just leave her—" I started to argue, but Beckah cut me off.

"You're not leaving me behind!" She struggled against his hold on her dress, finally managing to squirm out of his grip. "He's my daddy. I'm going!"

Beckah didn't seem afraid anymore. She swung her legs over the side of the windowsill and was hanging onto the ledge while the wind snatched at her skirts. She gave me a look of determination, like she was trying to convince me that she really wasn't scared.

I looped an arm around her waist, and pulled her toward me. I figured I had about two seconds before she got scared again and did something to mess up my aim. So before she could figure out what I was about to do, and right when Mavrik was circling back toward us ... I jumped. I jumped off the ledge ten stories in the air, and I took her with me.

Beckah screamed, but I could barely hear her as the wind rushed past my ears. I just held onto her as tightly as I could as we fell, and braced myself for what was coming; either death from the fall or what I hoped would be a dragon catching us.

Mavrik did catch us. He came darting through the air, wings spread wide, and hovered just long enough for us to crash into him. We hit hard, and it knocked the breath out of me at first. I was dazed, relieved, and trying to get my bearings.

We landed on Mavrik's back just a few feet away from the saddle, and I started dragging Beckah toward it with all my might. She didn't fight me at all. In fact, she was clinging to my chest like some kind of frightened baby animal. I had to pry her off me when I finally got into the seat and crammed my feet down into the leg sheaths on either side of the saddle. With Beckah sitting in my lap, I kept one arm wrapped tightly around her waist, and finally got a chance to look back at Felix.

He was standing on the ledge now, looking at Nova as she circled around the tower. I saw him make some kind of prayer sign with his hand before he jumped. I heard him yell, saw him drop, and Nova dove after him with a trumpeting roar.

She was bigger and slower, so she missed him at first. As she zoomed past, she stretched out one of her strong hind legs to snatch him out of the air by the boot. He hung upsidedown, screaming and flailing until Nova tossed him back up into the air like a cat playing with a dead mouse.

He flipped end over end, and came back down to land right in the saddle with a hard thud. He had his arms and legs wrapped around her scaly body, and sat there clinging to her until he finally realized he wasn't about to plummet to his death. Then he got himself situated in the saddle, and we veered away toward the horizon.

Where are we going? Felix asked me with the sign language we'd learned to use in the air.

I only had one free hand since I was hanging onto Beckah, but I still managed to sign back to him, *Halfax.*

I've got the lead, he signed. *We'll fly low and watch the roads. Maybe we can catch them before they get too far away.*

I nodded, and was glad to let him lead since I really had no idea how to get to Halfax from here. I was starting to let myself hope. If we could find Sile, then surely we could find some way to save him. Maybe, just maybe, this would work.

CHAPTER SIXTEEN

It was a pretty good plan in theory. We were going to do low passes along the roads, looking for any sign of recent travelers and the men wearing white masks. But as the hours began to drag on, we had to broaden our search, and still didn't find any sign of them. It was as though they'd disappeared completely.

The sun was starting to rise, and the early morning wind was bitter cold. Beckah was shivering, and I could hear her teeth chattering. She definitely wasn't dressed for this altitude, so I took off my cape and wrapped it around her to keep her warm.

"Jae?" She whimpered and grabbed one of my hands as I reached around her for the saddle handles. "What if we can't find him?"

I clenched my teeth because now I was beginning to worry about the same thing. "We'll find him, Beckah." For her sake, I tried to sound sure about that. "Don't give up."

Felix and Nova swooped in close, and he started giving me hand signals again. *We need to land and come up with a new plan.*

Right, I agreed. *Let's stick close to the roads, just in case.*

He nodded, and Nova veered away to find a good place to land. Mavrik and I followed, keeping close on his tail. We found a good spot where the main road leading toward Halfax dipped down through some low marshlands. There were lots of big trees covered in hanging moss, and just enough room for the dragons to drop down and land. Our dragons could hunker down under the trees so no one could see them, even from the air. It was the perfect hiding spot to rest and keep a lookout for any passing traffic without giving ourselves away too easily.

As soon as we dismounted, the dragons rooted around in the mud to find places to lie down, but neither one of them looked happy about it. The mud stank like rotting compost, and it was slimy and thick. It was miserable to walk around in it because it would just about suck your boots right off your feet. Finally, we found a spot dry enough to at least sit down.

"If you're right about them going to Halfax, then they'll have to come by this way," Felix grumbled as he plopped down and started trying to rake the disgusting silt off his boots with a stick. "This is the only road through the marshlands. Any other way would take you days to get around it."

"I don't understand how we could have missed them. Maybe we should have been flying lower." I was helping Beckah hobble through the sludge. She had to hold her skirts up to keep from tripping, but they still got caked in mud.

"We should have been plenty low enough to see them on the road." Felix sighed as he gave up trying to get the mud off his shoes. He was leaning back against a tree trunk, staring up at the morning sky. "We have no armor, no weapons, and no food. This is definitely a new level of stupid for me."

I sat down beside Felix, and Beckah settled in right next to me. She leaned against me, and was already sound asleep before I had even gotten comfortable. It was weird to have her clinging to me like this.

"I didn't mean for you to come with me, Felix. I know this'll probably ruin my career and get me kicked out of the academy. I didn't want it to ruin everything for you, too," I told him. "If we get caught just blame it all on me, okay?"

He chuckled, and gave me a teasing punch to the arm. "Nice try, small fry. We're in this together. I couldn't let you run off and get yourself killed, not after what happened with the saddle last time. You're right. I should have believed you then. And I do believe you now."

I smirked back at him; that made me feel a little better. "So what's the plan?"

Felix let out another loud sigh, and put his head back against the tree trunk. "I was about to ask you the same thing. I guess you should tell me exactly what you saw, first."

So I did. I told him everything I could remember about sneaking out of the room, about seeing Sile with his hands bound, and the four men in white masks that had him at knifepoint. It hadn't looked good, and we'd lost critical time trying to find someone to help us.

"I know it sounds crazy," I said, trying to get comfortable with Beckah leaning against me. She was sleeping so hard she didn't even quit snoring when I pulled her legs over my lap so she was resting with her head against my shoulder.

"After what happened with the saddle, not really." Felix was chewing on the inside of his cheek, looking thoughtful. "The white masks do sound like the king's private guard, though. I've only ever seen them around when someone from the royal family is visiting. But, if anyone could pull off a kidnapping like that in the middle of a ball, it'd be them. They're an elite guard trained in extreme stealth and hand-to-hand combat. They're usually handpicked from the military, and then completely removed from society. No one knows much about them because everything about their training is totally secret. It's like a cult, I guess."

My heart sank a little. "Why would they want to kidnap Sile?"

Felix just shook his head, and we both sat there for a long time in silence. This was bad. If these guys were the king's elite guards, what chance did a couple of fledgling dragonriders stand against them? Even if we could find them, we probably wouldn't be able to free Sile. We really had no idea what we were getting ourselves into.

"How did you do that earlier?" Felix asked suddenly. He was staring over at me with a weird look on his face. "How did you call Mavrik to you? And from that distance? It was incredible! I've never even heard of someone doing that before."

I blushed. "I don't know. It just felt like what I had to do. It was just an idea. I wasn't even sure he'd hear me."

"You're really weird sometimes, you know that?" Felix laughed, but I could still see that strange look in his eyes. It almost seemed like he was a little bit afraid of me now. I wasn't sure how to feel about it either, but it kind of bothered me that he seemed disturbed by it.

Felix offered to take the first watch while I slept. As much as I wanted to rest, I just couldn't get comfortable. Every little noise woke me up, and I had terrible dreams of darkness and creatures slithering through the marshes toward us. When it was my turn to keep watch, I knew I had to get up just to walk off my nerves. I carefully moved Beckah over so she could lean against Felix instead.

"Sile's gonna kill us for bringing her along," Felix muttered sleepily as he licked his thumb and wiped some mud off her cheek. "He won't want her around the dragons. He probably doesn't want her around us, either, but I guess he didn't have much of a choice when you volunteered to watch her tonight."

I was surprised he knew anything about her, especially since Sile had never mentioned her before to me. "How do you know that?"

"That's how it always is, Jae. You can't be a dragonrider and be a family man, too. Trust me. If dragonriders do get married, it never lasts long." Felix had a hollow sound to his voice, like he sort of understood. "If you bring people you care about into a world of war and danger, then someone is going to get hurt. Usually, it's us. We have one of the most dangerous jobs anyone can have. Most dragonriders just decide it's better not to have people in your life like that— people you can't stand to lose or who depend on you. That's why you'll see a lot of them with broken families, more than one failed marriage, or no family at all."

As I stood there over them, watching Beckah sleep against Felix's shoulder, I started thinking about what she'd told me about her own family. "She said her parents aren't getting along. That's why she ended up at the duke's house in the first place."

Felix looked down at her, too, frowning like he felt bad for her. "I guess those of us from noble families kind of dodge the worst of it because we don't expect our parents to pay much attention to us anyway. I mean, my dad was never around to begin with, even though he's not a dragonrider. He has always had problems with his vision, so he never would have made it through the academy. It didn't make any difference, though. He's never had any time for me." He hesitated, and I could tell just by the way his expression darkened that he must have felt a lot of anger toward his father. "The worst part is being alone. She'll hate that, you know?"

I did know. I knew exactly what it meant to be alone. Finally, I thought I understood why Felix had wanted to be friends with me in the first place. I was probably the only one who could understand the value of having someone be there for you, especially when your family wasn't.

"Yeah, but we'll be there for her." I gave him a half-hearted smile. "Someone should be. It might as well be us."

Felix just smirked and closed his eyes. "Speak for yourself, nanny."

He had no room to be cracking jokes at me for babysitting. "Well, you still have lipstick on your face, you know." I snorted.

Felix started blushing and wiping his face. "Yeah, yeah, you just go keep watch and let me sleep. We'll start the search again in an hour. Those guards couldn't have just vanished. Maybe we just missed them. We'll check every road between here and Halfax if we have to."

I tried to let that give me some hope as I walked away. We weren't giving up yet. There was still time to find Sile. It was already late in the morning, and my stomach was growling. The few hours of restless sleep I'd gotten only made me even more tired, but I knew there was no way I would be able to relax until I knew Sile was alive.

I paced a wide circle around where they were sleeping, keeping them in eyeshot at all times while I explored. The marsh went as far as I could see in every direction. I could hear strange sounding birds cawing in the trees. Frogs made high-pitched ringing noises in the tall reeds. Sometimes I heard something splash in the water nearby, and it made me jump. It was an eerie, smelly place.

Through the trees and hanging moss, I could see the road close by. It was built up on top of a dirt levy so wagons and horses didn't have to fight through the mud to get across the marsh. I climbed up to the top of the levy and stood in the road, looking down both ways without seeing anyone. Something about this place gave me the creeps, like maybe something was watching me that I couldn't see.

I walked down the road for a few yards, swatting flies away from my face.

Even though I was worn out, and worried about Sile, it was nice to have a few minutes to myself to think. I thought about the things I'd heard Sile say. Something about tampering with gods. I wondered what that meant, and what it had to do with him. What could he possibly have done that would make anyone want to kill him?

It was quiet except for the birds and frogs, and that's when I heard Beckah scream. It almost made me jump out of my boots. My heart started to pound, and I started running as fast as I could through the mud and slop to get back to them. I hadn't let them out of my sight for more than a few minutes …

But I was already too late.

There were six big men standing in our small clearing, and all of them were armed with swords and crossbows. But there was no way these guys were soldiers. They were wearing black cloaks, and mismatched pieces of armor. All of them looked filthy and sweaty, and they laughed at me when I stumbled into the clearing.

"That's it? That's the best yah got?" A man with a long curly beard had Beckah by her hair, and was holding a long dagger against her throat. He laughed at me and grinned with his crooked yellow teeth. "A halfbreed wearin the king's colors? Now that's a joke I never heard before!"

A few of the other men laughed again, and it made our dragons snarl. Nova and Mavrik were crouched together, hissing and showing their teeth as the men pointed crossbows at them.

"Let the kids go," Felix growled suddenly. He was standing with his back to the tree where he'd been sleeping earlier. Another man had a sword pointed at him, and Felix had his hands raised in the air. "You'll get a ransom for me, but you'd be wasting your time with them. A halfbreed and the daughter of a poor country knight don't go for much."

The bearded man cackled another gravelly, rasping laugh. "You think I'm interested in ransomin' any of you? Don't be stupid, boy."

"We don't have any money!" I yelled at him, feeling my face burn with fury. "We don't have anything for you to steal!"

When they all laughed at me again, I realized what they were. Slavers. I'd seen these kinds of people before. Filthy liars who captured anyone they could to be sold in the slave market. They weren't going to care who we were, or what we had; they would sell us off as workers for the mines, or worse.

"The halfbreed won't fetch much," one of the men pointed out. "He looks sickly. We'd be better off dumping him at one of the prison camps."

The bearded man seemed to agree. He pulled Beckah's hair and it made her whimper in pain. "We'll more than make up for the loss with her. A pretty young thing like this? There are plenty of pleasure houses in Halfax that'll pay twenty in solid gold for her. I bet no one's ever even kissed those soft lips of hers yet."

"Leave her alone!" My face burned. I was seeing red. Beckah was looking at me with her big green eyes begging me to do something.

One of the slavers aimed a crossbow right at me, and gave me an evil smirk like he would shoot me just for fun. It made Mavrik roar with rage, snapping his teeth and making the guys pointing their crossbows at him a little nervous.

"Call off the dragons, halfbreed," the bearded man commanded. He was looking right at me. "And I won't cut her throat open right here."

I wanted to tell Mavrik to burn them all to dust. The arrows from the crossbow wouldn't have hurt him much, not with his thick scales to protect him. But I wasn't going to risk Beckah's life. I couldn't risk her being burned along with them.

"Go, Mavrik." I told him. My dragon looked at me like he couldn't believe I was agreeing. His yellow eyes narrowed, and he hissed again in defiance. "It's all right. I'll be fine. Just go. Take Nova with you."

Mavrik didn't like it, but he obeyed. He growled and glared at them as he retreated backward into the marsh. Nova followed, and after a few minutes, I could hear their thundering wing beats as they took off into the sky.

"Tie 'em up, boys! And bring the wagon around!" the bearded man bellowed, throwing Beckah down into the mud at his feet. She hit the ground hard, and I saw her arms shaking as she tried to sit back up.

Felix cursed and fought them until a slaver kneed him hard in the gut, making him fall to his knees and groan. He couldn't fight anymore after that, and they tied his hands behind his back with ropes. They tied Beckah up, too, and then they started after me.

I backed up a few paces, tripping over my own feet in the mud. I could try to run, but there was no way I could outrun their arrows. Besides, I wasn't going to abandon my friends like that. I raised my hands in surrender, and went down on my knees before I gave any one of those slavers the satisfaction of getting to kick or punch me, too. They tied my wrists behind my back so tightly I could feel the circulation being cut off immediately.

The slavers were traveling in a big group of ten or so armed men. The bearded man, who they called Grothar, was obviously in charge. He ordered us to be taken up to the road, and we stood there waiting with slavers guarding us on all sides while two wagons pulled by a team of horses galloped toward us. I still didn't know how they'd found us, but that was the least of my worries now.

The wagons stopped right in front of us, and I got my first good look at the slave caravan. Both the wagons were made of solid black metal, with only one long, narrow window cut into the top of the door. It was barred, so no one could escape through it.

We came to the first wagon, and Grothar started barking out orders to his men. "Hurry it up, boys! I don't pay you to stand around runnin your mouths!"

Grothar opened the door to the first wagon with a big ring of keys he wore clipped to his sword belt. The slavers shoved Beckah into it. The inside of the wagon was totally dark, so I couldn't see into it, but I heard the panicked cries of other girls inside. It made fury boil in the pit of my stomach. There was nothing I could do as they slammed the door and locked it again.

Felix and I were tossed into the second wagon. It was just the same as the first, except there were men and boys in it instead of girls. It smelled like rotten hay and sweat, and I could hear other people moving around close by. When Grothar shut the door, it was pitch black, and the wagon groaned and rattled as it started moving again.

"Jaevid?" I heard Felix wheezing my name. He must have still been in pain from the blow he'd taken because his voice was raspy and faint. "Call Mavrik back like you did before! Get him to burn these guys to ash!"

I was struggling to sit up with my arms tied. I couldn't even move without bumping into someone close to me in the dark. It was terrifying, and it made it impossible think about anything except how afraid I was. I tried to find that same kind of calm I'd had before, to get that knot of heat back in my chest. But I couldn't focus. It was like my fear was jumbling my thoughts, making me confused. I worried about where we were going, I worried about Sile, about Beckah, and how we were going to get out of this mess.

Of all the bad things that might ever happen to me in my life, going to a prison camp was the worst possible option. Most Gray elves got to live in the ghettos, but if they ever broke any rules or were caught doing anything illegal, they were put in shackles, loaded into wagons just like this one, and shipped off to the prison camps. Not one of them was ever heard from again. I had seen it happen before. Mothers and fathers torn from their shacks, separated from their children. Anyone who tried to help them ran the risk of being shipped off, too. Those images played through my mind over and over, and I was so afraid that I couldn't breathe.

"I-I can't," I stammered and choked. "Felix .... what's going to happen to us? I can't go to a prison camp! Felix, p-please! They'll kill me in there!" Tears were starting to well up in my eyes, and my chest felt tight. I was fighting for every breath.

Through my fear and panic, Felix's voice reached out to me in the darkness. He still sounded hoarse, but he was totally calm. "Jaevid, listen to me. You have to calm down right now. You're a dragonrider. You can beat this. But you can't let yourself surrender to fear. So pull yourself together. It's time to man up. You're not a kid anymore."

I could hear the whispering of other voices around us. There were at least a dozen other people in the back of the wagon, but all I could see of them was faint shadows and occasionally the gleam of their eyes. They were like ghosts in the darkness.

I shut my eyes to block them out, and tried to concentrate on my breathing.

Felix was right. I had to pull myself together. Beckah needed me. Sile needed me. Dragonrider or not, I couldn't let this be the end. I had to survive.

"You still with me?" Felix asked.

"Y-yeah. Yeah. I'm fine." I answered.

"Good." His voice was getting a little clearer and stronger. "Because I have a plan."

17

CHAPTER SEVENTEEN

I was smaller and more flexible, so I started working my way out of the ropes first. The slavers had tied me up tight, but I was able to curl my legs up to my chest and slip my arms under my feet. Once I had my hands in front of me, it was much easier to move around. My eyes were getting used to the small amount of light that trickled in from the narrow window at the top of the door, and I could see Felix sitting nearby.

"I've got it," I whispered to him. I didn't want to run the risk of the slavers outside hearing me. "Hurry up and turn around."

He scooted closer and sat with his back to me. I had to feel around in the dark to find the ropes tied around his wrists, which was awkward since my hands were still tied together, too. I started untying him, and when I got the ropes loose, Felix was able to work them off himself. I heard him let out a loud sigh of relief.

While he untied the ropes on my wrists, Felix was looking around like he was plotting. I had no idea what he was going to do. Things didn't look so good from where I was sitting. We were outnumbered, locked in what was basically a metal box on wheels, and neither of us had a weapon.

"F-Felix?" a familiar voice whispered from the dark. It startled me because even though I couldn't see him, I knew who it was immediately. Lyon Cromwell was tied up in a corner of the wagon with his wrists and ankles tied up. While I couldn't be sure in the faint light, it looked almost like he had a black eye.

"Lyon?" I had to ask because I thought maybe my mind was just playing tricks on me. Why would he be in the back of a slaver's wagon?

"It's really you!" His voice was shaking, and he started sobbing. "Please, you have to get me out of here. Don't leave me here!"

Felix untied my hands and went to start doing the same for Lyon. I followed, but I kept my distance. After all, I hadn't had very good experiences with Lyon in the past. In fact, he had tried to beat me to death both times.

"You idiot," Felix growled at him as he pulled at the ropes. "How did you wind up in here?"

Lyon was sobbing hysterically. "H-he promised me I'd get promoted straight to captain!" I could barely understand him as he sniffled. "But he tricked me! They all lied!"

"Who?" I dared to ask.

He shuddered. "The king's Lord General. He came to me while we were at Blybrig, before training ever started. He said if I did what he told me, if I cooperated, he'd make sure I was promoted to captain straight out of the academy."

"You really are an idiot," Felix growled as he finished untying him. "You fell for that?"

"He's the Lord General! I had no reason not to trust him!" Lyon barked back defensively.

"Why is he trying to kill Lieutenant Derrick?" I tried to cut off their argument before it got started. After all, it wasn't like we had a lot of time. "And where are they taking us?"

"I-I don't know the details. At first, he just wanted me to sabotage Lieutenant Derrick's saddle. He wanted me to make sure that ... well, you know. But he came to me again before we left for Duke Brinton's. That time he just wanted me to lure Lieutenant Derrick out of the ballroom. Those guardsmen in masks jumped us as soon as we were alone." Lyon stammered and sniffled. He sat up and started rubbing his wrists. I could see him a little better when he leaned into the light from the window. He definitely had a big, shiny black eye.

"You don't know anything about why they'd want to kill a decorated, seasoned lieutenant like that?" Felix growled at him threateningly. "That didn't sound the slightest bit suspicious to you?"

Lyon actually looked a little afraid of him. "I don't know why, I swear! They didn't tell me anything. But I overheard the Lord General talking to those guardsmen from the king. They were saying something about a stone. They called it the god stone."

Felix and I glanced at each other. I had no idea what a god stone was, and I got the feeling he didn't either. But this couldn't be good—not if it was worth killing over.

"Do you know where they're taking us?" I asked him again.

Lyon started wiping his nose, but he was beginning to pull himself together. "The prison camp outside of Halfax, I think. I heard some of the slavers talking about it."

Felix grabbed the front of his tunic suddenly. It surprised me, and it made Lyon tremble and throw his hands up in surrender.

"This is all your fault, you little worm," Felix growled through his teeth. "Where is Lieutenant Derrick? Where did they take him? You better start talking, or so help me, I'll make both your eyes black!"

"Felix!" I touched his shoulder hesitantly. I was kind of afraid he'd hit me too, just out of blind fury. "Let him go. Just calm down. This isn't going to help." I hoped Lyon didn't change his opinion of me too much, just because I was saving his neck now. If Felix still wanted to beat him up after this was over, I wasn't sure I'd be so quick to stop him.

As soon as Felix let him go, Lyon started backing away from us frantically. His eyes were wide, and he looked terrified. "They separated us," he started to explain. "I saw them put Lieutenant Derrick in the back of another wagon. We only stopped once, outside the marsh. I guess they must have seen you guys flying over, because they started shouting orders and split up the caravan. The Lord General and the king's guardsmen took the lieutenant the long way around the marsh."

Felix cursed. It was a big mess, but at least now we knew how the slavers had found us in the first place. They'd probably been lying in wait for us to land. "Well, at least we're going in the right direction." He snorted.

I wasn't nearly as glad about that as he was. I didn't care which direction we were going—all I wanted to do was get out of this wagon. "So what's your plan for getting out of here? There's only one door, and it's locked from the outside."

Felix shot me a dangerous look. It made me wonder if he was going to punch me in the face, too. "You get to work on calling Mavrik back. You did it once before, you can do it again. You have to. Because if I have to go with my fallback plan, it's basically guaranteed to get all or most of us killed in the process." I swallowed hard when he turned away again. "Lyon, help me cut loose the rest of the prisoners."

Lyon hesitated. "But ... they're Gray elves."

He was right about that. There were three other men in the back of the wagon, and all of them were Gray elves. They were just staring at us with their diamond-colored eyes as big as saucers. They didn't say a word, and I knew that was because they were probably terrified of Felix and Lyon. One of them was elderly, his skin sunken against his cheekbones, and another looked like he was about Sile's age. The last seemed to be about Felix's age, and he just kept staring right at me.

"So?" Felix challenged. I saw him turn on Lyon, using the fact that he was bigger and definitely stronger to dare him to say something about it. "You see anyone else in here who can help us?"

Lyon did not look happy. I could see the disgust on his face as he went to help Felix untie the other prisoners. I could also see how afraid the Gray elves were.

They were terrified, and began pleading with us in the garbled elven language not to hurt them.

"Can't you get the halfbreed to tell them to shut up? They're going to give us away if they keep jabbering on like this," Lyon grumbled.

Felix didn't get a chance to jump to my defense. I beat him to it. "I don't speak elven," I snapped at him.

Even Felix looked surprised about that. The way they were both looking at me in stunned silence made me blush until the tips of my pointed ears burned.

"At least, not very well anymore," I clarified. After all, I could understand it. I had spoken it once, when I lived with my mother, but that seemed like such a long time ago. "My father didn't allow it. I haven't spoken it in years. I don't remember much."

The silence was awkward. Now the Gray elves were staring at me, too. They probably hadn't understood anything I'd said, but I knew why they were staring at me. I was a halfbreed, after all. They didn't like my kind, either.

"Just get to work," Felix commanded.

I didn't argue. I sat on the floor of the wagon, and tried to get my mind to be quiet like it had been before. I tried to push away the fear, and find that knot of warmth in my chest that sent chills over my body like a cold shiver. I focused so hard that sweat started to run down my forehead and get into my eyes. I concentrated as hard as I could, but the jarring motion of the wagon interrupted my thoughts. It made me wonder if Beckah was okay, and worry about if we would even be able to get to Sile in time now. As easy as it would have been to just blame Lyon for everything, I didn't. It was the Lord General, the supreme leader of all the dragonriders in the kingdom, who had started this. It was his fault.

I started to get frustrated with myself. I was getting angry, and my hands shook as I clenched them into fists. *"Just get me out!"* I yelled, slamming my fists down onto the floor of the wagon. It made a loud metallic thump.

Just like last time, nothing happened at first. Minutes passed, and Lyon was staring at me like I was out of my mind. Felix just looked worried, but the second he opened his mouth to say something to me there was an earth-shaking rumble from underneath the wagon.

All of a sudden, the wagon stopped. Outside, I could hear the sounds of men yelling and running past. My heart pounded in my ears as I strained to hear Mavrik's thundering roar coming to our rescue.

I did hear a roar. It was a bellow so deep that it made the wagon shudder, and the horses outside began to whinny in terror. It definitely wasn't Mavrik or Nova.

"What was that?" Lyon whispered shakily.

Felix was still staring at me with eyes wide and afraid. "Not a dragon," he whispered back. "Jae ... what did you bring here?"

I had no answer. I didn't know. The earth shook again, and the bellowing roar shook the wagon again. The Gray elves started praying in frantic voices, and clawing at the walls of the wagon. We were stuck inside, only able to listen as men shouted and fought outside. I could hear arrows from crossbows pinging against the side of the wagon.

Felix covered his nose with his hand, and he frowned hard. "What is that smell?"

I smelled it, too. It reminded me of the silt mud from the marsh; the reeking stench of old rotting plant life. It was putrid, and it made my eyes water.

Suddenly the back half of the wagon blew open. Shards of metal flew, and I was ripped right off my knees and sent flying out into the sunlight. I bounced off the ground like a stone off the surface of a pond, and when I finally landed, I couldn't catch my breath. I gasped and wheezed, looking up through the spray of mud and the chaos of slavers running back and forth.

What I saw made my jaw drop. I was too afraid to move. Never in my life had I even heard of something like this before, but there it was—a massive, incredibly huge, utterly giant turtle.

It was as tall as four horses stacked on top of each other, with massive claws on its feet and a big, diamond-shaped head. Its shell was covered in jagged, sharp spines, and there was old moss and vines hanging off it. When it snapped its jaws at the slavers, its neck shot out like a snake's strike, and I saw it split shields in half like crackers. It was fast, huge, and covered in thick plated scales. None of the slavers' arrows even pierced it, but they kept firing anyway.

"Gods and Fates!" I heard Felix shout in horror. He was running toward me, but he didn't take his eyes off the giant turtle. "Jaevid, why would you bring something like that here?"

Lyon was right behind him, running for his life and screaming, "It's a paludix turtle!"

I staggered to my feet. "Try to find a weapon," I yelled at Felix over the chaos. "I'm going after Beckah!"

Immediately, I started to search the chaos for the other wagon. My heart hit the back of my throat hard when I finally saw it. The horses pulling it had spooked and charged right off the levy into the swamp. They were panicking in the deep mud, and the wagon was turned over on its side. I could see hands sticking out of the barred rear window, and hear the women inside crying for help.

I ran like mad straight for the toppled wagon, skidded down the steep side of the levy, and splashed into the waist-deep muck. By the time I got to the back door of the wagon, adrenaline was pumping through my veins like fire.

"Beckah!" I screamed her name at the top of my lungs.

From inside the wagon, I heard her answer. "Jaevid!"

She was alive, and for a moment I saw her face through the narrow window. She stuck a hand out through the bars, and I grabbed it. "I'll get you out!"

I had no idea how I was going to keep that promise. The door was still locked with a big iron padlock, and about the time I thought to look back for Grothar and his ring of keys I saw his legs disappear down the paludix turtle's throat.

I pulled at the lock, yanking at it futilely and trying to think of some other way to get the door open. I needed something to pry the lock off, something strong and narrow enough to fit through the loop in the padlock. I waded through the mud as fast as I could, and climbed up into the driver's seat of the wagon that was tilted on its side. I had hitched up Ulric's horse and wagon plenty of times. I knew where all the parts and pieces should be, so as soon as my hand hit the big iron pin that connected the horse harnesses to the wagon, I yanked it out. The horses whinnied in triumph, and began to gallop away through the swamp.

The pin was perfect. It was made of iron, long and narrow just like a big stake, and I carried it back to start trying to pry the lock off. It probably would have worked for anyone else right away. But I wasn't big enough. I couldn't get enough strength against it to crack the lock. I fought and struggled, slipping in the mud and cursing out loud.

I was about to give up and try something else, when two sets of bigger hands grabbed the iron pin right next to mine. I was surprised to see Felix and the younger Gray elf boy standing beside me. They pushed with me, putting all our strength against the lock. With a sudden lurch and a loud crack, the lock popped off, and Felix pulled the door open.

Four Gray elf women came rushing out, tripping over their skirts in the deep mud. I searched for Beckah in the crowd, and finally found her still crouched in the back of the wagon. She had a little girl in her arms, a Gray elf toddler who was crying and clinging to her desperately.

"Come on!" Felix shouted at her.

Beckah looked at him with fury in her eyes. "I won't leave her!" She was not very big herself, and she could barely carry the toddler much less run with her.

Before anyone else could speak, the Gray elf boy that had been helping us with the door rushed in and took the child from Beckah. I heard him muttering under his breath, trying to comfort the frightened little girl. I couldn't understand much of what he said, but I did recognize a few words: my sister.

Beckah came out willingly then. She threw her arms around my waist and squeezed me so hard I couldn't breathe. I was so relieved to see her, to have her back in one piece, that I hugged her back as hard as I could.

"What are you waiting for?" Lyon shouted down at us from the top of the levy. "We have to get out of here!"

The slavers were so caught up in their battle with the massive swamp turtle that they didn't even notice all their prisoners running free. We ran through the marsh, and the Gray elves ran with us, trying to get as far away from the slavers and the giant turtle as we could. The sounds of the battle started to fade into the background until all I could hear was our footsteps sloshing in the mud, the sound of the frogs, and my own panting.

We didn't stop or slow down until it was dark. When we finally came to a patch of dry ground, one by one we all collapsed to sit down and catch our breath. We were a muddy, soggy, exhausted mess. But we were alive, and right then, that's all I cared about.

The Gray elves all grouped together, leaving Felix, Beckah, Lyon and me to sit off to ourselves. They hugged one another and spoke in hushed voices. I didn't try to eavesdrop on them; I could see the relief and happiness on their faces. They were free, for now.

"I can't believe it," Lyon panted. He was lying on his back with his arms and legs sprawled out. "First I get sold to slavers by the Lord General, then nearly devoured by an extinct species."

I glanced at Felix, and the look on my friend's face was enough to give me cold chills. His eyes were focused on me, but they were haunted. There was something about his expression that made me feel like he really was afraid of me now. "The great paludix turtle has been extinct for hundreds of years," he muttered in a hushed voice. "Or at least, we thought it was."

Lyon raised his head up to shoot me an accusing glare. "What exactly did you do, halfbreed?"

"It must have been in hiding for decades," Felix spoke up in my defense. Or at least, that's what I thought until he added, "Until you called it out."

Now I felt cornered. Everyone except Beckah was looking at me like I was some kind of monster—like I had done something terrible. I knew why, of course. Humans had always suspected Gray elves of using wicked magic and mischievous spells to manipulate people. They'd even called my mother a witch because of the way she could make the plants grow when she was alive. I didn't know if what I could do—calling out to animals with my thoughts—even qualified as something magical. But it was enough to get some accusing, disgusted looks from my so-called friends.

"I only did what you told me to," I reminded Felix angrily. I couldn't help it. It felt like he was turning on me, which was the last thing I expected. "How was I supposed to know that thing would hear me?"

I got up and stormed away from them, going to sit on the edge of our dry little patch of land by myself. I just couldn't stand to be around him when he was looking at me that way. It was one thing for Lyon to treat me like a traitor, but Felix was supposed to be my friend.

For a long time, I just sat there and watched the sun set over the marsh. The crickets and frogs sang in the tall reeds. Fireflies started blinking in the dark like warm orange spots of light. I took the necklace my mother had given me out from under my shirt, feeling the smooth polished bone while I thought about her. It had been a long time since I'd seen other Gray elves, and now it was starting to catch up to me. It made me miss my mother. She was the one person in the world who had loved me unconditionally.

I didn't say anything when Beckah suddenly came over. She sat down beside me with her legs crossed under her stained blue dress. For a few minutes, we just sat there and didn't say anything, even though I could tell there was something she wanted to say.

"What's that?" She pointed to my necklace.

I glanced down at it, running my thumb over the smooth white pendant. "My mother gave it to me before she died," I grumbled. I didn't feel like talking at all, much less about my mother. It just made me miss her more.

"It's beautiful," she said in a quiet voice.

I started to feel bad. I was being cold to her, and none of this was her fault. She didn't deserve to be treated like that. I let out a heavy sigh, and gave up being mad at Felix. "She said it would protect me." I glanced over at Beckah, and tried to give her a convincing smile. "I guess it doesn't work very well."

Beckah smiled back at me. She had mud in her hair, all over her dress, and even smeared on her face. But her green eyes still shone brightly. "You made it into the academy to be a dragonrider. You jumped off the top of a tower at the duke's estate and lived. And now you saved us all from slavers and a giant man-eating turtle. I think it works pretty well." She laughed a little.

I couldn't help but laugh, too. Maybe it did work, after all. "So, how did everyone in your wagon get out of the ropes?"

She smiled proudly. "My daddy does teach me a few things when he comes home. He didn't give me a magical necklace, but he taught me how to escape ropes and shackles when I was little. He made it like a game, you know? It was really fun. And it made my momma furious. He started teaching me how to shoot a bow, but Momma put a stop to that. She said girls don't shoot bows."

I had underestimated her. She was a kid, sort of, but she was brave, and she was definitely a lot smarter than I was. "Your dad is a good man, Beckah," I told her. "No matter what else happens, you should know that."

"You are too, you know." She gave me a meaningful look. I could see on her face that this is what she'd really come over to talk to me about. "Whatever you did back there, I know you just wanted to help us. You're a good person. And if Felix and that other guy can't see that, well, then they're too dumb to be dragonriders anyway."

I blushed. "It's not because they're dumb, Beckah. It's because I'm a—"

"No, she's right,." Felix butted in suddenly. It startled me, and I turned around to see him standing behind us with his arms crossed. He didn't look angry, or even wary of me anymore. In fact, he looked frustrated and embarrassed. "I'm sorry, Jae."

I was so surprised I couldn't even say anything back at first. All I could do was just nod at him a little and smile awkwardly. How could I not forgive him?

Felix was my friend, and one of the best ones I'd ever had. If I lost him, I probably wouldn't last very long in the academy. The other fledglings would eat me alive and toss whatever was left to their dragons.

"It's okay," I told him. "This whole calling to animals thing is weird for me, too."

"Did your momma ever tell you anything about it?" Beckah looked worried. "Is it something all Gray elves can do?"

I shook my head. "No, she never mentioned this. I've never even heard of it before."

"Well, whatever it is, we should probably keep it between us," Felix suggested. "It'd freak the instructors out."

I couldn't argue with that. He was definitely right. The last thing I needed was to give the instructors at Blybrig one more reason not to trust me. Until I figured this out, we had to keep it a secret. I couldn't use it unless it was absolutely necessary. If anyone else found out, at the very least it could get me kicked out of the academy.

"But what about that other guy?" Beckah cut a suspicious glance over to Lyon, who was still sprawled out on the ground.

Felix smirked and started cracking his knuckles. "Leave Lyon to me."

18

CHAPTER EIGHTEEN

The Gray elves were doing a lot better surviving in the marsh than we were. They built a small fire, and were sitting around it together roasting something that smelled amazing. I was already starving, and the smell of whatever they were cooking made my mouth water. It must have had the same effect on Felix because he was just sitting there, staring at them, with a miserable expression on his face.

"We should just demand that they give us a share," Lyon growled. "After all, we were the ones who did all the work."

"Yeah, sure." Felix rolled his eyes. "Why don't you go over there and tell them that yourself? Let us know how that goes."

"Send the halfbreed, then," Lyon bargained. He seemed determined not to use my name.

I shot him a glare. "They hate me just as much as you do, you know."

That seemed to surprise Lyon. "What? But you're—"

I cut him off before he could finish. "—half human. They don't like me for the same reasons you don't."

"I'll go," Beckah offered. She was licking her lips hungrily. It might have actually worked to send the most innocent and vulnerable of our group to beg for scraps, but I wasn't about to let Beckah risk herself on that chance. I didn't know what the Gray elves might do.

About the time Felix and Lyon started arguing over who should go, I noticed that the younger Gray elf man from before was walking our way. He didn't look much older than Felix, but his hair was already that shining silver color. The Gray elves were all born with black hair that turned silver once they finally hit puberty, so he had to be at least eighteen for his hair to already look like that.

He stood awkwardly on the edge of our pitiful excuse for a camp, which was basically just the four of us sitting in a circle, holding something that was wrapped up in charred leaves. His diamond-colored eyes flicked from one of us to the other, and he finally started to speak. Of course, he didn't speak the human language, and when he talked he looked right at me like he expected me to understand him.

I did understand some of what he said. He told us his name was Kiran, and then he offered what he had in his hands. It was roasted roots that they had dug up out of the earth, wrapped in damp leaves, and baked in their fire. The smell was fantastic, even for something that came out of this smelly marsh.

"These are gifts for us," I translated, giving Felix a hesitant look. "For helping them, I guess." The Gray elf language was very complex and I hadn't heard it, much less spoken it in years.

Felix smiled tiredly at him, and got up to take the food from him. Beckah and Lyon did the same, while Kiran kept eyeing them warily. It was like he half-expected a sneak attack.

When I got up to take some of the food from him, Kiran's expression went from uncomfortable to total disgust. He looked me over from head to toe, like everyone did, and I saw his nose wrinkle. The Gray elves didn't want me anywhere near them, just like the humans. I was both, and I was neither.

He didn't say a word to me as I took the food from his hands. I began to turn away, ready to go sit with my friends, until I saw his eyes go straight to the necklace my mother had given me. I'd forgotten to tuck it back under my shirt.

"Where did you get that?" he snapped at me in the elven language. He was pointing at my necklace.

I glanced down at it before tucking it back under my shirt collar. I didn't want him to get any ideas about taking it. "A gift," I answered. I spoke to him in English because I had a sneaking suspicion he could, too. He was young enough that he'd probably been born in an elven ghetto, just like me.

Kiran's lip twitched and his eyes narrowed. "Who gave it to you?" he demanded—in English this time.

I glared at him with as much courage as I could muster. "It's none of your business."

He got a mean smirk on his lips that made me nervous. Fortunately, Felix was sitting not too far away, and I could see him watching us out of the corner of my eye.

"I know that mark," Kiran said as he pointed to the king's eagle stitched onto my tunic. "You wear the clothes of the human warriors, but you're too young to even remember who started this war." The way he said it made it sound like an insult.

As much as I just wanted to turn my back to him and walk away, something about the way he talked down to me really got on my nerves. I was used to being treated that way by humans, but usually Gray elves just ignored me like I didn't exist. Kiran was the first one to go out of his way to pick on me. If my mom had been alive, she would have smacked him across the face. But me? Well, I had had enough of being pushed around for one day.

"I don't care who started the war," I told him. "And I don't care who wins it."

Kiran gave me a funny look, like that wasn't the answer he'd expected. "Why do you fight with them, *caenu*?"

I didn't have a good answer for that, so I just glared at him for a few seconds and then looked away. It was a difficult question to even think about. I hadn't really considered the idea that eventually I would be on the battlefield with a sword in my hand, trying to kill Gray elves like Kiran. And they would be trying to kill me, too.

When I didn't reply, Kiran went back to his own circle around the campfire with the other Gray elves. I looked at the food in my hand, and felt uneasy. I knew the Gray elves had a social custom that demanded all debts be paid. So this must have been their way of repaying us for letting them all free, even if that had only been a side effect of our own escape.

Lyon was eyeing his roasted potato skeptically. "What if this is poisonous? How do we know they aren't trying to kill us?"

Beckah glared at him. "Don't be stupid. Of course it isn't poisonous."

He glared back, though he seemed a little stunned that a kid was talking back to him like that. "How do you know?" he challenged.

"Because they're eating it, too," she replied with a mouthful of potato.

We all looked over at the same time to stare at the Gray elves. They were cozy, sitting close to their fire while they shared their own roasted potatoes. Beckah was right, and I was willing to chance it for the sake of my cramping hunger pains.

"What does *caenu* mean?" Felix asked as I sat down beside him and started unwrapping my own ration. "That elf, I heard him call you that. What does it mean?"

I was really rusty when it came to speaking the Gray elf language, but there were a few words that stuck into my mind like thorns. Those were words I'd come to hate; words I could never forget. *Caenu* was one of them.

I just focused on eating my piping hot potato while I answered because I didn't want to see the look on his face. "It's what the Gray elves call halfbreeds." I tried to sound as matter of fact about that as I could. I didn't want him to know how much it bothered me. "It means 'filth' in their language."

I could feel Felix's eyes on me for a long time. Maybe it had never really occurred to him that when I said the Gray elves hated me as much as most humans did I really meant it. They didn't want me around them, either. My mother had been the exception. She had loved me. But I knew better than to hope I'd get that kind of reception from the rest of her kin.

"He was asking you about the war, wasn't he?" Felix questioned me again. "He was asking you why you want to fight with humans instead of elves?"

I swallowed hard and finally dared to meet his eyes. "Yeah."

His eyes narrowed some, and I saw his jaw tense. "And you really don't care who wins this war?"

Again, that question crept up on me and stunned me. I'd answered Kiran before without really thinking about it, and now that I had a chance to really mull it over, I realized my answer wasn't going to change. "No, I don't."

"How can you say that?" Felix sounded worried, maybe even a little insulted.

I shrugged and took another bite of potato. "Because it doesn't matter to me. Neither side wants me, and no matter who wins, that probably won't ever change. I'll always be hated by both humans and elves because of what I am. So why would I want to fight for them?"

"So you're just fighting for the sake of having a job? Or so you won't have to go to a prison camp?" His brows were furrowed, and he was frowning at me hard.

"No that's not the reason," I corrected. "Well, maybe it is *a* reason, but it's not the *main* reason."

"Then what is?"

I looked at Felix squarely in the eye. "I'm going to fight for you. You said it yourself, that we're in this together. We're partners, right? So I'll fight to watch your back. It's the same reason I'm out here trying to save Sile. There aren't very many people in the world who care what happens to me. You, Sile, Beckah, Katty, even Mavrik are pretty much the only ones. So I'll do what I can to protect you, even if that means fighting in a war that'll end up being a no-win situation for me either way. It's worth it."

Felix's expression wavered. I saw that he wanted to smile, but he didn't. There was sadness in his eyes, deep heavy sadness. He just nodded some before he went back to eating.

Even with warm food in my stomach and no strength in my body, it was hard to sleep. I had nightmares about giant turtles and slavers. Early the next morning, I woke up with my heart hammering because I thought I heard the sound of hoof beats. But we were alone—completely alone.

The Gray elves were gone. All that was left of them were a few tracks in the mud, leading away across the marsh. They'd left us there to fend for ourselves, not that I was sad to see them go. Being around them was sometimes worse than being around humans.

What I'd mistaken for hoof beats started to get louder. When I realized what that sound actually was, I started shaking Beckah awake and yelling for Felix to get up. The sound got even louder and closer, and I heard the familiar bellow of Mavrik's roar from above the trees.

Seeing a flash of his blue scales and the sound of his roar made my heart soar. He'd come back for me. I certainly wouldn't have blamed him for just leaving me there to fend for myself, after the way I'd dismissed him before.

He and Nova were circling above us, looking for a good place to land. With so many trees growing so close together, there wasn't a place big enough for them. Suddenly, I got another one of those radical ideas.

"Come on, I'll give you a boost." I said as I pulled Beckah up to her feet. She was still rubbing the sleep from her eyes, blinking up at the sky. I don't think she really understood what I was doing until I was pushing her up toward the lowest hanging limb of a nearby tree.

"Are you crazy?" Lyon was awake and already protesting.

Felix just laughed, and started climbing up after me. "Better stay down here, Lyon. We wouldn't want you to risk hurting yourself just to follow us, would we?" The sarcasm in his voice made me laugh, too.

"You're not leaving me behind!" Lyon declared as he started climbing up the tree after us.

When I got to the top, to the very skinniest of the limbs that would hold my weight, I looked out across the marshland. I could see the tops of the trees for miles and miles around us. Far in the distance, I could see the mountains like ghostly blue shadows on the horizon.

Mavrik made a loud screeching noise as he swooped in low and circled around me. Now it was time for my plan. I got Beckah as close to me as I could to wrap an arm around her waist.

"You have to hang on to me," I told her.

She nodded and wrapped her arms around my neck. "I'm not afraid. I trust you."

When Mavrik came swooping low again, his powerful wings spread out wide, I gave him the hand signal for doing a roll. I wasn't sure he'd get it, I mean, we'd never really perfected his understanding of the hand signals we riders used in the air. But as he started to get dangerously close, he whipped over with his back facing down toward us.

I jumped straight up with all my might, reaching for the saddle handles. Not in a million years did I think I'd actually grab them. He was moving fast, like a streak of blue lightning. My timing had to be absolutely perfect.

And it was.

I grabbed the saddle handles, hanging on for dear life as we were suddenly snatched off the top of the tree. Mavrik rolled over, and I quickly got myself settled into the saddle with Beckah sitting right in front of me. We cruised over the tops of the trees, making a wide turn to go back and make sure Felix and Lyon were able to get on Nova.

I'm pretty sure Lyon was crying when they were finally sitting on Nova's back, him hugging Felix as he sat in the back of the saddle. Felix gave me a thumb's up, letting me know they were okay.

Take the lead, I signed to him. *We've got to get to Halfax before they do.*

Felix smirked, and I saw him lean down closer to Nova's neck. He put on the speed, and Nova shot forward like a brown and gold bullet. Mavrik roared at her, and I felt his body go tense and solid beneath the saddle. He beat his wings hard, and we went hurling forward with a new burst of speed.

Beckah reached to grab my hand, squeezing it until her knuckles were white.

"It's okay," I yelled to her over the rush of the wind. I thought she was afraid, but when I saw her face I could see that she was smiling.

Her eyes were wide, and she was looking out across the trees that blurred past. She looked at me with a huge grin. "This is amazing!"

I smiled back at her and brushed some of her hair away that was blowing into my eyes. I wasn't sure if I'd ever noticed before, but Beckah was really pretty— even if she did look a lot like her father. When she smiled at me like that, it made me blush.

Mavrik snapped his wings in sharp, quick beats that sent us bolting forward until we caught up to Nova. We kept our pace fast and our position as low to the ground as we dared. When we reached the other side of the marsh, I could see the royal city of Halfax far in the distance. I knew it right away because of the tall, swirling spires of the king's castle set back from the rest of the city against the side of a huge cliff. You could see the castle from just about anywhere in the city, even from the Gray elf ghetto where I'd lived with my mother.

Beyond the city's outskirts and surrounding farmlands was the prison camp. I'd never actually seen it before, but I knew what it was right away. From the air, it looked like a dark patch on the horizon. It was a big complex surrounded by high, black stone walls. The stones for those walls had been mined from the volcanic cliffs along the coast, so they were rough, uneven, and nearly impossible to climb without cutting your hands and feet to shreds. On the tops of the walls, tar mixed with shards of broken glass had been spread over it to keep people from trying to escape.

The prison camp was built in a big diamond shape with eight watchtowers looking down at the prisoners inside. From where we were, it just looked liked a big tangled mess of scrap surrounding one dark crater in the middle. The crater must have been an abandoned quarry, with layers of rock carved away to the glaring sunlight.

Seeing it, even from a distance, made my stomach tangle into painful knots. Ending up in a place like that was my absolute worst fear. I didn't want to go anywhere near it. I wanted to turn Mavrik around and bolt in the opposite direction. But Sile might already be there, trapped in that horrible place. We had to save him. I had given Beckah my word that we would, and I was determined to keep that promise.

"We've got to find a way inside," Felix said as soon as he dismounted. "If we try to take them from the air, chances are, the dragonriders stationed at the castle will come after us, and we'll all be arrested before we even get a chance to find Sile, that is if the bowmen in the watchtowers don't shoot us down first. Being stealthy will give us our best chance."

We had landed in a big open wheat field outside Halfax, about three miles from the prison camp. From where we stood, we had a straight view of it. Smoke rose up from beyond its tall black gates, and I was beginning to feel sick with dread.

"Break into a prison camp?" Lyon scoffed. He crossed his arms, and sneered at the idea. "You're all crazy. I'm not going in there. As if we could even get past the guards in the first place."

"It's your fault Sile is in there in the first place," Felix reminded him with a threatening growl. "You're coming with us, one way or another."

The two were about to start arguing again, glaring at each other and squaring off. I could sense the tension rising, but I wasn't eager to jump in the middle and break them up. It wouldn't exactly hurt my feelings if Felix beat Lyon to a bloody pulp.

"Y-you did this?" Beckah stammered suddenly. "But you're a dragonrider too, right?"

I flinched. Felix and I exchanged a glance. We hadn't told her Lyon was the one responsible for her father's abduction. I wasn't sure how she as going to handle that news.

Beckah was looking up at him with wide eyes. At first, I thought she might start crying. I could see revelation come over her whole demeanor as she started piecing it together that there was a traitor in our midst. Lyon had betrayed her father, and the reasons why didn't really matter.

But Beckah didn't cry. Instead, she balled her hands into fists and started for him with violent intent blazing in her eyes. "You! You did this! You're a traitor!" She screamed at him. "What did my daddy ever do to you?! You ... you selfish coward!"

I grabbed her by the shoulder before she could actually start hitting him, pulling her back and holding her while she kicked and fought to get away from me. I wasn't going to take the chance that Lyon wouldn't hit her back just because she was a girl.

Lyon was staring back at her, and his expression was difficult to read. If he could have felt any remorse for what he'd done, maybe he did in that moment. I didn't know Lyon well enough to be sure.

"I hope you die!" Beckah screamed at him. "You deserve to die!"

I put a hand over her mouth, holding her tight against my chest as she kept on fighting me. "Hush, Beckah. Don't say that." I told her as calmly as I knew how. I started forcing her to walk a few yards away with me. She needed to cool off.

"How can you defend him?" She turned on me next, and I saw angry, frustrated tears starting to brim in her eyes. Her cheeks were dark red, and her whole body was trembling.

As soon as we were far enough away that Felix and Lyon wouldn't be able to hear us, I grabbed her as tightly as I could. I hugged her. I held her that way, even though she fought me at first.

"I'm not defending him. He'll have to pay for what he did. But right now isn't the time. Right now, we have to concentrate on saving your dad. That's what's most important." I tried to talk gently to her to calm her down. She was just a kid, and even if I wasn't that much older than her, I felt like it was my responsibility to help her understand. "So just take some deep breaths. I know you're angry. Just calm down."

I heard her start to cry, and she quit fighting me. She put her arms around my waist and hugged me back, hiding her face against my shoulder.

"I hate him, Jae!" She whimpered.

"I know." I patted her head awkwardly. I wasn't sure what else I was supposed to do. My experience in comforting girls was pretty limited. "I'm not all that wild about him, either. He's used my face as a doormat before, you know."

"You'll make sure he doesn't get away with this, right?" she asked, looking up at me with her chin trembling.

I had already made some steep promises to her—promises I wasn't sure I could keep. But I'd try. After all, she deserved the very best effort I could give.

I nodded. "I'll try."

That seemed to satisfy her, and she pushed away from me a little. "People like that, who betray their own kind, they don't deserve any kind of justice. We should just throw him in the prison camp and see how he likes it."

I frowned at her. "You know, that's exactly the reason humans and Gray elves don't like me, Beckah. They both think I'm a traitor to my race."

I saw her expression fall. Her shoulders hunched up some like she was embarrassed, and she looked away uneasily. "That's not the same thing," she mumbled stubbornly.

I knew she was still upset, and most of what she said was just out of anger and frustration. But it still stung. "You can't just condemn someone, no matter what they've done. Everyone deserves justice, even traitors."

19

CHAPTER NINETEEN

I had a feeling Felix was going to get us all killed. We had given our dragons the signal to lay low and wait for us to come back, but that didn't make me feel any better as we snuck into a barn outside one of the little farmhouses nearby. It was a few hours after dark, and Felix had decided we needed to find some weaponry before we tried to get into the prison camp.

As Felix pushed the barn door open a crack and we all rushed inside, I started to get a queasy feeling. The moonlight filtered through the slats in the ceiling, revealing harvesting scythes, axes, and a whole collection of farm tools hanging on the walls of the barn. There were big clay jugs crowded against the walls, crates stacked to the rafters, and big sacks of grain and feed for horses. Felix went straight for a big hunting knife that was lying on a table that looked like it had been used for butchering and dressing game.

I picked up a sickle and held it awkwardly, wondering if I could actually hurt anyone other than myself with it. "Felix, how is this going to work?" I turned around to face him. "How can we fight the king's elite guards with farm tools?"

He was shoving an axe in Lyon's hands. But Lyon dropped it as soon as Felix looked away. "Better to have something than nothing at all," he answered. "Look, hopefully it won't even come to that. Quick, take off your cloak and shirt."

I watched him pick up an empty feed sack off the floor and start cutting holes in it until it looked suspiciously like a tunic. "What for?" I frowned as he handed it to me, and then started making another one for himself. I did as he told me, stripping away my mud-caked tunic and putting on the scratchy burlap sack.

"We need to blend in. If they see us in fledgling uniforms, they'll know right away who we are. You, Lyon, and I are going to sneak in first. Once we're inside, Beckah and the dragons are going to create a diversion for us. We'll cut Lieutenant Derrick loose in the chaos while Lyon is getting the main gate open, and hopefully the guards will be so distracted, they won't even notice us escaping," Felix explained. "Jae, you speak enough elven that we should at least be able to talk to the other prisoners and figure out where they're holding him."

It sounded good, but I was still confused about how we were actually going to get inside in the first place. He didn't explain that part, and I was sort of afraid to ask.

"How do we know they've even arrived yet?" Beckah was watching us, and she looked really nervous. Not that I could blame her. If everything went according to plan, she'd be the one being shot at by guards and hunted by the dragonriders from the castle. I didn't like it. I didn't want to put her in danger, much less imagine what Sile would do to me if she got hurt. But I also trusted Mavrik. I knew he wouldn't let anything happen to her.

Felix made himself a crude-looking tunic to match mine out of another empty feed sack, and put it on. Then he took the sickle I'd picked up, and a long coil of rope. "We don't," he answered sharply. "But we can't afford to wait. By now, Commander Rayken has realized we're missing from Blybrig. They'll be looking for us. And if we get caught, then there's no one left to help your dad. This is our one and only chance."

Beckah nodded, and I saw her swallow hard. Our eyes met, and I tried to show her a confident smile. "It'll be fine," I told her. "Don't worry. Mavrik is the fastest dragon in Blybrig. Nothing will be able to catch up with you."

"*You* quit worrying," she insisted stubbornly. "I can do this."

Felix stooped down to pick up one of the clay jugs on the floor, pulling the cork out of the top and making a face like it smelled bad. I could smell it too, even from a few feet away. They were jars full of lamp oil. He handed it to her, and gave her a serious look.

"You better be able to do it," he warned. "Because it's our lives on the line."

Outfitted with our makeshift farm tool weapons and empty grain sacks for tunics, Felix, Lyon, and I hunkered down in the shadows only a few hundred yards away from the huge black wall of the prison camp. Beckah was already with Nova and Mavrik, waiting for our signal to start her diversion. I'd given her the best crash-course in flying I could, showed her how to sit in the saddle, and felt like a complete jerk for leaving her like that. Felix had tied about a dozen of those clay jugs full of oil to Mavrik's saddle, going over the plan with her several times. She kept insisting she wasn't scared. At least that made one of us.

After creeping in as close as we dared, Felix, Lyon and I were laying flat on our stomachs, side by side on the ground, and watching through the tall grass. There was only one gate, just one way in and out of the prison camp, and it was heavily guarded. More armed guards stood at each of the eight watchtowers, looking down over the inside and outside of the walls. Even more of them marched around the wall to keep watch for people trying to escape from inside.

"It looks like the perimeter patrols are set about five minutes apart," Felix whispered. "That doesn't give us much time to climb the wall."

"We'll have to do it one at a time, then. That's going to take too long. They might see us." I frowned over at him, hoping he had a better idea.

"There's no other choice. We'll just have to go as fast as possible." Felix reached to pull the bundle of rope and sickle out from where he'd tucked them in his belt. He started to tie one end of the rope to the sickle, like a makeshift hook and line we'd be able to use for climbing up the wall. "I'll go first, then you, Jae. After Lyon comes up last, we'll split up and then give Beckah the signal."

When the next guard walked past, we waited a few seconds. It was long enough that I glanced at Felix, wondering if he'd lost his nerve. But suddenly he took off, sprinting toward the wall and swinging the rope and sickle over his head like a lasso.

The wall was about two stories tall. If he didn't hook the top on the first try, he might not have enough time to climb up before the next guard came by. He swung the rope harder and harder, and finally let it go, sending the sickle howling through the air and clattering against the stone. The sickle cracked against the shards of glass on top of the wall, scraped, and finally snagged with a loud crunch. It made me cringe. Someone definitely would have heard that.

We all waited, and I held my breath. But no one came. The guards hadn't heard us. Felix started reeling in the rope as fast as he could, giving it a few hard tugs before finally leaning his weight into it. When it held fast, he turned around and gave us a quick thumb's up. So far, so good.

He started to climb, using the side of the wall as leverage while he scaled the rope. Just as the last few inches of his boots disappeared up into the dark, the next guard came strolling by on patrol. I held my breath again, waiting to see if the guard would notice anything suspicious.

The guard walked past without even stopping, and all of a sudden it was my turn to climb. My heart was hammering. My hands were sweaty. I was petrified. But I set my jaw, balled my fists, and didn't give myself a single second to hesitate.

I bolted toward the wall, feeling around in the darkness for the rope. When I found it, I gave a tug. From somewhere above me in the dark, I felt Felix tug back. The coast was clear, so I started to climb.

I didn't dare look back to see if the next guard was coming. I just tried not to think about that. The climb was a lot further up than I'd thought. From the ground, it had looked pretty high, but by the time I got to the top of the wall, I was sweating and heaving for breath. Felix grabbed my arms when I got within reach, and hauled me up the last few feet. The top of the wall was slathered in tar mixed with shards of glass, but Felix had spread out his cloak to keep us from getting cut up. He made sure I was steady before he gave me a pat on the back.

Next, it was Lyon's turn. Felix got himself braced, holding the end of the rope that was hooked to the top of the wall, just for good measure. And we waited.

Minutes passed. Two guards walked by down below, and I held my breath each time, expecting to see Lyon come sprinting up to the wall to start his own climb. Maybe it was just taking him longer to work up the nerve. But he didn't come, and it was too dark to see where we'd been hiding in the grass before.

A few more minutes passed, then another guard, and Felix cursed. "That little worm! He ditched us!"

I was stunned. Lyon hadn't exactly been a friend of ours—more like an enemy that was stuck with us for survival purposes—but this? This was twice he'd betrayed the dragonriders, twice he'd proven to be nothing but a lying coward. I cursed, too. Lyon was supposed to be the one who opened the gate to let us out once Beckah and the dragons stirred things up as a distraction. Now we were short one set of hands.

"We can't wait any longer," Felix growled under his breath as he reeled the rope in. "We'll just have to find some other way to escape. Maybe we can climb back down."

Felix had dismissed that idea originally because of the arrows that were sure to be flying in the chaos. One of us could get shot. I knew if he was considering that as our best option now, then we were in real trouble.

"You go," I told him. "Go get ready to open the gate. I'll get Sile."

His eyes got wide. "Jae, you can't go by yourself. What if something happens? What if you need me?"

"You said yourself that I've got the better shot at finding him. I'm the only one who can speak elven and talk to the prisoners." I held out my hand for him to shake. Something in my gut told me this might be the last time we ever saw each other. "You know this is the only way."

I could barely see Felix under the starlight as he looked down at my hand, and instead of shaking it, he took the big hunting knife he'd stolen from the barn and put it in my palm. "Yeah, I know. Just ... try not to get killed." He clapped a hand against my shoulder roughly. "And remember, once the fire starts we only have a few minutes. Don't be late."

While Felix fixed the rope and makeshift hook so we could climb down the other side of the wall, I tucked the knife into my belt, making sure it was hidden under my scratchy burlap tunic. He let me climb down first. My head was spinning with fear as I repelled over the steep, jagged black stone. I prayed over and over that the guards wouldn't see me. None of them did.

When my feet hit the ground, I looked around to get my bearings. It was dark, but the torches burning the watchtowers gave off just enough light that I could see the faint silhouettes of the buildings all around. They weren't really buildings, though. More like shacks made out of pieces of garbage for prisoners to live in.

Everything was eerily quiet and still, except for Felix's boots scraping off the stone from overhead. He climbed down quickly, left the rope where it was, and hurried over to crouch down with me in the shadow of a nearby shack. My heart was pounding in my ears as I strained to see through the gloom. As my eyes adjusted, I could make out how all the garbage-made shacks surrounded the big crater in the middle of the prison camp. There were carved dirt stairwells leading down into the crater, and huge wheelbarrows that would take four or five people to move parked along the rim.

The inside of the prison camp smelled disgusting. It was like a mixture of filth, rotting flesh, and smoke that reeked like burning hair. There was also something in the air that left a mineral taste in my mouth. It was bitter, and made me want to spit.

"It's a salt mine," Felix whispered. "Can you taste it?"

"Yeah, but what's that smell?" I whispered back.

He just frowned darkly and pointed at the crater. "I'm not sure, but it's coming from in there. I don't like it, Jae. Something's not right."

Suddenly there was a metallic-sounding boom from the gate, and Felix and I tripped all over each other as we scrambled to hide. We ducked into a narrow crevice between two shacks, huddling in the dark and watching as the gate began to open.

The gate really was enormous, it was as tall as the walls, and made out of wood and iron. The only way to open it was by operating a crank in the heavily guarded tower. Just looking at it, I wondered if we really could pull this off. Strong as he was, I wasn't sure Felix could open it by himself.

The massive gate creaked and groaned as it opened. Horse hooves clattered in the dark. Out of the gloom, a wagon appeared and came to a halt inside the prison camp. It looked just like the slave wagon we'd been trapped in before, made out of solid metal, and pulled by a team of black horses. My breath caught in my lungs, and it felt like I had swallowed something hard that was stuck in my throat. Sitting on the driving seat, still wearing those white masks, were two of the elite guards from the king.

My hand went to the knife hidden under my tunic, and I gripped the hilt tightly. Even though I couldn't see him, I knew that Sile was in that wagon. He just had to be. That is, if Lyon had been telling us the truth. A wave of nausea hit me when I realized just how much was riding on our assumption that Lyon hadn't been playing us the entire time.

As I watched the gate begin to roll closed again, it felt like someone was slowly choking me. It was like watching my freedom slip through my fingers, leaving Felix and me trapped in this horrible place. I wondered if that would be my last glimpse of the outside world beyond these prison walls.

Then, something else distracted me completely.

From overhead, I heard another sound like the deep, thunderous concussion of wing beats. But I knew this sound right away—it was the drumming of dragon wings in the air. Only this time, they sounded larger than any dragon I'd ever heard flying before.

The dragon was as black as the dark side of the moon, so the only way I knew it had landed was because I felt the earth rumble under my boots with the impact. I could see the shadows cast over its gleaming scales by the torchlight and the faint silver glow of the moon. It was a monster that looked like something from a nightmare. It was twice the size of Mavrik, with two red eyes that gleamed against the night like smoldering coals.

"Gods and Fates," Felix gasped. I saw his eyes look up as an enormous dark shape descended from the night sky. "It's Icarus."

"Who?" I didn't recognize the name, but I could see the horror and fear on his face.

"He's the Lord General's dragon. A king drake," Felix answered, and I could hear his voice quivering with fear. "When a dragon lives to be over a hundred years old, it becomes a king drake or grand queen. They're the largest and most powerful dragons alive. There's rarely ever more than one in existence at a time."

"Great." I groaned. There was only one king drake in the whole world, and it was crouched between Sile and me. As if the king's elite guards weren't enough. We hadn't planned to do battle with a dragon like this.

Felix nudged me with his elbow. "Look!"

Icarus was crouching down to let his rider off, and a man wearing golden armor dismounted. The Lord General was a tall man, as tall as my father. He wore a helmet topped with a long red mane of horsehair, and a red cape that swept the ground at his heels as he moved. The Lord General walked around his enormous dragon toward where the wagon was waiting.

The elite guards driving the wagon had gotten down and unlocked the back door, and I found myself gripping the hilt of my knife again. When the door opened, the Lord General stepped in and blocked our view. I saw people getting out, and I clenched my teeth. I couldn't see who it was, and it was making me furious.

Then the Lord General stepped aside, and I saw him. Lieutenant Sile Derrick staggered in front of all four of the king's elite guards. They pushed him on, making him trip and fall. He couldn't even catch himself because his hands were still tied behind his back, so he hit the dirt face-first. They had tied a gag in his mouth and there was blood on his tunic. But he was alive.

I couldn't even be proud that I'd been right again about something happening to Sile because things were looking more hopeless than ever. We had come here to save him, to set him free, but not only were we trapped in a prison camp, we were also facing the Lord General, his king drake, and four of the king's most accomplished private guards—not to mention all the regular prison guards who were standing watch with bows and arrows in the towers, ready to make us look like pincushions. It looked impossible.

"All right." Felix took in a deep breath and I saw his shoulders flex. "We don't have much time. I've got the gate; you follow them and when you think you've got the chance, give Beckah the signal and get Sile out of there."

I nodded, but my whole body was starting to feel numb.

"We're about to die aren't we?" he asked me suddenly, glancing back and catching me off guard with that question. He was usually so confident.

I gave a small shrug, and tried to smile. "Maybe. But remember, you were the one who wanted to see what amazing, unexpected thing I'd do next."

Felix didn't answer, but I saw his cheek turn up in a smirk as he started slinking out of our hiding place. I watched him slip from shadow to shadow, making his way carefully toward the gate.

Now it was up to me. I couldn't turn back; too much was at stake. Alone in the dark, I watched them drag Sile back to his feet and lead him deeper into the prison camp. I took a deep breath to steady myself and balled my fists.

It was time to shake off my fear. I had to be brave. Sile was counting on me.

20

CHAPTER TWENTY

The elite guards were leading Sile deeper into the prison camp, pushing him whenever he stopped, and keeping a knife at his back. He wasn't fighting them as much anymore. As I crept in closer, I saw that one of his arms looked wrong. From the elbow down it was bloody, and there were pieces of white bone sticking up through the skin. Somehow, they had broken it, and I didn't want to think about how much that must have hurt.

They forced him down the stairs that led into the mining pit and disappeared. I hesitated. If I followed, I might get caught out in the open. I didn't know if there was anywhere to hide down there. I waited, looking back at the prison guards who were milling around the wagon still. They weren't looking my way. My only worry was the dragon, but with that horrible stench in the air, maybe he wouldn't smell me.

I made a dash for the nearest stairwell. As soon as I got a few steps down, I dropped into a crouch and hunkered down, trying to duck against the shadows. None of the men working below seemed to notice me. The Lord General had his back turned, saying something to Sile that I couldn't hear from so far away. All the elite guards were standing nearby, watching. But as my eyes tracked over the inside of the crater, I started to get a bad feeling.

The smell hit me like a kick to the stomach, and when I saw where it was coming from, I started to gag. The crater went down at an angle, with those dirt-carved stairwells on all sides, leading down to where the prisoners had been mining the salt out of the ground and loading those oversized wheelbarrows with it. In the very middle was a big pile of smoldering ash and debris. The embers were still burning bright red and putting off an eerie glow that made it easier to see what was going on. I didn't think much of it at first. I mean, I assumed maybe they'd just been burning trash or waste. But as my eyes adjusted to the change in light, I started noticing the white shapes in the ash.

Bones. They were bones.

There were hundreds of them, piled up like a big pyre. They had been burning the bodies of the prisoners there. The horrible stench in the air was the smell of burning flesh. As soon as I realized that, my skin got clammy and I felt like I was going to throw up.

Suddenly, I got that strange feeling that someone was watching me. Then a big hand grabbed a fistful of my hair. "What have we here?" someone spoke over me in a rough, grumbling voice. "Out after dark, are we? Looking for a good show?"

I heard a chorus of laughs as I kicked and fought, managing to turn around and get a glimpse of the man who had me by the hair. He was a big, pear-shaped man with narrow shoulders and a belly that was being mashed into a chest plate two sizes too small. He had a trimmed beard, dark eyes, and a big scar that ran down the side of his face onto his neck. The crest on his armor was the king's eagle, but I knew he wasn't a dragonrider. Except for that crest, his armor looked like the other prison guards.

"Well, why don't we just give you a front row seat?" He grinned down at me, and his teeth were covered in yellow tobacco stains. I could just feel the evil aura coming off him like smog. He started dragging me the rest of the way down the stairs, and I fought him every step of the way. When we got close to the big pile of charred bones, I fought even harder.

The Lord General turned around to see what the commotion was. He scowled down at me, curled his lip, and sent the guard a disapproving frown. To him, I must have looked like just another prisoner here. I wasn't wearing my Fledgling's tunic and cape anymore.

"What is that, Warden?" the Lord General asked.

"A halfbreed," the man holding me by the hair chuckled. "Haven't you ever seen one before? Sneaky little rats. Some of them could about pass for human, but I can smell that elf blood in their veins a mile away. They can't fool me. And this one's decided to test my rules. Looks like he'll be meeting his ancestors sooner than scheduled!"

The Lord General just rolled his eyes, and didn't even give me a second glance as he started removing his riding gauntlets. "Do what you want, but only after the ritual is complete. I don't want you botching it. You have no idea what a chore this has been." He moved away, angrily muttering under his breath something about small favors.

When he stepped aside, I saw Sile up close for the first time since the officer's ball. He was lying on his side, his mouth bloody like someone had hit him across the face really hard. Our eyes met, and I saw something in his face I hadn't expected. Oh sure, I had expected surprise, confusion, maybe even a little anger ... but Sile looked at me with absolute terror.

He tried to speak, but his voice cracked. He just lay there, staring at me with a look that drove an ice-cold spike of panic into the center of my chest. Something was wrong. I just didn't know what it was, yet. It was as though he wanted to tell me something—something important.

The warden threw me down onto the ground only a few feet away from Sile. He put a foot on my chest to keep me from getting up, and stood there with his arms crossed. He was so big and fat I couldn't get his foot off me no matter how I tried. He smirked down at me, and ground his heel into my ribs. It hurt, but I clenched my teeth and refused to give him the satisfaction of crying out in pain.

I knew I had one choice now, just one chance. Maybe things weren't exactly going according to plan, but our plan had been pretty much ruined the moment Lyon abandoned us. I was playing this by ear, and now it was time for a diversion.

I tried to relax, to let my mind get quiet. It was easier this time, which was strange considering the last time I was in a situation like this, I'd accidentally called out a giant man-eating turtle. Something trickled down the back of my brain like a warm shiver, making my skin prickle and my whole body shudder at once. It grew more intense, until I was shivering like I was cold.

"Put it down over there," I heard the Lord General say.

I opened my eyes to see the king's elite guards carrying what looked like a big, gold-plated box. It must have been heavy, because even with four of them helping, they were still having a hard time managing it. They set it down near the smoldering pit of bones, and the Lord General stepped forward to run his hands over it thoughtfully. He stroked the intricate carvings on the lid, and a strange look of pleasure flickered across his face. He glanced up, like he was looking at someone for approval. But the only people there to look at were the elite guards, and their masked faces hid their expressions, and none of them moved an inch.

"Open it," he commanded again. "Let us begin the ritual."

My head was starting to feel uncomfortably hot. That intense shivering heat in my mind spread all over my body, and made it feel like my muscles were tingling. It definitely seemed to be coming from whatever was inside that big golden box. My heart started to pound in my ears. My body shivered, and I tried to clear my mind again.

I reached out for Mavrik with my thoughts, calling to him just like I had before. I waited until I felt that sensation of weight in my chest to open my eyes toward the sky. *"Mavrik, it's time. Let them taste of your flame!"* I spoke in the elven language, hoping that it would still work and that none of the guards standing around me— particularly the one with his foot on my chest—would be able to understand.

The warden looked down at me with a menacing smirk. "What did you say, whelp?"

Mavrik answered him for me with a deep, bellowing roar from overhead. It was a sound I knew all too well. Everyone looked skyward, including the Lord General, who clearly hadn't been expecting any other dragons to be cruising the area.

Mavrik roared again, with Nova joining him in a chorus of fury from the air. There was an explosion of flame somewhere outside the prison camp. All the guards began to scream in alarm.

Dragon flame isn't what most people imagine. It isn't like the flames from an oven or a fireplace that stops burning once you douse them with water. Dragons spit is a sticky, very acidic venom that reacts with the air and starts to burn instantly. They have two jets in the back of their throat, and can spit that potent mucus about twenty feet. It sticks to whatever it touches like milky-colored tar, and even if you manage to snuff out the flames with water, the acid will still eat away your skin in a matter of seconds. It's pretty awful stuff. Sile had once explained to me that dragons rarely spat flame unless commanded to. They used it as a defensive mechanism, to protect themselves or their eggs on the ground where they couldn't walk or run as quickly as other predators.

I smelled the pungent odor of the dragons' flame burning in my nose, and I heard men shouting, the sounds of bowstrings snapping as arrows were fired. I knew that now was my chance.

The warden wasn't looking at me. He was staring up at the sky like everyone else, looking for the dragons that were showering the ground outside the prison camp with their burning venom. I pulled out the hunting knife hidden under my tunic, and rammed it as hard as I could into his calf. Before he could react, I ripped the knife back out again. I stabbed him twice, and the warden howled in pain. He went stumbling back and finally fell over as he clutched at his bleeding leg.

I was back on my feet in an instant, rushing to where Sile lay on the ground. I cut the ropes on his hands, and pulled the gag off his mouth.

"We have to get out of here now!" I shouted over the chaos.

He was still looking at me with that weird, haunted look of terror in his eyes. I decided maybe he was just in shock. Maybe he was confused, worried he was seeing a ghost, or had been beaten to the point of being delirious.

"How ... ?" he spoke in a weak voice.

"I'll explain later," I told him. "We've only got a few minutes! Hurry, you have to get up!"

A sudden rush of heat sucked all the air right out of my lungs. Something exploded on the ground only a few yards away, bursting into flame as it was showered with sticky dragon venom that caught fire immediately. It burned my eyes, and I had to shield my face. I recognized the shards of a clay jug that landed on the ground near my boots, and knew it had been Beckah. She was using the jugs of oil as explosives, keeping the guards occupied and confused while we tried to make our escape.

"It's those little fledglings from Blybrig. Don't just stand there, you fools! Shoot them!" the Lord General bellowed with fury.

At that moment, he seemed to realize who I was. He turned around slowly, leveling a burning glare on me as I was helping Sile up to his feet. I met his gaze, seeing the reflections of the flames in his eyes.

"Ah," he growled, showing me a wicked smirk. "So *you* are the little piece of halfbreed filth that has infected my ranks. I heard about you and your wild, mongrel of a drake."

I squeezed the hunting knife in my hand, putting myself between the Lord General and Sile. "No," I said. "I'm the little piece of halfbreed filth that isn't going to let you murder my sponsor!"

"A mistake you won't live to regret, I'm afraid." His smirk broadened, and he pulled the biggest sword I'd ever seen from a sheath at his hip. It was almost as long as I was tall, made of black metal, and had the head of a dragon that looked a lot like Icarus engraved on the hilt with two red rubies for eyes.

He started to advance on me, and I got a much better appreciation for just how tall he was. My head almost came to the middle of his chest. Almost. A sense of doom loomed over my head as he started to size me up, looking over me like he was deciding which part of me he wanted to chop off first.

The dragons kept raining fire down from the sky, and I heard Icarus bellow a roar of challenge to them. Men shouted orders or screamed in pain as the acidic venom burned them. And through it all, the Lord General came striding toward me with the fires of battle reflecting off his bronze armor. Behind him, I saw the ghostly figures of the elite guards through the flames.

I braced for impact, trying to remember all my combat training. Of course, we hadn't trained for anything like this before. The Lord General outclassed me in every way possible, and I knew this was going to be my end. But if he was going to kill me, I wasn't going to let him do it without a fight—however brief it might be.

Suddenly there was another crash, another explosion of flame as Beckah threw another jug of oil. It hit that big gold-plated box, and fire belched up into the sky as it was smashed into a million pieces. The Lord General let out a primal yell of frustration, running to the remains of the box and trying to look through the wreckage like he was searching for something.

That *something* rolled across the ground toward me and came to a stop right in front of my feet.

It was some kind of orb, a big round stone the size of a grapefruit. It laid at my feet, peeking out from a charred cloth it had been wrapped in, and I could see that it was a milky, bright green color. There were strange markings on it like splotches of gold, but it didn't look like anything that had been drawn onto it by hand. The marks looked natural, like they had just formed that way somehow, but I couldn't see enough of the stone to tell if the marks made any patterns or designs.

The minute I saw it, I felt like I couldn't move. It was splattered in burning oil from the jug, and I got this eerie feeling that the stone was *looking* back at me. My whole body got cold. My hair stood on end. I felt short of breath, and suddenly that pressure in my chest became so intense that it hurt. My head started burning again. But I couldn't look away. I was caught up in staring at the stone, feeling like I was drowning under its pale green surface.

"Don't look at it!" Sile was right behind me. He smacked his only working hand over my eyes and started pulling me away.

Immediately, I snapped out of my trance.

He was right. This is the chance we'd been hoping for.

Together, Sile and I ran for the front gate. We dodged screaming prisoners who were running from their burning shacks, guards trying to put out the fires, and falling jugs that exploded into new bursts of flame. Sile was hurt badly. He had a hard time running, but he couldn't exactly lean on me since I was half his size. He staggered and stumbled, and a few times I had to use all my strength to keep him from falling.

Finally, I saw the gate. It was cracked open already, and Felix was standing just outside it with his eyes wide in horror at the chaos we'd unleashed. I saw him looking through the blazing madness, desperately searching for us. When he spotted us struggling to get away from the chaos, he didn't hesitate for a single second. He sprinted toward us and put Sile's good arm around his shoulder, helping him along as we made our final dash for the open prison camp gate.

As we ran out of the prison gate, my spirits soared with new hope. We had made it out. Sile was with us. We had rescued him. And I thought for an instant that it was over. I thought we were free.

I was wrong.

When we stopped to catch our breath, waiting for Beckah to descend with Mavrik and Nova and carry us away into the night, I made the mistake of looking back. From back inside the prison camp, I heard a deafening roar that shook the ground under my feet. Dragon flame burst through the prison camp gate, melting the iron and turning it to a pile of molten mush in a matter of seconds.

Icarus came crawling out of the inferno like a demon straight out of the pits of hell. His red eyes gleamed, and the flames danced over his glossy black scales. He hissed, baring rows of dripping fangs as he charged straight for us, ready to burn us all to ash. On his back, I could see the Lord General sitting in the saddle with his sword still drawn. I could have sworn I heard him laughing over the roaring of his dragon and the rush of the flames.

Icarus was coming for us, and there was no way we could outrun him. Huddled together, looking into the fires of doom, Felix, Sile, and I exchanged a meaningful look. This was it. We were trapped like rats, with nothing to cling to now except each other.

I closed my eyes again for a moment, and then looked up to the sky. Finding that quiet place in my mind was easy for some reason, even in the face of certain death. The sound of Icarus growling became distant, and my thoughts were crystal clear.

"Don't come down here, Mavrik," I told him. I knew he would hear, and he'd be furious that I was refusing his help again. "We can't let Beckah get hurt. If you bring her down here, she would be killed with the rest of us. I can't let that happen, so don't land. It's all right."

Then something strange happened, something that had never happened before.

Mavrik answered me.

It wasn't with words. I saw a flash of images in my mind, like a dream only I wasn't sleeping. Mavrik was sending me these images, communicating with me through pictures and colors. First, he showed me a flash of our first encounter, when I'd made my deal with him. Then he showed me the giant paludix turtle that I'd called out of the marsh. Finally, I saw myself standing in front of Icarus, while the huge king drake lowered his head in submission.

Suddenly, I knew what I had to do. Mavrik had given me the answer. I stood up, pushing away from the others and beginning to walk toward Icarus.

Felix shouted after me. "What are you doing?"

I didn't look back at him. "I'm going to have a word with the king."

Icarus came to a halt directly in front of me. He towered so far above me that he blended into the night sky, and all I could see of his head were his two glowing red eyes. He snarled, his lips curling back to show me rows of jagged teeth that were dripping with that burning venom.

"Crush his bones," the Lord General commanded. "Leave nothing but ash for his friends to bury."

Icarus hissed and seemed happy to oblige. He started to lower his massive spine-covered head down toward me. I could hear him taking in a breath, preparing to blast me with a spray of his flame.

I knew what I had to do. Icarus was a king drake, the most powerful of his kind. Sile had told me before that once dragons chose their riders, that they shared a bond of comradery, but now they were treated more like livestock. That was why my connection with Mavrik was so special; he had chosen me and accepted me as his rider of his own free will. But chances were, that hadn't been the case for Icarus. Now, I was about to put that to the ultimate test.

"Great king, please hear me," I called out to Icarus. I went down onto one knee before the king drake, showing him reverence he'd probably never been given before. "Why are you taking orders from a rider you didn't choose? He's ordering you to kill me, but I come to you with respect and ask you to show me mercy. Remember who you are. Don't let this human rule you. You owe him nothing!"

Icarus paused. His bottomless red eyes were staring right at me, boring into my soul. I could sense how powerful he was, how wise and old. And now he was listening to me.

"What right does he have to command you?" I continued. "A king should have the right to choose who rides upon his back. No one should force that choice upon you, or any of your kin! Take back your freedom!"

The king drake growled. I saw his big nostrils puff, sampling my scent with a deep breath that made my hair blow wildly around my head.

"What are you doing?" The Lord General screamed with rage. "You stupid beast, do as you're told! Burn him until his bones are nothing but charred coals!"

All of a sudden, Icarus turned on him. He spread his leather black wings, reared back onto his hind legs, and let out another booming roar. But this time, it wasn't directed at me.

As I started to run back toward Sile and Felix, I saw the king drake whip his head around and strip the saddle off his back with his teeth, taking the Lord General with it. I heard the sound of screaming, pleading, and dragon teeth against armor. I couldn't bear to watch Icarus devour his own rider, so I just ducked my head and kept running.

Felix and Sile were already hobbling away as fast as they could. When I caught up to them, I tried to help Felix carry Sile's weight. We made it away from the burning prison camp safely to the rolling grassy hills of the farmland beyond. By then, the dragonriders from the castle were circling overhead, looking for what had caused this mess, but Mavrik and Nova were already long gone. Soldiers and people from the city were trying to put out the blaze.

I, for one, wasn't sad at all to see that horrible place go up in smoke.

We laid Sile down in the grass and sat down to catch our breath. We didn't speak at first. Instead, we just sat there watching the prison camp burn against the night sky.

Sile grabbed my arm and squeezed it tightly, looking up at me with a sense of urgency. "Never do that again," he growled.

"Call to a dragon?" I wasn't sure what he meant. I'd done a lot of things recently I probably shouldn't have.

"No," he said hoarsely, and his grip on my arm weakened a little. "Risk your life for mine."

21

CHAPTER TWENTY-ONE

Beckah was waiting for us at the corner of the same farmer's field where we had stolen the tools. She was standing between Mavrik and Nova with the night wind blowing in her long dark hair. When she saw us coming, her eyes filled with tears, and she ran toward us with her arms open wide.

Beckah hugged her father tightly, and he put his good arm around her while he kissed the top of her head. "Beck!" His voice quavered, and I saw tears in his eyes as well. "What are you doing here?"

It was a long story, and there wasn't time right then to go hash it all out for him. It would just have to wait. We had to get as far away from that prison camp as possible. Sile saddled up with Felix, Beckah sat with me, and we took off into the twilight and left the prison camp far behind.

As she sat in front of me, I saw Beckah smiling again. It made my stomach swim with nervousness. She took my arm and wrapped it around her waist so she could squeeze it tightly, and my insides just squirmed harder.

"Thank you so much, Jae," she said, looking back at me over her shoulder. "You're amazing." She was sitting so close to me that her nose almost touched mine when she turned back to see me. I could count every freckle on her cheeks and nose.

I blushed so hard I could barely see straight. "You're welcome." I didn't know what else to say.

Over on Nova's back, I caught a glimpse of Sile staring at us. He didn't look very happy. In fact, I could have sworn he was glaring daggers at me. I quickly leaned back away from Beckah, and took my arm out from around her waist.

It was a long trip back to Blybrig. We flew all the way without stopping, finally landing outside the breaking dome as the sun began to set. There was a big group of instructors and students waiting there for us as soon as we touched down. I noticed that there were also armored city guards from Halfax standing around, men the king must have sent. I recognized the style of their armor from when I lived with my mother in the ghetto. That made dread hit me like a kick to the gut.

The other instructors were quick to help us get Sile down out of the saddle. They carried him toward the infirmary, because he was so weak. As he disappeared through the crowd, Beckah followed closely behind and held on to his good hand. Felix and I were left standing there awkwardly by our dragons, wondering what would happen to us now.

Everyone was staring right at us. Students, instructors, even the guards were just standing there with expressions I couldn't interpret. No one said a word.

Felix and I looked horrible. We were both still wearing the tunics Felix had cut out of old grain sacks, and we were caked with smelly mud from the marsh. We were filthy, hungry, and completely exhausted. But no one was looking at us with pity or sympathy. No one seemed glad to see us, either. I couldn't help but wonder if we were about to be kicked out of Blybrig, or arrested. I didn't even want to think about how many rules we had broken.

Finally, the somber-faced instructor standing nearest to me went down onto one knee, putting a fist on the ground as he bowed to us. Like a ripple, all the others in the crowd began to do the same—even the guards from Halfax. Felix and I exchanged a wide-eyed glance. I couldn't believe what I was seeing. I was pretty certain no one had ever bowed to a halfbreed like this before.

No one tried to stop us when we finally went to put our dragons away in the Roost. I took my time removing Mavrik's saddle and feeding him big hunks of raw meat. I ran my hands over his scaly head, scratching him behind the ears until I heard him begin to purr. He looked at me with his bright yellow eyes. I got an eerie feeling when I remembered how he'd spoken back to me at the prison camp. He really did understand it when I talked to him, and he now could communicate back.

"Thank you," I said as I rubbed his snout. "I'm lucky to have you as a partner."

Mavrik made a happy chirping noise, and the image of us flying together flashed through my mind. It startled me. I couldn't stop grinning at him. "Get some rest. I'd say we've both earned it."

He didn't waste any time. He bedded down in his nest of straw, putting his nose on his tail and closing his eyes. I could still hear him purring to himself as I left his stall and went back down the stairs.

I knew that sooner or later, Felix and I were going to have to answer for what we'd done. It wasn't like no one had noticed we were missing. But thankfully, training had been suspended until we were found. And now that we were back,

Academy Commander Rayken gave everyone a few days to settle down before training resumed. It gave me time to eat and sleep as much as I wanted.

Three days later, early in the morning, Felix and I got the order that Commander Rayken wanted to see us immediately. Felix looked nervous, but I had already come to terms with the fact that this was probably the end of my career as a dragonrider. I was going to take all the blame, since it had been all my idea in the first place, and Commander Rayken was going to formally dismiss me from Blybrig. At least, that's what I was expecting.

Dressed in clean fledgling uniforms, we walked together to his office without saying a word. We didn't look at each other as we climbed the stairs and waited outside the door. Felix knocked, and I heard Commander Rayken's voice telling us to come inside.

We stood side-by-side at attention in front of his desk with our hands clasped behind our backs. I didn't dare meet his eyes as Commander Rayken looked us over with a steely expression. It was hard to tell what kind of mood he was in, since I had only seen him a few times before, and he apparently never smiled. He had hard lines on his face from his constant frown, and something about his features reminded me of an old cranky owl.

"You two have made my life very complicated, as of late," he said at last. "First with the saddle nonsense, and now this."

"Sir," Felix spoke up suddenly. "Permission to speak freely?"

The Commander narrowed his eyes and nodded.

"This was my fault, sir. I take sole responsibility for what happened." He squared his shoulders, looking like he was having a hard time holding himself together.

At first, all I could do was stare at him. I didn't even realize my mouth was hanging open until a few minutes had gone by. "B-but that's not—"

Felix shot me an angry look. "It was, Jae. I could have stopped you from leaving Brinton's estate, but I didn't. I'm the oldest, so I'm responsible."

"It's admirable to try and spare him from punishment," the Commander interrupted us suddenly. "But I'm afraid your friend came to me personally in the ballroom asking for my help. You were nowhere in sight, Mr. Farrow."

Felix's face flushed, and he glared down at the tops of his boots. He didn't say anything else.

Commander Rayken's gaze turned on me then, and I found myself wrenching my sweaty hands together behind my back. "Do you remember when you first came here?" he asked me. "Lieutenant Derrick was adamant that I should allow you to join our brotherhood. He insisted that having you here would help restore our fading legacy of honor and discipline."

I tensed, waiting for the axe to drop. As ready as I'd thought I was before to hear him kick me out of Blybrig, I was so nervous I was shaking. I didn't want my time as a dragonrider to be over.

Commander Rayken sighed as he leaned forward to rest his elbows on his desk. "As much as it pains me to admit it—he was right."

I was stunned. For the second time, I couldn't speak. All I could do was stand there, staring at him with my mouth hanging open again.

"You have demonstrated courage that only befits a dragonrider," he went on. "Apparently, in saving your sponsor, you also prevented the success of a plot to defile a sacred artifact that would have granted the Lord General immortality. That power hungry fool stole from the king, paid off some of the royal elite guards to join his cause, and infiltrated my academy. He betrayed his own brothers, whom he had sworn to protect and lead as Lord General, in the most profound way imaginable. It's only fitting that his own dragon went mad and devoured him. Good riddance."

Felix and I exchanged a meaningful glance. We both knew Icarus hadn't really gone mad. I had been the one encouraging the king drake to rebel, although eating the Lord General was entirely the dragon's idea.

"You're talking about the god stone?" I dared to ask.

The Commander just sighed again, fidgeting with papers on his desk. "Yes. Some call it the god stone. The king prizes it as the crown jewel of his reign. It's all magical nonsense, really. It's ridiculous, thinking a rock could grant anyone immortal life."

I felt a little queasy when I thought about the stone I'd seen through the flames in the prison camp. That milky green orb wrapped in a cloth had lain right at my feet. It entranced me somehow, as though it had some sort of force to pull me in. Remembering it gave me chills.

"But why did he want to kill Sile?" I murmured under my breath. I recalled that the Lord General had said something about a ritual that needed to be performed. "What did Sile have to do with a ritual like that?"

"Why don't you ask him yourself?" Commander Rayken grumbled. "He's leaving this afternoon. The infirmary has declared him physically unfit for duty. He's being medically discharged as of today. From now on, you will both be sponsored by Lieutenant Rordin."

It took a moment for that to sink in. Sile wasn't coming back. He wouldn't be my sponsor anymore. The minute I got that news, it felt like my career was doomed. Sile had looked out for me and been forgiving to my small size and pathetic strength. He'd never cared that I was a halfbreed. I didn't know who Lieutenant Rordin was, but I seriously doubted he was going to approve of me.

I looked at Felix, wondering if he'd known about this already. Judging by the total shock I saw on his face, clearly he hadn't.

"Training will formally resume tomorrow, so I suggest you both prepare," Commander Rayken said, wafting his hand at us as though he were shooing us away. "You are dismissed."

As soon as we got back outside, Felix turned to me with a sly grin. He grabbed my shoulders with excitement, and started shaking me like a rag doll. "Can you believe that? Do you have any idea how lucky we are? I thought for sure we were both about to get the boot!"

I smirked back at him. "So did I, but we should probably go talk to Sile."

His smile faded a little, and he let me go. "Yeah. He's bound to be pretty upset about getting medically discharged."

To be honest, the idea of seeing Sile again made me nervous. I didn't know what would be left of the man I'd looked up to like, well, like the father I'd never really had. Sile had always been so dignified and proud, a true dragonrider in my mind. Seeing him battered, broken, and now officially dismissed from service was going to be difficult.

We made our way to the infirmary building as the sun was beginning to dip below the mountains. When we arrived, a medic in a white tunic told us to wait in the foyer while he asked if Sile was willing to have visitors. I'd never been in the infirmary before, but it had a very pungent odor from all the medicines. When the medic returned, he told us to follow him and showed us the way up a flight of stairs to the second floor. There were lots of rooms for patients, but most of them were empty with only a single clean, white bed inside.

Sile was sitting on the edge of his bed with his whole left arm wrapped in layer upon layer of gauze. I could see that his forearm was splinted, and only the tips of his fingers peeked out of the dressings. His lip was still swollen, he had a nasty bruise on his jaw and around one of his eyes, but he still managed to look like the proud warrior he was.

He was talking to Beckah in a soft voice where she sat in a chair near the doorway. When we came in, they both looked up. Beckah's face brightened as she smiled at me. She stood up and threw her arms around my waist, hugging me tightly, and then doing the same thing to Felix. Sile didn't seem to approve of that, even though he didn't say anything to stop her. I could see his expression stiffen into a tense frown.

"Beck?" He cleared his throat to get her attention. "Why don't you go see about getting us some dinner before we get on the road back home? I could use a bite to eat."

She beamed at him before she went skipping out of the room, her long dark braid trailing behind her. Our eyes met as she passed, and she winked at me playfully. It made me smirk a little and blush again in spite of myself.

When I looked back at Sile, he was glaring at me like he wanted to hit me. "Would anyone care to explain to me why you took my little girl on your suicidal rescue attempt?"

I was getting the feeling he expected *me* to answer that. I opened my mouth to come up with some kind of excuse, but Felix beat me to it. "She insisted on coming," he said. "She refused to let us leave her behind."

Sile cut him a murderous look. "She is a fourteen-year-old *child*. You're nearly a man. Surely you can see how I have a hard time believing she forced you to do anything."

I swallowed hard. "Sir, we were afraid whoever kidnapped you might take her, too."

"She could have been killed," he snapped. I heard him sigh as he started rubbing his forehead with his good hand. "You all could have been killed, and that would be on my head. I would be standing before my ancestors with the blood of three children on my hands in addition to ..." His voice trailed away, and he just sat there staring vacantly ahead of him.

"Sir?" I started to ask. There were so many things I wanted to know that I really didn't know where to start. "Why you? If the Lord General needed some kind of a sacrifice for the ritual to grant him immortality, why did he pick you? Couldn't he have just picked an easier victim?"

Sile met my gaze again, and this time he looked confused. "Immortality? Is that what they're saying?"

Felix and I both nodded.

He chuckled hoarsely like that was ridiculous, shaking his head. "Lies," he muttered. "Lies, as usual."

"Sir?" I was anxious for him to explain.

Sile just kept shaking his head while he ran his fingers over the thick bandaging on his arm. "In this case, knowing too much can most certainly kill you. Let what happened to me be an example for you of what happens when you know too much. What I know has almost taken my life twice. It's better that you know nothing, for now."

I didn't like that answer, and judging by the sour look on Felix's face, neither did he. We'd been through a lot just to be shut down without any idea what was going on with Sile. I felt like he owed us something more than that vague explanation. "But what if they come for you again? If we don't know what we're up against—"

"They won't," he interrupted. "I'm not a threat to them anymore. The medics have said that my arm will heal, but I have lost almost all sensation in my hand. I cannot grip a fork without great effort, much less a sword or a dragon saddle. I am useless in the eyes of the king now. Valla will be released to join the other dragons in the wild, and I will go home to my family in retirement."

Sile didn't sound happy about that at all. His expression was somber as he stared at the floor, and I could see the look of distress in his eyes. I couldn't imagine how lost he must have felt, suddenly having his life's career ripped out from underneath him. Even so, when he sighed, I caught his eyes for just a brief second. It made me wonder if he really was telling us the truth. Was he really safe now?

"And we're being passed on to someone else. Lieutenant Rordin—whoever that is," Felix grumbled.

"Jace Rordin is a good man," Sile said. "I fought alongside him when I was a younger man. He's only just now retired from the front lines. If you're smart, you'll listen to what he has to say. He'll have valuable information and tactics to share with you that most riders don't have, because of his experience."

He paused then, looking over at me as though he could sense what I was wondering: Had Sile told him that I was a halfbreed? He smirked and gave a small shrug. "I told him you were unique, but you are the bravest fledgling I'd ever met. Brave to the point of suicidal, in fact."

Hearing that made me deflate. "I wasn't brave. I was terrified the whole time."

Sile gave me a strange look then, as though what I said disappointed him. "Bravery is not an immunity to fear, it is rising up to meet it with the hope that nothing is impossible."

I shifted uneasily where I stood as Sile just sat there staring at us. After a few uncomfortable moments, Beckah came back in carrying two plates piled with food. She glanced at all of us as she put the plates down on the bedside table. I could tell she was trying to figure out what was wrong. Finally, she looked at her father with a worried expression.

Sile just smiled at her. "Maybe you'd like to go eat with them in the dining hall, instead?"

Her face lit up suddenly, and she looked back at us hopefully. "Daddy, are you sure? I already brought something up here."

He just waved a hand at her dismissively, "I can eat both. I haven't had anything in days. I'll be fine. Go on."

I had a feeling he just wanted to get rid of us for a while. Despite the way he smiled at her, I could still see sadness in his dark eyes. This was hard for him; it just had to be. Leaving Blybrig meant his days as a dragonrider were over forever, and I could imagine how that would terrify someone who had been doing this since he was our age.

"I'll come by next year and see how you two are progressing," Sile called after us on our way out the door. "So don't disappoint me."

I swore right then that I would do my best not to. Out of every other dragonrider here, his opinion was the one I valued the most. I wanted his approval more than anyone else's. I wanted to make him proud of me.

22

CHAPTER TWENTY-TWO

Two days later, Lyon was back, and standing in formation at the call to arms. He looked pretty horrible—like he hadn't slept since he'd abandoned us at the prison camp. There were dark circles under his eyes, and he wouldn't tell anyone what had happened or where he'd been. It took me a while to talk Felix down from wanting to beat the life out of him right then and there. I thought I'd succeeded, but then I spotted Lyon in the dormitory hallway later that night and he had a fresh black eye. I didn't have to wonder who'd given it to him.

I was relieved when training started up again. It was comforting to be back where everything made sense, and all my days were planned down to the last minute. I had a warm bed, three good meals, and I got to train with Mavrik every day. I didn't tell anyone about my new ability to communicate with him, or that he could speak back to me by sending me images in my mind. Considering how most people were responding to me calling to animals, I decided it was probably best to keep that to myself, for now.

Felix and I got back into our old routines like nothing had ever happened, well ... except for our new sponsor. Lieutenant Jace Rordin was a lot different than Sile. When he met us for the first time, I got the impression right away that he wasn't going to put up with any nonsense. He looked like he was in his mid-thirties, but I would have never thought of him as old. He was a fairly normal height, with an average build, dark eyes under a serious brow, and dark brown hair that was beginning to turn gray along his sideburns and temples. He had a grim, somber look about him just like you would expect from a man who'd just returned from the battlefront.

When he looked at me, it made my shoulders seize up instinctively because I was always afraid of what he'd say to me. He'd just gotten finished killing Gray elves, and I knew what I looked like. But he never said a word about my heritage, which only made me more anxious.

Jace may not have looked like anyone extraordinary, but he was a very good swordfighter. He kept us doing the same drills every the morning Sile had started with us, only he made us get up even earlier and actually did them with us. He even ran laps with us. Then he started teaching us more about sparring and hand-to-had combat techniques, advanced stuff that the other fledglings weren't learning yet.

He pushed us to our breaking point every single day. I could tell that my size and lack of strength were annoying to him. He was constantly critiquing me, insisting that I needed to work harder, and shaking his head like I was a big disappointment.

I still wasn't any good with the weaponry we were learning to use. Swords were still too big and heavy, and I could barely pull back a bowstring. It was frustrating, but I muscled through. I wasn't going to give up. If Rordin was trying to break me by proving I wasn't strong enough to stay here, then he'd just have to toss my body out on the doorstep after I died from doing too many pushups.

"You need to keep up this regimen during the interlude," Jace growled at my heels as he ran behind us during morning laps. "Every day you should run, fly drills, and work on building your strength and stamina."

I didn't know what the interlude was. It seemed to be a pretty big deal though, because the whole academy started buzzing about it as training went on. Instructors looked more serious and pushed us even harder. The avian class ahead of us started to look more stressed and worried. You could practically taste the tension in the air.

On our last week of training before the interlude, Felix explained that while training for the older students went year-round, fledglings got a three-month break while the class ahead of us, the avians, learned ground survival techniques. It all focused around that final month where all the avian students were put through a rigorous final test they called the battle scenario.

"That'll be us next year, you know. It's the most intense training we'll ever do," he said. "They teach us how to endure interrogation, torture, and how to survive in Luntharda if we get shot down behind enemy lines. Students have died during this training. It's no joke. All the instructors have to be present to help out."

Now I was starting to understand why Jace was pushing me so hard. If that training was difficult, or even deadly, to normal students, I could only imagine what it was going to be like for me. Jace must have been concerned that I was too small to survive, and I couldn't really blame him for that.

"We won't have our dragons to help us. They'll have some kind of goal for us, usually it's to evade capture as long as possible, and you have to survive being eaten by monsters or starving to death. Then once everyone's been caught, the instructor's start the mock interrogation."

"Mock interrogation?" I didn't like the sound of that.

Felix just shrugged. "Yeah, but we'll get specialized training on how to handle it. It'll be fine."

I wasn't so sure. Well, I knew Felix would probably be all right. He was strong and probably one of the best hand-to-hand fighters in our class. My own skill set was still questionable, though. I wasn't sure talking to animals would do me any good.

When training finally began to wind down, the other fledglings made preparations to go back home for our three-month break. Felix was going back to his parents' estate. He kept asking me over and over if I wanted to stay with him and train. He insisted his parents wouldn't mind, or that they probably wouldn't even notice I was there at all.

"They barely notice me and I'm their only child." He chuckled as he packed his clothes and uniforms back into his bags.

"It sounds great," I said. "It's not because I don't want to. There's just, well, there's someone I need to see."

He turned a sly grin in my direction. "Your girl, huh?"

I blushed. "I told you, it's not like that. But I promised her I'd see her as soon as I could."

He kept grinning as he went back to packing. "Sure, sure. You've got quite a tale to tell her, huh? You think she'll believe any of it?"

"I don't know. I guess it is kind of a wild story." I rubbed my thumb over my mother's necklace, toying with it while I sat on the edge of my bed. I'd already packed all of my things up, but I didn't want to leave until I absolutely had to.

Going back home was bittersweet. On the one hand, I was excited to see Katty again and tell her about everything. But then there was my family. I wasn't looking forward to seeing them again, and being forced to sleep in the loft, or blamed for everything by my stepmother and her two little demon daughters. I knew being a dragonrider wasn't going to change anything when it came to them.

Felix finished packing and picked up his bags, nodding for me to follow him as we left our room behind. We walked together one last time down the stairs, out of the dormitory, and across the open grounds toward the Roost. I took my time putting Mavrik's saddle on. Out of the corner of my eye, I could see that Felix was doing the same. Neither of us wanted to leave, I guess.

When we met back outside the Roost, it was awkward. I didn't want to admit it to him, but I was going to miss Felix. He'd become my best friend to replace Katty when she wasn't around. Not having him there to watch my back, or tease me about my love life, was going to make it hard to get through three months of dealing with my family.

"Well, if you need anything, send me a letter. Or just show up, if you want." He was looking at me with a worried expression. "Hey, uh ... you're a dragonrider now. So don't let anyone push you around. You don't have to put up with that anymore."

I smiled at him. "I'll try to remember that."

"And keep training, like Lieutenant Rordin said," he added. "Next year will be twice as hard as this one. You need to be ready."

"Right."

"And, seriously, if you want to come visit for a few days—"

"Felix?"

He paused. "Yeah?"

I smirked, reared back, and gave him a punch in the arm as hard as I could. "I'll be fine. See you in three months."

He just rolled his eyes because my punch didn't even make him flinch. "Says the kid with noodles for arms," he mumbled under his breath. Finally, he just gave me one of his sly, crooked smiles and gave me a swat on the back of the head.

I stood there for a few moments and watched him walk away. He climbed up onto Nova's back, fastening down his luggage before he gave me one last wave and took off into the sky. I watched them go, climbing higher and higher, until they were nothing more than a tiny dark speck on the horizon.

Mavrik lowered his head and started making those curious chirping sounds and blinking his big yellow eyes at me. A crystal-clear image of Felix and I playing chase through the sky on the backs of our dragons flashed through my mind. I knew it came from Mavrik.

I turned around to pat his snout. "Yeah," I told him. "Don't worry. We'll see them again."

AVIAN

The Dragonrider Chronicles Book Two

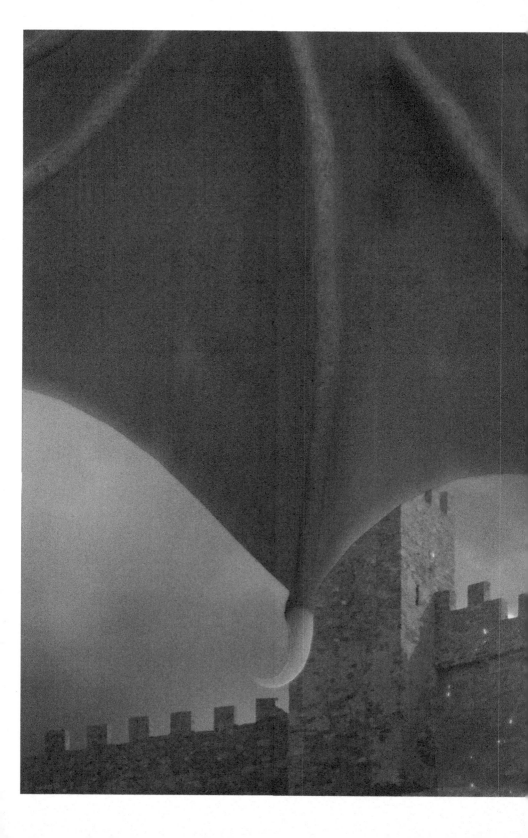

I

CHAPTER ONE

Not everyone can be a dragonrider. Not everyone can handle the stress or the physical demands of having the most dangerous job in the king's forces. My mentor, Lieutenant Sile Derrick, once told me that dragonriders are not born—they are made. He said that they have to be hammered, shaped, and baptized in fire, just like when a blacksmith molds a lethal sword out of a hunk of raw metal. Blybrig Academy is where all dragonriders are made. It's our forge. Never in a hundred years would I have guessed I would find myself there, facing the furnace of my destiny. But destiny has a funny way of picking you when you least expect it.

There was snow on the mountains when I left Blybrig behind for the three-month interlude in my training as a dragonrider. I hadn't been back home to Mithangol in almost a year. I wish I could tell you that I was looking forward to seeing my father, stepmother, twin half-sisters, and older half-brother again. But I wasn't. In fact, I was absolutely dreading it. The very thought of living with them put painful knots of anxiety in my stomach.

I looked into the cold wind from the back of my dragon, Mavrik, who stretched his wings out wide to catch the updrafts. He soared like a magnificent blue-scaled eagle. I was sitting between his strong neck and powerful wing arms in a saddle made of finely crafted leather. He could sense my uneasiness. Every now and then, he flicked a glance back at me with one of his big yellow eyes, making curious clicking and chirping noises.

"It'll be fine." I tried to sound confident. "I'm sure things will be different now."

In fact, I knew they probably wouldn't. If anything, now they would be much worse. My father had never liked me. He had never even wanted me to begin with. But after my mother passed away, there was nowhere else for me to go except maybe a prison camp. I'm pretty sure that's where I would have ended up if my mother hadn't left behind a letter that named Ulric Broadfeather as my biological father. That letter made him my only living relative, so he was duty-bound to adopt me. It was a law in Maldobar, so he couldn't refuse even though I was a halfbreed. It would have looked worse to abandon me than for him to have a halfbreed for a son.

Far below, tucked into the crevices of the Stonegap Mountains, I saw Mithangol. That was where Ulric and his real family lived, and where I'd been an unwelcomed guest since I was twelve years old. It was the dead of winter now, so all the roofs of the houses and shops were covered in a thick blanket of clean white snow. I could see the steep slopes dotted with dark fir trees and smoke rising up from all the chimneys.

I'd lost all track of time while I was in Blybrig Academy. It was close to the coast and cut off from the world by mountains on all sides, so the seasons practically stood still. It was always warm, dry, and sunny there. After spending so many months in the constant warmth of the desert, I'd forgotten what the winter cold felt like. I shivered hard, and Mavrik made an unhappy grumbling, growling sound. I guess he didn't like the cold, either.

Since I was sure no one at home was expecting me, I wasn't in any hurry to get back there right away. Besides, there was someone else I had to see first. Mavrik circled around the outside of the small city looking for a good place to land. Finally, he cupped his wings and lurched toward the ground, stepping awkwardly into the snow and growling as he hunkered down long enough for me to jump down out of the saddle. I took my bag off his back, and gave him a good scratch behind the ears.

"Go find a good spot in the sun," I told him. "At least until I can figure out how to fit you in the barn." I wasn't sure Ulric was going to allow that—especially since there was a good chance Mavrik might eat the horses. The only thing more dangerous than a hungry dragon is a bored dragon.

Mavrik blinked at me, snorted, and took off into the sky again. I stumbled back as the rush of wind off his wings hit me hard, making me lose my balance for a moment. I stood ankle-deep in the snow, watching him soar upwards and disappear into the low clouds. Even if I couldn't see him, I could still feel his presence like a buzzing warmth in the back of my mind. It gave me comfort as I started hiking through the thin line of pine trees.

I knew Mithangol like the back of my hand. I'd spent a lot of a time avoiding my family, and even more time getting into trouble with Katalina Crookin. Katty had been my best friend until I went to Blybrig, and so I started for her house right away. I still considered her one of my closest friends, even if I hadn't seen her in almost a year. Knowing that I'd be standing in her house soon, getting hugged and force-fed by her mother while I told them about my training, put a smile on my face. I was so excited to finally see her.

I walked down the side of the road that led past the Crookin's home. Further down that same road was Ulric's house, but I wasn't going to let myself think about that yet. Katty's father was a blacksmith, and I knew by the smell of scorched metal in the air that he must have been working in his forge. The sun was just beginning to set as I came up the drive toward the front of their house. I saw lights burning in the windows, and smoke puffing out of their chimney. The place looked cozy, and exactly how I'd remembered it.

I knocked on the front door, my stomach churning and doing excited back flips while I waited. I wanted to see Katty, and at the same time, I was so nervous. I wondered if she had changed since we last saw each other. I was fairly sure I hadn't grown at all, despite my best efforts. Finally, the handle lurched, the door opened, and I held my breath.

It wasn't Katty.

Mrs. Crookin stood in the doorway wiping her hands on her apron. When she saw me, she started to smile. Her eyes got bright, and she grabbed me before I could even remember to hold my breath. She always hugged me so tight I thought I might suffocate.

"Jaevid!" She crooned at me, and started kissing my cheeks. "Look at you! So handsome in that uniform! Katty told me you were taken in by the academy. Training to be a dragonrider, is it?"

I blushed as she held me out at arm's length. I was still wearing my fledgling uniform with the king's golden eagle stitched onto the chest. I hadn't bothered putting on my armor, though. It was still packed away in my bags. "Yes, ma'am."

"Oh, she's going to be so excited to see you. She read your letters over and over." Mrs. Crookin started wiping dirt from my face with her apron. "She's out at the forge, dear. You should go surprise her."

Katty had told me in one of her letters that she was going to be an apprentice for her father and learn to be a blacksmith, too. I knew that would definitely make her happy. She had always talked about wanting to learn her father's craft. It was her dream.

I left my bag in the doorway and started out across the snow toward the barn where Mr. Crookin had built his own forge and bellows. Black smoke belched out of the stone stack, and I could see the bright red glow of the fire inside shining from the crack under the door.

My stomach was doing more aerobatics than ever as I started to pull on the handle. I opened it just a little, barely enough to peek inside and see what she was doing. All of a sudden, my heart hit the back of my throat like someone was choking me. It hit me so hard I couldn't even think. I couldn't breathe. All I felt was a burning, angry heat in the pit of my stomach like I'd swallowed a mouthful of dragon venom.

Katty was there, and I didn't see her father anywhere. But she wasn't alone. She was standing with a boy who looked like he was eighteen or so—a lot older than I was. He was a lot taller than me, too, with coal-black hair pulled into a short ponytail. He was wearing a blacksmithing apron just like she was, and they were laughing together. I didn't recognize him, which bothered me the most. Mithangol was a very small city. Most of the younger men had bullied me at one time or another while I was growing up, so I knew who they were. But I had never even seen this boy before.

She giggled at him while he teasingly smudged ash on her cheeks, and when she turned around to start working again, I saw him put a hand on the base of her back. It made that angry fire in my gut burn all the way up through my chest. I couldn't even see straight.

They hadn't noticed I was standing there, so I shut the door and backed away. I went back to the house with my heart hammering in my ears. When I got inside, I picked up my bag and got ready to leave.

"Wasn't Katty working out there?" Mrs. Crookin sounded worried. She was leaning in from the kitchen, looking me over for an explanation.

I couldn't meet her gaze. I was sure if I did, she'd see how upset I was. "Yeah. But she's busy. I'll just come back some other time," I lied.

Mrs. Crookin didn't try to stop me as I gathered my bag and left. When the cold air hit my face, I realized just how angry I really was. I didn't even understand why seeing her with that boy made me so upset. But it did. It felt like some kind of betrayal, even if I had no justification for it. Katty and I were just friends. We'd always been just friends. I had no right to be upset about who she flirted with. None of that mattered right then, though. I was so furious I was seeing red.

In my mind, Mavrik sent me an image of him burning the barn to the ground with Katty and that stranger inside. I shook my head, and looked up to the darkening sky. "Don't bother," I muttered.

I knew he would hear me even if he were ten miles away. We were linked now in a way I didn't understand. While I was at Blybrig, I'd discovered I had a unique ability to call out to animals. They could understand me. But so far, Mavrik was the only one who could communicate back to me. That was our secret.

I dragged my feet through the snow as I walked down the road toward Ulric's house. My thoughts were clouded and confused. I wasn't even worried about seeing my family anymore. All I could think about was that stranger and how he'd touched Katty, smiled at her like that, and made her laugh. It made me so annoyed with her, and even more furious and frustrated with myself. I was so caught up that when I turned the corner to walk up the steep, muddy drive toward my family's home, I didn't notice the house.

Then I looked up.

There were no lights burning in the windows, and the house was completely dark. It was getting kind of late, though. Maybe everyone had already gone to sleep? Still, it was strange that there was no smoke coming from the chimney. As cold as it was, Ulric would have normally lit the fireplace to keep the house warm all night.

I hurried up the drive toward the porch, noticing that the garden was dead and covered in snow. My stepmother, Serah, usually covered the ground with pine straw to protect the plants from the cold until spring. Cupping my hands around my eyes, I peeked in through the front window to see if anyone was still sitting up in the parlor. Sometimes Ulric sat at the side of the dying fire to smoke his pipe until really late.

What I saw put another hard, painful knot in my throat. I ran to the front door and started beating on it. To my surprise, the door just swung freely in. It wasn't even locked.

The house was empty.

For a few minutes, I could only stand there in the open doorway while the cold winter wind howled past me. I stared through the darkness into the parlor and kitchen in front of me. There wasn't a stick of furniture anywhere. Judging by the dust gathered on the kitchen counters and windowsills, they hadn't been here for months.

Slowly, I began to realize the truth: they had left me. Ulric had taken his whole family, moved, and never said a word to me about it. Maybe it was naïve to expect him to tell me, but it still left me stunned.

"Jae!" I heard someone call out to me, and I recognized who it was right away. But hearing *her* voice didn't give me comfort like it usually did. I didn't turn around. I just kept standing there, staring into the empty house, wondering what I was supposed to do now.

Katty ran up behind me with ash still smudged on her cheeks. She was flushed and out of breath, wearing a dark gray dress and blacksmithing apron that were both covered in scorch marks. "Jae?" she said my name again.

I was going to have to face her eventually. At least now, she wouldn't know I was upset about what I'd seen with her. I had bigger problems. "They left," I muttered back, finally looking back at her.

Katty had grown. She looked different, and not in ways I necessarily felt comfortable with. The boys in town had always teased her and called her ugly because of her wild, frizzy curls and scrawny build. Her golden, curly hair was longer and it wasn't frizzy at all. It framed her round face and made her look... very, very beautiful. Her wide blue eyes glittered in the darkness, but I had to look up to see them because she was taller than me now. All her freckles were gone, and now her skin looked smooth and soft. She had adult shapes to her body now that were almost hidden by her thick leather apron.

She looked a lot more grown up now. And for some reason, that made me angrier and more frustrated than ever. Katty was only a few months older than I was, so I had always felt better about my lack of size because she wasn't all that big, either. But now I knew for sure that I was doomed to be a tiny scarecrow forever. Even girls were outgrowing me.

"I know," she said softly. "I came by a week ago to see if you'd come back yet, and they were already gone. This was left for you. I found it slipped under the front door. It's from your brother. I hope you don't mind, but I read it already. I wanted to know why they left without saying anything." She reached into her apron pocket and pulled out a wrinkled envelope.

I took it from her, scowling at it as I crammed it into my own pocket. Why they'd left didn't matter to me right then. All I cared about was that now I was alone here, in a big empty house. I didn't have any furniture. I didn't have any clothes other than my uniforms. I didn't even have food.

"Don't worry, okay?" Katty reached out to put her arms around my neck. She hugged me, but it didn't make me feel any better. In fact, it just felt awkward and wrong—like she was comforting a little kid. "We'll help you. We'll bring you anything you need."

"Thanks." I couldn't make myself say anything else. I was too upset. My jaw locked up and I clenched my teeth.

"I'm so sorry, Jae." She hugged me even tighter. "I've missed you so much."

For some reason, I didn't quite believe her. She'd obviously had some company to keep her from being lonely without me. "Yeah," I managed to answer dryly. "Well, I'm back now for three months."

"You can come stay with us tonight," she offered.

I backed away from her a little, looking into the empty house and trying to decide what to do now. Finally, I shook my head. "No, but thanks. I'll be fine."

She arched a brow at me suspiciously. I could see confusion in her eyes. "But Jae, there's nothing here. You can't possibly—"

"I'll be fine," I repeated. "Please leave me alone."

This definitely wasn't the welcome home I'd expected. Oh sure, I'd anticipated getting the cold shoulder from Serah and my siblings, being forced to sleep in the loft room again, and maybe even getting a beating from Ulric just for old time's sake. This had caught me completely off guard. I felt so lost.

Katty nodded a little, and started to look sad. "Okay, if you're sure. I'll come by tomorrow with something to eat. We'll catch up." She gave me a hopeful smile.

I couldn't smile back at her. I tried, but the ability wasn't there. As she turned to leave, I lingered in the doorway of the empty house and watched her walk away. I waited until she was far away, too far to see me through the darkness, to let my feelings show.

A few tears blurred my vision and left warm streaks down my face. I wiped them away quickly. Maybe if I were a normal-sized, halfway healthy-looking young man like that stranger she'd been giggling with, Katty would have noticed me first. But I wasn't. And I never would be. I swallowed my feelings quickly. No matter what happened, I was a dragonrider now. Dragonriders didn't cry.

It started snowing again. Fat white flakes swirled in the air around me when I turned back toward the house again. There really was no point in going inside. Not tonight, anyways. So I shut the door and started for the barn instead. I called out to Mavrik, telling him to land, as I pushed open the heavy barn door. All the horses were gone. So was the wagon, and most of the tools Ulric had kept on hand for his work as a tackmaster. There was old hay still piled on the floor, and it still smelled like the oils he used to season the leather for the dragon saddles.

The earth flinched under my boots as Mavrik landed, and I heard him chirp at me worriedly as he crawled my way. The barn was barely big enough to squeeze him in. He had to curl up into the smallest dragon-ball I'd ever seen. He laid down with his snout on his tail and his wings folded up tightly against his sides. If he stretched at all, he'd take out a wall or the roof. It definitely wasn't as comfortable as the Roost, but at least it was safe from the wind.

I rolled the door close again, and started looking around for anything left behind that I could use. I found a few half-burned candles and an old quilt that smelled like it had been used as a horse blanket. Using the piece of flint I kept in my saddlebag, and a hunting knife I'd stolen from a farmer a few months ago, I lit the candle and wrapped myself up in the blanket.

As I leaned back against Mavrik's side, I finally took out Roland's letter and held it up to the candlelight. His script was small, and it was hard to read, but what it said left my head spinning worse than ever.

Roland had officially joined the ground infantry about the same time Ulric and I had left for Blybrig last spring. He'd gone to training in Halfax, and been given a post as a cavalryman. Ulric and Serah had told him about their decision to move only a few weeks before they actually had. Apparently, Ulric had gotten an offer to buy a bigger house with a better workshop near Westwatch. They'd given this house to Roland to live in when he wasn't away with the infantry, but he didn't want it. So he was offering it to me, instead. He wrote that if I wanted it, it was mine, or I could try to sell it. He didn't plan on ever coming back to Mithangol if he could help it. I didn't blame him for that.

At the very bottom of the letter, in what looked like a last minute scribble, he wrote that he was being sent to the frontlines at Northwatch. He said that if I ever made it that far, I should try to find him. When I read that, I exchanged a wide-eyed look with Mavrik. Roland had never wanted anything to do with me before. He had always acted like I didn't exist. I wasn't sure what to think of that.

I read the letter over and over to be sure I hadn't missed anything. All the while, my mind was racing with the question of what to do about the empty house. I didn't know if I could sell it and leave Mithangol like he had, or if I should try to stay and make some kind of a temporary life for myself here. I only had three months. For a long time, I sat there staring at the letter while Mavrik purred himself to sleep. I scratched at his big ears and rubbed his scaly snout.

Finally, I folded up the letter and blew out the candle. There wasn't anything I could do tonight. I was tired from traveling, and my mind was foggy with so many confusing emotions. I curled up closer to Mavrik's warm side, putting my head against his neck and closing my eyes. I listened to him breathing as he slept.

I knew I couldn't express to him with words how glad I was to have him there. Still, I knew he'd probably be able to sense my emotions the same way I could sense his. He probably knew I needed him now, when I had no one else to turn to. He wasn't just my mount; he was my friend, my partner, and my greatest ally. Whatever happened to me now, I knew he would be there.

I would never really be alone.

2

CHAPTER TWO

I woke up the next morning feeling stiff. It was still cold outside, but I was warm where I lay, snuggled up beside Mavrik under the old horse blanket. I wasn't eager to get up and face the day, or the winter weather outside.

It was easy to feel hopeless. It was easy to look at my situation and want to give up. I could just go live with my best friend Felix for the interlude, like he'd wanted. He was the son of a rich duke, so I would have plenty to eat, a nice warm bed, and lots of time to train if I went to stay with him. The only reason I'd bothered coming back here was to see Katty, and now that was completely ruined.

Then it hit me.

It hit me so suddenly, I glanced at Mavrik to make sure that he hadn't put that thought in my mind, but he was still asleep. I'd spent too much of my life feeling sorry for myself. I wasn't going to make anyone proud moping around. I was done taking the easy road, and sitting back wishing things would get better. I hadn't just spent a year in training to be a dragonrider to let something like this defeat me. This was an opportunity to show everyone else that I wasn't helpless, that I could fend for myself, and I intended to seize it. For me, nothing was ever going to be easy. The only thing I had control of was how I handled it.

I got up, brushed the straw off my clothes, and started pushing the heavy barn door open to let the morning light stream in. Usually winter days in Mithangol were overcast and bleak, but today the sun was shining through the thick cloud cover. It sparkled over the freshly fallen snow, and a blast of cold wind cut me right to the bone.

Behind me, Mavrik growled sleepily as the morning sun filtered in. He squinted, snorted, and rolled over to face away from the light. Apparently, he wasn't ready to get up yet. It had been hard enough to pack that much dragon into this small barn to begin with, so I decided I would let him sleep. There wasn't much he could do for me today, anyway.

"I'm going to get things cleaned up," I told him as I tied my cloak under my chin. "Don't eat anyone, okay? And don't burn down anything, either. We're keeping a low profile."

He just flicked the end of his long tail and started snoring again.

The house didn't look any less bleak or empty even with the sun shining through the windows. I decided to go in and see exactly what I had to work with before I started cleaning. Ulric and Serah hadn't left me much, though. I opened all the doors and windows to let the cold wind blow through. It made it freezing inside, but I had to get rid of the musty smell.

I hadn't spent all that much time inside the house itself before, so it was weird to be standing in it alone. Serah had never liked me touching her things, and she had forbidden me to be inside without her supervision. It wasn't a big house, and it wasn't fancy at all. The floors were bare wood, and the walls were covered in old plaster that was chipping in places. Downstairs there was only a small parlor with a fireplace, a kitchen with a wood stove, and a single washroom with a big copper basin for bathing.

There was basically nothing left in all the kitchen cabinets except a few old breadcrumbs and some old empty jars. There were a few split logs stacked up beside the stove, but I had a feeling I was going to have to learn to cook for myself now. I had never cooked anything before in my life. I didn't know how to make bread, or anything like that. This wasn't going to be easy. I knew I had a lot of learning to do.

Up the narrow staircase were the three bedrooms. They were all about the same size, and I had never slept in any of them. I was surprised to find that they left all the bed frames and old, lumpy mattresses behind. There was a fireplace in the room that used to belong to Ulric and Serah. It also had the biggest bed and a window that overlooked the front drive. I decided I would take that room for myself, since this was going to be my house now.

The second room had been Emry and Lin's. There were two much smaller beds set on either side of the space, with a window in the middle of the far wall. The rest of the furniture was gone. The only trace of my horrible twin sisters left was a hole in one of the walls leftover from when Emry had thrown a fit, accused me of stealing a pair of earrings from her, and hurled a jewelry box at me. She'd missed me, thankfully, but managed to put a big dent in the plaster. Naturally, that had invited Ulric's wrath down on both of us—well, mostly on me.

Roland's room had the only other decent sized bed. Since they were expecting him to be living here from now on, it still had a lot of his stuff left in it. His bed still had all the sheets and pillows on it, and his armoire still had his clothes inside. They were all bound to be way too big for me, but at least now I had the option of something to wear other than my academy uniforms.

I had never been inside his room before, and it was weird to be standing there with his belongings. He had sounded very sure in his letter that he wasn't coming back, though. I guess none of this stuff mattered enough to him to come back for it.

At the end of Roland's bed was a large wooden trunk with iron clasps and hinges. The old padlock on the front wouldn't budge, no matter how I picked at it. Considering there was no one here anymore to beat me senseless if I broke into Roland's private property, I didn't waste any time using my hunting knife to pry the hinges off the back of the trunk and open it.

Inside, buried under an old blanket, was a collection of things I knew must have been special to him—things he hadn't wanted anyone else to touch. Lying on top was an old scimitar that looked like it must be some kind of heirloom. But as far as I knew, our father had never been a soldier, so I didn't know where Roland would have gotten a blade like that. I didn't remember ever seeing him carry it around.

I picked it up, feeling how light it was in my hand. The more I looked at it, the more I realized what a beautiful weapon it truly was. It had ivory and silver inlaid into the hilt with designs that looked like the head of a stag. The curved blade needed to be sharpened and polished, but it was slender and had a beautiful shape. It looked like it had probably been a very expensive blade whenever it was originally forged. Even the scabbard was covered with a sheet of hammered bronze that had the same engraving of a stag's head on it.

I'd never seen such an ornate weapon before. All the weapons we used at the academy for training were blunted or made out of wood so we didn't accidentally kill each other. None of them looked like this. None of them had been crafted so carefully, with such attention to detail and beauty.

I grasped the leather of the grip and took it out of the sheath, holding it firmly. I had practiced with lots of different weapons at the academy in the past year. None of them suited me well. I fumbled clumsily with the swords that were too heavy or too big, struggled with bows that I didn't have the strength to draw, and made all the instructors look at me like I was a dead man walking.

But this scimitar was different. I could feel it right away. Something about the way it fit into my hand, even if it was still way too big, just seemed right. It felt comfortable in my palm, and I liked the way the light danced over the unique curved shape of the blade.

I put the scimitar back into the sheath, and set it aside to keep going through the trunk. Roland had been keeping his savings from working odd jobs around the city in a leather purse. I counted out twenty gold pieces, ten silver, and fifteen coppers. I had never seen that much money in my life. As wrong as I knew it was to take his life's savings without asking, I needed to buy food. I would have to pay him back later. Eventually, though probably not anytime soon, I would start getting paid for my work as a dragonrider.

The only other item buried in the trunk was a leather-bound book. I untied the strings that held it closed, and discovered it was a journal. Immediately, I closed it and put it back into the trunk without reading a single word. Maybe I'd borrow his savings, and keep the scimitar, but I drew the line at that. I wasn't going to rifle through his personal thoughts. It felt wrong to even hold the thing.

Picking up the purse of coins and the scimitar, I shut the trunk again and looked around the room. I couldn't shake that eerie feeling I got from standing in there. Roland and I had never been close. We'd only exchanged a handful of words in three years. We were basically strangers, but he must have found some reason to reach out to me. He was the last person in the world I had expected that from. It was a humbling surprise to know that he even thought about me.

I turned around to leave the room with my new treasures in my hand, and almost smacked right into Katty. She was standing in the doorway watching me. She hadn't made a single sound. It scared me to death.

"What are you doing here?" I asked, doubling over to recollect my nerves. For a moment, I'd thought she was Ulric or Serah about to catch me going through Roland's stuff.

She had her arms crossed, and her golden curls bounced around her face when she shrugged. "Momma sent some food for you. I told you she would last night." Her tone was sharp, and I noticed she was scowling a little. I was about to ask why, but she beat me to it. "I know you saw me with Bren last night. Momma said you went out to the shop, so I know you saw. Don't try to deny it. Tell me the truth, is that why you're acting so weird?"

That caught me off guard. I stared up at her, since she was now several inches taller, and fumbled for words. "I'm not acting weird."

"Yes, you are. I've seen you hurt, sad, and upset because of your family plenty of times. But you've never been this way toward me." She took a demanding step in my direction. "You've never not wanted me around. So why don't you go ahead ask me what I know you want to ask?"

I frowned hard. "There's nothing I want to ask."

She matched my firm look with an even angrier one of her own. "Fine. Be stubborn, then. I'll tell you, anyway. My father took Bren on as an apprentice at the same time I started. We've been working together every day since then."

"Great," I growled back through clenched teeth. I was starting to feel that furious heat rising up in my chest again. "I'm sure he's a swell guy, too."

"He is!" She snapped. "And it just so happens that I like him!"

"Good!" I yelled as I stormed past her. I was so angry my hands were shaking. I wanted to get away from her. I stomped down the stairs to the kitchen and started heading for the front door. I'd almost made it there when she grabbed me by the back of the shirt and yanked me to a halt.

"Jaevid, talk to me about this!" She started shouting, too. "I know you're jealous. But can you blame me? He's going to be a blacksmith, too. He'll be able to help me take over my father's business. He comes from a good family. And he's—"

"—not a scrawny little halfbreed," I finished for her. I was losing my ability to keep my anger under control, so she got a full-forced glare when I turned back to face her.

Her expression went totally blank, and I saw her blue eyes go wide. Anyone who didn't know her well would think she was just surprised, but I'd been around Katty long enough to pick out those faint traces of guilt in her expression. I'd hit the nail on the head.

Even if I wasn't puny-looking, I doubted she would ever see me as more than a friend because I was a halfbreed. She was willing to be seen with me, to associate with me, but only as a friend. She had drawn the line at that, but had failed to let me know about that little detail. I'd never be anything more to her, and I was just now figuring that out.

I took a few seconds to breathe. I was trying to keep my temper in check as best I could before I said anything else I'd probably regret later. It didn't work.

"Well, I'm glad we've finally cleared that up. Now I know where I stand. Just get out, Katty." I growled at her again.

Her eyes went steely, and she recoiled a little. I guess she was waiting for me to reconsider or apologize because she kept standing there, staring at me.

I couldn't stand it. I hated knowing that every second we had spent together was basically a fraud. I already had to fight to earn any acceptance and respect from the other riders at Blybrig; I wasn't about to do the same thing for her attention. If she wanted Bren so badly, then she could have him.

I left out the front door without saying anything else. I already felt bad for letting my true feelings show. I hated that I knew how she really felt about me now. I felt like a fool for ever thinking I had a chance with her.

Katty didn't try to talk to me again. I caught a glimpse of her storming toward her house as I ducked into Ulric's workshop. I'd known her so well before, or at least that's what I thought, but now she looked like a stranger. It felt like the Katty I used to know was gone... and I'd never even gotten to say goodbye.

I didn't know what else to do with my frustration, so I went to work. There was a lot left to do, anyway. Ulric's shop was basically empty. There wasn't anything left downstairs except for some scraps of leather and a pair of wooden sawhorses. It still smelled like the oils and hides he'd worked with, and I couldn't shake a sense of tension in the air as though his presence had left an invisible stain on the place.

My stomach was churning as I climbed the ladder up to the loft room where I had lived like a stowaway for three long years. All the old crates and boxes being stored up there were still sitting around, right where they had been before. My cot was there, too, with the same old quilts piled on it and a candle burned down to a nub. It was drafty and cold because of the cracks in the walls, and as I stood there staring at my old room, I started to think about my mother. So many nights I had lain awake in that bed, missing her. Now, she felt further away than ever. My memories of her were beginning to fade. I couldn't remember her smell anymore, or the sound of her laugh. It chilled me to the bone.

There were rusted old garden tools, rakes and shovels, and old scraps of wood leaned up against the walls in the loft room. Long-forgotten pieces of furniture were pushed into corners and covered with sheets. One by one, I started going through the storage crates. They were stuffed with moth-eaten clothes, a set of cast-iron pots and pans that looked like they were several generations old, and odds and ends that were probably worthless to anyone else. But these were my treasures. They were the only things in the world, except for the clothes on my back, that actually belonged to me.

What interested me more than anything else I found was an old carpenter's toolkit in a solid, handmade wooden box. I had known Ulric was a craftsman, from a family of craftsmen, but I had never seen anything like that before. There were tools for boring holes, saws of all shapes and sizes, files, chisels, a hatchet, and a hammer. I held each one, and wondered how you could use such simple instruments to make things like tables and chairs. Something about it made me want to give it a try, just to see what I could do.

After emptying the loft room and moving my new housewares onto the front porch, I went to close all the windows and doors again. I brought some firewood from the stack behind the barn and started a fire in the downstairs hearth, and in the kitchen stove. Using one of the big iron pots I'd found, I melted down buckets full of snow and used an old shirt as a rag to start washing the down windows, floors, and walls. I washed away months of dust, years of bad memories, and all my anger.

When everything was clean, I started moving the old pieces of furniture in. There hadn't been much, but it was enough to get me by for three months. There was a rocking chair that must have been for a nursery because it was made from the same color of wood as an old baby crib I'd also found in the loft room. I'd left the crib up there, but the chair I put in the parlor near the fireplace.

I put an old washstand up in my new room, and stacked the iron cooking ware in the kitchen cupboards. It took me almost all afternoon to push Roland's big armoire from his bedroom, down the hall, to my new room. I stripped down the sheets, blankets, and pillows from his bed and put them on mine. Then I took his trunk, too, and put it at the end of the bed. Among the knickknacks left behind in the loft room were a few old oil lamps that I put in my bedroom and down in the kitchen.

By the time I finished arranging everything, it was already dark outside, and I was absolutely starving. I finally sat down on the floor in the parlor, warming myself in the light of the fire, and unwrapped the food Mrs. Crookin had sent. She had packed up a big wedge of cheese, roasted meat, fresh loaves of bread, and some dried fruit in paper packages—enough to last me a few days if I rationed it. So I ate all I dared, and put the rest away in the kitchen.

When I went back out to check on Mavrik, he was gone. He had squeezed himself out of the barn door somehow. Under the moonlight I could see faint silhouettes of dragon-shaped footprints in the snow. I wondered where he went. I had been so busy all day; I hadn't even stopped to check up on him.

The image of Mavrik chopping happily on the leg of a freshly killed deer flashed into my mind. It made me gag a little, hearing the sounds of bones crunching between his teeth in my mind like that. I glared up at the sky and called out to him, knowing he'd hear me no matter how far away he was, "Keep that kind of stuff to yourself next time, will you?"

I left the barn door open for him whenever he decided to come back, and stomped through the snow back to the house. It was warm inside now, and even though there wasn't much in the way of furnishings, it still felt cozy to me. I took the liberty of barring the front door with the big wooden beam Ulric had left leaning in its usual place. When I locked myself inside, I finally felt safe.

I shoveled some logs and embers out of the parlor hearth into the iron pot, and carried them upstairs to start another fire in my bedroom hearth. It was strange to be alone in an empty house, and yet at the same time it made me feel calm. It was a lot better than sleeping in the barn or the loft room. It was actually the nicest place I'd slept in so far.

I settled down under the mound of old quilts I'd borrowed from Roland's bed, and watched the fire cast flickering shadows on the ceiling. There was still a lot left to do. I had to find some way to feed myself. It would have been a whole lot simpler if the garden weren't frozen solid. My mother had taught me a lot about how to grow all kinds of things, but there was no way I would be able to grow anything to eat in the dead of winter.

I was hoping that if I carefully budgeted the little bit of money I had, I could make it last until training started again without having to find a job somewhere in the city. I could buy cheap grain, and try to set snares or hunt for squirrels and rabbits in the woods. Mavrik might even let me steal a few scraps from his kills, since he clearly didn't have a problem finding his way to a deer when he wanted one.

One way or another, I knew I would make it. I had to hold out for three months.

Until then, I would learn to survive on my own.

CHAPTER THREE

Before I left for the interlude, Lieutenant Rordin had insisted that I keep training during our three-month break, even though I wasn't at the academy. I knew he was right. I was doomed to be smaller than all the other riders, so I was going to have to work a lot harder in order to keep up. I was going to have to train more than everyone else. So every morning, I did.

The minute my feet hit the floor, I did as many push-ups and sit-ups as I could until I was soaked with sweat. Then I layered up in three or four shirts and two pairs of pants before braving the cold to run. I didn't have a good gauge of how far I was going compared to how far we were running at the academy, so I just ran until I was too tired to go on. When I finally staggered back to the house, I ate a quick breakfast from my stores of food while I heated up water in the copper basin in the washroom. Then I bathed, changed into fresh clothes, and started the rest of my rigorous morning routine.

Over the weeks, I set up a network of snares in the pine forest around the house. Since I was determined *not* to run into Katty, I avoided their property altogether. I baited my traps with little piles of seeds, or pieces of dried fruit, and was lucky enough to get a couple of rabbits or some squirrels almost every day. That paired with the big sack of dried apple chips, three wheels of cheese, and sack of grain I'd bought in the city made for good eating. After some vague instructions from the baker in town, I could even stagger through making crude loaves of bread. They didn't taste great, not like the heavenly bread Mrs. Crookin made, but they were at least edible.

During the day, I took up learning woodworking and carpentry. Those old tools I'd found in the loft room became my friends, and I spent hours in Ulric's workshop learning how to use them through trial and error. I learned to chisel, to shape wood, to craft whole pieces of furniture without having to use any nails. It wasn't easy, and my hands blistered from handling the tools. I managed to cut myself a few times and bust my knuckles open with the hammer, but I was determined. I wasn't giving up.

My first few creations were pretty awful. I made a table with one leg that was shorter than all the others, so it wobbled and was basically useless. The first chair I made fell apart the minute I sat down in it. But I kept practicing. I loved it, even if I wasn't good at it yet. I worked every day, and savored every second I spent shaping something useful out of raw pieces of wood. Eventually, my chairs didn't fall apart. I could add extra details to the pieces I made, like intricate carvings, or claw-like feet to the bottoms of chair and table legs.

I sold my first rocking chair to the baker in the city. It took me forever to carry it there on my back, but I didn't want to risk anyone seeing me on Mavrik. That was a whole lot of attention I didn't need. Once I got the chair to the bakery, I was careful not to say that I was the one who'd made it. But the baker's wife was thrilled with it. She insisted on buying it the second she saw it. So I sold it for two silver pieces. It was the first time I felt like I'd done anything worthwhile, except for saving Sile's life a few times the year before.

Selling something I'd made boosted my confidence. I started making things that were more complex, and buying better pieces of wood to use with the money I made. I bought nails, new hammers, and sanding tools. I spent all day drenched with sweat, creating new projects in my father's old workshop. My hands got rough, and they got stronger and tougher every day. But as soon as the sun began to set, I knew it was time to get back to reality.

At dusk, I saddled up Mavrik and took off to fly drills. I didn't want anyone to see us, sweeping low over the mountains, flying patterns, and diving along the steep cliffs, so we always waited until dark. We flew for hours, until I was too tired to keep my eyes open anymore. Then we landed, and I went inside to eat dinner before I went to bed.

I fell into a routine. The days ran together. The only thing that kept me conscious of the time was how often I bumped into Katty—which happened less and less. I saw her a few times in the city, and of course, she was always with Bren. She stared at me from afar like she was waiting for me to do something. She always managed to look angry and sad at the same time, like she wanted to choke me until I apologized to her. But I never spoke to her. I never went near her, or even waved. There was a distance there I didn't think I could breach. It still hurt to think about her, and seeing her only made it worse. It was like there was a big, rotting hole in the middle of my chest. I knew I missed her, but I couldn't decide if it was because she'd been *that* special to me, or if I just hated being alone.

I was working on a new kitchen table for my house. Right away, I knew it was going to be one of the nicest things I'd made so far. I was taking my time, smoothing out the top with a big strip of rough sandpaper, when I heard a horse whinny outside. Immediately, I put my tools down. I wasn't expecting any visitors, and I knew how a horse would respond to the sleeping dragon curled up in my barn if Mavrik decided to get curious. Horses and dragons didn't get along.

"Stay put," I murmured to Mavrik, knowing he would hear me.

I pushed the workshop door open and went out into the snow. The wind was frigid, and the snow was so deep it came up to my knees. Mithangol was not a great place to be in the winter months.

A mail courier was riding up the drive toward my house. It had been weeks since I had even seen one carrying letters past my house, and none of them had delivered anything to me. When he saw me, the courier stopped and started rifling through his saddlebags. He was waving a letter in the air by the time I met him.

"From Saltmarsh, outside of Southwatch," he said as he handed me the letter. "Anything for delivery?"

I shook my head and took the letter from him.

The courier didn't waste any time. He turned his horse around and trotted off back down the drive.

Looking down at the weathered envelope, I saw the address scribbled onto the front. It didn't say whom it was from, though. I knew where Saltmarsh was only because I had to memorize very detailed kingdom maps as part of my training at the academy. It was a small port city about ten miles to the west of Southwatch, along the coast. I didn't know anyone living there, though.

I had some hopes the letter would be from Roland or Felix as I opened it. But as I unfolded the thick parchment, I got a sick feeling in the pit of my gut. All it said was:

I need you. Come quickly. – B.D.

The message was vague, but I still knew who it was from right away. I only knew one person in the whole world with those initials, and I didn't think she would go to the trouble of sending a letter like this if wasn't an emergency.

Beckah Derrick was the daughter of my former sponsor at the academy. She was one of the smartest and bravest people I knew, and she was also one of my best friends. If she needed me, then I wasn't about to hesitate.

"Looks like we're taking a trip," I muttered as I stood there in the snow, staring at the letter.

Mavrik came crawling out of the barn, yawning and making curious chirping noises. He leaned his big head down to look at the paper, too. His hot breath blasted past my head as he snorted, and sat back on his haunches.

I scratched his chin, making him purr and flick the end of his tail. "Don't worry. I bet you'll like Southwatch. It's probably a lot warmer there."

It didn't take me long to pack because I didn't have much to take. I gathered up enough rations of food to last a few days, some of Roland's old clothes that were still several sizes too big for me, my armor, and my hunting knife. Once I had everything tied down to the saddle, I locked up the house, closed the barn, and climbed onto Mavrik's back.

We leapt into the sky just after midmorning and headed south along the coast. It was freezing cold, and I hunkered down as close to Mavrik's neck as I could to keep out of the wind. He was warm, and it kept me from freezing to death, but my teeth were chattering until we finally got out of the mountains.

As we soared past the last few peaks, I got my first look at the ocean. A blast of salty wind filled my lungs, and made me smile. The whole horizon was covered in blue, as far as the eye could see. Down below, the waves lapped at white sandy beaches. I could see fishermen dragging nets out of the surf. We passed little cities and towns nestled right close to the coast, rolling green farmland with cattle grazing, and huge marshes. In the distance, I could see the tiny dark shapes of ships going in and out of the ports. The cool wind didn't bother me anymore, not with the warmth of the setting sun on my face.

We followed the coastline, flying low and fast as I kept an eye out for Saltmarsh. My internal map was telling me we should be getting really close. Just as the sun was about to set over the ocean to the west, I saw the lights of a city down below. There was a big port stretching out into the ocean, with three-mast ships docked. I knew it had to be Saltmarsh. It was supposed to have one of the biggest shipping ports for goods going in and out of Maldobar, second only to Southwatch itself.

I urged Mavrik to swoop lower, keeping a lookout for a good place to land. He let his wingtips brush the ocean, roaring happily as we swept over the beach and stirred up flocks of seagulls and pelicans. As we cruised the outskirts of the city, I picked a good spot on the open beach to touch down, and Mavrik started to flare his powerful wings to slow us down. He stretched out his hind legs, ready to grip the sand.

Suddenly, I got a queasy feeling in the pit of my stomach.

Something wasn't right. It hit me full-force, and sent a swirl of panic through my body like a cold shiver. Mavrik felt it, too, and he faltered in his landing. It was rough, and I had to cling to the saddle to keep from being thrown over his head.

A dark shadow passed over us. I heard a sound; a deep thundering roar that made my heartbeat stop for a few seconds. I knew that roar, even though I'd only heard it once before. It was the kind of sound you never forget.

The earth flinched as Icarus landed right in front of us. He bared his jagged teeth, his broad wings spread wide, and his red eyes burning like fiery coals. He flared his spines, puffing out angrily and making himself even bigger than the humongous beast he already was.

The king drake was every bit as terrifying as he had been the first time I saw him. He was like a monster that had crawled right out of someone's nightmares. His scales were as black as volcanic glass, and he was at least twice Mavrik's size. I had watched him devour his own rider, the Lord General, in a fit of fury only a few months ago. But I had no idea why he was here now. Apparently we had some unfinished business.

Mavrik snarled back at him, slicking his ears back against his skull and letting the spines on his back and tail raise up like hackles. He flared his wings and hissed, snapping his jaws threateningly at the king drake. In my mind, I saw the flickering image of myself getting out of the saddle. Mavrik wanted me to escape.

I squeezed the saddle handles. "No way," I growled through my teeth. "If it's a fight he wants, then he'll have to take on both of us. I'm not leaving you."

Mavrik let out a thundering roar, but Icarus wasn't afraid. Why should he be? He was bigger and definitely stronger. The king drake bellowed back, and started to lunge for us with his jaws open wide.

I yelled out in anger, and Mavrik spat a column of burning venom right in Icarus's face.

It made the king drake hesitate, and gave us just enough time to get back in the air. I knew we'd have the advantage there. Icarus might have been stronger, but we were faster. No one was faster in the air than Mavrik.

Icarus started chasing us. His wing beats sounded like claps of thunder, and I could feel his eyes on us. I was too scared to look back and see how close he was. Mavrik poured on the speed, zipping through the air and giving us enough space to whip around and make a calculated attack dive.

It seemed like a good idea at the time. We had a brief window, a speck of leverage, and one shot to use it. But my training in aerial combat like this was... well, I hadn't gotten *real* training yet. I was going on instinct and prayers. Neither were enough.

Icarus was ready for us. As a king drake, I had no idea how many battles he had already fought in, or how many riders he had crushed like twigs. As soon as we got close, he swirled out of our path, and reached around to clamp his jaws onto one of Mavrik's legs as we zipped past.

Mavrik shrieked. I could feel his panic and pain like it was my own. It made me cry out with him. Icarus bore down with his teeth, and flung us toward the ground like we were a scrap of meat.

Mavrik tried to recover. He tried to flare, to brace for an emergency landing, but there wasn't enough time. We had only seconds before we hit, and he used that time to make sure I wasn't crushed under his weight. He landed on his side, skidding across the sand. It hurt, and at that moment, I wasn't sure which was his pain or mine.

When we came to a halt, Mavrik tried to get up. His leg was bleeding. The punctures were painful, but it didn't look like any bones were broken. We were lucky, so far. He struggled, growling and whimpering. Quickly, I started unbuckling myself from the saddle.

Another loud boom made the ground shake again as Icarus landed not far away. Burning venom dripped off his jaws as he started prowling toward us slowly, watching us with those horrible glowing eyes. He was taking his time, deciding how best to tear us both to shreds.

I scrambled off Mavrik's back as soon as I got the last buckle undone. I grabbed the hunting knife from my saddle, and started running headlong for the king drake. Mavrik howled in protest, floundering and limping as he got back to his feet.

"Stay back!" I yelled, brandishing my knife. "If you want to kill him, you'll have to get through me, first!"

Icarus seemed to consider that. I probably looked like a good appetizer to him. He tilted his head to the side, his nostrils flaring as he breathed in my scent. Behind me, I heard Mavrik snarling and roaring desperately. He was not in any shape to fight a king drake.

Icarus stood over me like a towering black demon. He roared so loud it made my teeth rattle. I could smell the venom on his breath. I saw my death in his bottomless red eyes. This was it, I guessed. He wasn't going to let Mavrik and I get away with challenging him. You didn't just challenge a king and walk away unharmed.

Suddenly, I heard a scream. But it wasn't a dragon scream. It definitely wasn't me, either. It came from down the beach, and sounded a lot like a girl. All three of us stopped, turned, and looked in surprise.

Beckah Derrick was running as fast as she could over the sand, stumbling and tripping all over her white nightgown. Her dark hair was tied into two long braided pigtails that whipped behind her as she sprinted toward us. She waved her arms, screaming at Icarus at the top of her lungs. The huge black dragon regarded her with a snarl, and I prepared myself to fight to the death to save her and my dragon—a fight that probably would have lasted about two seconds.

But all of a sudden, Icarus started backing away from me. He lowered his head and hissed, still growling and glaring at me like he wanted to finish me off in one bite. Beckah was yelling at him like she was scolding a naughty puppy. She walked right up to the huge black dragon and swatted him on the snout. It made him flinch, hiss, and turn his head away like he was ashamed. He wouldn't look her in the eyes.

Speechless didn't even begin to describe how I felt.

Shocked. Stunned. Completely blown away—those were a little more accurate. I exchanged a wide-eyed look with Mavrik. He looked like he couldn't believe what he was seeing, either.

"I told you that is a no-no!" She said with her hands on her hips. "You can't just eat people. It's not nice. Those are my friends! Stop being such a bully!"

Icarus hunkered down in the sand, making himself as small as a monstrous black king drake could. He curled his long spiny tail around his legs and snorted at her in frustration. But when she started rubbing his neck and snout... he actually started to purr. His red eyes closed, and he pushed his nose against her affectionately.

At that point, I was pretty sure my heart had stopped beating entirely.

Beckah turned to look back at me with a big grin on her face. My mouth was hanging open, and not just because she was petting Icarus like he was an overgrown housecat. She had grown, too. The last time I'd seen her had been almost six months ago. She had looked like a little kid then, and I had thought of her like she was the little sister I needed to protect. But apparently everyone else in the world was growing up except me.

Beckah walked toward me with the wind in her hair. Her fluffy bangs puffed over her face, and the light of the setting sun made her green eyes the same color as the ocean. She was as tall as I was now, and so beautiful it made the back of my throat feel like someone had punched me in the neck.

When she put her arms around my waist to hug me like she always did, I hesitated. I wasn't sure if I was allowed to touch her anymore. I almost forgot who she was. That is, until she squeezed me so hard it made me choke.

"I knew you'd come," she said.

I smiled in spite of myself, and hugged her back. She smelled really good, like a mixture of the ocean and flowers. "Of course I'd come." I studied Icarus from over her shoulder, who was still glaring at me like he wanted to eat me. "I guess this is what you were talking about?"

She leaned back to look at me with a big, happy smile that put dimples in her freckled cheeks. "You don't know the half of it, Jae."

4

CHAPTER FOUR

Beckah had started building a little campfire with pieces of driftwood further down the beach. It was about a mile away, and we walked there together with our shoes off, letting the waves lap at our bare feet. I carried my boots and socks in one hand, and she held onto my other one tightly. Whenever I looked down, I couldn't tell which fingers were hers and which ones were mine. It gave me a strange feeling.

When we got to her campfire, I helped her drag up more pieces of driftwood to burn, and spread out a quilt she'd brought from her house on the sand. I used the flint stone in my saddlebag to start the wood burning while our dragons settled in, curled around us like a living wall of scales and wings.

Mavrik was licking his wounds, and he didn't look happy at all that Icarus was so close to us. Every now and then he'd snarl at him a little, like he was warning him not to try anything. Icarus ignored him. I was just glad they weren't trying to kill each other anymore.

"He's been following me ever since the prison camp," Beckah said as she sat down on the quilt. "I don't know what to do about him, Jae. He won't leave. I've told him to go at least a hundred times. You have no idea how hard it is to hide a dragon."

I laughed as I sat down next to her. I tried not to blush when she scooted over closer to me and leaned her head against my shoulder. "Does your dad know about him?"

She shot me an exasperated look. "Absolutely not. Can you imagine what he'd do? You know girls aren't allowed to ride dragons."

"You already have," I reminded her.

Beckah sighed. "That was different. It was an emergency. Momma and Daddy were so furious about all that. If they knew about this, it would be much worse. But I can't keep him a secret for much longer. Some of the people in the city are already talking about a big black dragon that's been swiping cattle. Sooner or later, they're going to find out."

She looked up at me, and the light from the fire made her green eyes sparkle. It made me nervous. "Can't you talk to him?" she asked. "You know, like you did before? Please, Jae, just tell him to go away. I can't keep him, and I certainly can't ride him." She was telling me one thing, but I could see something completely different in her expression. She didn't really want him to go—she was afraid of what would happen when her parents found out.

"I'll try," I promised.

She put her head back against my shoulder. "There's so much I want to tell you, Jae. I don't know where to start."

"You mean more than being followed around by a king drake?" I asked.

It made her giggle a little. "I'm so glad you're here."

"Yeah, me too." Talking about everything that had happened since I'd gotten back to Mithangol was hard. None of it was easy to admit. I mean, being abandoned by your entire family isn't exactly something to be proud of. But she didn't make me feel embarrassed when I started explaining it to her. I told her about everything except for what had happened with Katty. For some reason, I didn't want Beckah to know about that. It really was embarrassing to think about, let alone tell her about it.

"Well, at least your brother left you a letter," she said with a sour look on her face. "I just can't believe what they did. How could they leave like that? It's horrible."

I shrugged. "It's over and done, now. If I hung onto every bad thing anyone's ever done to me, I'd be dragging around a lot of extra weight."

She was quiet for a few minutes. Then scooted away a little, far enough to turn around so that she was facing me. She grabbed my hands and started looking at them in the light of the fire, tracing her fingers over my palms. "So all this is from the woodworking?" She asked, rubbing her thumb over one of the thick calluses on my hand. "I noticed it before."

I tried not to think about how soft her hands were. "Yeah. Maybe I'll make you a chair or something."

She grinned at me. "I'd *love* that!"

I blushed so hard I couldn't even look at her. "How is your dad doing with retirement? How's his arm?"

I should have known better than to bring that up. She let my hands go and her expression fell. She sat back some and stared at the fire with a far-away look in her eyes. "That's the other reason I asked you to come here. Something is wrong with him, Jae. Something he isn't telling anyone about. He's so nervous ever since that whole mess at the prison camp. It's almost like he's afraid someone is watching us. He's always been a little paranoid, I guess. But never like this. It's scaring me."

"What do you mean?" Hearing that made me worried.

"We used to live in Southwatch, you know. He moved us out of our nice house in the city as soon as we got back. Momma was furious, and they argued about it for weeks. He wasn't going to take no for an answer," she said. "Now we're living in a much smaller house out here in the middle of nowhere. We weren't allowed to tell anyone where we were going. He's going to be so mad when he finds out I told you, but I didn't have a choice."

I took her hand again and squeezed it a little. "I won't tell anyone, Beckah."

She smiled at me weakly. "I know. I trust you more than anyone."

The silence got awkward as we sat there, staring at each other in the light of the fire. I got this weird feeling like I should do something, but I wasn't sure what. She was looking at me like she was waiting for something to happen. It put nervous knots in my stomach and I didn't understand why.

"We'll figure it out," I promised her. It seemed like whenever I was around her, I started making promises like that.

She looked a little disappointed, and sighed as she looked away back toward the fire. "I hope so. Maybe you can talk to him about it. He trusts you, too, you know."

I wasn't sure what to think about that. I knew how much I respected and admired her father, Sile Derrick. It was hard to believe that he thought of me as anything more than a scrawny kid he'd had to protect from being pummeled by the other students while he was my sponsor and instructor. Sure, I'd saved his life a few times, but I didn't consider that to be anything other than my duty as his student. I didn't expect any praise or respect because of that. If anything, I still felt like I owed him for all the time's he'd stuck his neck out for me.

"I want to understand why, Jae." Beckah whispered. The emotion in her voice surprised me. I noticed there were dark circles under her eyes. She looked haunted, and her voice trembled when she spoke. "I don't believe what they told us, that it was just some kind of plot by the Lord General. They didn't choose my daddy at random. It was planned. There's a reason they tried so hard to kill him twice. If it was only a plot to use him as some kind of a sacrifice, they could have picked anyone. They could have plucked someone else off the street and no one would have even noticed. They came after him for a reason, and now I think he's afraid they'll try it again. I think that's why he moved us like this. I think he's trying to hide from them."

I could tell she'd been beating herself up over this. I couldn't imagine what it had been like for her, but I wanted to make her feel better. I put an arm around her shoulders and pulled her toward me to hug her again. "I don't believe what they said, either. It'll be okay. Your father is the best man I've ever met. You have to trust that he knows what he's doing."

Beckah hid her face against my shoulder. "I've felt so alone," she whimpered. "I've missed you so much."

My face burned and I was glad she couldn't see it. No one had ever said that to me before. Not like that, anyway. It made me blush until the tips of my ears felt like they were on fire.

"What about Felix?" I have no idea why I even said something like that. It was stupid, and I knew it the moment the words left my mouth. I regretted it immediately.

She pulled back and looked at me strangely, like I'd suddenly grown a third eyeball. "What about him?"

I swallowed hard. "Well, I mean he was there with us through everything. Do you miss him, too?"

Beckah frowned. "That's different."

I opened my mouth to speak, but I didn't get a chance. She grabbed my chin and kissed me on the cheek.

It seemed like the world was moving in slow motion. I just sat there, staring at her. At first, I wasn't sure what to think. But as the seconds passed, I realized I liked it. I *really* liked it.

"We should go back to the house," she said as she stood. She offered me a hand to help me up, and then started folding up the quilt. "Momma's probably already gone to bed, but Daddy will still be up. We have to tell him you're here." She sighed shakily and looked at Icarus. "Do you think you can get him to leave me alone?"

I was still having a hard time thinking about anything except that kiss. But I looked at Icarus, and he shot me another disapproving dragon glare. "I'm not sure. I guess we'll try to discuss it in the morning, though."

I took my one bag off of Mavrik's saddle and followed Beckah across the grassy dunes. The moonlight was bright enough to see by, and the wind was strong coming in off the ocean. In the distance, I could see the lights of the city a few short miles away down the coast.

The Derrick's house wasn't small, like Beckah had made it sound. At least, not to me. It was two storys tall, made out of dark stacked stone, and there were a few candles burning in the arched windows. I could barely make out a stable behind it as we walked up the sandy drive toward the front door.

I started to get nervous because I wasn't sure how Sile was going to react to me being here. I was anxious to see him and talk to him about what had happened. I might even get some real answers this time. But at the same time I knew he might slam the door in my face and tell me to mind my own business. Beckah also looked nervous as she opened the front door and let me go in ahead of her.

The house was nice and cozy on the inside. There were pictures on the plaster walls, and rugs on the floors. A narrow entryway led into the parlor where Sile was sitting with his feet propped up by a smoldering fire in the hearth. He didn't even look back at us as we stood in the doorway.

"I've told you about sneaking out, Beck." He grumbled.

"I'm sorry," Beckah muttered back. "Daddy, we have a guest."

He turned and looked back then, his piercing glare hitting me full force. At first, I was definitely afraid he was going to come at me swinging. When he saw it was me, his expression changed into confusion and frustration. He seemed annoyed that I was here.

He shot Beckah a punishing look. "We talked about this."

She cringed and looked way. "I know, Daddy, but—"

"Go back to bed. Right now," he growled at her.

Beckah nodded, gave me a worried smile, and hurried away up the stairs.

The silence was uncomfortable. I stood in the doorway for a few minutes, wondering what I was supposed to do or if I should even stay. Maybe these were valuable minutes he was giving me as a head start before he forced me out the door. Then I heard him sigh, and he settled back into his chair to stare at the fire again.

"I was hoping you would have at least grown an inch by now," he muttered.

I was instantly humiliated. "S-sir, please don't blame Beckah for—"

"Sit down," he cut me off.

I shuffled across the room and sat down in the chair across from him. His expression was unreadable and intense. He had the same dark circles under his eyes Beckah had, like he'd sat up every night just like this, waiting for someone to come pounding on his door to take him away again. I noticed his arm wasn't wrapped up in a cast anymore.

"She thinks I don't know about the dragon," he said darkly.

I was too surprised to answer.

"I may be old and retired, but I'm not stupid. I've been around dragons longer than you've been alive. I know when there's one stalking around my house." He glanced at me again, looking me up and down like he was searching for any sign of growth since last year when I'd started training. "Well, there's a little more meat on you, at least. Not enough, though."

My face burned with embarrassment again. "I've been training every day."

He nodded. "Good."

"She asked me to come here because she wants me to... tell Icarus to go away." I blurted. I sincerely hoped Beckah wasn't hiding outside the room eavesdropping on us. I felt like I was betraying her by telling him everything.

"He won't listen to you, boy. Maybe you can talk a king drake into rebelling against a rider he didn't choose, but when a dragon picks its companion the way

Mavrik picked you, there's nothing you can do to change it. It's like fighting gravity."

Sile always had a way of teaching me things even when he didn't mean to. I'd never questioned Mavrik's attachment to me, much less tried to understand it. Hearing that Icarus, the most powerful drake in the world, had picked Beckah—that was amazing news.

"She's a dragonrider," I whispered under my breath.

He shot me the same punishing glare he'd given her earlier. "No. She's a girl. Women are forbidden to join the brotherhood of dragonriders. You know that."

"But... I thought you said that being chosen automatically made someone a dragonrider, regardless of who they are," I argued. "What if she wants to be one? How is it any different than when Mavrik chose me?"

"Because there are some things women are not meant to see, let alone experience," he snapped angrily. "You really want my daughter, my precious little girl, holding a sword and riding into a line of enemies that want to slaughter her? As her father, I am supposed to protect her. That is my duty as a man. It's not something a boy can understand."

I bit my tongue. He was right. The idea of her doing something like that, something that would most likely get her killed, cut me right to the core. I didn't want anything to happen to her. I wanted to protect her, too.

"Things are the way they are for a reason, Jaevid," he said. "They may not be fair, but we must choose our battles wisely. We have to do what we can to protect what matters most."

I got the feeling he wasn't just talking about Icarus anymore. Everything Beckah had said to me about how he'd moved them here in secret started nagging at my brain again. "What are you protecting them from?" I asked. "Beckah said she thinks you're hiding out here—that you're afraid someone is looking for you."

He flicked me another irritated glance before he reached over to a table beside his chair and started filling a pipe with tobacco. "You know everything you need to know right now," he answered coldly. "You should be less worried about my affairs and more concerned with the training that awaits you this year. The avian year at the academy is the most difficult, and it's the year when the weak or stupid often die. Everything they do is to prepare you for what might happen when you step on the battlefield. They will beat you hard because war is going beat you even harder."

Felix had said something similar to me about what lay ahead in our avian year. He had mentioned that we'd have to endure interrogation training and how to survive in Luntharda if we found ourselves stranded behind enemy lines. That put a hard knot of anxiety in my chest as I sat there, staring down at the tops of my shoes.

"I was hoping you'd have at least gained an inch or two, or a few more pounds of muscle. Maybe then you'd be less of an easy target for them during the interrogation portion." Sile sighed, shaking his head some before he started to light his pipe and puff rings of gray smoke into the air. "They're going to come for you, Jaevid. You're the weakest link. You need to start asking yourself if you're ready for that."

I clenched my hands into fists. "I've been the weakest link my whole life, sir. I can handle it."

He snorted, and I saw the corner of his mouth twitch at a smile. "That's why I like you, boy. You're brave to the point of insanity. You'd walk into the abyss without a second thought."

I wasn't sure if I should take that as a compliment or an insult. It kind of sounded like both. "I just do what I think is right, sir."

Sile looked at me then, and there were a thousand thoughts in his eyes that I could sense, but I couldn't understand any of them. Somehow, it made me feel very small. There was a lot he knew, a lot of things he wasn't telling me. And when he looked at me like that, it made me wonder what would be waiting for me back at the academy.

"Sometimes what you know is right isn't what everyone else wants to do," he said. "Then you have to ask yourself if you're willing to live with the consequences of doing what you know is wrong just to keep the peace."

I swallowed hard. "I couldn't do that."

He smiled darkly. "Is that so? Why?"

I tried to square my shoulders and look more confident than I was. "Because I'd rather be seen as a traitor by everyone else than betray myself like that."

Little by little, the edges of his grim smile began to fade, and I saw those hundreds of thoughts come rushing back like an ocean tide. "I hope you always feel like that, Jaevid," he said softly and turned away to look back at the fire again. "There's a guest room upstairs. Third door on the right."

"S-sir?" I hadn't expected him to ask me to stay.

"I suppose it's good to have someone as idiotically brave as you are around now and again. If anyone can change that dragon's mind, it's you. We'll address it later." He wafted a hand at me, waving me out of the room. "Goodnight."

I started for the doorway with my bag in my hand. My head was still spinning like a top after everything he'd said to me. I was almost out of the room when he cleared his throat to get my attention again.

"And if I catch you sniffing around my daughter's room, I'll pull those pointed ears right off your head."

CHAPTER FIVE

Being in Sile's house was weird. He had never talked about his family to me before, so everything I knew about them had mostly come from Beckah. I wasn't sure what I was allowed to touch, or where to go, but I found the guest room right where Sile had told me it was. The room was spacious and a lot better decorated than my house. There were curtains on the windows, a big bed with comfortable looking blankets, and a soft wool rug on the floor.

I shut the door behind me as quietly as I could, and put my bag down on the floor at the foot of the bed. The two tall windows faced the front of the house. In the distance, I could see the ocean glittering in the moonlight. I cracked one open to let the cool, salty breeze flow in. The house was so quiet that I could hear the surf. It was a beautiful sound that slowly lulled me to sleep.

The lonely cawing of seagulls woke me up early the next morning. I rolled over, squinting at the beautiful view of the sea over the dunes... and that's when I realized I wasn't alone. I saw a few locks of golden hair peeking over the blankets in the bed next to me. Suddenly, I was aware that there was a very warm, very alive *something* sleeping next to me.

I bolted upright in bed. Before I could figure out what had happened, I was sitting nose-to-nose with a big shaggy dog. He looked at me with warm brown eyes, and swiped his slobbery tongue right up my face.

From the doorway, I heard someone giggling. I looked to see Beckah standing there, watching us with the bedroom door cracked open. She whistled and the dog bounded off the bed, trotting to her with his tail wagging. She ruffled his ears as he went past.

"I forgot to warn you last night," she laughed. "Eddy can open doors... and he also really likes to sleep on the bed."

I laughed. "Smart dog."

Beckah shrugged a little and started twirling a lock of her dark hair around her fingers thoughtfully. "So Daddy talked to me this morning. He told me he knew about the dragon already. And he's going to let you try to convince him to leave."

"Yeah," I admitted. "We sort of discussed that last night."

She stood there quietly for a moment, still twirling her hair, and finally looked up at me with a hesitant look in her eyes. "I'm not sure I want him to go."

I was afraid of that. Icarus had chosen her. He listened to her. They had the potential for the same kind of bond I had with Mavrik. And for me to step in and try to drive them apart, well, it felt wrong. I wasn't sure I could do it, or if Icarus would even listen.

"What do you want me to do?" I asked her.

She sighed shakily and nibbled on her bottom lip. I could see that she was struggling with this. For her to keep Icarus was definitely counterproductive to Sile's efforts to keep his family hidden. People were already talking about the king drake in the city. He was sure to attract all kinds of attention. Not to mention the fact that she was a girl, and girls weren't allowed to be dragonriders. But at the same time, I couldn't think of any better protection than an angry dragon. Icarus wasn't going to let anything happen to Beckah—not if he could help it.

"Daddy took Momma to see the doctor this morning. She was having pains all night," she said finally. "So I have a little time to think it over. They probably won't get back until late this afternoon."

I nodded. "Okay."

"I thought we could go to the beach." She smiled a little and came in to plop down on the edge of the bed. "So hurry up and get dressed!"

I noticed she was already wearing something she could swim in. It was a white cotton dress that came to her knees with no sleeves and little purple flowers stitched on it. She had sandals on her feet made out of knotted strips of cloth, and her long hair was hanging in two loose braids down her back.

I threw off the blankets and started rummaging around for my shoes. I didn't have anything to wear other than what I had on. I definitely didn't have anything that was made for swimming, but I figured I could make it work.

While I was hurrying through lacing up my boots, Beckah came crawling across the bed. Before I knew it, she was braiding my hair. I could just imagine what Felix would've said if he could see me sitting there with a girl fixing my hair.

"It's gotten so long," she said. I could hear the smile in her voice.

It made me really nervous to have her touching me like that. She'd always seemed fascinated by my hair. Human men usually kept their hair cut short, and mine had gotten very long over the past few months.

"My mom wanted me to keep it like this." I told her.

She kept tugging on my hair, winding it down into a long braid before she finally tied it off on the end. "Is that something all Gray elves do?"

"Yeah," I said as I looked back at her. "Having long hair is one of their sacred traditions. Different tribes do different things, like weave beads into it for every year of life or major accomplishment. It's a symbol of pride."

She smiled at me and gave my braid a playful yank. "Okay then, Mr. Pride, let's go to the beach."

I helped Beckah carry a quilt, a bag of snacks, and a few towels back down the winding path that led across the dunes toward the beach. Eddy went with us with his tail wagging the whole way. He ran on ahead and barked like crazy while he chased flocks of seagulls.

The sun was warm on my back as we worked together to spread out the quilt. We anchored down the corners with rocks so the wind wouldn't blow it away. The sand was so soft and clean that it literally squeaked when we walked on it. We sat together on the quilt, taking off our shoes, and talking about everything that had happened since we'd last seen each other. I was so busy telling her about all the new pieces of furniture I wanted to make that I didn't notice she was packing together a ball of sand in her palm—until she threw it and hit me right in the face.

Beckah took off running into the waves, laughing wildly, and I chased after her. We spent all day in the surf and sun, chasing crabs and the little fish that darted in around our legs. She showed me how to make sandcastles by squeezing watery sand through my fist, and I let her bury me up to my waist. Beckah was a great swimmer, and she taught me how to dive down and find seashells in the deeper water. It was the most fun I'd ever had in my life.

When lunchtime came, we went back to sit on our quilt and eat some of the food she'd packed. She'd brought some leftover biscuits from breakfast stuffed with blackberry preserves, some pieces of cheese, and four huge, juicy peaches. We talked while we ate, leaning back on our elbows with our feet in the sand. Eddy was still running around, digging holes and begging us to throw a stick so he could retrieve it.

We talked about anything and everything. She wanted to know about my mom, and for once, it didn't hurt so bad to think about that. I asked about her parents, things I knew Sile would never tell me even if I had the nerve to ask him.

"So is she going to be all right?" I asked. "Your mom, I mean. You said she was having pains."

Beckah took a big bite out of a peach. "I don't know. Daddy said she's having a hard time with this baby. She's supposed to have it any day now, but she's been like this the whole time. She barely eats, barely sleeps, and she says she feels sick all the time. The doctor says there's nothing more he can do. She just has to stay off her feet as much as possible and hope for the best."

I looked down at the half-eaten peach in my hand. "I'm sorry, Beckah."

"It's okay. Momma's strong. She can make it." She got quiet for a moment while she chewed, and I could tell she wanted to change the subject. "So where are the dragons?"

I had wondered the same thing. Mavrik flashed an image of himself and Icarus sunning themselves in a grassy field, preening their scales, and basking in the warm air. I guess they'd worked out their differences, for now. "They're close by. I think they've finally called a truce."

I caught Beckah staring at me with a weird look on her face, like she was amazed. "Can you really talk to him with your mind? What does he say to you? What does he sound like?"

"He doesn't *say* anything." I blushed. "It's more like pictures. He shows me things, sort of like I'm dreaming only I'm not asleep."

"Will I be able to talk to Icarus like that?" she asked.

I shook my head a little. "I don't know."

Slowly, a big grin started to inch across her face. "That is *so* awesome!"

I rolled my eyes at her and laughed. "I'm glad someone else thinks so."

She took another bite out of her peach as she lay back on the blanket. For a few minutes, she didn't say anything and we sat there together listening to the roar and crash of the surf. It was peaceful, and I felt so calm. I didn't want to go back to Mithangol. I didn't even want to go back to Blybrig.

"I don't want Icarus to leave," she said as she lay there, wiggling her toes in the sand.

I turned to look down at her. I had sort of been expecting this, but it was still surprising to hear that she'd made that decision so suddenly. "What changed your mind?"

"You," she said matter-of-factly. "You always make me feel braver. And I can't help but feel like he chose me for a purpose. Maybe there's something I'm supposed to do for him. He wouldn't choose me for no reason, would he?"

She got quiet then, and I wasn't sure what to say until she sat back up and nudged me with her elbow. "When you're at the academy, do you ever get afraid? I mean, I know they do some terrible things to you during training. I've heard Daddy and his friends talk about it. Does it scare you?"

I had to think about that. I had been through a lot during my first year of training, a lot of new experiences and challenges I hadn't been sure I would survive. Now everyone was telling me the worst was yet to come.

"Yes," I answered. "But when those times come, I just try to think about something good. Good memories always give me hope—like the times I spent with my mom when I was little."

She reached over and took my hand. Her fingers were still sticky from peach juice, but when she looked at me and smiled, it was like seeing the sunrise for the first time. There was so much warmth and hope in her eyes.

"When things get tough this year, when you start to feel afraid, I want you to think about today," she said.

"I will," I promised.

We packed up our stuff and started back for the house. Being in the wind and sun all morning had worn me out, even though it was the first day in months I hadn't gone straight from bed to a grueling workout routine. My arms and legs felt heavy, but my heart was full. I'd never smiled this much before in my life. It made my cheeks hurt.

"Look! Momma's home!" Beckah pointed excitedly to where a horse and carriage were parked in front of the house. She went running on ahead of me, tripping over herself with her braids flying.

I could see Sile helping a very fragile-looking woman out of the carriage. I had never seen his wife before, but it didn't surprise me that she was pretty. Or at least, she might have been. Now I understood what Beckah had said about her pregnancy being hard on her.

Her belly was hugely swollen, and she was so petite that it looked like might cause her legs to break under the weight. She had dark, reddish brown hair and soft blue eyes. Her skin looked almost ashen, and her cheeks looked sunken. Sile handled her like she was made of glass, easing her down the steps from the carriage to the ground.

When she saw me, Mrs. Derrick paused. Our eyes met, and I wasn't sure what to do. I didn't know how she'd react, or how much Sile had actually told her about me. She leaned a little closer to her husband and whispered something, Sile nodded, and then, very slowly, she started to smile.

It made me stop because when she smiled, even though she basically looked like she might collapse at any moment, I could see how much Beckah favored her. They had that same familiar gentleness in their eyes. She curled a finger at me to call me closer.

I went toward them hesitantly, not sure if I was allowed to talk to her. Sile was eyeing me over again like he was still looking for some sign of growth. I hated to keep disappointing him.

"He's absolutely darling," Mrs. Derrick said. She had a very soft, breathy voice.

"It's good to meet you, ma'am." I stopped a few feet away from her, and was about to bow... but she took a few hobbling steps toward me and put her hands on my cheeks. They felt cold to the touch, which was a little disturbing.

"Aren't you just the cutest thing? Like a little lamb," she crooned. "Such good manners. You should thank your mother for that every night in your prayers. Only mothers teach such good behavior to their little boys."

I was beyond embarrassed. Out of the corner of my eye, I saw Beckah giggling at me, and Sile was rolling his eyes.

"Don't patronize him, dear. He's seventeen now, right? Not a kid anymore," Sile said. He was at least trying to defend my masculinity. I couldn't thank him enough for that.

"A-actually, I'm sixteen, sir," I stammered.

"Sixteen is hardly a grown man, Sile. Look at him. Such a sweet little boy." Mrs. Derrick gave my cheeks a tug before she let me go. "It looks like you've both had too much sun this morning. Beck, dear, you're as red as a cherry. Come inside and help me get settled. We should make a good supper for our guest tonight, don't you think?"

She started trying to walk to the house, and I realized then why Sile was so intense about helping her. She could barely take a step without shaking. Her body looked incredibly weak. It was worrisome to me, and I'd only just met her. I couldn't imagine how it must have made him feel to see her that way.

Gently, Sile took his wife by the arm and helped her up the front steps into the house. As I stood there watching them go, Beckah came up beside me and nudged me with her arm.

"I knew she'd like you." She winked at me. "Don't take it too hard, little lamb. It's because she's got babies on the brain. She talks to everyone that way."

I couldn't help but laugh. "Well, I guess I've been called worse."

We followed them inside and Beckah took all our things to put them away. It took Sile a long time to get Mrs. Derrick settled in a big chair at the head of the dinner table. The chair was covered with blankets and cushions so she was comfortable, and he wrapped her up in a quilt carefully. I watched him kiss her forehead.

There was love between them—I could sense it. But I could also sense a lot of tension and frustration. There was something distant in their eyes when they looked at each other. I didn't understand why. He regarded her like she was an artifact to be preserved. There wasn't much tenderness in his expression whenever he gazed at her. It was like he was just going through the motions, doing what he knew he should because he didn't know what else to do. And when she looked at him, it was like she wanted to say something, but didn't know where to begin. She just seemed so lost.

Sile started making dinner while Beckah helped him. They were washing and peeling vegetables, stoking the cooking fires, and working together like a well-trained unit. They'd obviously done this before. I wasn't sure what to do with myself. I felt like I should be helping, too.

"Come have a seat, dear." Mrs. Derrick was smiling at me as she patted the chair next to her at the table. "Your name is Jaevid, isn't it? Beckah told me all about what you did for my husband. You must be a very brave little boy."

"He's not a little boy, Lana. He's about to start his avian training. He'll be a war-hardened soldier this side of next year. Quit babying him." Sile growled. His tone was harsher than it should have been for talking to someone as fragile as she was, but his wife didn't seem to pay him any attention.

"You know, of all Sile's students I've met, I think you must be the first one that's ever come to visit," she said as I sat down next to her. "You'll make such a handsome little soldier. Honestly, those no-good rich boys that take up dragonriding these days could stand to learn a thing or two from you. They've never had to do an honest day's work in their lives! They can't appreciate how hard others have to work to get where they are."

I wasn't sure if it was safe to answer. Sile kept shooting us glares out of the corner of his eye. "Thank you, ma'am." I decided that was the safest thing to say.

She reached out to brush some of my hair out of the way, just the same way Beckah had when we'd first met. She touched the pointed tips of my ears with her cold fingers. "Fate was cruel to have cursed you with mixed blood. Look there, dear, and hand me my stitching."

She pointed to a basket sitting near the fireplace. I brought it to her and she started to take out little pieces of soft fabric, needles, and thread. While she talked to me, Mrs. Derrick sat beside me sewing baby clothes by hand. I recognized the same stitched flowers that Beckah had on her beach dress.

"You shouldn't be worrying with that," Sile grumbled as he filled a pot with water. "We can afford to buy clothes, Lana."

She frowned down at her work. "Things like this should be made with love—not that you care to understand anything that's important to me." The sharpness in her tone startled me a little. It made things awkward immediately.

Sile glared at her, but he didn't say anything back. It was uncomfortable. I caught Beckah looking at me with a hopeless look on her face while she was chopping carrots. She seemed so sad. It must have hurt to see her parents acting that way.

"Beck is learning to stitch, too, you know," Mrs. Derrick said. "Someday, she'll be able to make her own dresses for her children. She might even get a good job at a tailor's shop in the city. The city's a much better place to meet husbands. Like a good merchant, or maybe a grocer. Wouldn't you like a grocer, dear?"

Beckah's cheeks got so red you couldn't see her freckles anymore. "Momma!" She squeaked in protest.

Mrs. Derrick smiled at her affectionately. "You'll have to practice, though. No one wants knots in their embroidery. Fine men want polished wives, so they look for that sort of thing. Details always matter."

Beckah blushed even harder and turned her back to us to start stirring a big pot of stew. I heard her mumble, "I'm not even good at stitching."

Sile set the table for us with bowls and spoons. He helped Beckah bring over the bubbling pot of thick vegetable stew. It smelled so amazing it made my mouth water. I hadn't eaten this good since I was at the academy. We had freshly baked bread with fruit preserves, and the leftovers of an apple pie from the day before with big glasses of milk.

I didn't say anything to them about it, but that was the first time I'd had a family meal with anyone since my mother died. I was never allowed to eat with Ulric and his family when I lived with them. It always upset his wife for me to be sitting at the table with her *real* children. Even Mr. Crookin had seemed uncomfortable with it whenever he caught me eating at their table with Katty. I'd never been welcomed at anyone's family table until now.

Even though Sile didn't say much during dinner, we still had a good time. Beckah and I told them about what we'd done at the beach all morning, and Mrs. Derrick teased us about our matching sunburns.

I felt something warm and wet on my leg, and looked down to see Eddy sitting at my feet. He was drooling all over me, watching me take every bite. When I noticed him, he licked his lips hopefully. I snuck him a few little pieces of bread.

After dinner, Sile started helping his wife upstairs to their bedroom while Beckah and I cleaned the kitchen. We cleared the table, wrapped up the leftovers in paper, and started doing the dishes. Beckah passed me the freshly scrubbed dishes so I could dry them with a towel. I stood beside her, trying not to think about what her mother had said about merchants and grocers. I couldn't figure out why that bothered me so much.

"How long can you stay here?" she asked.

I didn't want to think about that. I was having such a good time here with her, the last thing I wanted to do was go back to the bitter cold in Mithangol and sit by myself in an empty house. "As long as you want me to, I guess. Until I have to go back to the academy."

"I wish you didn't have to go." Beckah's voice sounded sad.

"I'll come back," I said.

She sighed. "I know."

Neither of us said anything else as we stood there, finishing up the dishes and putting them away. I was realizing how hard it would be to leave. I knew Sile probably wouldn't like it one bit, but this place had already begun to feel like home to me. It was warm and comfortable, and it was filled with people I cared about. I didn't feel unwanted here, which was definitely a first.

"I'm scared to talk to Daddy about Icarus," Beckah said. She looked at me with worry in her eyes. "He won't understand. He'll tell me I can't keep him because I'm a girl. You know how he is. It's impossible to argue with him once he's made up his mind about something."

I smiled at her. "I think he'll understand better than you expect. Besides, you have to try, right? Icarus is counting on you."

She smiled back a little, and for a few moments, we stood there and stared at each other. Once again, I got that nagging feeling in the pit of my stomach that I should do something. I just couldn't figure out what.

A loud scream from upstairs made us both jump.

Our eyes went up to the ceiling, hearing the thumping of someone running over the floorboards overhead. Sile started shouting for us at the top of his lungs. Maybe it was what had happened to us last year at the prison camp, or maybe it was my training finally starting to sink into my subconscious, but I grabbed Beckah's hand right away and started dragging her up the stairs as fast as I could.

6

CHAPTER SIX

I had never seen so much blood before in my life. It started at the doorway to their bedroom and made a slippery trail all the way to the bed. Mrs. Derrick was lying on her back, clutching her belly in pain, and screaming at the top of her lungs. Sile's hands were covered in blood, and there was no color at all in his face. He stood there looking absolutely terrified. He appeared too shocked to know what to do, which definitely didn't make me feel any better. If he was panicking, then I should be petrified.

"It's the baby," Sile stammered. His voice was broken and I could see desperate grief on his face. Not even he was trained for something like this.

Beckah was pale. She looked like she might collapse at any moment. "We need the doctor!" she managed to cry out.

Sile grabbed her by the shoulders suddenly, forcing her to look at him. "Go downstairs. Get as many towels as you can."

"B-but, Daddy! The doctor!" She started to sob.

"There's no time. It takes two hours just to get to the city. She won't last that long." He told her firmly. "Go! Do as I tell you!"

Beckah ran out of the room crying, and I was left standing there staring at Mrs. Derrick as she writhed in pain. When I looked at Sile, I knew something was seriously wrong. This wasn't the way it was supposed to happen. Her life was in danger.

Sile went to her bedside and held her hand, whispering to her softly as she whimpered and sobbed. I could see his hands shaking, and I could have sworn I saw tears in his eyes. It hurt to see him like that, but I didn't see how I could do anything except get in the way. I had no medical training when it came to things like this.

From outside, I heard a roar like thunder. The house shuddered under a sudden blast of wind. Too late, I realized what was happening.

I ran to the window, looking out just in time to see Icarus sailing into the darkness toward the city with Beckah clinging to his back. She was going to get the doctor. For a few seconds, I couldn't breathe. I watched her disappear into the night with the sounds of Icarus's wing beats fading in the distance.

"I have to go after her!" I started for the door. "She doesn't even have a saddle!"

Sile caught me by the back of the shirt, yanking me back into the room. "Even if she finds the doctor, he won't make it here in time!" He yelled right in my face. "I know *you* can fix this. So do it! Save her!"

I stared up at him in terror. I had no idea what he was talking about. What could I do? I wasn't a doctor! I'd only had a little bit of training when it came to treating wounds—and he was the one who had taught me all that stuff in the first place!

Behind us, Mrs. Derrick screamed in pain again. It made Sile tighten his grip on me.

"She told me what you'd be able to do," he growled furiously. "I won't let my wife die. Heal her!"

I raised my hands up in surrender. I tried to speak, but all I could do was choke on my words. Sile pushed me toward the bed and grabbed my wrists. He forced me to touch his wife's face, putting my palms on her forehead. He held me there with all his strength no matter how much I struggled.

"Do it!" He shouted again, right in my ear.

Mrs. Derrick looked up at me through her tears. She was trembling, and I could see the pure panic in her eyes. She grabbed my arm and squeezed it hard.

"P-please," she sobbed.

I was at a loss. Sile was looming behind me, ready to rip my head off if I didn't do something. She was looking up at me pleadingly. And I was just standing there with my hands on her face, trying to figure out what they wanted from me. This woman was going to die right in front of my eyes and they were both acting like I could somehow stop it.

I did the only thing I could do: I thought about my own mother. Seeing Mrs. Derrick like that brought back those horrible memories of watching my mother slip away, lying in her bed with her body burning up with fever. I'd never felt so helpless before... until now.

Tears started to run down my face. I didn't want to watch anyone else die like that—like their life was slipping right through my fingers.

Then it started like a tingling warmth in the back of my mind. Just like the first time I'd called out to Mavrik, I felt that twinge of pressure in my chest.

Unlike all the times I had felt it before, this time it began to spread. It grew and grew until I could barely breathe. All around me, the sounds of Sile yelling and Mrs. Derrick crying seemed to fade away to white noise.

My ears were ringing. Everything got fuzzy. Time seemed to slow down to a crawl. I could feel my palms getting hotter and hotter until it was like my hands were stuck into red-hot coals.

All of a sudden, the room was spinning out of control. I heard a sound like a concussive boom, but I couldn't tell if it was real or only in my head. Something inside me snapped. I couldn't breathe at all anymore. I couldn't think. I could barely even feel myself falling.

Before I knew what was happening, I was lying on the floor while the ceiling spun above me. I still couldn't hear anything except a high-pitched ringing in my ears. I didn't know how long I lay there. It felt like hours, but I really had no idea. My body felt like a slab of lead. I couldn't move my arms or legs. My lungs started to ache, and I realized I still couldn't breathe.

Suddenly, Sile crouched down over me. I could see his lips moving and the worry on his face, but I couldn't hear anything he said. He picked me up like a ragdoll and started carrying me out of the room.

I managed to catch a glimpse of Mrs. Derrick before we left. She was propped up in the bed cradling a squirming bundle of cloth in her arms. There were still tears in her eyes, but they were tears of joy now. She was smiling, kissing her newborn baby. Seeing her like that gave me a little hope. I figured if I was about to die from whatever I'd done, at least I was able to help her somehow. At least she would be happy and her baby would be safe.

Then my air ran out. Darkness swallowed me before I knew what was happening. It felt like drowning in black water. It was quiet, so quiet. About the time I started to wonder if I was dead, I sputtered awake again. Sile was leaning over me, pumping my chest with his hands and forcing his breath into my lungs. He saw me stirring and started smacking my cheeks to try to wake me up.

I choked, taking in as much air as I could. For an instant, I was relieved. I thought I was going to be okay. I could finally breathe normally again. I could hear, even if things were still a little fuzzy. And then I realized I still couldn't move my arms and legs.

Pain hit me so suddenly that at first, all I could do was scream. As it got more intense, though, I couldn't even do that anymore. White-hot agony shot through me like someone had rammed a dagger right between my eyes. My skin was on fire. My blood boiled. It took everything I had to grit my teeth and bear it.

"Jae!" I heard Beckah's voice call my name, but I couldn't will my eyes to open long enough to see her. The pain was too much.

"Where's the doctor?" Sile asked her. He was sliding his arms under me again to pick me up off the floor.

"H-he's on his way. He promised he'd hurry. Daddy... w-what happened?" I could hear Beckah crying. She was following him, whimpering my name pleadingly. I couldn't see her, but I could sense her nearby. I wished I could move, or at least open my eyes and look at her.

"Go and see to your mother, Beck," Sile ordered as he put me down on the bed. He pushed a hand against my forehead, and that was when I realized I was burning up. His hand felt really cold against my skin. He pulled my eyelids open with his fingers, and I could see him looking down at me with concern.

"But, Daddy—" she started to protest.

"I said go!" he yelled.

I couldn't see anything when he let my eyelids close again, but I could hear the sound of footsteps leaving the room. The bed flinched, and I could hear Sile's ragged breathing near me. It almost sounded like he was... crying.

"The gods will never forgive me," he whispered shakily. "I gave her my word and now I've failed her."

Time passed with those words echoing across my mind.

The pain didn't let up for an instant, although I seemed to get used to it enough that I could think through it somewhat. I wanted him to explain. What had I done? And how had he known I could do it? Would I even survive this? I had so many questions, and no way to ask them. The pain sizzled over my body like someone was skinning me alive. It even made my bones ache right down to the marrow.

Once, I thought I heard another voice nearby. It wasn't anyone I recognized, though. It sounded like an older man, and I could vaguely feel him poking at me, like he was examining me.

"Sixteen you said?" I heard the stranger ask. He must have been the doctor. "A bit late, but I've seen this before. These halfbreeds are a strange sort. It's that elf blood, you see. It throws off their growing patterns. The Gray elves don't mature slowly like normal human children do. Instead, it happens all at once. As best we can tell, it's much like an insect bursting from a cocoon. Sudden, rapid change that takes an incredible physical toll. Just imagine every part of you being stretched at once."

There was an uncomfortable silence. The room felt heavy. Even though I couldn't see, I could sense everyone was looking at me.

"Those Gray elves are a notoriously tough breed, though," the doctor continued. "Their bones are like metal, and wounds to their flesh tend to heal much faster. So their purebooded offspring can handle such a radical change. But having human blood in the mix weakens these halfbreeds too much. Think about it. How many adult halfbreeds do you see walking around? Not many at all. So few of them survive this."

"Is he going to be okay?" Beckah's voice asked. It sounded like she was sitting very close by. Vaguely, I could feel her hand holding tightly onto mine.

There was another tense silence. I wanted so badly to answer, to sit up and assure everyone that I was fine. I just needed to rest and then everything would be okay. But I couldn't.

"Lieutenant Derrick, you're a good man, so I'll be perfectly honest," the stranger answered. "I've only ever witnessed this once before. So few of them even survive to adolescence at all. His body probably won't be able to stand the pain. But even if it could, he is starving for nutrients as we speak. All children need food to grow, and what he's going through is basically years of physical maturity packed into a very short amount time. He's already thin and has obviously suffered from some malnutrition. He will probably starve to death in the next day or so. You should... make the necessary preparations. I can send word to the minister for you. He doesn't like presiding over the burial rites for elves, but in your case, I think I could convince him to make an exception."

Beckah started to cry. I wanted to yell in protest. I was alive. Couldn't they see that? I wasn't even dead yet and they were already planning my funeral!

"Isn't there anything we can do?" Sile sounded determined.

The stranger sighed. I heard footsteps going toward the door. "You could try forcing him to eat, though in his current state, I'm not sure it would help even if he ate constantly over the next few days."

"Thank you, doctor." Sile and the man kept talking as they left the room. Soon I couldn't make out anything else they said.

Suddenly Beckah put her arms around me. She buried her face against my neck and I could feel her shaking as she cried. "I won't let you die," she said. "So don't you dare give up, you hear me?"

She got up and left the room, and I was left there wondering what was happening to me. I had always hoped and prayed that I would grow some. I had anticipated getting a little taller, especially since my father was practically a giant compared to most other men. I had expected my voice to get deeper, or that I would at least fill out to look less like a skeleton. But nothing could have prepared me for this. Now, I was just hoping I would survive.

Each day that passed felt worse than the one before it. Instead of getting better, the pain seemed to get worse and worse. Everything ached. My stomach felt like it was grinding against my spine. I was so hungry I couldn't think, and so thirsty that it hurt to even breathe.

Every time I started to lose my will to go on, Beckah was there. I always knew it was her because I could recognize the feel of her hands. She forced me to eat by prying my mouth open and pouring something like soup down my throat. I don't know how often she did it. It seemed almost constant. And each time she finished, the effects were immediate. I felt a little better for a few minutes. My stomach didn't ache so badly, and I got some relief from the agony in my bones. Then the pain would return with a vengeance.

I was living in a nightmare. The doctor's words kept gnawing at the back of my mind. He had said I wouldn't survive this. He even told Sile to go ahead and prepare to bury me. I didn't want to die. Not yet. But it was getting harder and harder to remember anything other than suffering.

As more time passed, my mind started to fray. My thoughts were less clear. I couldn't tell who was touching me or feeding me anymore. I couldn't feel anything except the pain.

Mavrik gave me some relief in my darkest moments. He sent me images of us flying at the academy; memories that sometimes found me in that dark place. I could sense his concern, and it brought me comfort to know that he hadn't left me to go through this alone. After a while, though, I couldn't even make myself focus on that either. I was numb inside and out. I started to lose my will to go on.

I started to hope I would die, just so the pain would finally stop.

7

CHAPTER SEVEN

It was peaceful when I opened my eyes. At first, I thought I might be dead. I could faintly hear the sound of the surf in the distance. I could smell the salty ocean wind coming through the open windows. The air was cool against my skin, and everything felt calm.

The pain was finally gone.

At first, I just assumed I was dead. It was the only thing that made sense. That is, until I realized I could take a deep breath, and nothing hurt. I could wiggle my fingers and my toes. Slowly, I started trying to raise my head up to look around. My body was stiff and sore all over, like I'd been run over by a herd of horses. There wasn't a single part of me that didn't ache. My joints felt like someone had poured sand into them. My head throbbed when I looked into the glare of the sunlight.

But I could do it—I could move. I could think. And even that intense soreness was nothing compared to the pain I had been in before.

Then I saw Beckah curled up on the bed next to me. She was slumped back against the headboard, sound asleep, with a half-finished bowl of soup in her hands. I could tell by the look on her sleeping face that she was exhausted. There were dark circles under her eyes and her hair was frazzled. She probably hadn't let herself rest in days. Or had it been days? I wasn't sure. My sense of time was distorted. Everything had felt like one long nightmare.

I sat up slowly, and reached out to carefully slip the bowl of soup out of Beckah's grasp so she didn't spill it in her sleep. Suddenly, I noticed my hands. I stared at them, and it was surreal.

They were... huge!

Or at least, they were a lot bigger than they had been before. I started wiggling my fingers to make sure they were actually my fingers, and not some kind of illusion.

A surge of adrenaline made me forget all about Beckah and the soup. I got out of bed and almost fell flat on my face. My legs were still weak. I could barely walk, so I leaned against the bed as I staggered across the room toward the mirror.

The young man looking back at me was barely recognizable. I didn't believe it really was me until I saw him moving whenever I did. It just didn't seem possible. It couldn't be real.

The man in my reflection looked a lot like my father, with a squared chin and piercing pale blue eyes. His hair wasn't black, but it wasn't white like a Gray elf's either. It was somewhere in between, like the color of ash. All traces of boyhood were gone from his face, and when he narrowed his eyes back at me... his gaze was disturbingly piercing. It made my skin prickle because it was the same harrowing, fierce look my father had on his face almost constantly.

Slowly, it started to sink in. That was me. I wasn't a puny, half-stuffed scarecrow anymore. I actually looked older than I was, maybe nineteen instead of sixteen. I didn't look like a kid, I looked like a man!

I must have grown out of my clothes because I was basically just wearing underwear and they definitely weren't mine. I guessed I was borrowing some from Sile, which was kind of embarrassing and awkward. I didn't dare take them off, though. I wasn't wearing anything else.

I looked down at my arms, my legs, and it actually got me choked up. I wasn't a skeleton. Well, at least not as much as before. I was still lean, still skinny compared to someone like Felix who was all brawn, but now I looked mature. I looked healthy. I was so grateful for every single ounce of muscle I could get. I still wasn't totally convinced this wasn't some kind of dream. It seemed too good to be true.

"Jae?" Beckah said my name.

I turned to see her sitting up on the bed, wide-awake, and staring at me with eyes as big as saucers. She almost looked scared of me. I tried to speak but it came out as a bunch of excited sounds.

"Is that really you?" she asked shakily.

"I-I'm not sure," I stammered as I glanced back at the mirror to make sure. My voice sounded different, too. It was deeper. "I think so."

She put the bowl on the nightstand and started creeping toward me cautiously. When I turned to face her, she jumped back a little. I noticed she was looking up at me—way up. I was a lot taller than her now. She was trembling a little as she eyed me up and down.

"Beckah." I hated to see her be afraid of me. I wanted her to know it was still the same me. On the inside, I didn't feel any different than before. "It's okay."

She didn't look convinced, even as she started to inch toward me a little. At any moment, I half expected her to bolt out of the room screaming. I could see her looking me over, like she was searching for traces of the scrawny little Jae she'd known before. When she finally met my eyes again, the corners of her mouth were twitching at a smile.

"Well, you're definitely not a lamb anymore," she said uneasily.

I smiled, and before I could think about it, I hugged her. Probably not the best idea since I wasn't exactly wearing much in the way of clothes. But I knew she was the reason I was still alive and breathing. I had survived because she never gave up on me. I knew I would spend the rest of my life trying to find some way to repay her for that.

She didn't seem to mind if I was mostly naked or not; she put her arms around my waist like she always did and hugged me tight. She wasn't strong enough to choke me anymore, though. The hug was a lot different from before. I was so much bigger than she was now. Her head only came up to my chest, and I could easily swallow her up in my arms. She felt so fragile.

Her angry-looking father definitely minded the hugging, though. Sile was standing in the doorway. He arched a brow at me and cleared his throat, narrowing his eyes into lethal slits. Somehow, it reminded me of the way Icarus glared at me. I knew that was probably going to be my only warning. I had about two seconds to let his daughter go before he made good on his promise to rip my ears off. Growth spurt or not, I was well aware that Sile could still beat me within an inch of my life without ever breaking a sweat.

We jumped apart immediately. Beckah was blushing as she hurried over to pick up the bowl of soup. She skirted around her dad as she went out of the room like she couldn't get away fast enough.

"Oh by the way, he's awake," she added quickly.

Sile gave her a hard look as she disappeared into the hallway. "I can see that," he grumbled. When she was safely downstairs and out of earshot, he curled a finger at me to follow him. "You can't walk around naked in my house, boy."

I followed him to his room, keeping a hand on the wall because my legs were still wobbly. They tingled like they had been asleep for a long time. As I walked behind him, I noticed I was taller than he was now. That startled me a little, and it made me want to shrink down some. I didn't feel like I deserved to be taller than Sile.

"They're going to be too short," he said as he opened his armoire and started throwing clothes in my direction. "But they'll do for now. Figures you'd inherit *his* stature."

I pulled a green tunic over my head and stepped into a pair of pants. They were definitely too small. The shirt was tight across my chest and back because my shoulders were bony, but broad. The pants were so short they came up above my ankles. The waist was a little too big for me, though, so I kept pulling them up until Sile finally tossed me a belt. When I finished dressing, I noticed Sile was still standing there with his arms crossed, sizing me up like he always did.

"You feeling all right?" he asked.

His concern caught me off guard. "Yes. I'm a little sore. It's already getting better, though."

I met his gaze. For a few long, uncomfortable minutes, we just stood there staring at each other. His brow was furrowed, and he was frowning like he wanted to yell at me. I wasn't sure why.

"You know I had to buy a coffin. It's leaning up against the side of the house outside." He snapped. He acted like I had forced him to do that.

I didn't know what to say. I wondered if I should apologize or not. I wasn't sure what I'd be apologizing for, though. Almost dying?

"Don't do that to us again," he warned.

I nodded, even if I wasn't completely sure what he was talking about. "Yes, sir."

He snorted and looked away, scratching at the back of his neck uncomfortably. "I suppose I should thank you."

"For what?"

He started toward me, and I couldn't tell if he was about to hug me or punch me in the face. I cringed because both options seemed uncomfortable. When he got close enough, he put a hand on my shoulder. "It was my fault. I forced you to do something you weren't ready for, and it almost cost you your life. But what you did—"

Like a bolt of lightning, the memories of what had happened burst into my head. His wife had been dying right in front of my eyes. Then Sile had insisted I do something about it. And… I *had* done something, I just didn't know what. I couldn't stand it anymore; I had to know.

"What did I do?" I interrupted.

Sile smirked at me and shook his head some. "Why don't you go downstairs and see for yourself?"

Sile followed me as I went down to the first floor. The more I walked, the steadier my legs got. I was stiff, and parts of me were sore, but it was getting better by the second. The more I moved, the better I felt.

I could hear singing coming from the kitchen, and I thought I recognized Mrs. Derrick's voice. Something smelled fantastic, like freshly baked pie. It made my mouth water.

As I started to peek around the corner, Sile gave me a shove from behind. I came stumbling into the kitchen, almost tripping and falling on my face. Beckah was sitting at the table with her sewing tools spread out around her. She smiled at me, but I had a feeling she wasn't practicing her sewing because she wanted to.

"Jaevid!" Mrs. Derrick's voice sang my name.

When I turned around to see her, I barely recognized her. Her eyes were shining and her skin was glowing. She looked healthier than all of us. There was rosy color in her cheeks, and she had more meat on her bones. She looked ten years younger, and her smile was so bright that it made me blush.

There was a squirming lump cradled against her chest in a sling made out of soft pink fabric. I didn't even notice until I heard it whimper and start to cry. It was a tiny, wrinkly baby. She patted and stroked it, cooing softly until the baby became silent again.

Mrs. Derrick looked up at me and smiled again. There were tears in her eyes, but she didn't look sad. Before I could smile back, she started hugging me. She kissed both my cheeks until they were wet, and combed her fingers through my hair.

"What a beautiful gift fate has given you, my lamb," she whispered.

I blushed because I didn't know what she was talking about. I couldn't figure out how I had caused any of this. How had I saved her? What gift was she talking about?

Mrs. Derrick seemed to notice my confusion. She put her palm against my cheek and stroked my face with her thumb. "Someday you'll understand. In the meantime, sit down! Look, I've been baking all morning. There's a blueberry pie just for you. Go on!" She basically shoved me into a chair across from Beckah.

Before I could protest, there was a piece of pie and a fork in front of me. It distracted me immediately. Who can argue with pie?

I was too shocked to start eating, though. Mrs. Derrick was... better. Much, *much* better. I didn't know if that was my fault, or just because she'd finally had her baby. I looked at Beckah for answers, but she only grinned shyly and went back to her sewing.

"He can eat later," Sile said. He was leaning in the doorway watching us with a strange smirk on his face. "I need to talk to him outside."

Mrs. Derrick swatted at her husband with a wooden spoon teasingly. "He hasn't had anything but soup in nearly two weeks! Let the poor child have a bite or two! Look at him, still as skinny as a rail. He needs some meat on his bones."

Sile rolled his eyes, but he never quit grinning.

"I'll get you a piece, too," she crooned to him. It must have worked because he grabbed her spoon and pulled her in close enough to kiss her on the mouth.

Watching them made me blush, and suddenly I had a good reason to stare down at the steaming hot piece of pie in front of me. Looking at it made it impossible to think about anything else except how hungry I was, so I started eating.

"Now see what you've done?" Beckah whispered.

I looked up with a mouthful of food in my cheek. She was kidding, I guess, because she winked at me and grinned.

Warm, solid food felt amazing in my stomach. I ate four slices of pie and two pieces of berry cobbler before I finally felt full. Mrs. Derrick wanted to keep feeding me, but thankfully Sile waved her off.

"Let's go outside," he said to me with a dark twinkle in his eyes.

I started to get nervous. That was same look he got at the academy whenever he was about to force me to do something unpleasant in the name of training.

"But I don't have any shoes," I protested. My old boots were definitely not going to fit anymore.

"You won't need them." He pointed to the front door. "Hurry up. You don't realize it, but you're due back at the academy in two weeks. Time is running out, and there's still a lot you need to learn."

Sile was right. I would have to go back early and have new armor made. Probably a new saddle, too. No way my stuff from last year was going to fit me now. I wondered if I'd have to come up with the money for all that myself, or if Sile was still going to be my sponsor. My new instructor, Lieutenant Jace Rordin, was about as nice as anyone could expect from a war dog that had just been dragged off the frontlines. He didn't act like he hated me. But I seriously doubted he was going to buy me any new equipment. Armor was expensive. The little bit of money I had saved up from my carpentry work wasn't enough to even buy myself a new helmet.

I followed Sile out the front door and toward the little stable behind the house. I tried not to look at the coffin that was still leaning up against the side of the house. He had said it was supposed to be for me. I couldn't help but notice that it would have been way too small now. Still, seeing it gave me a creepy feeling.

Sile opened the stable door and disappeared inside. While I waited for him, I tried to get a grip on my nerves. I needed some answers, and I knew Sile was holding out on me. He knew more about me than I did, apparently. I needed him to tell me what I'd done to his wife to heal her like that, and how he knew I could even do it in the first place. I had a feeling he wasn't going to just throw up his hands and confess everything. He had been keeping these secrets for a long time, and there had to be a reason.

Sile came out of the stable with a long wooden carrying pole and an old, banged up helmet. He smirked at me as he dropped them at my feet and went back inside to bring out two fifty-pound bags of grain. I watched him tie the bags to each end of the pole, and then he snapped his fingers and pointed at the ground.

I knew what that meant. I squatted down and braced myself as he put the carrying pole over my shoulders like a yoke. Once upon a time, a few weeks ago, those bags of grain would have weighed more than I did.

"There's a pier for local fishermen three miles down the beach to the east. There and back twice. The sand near the surf is firmer. Try not to fall and ruin the grain, if you don't mind." he said as he picked up the old helmet and mashed it down onto my head. "And I better not catch you walking."

"Yes sir." My answer was automatic. It was easy to fall back into the state of mind I had been in during training. Even though Sile hadn't been my instructor for a while now, I knew better than to argue with him. He didn't like excuses.

Sure, I had kept up my own workout regiment every day since I left Blybrig, but that didn't help me at all. Running down the beach with a hundred pounds on my back was more than exhausting. I wasn't used to my new body, and all my joints ached. My muscles were still sore. Every step hurt.

It was nearly dark by the time I finally finished, and I was exhausted and starving again. I dropped the pole and bags back outside the stable before I sat down to catch my breath. I was dripping sweat and my feet were throbbing. All I could think about was food. I really hoped there was some pie left.

"Here." Sile appeared behind me with a big piece of fresh-baked bread and a canteen in his hand. He tossed both of them to me. "Took you long enough."

"I *have* been training," I insisted as I took off the helmet and gulped down big bites of the bread. "I'm still weak. I'm not used to this body yet."

"That's not going to be an excuse at the academy. You know that," he said, walking around me to pick up the bags and carry them back into the stable. When he came out again, he had two wooden practice swords in his hands like the ones we used in training. He dropped one of them at my feet and nudged it toward me with the toe of his boot. "Get up."

"Sile," I protested. "I have some questions."

He turned his back to me and walked a few feet away, spinning the sword over his hand with expert speed. I seemed to recall hearing him say that the arm injury he had gotten at the prison camp last year would keep him from ever being able to hold a sword again. That didn't seem to be the case. He was whipping the practice sword around like there was nothing wrong with his arm at all.

"There'll be time for questions later," he growled. "Besides, the answers aren't important."

"They're important to me!" I couldn't keep myself from lashing out at him. It was one thing for him to brush me off, but he was keeping things from me on purpose and trying to make it seem like none of it mattered. It did matter. It mattered a *lot*. "How do you know so much about me? How did you know I could heal your wife like that? What's wrong with me?"

When Sile turned around, he had a dangerous look in his eyes. It actually scared me a little. He pointed his sword at me threateningly. "What should be important to you right now is learning how to survive because what is coming your way will, in all likelihood, kill you. Now get up."

I obeyed, snatching up the sword as I stood. But I didn't take my eyes off him; I wasn't backing down yet. "Saving your life last year almost killed me. I think you owe me a few answers."

I saw his jaw tense and his knuckles turned white as he gripped his sword more tightly. "I didn't ask you to save me," he growled through clenched teeth.

"You didn't have to," I growled back. "Beckah did. And she suspects that you've moved them all here because you're trying to hide from someone—and I think she's right. It's all connected somehow, isn't it? I'm not stupid, you know. I know it wasn't coincidence that you stuck your neck out for me so I could become a dragonrider. No one else would have done that for a halfbreed. Not even my own father cares about me that much. So why won't you tell me what's going on?"

Sile lunged at me so suddenly I was caught completely off guard. I almost fell backwards as he brought his sword down toward my face. I moved to block, and the impact rattled my teeth. So much for that "crippling injury" he was supposed to have. He still hit like a hammer.

But I had changed some since the last time we'd crossed blades. I was stronger, and I could hold off his attacks. My own strikes were faster, steadier, and I could see him having to focus harder to keep up. He couldn't toy with me like before.

Something had definitely clicked in my brain. The sword felt good in my hands. I stepped easily through parries and strikes that had been so difficult for me last year because I lacked the size to match my opponent's reach. It didn't feel like a struggle anymore.

I could sense that Sile was getting more and more aggressive. His attacks came faster, and he was using tricks that he'd never used before. I thought I had him on a downward swing, and he locked his hilt with mine, and twisted the blade out of my hand. Before I could even process what happened, there was a boot in my chest. Sile kicked me to the ground.

Suddenly I was lying on my back with both swords pointed at my throat. I was forced to tap out in surrender.

"Why won't you tell me?" I glared up at him. "It's my life. I have a right to know."

"Because I promised her I wouldn't," he snapped.

"Who?"

I saw the rage in his eyes. He'd said too much. "I told you, it doesn't matter!"

While he was busy being angry with himself for giving something important away, I used a leg sweep to knock him down. I didn't give him a chance to recover. I threw myself at him and tried to get him into a grappling hold.

It was a good idea, in theory. But I was very rusty on the grappling maneuvers. I had been so terrible at hand-to-hand combat before. I was basically just a practice dummy for Felix. I had no good experience to go on.

Sile pinned me with a knee across my neck in a matter of seconds.

"Quit worrying about answers and focus on what you have to do to survive." He bore down with his weight so hard I could barely breathe. "And don't tell anyone about what you can do. I mean no one. Not even Felix. Don't even try to do it again. You can't tell anyone what you can do."

Part of me really wanted to punch Sile in the face—maybe even break his nose for good measure. But I was having a hard enough time staying conscious as he crushed my windpipe. All I could do was nod, and he finally let me up.

I sat up coughing and rubbing my neck. I was so furious I couldn't see straight. I already knew better than to tell anyone about what I had done to his wife, just like I knew better than to tell any of the other riders that I could talk to Mavrik with my thoughts. I was starting to collect a lot of big, dangerous secrets. "And what exactly am I supposed to survive? Felix already told me about the interrogation stuff. So they'll use me as a punching bag for a few weeks? Big deal. It's not like I'm not used to that already."

Sile cracked a smirk and rolled his eyes, offering me a hand to pull me back up to my feet. "Felix is a good friend to you, however not even he can fully appreciate what's about to happen. I've done everything I can to protect you. But when you exposed yourself last year and risked saving my life, everything I've done in that regard became pointless. Now there's nowhere you can hide, and I can't be there to protect you anymore. You should try growing some eyes in the back of your head."

Something about the way he said that made me very uncomfortable. "You mean someone's going to try to kidnap me now? For some kind of immortality ritual?"

Sile glared at me like that was a stupid thing to ask. It made my face feel hot. I was embarrassed and frustrated because I didn't know what questions I should be asking. Most of the ones I did ask, he refused to answer.

"Go inside, get some dinner, bathe, and go to bed," he commanded, picking up both swords and starting back into the stable. "Be back out here at first light. Your vacation is officially over."

CHAPTER EIGHT

There was a sense of urgency in the way Sile trained with me every day. I was running out of time. He pushed me harder than I had ever been pushed before, and still wouldn't tell me exactly why. He didn't give me a spare minute to question him, either. I barely even had enough time to think.

Sile got amazingly creative coming up with ways for me to build up my strength, which frankly hadn't exactly blossomed like I'd hoped it would. At first, it was a struggle just to make it through one exercise. But after a few days, I could already feel myself getting stronger. I could run further and faster without getting tired. He had me doing pull-ups and chin-ups on an exposed beam in the stable. I did push-ups with those bags of grain piled on my back, and sit-ups until I felt like I was going to puke.

We sparred for hours, practicing with swords, scimitars, and drilling through grappling techniques. He even tied me to the family carriage and had me pull it around the house in circles a few times. All that work made it hard to keep track of time, but I could tell his intensive training was starting to work. Even if I hadn't gained much muscle, I was getting more and more comfortable in my new body every day.

I felt bad for how much I was eating. I knew I was costing them a lot of extra money. But I was starving all the time. My appetite was out of control, and I couldn't do anything about it. It made the training Sile was putting me through show with quicker results, but it also meant I was eating them out of house and home. I could eat more than the rest of the family combined. Mrs. Derrick teased me about hiding it under my chair, because even though I could eat a whole roast by myself, I never gained a single pound.

While we trained, Beckah brought us water and food regularly. I could tell by the look on her face that something was wrong. She seemed nervous just to be around me. I wondered why. I wanted to think that my sudden growth spurt wouldn't change anything between us—but it already had. She was right there in the same house with me, and I missed her like she was a thousand miles away. We didn't talk much, and she barely made eye contact with me.

After a week and a half, I knew my time with Sile's family was up. As much as I hated the idea of going back to Mithangol, I needed to do a stopover at my house to check on everything. Then I had to get to the academy in time to have more armor and a new saddle made. My legs were way too long for the one I had now. Sile had wrestled with it, trying to find a way to rig it so I would fit without looking like a man trying to squeeze into a baby's highchair, but it was a lost cause.

"Just take it off," I told him. "I can ride without it. It's only a day's flight."

Sile frowned. He obviously didn't like that idea. "It's dangerous to ride without a way to anchor yourself to him. If he banks too steeply you'll slide off. I've already demonstrated for you what it's like to fall off a dragon's back."

"Lucky for me, I can talk to him. Besides, Beckah did it and she's never even had training. I'll be fine," I countered. Mavrik chirped with agreement, and I started unbuckling the saddle from between his neck and wing arms.

Sile was strangely quiet as I removed the saddle. He stood back and watched, rubbing his chin and following me with his dark eyes. "You need to start a fight," he said at last.

I stopped and stared at him. "A fight? With who?"

He shrugged a little. "It doesn't matter. The bigger the better, though. That way they can't say you were just using your new size to pick on someone smaller."

"But why?" I'd spent most of my life avoiding fights because of the guarantee that I would be crushed. The idea of starting one on purpose was not something I was excited about.

Sile moved around to Mavrik's other side and started helping me unbuckle the saddle. "At survival training, they always target the weakest link and use him to exploit and antagonize the rest of the class. They want to get a reaction. Unfortunately, there's only one other person in your class who cares what happens to you. And trust me, the last thing you want is to put the spotlight on him. So you need to prove that you aren't the weakest link anymore. You don't have much time to do it, though."

"And the best way to do that is to get into a fight?" I didn't like the sound of this at all.

"Yes. And I would strongly encourage you to win." He gave me a meaningful look over Mavrik's back.

"What am I supposed to do? Walk up and punch someone?" I tried to think of a good reason to do something like that. There wasn't one.

"I'm sure you'll come up with something. You were essentially a doormat for most of your peers last year. Surely there's someone you'd like to get revenge on," Sile said as he hoisted the saddle away and flung it over his shoulder.

I stood there thinking about that while he carried my old saddle away into the stable. Mavrik got up and shook himself. We exchanged a glance, and a vision of Lyon Cromwell flashed across my mind.

"I'm not going to punch Lyon for no reason," I told him.

Mavrik made an irritated grumbling noise and stared preening his scales. I knew what he was thinking, and not just because he started showing me images of the fight at the prison camp last year when Lyon abandoned us. I had plenty of reasons to do more than punch Lyon. He was not my friend. He hated me, and he had spent a lot of his spare time bullying me in the past. I would have been lying if I told anyone I didn't resent him for that, but that was a far cry from wanting to go out of my way to pick a fight with him.

"Forget it. We'll think of something else," I grumbled.

Mavrik yawned and started crawling away, looking for a shady spot to stretch out for a nap. Sile came back and followed me to the house. I still had to pack up my stuff and say my goodbyes. I was hoping to get back to Mithangol after nightfall. If I could get in and out of there without anyone seeing me, I would be happy.

It was awkward to eat my last lunch with them. Or at least, it was awkward for me because Beckah wouldn't even look up from across the table. She sat there, swirling her fork in her food, and didn't say a word. It was killing me. I needed to talk to her before I left for this year of training. She was the only person who gave me any confidence in myself.

Mrs. Derrick was caught up with her new baby girl. The chubby little thing was wrapped up in layers of pink blankets. She squirmed in her mother's arms, making strange baby-noises. Every now and then, though, Mrs. Derrick would look up at me and smile again, reminding me to eat as much as I wanted. I decided that was probably her way of thanking me.

Sile was uncomfortably quiet, too. He looked like he was lost in thought, or maybe even worried about something. I hoped it wasn't me. I wasn't small anymore. I could survive. I wasn't doomed to be the weakest link everyone would prey upon. At least, that's what I was hoping.

After dinner, I went up to the guest room and packed up the few things I'd brought. Mrs. Derrick told me to leave my old clothes and boots, since none of them fit now. I didn't have much else to take. My belt, vambraces, helmet—none of it would be any use to me anymore. So I tried to fold it all up neatly and put it on the dresser. Sile had bought them all for me, so it only seemed right to give them back now.

The door shut behind me suddenly and I almost jumped out of my skin. I half hoped it was Beckah, but instead Sile was standing there with his arms crossed. He was looking at me like he had something to say. Immediately, my stomach started to squirm nervously.

"I've decided to let the dragon stay," he told me. "Icarus, that is."

I swallowed hard. "I think that's a good idea."

He frowned. "Because Beck wants to keep him?"

"No," I answered quickly. "Because if you want to keep something around for security, a king drake is the best guardian anyone could hope for."

He snorted and looked away again. "I kept hoping Valla would come back. But I'm a fool for even expecting that from her. She didn't choose me the way Mavrik chose you. I was a taskmaster to her, nothing more. Despite all we've been through, she's better off without me. She didn't even look back."

"You let her go?" I wasn't all that surprised. Sile had mentioned before that his dragon wasn't bonded to him like Mavrik was to me, or Icarus was to Beckah. He'd also said he was going to let her go, since he wasn't a dragonrider anymore.

"I owed her that much," he said. "Look, Jae, regardless of what's been said and done, I do owe you an apology."

I froze and stared at him. I was beginning to suspect I might be hallucinating. "For what, sir?"

"For keeping these things from you. For pushing you too far and almost getting you killed." He looked at me uneasily. "But I'm a man of my word, and I gave someone a promise that I'd only tell you what you needed to know. This isn't the right time. You'll have to trust me about that."

I did trust him. But that didn't make me feel any better right then. I was starting to get nervous. Just thinking about going back to Blybrig had my stomach tied up in painful knots.

On the one hand, I wanted to see Felix again and get back into the saddle. I wanted to start training like I had been before. Then on the other hand, I dreaded what was coming. I hated the discriminating way everyone looked at me, and knowing that I basically had no allies there other than Felix and maybe Lieutenant Jace Rordin. We were all supposed to be brothers at arms, and yet I knew I was still an outsider. That would probably never change no matter what I did.

"I'm still trying to believe that I can do this," I told him. "I knew it wouldn't be easy, but it's hard enough trying to have faith that I'll make it to the end of training."

Sile walked toward me and put a hand on my shoulder like he had before. It was still strange to be able to look at him eye-to-eye now. "Faith won't make things easier for you, Jaevid. But it will make them possible."

He reached into his pocket, taking out a small leather bag. I could hear coins jingling around inside as he handed it to me. "For your new armor and saddle," he told me. "There should be enough there to get you fully outfitted."

"Sir," I started to protest. I didn't want to take any more of his money. He'd already paid for the equipment I'd used last year. He'd volunteered to sponsor me because my father wouldn't, and I knew there was no way for me to ever pay him back.

Sile shoved the bag into my hand anyway. "Just shut up and take it."

We exchanged an awkward moment of silence, staring at one another. I had an eerie feeling we were both thinking about the same thing: what was going to happen to me this year at training? Was I going to be able to survive it? Sile acted like there was something greater at work here—something I was supposed to be a part of. If I didn't make it, if something went wrong, what would happen?

I cleared my throat, put the coins into my pocket, and picked up my nearly empty bag. "I should get going." I paused on my way out the door and looked back. "Where's Beckah? She's been avoiding me, hasn't she?"

Sile scowled at me. "Still sniffing around my daughter, are you?"

I felt my ears start to burn with embarrassment. "S-she's my friend, sir."

"She was headed to the beach, last I saw her," he grumbled at last. "She doesn't like goodbyes."

He sounded like he knew that first hand. It made me think about all the times she'd had to say goodbye to him as he left for training or war. She never knew if she'd see him again every time he left. Now, it was starting to be that way with me, too.

Then I realized why she might be acting so weird.

After thanking Mrs. Derrick for all her good food, I left the house and headed for the beach. Overhead, Mavrik was wheeling in slow circles with his blue scales sparkling in the sunshine. The salty sea air blew in hard from the water, and the sun was warm on my skin. As I came over the last grassy dune, I could see the dark shapes of ships on the horizon, the powdery white sand stretching along the coast, and the glittering waves crashing against the shore.

Beckah was standing near the water with the wind in her hair. Icarus was crouched beside her, his huge body compacted up like a crouching cat, and his long tail wrapped around him. It looked like they were having a secret conversation. They both looked back at me at the same time when I got close. That's when I noticed that Icarus was wearing my old saddle—the one I'd grown out of. It didn't look like it fit Icarus very well, after all he was a lot bigger than Mavrik, but it was probably about the right size for Beckah.

"You're angry at me, aren't you?" I asked her. "For leaving, right?"

Beckah frowned. "No."

"Then it's the way I look now? You don't like it?"

She didn't answer right away, and I got a sick feeling in my stomach that maybe I'd been right. I could handle her being upset with me for leaving. But if she was shutting me out because of how I looked—I wasn't sure I could stand going through that again. It wasn't something I could change. I couldn't help the way I looked.

Finally, she turned back toward the ocean and let out a loud sigh. "I'm not angry at all, Jae. It just seems like the war and the academy both keep taking away the people I care about the most. There's never anything I can do to stop it. I wish you weren't going. I wish you'd stay here with us. And at the same time, I wish I was going with you," she confessed. "I feel like I *should* be going with you. I can't explain it. But ever since Icarus chose me, I've had this feeling that there's something I'm supposed to be doing. It's getting stronger and stronger, and I'm afraid. No one's going to accept me as a dragonrider because I'm a girl."

"You told me once that it didn't matter what anyone else thinks," I reminded her. "You said that if it was something I really cared about, then nothing else mattered."

Beckah started to fidget. I could see that she was thinking hard about this, and that she was obviously worried. It was a big chance to take. I still wasn't comfortable with the idea of her riding into battle or trying to become a dragonrider, but I wasn't going to try to hold her back. If she wanted to fly, I knew nothing was going to stop her.

"It is weird to see you this way now," she mumbled. "I know it's silly, but it makes me wish I could look more grown up, too. Maybe then you wouldn't forget about me, or think of me as a little kid anymore."

"Forget about you?" I put my bag down and went to stand next to her. She flashed me a stubborn look, but all I really noticed was how her eyes were the same sea-green color as the ocean.

"I'm still the same person, you know. I don't feel any different on the inside. And besides, I like the way you look." Admitting that made me blush. "I'll come back, Beckah. You'll see me again. I won't forget."

She reached down into the pocket of her apron and took out a square piece of thin, white cloth. It was handkerchief. When she put it in my hand, I saw that there were two dragons stitched on it. One was blue like Mavrik and the other was black like Icarus. They were flying together with their necks and tails intertwined and their wings spread wide.

"Momma says that in the old days, ladies would give knights tokens for good luck to carry with them into battle," she explained. "I know the stitching isn't very good. I guess Momma's right, I should have practiced more."

"You made this for me?" I smiled at her, and took her hand. "It's amazing."

She grinned back at me, and her freckled cheeks looked slightly more rosy than usual. "Keep it with you, okay?"

I nodded. "Of course."

"Please be safe," she said earnestly. I felt her squeeze my hand.

Something stirred in me, seeing her that way. The urge to protect her shot through my body so suddenly, it was startling. Just knowing that I would be at the academy, too far away to do anything for her if something happened, was now unbearable.

"If anything goes wrong, tell your father to go to Mithangol," I said.

She tipped her head to the side like she was confused. "Why?"

"My house is empty now, and no one would think to look for you there. Sile knows where it is; he's been there before. My family won't be coming back, and yours might need a place to hide. You'd be safe there. You'll tell him, won't you?"

Beckah nodded, but I saw sadness in her eyes. She squeezed my hand again before she let it go. "Goodbye, Jae."

Behind us, Mavrik landed and started making insistent chirping sounds as he tossed his head. It was time to go. By the time I finally thought about hugging her one last time, I was already sitting on Mavrik's back, trying to find a good way to hold onto his scaly hide. It was way too late then, and I cursed myself all the way back to Mithangol for not thinking of it sooner.

9

CHAPTER NINE

It was dark when we landed in Mithangol. I was sore and exhausted from hanging onto Mavrik's back for dear life the whole way. Dragon scales are not built for comfort at all. I was definitely not looking forward to another long ride without a saddle. The sooner I got some new equipment, the better.

The house looked the same as I'd left it—dark and basically empty except for the furniture I had made myself. As soon as I got inside, I built a fire and started cooking a quick dinner. I ate alone at my kitchen table and thought about Sile and his family the whole time. It was so quiet. There was no life, no happiness in my house like there had been in theirs. No baby noises. No sounds of laughter. It made me miss them a lot. The time I'd spent with them was the first time I'd ever really felt like part of a family. Now that I was by myself again, I realized how alone I felt in this house.

After a hot bath, I started going through Roland's old clothes in his room. His clothes had once been enormous, but now they fit me just right. I was relieved to finally have a decent pair of boots that weren't uncomfortably tight.

I packed up several extra changes of his clothes, belts, and socks into my bag, along with the coins Sile had given me. I took out Beckah's handkerchief and looked at it again, running a thumb over the stitching of the two dragons. It made me smile and think of how much I already missed her. Carefully, I folded it up and tucked it back into my pocket.

It was late by the time I settled into bed. The fire burning low in my bedroom hearth put long shadows across the room. Even though it was peaceful and I was warm and comfortable, I had a hard time falling asleep. Something made me feel restless and uneasy. Then I finally did start to drift off, and I had the worst nightmare of my life.

As soon as my eyes closed, the dream pulled me under like someone had yanked the rug of reality out from under me. It didn't start out bad right away. I dreamt was sitting at the kitchen table in my mother's old house in the war refugee ghetto in the royal city of Halfax. The smell of flowers, plants, and warm fresh earth filled the air and took me back to the only time in my life I had ever really been happy. The rush of familiar sounds and smells made my head spin.

My mom was standing there with her back to me, preening a plant that was growing out of a big clay pot on the kitchen counter. It was a weird-looking plant, not one I'd ever seen growing in Maldobar before. There were huge red and yellow blossoms on it that were as big as my palm. Mom's silver hair was tied up in a braided knot, and I could hear her singing in her native language. It had been so long since I had heard her voice. It put a sharp pain in my chest like someone was twisting a knife in my heart. When I was little, I would have given anything for a dream like this—just so I could see her one more time.

"M-mom?" I tried to speak but my voice cracked with emotion.

She turned around like she was surprised to see me sitting there. Then she smiled, and it left me reeling. I'd missed her so much. Even though I knew it wasn't real, seeing her face was like taking a breath after holding it for all these years.

"Jae? Spirits and Fates! You've gotten so big!" She beamed at me as she wiped her hands on her tattered apron.

I tried to get up. I wanted to run to her and put my arms around her, but I couldn't move. Something held me in place like I was sinking in quicksand. It was a reminder: this wasn't real. It was a dream. It wouldn't last for long.

Her smile started to fade some, and I saw traces of sadness in her eyes. She came closer, just out of my reach, and sat down at the table across from me. "I know it's been hard for you, dulcu."

She spoke with the same heavy accent she'd always had. My mother had struggled with learning the human language, so she'd always mixed in elven words whenever she couldn't remember human ones. She had called me "dulcu," which was like calling someone "sweetheart" or "darling," all the time. I couldn't believe I had almost forgotten that.

There was so much I wanted to ask her. But right then, all I could do was stare at her and try to drink in every detail. I didn't want to forget again. She had her bangs tucked behind her long, pointed ears, and there were little wrinkles in the corners of her diamond-colored eyes. Her heart shaped face was aged, and still beautiful and ethereal looking.

"I'm very proud of you," she said. "You know that, don't you?"

I finally managed to speak. "But I'm a dragonrider now. I'm learning to fight—to kill your people—for the humans. How can you be proud of that?"

She looked sad again. "Some things are not simple because they aren't made to be that way. That is you, too, dulcu. You were not made to be simple, so things will never be easy for you. I'm very sorry for that. I wish I could be there to help you."

Mom stiffened suddenly, and her eyes got wide. She glanced back as though she could hear someone whispering in her ear. I got an extremely bad feeling, like someone was breathing down the back of my neck. It made my skin prickle.

In the corner of the room shadows were starting to gather in a big, boiling mass. They grew larger and darker, growing to climb the walls like inky black vines. The bigger they got, the more the tension in the room rose. It was like someone was dragging their icy fingertips up my spine.

"He knows," my mother whispered. When she looked back at me, I saw fear in her eyes. "You must keep learning, Jaevid. Don't be afraid of what you can do."

"But, Mom," I protested. Somehow I could sense that the dream was about to collapse on itself. "Will I ever see you again? Like this?"

My mom just smiled gently. It was one of those looks only mothers can give.

The dream shifted as the black vines spread, consuming the room and choking out all the light until there was nothing except darkness. I was cold and lost, not sure which way was up or down. It was scary, but what came next was much, much worse.

When the darkness cleared, I was standing on a muddy road in an open valley. At first, I was relieved. After all, the place was beautiful. The sun was shining over rolling hills covered in a blanket of clean, white snow. There were huge mountains crowned with snow on either side of the valley, but they were miles away.

Before me, I could see what looked like a huge forest with a dark tree line that marched off in both directions for miles and miles. It was like standing on the boundary of two completely different worlds. The trees were enormous—about three times the size of a normal tree. The road I was standing on wound away into the distance, snaking along the backs of the snowy hills until the dark forest swallowed it up.

Suddenly, I heard the shrill whinny of a horse. I looked back as a company of horsemen came trotting down the road. There were sixteen of them dressed in shining bronze armor, carrying the banner with the king's golden eagle on it. They rode surrounding a beautiful gilded carriage that was drawn by four white horses with blue ribbons woven into their manes and tails.

They were heading for the forest with their banners fluttering. I tried to step out of their way, but once again, I couldn't move an inch. My feet were stuck and I braced, expecting the carriage and horsemen to plow right into me. Instead, they blurred right through me like I wasn't even there. All I felt was a slight chill. As real as it all seemed on the surface, I realized this was just a dream as well.

The company went on, leaving me behind without a second glance. It was like they couldn't see me at all. I caught a glimpse of one of the guards as he passed—something about him seemed vaguely familiar. I couldn't be sure because his helmet covered most of his face.

As soon as they got past me, a shout went up. The company came to an abrupt halt. From where I was standing, I couldn't clearly see why they'd stopped. I only caught a few glimpses of what looked like a man in a heavy brown cloak, standing right in the middle of the road. Had he been there the whole time? I didn't remember seeing him there before. Immediately, the mere sight of him gave me a cold feeling. The hood of his cloak was pulled down to hide his face, and he didn't move at all.

"Stand aside for his majesty, the King of Maldobar, who seeks peaceful court with those who dwell in the wild forest!" The leader of the guards announced.

I heard a raspy voice begin to chuckle from under the stranger's hood. It gave me a pins and needles sensation in my arms and legs. All my hair stood on end. I didn't know that voice, I was sure of that. But something told me I *should* know it.

"Peaceful? You don't even know the meaning of the word." The stranger sneered. "You human fools. You're all so ignorant, and yet so sure of what you think you know. It's your greatest flaw. But it could be useful. Yes, you will be very useful to me."

I could sense the tension rising. Some of the guards were touching the hilts of their swords. Their horses shifted uneasily.

"Stand aside!" The guard tried again.

The next thing I heard was screaming. Chaos erupted all around me. Horses shrieked in panic and threw their riders off, galloping away in all directions. I saw the shadow of something streaking down from the sky as fast as an arrow. It was huge, although not as big as a dragon. I had never seen any dragon move that fast. The creature was too quick to even be seen clearly, and it made a terrifying screeching sound like the piercing cry of an eagle.

I could smell blood and hear swords clashing, but I was helpless to do anything about it. I couldn't move. I finally saw the man in the brown cloak as he butchered two of the guards through with a sword that looked like it was made out of white wood. The hood covered most of his face, so I only caught a glimpse of his features as he turned past me. I saw his diamond-colored eyes flashing with anger, and a few locks of his platinum-colored hair. His lips curled into a brutal snarl.

He was a Gray elf.

Just meeting his eyes put a stabbing pain in my chest that made me choke. A smothering sense of chaos started bubbling over my brain, twisting my thoughts and making me furious. But as soon as he looked away, the feeling subsided.

The way he fought was unlike anything I had ever seen before, even at Blybrig. He moved like a ghost. Every stroke of his strange white sword was smooth and effortless. In a matter of seconds, he was the only one left standing.

The Gray elf warrior stepped over the broken, slashed-up bodies of the guards with no sign of remorse. He wrenched open the door to the carriage. All I could do was watch in horror as he started dragging out the people hiding inside. The king, a middle-aged man with graying hair, came out fighting. But he didn't last any longer than his guards did.

Panic surged through my body, turning my blood to ice when the Gray elf rammed his sword into the king's chest. The warrior watched the king gasp and die with a burning look of malice in his color-changing eyes.

The warrior dropped the king's dead body into the mud, kicking it aside and going back into the carriage again. I watched him do the same thing to the young queen and her two small children, leaving them all piled there in the sludge as though they were nothing but trash. I had witnessed plenty of horrible things in my life. This was different. This made my whole being cry out for revenge. Nothing about this was right. It was murder—senseless murder!

Then I heard a sound that made my heart stop cold.

One of the guards was back on his feet. It was the one that had looked so familiar to me, though I still couldn't figure out who it was. It seemed like his face was intentionally skewed to hide his identity, but I could still tell that he was fairly young. He stood shakily with his sword in hand, shouting out a challenge to the murderous Gray elf that had just slain the whole royal family in cold blood.

The guard was the only one left alive, and he was bleeding from a deep gash on his leg. His bronze armor was spattered with blood. He could barely stay on his feet. A sense of comradery thrummed through my chest like a surge of heat and energy. More than anything, I wanted to step in and stand beside him. We could both fight and die together, side by side.

The Gray elf warrior turned around slowly, his face still mostly hidden underneath his hood. I could see his mouth. He was smiling wickedly. He spun his white blade over his hand again and again with expert speed, taking slow steps toward the lone guardsman. I was no master swordsman, and even I could tell he was toying with the guard. This wasn't going to end well.

"Aren't you brave?" he hissed with pleasure, like this was all amusing to him. "Tell me, little soldier, just how brave are you? What would you do to save your own life?"

The two men squared off, preparing for a final fight. I could feel my pulse racing. Dread was building up, like hot stones were being stacked on my chest until I could barely breathe.

Something important was about to happen. I didn't understand how, but I *knew* it. The Gray elf started to take his first step, his sword drawn back to strike...

I bolted awake.

I sat up in bed with my mind racing and my pulse still hammering in my ears. I was soaked in a cold sweat. Immediately, I felt sick. I barely made it to the big iron pot by the fireplace before I threw up. When my stomach was empty, my thoughts finally started to clear.

For a long time, I just sat there leaning against the wall. The heat from the coals smoldering in the fireplace was warm against my face, but I was still shivering. I tried to remind myself that it was only a dream. It didn't help at all.

It was so early in the morning that the sun wasn't even up yet. The air was bitter cold, and there were snowflakes falling from the dark sky. I was more exhausted than ever, and I knew I'd never be able to go back to sleep—not with dreams of gore and bloodstained snow still burning in my mind. I needed to get up, move around, and do anything to keep my mind off of that stuff. I couldn't afford to get distracted by nightmares now.

I started to get dressed, pulling on a pair of Roland's old boots and vambraces, two thick wool tunics, heavy canvas pants, and a belt. I clipped my hunting knife to my hip, tied my hair back, and clasped an old traveling cloak around my shoulders. It didn't take me long to pack up the rest of my gear, including the old scimitar I had found in the Roland's trunk. I tucked Beckah's handkerchief into one of my vambraces where I knew it would be safe, and started downstairs.

The snow was falling heavily when I came outside. Mavrik was growling about the cold and flicking his tail as I pushed the barn door open. He stayed hunkered down in the hay, his wings and legs folded up close to his body, watching me as I looked around for something to use as a makeshift saddle. I found a length of rope and I used it to tie my bag onto his back, but there wasn't much else to work with. My safety would depend on Mavrik. It made me extremely anxious. We would be flying higher and further to reach the Devil's Cup, a small crescent-shaped valley where Blybrig Academy sat looking to the western seas. I would have to ride carefully and take things slowly.

It took a few minutes of coaxing to get Mavrik out of the barn. He hated the snow, not that I blamed him. We hadn't been in Saltmarsh for very long, but I was already missing the warmer coastal temperatures, too. Unfortunately, that wasn't the only thing I missed about Saltmarsh.

Once we took off, soaring above the heavy clouds that smothered Mithangol in winter, the air was much clearer. In the distance, the sun was just beginning to rise, and it turned the tops of the clouds a warm pinkish golden color. It looked like a sea of color spread out before us, breaking against the peaks of the Stonegap Mountains that stuck up through the clouds like castle spires. The air was still chilly, and it cut right through all the layers of my clothing. Still, it was good to breathe in the clean, free air.

"Ready to get back to business?" I asked as I gave Mavrik's scaly neck a pat.

Even over the rush of the air humming past us, I knew he would hear me. "I bet Nova's already there waiting for you."

He tilted his head to the side some so he could look back at me with one of his big yellow eyes. He gave a trumpeting roar, and beat his wings harder. We lurched forward with more speed. It made me smile and lean down against his neck. After months of dreading what was waiting for me at Blybrig, now that I was finally going there...I just couldn't wait.

10

CHAPTER TEN

We were already making good time. I used the peaks of the mountains as markers, so I knew exactly which way to fly as we made our way toward Blybrig. As the day wore on, the temperatures on the ground started to rise and the clouds began to clear away. I could see the cliffs and steep ravines dotted with fir trees far below. Everything was still covered in snow. It reminded me of the long, grueling journey through the mountain pass I had made with my father last year. I was more than happy not to be on foot again this year, let alone traveling with Ulric. He wasn't exactly good company.

"I wonder if Felix will even recognize me," I wondered out loud. The air rushing by was so loud I could barely hear my own voice.

Mavrik snorted, and glanced back at me again. In my mind, he showed me an image of when Felix and I had parted ways last year, awkwardly exchanging a few friendly punches on the arm. Felix had been so worried about letting me go back home by myself. He had also spent a lot of time sticking up for me last year, and making sure none of the other students beat me to death when the instructors weren't looking. Boy, was he in for a surprise.

Suddenly, Mavrik's body shuddered underneath me. He went completely tense, all the muscles in his body becoming as solid as stone. I barely had time to brace myself before he snapped his wings in tight against his body and started a frantic dive straight down.

"Stop it! What are you doing?" I shouted at the top of my lungs. I pulled on the knobby spines that ran down his back with all my might, trying to get him to level off again.

Mavrik ignored me. He started making swift, jerking twists to avoid cliffs as we rocketed down toward the earth. Fear burrowed deep into my gut like a cold knife, but I clenched my teeth and tried to flatten out against his neck. Without a saddle to anchor me down, it took everything I had just to hang on.

Then an image flashed across my mind. It was garbled and hazed with frantic color, but I saw it clearly for an instant. I saw the faces of Katty, Bren, and Mr. Crookin, all pale with terror. I saw blood on the snow, and something big closing in for the kill.

Then it made sense. They must have been somewhere far below us on the Stonegap Pass, making their way to Blybrig as well. Mavrik could smell them, even from a few miles away. I felt like an idiot for doubting him. He showed me another flurry of images, and this time I saw the knife in my belt, the scimitar, and the maneuver he wanted to try.

"All right," I muttered as I reached down to pull out the hunting knife. "Get me as close as you can."

Mavrik spun downward, bursting through the last layer of clouds that hugged the lowest parts of the mountains. Rocks and steep cliff sides seemed to appear out of nowhere, so close that a few more inches would have taken my head off.

I saw them a few hundred yards away. Mr. Crookin's wagon was stuck in the deep snow on the side of the road. It looked like it had a broken axel, and the horses were panicking, pawing the air and bucking against their harnesses. Katty was huddled over her father, who was lying motionless on the ground. The snow around them was stained red with blood. Bren was still on his feet, holding a sword at arm's length to keep three big wolves at bay. The wolves were pacing and snapping, looking for the right moment to strike.

Mavrik's thoughts raced across my brain, showing me scenarios and where the other wolves were. He smelled eight in all. I tightened my grip on my knife. The scimitar was old. I wasn't confident it would hold up in a fight, so I decided only to use it as a last resort.

We burst through the heavy fog, and Mavrik let out a bone-rattling roar. It startled the three wolves who were squaring off with Bren, sending them scurrying to the thickets on the side of the road. I knew they would be back.

I gathered my courage, and waited until the very last second. The ground rushed up, and Mavrik flared his wings in the blink of an eye. He stretched out his hind legs, touching down for only a flash of a moment before kicking skyward again.

As Mavrik touched the earth—I jumped off his back. I hit the ground and dropped into a roll so that the impact didn't break my legs. When I got up, my head was spinning and it took a second to get my bearings.

Someone behind me shouted, "It's a dragonrider!"

I spun, spotting Bren first because he was standing closest to me. He was still armed with a sword. Then I locked eyes with Katty. It only lasted a second or two, but the minute she saw my face, I knew she recognized me.

"Look out!" Bren shouted again.

I turned around, just in time to see fangs flashing in my face. A wolf lunged at me, and I didn't hesitate. All that training with Sile clicked into my brain instantly. I dove, spinning to dodge the wolf's attack, and swinging around to drive my hunting knife into the back of the animal's neck. The wolf yelped, whined, and collapsed onto the snow.

"On your left!" Bren was standing with his back up against mine, giving us a circle of protection to watch on all sides.

The mountain wolves closed in, emerging from the thickets like ghosts. There were seven in all, each one easily two hundred pounds. They encircled us, pacing around to look for the perfect opening to make an easy kill. They were wild with rage, lashing out recklessly like they were rabid. Something about it didn't seem right. I had never heard of wolves acting this way, and when I looked them in the eyes, I got a sick feeling that scrambled my thoughts. It made it impossible to try to speak to them like I had with other animals.

Bren caught one in the leg with his sword, and jumped on it quickly to drive his blade through its ribs before it could get away. I had the smaller weapon, so I knew I would have to get up close and personal. I was prepared for that.

A big wolf lunged at my front while another came from the side. I managed to throw my knife, hitting the first one right between the eyes. It dropped to the snow immediately and didn't move again. The second one hit me like a brick wall. I felt its jaws clamp onto my thick leather vambrace, beginning to jerk and flail like it wanted to rip my arm off. Its teeth couldn't touch my skin because of the thick leather, and I quickly reached for my scimitar.

The instant the blade left the sheath, it filled the air with a metallic humming sound. I was only barely aware of it, like a faint chime on the wind. But all of a sudden, the wolf let me go. Immediately it started backing away with its ears pressed back, whining like it was in pain. I was stunned, staring at the cowering creature.

Then another wolf hit me from behind. I felt its jaws on my shoulder, tearing at the layers of my clothes to get to my skin. Immediately, I threw myself backwards with all my strength and hit the ground so my weight bore down on the wolf, pinning it underneath me. I spun the scimitar in my hands, jabbing it backwards and catching the beast in the stomach. It shrieked in pain and finally went limp.

Looking up from where I was sitting in the snow, I saw the eyes of three big wolves still standing. They started closing in. Bren was right next to me, shaking like he was terrified but still holding his sword. He kept looking over at me as though he expected me to give him orders.

Suddenly, an image flashed across my mind.

"Get down!" I yelled at the top of my lungs. I threw myself at Bren, grabbing him from behind and wrestling him to the ground a second before it hit.

I heard Mavrik's roar, the wind buzzing over his scaly hide, and the sound of him breathing flame. I felt the heat of it on the back of my neck, singing a few hairs as he passed right over us. When I looked up again, Mavrik had disappeared back into the fog, but the wolves were nothing but three mounds of burning fur in the middle of a big puddle of sticky venom.

It was over. Everything was strangely quiet, except for the popping of the flames. The wolves lay motionless all around us, and I let Bren up as I staggered back to my feet. He stared at me with a mixture of shock, horror, and surprise. I was about to explain, but another sound made us both turn. We raised our blades, ready to fight.

But it wasn't a wolf this time.

What came out of the woods looked like some kind of cat. It was huge, as big as a fully-grown bear, and covered in shaggy silver fur. It had a bobbed tail, big muscular legs, and two long fangs that dripped down below its jaws. It stalked toward us with its head low, snarling with rage.

"W-what is that?" I heard Bren whisper from beside me.

I was too stunned to answer.

Its blue eyes were focused right on me, like it was looking right into my soul. When I looked back, it was as though I could feel chaos boiling inside the creature. It was the same feeling the wolves had given me, and I couldn't figure out why. It was a wild, angry, primal chaos. It didn't have any sense of right or wrong. It only craved violence and blood. I knew I had experienced this kind of reckless fury before, I just couldn't remember where. I didn't have time to think about it then.

Slowly, I reached a hand out toward Bren. "The sword," I said. "Give it to me."

Bren didn't argue. I felt him put the hilt of the sword in my hand. I squeezed it hard.

"Now move away. Don't look into its eyes," I told him, keeping my own gaze fixed upon the huge silver cat. I couldn't explain why, somehow I knew it was only interested in me. This was personal.

I stepped toward the beast, meeting it in the snow with Bren's sword in one hand, and my scimitar in the other. I gripped both weapons and squinted into the cold mountain wind, watching as the animal moved with me. It stepped when I did, and smelled the air. I could feel it looking me over, searching for a weakness.

I got no warning. The cat charged before I even had a chance to try to speak to it. I wanted to talk it down, to settle things without spilling any more blood, but now that option was completely off the table. The cat sprang toward me as fast as a bolt of lightning. I saw its jaws opened wide, rows of jagged fangs ready for the kill. There wasn't time to hesitate. I had one chance, and one plan.

I dove toward it.

Behind me, Katty screamed.

My body moved, acting on pure instinct. I wasn't even afraid. I ran toward the cat and dropped to my knees, skidding under its body and swinging both blades out wide to strike its legs.

The beast howled in pain. I felt the impact as the cat's huge body collapsed into the snow. It flailed around on the ground, snarling and snapping as I got back on my feet.

Even when I stood over the cat, it was still trying to get to me. It couldn't even move its hind legs anymore, since I'd nearly cut them off, but its rage was so intense that it wouldn't surrender. For whatever reason, the cat *needed* to kill me. It was like some kind of crazed sickness. I could feel that boiling wrath starting to leak into my own mind, just by looking at the cat. Something about it disgusted me beyond words.

I jabbed my scimitar into the animal's heart. Immediately, it went still and that sick feeling of fury drained out of the air. I stood there, watching the last few breaths of life leave its body, and I realized today was the first time I had ever killed anything with my own hands. I wasn't necessarily proud of that. I didn't want to kill anything, but there wasn't any other choice.

Everything was quiet again. Slowly, I turned around to look at Bren and the others. They were all staring back at me with wide eyes. Even Mr. Crookin looked completely dumbstruck. I bowed my head some, and sheathed my scimitar.

Behind me, I heard the sound of wing beats and felt the ground flinch as Mavrik landed. He let out a deep growl, and sent an image into my mind that made my hands curl up into fists. He was reminding me that these people might not be my friends.

I looked straight at Bren. He looked about eighteen. His black hair was pulled back into a short ponytail like before, and his features were soft and almost babyish. His dark eyes stared at me with a mixture of awe and relief. He wasn't very tall, but he was stocky and must have been pretty strong. He was a blacksmith's apprentice, after all.

I thought about what he had done during the fight. He'd obeyed my every order, and fought bravely at my side. It was strange, but out of the three of them, I got the feeling he was the one I could trust the most.

"It's all right," I said. "He's fine."

Bren blinked as though he were trying to make sure he wasn't dreaming. "Y-you sure about that? He's snarling at me."

"I wasn't talking to you." I glanced back at Mavrik, who was still swishing his tail angrily. He hadn't forgotten what had happened the last time I saw Katty and

Bren together. Seeing them flirting with each other had filled me with anger and confusion before. But when I looked at them now, something was different. Without speaking, I tried to tell him that.

I locked gazes with Katty again and I felt... nothing. No pain. No resentment or anger. I wasn't sure if that was a good thing or a bad thing.

"The dragon understands you?" Bren still looked amazed.

I nodded and handed Bren his sword back. So much for keeping my special ability a secret. "Usually he listens to me. I'm not making any promises, though. You might want to keep your distance."

Strolling over to one of the dead wolves, I put my boot on its neck and pulled my knife out of its head. That simple hunting knife was turning out to be awfully handy. It had saved my life more than once now. It was like a good luck charm.

I could feel Katty staring at me as I walked toward where she was sitting in the snow. She was holding her father's head in her lap. It was hard to tell if she was happy, sad, angry, or just confused. Maybe she was trying to process the situation. Or maybe she was trying to figure out how I had grown almost two feet taller in a few weeks.

Mr. Crookin was conscious, but I could tell he was in a lot of pain. I saw right away where he had been bitten by one of the wolves. The bite was deep, and his leg was bleeding badly. I used my knife to cut away his pant leg to get a better look. Even though my medical training wasn't very extensive, I knew I could treat something like this. At least, I could make sure he wouldn't bleed to death before they made it to Blybrig.

"Get me a belt, or a strap. Something to stop the bleeding," I ordered.

"Right!" Bren ran off obediently.

I tried to smile at Mr. Crookin, who was staring at me with a glazed look in his eyes. He had snowflakes in his bushy beard, and even from that distance I could smell the scent of scorched metal on his clothes. It brought back memories of being in the forge when Katty and I were younger.

"I'll get you fixed up. You can be back on the road by morning. They'll be able to see to it properly at the infirmary," I told him. Then I looked at Katty. It made her flinch, as though she were afraid of me. "Try to get him into the back of the wagon. We need to move away from here. The smell of blood might bring other predators."

She stared and didn't say a word. It was really uncomfortable.

I left them to retrieve my bag from Mavrik's back. He snorted at me when I came close, flashing me a look that I understood even without the visual aid in my mind; an image of the last time I'd talked to Katty. We had argued, and it hadn't ended well. I wasn't the sharpest person when it came to girls, but even I could tell things still weren't okay between us.

"I know, I know," I muttered as I slung my travel bag over my shoulder. "I'm not exactly thrilled about it either, you know. But I can be civilized. Hopefully she can, too. Besides, I'm not going to let Mr. Crookin bleed to death. So just stay close, okay? Make sure we don't get any more surprise guests. And don't eat Bren."

Mavrik chirped at me and took off, stirring up the snow as he went. When it settled, I found myself staring at the huge cat's dead body again. All my life, I'd heard of animals like this living deep in the mountains. This was the first time I had ever actually seen one, though. Even when I traveled on the same path through the mountains alone with my father last year, we hadn't seen anything like this. Ulric always kept a fire going when we made camp. He'd told me once that fire and the smell of humans was enough to keep anything dangerous away. These kinds of animals weren't used to the smells and sounds of people.

I stared down at the cat's body and remembered the sense of chaos that had come off of it. Something about it wasn't right. I just couldn't figure out what.

When I climbed into the back of the covered wagon, Mr. Crookin was talking quietly with his daughter. I couldn't hear exactly what he said, but I know I heard him mention my name a few times. As I approached them, they both went silent and stared up at me. It made things even more awkward.

Katty helped her father into one of the small beds, and started taking his boots off. She scooted as far away from me as she possibly could when I came over and put my bag down. I tried not to pay her any attention. In such close quarters, it was difficult. She was acting like I might decide to hit her or something, even though I had never once tried to hurt her in my life. I knew better than to ever raise a hand against a girl. I'd seen my father do it enough times to understand no good came of it.

I took out my small first aid box, and carefully laid out all the tools, gauze, and salve I would need. I didn't have much. This kit was supposed to be for emergencies. I wondered if I should try healing him the same way I had healed Sile's wife. But I quickly shook those thoughts from my mind; I'd already revealed one secret today. I wasn't even sure I could trust these people anymore. And compared to talking to dragons and animals, healing someone with my touch was bound to raise a few eyebrows. It might even get me in serious trouble if someone at Blybrig found out.

"Bring hot water," I told Katty. "I have to sterilize the needle before I can start."

She still didn't speak to me. She got up, and left the wagon without a single word. Even though I wanted to ignore her, I couldn't help but watch her go. She had changed so much since last year. Sure, she was beautiful, but her personality was totally different. I wasn't sure I liked it. She was like a stranger to me now.

"She's a stubborn girl," Mr. Crookin said in his gruff voice. I guess he felt bad about the cold way she was treating me.

"It's fine." I started inspecting his wound, trying to wipe away the blood so I could see where I needed to stitch.

Mr. Crookin made a snorting noise. "Well, it seems you haven't changed much after all," he said. "You know, you might do better in life if you got angry every now and then. Especially when people deserve it."

I didn't answer.

Bren came in suddenly, holding a leather belt out to me. "Here. This is what you wanted, right? We got a small fire going outside using some of that dragon venom. We should have hot water soon." He sat down nearby, and I noticed that he couldn't even look at the wound without his face getting pasty white. The sight of blood must have made him sick.

I used the belt to make a tourniquet. When Katty came in lugging a pot of steaming hot water, I sterilized the needle and used a wet washcloth to clean the wound. Then I started sewing it shut. I have to give Mr. Crookin some credit for being a tough old man. He didn't flinch even once. When I finished, I smeared some smelly herbal salve over the wound so it wouldn't get infected. Finally, I wrapped it in a few layers of gauze.

"That should hold you for a few days." I smiled at Mr. Crookin as I finished bandaging his leg. "Sorry if it hurt. This was my first time treating a real wound."

Mr. Crookin nodded in thanks. "You did fine, boy."

"I checked the axel, Master Crookin." Bren piped up suddenly. He was looking better now that the bloody part was over. "It's not broken. It came out of line. If we can readjust it, then we could get back underway."

"I'll help you. He shouldn't move around too much. It might pull the stitches out." I offered as I packed up my first aid kit and put it back in my bag. "Then I'll be out of your way."

Bren frowned like he was disappointed. He looked toward Katty as though he hoped she would say something to stop me. She didn't. She still refused to speak while I was there.

"At least let us feed you a meal before you go," Bren insisted. "You saved our lives. Those wolves came out of nowhere. I've never seen them attack a wagon like that."

I shook my head. "Neither have I."

"And then the mountain cat." Bren was starting to sound nervous. "It's just like those guards said..."

"Guards?" I asked.

Bren's expression was grim. He fidgeted with his hands while he started to explain. "We passed a few guardsmen as we were leaving Mithangol. They warned us to be careful. There are rumors spreading throughout the kingdom of wild animals going crazy like this. They're attacking people for no reason. And not only predators like wolves and mountain cats. Peaceful animals like deer are doing it, too."

His story sounded a little too unbelievable. I couldn't visualize a herd of deer attacking anyone. Deer were supposed to be peaceful, timid animals. Still, my mind kept racing back to that feeling of chaos I'd felt from the wolves and the huge cat. If the deer were possessed by that same kind of rage, then they might actually do something like that. It was terrifying to think that it might really be some kind of sickness that was spreading through the kingdom. I dreaded to think of what would happen if people started getting infected.

"I'll help you fix the wagon," I decided out loud. "And stay for dinner, if you're sure that's what you want."

Bren smiled and stood. "Okay!" He still had a lot of energy for someone who'd just been in a fight for his life.

I left my bag in the wagon and went out into the snow with him. While he unhitched the horses, I looked around for a good, sturdy tree branch we could use to lift the wagon long enough to reposition the wheel axel. Lucky for us, the wagon wasn't very big. It was heavy, though, thanks to all the tools and supplies inside.

Once the horses were clear, Bren crawled under the wagon and got ready to move the axel back into place while I used the long branch to wedge under the wagon and lift it. It was incredibly heavy. My arms were shaking as I pushed down on the branch and tried to keep it steady. Thankfully, it only needed to be raised a few inches. Bren wiggled the long metal axel back and forth, trying to position it.

Then something cracked.

Bren yelled as the branch snapped in half and the weight of the wagon started to collapse down on top of him. I reacted in the blink of an eye. I grabbed the wagon right under the wheel and lifted with all my strength. My arms ached. My back creaked. The full weight of the wagon seemed to be bearing down on me, but I couldn't let it fall or Bren would be crushed.

"Hurry and get out!" I yelled. My fingers were starting to slip. I could feel the wood scraping on my skin, setting my palms on fire. It was like trying to hold up a small house with my bare hands.

"No!" Bren shouted back. "I-I've almost got it!" I heard him frantically trying to wiggle the axel again.

"You idiot! Do you want to die? I can't hold it!" I started to yell again. My fingers were definitely sliding. I knew I had maybe three more seconds left before I lost my grip.

Suddenly, the load lessened. Katty appeared right beside me out of nowhere, helping me hold the wagon up. She was a girl, but she had always been tough. Apparently now that she'd been working with her father in the forge, she was even stronger. She helped hold the weight of the wagon long enough for me to get a better grip.

"Got it!" Bren immediately scrambled out from under the wagon. I dropped the weight back onto the axel, and the wagon settled with a groan.

"You almost got crushed, you know." I grumbled, trying to catch my breath and watching as Bren dusted the snow off his clothes. My fingers were still throbbing.

"Lucky for me you caught it, huh?" He smiled cheerfully. I was starting to wonder if he was dumb or something. "Anyway, we can hitch the horses back up now. Good work!"

I glanced sideways at Katty. She was actually smiling back at him. Seeing her in a good mood caught me off guard. Bren strolled away to fetch the horses, and she stood there beside me, shaking her head.

"I know what you're thinking," she said. I was stunned that she was actually talking to me. "No, he isn't stupid. He's just a happy person. Nothing ever gets him down. And I like him that way."

I crossed my arms and shrugged. "Stupid or not, I suppose he does seem like a nice guy." I couldn't help but smile a little myself.

"Are your hands okay?" she asked. "You could have broken your back like that, you know."

Her concern surprised me even more. I glanced down at my fingers. "Sore. Maybe a little bruised. But fine."

She was quiet again. I watched as she helped Bren fasten the horses back to the wagon. We worked together again to get the heavy wagon out of the snow and back onto the side of the road. It took almost an hour because of how far into the deep drifts the wagon had gone. But eventually, we got underway.

Katty and Bren sat on the driver's seat next to each other. From inside the wagon, I could hear them talking and laughing together. I sat on the floor beside some crates of raw metal slabs, feeling awkward and out of place again. I didn't like Katty that way anymore, but I still didn't like the feeling I got when I saw them together. It reminded me of how she had dismissed me because I was a halfbreed. That still hurt to think about. In fact, it hurt way worse than being rejected just because she didn't like me that way.

"I hear that instructor of yours, Sile Derrick, has been relieved of his duties as a dragonrider." Mr. Crookin was lying on his bed. Hearing his voice made me jump a little because I thought he was asleep.

"Yeah," I answered. "He got hurt last year. He can't ride anymore."

"Convenient. But it's a good thing." Mr. Crookin made a thoughtful, grumbling sound like a sleepy old bear. "Rumor is that he's a dead man walking. Any man who goes into that wicked forest and comes back alive and unharmed must have some kind of dark magic in him. That kind of thing always ends in bloodshed. It's better if he doesn't take anyone else down with him."

I sat up a little. "What do you mean? Wicked forest...are you talking about Luntharda? Sile has been there?"

Mr. Crookin let out a throaty, coughing noise. "Yes, well, that's the rumor. It was years ago, not long after the war first began. They say he deserted his fellow riders on the eve of battle and went into the forest alone, only to return three days later completely untouched. Either he has the luck of the gods, or there is something wicked in him, as well. Luntharda takes no prisoners. It wouldn't simply let a human man go like that."

I was so surprised that I sat there, staring at Mr. Crookin while the wagon jostled and bounced. Sile had never said a word about this to me before. I wondered if Felix even knew about it.

Thoughts were still racing through my brain when Mr. Crookin added, "I worried he might be trying to work a bit of that dark magic on you. It's strange that he took such a liking to you. That forest has already fouled your blood, but you do seem to have a decent heart in spite of that. My wife insists that you're a good boy."

I still couldn't say a word. My brain was stuck on the news that Sile had gone into Luntharda all alone and yet somehow he'd survived. Last year, I had done a lot of reading about Luntharda. There were more horrible things in that forest than I could even count. Imaging that Sile had gone into the forest alone and survived—let alone walked away from it without a single scratch—didn't seem possible. It had to be a rumor.

"Do you love my girl?" Mr. Crookin asked suddenly.

I snapped out of my daze. "S-sir?"

"Katalina. My daughter. Are you in love with her?" he asked again.

I swallowed uncomfortably. Mr. Crookin had never spoken to me this much before, and how I felt about his daughter was the last thing in the world I wanted to discuss with him. Still, I decided it was best to give him an honest answer. "No. Maybe I did love her once, a little. But not anymore." My throat was stiff with embarrassment.

Mr. Crookin was quiet then. I thought maybe he was trying to decide what to say, or that he might be offended by my answer. Then I heard him start to snore. I slumped back against the side of a crate, and let out a sigh of relief.

I glanced back toward the front of the wagon where Katty and Bren were sitting side-by-side on the driver's seat. I couldn't help but wonder why Mr. Crookin had asked me that all of a sudden. Just by the way she blushed and smiled at Bren, it was obvious that she liked him, not me. She'd never been that way around me. At least, if she had, I'd never noticed it before.

The fact that Bren wasn't such a bad person was still sinking in. Part of me had been hoping he would turn out to be a jerk because then it would be a lot easier to hate him. He was so cheerful all the time it seemed like he might have brain damage. I could tell he liked Katty a lot, too. They seemed happy together, and that didn't upset me like it had before. I didn't love her. She was just a memory. If they could be happy together, then I could be happy for them.

For some reason, the only person I could think about at that moment was Beckah. I reached into my vambrace and took out the handkerchief she'd made for me. I ran my fingers over the stitching of the two dragons, a black one and a blue one. Mavrik and Icarus. The more I thought about her, the more I realized I missed her. It made me smile.

Then I noticed Katty was turned around in her seat. She was staring right at me. Her eyes were locked on the handkerchief I was holding ...

... and for whatever reason, she looked absolutely furious.

11

CHAPTER ELEVEN

We stopped after nightfall and made a small campfire. Mr. Crookin was sound asleep. He wasn't running a fever, so for now it seemed like he would be all right. Bren and Katty were worried about him, and I tried my best to assure them that he was probably exhausted from so much blood loss. It was better to let him rest for now.

Bren and I sat by the fire while Katty prepared food for us. She threw together a simple stew with dried meat and vegetables in a big iron pot. It smelled so good, and I was starving. I didn't hold back my appetite. After three big bowls and a small loaf of bread, I finally sat back and sighed.

"You were hungry, huh?" Bren chuckled.

I blushed. "Yeah, I guess so."

"You know, I had a totally different picture of you in my head." Bren kept talking between bites of stew. "You don't look at all the way Katty described you. It's great to finally meet you."

I saw Katty's shoulders flinch slightly, but she didn't look up at us. She kept staring straight down into her own bowl.

If this conversation was making her uncomfortable, Bren was totally oblivious to it. "You're so tall! I swear, you look like you should be in your twenties."

"Actually, I'll be seventeen soon," I answered.

"Geez! I can't believe you're younger than me!" Bren laughed and grinned. "And you're a dragonrider. That is *so* awesome. I'm jealous! I bet you get a ton of love letters, huh? I swear, if anyone even mentions dragonriders, girls swoon all over the place. It must be nice to be so popular."

Immediately, the atmosphere became tense and awkward again. Out of the corner of my eye, I watched Katty. She had stopped eating, and was squeezing her spoon in her fist until her knuckles were white.

I swallowed hard, and looked down at the tops of my boots. "Not exactly."

Bren looked confused. "Why not?"

I didn't want to answer. How could he not know? Was he really that dense? I was a halfbreed—it didn't matter what job I had. Women would continue to treat me the same way Katty had. I would never be good enough. I would always be disgusting to them. I couldn't believe Bren didn't realize that.

"Ah, I get it," he said suddenly, like it was all clear to him now. "You're old fashioned! The romantic type, right? So then there's just one special girl. What's she like?"

For some reason, I was blushing like crazy. I kept staring down at the ground, trying to decide how to change the subject. I didn't know how to describe to anyone else how Beckah made me feel, and I didn't want to try. Not in front of these people.

Before I could answer, Katty stood up. "You're both idiots. This is a stupid conversation." She slammed her bowl down on the ground and stormed away from the campfire. Without another word, she disappeared into the back of the wagon.

Her sudden reaction left me in shock. For a few minutes, Bren and I sat there in stunned silence. Katty hadn't even finished her dinner. It didn't look like she was coming back for it, either.

"Sorry about that," Bren mumbled with a concerned frown. "I always do that."

"Do what?" I wasn't sure what he meant.

He sighed. "Say stuff without thinking. I guess I shouldn't bring that kind of thing up in front of her. I know you two had some kind of a relationship, right? She always told me it was nothing. She said you were more like a little brother to her. I didn't think she would care."

Even though I was totally embarrassed, I tried not to let it show. I shrugged, and forced a smile. I didn't want him to feel bad. It wasn't his fault, anyway. "It's okay. Don't worry about it."

"I should have told you already," he said. "Thanks for saving us today. I can make swords all day long, but when it comes to fighting... I guess I've never been good at that kind of thing. I was so relieved when you showed up."

Bren reached over to shake my hand, and I caught myself hesitating. People didn't thank me for stuff like that very often. Even Sile, after going through so much last year to save his life from being sacrificed by the Lord General, had just growled angrily that I shouldn't risk myself for his sake.

"It's my duty as a dragonrider to fight and protect citizens. You don't have to thank me." I finally shook his hand, and we exchanged a smile.

"That reminds me." He perked up suddenly, pointing to the scimitar at my hip. "Can I see your weapon? I noticed it before, but I couldn't get a good look."

I unbuckled the scimitar from my belt and handed it over to him. "It's pretty old and beat up." I almost felt like I should apologize for that, since he was a blacksmith. He was bound to notice how worn and dull it was. It probably looked like I hadn't taken care of it.

"Wow," he breathed in awe as he looked over the scabbard. I saw his eyes grow wider. He handled it carefully, looking over the details on the hilt and blade. "I've never seen anything like this before."

His reaction confused me. Sure, it had an intricate design on it, but it was so beat up you'd barely notice. "What do you mean?"

Bren scooted a little closer so he could show me. "Well, look here. The shape of it means it was definitely made by a human. Humans always make blades in this style. They're straight and slender. You can see the blade is only slightly curved, right?"

I nodded. It was definitely a scimitar, but the curve was gradual and elegant, rather than severe and dramatic.

"Elves always make their blades leaf-shaped. And they never put cross-guards on it, like this one. So whoever made this blade was definitely a human." He turned it over, brushing his fingers over the faded designs on the hilt and pommel. "Look here, you can see words used to be engraved on the blade itself. Humans rarely do that. Not unless it belonged to a very important family. And the stag," he hesitated. "The stag is the emblem of the Gray elf royal family. Kind of like our king uses the eagle as his symbol. I've never seen the stag on a blade before. Elves are very possessive of their weapons, you know. Very few of them ever fall into human hands."

I hadn't noticed the words engraved on the blade itself before. They were so faint, almost rubbed down until they were completely gone. I couldn't make out what they said. The more he talked, the more I started to understand why he was so amazed by this scimitar. It was stranger than I'd ever realized.

"So maybe it was a human blacksmith that made this scimitar." Bren was almost whispering now. "But it looks like it was made it for an elf. Why else put that stag on it? I've been studying weaponry and armor my entire life. I've studied every style and method of making all kinds of weapons, and I've never heard of a blade like this before. Look at all the details and effort they put in to make it look like the perfect blend of human and elven design. It's incredible! Where did you get it?"

I cringed. I didn't want to tell him I'd taken it from my brother's belongings. "Well, I think it's some kind of family heirloom. I found it buried at the bottom of a trunk in my father's house."

"It's a shame you don't know anything else about it. I bet it has quite a history." Bren started to hand the scimitar back to me. Then he stopped. His eyes met mine directly. "Let me fix it for you. You know, as a way of saying thanks for saving my life today. I can repair the damage and make it look like new again."

"I-I can't let you do something like that for free," I stammered. "That kind of thing is usually expensive, right?"

"I want to!" He started insisting. "Besides, I haven't made a name for myself as a blacksmith yet, so I need all the practice I can get. And I promise, I'm very good with swords and armor. I won't mess it up."

His mind was made up, and I decided it was probably best not to try to talk him out of it. He seemed determined. So I smiled and nodded in thanks. "I appreciate it."

Bren grinned from ear to ear. "Great! I'll have it finished for you before we leave Blybrig, I promise."

"I'd ask about hiring you to make me some new armor, but I don't want to cause any more problems between you and Katty," I said. "Seems like she's had enough of me to last her a lifetime."

His smile faltered a little, and he sighed loudly again. "She's hard to understand sometimes. It's too late for me, though. I'm already in love with her."

I didn't know what to say. He was so honest about everything; it was kind of intimidating. I shifted uncomfortably, and looked up at the dark sky. "I should get going before the sun rises."

"You're sure you don't want to rest here for the night?" Bren gave me a concerned look. "It's late. You've got to be tired after what happened today."

Honestly, I should have been about to drop. I hadn't slept well in days. Instead, just knowing I was this close to Blybrig made my head buzz with energy. And thinking about what Mr. Crookin had told me about Sile didn't help either. I was restless. I knew I wouldn't be able to sleep now, even if I tried.

I smirked at him and gave him a thumbs up. "I'm fine. See you in a few days. Try not to get eaten by anything."

Bren smiled back at me, and gave me a thumbs up in return. "May you have safe travels, dragonrider."

I GATHERED UP MY BAG AND LEFT THE CAMP AS QUICKLY AS POSSIBLE. MAVRIK and I took off into the midnight sky, leaving the ground far below. Once we broke the cloud cover again, the heavens opened up overhead. The moonlight was so bright. It washed over everything, making the world seem like it was made out of platinum. We chased the shooting stars, skimming the tops of the clouds and racing toward the dawn.

As the sun began to rise and turn the horizon soft shades of pink, I got my first look at the Devil's Cup since last year. It put a big smile on my face right away. I could sense Mavrik's excitement, too. He let out a booming roar as we started our descent down toward the valley.

It was early in spring, but all the prickly plants and cacti were already in full bloom. They brought an unnatural amount of color to a place that was usually nothing but hot, arid desert. In the very middle of the crescent-shaped valley, Blybrig Academy stood proud. I could see the sunlight glinting off the roof of the breaking dome, the place where I had first met Mavrik. I saw the Roost, crowded with dragons and riders like always.

I was so busy looking down I forgot to look up. A sudden roar almost made me have a heart attack. Nova swept in beside us, chirping a greeting to Mavrik. She was the big, beautiful female dragon that belonged to Felix. Her coppery colored scales gleamed with patterns like a jungle snake.

Her saddle was empty, and I reached down to pat Mavrik's neck to get his attention. "Where's Felix?"

Mavrik chattered to Nova, who roared in reply and veered away, sailing through the sky down toward the academy. Mavrik sent me a mental picture of the student dormitory. I guessed that Nova was just out exploring while Felix was getting settled into our room.

"Well, let's hurry then!" I patted his scaly neck again, and he growled in agreement.

Mavrik was eager to join Nova. When we finally landed outside the academy, he barely gave me enough time to untie my bag from his back before he was taking off again to chase her through the clouds. The burst of wind off his wings made me stagger back. I tripped over my own feet and landed on my rear end. Mavrik didn't care. He was too busy nipping playfully at Nova's tail.

"Flirt!" I yelled after him.

He didn't answer.

I got up, dusting the dirt off my pants and slinging my bag over one shoulder. Suddenly I heard a familiar voice from behind me.

"Riding in bareback. That's a first." My new instructor, Lieutenant Jace Rordin, was standing right inside the academy's front gates in full armor. By the way he was glaring at me, anyone else would have thought he was about to chew my head off... but that was the way Jace looked at everyone. I'd never seen him smile.

"Trying to show off?" he growled.

I stopped and saluted him by putting a fist across my heart and bowing slightly. "Almost dying every time he decides to take a steep turn isn't showing off, sir."

Jace snorted. His eyes scanned me over from head to toe. That's when I realized he actually had to look *up* to meet my gaze now. I was taller than him. He still had a much stockier build, but this was definitely new.

"What happened to you?" I could sense him still sizing me up.

I shrugged, and it was hard not to smile. "A lot. It's kind of hard to explain."

"Humph." He just scoffed and turned away, walking ahead of me into the academy. "Well, at least I won't have to worry about someone accidentally stepping on you during morning drills anymore. I was getting tired of scraping you off the bottom of everyone else's boots."

"Yes, sir." I decided this was probably Jace's attempt at being happy for me.

"Go ahead and get settled into your room. Third floor this time. That sidekick of yours already picked up your books and maps." He started barking orders at me right away. "See that you get all your equipment on rush order. You need to be fully outfitted when training starts."

"Yes, sir," I repeated.

"Morning drills start at dawn on the first day of training. You don't have a saddle, so I don't expect you to fly drills until then. But I better see you working on your ground combat maneuvers. Have that friend of yours help you." He went on and on. For some reason, it was a huge relief to have someone breathing down my neck, growling orders at me again. It was familiar, and it put my nerves at ease.

"Yes, sir. Thank you, sir." I stopped to salute him again.

He gave me a cold look. "What are you thanking me for, avian?"

"I-I guess for not treating me any differently," I stammered. "You know, because I look like this now."

Jace frowned. "Why would I treat you any differently? I don't care if you have six eyes and hooves for feet. You better have your butt in that saddle as soon as possible, understood? No excuses."

I nodded and turned toward the dormitory. Once I had my back to him, I couldn't keep from smiling anymore; it was *so* good to be back. The world made more sense here. I knew what I had to do, where I was supposed to be, and what was expected of me. That was the best kind of therapy a man could ask for.

I walked past the armories on the way to the student dormitory. Some of the blacksmiths and tackmasters were already there, heating up their forges and taking orders for saddles and gear. I knew I needed to get back there soon and place my orders so my equipment would be ready before training started. I didn't have any time to waste.

I tried not to look for my father. He'd moved to a different city, but I knew he would still come back to Blybrig for spring. It was when he usually made most of his money. Thankfully, I didn't see Ulric anywhere as I passed. It made me nervous to even think about running into him. I wasn't sure how he'd treat me now that he'd basically disowned me.

Groups of other boys were hanging around outside the student dormitory when I walked up to the door. They were fledglings, I guessed, and they stared at me with wide eyes as I went by. I was used to being stared at like that, but it almost seemed like those boys were actually afraid of me. Beckah had seemed scared of me, too, at first. I wondered if Felix would act like that.

The dining hall on the first floor was just how I remembered. It always smelled like fresh bread in there. I made a mental note to stop back by for a late breakfast as soon as I could. As I went up the stairs, I passed the second floor where I'd shared a room with Felix last year. There were more fledgling students clambering in the hall, looking for their names written on the doors. It brought back a lot of memories.

The third floor was much quieter. Only a few other avians were hanging out in the hallway, but I didn't recognize any of them. They were wearing a different style uniform than I had worn last year, and some of them had golden stripes stitched onto their shoulders. I wondered what that meant. I'd never noticed it before. Last year, my only focus had been survival, so a lot of things had just passed right under my nose.

My stomach started twisting into nervous knots as I walked down the hall, looking for my name on the placards that were nailed to all the doors. Each one had the name of an instructor and the names of his three students below it. Last year, we had only been in pairs of two. But the avian class was much bigger, so I assumed each instructor probably had to take on an extra student.

When I finally found the placard with my name, I stopped dead in my tracks. Shock hit me like a brick to the temple as I read the names carved into the placard over and over:

6
Sn. Lt. Rordin
Jaevid Broadfeather
Lord Felix Farrow
Lord Lyon Cromwell

All I could do was stare at it for a minute or two. I blinked and leaned closer to the door. I was seriously hoping my eyes were playing tricks on me. That couldn't be Lyon's name. Lyon Cromwell was going to be teamed up with us? Was this some kind of sick joke? Lyon had betrayed us not once or twice, but *three* times last year. He was a coward and a traitor. He'd also used me like his personal punching bag a few times. I wasn't even sure how he'd managed to get away with his betrayal and still be in the academy at all. He'd vanished right after he abandoned us to be mauled by Icarus and the Lord General, and as far as I knew, no one had said a word about where he went.

I started to get queasy and angry all at the same time. Then the door opened and smacked me right in the face. I dropped my bag and staggered back, holding my nose.

"Whoops!" A familiar voice was laughing from the other side of the door.

Felix stuck his head out of the room, grinning from ear to ear the same way he always did when he was up to something. "Sorry! Didn't see you there, man."

I stared at him. He hadn't changed much at all. His hair was a little longer, but it was still that same dark golden color. His wavy bangs swept across his forehead, and his light brown eyes glinted with mischief. He was looking back and forth down the hall like he was waiting for someone.

"Hey, if you see a little halfbreed coming this way, let me know, will you? Just whistle or something. I've got a bucket of water set up over the door and—"

"Felix!" I put my hand down and glared at him.

"Do I know you?" I watched him blink at me like he was confused. He didn't recognize me. Slowly, he started narrowing his eyes and tilting his head to the side a little. Then his mouth fell open.

"J-Jae!" he yelled.

I scowled and crossed my arms. "Seriously? You didn't recognize me at all?"

Felix punched me in the shoulder so hard it sent me rocking onto my heels. That's when I realized he'd been going easy on me last year whenever we sparred together. Really, *really* easy, apparently.

"You jerk! Why would you do that?" I yelled back at him as I clutched my shoulder. "That hurt!"

"You ruined my welcome home present!" He reared back to hit me again.

"Present?" I dodged his swing as he tried to punch me in the face. "You were going to drop a bucket of water on my head! What kind of stupid present is that?" I grabbed his arm as he swung at me again, stepping in close to throw off his balance before I slung him down onto the ground.

"I worked hard on it!" He was laughing as I tried to wrestle him into a headlock on the ground.

It didn't work. I was taller, but he was still much bulkier and a lot stronger. He jabbed another punch into the pit of my stomach. Immediately, I couldn't breathe. While I was choking for air, he flipped us over and pinned me to the ground with a knee in my back.

"Well, it's definitely you," he chuckled. "You're still terrible at this."

"Get off!" I rasped. I could barely talk because my stomach was throbbing from where he'd hit me.

"Fine, fine. But you lose." He stepped off, grabbed the back of my tunic, and tried to pull me back to my feet. He had a much harder time managing that now that I was taller than he was. "Seriously, though. What happened to you? You look like a twenty-year-old! Did you find a witch to cast a spell on you or something?"

I was still rubbing my stomach and my shoulder. I couldn't even stand up straight. "I finally hit puberty, I guess," I wheezed. "Do I seriously look *that* old?"

"Hit puberty?" Felix laughed loudly. Other students in the hall were staring at us now. "You didn't just hit it. You mugged it in a dark alley and left it to die. What are you now? Six foot three? Six foot four?"

I blushed and snatched up my bag. It was embarrassing to have him making a scene in the middle of the hallway. The other avians were staring at us like we were crazy. "I haven't measured," I grumbled as I hobbled toward our room.

"Your hair is different, too. Is that because of your Gray elf blood?" He started poking me in the back as he followed. "Too bad you couldn't manage to bulk up a little more, huh? Then someone might actually mistake you for a dragonrider this time around. But no one can have everything, I guess. Look at you, you're so lanky—like a flag pole."

I knew he was teasing me. No one liked watching me squirm more than Felix Farrow. And if I fought back, it would only make things worse. The teasing never stopped once he knew he had some leverage that embarrassed me. I'd already made that mistake last year when he found out I was writing "love" letters to Katty.

"Shut up! It's not that big of a deal!" I grabbed the doorknob and started to go inside.

Felix tried to stop me. "Hey wait a min—"

It was too late.

The bucket fell from where he had it balanced over the door, landing right on my head. Ice-cold water splashed everywhere, drenching me from head to toe.

Felix was laughing like a maniac.

I sputtered and pulled the bucket off my head so I could throw it at him.

"It's not my fault! I did warn you." He grinned, grabbing my shoulder and giving it a friendly shake. "By the way, welcome back."

CHAPTER TWELVE

My boots and socks were still squishing with water as I walked out of the dormitory. Felix was hot on my heels, and he hadn't stopped talking since I hit the doorstep. I could feel him staring at me. Every now and then, he poked at me again like he wasn't sure I was real or not. Finally, I couldn't take it anymore.

"Would you stop that? It's getting annoying," I growled in frustration.

Felix looked up at me with amazement still written all over his face. "Sorry. It's kind of hard to believe this is really you. I keep expecting to blink and suddenly you'll be back to your old scrawny self again."

I could feel my face starting to get hot with embarrassment. "Tell me about it. I still don't recognize my own reflection."

"And you honestly don't know what did this to you?" he asked. "Are you going to come back looking like an old man the next time we get a break from training?"

I shot him a glare. "I don't think so. Look, it's not like I know all that much about Gray elves either. You know I wasn't raised in Luntharda. I was a kid when my mom died, and she had sheltered me from everyone my whole life—including other Gray elves. I only know what I heard the doctor say, and who knows how much of that is even true."

"And what did the doctor say?" He looked interested.

My memories of what had happened were blurred because of the pain I'd been in. It was like trying to remember a dream, so I just told him what I could. The Gray elves all grew that way, apparently. They grew fast, in short bursts, instead of gradually over time. All I knew for sure was that it had hurt—a *lot*—and I wasn't looking forward to it ever happening again.

"I can't believe your mother never mentioned any of this to you." Felix sounded skeptical, like he didn't quite believe me.

"I was twelve when she died, Felix," I snapped at him angrily. "We were just trying not to die of starvation. We didn't exactly have the time to discuss my future."

Felix raised his hands in surrender. "Geez. Relax. You're kind of cranky now, you know that? Did all that growing give you mood swings or something?"

I scowled and elbowed him in the ribs. "I'm not cranky."

We walked together toward the armories where craftsmen were hard at working making armor, saddles, and weapons. I had Sile's bag of coins in my hand, and I was trying to ignore the way the other students and instructors were staring at me as we passed. It was bad enough to have them look at me that way; Felix could have at least been a little more sensitive about it. It made me irritated that he was being this way. I wanted things to go back to normal.

We went to the blacksmiths' side of the armory first, and I looked for the same old man who'd made my armor last year. It seemed like a good idea to stick with someone who'd already worked with me before. At least I knew he wasn't going to intentionally compromise my equipment. I'd seen last year how badly things could go if something on a saddle broke during flight.

On our way, we passed another group of avian students. Once again, I didn't recognize any of them, but I did notice they looked a little older than us. They were also wearing those same golden stripes stitched onto the shoulders of their uniforms.

I leaned over to Felix. "What are those stripes for? Do they outrank us?" I still wasn't familiar enough with the order of power amongst the dragonriders to know who outranked me. I just assumed I had to salute everyone except for fledglings and other avians.

"Hah! They'd like you to think so. Don't let them talk down to you." Felix smirked. "We get four tries to pass this year in training. Didn't you know that? If you fail the battle scenario, or you don't perform well in interrogation training, they give you a stripe and you get to try again next year. After three stripes, they put a circle on your shoulder, and that means it's your last chance to pass. Trust me, you do not want to get a circle. They always give those guys the hardest time."

"Does anyone pass on the first try?" I asked. I had to wonder. There seemed to be a lot of avians walking around with stripes on their shoulders.

Felix shrugged. "Sure, I guess some do. But it's not the end of the world if you don't. The whole point of this training is to learn how to hold up under pressure, so the more you endure, the stronger you are."

I let that sink in as we walked the rest of the way to the blacksmith's shop set up in one of the small forges. So even if I messed up this time, I could try again next year? Hearing that left me puzzled. Sile had always made it sound like this was the only chance I'd get.

The blacksmith from last year didn't seem to even notice that I had basically doubled in size since he measured me before. Or if he did, he didn't say a word about it. He worked, grumbled, and scratched at his beard while he jotted down my information.

When he started fitting me for a helmet, I noticed that there were a lot of different styles. Last year, all his samples had been plain and basic. Fledglings didn't really need nice armor for training. Each one of these helmets had a different shape and design. He picked them up one by one, taking his time to fit it onto my head, and then examine carefully how it looked. Finally, he seemed to settle on one he liked. It fit my head snugly, and the glass slit for my eyes was a little wider, so I could see more.

"Going traditional?" Felix asked. I could see his expression through the glass eye-shield, and he didn't look happy. "The style seems a little old-fashioned to me."

The blacksmith made an annoyed, barking sound as he yanked the sample helmet off my head. "Bah! What do you know? Who is the armor master here, you or I?"

"It's okay." I didn't want Felix to start an argument over something like that. Maybe he didn't realize how personally these craftsmen took their work. After years of watching Ulric make dragon saddles, I knew better than most not to question them like that. "Traditional is probably best. I stand out enough already as it is."

Felix frowned like he didn't agree. "At least do some engraving. Otherwise, I might as well just loan him my grandfather's armor."

The blacksmith made another angry sound, like a mixture of a growl and a cough, but he didn't answer. Instead, he went back to work. When he finished, he held up his notes for me to see.

"Sign there. Then pay up," he ordered, jabbing a gritty finger at the bottom of the page.

I scanned over the notes. I couldn't read his jumbled writing at all, but I signed my initials at the bottom anyway. When I counted out his payment, I ended up handing over a third of the coins from the stash Sile had given me. It made me anxious about how much money I was costing him. How long did it take to earn this much? Shouldn't this money be spent on his own family?

"Never seen anyone jump from a size three to an eight in a year," the blacksmith muttered. It caught me off guard. Even though he probably didn't get many halfbreed customers, I'd assumed he didn't remember me. He crammed the coins in his apron and waved me off. "It'll be ready in two days."

It took a little longer to find the tackmaster who had made my saddle last year. After we did, and got Mavrik to agree to being fitted with the wax mold again, the exchange went basically the same way. I picked out a more basic, traditional design made out of black leather, and Felix complained that it was too plain. Apparently, I was expected to have a more ornate saddle since this would be the one I used in battle someday.

In the end, I insisted on sticking with the most basic style. I still couldn't shake off my guilt about spending all Sile's money that way. It seemed like a waste. I didn't really need all the frills and details that Felix kept insisting on. They were just for decoration.

"It's fine," I told him. "It probably took Sile a long time to earn this money. I can't blow it all on stuff I don't even need. I'll get the basics, and send whatever money is leftover back to him. He's got a family to feed, you know."

"He gave you that money so you *could* blow it on outfitting. A rider's saddle is supposed to be his pride. It's a mark of accomplishment." Felix crossed his arms stubbornly. He didn't get it. He was the son of a powerful duke, so I knew money was probably never an issue for his family. But I had experienced firsthand how much difference a little bit of money could make. It could mean the difference between eating or going to bed hungry.

I rolled my eyes and paid for the plain saddle anyway. "It's just a saddle, Felix. My bond with Mavrik is my pride. It's all I need. Anyway, I haven't exactly accomplished anything yet, have I?"

Felix couldn't really argue with that, but he sulked the whole way back to the dormitory. When we sat down in the dining hall, he slammed a tray of food down between us. There were two big plates piled high with food. For the first time since my weird growth spurt, I didn't feel guilty about eating as much as I wanted. I didn't waste any time diving into the fresh baked bread and roasted meat.

"You're different now." Felix was still glaring at me over the huge leg of turkey he was holding.

"How so?" I asked.

"I don't know. I can't put my finger on it. Something's definitely changed, though," he answered with a mouthful of food. Then, in the blink of an eye, his sulky demeanor vanished like he'd forgotten all about the saddle and armor. He started grinning at me with that mischievous twinkle in his eyes again. "So. How's your girl? I bet she was surprised to see you like this, eh? Did you finally kiss her?"

"No." I'd given up trying to explain to him that Katty and I had never been a couple a long time ago. He assumed that because we'd written letters to each other. I just decided to go with it. "She basically dumped me right when I got back."

"Aw, that's rough." He looked genuinely sorry for me. "Did she say why?"

"Not exactly. I sort of came home and found her with someone else." It still stung to admit that. Not because I had any feelings for her anymore, though. "She's here with him, now. They're both working for her father as blacksmith apprentices."

Felix sat straight up in his chair, and looked like he was about to choke on his food. "You're kidding! She's here? Why didn't you say so before? I want to get a look at her."

I shook my head. "No way. She doesn't want me anywhere near her."

"What about the new guy?" he pressed. "Why don't you try to fight him for her? You'd probably win now that, well, you're practically a giant."

I frowned down at the half-eaten loaf of bread in my hand. "Because he's actually a nice person. It wasn't his fault. She told him I was like her little brother." My pride took another hit.

Felix cringed. "Ouch."

"Yeah. Tell me about it." I took a big bite of bread and chewed while I thought it over. "I'm not that upset, though. I was before. Now I think it's better this way."

He looked stunned. "Seriously?"

"Yeah." I shrugged.

Felix started eyeing me suspiciously. I could see the wheels turning while he tried to figure out why I wasn't more upset over being rejected like that. I'm sure anyone else would have been. But whenever I thought about my feelings, or girls, or any of that stuff... it wasn't Katty's face that came to mind.

I could feel the lump under my vambrace where the handkerchief Beckah had made for me pressed against my forearm. It reminded me of the last time I'd seen her, standing on the edge of the ocean. I did *not* want Felix to know about any of that. I knew if he ever found out, the teasing would never end.

"So what about you? How was your time at home?" I changed the subject before he could start interrogating me.

Felix's eyes got dark, and he started picking at his food. He stabbed at his boiled potatoes like he was trying to murder them. "Terrible, as usual. I don't want to talk about it."

I was speechless. Felix had never shut me out like that before. But when it came to my personal life, I knew he would never let me dodge questions like that. I wasn't about to let him get away with it, either.

"You might as well just say it," I said. "I'm not going to let it go. So talk."

His lip curled some, like he was fighting back a snarl, and he stabbed another potato. I could see rage burning in his eyes. "Seriously, leave it alone."

I was willing to call his bluff. I leaned forward and stole a potato off his plate just to spite him. "Talk," I demanded again.

He shot me a dangerous look and stayed silent for a few minutes. I didn't say anything, either. Finally, he let out a loud sigh and surrendered. "Dad's got some kind of nervous illness. He won't even come out of his room. My mother tells me he's sick with worry that I won't uphold my duties as his heir, or that I'll be killed in battle and there'll be no one left to take over the estate. She says if I acted more like an adult and took more responsibility, he might get better."

I hoped I was hearing that wrong. "You mean, they're saying it's your fault he's sick?"

Felix didn't look up. His expression was so bleak, I barely recognized him. I'd never seen him look like that. "Jae, it's always my fault when it comes to them. Dad was furious when I chose to become a dragonrider instead of staying home and learning to run our estate. If I wasn't their only child, I know he would have already disowned me. He's told me before he doesn't think I can handle being duke."

"I'm sorry." I didn't know what else to say.

He shook his head. "Don't be. I'm not giving this up. I've worked too hard. It feels wrong not to be here, you know? Dad can disown me, if he wants."

I couldn't help but frown. "You're giving up being a duke? Just to be a dragonrider?"

"Of course not. He won't *actually* disown me. I'm the only heir to my family's name. When my dad dies, there's no one else to take over except me. If I don't take his place as duke, our estate will have to be broken up amongst our extended family. Sooner or later, I'll have to retire as a dragonrider and take his place. In the meantime, I'm going to do what I want. And I want to be here." He said it like it was nothing, but I knew giving up being a dragonrider was a big deal. I had seen the effect it was having on Sile.

I thought about that while we finished eating. It was hard for me to see Felix as a noble. We had been through a lot together last year, and he'd never acted like someone with a lot of power or influence. Looking at him from across the table, I tried to decide if I could even picture him as one of those fat, rich men wearing fluffy silk shirts, fur cloaks, and lace.

No. I definitely couldn't picture that.

As we left the dining hall to go back to our room, Felix brought up the dragonrider ranking system again. He was amazed that I still didn't know anything about it, and started rattling off information faster than I could follow.

"Once we pass our avian year, we'll be sworn in as lieutenants," he explained.

"You mean like Sile was?" It didn't seem right for me to be the same rank as Sile and Jace yet. They had both fought in the war and served as instructors for years.

"Hah! No, of course not. They were *seasoned* lieutenants. That's different. It means they've fought in combat more than five times, or have done something worthy of being promoted," he said. When we got to the door of our room, he paused to show me where the placard had the abbreviation "Sn." before Jace's name.

"And that stands for seasoned?" I hadn't paid much attention to it before.

He nodded. "Although, most people just call them lieutenants anyway. They like to group us all together because generally we are the ones who do the most fighting. It takes a long time to get promoted past seasoned lieutenant, and once you do, it means less time on the actual battlefield."

Felix went on tell me about the other ranks. After seasoned lieutenants came captains, colonels, and then there were only three higher ranks a dragonrider could achieve. Those were the most prestigious offices in all of the king's forces.

"The two sky generals are in charge of all the forces north or south of the royal city," he went on as he opened the door. "But really, they're basically glorified errand boys. They spend most of their time behind a desk, and answering to the lord general when something goes wrong."

We both fell silent when he said that title. We'd met the last lord general, and it wasn't something either of us wanted to talk about where someone might overhear.

When I looked at Felix, I could see the frustration on his face. I wondered if he had the same concerns and suspicions I did. I knew for sure that none of what Academy Commander Rayken had told us last year was true. Of course, I had no real proof of that. But anyone with holes for eyes could see that it was some kind of a cover up. Someone was working hard to keep the truth hidden about what the Lord General had been doing with that god stone.

I started thinking back to when I first saw that stone. Commander Rayken had called it the god stone. I didn't know what that meant, or anything about the stone itself, but I could remember clearly how looking at it had made me feel. Just one glimpse of it had pulled me into some kind of weird trance. It still gave me chills. Thankfully, Sile had been there to clamp a hand over my eyes and drag me away.

"So, what about being an academy commander?" I asked as I tried to shake those memories from my mind. "Where does that fall in the rankings?"

Felix shrugged as he wandered across our small room to flop down on his bed. "It's the same as captain, but there's only one academy so there's only one commander. The king hand-chooses the new academy commander himself. He usually gives it to a dragonrider who's shown good leadership in combat, or who's been injured such that he can't fight anymore. I'm actually surprised Sile didn't get it. It's not the most glamorous job in the world. I mean, he's basically a glorified babysitter for all of us, right?"

I got a sour taste in my mouth. Immediately, I remembered the rumor Mr. Crookin had told me while we were in the mountains. Thinking about Sile going into Luntharda made me forget how to walk. Before I realized it, I was standing in the doorway staring into space.

"What's wrong?" Felix was looking me over like he was concerned.

I wasn't sure how much I should tell him. Sile had warned me about saying too much. But I needed to know if the rumor was true or not.

"I saw Sile during the interlude," I finally admitted.

He frowned at me suspiciously. "What do you mean? He went to Mithangol?"

"No." I shut the door behind me before I dared to say anything else. "I got a letter from Beckah. She wanted me to come visit. They're living in Saltmarsh now. That's where I was when this growth spurt hit."

I started to explain as we went into our room. Our new dorm room wasn't that much bigger than the last one. It was more like a closet with three beds crammed into it, and a skinny window on the far wall. Felix had picked the bed in the middle, and I knew why without even having to ask. He wanted to put himself between Lyon and me in case our old enemy tried anything suspicious.

But now Felix was glaring at me like he might reconsider that. "You've been holding out on me," he said accusingly.

I winced and shuffled to sit on the bed next to the window. "Sile didn't want me to tell anyone. You know how he is." I knew that wasn't a good excuse.

"So what's going on?" he demanded.

It took a while for me to tell him about what had happened during the interlude. I didn't go into too much detail about how my family had abandoned me. That didn't even bother me that much; they'd never felt like a family to me, anyway. I was way more concerned about what had happened at the Derrick's house.

I told him everything about Beckah and Icarus, and how Sile didn't seem like he was wounded at all. He had been plenty capable when he sparred with me. I told him about my suspicion that someone was still after Sile. Whoever it was, Sile was running scared, and he had a lot to lose if they ever caught up to him. It had to be more than some dumb plot about an immortality ritual. I'd never even heard of a god stone, or whatever they called it.

I kept the details about what had happened with Sile's wife to myself. I didn't want anyone to know about how I had somehow healed her. I wasn't sure how it happened, or if I could even do it again. I wasn't ready to talk about it. I needed answers first. I knew if I said anything now, Felix would probably give me that weird look again—like I was transforming into some kind of monster right before his eyes. I hated it when people looked at me like that, but it hurt even more when Felix did it.

I told him about what had happened in the mountains, and how I couldn't talk to the wolves or the big mountain cat that had attacked me. I repeated everything Bren had told me about other animal attacks that were happening throughout the kingdom, but when it came time to ask him about the rumor... I choked. I didn't know how to ask. It sounded like an accusation, and I didn't want to be the one pointing fingers at Sile's back.

"So," Felix sounded overwhelmed. He paused to take a breath. "Basically Beckah's a dragonrider, the animals are all going rabid, and Sile is still being hunted by some unknown enemy who wants to murder him and his family?"

I couldn't answer. It was a lot to think about, even when he summed it up like that.

"And you seriously thought you could handle all that by yourself?" He laughed, but the atmosphere was still tense. "Well, I don't know anything about crazy animals attacking people. I haven't heard anything about it. Sile's probably right about you getting too involved in his personal affairs. You'll get distracted from what you should be focused on. We're here to train. This is what's most important now, right? Just forget everything else. If you're constantly worrying about something a hundred miles away, you're liable to get killed by something two feet in front of you."

He did have a point. I already had so much on my mind. It was hard to keep my eyes on my goal when the rest of my life felt like it was spinning out of control. Somehow, I had to get it together. I had to focus.

"Besides," he said. I could hear the mischievous grin in his voice without ever having to look at him. "You were holding out on the most important detail of all. How long did you think you could hide it from me?"

"Hide what?"

He chuckled wickedly. "That you're in love with Beckah."

I wanted to deny it. I also wanted to punch his lights out. But I couldn't do anything except look away with my ears burning like they were on fire.

Felix saw my reaction, and it made his eyes gleam dangerously. "You're not even denying it!"

"What's the point?" I tried to deflect. "You'll tease me about it no matter what I say."

He wasn't listening. He'd already launched into harassing me, and I knew nothing would stop him now. "You know, I kind of feel bad for telling everyone you weren't stupid. You should know better than to go after an instructor's daughter. Do you have a death wish?"

"I'm not going after her," I snapped. It wasn't a lie, but I wasn't necessarily proud of that. I kind of wished it had been.

"Yeah, right." Felix rolled his eyes. "Take a little advice from someone who actually has experience with girls, okay? Stay away from her. Sile will literally kill you if he ever catches you two together. And considering how many friends you have in the world, it'd probably be best not to lose the one who's paying for all your stuff."

13

CHAPTER THIRTEEN

I still couldn't figure out how to ask Felix about the rumor. After he fell asleep, I couldn't stand to stay cooped up in our room either. I was restless, and listening to him snore wasn't helping at all. So I laced up my boots and went down to the dining hall to swipe a few spare beef bones from the trash bins. Then I started for the Roost.

The night air was cold, and the moon was so bright it put shadows on the ground. All the other students and instructors were closed up in their rooms, resting for the next day. The craftsmen had already put away their tools and shut down their work for the night. I caught a glimpse of the red-hot coals still smoldering in a few of the forges as I passed the armory. It made me wonder if Mr. Crookin and the others had ever made it here.

When I arrived at the Roost, a few avians were still doing the cleaning detail rounds. As fledglings, we'd gotten away with not having to do much in the way of care when it came to our dragons. But according to Felix, this year would be different. We would have to take turns cleaning all the stalls and lugging around big buckets of raw meat to feed the hungry dragons. We would have to oil our own saddles, and clean our own weapons.

None of the other avians paid me any attention as I made my way to Mavrik's stall. It wasn't a very large room, but it was just big enough for a dragon to nest in. The floor was covered with soft hay, and there was a trough of water along one of the walls. The Roost was built like a giant honeycomb, with no walls on one side so the dragons could fly in and out. Through the opening in Mavrik's stall, I could see the whole academy shimmering in the night. I could see the moonlight shining off the snowy mountain peaks in the distance, and thousands of stars.

Mavrik was curled up like a mound of blue scales. His wings were folded up tight, and his snout was resting on the tip of his tail. When I came in, he opened one of his big yellow eyes and studied me. I saw an image of myself sleeping in my bed flash through my mind.

I smirked and gave him a shrug. "I tried. I can't sleep. You know how Felix snores. It's like listening to a bear try to cough up a hairball."

He made a grumbling sound and closed his eye again.

I tossed the cow bones right in front of his nose as I sat down in the straw next to him. Immediately, his big nostrils puffed open wide as he smelled the scraps of meat and cartilage still left on the bones. He opened his mouth lazily, snaking out his long black tongue to twist it around one of the bones and drag it into his jaws. The sound of his teeth crunching the big bone into splinters made me cringe.

"You're welcome." I shuddered and looked away.

Leaning against his scaly neck, I could feel him breathing and moving as he chewed. It made me feel calmer, like I could finally hear myself think, and I didn't have to hide anything anymore. Mavrik knew all these secrets and rumors were beginning to smother me. I couldn't hide anything from him.

"Being back here like this reminds me of when we met," I murmured.

Mavrik made a few low, clicking sounds as he crunched on another bone. The image of our meeting, of when I first came into the breaking dome and saw him, came into my mind. It was bizarre to see myself from his perspective. I had looked so terrified, small, and pathetic. My face was covered in bruises from the beatings I'd taken. But for whatever reason, Mavrik had chosen me.

"I'll keep my promise," I told him. "When this is over, maybe we'll both be free to find our own peace somewhere."

Mavrik started to push his big snout up against my arm, insisting that I rub him. He purred as I scratched at his snout and ears, resting his big head on my leg. It was so heavy it started to cut off the circulation, but I didn't want him to move. Being so close to him made me feel safe.

I took out Beckah's handkerchief and rubbed my thumb over the embroidery of the two dragons. I wondered where she was. Maybe she was standing on the beach with Icarus again, or talking to some grocer about how well she could stitch.

"A girl gave that to you, right?" An angry voice hissed at me suddenly.

When I looked up, I was shocked and a little relieved to see Katty was standing in the stall's doorway. After what had happened with the wolves and the mountain cat, I was concerned about what would happen if they got attacked again.

Katty didn't look happy at all to see me, though. Her arms were crossed, and she looked every bit as furious as the last time she'd caught me staring at that handkerchief. I quickly put it in my pocket.

"You look at it a lot." Her nose wrinkled up like she had smelled something terrible.

Behind me, I felt Mavrik's side vibrate as he growled. He lifted his head off my leg to look at her, showing his teeth and twitching the end of his tail. Apparently, he still hadn't forgiven her.

I put a hand against his snout to try to calm him before I answered her, "Yeah. Why does that matter to you?"

She blinked like someone had spat in her face. I saw her cheeks start to get red, and she dropped her hands to her sides. The rage on her face finally broke, and she started to look sad. Tears welled in her eyes. I wasn't expecting that.

"I made a mistake," she whispered. It sounded like she was clenching her teeth. "You're not like a brother to me. I don't know why I said that. It's not true."

I was starting to get uncomfortable. "Katty, it's fine. I lost my temper, too. But everything's okay now. We can still be friends."

She started to get angry again. Her hands curled up into fists. "That's not what I mean," she snapped.

Before I could ask her what she was talking about, Katty came stomping across the stall and dropped down onto her knees in front of me. She grabbed my face in both of her hands, and glared at me like she was expecting me to do something. When I didn't move, she made an annoyed huffing sound and started leaning toward me.

Alarm bells were ringing in my head like crazy. Nothing about this was right. I couldn't go through with it. Before she could kiss me, I put a hand against her shoulder to stop her. Our noses were only a few inches apart.

"What are you doing?" I demanded.

Her eyes popped open like she was stunned. I could feel her breath on my face. "Don't you want to kiss me? It feels good. You'll like it, I promise."

"No." I slowly pushed her back away from me. "You know this isn't right. What about Bren? I thought you liked him?"

She scowled. Her chin started trembling. "How can you reject me like this? Like I'm nothing!" Her voice was shaking, and her eyes were glaring right into mine. It felt like I was staring into a churning black abyss. It felt like chaos. "You think just because you're some big shot dragonrider now, you can toss me aside and have any girl you want? You think the girl who gave you that handkerchief cares about you?"

"What are you talking about?"

I didn't understand where all this anger was coming from. I was so bewildered by what she was saying; I didn't notice she was rearing back to hit me until it was too late. She slapped me hard across the face. "You're wrong! I'm the only one who will ever care anything about you. It doesn't matter what job you get, what you look like, or where you go. You'll always be a halfbreed. No girl will ever love you like I do. You'll never have anyone. It's me or no one."

She started to slap me again, but I caught her wrist. Behind me, Mavrik was snarling again. His ears were slicked back, and he was sending me mental images of how he wanted to bite her head off—literally. I wasn't sure how long his patience was going to last.

"Katty, stop it!" I held onto her wrist tightly as she started to fight me.

She was strong because of her work as a blacksmith's apprentice, and it didn't take long for her to pry herself away from me. She stood up and started trying to hit me again. I had to use a few sparring moves to hold her off so I could get to my feet.

I didn't want to fight her, but this had to stop. When she started to attack me again, I spun her around into a grappling hold with her arms pinned behind her back. I made sure I did everything I could to hold her still without hurting her. She started cursing at me as I forced her to walk out of the stall. Once we were in the hallway, I let her go and took a step back.

"Go back to your father," I growled at her. "I don't know what made you change like this, but you're not the Katty I used to know. Whatever you've become, I don't like it. Stay away from me. Don't come see me ever again."

For a few seconds, we just stood there glaring at each other in the darkness. I knew by the look on her face that this wasn't over. She was still angry. She wanted to hurt me. I didn't understand where all this was coming from. She'd already picked Bren instead of me! Wasn't that supposed to be the end of things between us?

Finally, Katty spun around and ran. When I heard her footsteps going back down the stairs, I could finally breathe. My cheek was stinging from where she'd slapped me as I returned to the stall and sat down again.

Mavrik was still growling. The very tip of his tail twitched back and forth, and he was staring at me with his cat-like eyes glowing in the moonlight. He sent me another image of himself snacking on Katty's head.

I cringed and pushed the image away. "Quit that. It's grossing me out."

When I sat back down against his side, his growling started to fade. He sulked and refused to look at me. "I always do that, huh?" I asked as I scratched him behind his ears and horns. "You try to stick up for me, and I tell you no."

Mavrik made an annoyed, grumbling noise like he agreed.

"It's not that easy, you know. You can't eat people every time they make you upset." The more I scratched, the more I felt him start to relax. Soon I had him purring again, and his big yellow eyes started to close.

I tried not to think about the things Katty said about girls never caring about me. I knew Beckah wasn't like that. She cared about me. But doubt started creeping in anyway.

Beckah was growing up. Even I could see that. She might start to change. She might meet a grocer... or a Bren. And then I might become like a little brother to her, too.

I HAD FORGOTTEN ALL ABOUT MY NIGHTMARE. I WAS SO EXHAUSTED, IT DIDN'T even dawn on me that this was the first time I'd gotten to sleep since that night. But as soon as I felt myself starting to nod off, leaning against Mavrik's side, I got a jolt of panic. I didn't want to have that dream again.

Unfortunately, I didn't have a choice.

As soon as I dozed off, I could feel it coming. I fought it as hard as I could, but the dream held me under. I could feel the cold of the wind. I could see the giant trees of Luntharda looming before me as I stood on the muddy road. I saw the king's company coming toward me, heading for the forest with their banners fluttering in the sunlight.

The scene played out just like before. The Gray elf warrior emerged, cutting through the ranks like an angel of death. He butchered the king in cold blood. And then that single guard rose up from the bloodstained snow, barely able to stand, to fight him.

My heart was pounding in my ears. I knew it was a dream. Even so, I couldn't force myself to wake up no matter how I tried. I didn't want to see what happened. I was afraid and angry because there was nothing I could do to intervene. My body was stuck in one spot. All I could do was watch.

I saw the Gray elf take his fighting stance, sneering at the guard and beginning to advance. The guard's hands were shaking so badly he could barely grip his sword. They started to lunge at each other, and I tried to look away. I didn't want to see what happened next.

Then the dream started to fall apart again. I was sinking into the earth, being swallowed by the darkness. I never saw who struck first. My last glimpse of the dream was the Gray elf and the guard running toward each other, prepared to fight to the death.

All of a sudden, I heard my mother's voice. It seemed to be coming from everywhere at once, booming like thundering in my mind.

"Return it."

It was so clear, and so loud, that it made me bolt awake. I was drenched with a cold sweat, and my mind was racing. I felt sick immediately, but I was determined not to throw up this time.

I sat against Mavrik's side, gasping for breath and trying to calm down. Mavrik was looking at me, and I could feel his big puffs of hot breath blasting against my face. He started chirping with concern as he pushed his snout against my chest. He sent worried colors of blue and yellow swirling into my thoughts.

Without thinking, I reached to close a fist around my mother's necklace. I was used to feeling it around my neck, but when I touched it... it felt like it was on fire. It burned me, and I jerked my hand away from it. I'd worn this necklace for most of my life. It had definitely never done anything like this before. It was a piece of carved bone.

Mavrik and I exchanged a stare. My hand was red and throbbing where the necklace had burned it. Since I could see his thoughts trickling through my brain like a shower of worried blue color, I knew we were both thinking the same thing: what the heck was going on?

JACE FOUND ME ON MY WAY BACK TO THE DORMITORY. IT WAS STILL DARK outside, but I knew the sun would be rising soon. I hadn't intended on spending the night in the Roost. I was stiff from sleeping upright, and cold because my clothes were damp with sweat. All I wanted to do was take a hot bath and try sleeping in my bed for a few more hours.

But when I saw Jace, it stopped me dead in my tracks. I knew I was busted.

"Where have you been?" he demanded.

I winced. I knew students weren't supposed to be outside their rooms after dark. Technically, training hadn't started yet. I also knew better than to think Jace would give me a pass because of that. "I'm sorry, sir. It won't happen again."

Jace narrowed his eyes like he didn't believe me. "It better not. Four extra laps this morning might help you remember."

I nodded. "Yes, sir."

"Go on. You have plenty to keep you busy, avian." He brushed past me on his way out of the dormitory. I turned to watch him go. Jace was a hard man to read. He never made any expression except for that grim, sour-looking frown he wore all the time. I honestly couldn't tell if he was grumpy, angry, or just bored out of his mind.

Felix was already getting dressed when I got back to our room. He was hopping around, trying to wedge his foot down into one of his tall riding boots. "Well, you look awful. Busy night, I take it?"

"I don't want to talk about it." I sighed and sat down on the edge of my bed.

"Your old girl came by here last night. She's pretty, but man, she's gotta nasty temper," he said. "Apparently, she thinks someone gave you a love token. She was demanding to know who it was from."

"Katty came here?" I frowned. Apparently, I'd been right about her not letting it go. This was getting out of control. I leaned forward and rubbed my face. My head was throbbing from my nightmare, and my skin was sticky from sleeping in sweaty clothes. "What am I supposed to do?"

Felix slapped a hand against my back. He was laughing. "You're supposed to get ready for morning drills, dummy. Get your priorities straight. Work first, girls later."

I groaned. He was right. There was nothing I could do about it now, anyway. Felix kept laughing at me right up until I told him about the four extra laps I'd earned us by sneaking out of the room after dark. For some reason, he didn't find that quite as funny as my lousy love life.

He shot me a dirty look on our way out of the dormitory. "You seriously need to figure out how to keep a low profile. Remind me not to stand too close to you during the mock interrogation."

I punched him in the arm for spite.

It might have devolved into another sparring session, but we had work to do. As the twilight turned the horizon purple, we started running. We ran laps around the academy's outer wall until we were staggering with exhaustion. Then we started repetitions of push-ups, sit-ups, and grappling holds.

Jace met us armed with wooden practice swords. He shouted at us, giving commands to demonstrate parries, strikes, and disarming techniques until it felt like my arms were going to fall off. I'd never felt more confident in my life. I was still skinny—like a flag pole even—but I wasn't the weakest link anymore. This was my chance to prove it.

Our morning drills went on until way past breakfast. Official training hadn't started yet, so there was no call to arms to signal the start of the day. Jace could hold us hostage as long as he wanted. Finally, after four long, grueling hours, he called us to a halt. My hands were buzzing with energy. My heart was pounding. Sure, I was starving and completely exhausted, but I hadn't felt this alive in months.

"Well, it seems you haven't forgotten everything from last year. But it's not good enough," Jace growled as he walked around us. I could feel him sizing me up again. He never looked at Felix that way, which was annoying and unfair. I knew it was probably because I was a halfbreed. "Go clean yourselves up. I've signed you both up for tack detail until training starts. You'll be checking every saddle, oiling every scrap of leather, and polishing every bit of brass. Understood?"

"Yes sir!" We both shouted in unison.

Jace dismissed us, and Felix and I glanced at each other. Tack detail didn't sound very fun. It could have been worse, though. I was more than happy to take the smell of oil and polish over the stench of dragon manure any day.

We ate breakfast without talking at all. I was too exhausted to say anything, and Felix was too busy shoveling as many pieces of bacon into his mouth as possible. He acted like he'd never seen food before. He always ate like that in the morning.

I took my time bathing. Every muscle in my body was sore, but it didn't bother me. I noticed that I was starting to get very distinct calluses on the palm of my sword hand. When I got out of the tub, I hurried through combing out my hair and tying it back into a ponytail. It was getting so long and hard to manage. I caught myself wishing Beckah were there to braid it for me like before.

Looking at myself in the mirror still made me uncomfortable. I hated how much I looked like my father. I'd always favored Ulric a lot more than I did my mom, but now it was like seeing his ghost in my reflection every time I looked in the mirror. It was creepy, and it made my heart skip a beat with panic every time.

I was entertaining the idea of trying to sneak in a short nap before I started tack detail as I walked back to our dorm room. Having nightmares every night was starting to take a heavy toll on me. If I couldn't get any sleep, I wasn't going to last long once our real training started. I'd almost decided it was worth getting my head chewed off if Jace found out when I walked in.

Lyon Cromwell was standing in the middle of the room. By the look of things, he had just arrived. He was still holding his travel bag in one hand, and wearing special riding gauntlets with resin palms made for gripping a dragon saddle.

He and Felix were squaring off, standing less than a foot apart, and glaring right into each other's faces. No one was saying a word, but I could sense that things were about to come to blows. This wasn't going to end well.

"Hey!" I slammed the door behind me to get their attention. "Knock it off! If Lieutenant Rordin hears about you guys fighting—"

Felix cut me off before I could finish. "He won't. It's hard to run off and tattle with a broken jaw, isn't it Lyon? Step back outside, Jae."

"That's right, rich boy." Lyon sneered. "Send your little sidekick away while the grownups talk."

I rolled my eyes. Apparently, nothing about Lyon had changed since last year. He was still a bully. And he still hated my guts. "I'm not going anywhere. You're both being stupid. We're supposed to be working together."

Lyon shot me a glare. "Save your preaching, halfbreed. He's the one who jumped me as soon as I walked in."

"I have a name, you know." I glared back at him. "And I'm not preaching for your benefit. Felix, back off. It's not worth it."

I could see Felix thinking it over. I knew him well enough to tell that he was weighing the risk of being caught and punished by Jace against how good it would feel to punch Lyon in the face a few times. I didn't blame him for wanting to. I wasn't exactly Lyon's biggest fan. But if we were all going to have to spend the rest of the year living, training, and doing cleaning rotations together, then it was probably best not to start off by beating each other's faces in.

"We don't have to like it." I took the risk of getting caught in the crossfire and stepped between them. "We just have to tolerate one another. So let's suck it up and get through this."

Felix met my gaze. He let out a deep, growling sound and scrunched his mouth up angrily. "Fine."

I let out a sigh of relief when he turned away and left the room. For a minute there, I thought he might decide to hit me instead. He slammed the door so hard it made my teeth rattle.

"You're not winning any points with me, you know," Lyon said. "I don't need you to stick up for me. I don't need you at all. No one here does."

I'd already heard this speech from him last year. It was old news. "Yeah, yeah. I know. Because I'm a halfbreed, right?"

Lyon fumed silently. He glared daggers at me for a few seconds. I could sense that he was looking me over with the same sort of amazement Felix had. I looked a little different than the last time he saw me. I wouldn't be easy prey for him anymore. Now I was several inches taller than he was.

"We're on tack detail," I told him as I went to drop my dirty clothes in the basket by my bed. "Jace's orders."

I didn't stick around to hear anything else he had to say. It was hard enough to stand close to him. All I could think about was what he'd done to Sile last year. I wanted to punch him myself. It wasn't worth it. Hating him and trying to make him pay for what he'd done wasn't going to get me anywhere. I couldn't let myself get distracted by those feelings right now.

When I caught up to Felix, he was throwing tack around in the Roost's saddle room like a hurricane. He still looked furious, and didn't say a word when I came in. He was stacking saddles and slamming bottles of polish onto the workbenches. His jaw was tense. I could see a vein standing out on his forehead.

"Are you gonna stand there and watch me do all the work?" he snapped suddenly.

I shook my head and started helping him stack the saddles up, moving them all onto one side of the room so we could go through and check, polish, and recheck them all one by one. "I wasn't doing that for his sake, you know," I muttered. "I know you were trying to stick up for me."

Felix didn't answer.

"Things are different this year. You don't have to be so worried about me. I can take care of myself now." I picked up a couple of oiling rags and tossed one to him.

He paused, staring at me as he caught the rag. We studied each other awkwardly from across the room without saying a word. After a few minutes, Felix's shoulders sagged. He let out a sigh. "Old habits die hard, I guess. I had no idea if you'd even come back this year. You don't know how many nights I stayed awake wondering if that scumbag father of yours had murdered you and tossed your body in a ditch somewhere."

I smiled and started setting up three workstations for us with stools and sawhorses. "Well, now that you don't have to worry about being my bodyguard, worry about yourself for a change. Don't let the stuff Lyon says get to you. He's just trying to start a fight. By the way, do you think he'll actually come help us?"

Felix went over to the stack of saddles. He took the first one off the top of the pile and threw it at me. It was like tossing me a small cow. I managed to catch it, but it almost knocked me over.

He laughed. "Who cares? We already know we can't trust him, right? So I'm not gonna rely on him for anything. Fool me once..."

I couldn't argue with that logic. Last time we had relied on Lyon, we'd ended up trapped in a prison camp with royal guards and a king drake standing between the exit and us. I dropped the saddle onto the sawhorses and started checking all the straps and buckles. If anything looked bent, torn, or loose it would have to be fixed before the rider could use it again.

Felix started doing the same with another saddle. As the hours ticked by, we checked each one over and over, and then cleaned them with leather oil and brass polish. Of course, Lyon never showed up to help. By the time the sun was starting to set, there were still a dozen saddles left in the pile. My hands were aching, and I was beyond starving.

"Let's finish up after dinner," Felix grumbled. "If I look at another buckle my eyes are going to turn to mush."

I agreed and stood up to stretch. We still had a lot left to do, but I couldn't imagine starting on another saddle until I had something to eat. Thinking about some fresh, hot bread and roasted meat made my insides squirm happily.

Felix and I left the tack room and started for the dining hall. It was late in the evening, but the academy was still bustling with activity. Students were running around in groups, following instructors. Most of them were wearing their uniforms, but Jace hadn't given us our new avian tunics yet. The fledglings all looked so young to me now. It was hard to believe I'd been one of them last year. It seemed like so long ago.

The craftsmen were still working in the forges and armories, making new equipment while their apprentices ran errands. Tackmasters poured wax for saddle molds while riders struggled to get their dragons to cooperate. I still didn't see my father anywhere, but I wasn't going to go out of my way to look for him. After all, it's not like I had anything to say to him, and I knew better than to think he even wanted to see me.

I was about to take my first bite from a big piece of roasted pork when Felix drummed up the topic of the annual officer's ball. Immediately, he had a captive audience. Other avians sitting close to us scooted in closer, grinning like we were sharing in some big secret. They were more than willing to ignore me altogether if it meant they'd get some useful information about girls. Felix apparently knew a lot about them and he was always more than happy to talk about it. He loved the attention.

Training hadn't even started yet, but Felix was already planning out our evening like the ball was tomorrow night. He rattled off the names of noble girls he wanted to dance with, and people I should avoid. None of those names meant anything to me. I didn't know any nobles except for him and Lyon, but some of the other avians seemed interested.

"Julianna Lacroix," he whispered like her name was a curse in some foreign language. "You'll know her because of her teeth. They're so big she can't say two words without spitting on everyone in a two-foot radius. If you can't avoid dodging a dance with her, at least try to hold her out at arm's length to avoid the spray."

I scowled at him. "That's rude."

Felix glared right back at me challengingly. "Says the one who's never even met her. It's like dancing with an angry camel. You'll see at the ball."

I rolled my eyes and went back to eating. The other avians were much more interested in his detailed descriptions of the noble girls. They asked him questions, and Felix went on and on about who would most likely step on their feet, try to trap them into boring conversations, or would be the most willing to fool around with a few meaningless kisses.

When I didn't join in, Felix started scolding me again. "You should take this more seriously." A few of the other students sitting near him nodded in agreement. "We're expected to interact this year. We have to make an impression."

"I'd rather not make an impression as a moron, if it's all the same to you," I growled at him. It came off a lot harsher than I meant it too. I regretted it instantly, and Felix actually looked a little stunned that I had lashed out at him like that.

He sank back in his seat, frowning at me like he couldn't decide if I was kidding or not. I shrugged and waved a hand at him to try and brush the subject away. "Look, it's not a big deal to me. No one's going to ask me to dance, you know that. So why worry about it?"

Felix pursed his lips. "You never know. Halfbreed or not, you're still a dragonrider."

I was starting to hate it when he said things like that to me. My heritage didn't matter to him, but it mattered to everyone else—especially girls. Katty had made that fact very clear. Her angry words were still ringing in my ears. As much as I didn't want to admit that she was probably right, I had to face facts sooner or later. When it came down to it, I was still a halfbreed. Beckah was probably going to end up with a grocer after all, and there wouldn't be anything I could do to stop it.

"That's the stupidest thing I've ever heard." Lyon piped up right on cue. I hadn't even noticed him coming into the dining hall. He sat down with a tray of food a few seats down from me. "Don't even get his hopes up. The noble girls will take one look at him and probably faint in terror."

I flashed a look of warning to Felix. I could see him gritting his teeth already. His shoulders were hunched up aggressively, and his biceps were bulging under his sleeves.

Lyon apparently had a death wish, because he didn't stop there. "I mean, come on. We were all told the same stories as kids. Gray elves are blood-thirsty savages squatting in the mud of that wicked forest, weaving evil magic and eating the hearts of fair maidens. That's all those noble girls will ever see when they look at him. It doesn't matter what uniform you put him in. You can't make dung into diamonds, and you can't make a halfbreed a hero."

There was silence at the table. The other avians sitting around us were looking back and forth between the three of us, not daring to say a word. The tension was so thick you could practically see it. Felix might as well have had steam coming out of his ears. Frankly, I didn't care what Lyon said about me anymore. He probably knew that, too. He was just trying to get a rise out of Felix. Unfortunately, it was working.

Anyone could have seen that Felix was on the edge. His hands were balled into fists that made the veins on his arms stand out. His jaw was locked, and his nose and mouth were twitching at a snarl. I knew we had a few seconds before he snapped and dove over the table.

Suddenly, something inside me clicked. I'm not sure what it was. Maybe I was thinking of what Sile had told me before—that I was viewed as the weakest link in the academy and the others would try to take advantage of that. Or maybe I had grown into a moody jerk with a really short temper. Either way, something came over me and I was helpless to stop it. I saw what was happening, and instead of keeping my head down for the sake of appearances, I acted.

Lyon was using me to get to Felix. That was going to stop.

I put my hands on the table and stood. All eyes turned to me. I only focused on Lyon. "You and me. Outside. Right now."

Lyon choked on his food. "What?"

"You heard me." I couldn't believe how calm I sounded. "If you've got something to say, say it to me. Don't talk like I can't hear you, or like I don't understand. I know what you're trying to do. You think you can keep using me to provoke him? Like he's my keeper or something?" I leaned down to put my face uncomfortably close to his. "Big mistake. I'm nobody's sidekick. I'm definitely not your doormat anymore. So let's go outside and clear the air, shall we?"

A chorus of *oooh*'s went up all around the dining hall. I could feel the excitement rising with the anticipation of a fight. Everyone was hoping for a show.

It was a stupid thing to do. Even I knew that. But Sile had been right all along when he told me I had to pick a fight. I saw that now. I had to establish myself as a capable member of this academy, especially if I wanted to make sure Felix didn't go around swinging wildly at anyone who said something bad about me. I knew Felix would fight to the death defending me against everything and everyone. It sounded great in theory. In practice it put a huge target on his back. It made everyone look at him like an obstacle that had to be overcome in order to get to me. I had to make a stand for myself now.

Lyon sat there, glaring up at me. I could tell he was thinking it over. He probably didn't want to fight me, but I'd left him no choice now. If he backed down now, he would look like an even bigger coward.

He pushed his tray of food away and stood up to meet me nose-to-nose. "Fine," he agreed. "Outside it is."

14

CHAPTER FOURTEEN

A huge crowd of students followed us out of the dining hall. I knew it was only a matter of time before the instructors noticed and stepped in to stop us. I had a plan. This had to be fast.

We gathered right outside the dormitory, and slowly everyone started forming a big circle around Lyon and me. Last year, Lyon had kept company with a group of lackeys who always showed up whenever he wanted to push me around. As he emerged from the crowd, I noticed that he was alone now. In fact, I hadn't seen them around him at all since our incident at the prison camp last year. Maybe he'd lost his friends?

As I started toward him, I felt a strong grip on my elbow. "Have you lost your mind?" Felix muttered furiously.

I wasn't sure how to answer that.

"Jace is going to beat your face in," he warned. "Call this off. You've made your point."

I pulled my arm away and smirked. "No, not yet. You don't get it, do you? If I'm going to survive here, and if you're going to keep being my friend, then I have to do this. Besides, what's the worst he can do? Make me run a few more laps?"

The color was draining out of Felix's face. I knew why. I joked about it now, but the chances that Jace might actually beat me for this were good.

I tried not to think about it as I turned back toward Lyon. I knew there was a lot worse Jace could do than hit me a few times. He could get me kicked out of the academy. "Yeah, like that's anything new." I muttered to myself. The fear of getting kicked out had been my driving force last year. Now, for whatever reason, it didn't scare me as much. I was trusting Sile's advice. Surely he wouldn't tell me to do something that would get me in that much trouble.

The crowd around us had started yelling and cheering as I squared off with Lyon. The realization of exactly how stupid this was started crashing in on me. Not just because it was unnecessarily barbaric, but also because I was pretty much the worst hand-to-hand fighter in the world. I couldn't remember if I'd ever actually seen Lyon spar before, so I didn't know what his strengths were. It was a safe bet to assume that whatever he could do, it was better than anything I could come up with.

I widened my stance, put up my fists, and braced for impact.

For a few seconds, we paced around in a slow circle and sized each other up. It was almost like a dance. I was studying how he moved, trying to find a weakness. Lyon was short and husky, so I knew he'd probably hit hard. I'd have to use my speed and reach to keep from taking too many blows. After all, part of my plan was to draw this out as long as I could.

Lyon lunged first. He dove at me and started swinging his fists. The crowd roared with excitement. I only heard one person cheering for me, and I didn't have to look to see who it was.

I dodged and weaved around Lyon's attacks easily. He was a lot slower than I expected. I easily darted in to jab at his face, pounding his cheeks and then jumping back out of his reach again before he could retaliate. It started to frustrate him. I could see his anger mounting. Even if his heart hadn't been in this fight before, the idea that I might beat him in front of everyone was starting to wear him down.

He started getting reckless. He lunged at me and grabbed the front of my tunic. He pounded his fist into my face so hard it made my brains feel scrambled. I was stunned, but not for long. I hooked a leg through his and drove my elbow into his gut, sending us both sprawling into the dirt.

I knew I wasn't much of a match for him when it came to grappling. My height and speed wouldn't serve me much. On the ground, he had the advantage, and he refused to let go of my tunic so I could get away. Lyon got me into a headlock from behind and started to squeeze. My vision blurred. I could taste blood in my mouth.

Through the haze, I saw Felix squatting down a few feet away from me. He was yelling at the top of his lungs, but I couldn't make out anything he said over the noise of the crowd. I tried to get my legs back under me. If I wanted to win, I had to get back on my feet somehow.

Lyon was so heavy. His arms were thick and strong, squeezing my head tighter and tighter. It was hard to move at all. No matter how I squirmed or clawed at his arm, he kept adding pressure to my neck until I could barely breathe.

Then, something inside me broke like a floodgate of anger. It wasn't anything like that sense of calm that had come over me in the dining hall. This was something a thousand times worse. I'd never felt anything like it. White-hot rage filled my veins like fire. My vision snapped into focus. My body surged with energy. The pain from being hit and choked was gone.

I went absolutely crazy.

Without warning, I slammed my head back against Lyon's. It hit so hard I heard the crack like someone snapping a tree in two. Immediately, he let me go.

Normally, I would have taken that chance to get back on my feet so I was in a better position to keep the fight going. After all, that had been my plan all along: to show the others that I could hold my own until an instructor stepped in to break things up. No one had to get seriously hurt. Worst case scenario, Jace would make Lyon and me run laps all day.

But now things were out of control... and I couldn't stop myself. My body moved without my permission, doing things I didn't even know I could do.

I was like an animal. I dove after Lyon and whipped him into a lethal hold, bearing my knees down on his shoulders and locking my ankles under him. I saw the fear in his eyes as I snarled down at him, and drew back to begin pounding my fists into his face again and again. My knuckles were coated with blood, and I wasn't sure how much of it was his or mine.

The crowd went completely silent. All I could hear was the gory sound every time my fist met his face. Lyon wasn't moving anymore, but I kept hitting him anyway.

Someone grabbed me from behind. I knew it was Felix by the strength of his hold. He tried to pin my arms and drag me away, but I whipped around, stepping easily through complex sparring moves like they were nothing. I moved like a ghost, and not even Felix could keep up.

I had him pinned on his stomach in matter of seconds, wrenching his arm behind his back and adding pressure that would break it if he didn't surrender. But he wouldn't tap out. Felix would never surrender like that, and part of me knew it. I'd have to break his arm.

That should have been more than enough to make me stop. Felix wasn't my enemy. He was my best friend. I didn't want to hurt him. But I couldn't shut my brain off. I couldn't stop. My body kept moving, getting closer and closer to snapping his arm.

Suddenly, I felt the point of a knife at my throat.

"Let him go, demon," an unfamiliar man's voice boomed at my back.

Immediately, I let Felix go. My mind started to clear. The prick of that knife had been enough to jar me free of that horrible trance. I could think again. Underneath my tunic, I could feel my mother's necklace burning hot against my skin again.

My hands were shaking as I started to raise them in surrender. Before I could speak, a big boot kicked me to the ground. Someone started roughly tying my hands behind my back, binding me up like a prisoner. Fear poured over my body like ice water.

I could sense incredible strength in the arm that yanked me to my feet. The other students still gathered around all looked at me with different expressions of horror, fear, and awe. Some of them were checking on Lyon. He was sitting up and moving. I was so relieved that he was alive, even if his face was a pulverized bloody mess. I hadn't killed him, and that was enough to make me thank the fates.

Felix was standing a few feet away, rubbing his arm. I couldn't bring myself to meet his gaze. I was so ashamed and disgusted with myself. I had never intended for the fight to get this bad. I hadn't wanted to hurt Lyon like that.

"Who let this piece of filth into our midst?" The man holding my arms shook me violently and roared. He sounded like an angry bear. It terrified me. Even though I couldn't see him, I could sense his size and incredible strength just by the way his massive hand gripped me. The other students looked afraid of him, too. Their eyes were wide, and some of them were even slipping away into the dark.

"Commander Rayken has betrayed us by letting this creature into our brotherhood," he rumbled. "But it's easily fixed. Pay attention, all you little mutts. Let me teach you something useful. This is how you sever a demon's spine without getting any blood on your sleeves."

I felt the point of a knife press hard against the back of my neck, and hot breath against the tips of my pointed ears. I trembled, and squeezed my eyes shut.

"Lieutenant Thane." My knees almost buckled with relief when I heard Jace's voice. "That avian belongs to me. I'm going to have to ask you to let him go."

I opened my eyes, and he was standing right in front of me. Jace was looking at the mess I'd made with the same eerily blank expression he always wore. It wasn't comforting at all, but at least he wasn't going to let Lieutenant Thane—whoever that was—butcher me like a spring calf in front of the whole academy.

"This *thing* isn't an avian," Thane snarled ferociously. He squeezed my arm so hard I was sure it would snap in half. "Or have these months away from the battlefront made you forget what the enemy looks like? Here, let me remind you." He grabbed a fistful of my hair and jerked my head around to look at the crowd.

Jace stared at me for a few uncomfortable moments before he spoke. "I'm very aware of what he looks like. I'm his instructor. Now let him go. I won't ask you again." His voice was so calm it gave me chills. He still hadn't made any expression, but I could see something like cold fire burning in his eyes. It chilled me to the bone.

Almost all of the other students had found a chance to slip away by the time Lieutenant Thane finally let me go. I stumbled and almost tripped, but Felix caught me. He started untying my hands while the two lieutenants continued to argue. Thane's voice boomed like a dragon's roar, and when I finally got a glimpse of him, my stomach turned to mush.

Thane was a huge man. He towered over everyone like a mountain of muscle. His body was so bulky that he barely had a neck. He had a long, scraggly black beard, but no hair on his head at all. His eyes were as black as pitch, and they darted back and forth between Jace and me like he was looking for a chance to strike at one or both of us.

I swallowed hard. My whole body was still shaking. I couldn't tell if it was from fear or because I was still coming down off whatever had made me go crazy like that. Standing under the inferno of Thrane's glare, I could sense how much he hated me. He leered down at me, flexing his huge hands like he was imagining what it would feel like to break my neck. I held my breath and waited to see what he'd do. Finally, Thrane made a snarling sound and stormed away. Apparently, he wasn't willing to fight Jace over the chance to kill me—at least, not yet.

"What's wrong with you?" Felix whispered as he finished untying my hands. "First you challenge Lyon to fight, then you try to crack my arm off?"

"I-I don't know," I stammered as I rubbed my wrists. Thane had tied them so tight that it left deep red marks and bruises behind.

"You scared me to death." Felix grumbled. He smacked me on the back of the head. "Don't do that again, idiot."

"I'm sorry. I didn't mean to. I couldn't control myself. I couldn't stop it." I didn't know how else to explain it to him. I didn't even understand it myself.

"It's battle fever," Jace interrupted suddenly. I almost jumped out of my skin when I saw he was standing so close, listening to us. "The elves call it *kulunai*, or something like that."

I wanted to duck away, or hang my head in shame. I knew there was going to be some kind of punishment for this. Still, hearing Jace talk about it like he understood caught me completely off guard. I couldn't look away. I'd never heard of battle fever before.

"It's brought on by pain and adrenaline," he continued. "It's some kind of self-defense response. I've only ever seen it in adults on the battlefield. I don't think the kids are capable of it."

Felix let out an uneasy sigh when he sized me up again. "That explains why it's never happened before. Right, Jae?"

I couldn't speak. I was too humiliated and shaken up. All I could do was nod.

"I've heard rumors that the adults induce it before battle in some kind of ceremony. Who knows how much truth there is to that." Jace started to stroll away from us. As he passed me, I let myself hope that he might actually let me go without any punishment.

Then he slapped me hard across the cheek. It made my whole jaw hurt. He'd never hit me before, and it felt like someone had taken a plank of wood to my face. Normally, I would have been terrified or hurt that he would slap me like that. But after everything I'd done, I knew I deserved it.

"Don't do that again," he warned me in a deep growling voice. "You have to control it. You don't realize how lucky you are; Thane will not forgive you a second time."

I didn't say it out loud—I was too busy rubbing my cheek because it was stinging like it was on fire—but I knew Thane hadn't forgiven me at all. He wasn't willing to fight Jace in order to get to me. Jace had saved my life.

"Who was that other student you were fighting with?" he demanded.

Felix piped up first, so I kept my mouth shut. I knew he was eager to tattle on Lyon the first chance he got. "Lyon Cromwell. He's your third student, sir."

Jace's eyes narrowed. "What?"

"Yes, sir. Lyon Cromwell, son of Duke Cromwell. He arrived this morning. He was supposed to be cleaning tack with us today, but he never showed up to help."

"Is that so?" Jace's tone deepened, and he turned his cold eyes back on me. "Well, it seems you three need some encouragement in order to act like soldiers. Lucky for you, I'm very good at providing that kind of... *encouragement*."

Felix and I cringed at the same time. We knew what kind of encouragement he was talking about. Tomorrow was going to hurt.

"We're not finished with the saddles yet, sir," Felix said. "Being shorthanded put us way behind."

Jace had already started walking away. But Felix's comment made him stop and glance back at us. He gave us a hard, disapproving frown. "Hurry and finish them, then. But clean yourself up first." He gestured to my face. I'd forgotten all about the few good punches Lyon had scored on my nose. It was still bleeding a little.

Once Jace was out of earshot and we were alone, Felix let out a string of curses. I was still too overwhelmed to be angry. Between not getting any sleep because of my nightmares, worrying about running into Katty again, figuring out that rumor about Sile, and hiding all these secrets about my strange abilities, I didn't have room for anything else. My head felt like it was going to pop. I couldn't take it.

I took off toward the tack room. Before I could get to the door, a mountain of blue scales dropped from the sky and landed right before me. Mavrik chirped with concern as he lowered his head. I could barely concentrate. I was still shaking. He pushed his snout against my chest, and I leaned against him.

"I can't take much more of this." I muttered as I ran my hands over his scaly head.

Mavrik gave me a low growl. He could sense what I was thinking, and I guess he didn't like it. I was beginning to think maybe this wasn't the place for me, after all. So much was happening. I felt out of control. I couldn't even trust myself anymore. At any moment, I might snap like that again and end up hurting someone I cared about. How could I live with that? Jace told me to control it as though I actually could. But how could he understand? He was a human.

"You better not be going off to pout," Felix called after me. I could hear him running to catch up. "I'm fine. I'm not even angry. So don't worry about it."

I stood there frozen as I watched the green colors of concern Mavrik sent swirling through my brain. I was still thinking about leaving. How could I ever hope to keep my promise to protect my friends if I was going to end up being dangerous to them? I couldn't trust myself to fight next to Felix if there was a chance I might turn on him at any second.

"I'm not stupid, you know." Felix was walking up behind me. "I know when something's bothering you. You've got circles under your eyes like you haven't been sleeping. So what is it? What else aren't you telling me?"

I shut my eyes tightly and pushed Mavrik's head away. I didn't want to tell him about my nightmares. It was embarrassing and it made me feel weak. They were just dreams. "It's nothing."

"Liar. Quit being such a girl and confess. What's going on?" He slapped a hand down on my shoulder so hard it almost knocked me over. "You know you can trust me. I'm not going to judge you."

I bit down hard on the inside of my cheek. As much as I wanted to tell him everything, I couldn't. I was turning into some kind of monster, and I didn't deserve to be here anymore.

"I can't." I snapped at him. "Just stay away from me."

"Why? Because you think I'm afraid of you now? Nice try, kid. You'll have to do worse than break my arm if you want to scare me." He stepped into my path and crossed his arms. "Jaevid, come on. I can see that you're struggling. You can't carry all this on your own."

I was determined not to cave. I wouldn't give in, not this time. "I don't have a choice," I told him.

His expression fell some. He looked hurt. For a few minutes, we stood there silently until it was awkward.

Finally, he nodded and stepped out of my way. "Fine. Have it your way. You want to be the cool loner, so be it."

I DIDN'T WANT TO BE A LONER. THERE WAS NOTHING COOL ABOUT IT. I hated knowing I had hurt Felix by shutting him out like that. I needed him to be my friend like before. But Sile had warned me about saying too much, and now I was starting to understand why. There were things about myself—dangerous things—that I wasn't even aware of yet. In order to protect him, I had to keep this stuff to myself. If someone like Thane figured out that I was turning into some kind of mutant halfbreed sorcerer, then I couldn't let Felix be guilty by association. He'd defend me to the bitter end, even when I didn't deserve it.

The days leading up to training passed slowly, and each one was more miserable than the last. Felix didn't talk to me at all. He wouldn't even look at me. I'd never been so lonely in my life. I knew he was just sulking. It was probably killing him, too. But I wasn't going to give up now; it was much safer for him to keep his distance from me.

My nightmares continued every night without fail. As soon as I closed my eyes, I was pulled into that same vision. I fought it as hard as I could. It never helped at all. All I wanted was a few hours of sleep. The dream played over and over again in my head, startling me awake every time. I always woke up in a cold sweat with those eerie words ringing in my ears:

"*Return it.*"

After he was released from the infirmary with a broken nose, Lyon joined us in our early morning training drills. He struggled with the running because his old instructor had never required him to do anything like that. Jace spent a lot of extra time "encouraging" him.

The closer we got to the start of training, the more ruthless Jace was about our morning routine. He yelled until it felt like my eardrums were sore. One day, he even came out with a bullwhip while we were struggling through an hour of push-ups. If we slowed down at all, he cracked it in the air. He was incredibly accurate with it. He could pop it right at the tip of my nose. It never actually hit me, but I could practically taste the leather in my teeth.

After finishing our morning drills, the three of us worked through cleaning saddles. It took us hours to finish, but no one ever said a word. Felix was still sulking, so he wouldn't talk to me. Lyon looked terrified of both of us, and he never said a word. His face was bruised up, thanks to me. I felt really bad about that, but I couldn't bring myself to apologize. I couldn't find the will to try talking to either of them, not that they would have answered. It was depressing to work for so long in total silence.

In the dining hall, I sat by myself. It was painful to watch Felix sitting with the other avians, laughing and carrying on like always. The gnawing sense of loneliness in my chest wore on me. It was getting harder and harder to cope. I didn't want to be here anymore. I started thinking about leaving altogether, but I knew Sile would probably hunt me down to the ends of the earth if I gave up. He'd spent a lot of money and risked his honor and good name for me to be here.

The day before training, I got word that my gear was finally finished. It had taken a lot longer than I expected, especially since none of my stuff was that intricate. But after morning drills, Jace gave me permission to go and pick up everything before I started to work on cleaning saddles.

I went alone to pick up my armor first. I waited while the blacksmith brought it out piece by piece, laying everything out on a worktable so I could inspect it. He'd wrapped it all in rags to protect it.

About the same time I started unwrapping it, the blacksmith spoke up. "Took a little longer after you made those changes."

"Changes?" I held up one of the gauntlets. It was definitely the traditional style I'd chosen, but there were a lot more grooves cut into it than before. As I unwrapped each piece of my new armor, I noticed more and more of those same beautiful details. All the bolts holding it together were plated in gold. The breastplate was accented with grooves and etchings. The armor was much more ornate than I had asked for.

The helmet was the most detailed of all. There was a snarling dragon's head engraved on both sides of it, so that it looked like my face was coming out of its mouth. The engraved lines of the design had been inlaid with gold, so it shimmered in the light. It was beautiful, but definitely not what I'd ordered.

"I didn't ask for any of this," I said.

The blacksmith scowled at me. He dug through his box of paperwork until he found my forms, and shoved them at me roughly. The first few pages looked exactly how I remembered, but on the last page there was big paragraph scribbled asking for all the extra details. I knew that handwriting right away.

"It's already been paid for," the blacksmith grumbled.

I scowled at the paper. I had to fight the urge to crumple it up in anger. "It's okay," I managed to growl through my teeth. "I must have forgotten. I'll take it."

The blacksmith wrapped all the pieces back up for me, placing them carefully in a big canvas bag. I slung it over my shoulder and carried it away toward the tackmaster. I already had suspicions burning in my brain before I ever got there.

And I was right.

My saddle order had been changed as well. Instead of the plain saddle I had ordered, someone had gone right behind me and added details. They'd also paid extra for them. The saddle was beyond beautiful. It was made of dark, chocolate brown and black leather. The buckles were layered with an extra layer of brass so that they shimmered to match the gold details on my armor. The sides were engraved with intricate scrollwork like vines, images of dragons, and something that looked suspiciously like a turtle. The seat was padded with layers of soft deer hide, and the handles were made from engraved milky white ivory.

Even with the extra money I'd had leftover, there was no way I could have afforded something like this. I had only seen my father make a saddle this nice a few times in my life, and always for some high ranking official like a general. I was so shocked that I forgot to get upset about it.

Mavrik stretched out obediently on the ground when I asked him to let me fit the saddle to his back. He made a big show of yawning and groaning as I put it on, testing the fit of all the straps. It was perfect. The brown leather looked almost red against his dusky blue scales. And the black leather picked up on the onyx color of his horns. It didn't look like a saddle at all—it looked like a part of him. The sight of it made me smile.

Mavrik shifted and squirmed, testing the fit before he finally gave me a chirp of approval.

"It's good?" I asked him.

He answered with a blast of hot, stinking dragon breath in my face as he yawned again. I took that as a "yes."

"Fine, then. Try not to bang it up, will you? I can't afford to replace it." I patted his neck and sent him off. After I cleared everything with the tackmaster and thanked him for his work, I didn't waste any more time around the armories.

I owed someone a piece of my mind.

Felix was sitting outside the dormitory, picking food out of his teeth after breakfast. A few other avians were standing around talking to him, but they cleared out as soon as they saw me coming. I guess I had made an impression after all.

I took the bag of armor off my back and sat it on the ground between us. "Why did you do that?" I demanded.

Felix glared at my shadow. He wouldn't look up at me, and he didn't say a word. That stubborn, rich idiot. I'd recognized his handwriting on those order forms immediately.

I was getting really tired of his sulking act. "You know I can't pay you back for this. That saddle probably cost more than I would at the slave market."

"You're not paying me back," Felix snapped suddenly. "So don't even try. It was supposed to be a gift."

"Why?"

He finally met my gaze with stubborn fury in his eyes. "Because even though you're being stupid, you're still my friend. Because you're a dragonrider, and there's an expectation of how we should look when we go into battle. And because when you die, you'll be buried in that armor, and it shouldn't look like a rusted out tin bucket. You deserve better than that. Do I need any other reasons?"

I choked on my frustration. I couldn't even get a word out.

"I get why you're doing this. You think you're doing me a favor by keeping me in the dark. Don't you realize I know the risks of being around you?" Felix's body language relaxed some as he let out a heavy sigh. He started scratching at the back of his head. "I understand all that, and I don't care. If you're going down, then I'm going down with you. That's the way it is."

"But—" I started to object until he cut me off.

"Oh give it up, will you? If you're not ready to tell me what's really going on with you, then fine. I guess that's your business. But quit trying to protect me. It's weird and annoying."

For some reason, I had to smile. I knew Felix pretty well. He never liked admitting when he was wrong about anything. This seemed like his way of letting me know he felt bad about pushing me for information. He would let me keep my secrets for now.

"Fine. Quit buying me stuff behind my back." I added.

When Felix looked up at me again, he was finally grinning. The tension in the air was gone. Things were back to normal again. It felt like a weight had been lifted off me.

He stood up, and punched my arm. "That's the worst thank you I've ever heard."

15

CHAPTER FIFTEEN

Working through tack detail duties was so much easier now that Felix and I were back on speaking terms. Lyon never said a word, but he showed up and helped out as usual. I still felt a nagging sense of guilt whenever I looked at him. Lyon's blue, battered nose was wrapped up in gauze that went all the way around his head. I'd overheard some of the other avians joking that he would probably have a crooked nose for the rest of his life. I'd never meant for that to happen, and he seemed genuinely terrified of both of us now. I decided to try to find the right moment to apologize to him—preferably when Felix wasn't there to heckle me for it.

After we finished up with tack detail, there was still plenty of daylight left. It was the last day before the official start of training, so the academy was full of people. Craftsmen were packing up to leave in the morning. Instructors were showing the new fledglings where they had to go on their first day. There were dragons everywhere. Some circled overhead, riding in the updrafts or chasing each other. Others lounged on the ground, napping in groups like lazy housecats. More were climbing the walls and preening their scales, or basking in the last few rays of sunlight. There was so much energy in the air that it felt contagious. Sure, my brain was a scrambled, exhausted mess, but I was still excited for the first call to arms in the morning. I was ready to get started.

On our way out of the tack room, Felix started poking my shoulder excitedly. "Hey, let's go for a ride. We haven't flown together since last year, and you need to test out that new saddle."

I tried to resist. I'd already gotten in trouble with Jace twice. I wasn't looking to test how many chances he'd give me. "Will Jace get angry if we go without his permission?"

"Maybe not. I mean, we're not fledglings anymore. We can handle it if something goes wrong." Felix was a champion when it came to bargaining with me. He knew I wanted to fly as badly as he did. It didn't take much to convince me.

"Okay, fine." I stopped and glanced back. Lyon was still in the tack room pretending to put things away. He always did that. I guess it was so he would have an excuse not to walk out with us. "What about him?"

"Forget him." Felix scoffed and started climbing the stairs up to the Roost.

But I couldn't forget him. He was supposed to be our third man, now. He was our partner in training. It was bad enough his old lackeys from last year had abandoned him. If we shunned him, he'd be alone. I knew what alone felt like.

"Lyon," I called out to him.

He flinched, and looked over at me with wide eyes. His face was pasty white with fear, like he might suddenly bolt if I made a wrong move.

"We're going out for a flight. You should come, too."

Lyon stood there, motionless. He didn't say anything. We stared at each other for a long time, and finally I decided he wasn't going to answer me at all. I cleared my throat and took a step back toward the stairs.

"Well, if you change your mind, you should come find us," I said. I left him in the tack room and ran up the stairs after Felix.

Mavrik growled and chirped with excitement when I came into his stall. He chattered and grumbled anxiously while I strapped on some of my new armor. I didn't dress out fully since this was just a pleasure ride. I slipped the chestplate over my head and buckled it into place, then tightened the shiny vambraces and gauntlets over my arms. The palms of the gauntlets were coated in a thick layer of rubbery resin that made it easy to grip the saddle handles. I slipped the helmet over my head, tapping a finger on the long glass slit cut across the front so I could see without the wind blowing in my eyes.

I could tell this armor had been made with much more care and precision than the stuff I had worn last year. It fit snuggly, but it was so much lighter and more comfortable. It was made to fit me, and something about it felt right.

"Nice. It looks good," Felix muttered from the doorway. He was dressed out in a few pieces of his own armor. His was different than mine, with a much sleeker style. The metal had been stained to look almost golden brown, and there was a crest of black horsehair on the top of his helmet.

I gave him a thumbs up. "Fits good, too."

"Glad to hear it. I'll take the lead, if you don't mind." He chuckled and waved before going back to his own stall.

I smirked at Mavrik. He eagerly crawled to the edge of his stall and looked out to the steep drop below. I could see his armored sides moving in and out with his excited breaths. His powerful hind legs were coiled, ready to leap into the sky. The setting sunlight shimmered over his blue scales.

"He can take the lead," I muttered as I ran my hand over my dragon's side. I could feel the power of his muscles underneath his thick hide. "But let's see if he can keep it."

As I climbed into the saddle and got myself buckled in, Mavrik let out a booming roar. He didn't give me a second's chance to prepare. When the last strap was in place, he dove headlong out of his stall and we went rocketing toward the ground. Out of the corner of my eye, I saw Nova and Felix doing the same thing. We spiraled down like two bolts of lightning, and at the last second, our dragons flared and caught the wind with their powerful wings.

We soared into the sky, sailing on the winds like two armored kites. I could barely make out the sound of Felix laughing as he urged Nova to go faster, taking the lead as we left the academy behind. I could see other riders flying in pairs or groups all around us. Some flew high, scraping the clouds like they wanted to get a glimpse of the stars. Others were doing low passes, or weaving dangerously close to the steep cliffs.

The minute I got a deep breath of the free air in my lungs, I felt all the stress and worry in my mind melt away. None of it seemed that important anymore. I could fly away and leave it all behind. When we flew like this, I had a hard time telling which feelings were mine and which were Mavrik's—not that it mattered. When we flew, it was like our souls touched, and the spark could be seen for miles and miles.

Felix and Nova flew considerably fast, but they were no match for our speed. Mavrik caught up to them quickly. We zipped past, and rolled over into another steep dive. Nova chased us, and we started doing spirals and rolls as fast as we could. We flew up, punching holes through the clouds and getting a glimpse of the first few evening stars before we stalled and started falling. The freefall was incredible, and Mavrik roared with delight as we plummeted back toward the ground.

When we were all winded and exhausted, we landed on a nearby cliff to rest. The sun was beginning to slip down behind the distant ocean. From where we were sitting, we could barely make out the surface of the water, glittering like a mirror on the horizon. The cliff gave us a really great view of the academy, which stood out on the valley floor like a big stone circle. The dark shapes of dragons flew all around it.

I sat on the edge of the cliff with my legs dangling over the drop. Mavrik was crouched beside me, still panting with his mouth open. On the other side of me, Felix was drinking from a canteen he'd clipped to his saddle. Nova was preening her brown and golden scales. Everything between us felt calm. It felt right.

"Where did you get Nova, anyway?" I didn't know why I'd never thought to ask him that before. "Did she choose you?"

Felix wiped his chin and handed me the canteen so I could drink, too. "No, of course not. I bought her when she was a hatchling. That's the way it usually goes, these days. It's like when people breed horses, or dogs. Whoever owns the female pays a siring fee for a male to come and, well, you know. When she lays her eggs, people start bidding to get one of the hatchlings. The highest bidder gets first choice."

"And she was your first choice?" I looked up at Nova. I could see why he would choose her. She was big, for a female. She had beautiful markings, and there was definitely something regal about her.

"She was the dominant of the clutch. When dragons hatch, there's always a dominant baby. Just like with eagles, you know? There's always one that's bigger and stronger. They call it the dominant hatchling. Nova came out of her egg squawking like she owned the place, and she showed me her teeth when I tried to touch her. I can't explain it. I knew she was the one I wanted, even if she didn't like me. I knew I could win her over." Felix laughed and winked at me. "I'm great with girls."

I rolled my eyes. "I'm not sure that applies to dragons."

"Well, does she like me?" he asked.

"What do you mean?"

Felix arched a brow at me curiously. "I mean, you can talk to animals, right? So ask her if she likes me."

I eyed Nova uncomfortably. I'd never tried to talk to another dragon other than Mavrik except for Icarus. That hadn't ended so well for the rider. Besides, Mavrik was the only one who had been able to talk back to me.

"I-I'll try," I stammered and got to my feet. I started walking toward Nova.

As soon as I got close she turned her big head around to look right at me. Her intelligent, dark green eyes studied me. I swallowed back my fear, and reached a hand out toward her. She shied back, her pupils narrowing with distrust. I'd never tried to touch her before.

I started searching through my mind like before, looking for that quiet warmth that spread over my body. I felt her presence in that warmth, like a ripple on a pond. I could feel Mavrik, too, but his presence was so familiar to me now it was like second nature. Still, letting my guard down so I could sense these things gave me chills. My ability was getting stronger. I could focus faster. My fingertips buzzed and tingled with energy.

"It's okay," I said softly. "You can feel me, too, right? You know I won't hurt you. I just want to talk."

Behind me, Mavrik gave her some encouraging chirps.

Nova looked hesitant, but finally she pushed her snout against my hand. I could feel the blast of her strong breaths against my chest.

I couldn't keep myself from smiling. "You can understand me, can't you?"

She made a low, chattering noise. Her wise eyes focused directly into mine. It was silent except for the wind.

Then it happened.

Felix's dragon, Nova, spoke back to me.

It hit me like a tidal wave. It wasn't words, just like Mavrik didn't speak to me with words. It was a rush of emotion that poured into my thoughts like a dam had broken inside me. I saw visions, flashes of moments, and they blurred through my mind so quickly that I could barely understand all of it. But one thing kept leaping out, gripping me so that it stuck in my brain like a thorn: Danger was coming.

There was a strong sense of impending doom, like she knew something terrible was going to happen. I tried to ask her what it was. Even though I couldn't get a word out, she seemed to understand my question. She was reading my thoughts like Mavrik did.

But I didn't understand her answer. It was too jumbled; a furious mixture of images and feelings like a tangled mess of string. I cringed as I felt something familiar surge through our minds—that sense of chaos I'd felt from the wolves and mountain cat. I was starting to hate that feeling. It frustrated me, and dulled my senses. But now, thanks to Nova, I understood something new about it. The animals were afraid of this chaos that was trying to possess them. They could sense it coming, but they couldn't do anything to stop it.

Finally, Nova settled on one image. She showed me a deep, dark pit surrounded by trees. It was like a cavern in the earth that went straight down. There was a staircase overgrown with roots carved into the side of the cave that went spiraling around and around down into the dark. I didn't even realize that it really felt like I was standing there on the edge of the pit, until I almost tripped and fell in. Then I got that weird, panicked sensation like I was about to fall. It seemed so real.

Then I heard a voice. A voice echoed up from that dark place, and filled every corner of my mind.

"Return it."

Feelings of anxiety and genuine fear for my life surged through my body. I jerked away from Nova. The instant I took my hand away from her snout, my mind went quiet. The images and emotions were gone. Everything was calm.

Nova was still looking at me, her head tilted to the side like she didn't know why I had stopped our communication all of a sudden. I noticed my nose had started to bleed a little. My heart was pounding in my ears.

"Are you okay?" Felix rushed over. "What happened?"

I choked. My hands were shaking again. I got that cold, clammy feeling like I was going to pass out. Then my knees started to buckle.

Felix caught me before I hit the ground. He helped me sit down, and propped me up against the side of the cliff. He and the dragons gathered around, looking at me with concern.

"Just breathe. You're fine." Felix patted my shoulder roughly. "What happened? What did you see?"

My heart was still beating out of control. "I'm not sure," I managed to answer. "She *answered* me."

"Answered?" He looked confused. "Of course she did. Don't they all answer you?"

I shook my head and tried to wipe the blood off my nose. "Only Mavrik. Most animals seem to understand me, but he's the only one who has ever communicated back. But she answered me."

Felix started to look pale. "What did she say?"

I hesitated. Telling him what she showed me would definitely lead to questions. I would end up having to tell him everything. Well, almost everything. I hadn't told him anything about my dreams, but I couldn't deny that my repeating nightmare was somehow connected to whatever Nova had shown me. That voice that had spoken to me from the depths of that cavern—it was my mother's voice. There was no mistaking it.

I guess Felix could see me struggling, trying to decide what to tell him. He let out a sigh of frustration and sat down beside me. He leaned against the side of the cliff, rested his hands on his knees, and stared off into the sunset.

"You remember that time last year when you asked me why I wanted to be friends with you?" He said. "We had just gotten into a huge fistfight with Lyon and his buddies. You had been beaten to a pulp again, like always. I honestly didn't know if we could even win that fight. We were outnumbered. I guess it's a good thing we're both either too stupid or too stubborn to know when to run, huh?"

I'd been beaten up more times than I could count. That was a general side effect of being born a halfbreed. Even Lyon had found multiple opportunities to pulverize me. But I knew exactly which fight he was talking about. "You must be a lot more stupid than I am, though, since you still want to be friends with me even after everything that's happened."

"Probably. But I'm okay with that." He smirked. "We work best when we work together. Haven't you figured that out by now?" Felix looked over at me, and I knew he was right. Neither one of us would have survived last year if we hadn't been together. He needed me watching his back every bit as badly as I needed him watching mine.

"Fine." I surrendered. "But if you give me that look again like I'm turning into some evil Gray elf monster…"

He laughed so loud it almost made me have a heart attack. "You already did that once, right? And I survived, arm and all."

"That's not what I meant." My ears were starting to sizzle with embarrassment.

Felix punched my shoulder. I punched him back. We were both going to have permanent bruises on our arms. "I know what you meant. I already said I'm not gonna judge you. So relax and fess up."

BY THE TIME I FINISHED TELLING FELIX ABOUT THE DREAMS I WAS HAVING, the sun had set and it was almost dark. I couldn't bring myself to watch his reaction, but whenever he said something or asked a question, I could hear how serious he was. Something about my dream had him worried.

"Jaevid, did anyone ever tell you how this war got started?" Felix asked as we stood up. We started checking our saddles one more time, just to be sure nothing had bent or come loose during our last flight. We had to get back to the academy soon, or Jace would come looking for us.

"No." To be honest, it had never really mattered to me before. I assumed it was a problem a lot bigger and older than I was. I didn't see how knowing the details would make any difference.

Felix got quiet. The look on his face was intense. He started rubbing his chin, scratching at the beard that was starting to grow in. Finally, he started to tell the story.

"I mean, after twenty years or so, the details are muddy. Truth gets mixed with rumors. Pretty soon, it's hard to tell what's true and what's not," he said. "But the way I've always heard it was that the Gray elves struck first. They launched an attack against our northern border, started burning villages and killing townsfolk. The royal family was traveling up there and got caught in the crossfire. Only the king survived—if you can even call it that. His whole body was so badly burned and mutilated that to this day, he wears a mask and long baggy robes to hide the scars. They say his face was almost burned completely off by shrike venom. He doesn't come to balls or parties unless he has to. People rarely see him outside the castle. They say his whole mind has been consumed by the desire to win this war at all costs, not that I blame him. Look at what it's done to him, and to his people. Anyone would want justice for something like that. That's why he hates Gray elves so much."

I tried to think of what to say or how to respond. Nothing would come out. I stood frozen, staring at Felix. And he stared right back at me with a haunted look in his eyes. I knew we were both wondering the same thing.

"I'm dreaming about something that happened twenty years ago?" I forced myself to ask. I wanted to make sure this wasn't some kind of twisted Felix-style prank. He was totally capable of doing something like that just to watch me squirm. It was basically his favorite hobby.

Felix frowned and looked away. "No. Don't be ridiculous. That's not possible. It's a coincidence."

I was starting to panic. If he wasn't joking, then why was I dreaming about something like that? "But, Felix, the details are the same!"

He turned away and picked up his helmet. "No, they're not. You said the king died in your dream, right? Well he's not dead. I've seen him myself. He came to one of our solstice parties once. I was a kid then, but I remember it. He was definitely there, and definitely alive."

"Then why would I dream something like that? And why do I keep dreaming it every night?" I crossed my arms. I was ready to argue this until my ears bled, or until it made sense. Whichever came first.

"Maybe you overheard someone talking about it and you forgot." Felix shrugged off all my questions and crammed his helmet down onto his head. "I knew you weren't sleeping. You've got bags under your eyes big enough to store gear in. Don't let something like this distract you, much less keep you from sleeping. You can't afford to lose your focus now."

I knew I had never heard anything about this before, but I wasn't getting anywhere with Felix. I wasn't even finished telling him everything, yet. "I heard my mom's voice when I talked with Nova. She said the same thing: Return it. And she showed me a place with a cavern that went straight down into the ground."

"I've never heard of a place like that." His voice echoed from inside his helmet. "And return what? You haven't stolen anything, right?"

"No, of course not." I put my helmet on, too. "I don't know what she's talking about."

"It's probably some old memory of your mom that you've forgotten until now. That's all. Look, I've got something back at the dorm that'll help you sleep. You need it, especially tonight. Tomorrow is the first day of training, remember?" Felix gave me a thumbs up as he settled himself into the saddle. "They're only dreams. You're over thinking this. Not everything is a conspiracy, Jae."

I nodded. I didn't see how I had much of a choice. Not sleeping was killing me slowly, and tomorrow was guaranteed to be one of the hardest days of my life. Felix was right about that, at least. I couldn't afford to get too distracted. But as for the dreams... I didn't agree. It couldn't just be a coincidence. I wasn't that lucky.

Once we landed back at the Roost, I took off Mavrik's saddle and carried it down to the tack room to be stored with all the others. It was nice to walk in there and know that tomorrow we wouldn't be on tack detail anymore. Someone else would be cleaning and checking the saddles. Sure, we'd have to take another turn at it eventually, but not for a while.

Felix bumped into me as he came in carrying his gear. "So that was it? You're worried about some crazy dreams?"

My stomach squirmed nervously. "Not just that. There's something else I've wanted to ask you about. I heard a rumor."

"About me?" He looked amused, maybe even a little excited.

"No, about Sile."

Felix's expression fell. "What about him?"

"Do you know a lot about him? About his past?" I knew Sile liked his privacy. What little I had found out about him was probably more than anyone else knew. But then, dragonriders liked to talk—especially about each other. Someone was bound to know something. Felix prided himself on being involved in as much gossip as possible. Wanting to be involved in everyone else's business must have been a side effect of being born a noble.

"I know some. He's been on the battlefront lots of times, and most of the other instructors really respect him. His kill-count is in the hundreds. They say he and Valla were a real terror in combat back in the day." He put his saddle down next to mine and started staring off into space. "He was supposed to be a crack-shot with a bow. I heard he could take out the eye of a deer from a hundred yards away, while flying. Most riders wouldn't even bother with a bow, you know. It's not a good weapon for us because most people can't make accurate shots in flight. The wind and speed are too much."

"Have you ever heard about him going into Luntharda?" I asked quickly before I could lose my nerve.

Felix paused. Slowly, he turned around to face me. "No one goes into Luntharda. Not unless they have a death wish. If the Gray elves don't kill you, the forest definitely will."

I started telling him everything Mr. Crookin had told me about how Sile had supposedly abandoned his men, gone into the forest alone, and come back without a scratch. It sounded unbelievable, even to me. I'd never seen Luntharda for myself. Based on what I had read in my studies as a fledgling, I understood how dangerous it was. There were monsters and vicious beasts at every turn. The idea that anyone could survive it alone was crazy.

"I've never heard any of this," Felix replied. "It sounds made up. Sile may be a little unstable, but he's not insane. It has to be a lie."

"It isn't," someone interrupted.

We both looked back to see Lyon standing in the doorway of the tack room. He kept his head down, like he was trying to hide the fact that his nose was still basically being held together by gauze. "It's true," he mumbled.

Felix puffed up defiantly. "Yeah, right. Like you'd know anything about it."

"I would," Lyon snapped. It surprised me. I couldn't believe he was still willing to stand up to Felix, even after what I had done to him. "You know who my dad was. And my grandfather, too. I'm a third generation dragonrider. And I've heard this story before."

I took an eager step toward him. It was a stupid thing to do. It shouldn't have surprised me that he flinched and started backing away. He was terrified of me.

Immediately, I stopped and raised my hands to show him that I wasn't going to hurt him. "I just want to know the story. Do you know what really happened?"

Lyon glanced back and forth between Felix and me, like he was trying to figure out if it was safe to stick around. At last, he started to talk. "It was at the beginning of the war, I think. My dad flew in the same legion as Lieutenant Derrick. They weren't friends, but you know how it is; everyone knows everyone." He shrugged and fidgeted nervously. "I heard my dad talking about it once. He was pretty out of it that night. He'd been out till late with some of his old war buddies. They were telling stories. They talked about a skirmish they got into with some shrikes right outside the forest."

"Shrikes?" I stopped him long enough to ask. Felix had said that word, too, but I didn't know what it meant.

"Is it a happy place, this private little world you live in? Seriously, get a clue." Lyon scoffed like I was being intentionally stupid. "Shrikes are our enemy. We aren't the only ones who fly. The Gray elves ride on their own monsters. We call them shrikes."

"They're brutal monsters, too," Felix chimed in. "Small, quick as the devil, and almost impossible to see. Their bite is extra nasty. It's got some kind of poison in it that rots your skin away. The Gray elves tip their arrows and blades in the stuff, too, so that if you get shot... it's more likely to kill you."

Both of them were silent, looking at me and waiting for my reaction. I wasn't sure what to do with that information. I'd never known we would actually be fighting enemies in the air. I didn't even know what a shrike looked like, let alone that I was going to be fighting them soon.

When I didn't speak up, Lyon rolled his eyes and continued. "Anyway. The story was that they were mixed up in a skirmish with a few shrikes. Things weren't going so great. But in the middle of the fight, Sile lands and starts going into the forest. No one could stop him because they were locked in combat. Dad said he strolled into Luntharda like he was out for an afternoon walk. A few days later, he showed up back at the citadel. He didn't have a scratch on him. No one knew what happened to him, or how he managed to come out of there alive. The captains and colonels interrogated him, but it didn't make any difference. He never said a word. They said it was like he was under some kind of spell. Like he was in a trance. He wouldn't talk to anyone about what happened. That's why they took him off the frontlines and sent him here to be an instructor."

"It had to be some kind of torture," Felix said quietly. "Something the Gray elves did to him to keep him from talking."

Chills swept over me. I was trying to process it all. Felix seemed to be doing the same. He was frowning so hard it put lines on his forehead. I was so busy watching him and letting that new information sink in, that I didn't even notice Lyon was staring at me until he spoke.

"I came to make sure you weren't late for curfew." Lyon was already starting to walk away. "So hurry up. It's already dark, and I'm not running any extra laps tomorrow. And some guy came by our room looking for you, Jaevid. He left something for you. He said you'd be expecting it."

Felix and I exchanged a look. Since when did Lyon check up on us? I was starting to worry I was hallucinating, but then I saw Felix start to grin. Nope, I was definitely not imagining it. Usually Lyon called me halfbreed. But tonight, he had used my name.

16

CHAPTER SIXTEEN

I waited until Lyon and Felix were asleep to unwrap the scimitar. Bren had carefully bundled it up in a soft cloth, and left a note thanking me for saving them again. As I unwrapped it, my hands shook with excitement. I could see the faint glow of the metal in the candlelight. It was the most beautiful weapon I had ever seen.

Bren had fixed everything, even the carvings on the side of the blade that had almost been rubbed completely off. I still couldn't understand what they said, though. They were written in another language. The blade shimmered. The polished bronze looked like gold. The ivory shone like pearl. The soft leather grip felt comfortable in my hand, and the metal hummed a beautiful note as I drew it from the scabbard.

I ran my thumb over the emblem on the pommel. The head of a stag stared back at me. Bren had said it was the symbol of Gray elf royalty. My mind was still processing everything I'd heard that day. It was a lot to take in. But knowing that the rumor about Sile was true, that he had been into Luntharda, made my thoughts churn. He was definitely hiding something. His kidnapping last year, my place here as a dragonrider, the dreams—somehow, it was all connected. I just had to figure out how.

I put the scimitar away. I wrapped it back up in the cloth and tucked it under my bed where I hoped no one else would find it. I had a feeling that if anyone else knew I was carrying around a blade with the Gray elf symbol on it, they wouldn't be as calm about it as Bren was. Now was not the time to be pushing my luck. Now was the time for sleeping.

Felix had already given me a tiny square of folded paper before he went to bed. He called it a sleeping remedy, and told me to pour it into some water and drink it all. If it worked, he promised he could get more. So I went to the washroom and took it. The white powder wrapped inside the paper tasted horrible. It was so bitter it made my eyes water. But I choked it down.

I wasn't sure the remedy was even working until I got back to our room. While I was changing out of my clothes, the room started to spin. My head got fuzzy. I barely made it to my bed before I collapsed. I was still wearing one of my shoes, but I couldn't get my arms and legs to cooperate long enough to take it off. And then, I didn't care.

Sleep overtook me, and the next thing I knew, it was morning. For the first time in a while, there were no dreams or nightmares. That remedy, whatever it was, had definitely worked.

I knew it was morning because a boot hit me in the head. That was the way Felix usually woke me up when I was running behind. He had a good aim.

"Get up, moron!" Felix barked at me.

I pushed myself up from the bed. That's when I realized my face was cold and sticky. I had been drooling in my sleep.

Lyon and Felix heckled me the whole time while I got dressed. They were already outfitted and ready to go, so I guess I deserved it for lagging behind. It was still dark outside as we hurried out of the dormitory to meet Jace outside the academy walls. He was waiting for us, armed with that bullwhip he liked so much.

We ran until we were all soaked with sweat. We did push-ups and sit-ups until my bones ached. Jace cracked his whip, shouting out the names of different stances, parries, and strikes. If one of us got it wrong, he was right there in two seconds to yell at all of us until our ears were ringing. Then we had to start over and do it all again.

We were the first ones to drag our saddles out of the tack room that morning. We saddled up, strapped on our armor, and took off into the first few breaths of twilight. It was the first time I had ever seen Jace and Lyon's dragons, but I didn't have much time to admire them.

Jace's dragon was a sleek gray male with faint markings that were only visible if you were standing close. The color of his scales looked like smoke in the pale light of dawn. That, Felix told me, was partly what had earned him his name. They called him Ghost not only because of his color, but also because he flew so fast you were likely to be dead, engulfed in dragon flame, before you even realized he had flown over.

It was the first time I had seen a dragon up close who had been in combat recently. It must have been fore Felix, too, because he was full of awe and admiration. He pointed out the intricate striped grooves that looked like they had been engraved onto the horns on Ghost's head. I'd never seen that on another dragon before. Or at least, I'd never taken the time to notice it.

"It's his kill count," Felix announced. His eyes were shining like he could barely contain his excitement. "A notch for every Gray elf rider he's brought down. Look at them all!"

After that, looking at the engraved stripes gave me a strange, nauseous sensation in my stomach. It reminded me that Jace wasn't just an instructor. He was a soldier. He had killed people—lots of them judging by the amount of notches on his dragon's horns.

Ghost wasn't the only one with those marks, though. Lyon's dragon was a much older male named Demos. He had notches going down every inch of the long horns on his head. He was big dragon, closer to Nova's size than any of the others, and apparently had a bad temper. It made me wonder if dragons picked up on the bad habits of their riders over time. His scales were a burnt orange color, and he had black stripes like a cat all over his body. According to Felix, Demos had been in combat more times than any of the rest of us. Lyon's father and grandfather had both ridden him into battle. That explained all the notches.

Jace gave us hand signals in the air, directing us to break off into pairs and fly our usual drills. Felix and Lyon flew together in a pair, with Felix in lead. I took up the position of following Jace. Dragonriders called it being a "wing end" because I was supposed to stay in formation, right behind Ghost's left wing, as we flew through our drill patterns.

I had already flown these drills before. It wasn't supposed to be anything new. But right away, I figured out why Jace had paired us together. Ghost was fast —*unbelievably* fast. I doubted Nova or Demos could ever keep up with him. When he poured on the speed, I gave Mavrik a mental nudge to follow.

At first, we could keep pace, but as Jace started whipping through spins and spirals, Mavrik started lagging behind. He was huffing and puffing, beating his wings harder than I'd ever seen him just to keep Ghost in our sight. I heard him growling, and I could sense his frustration. It made me angrier than I expected. We had always been the fastest. Falling so far behind made our drills sloppy and frantic, and each passing second made me more and more aggravated. I was every bit as mad about it as Mavrik was.

By the time we landed, Mavrik was furious that he had been outdone. I was bitter about it, too. Still, I didn't put on a show about it the way he did. Mavrik bared his teeth, snapping at the air as I dismounted. I could tell he wanted to challenge Ghost again, but the gray dragon ignored him as Jace and the others landed nearby.

I expected Jace to say something to me about how sloppy the drills had been. After all, we'd been scrambling to keep up the whole time. I was braced for the inevitable chewing-out I deserved as he walked past us. But he didn't even look at me.

I was stunned. Jace had outright ignored me! Surprisingly, that hurt even worse than being yelled at. It stuck in my pride like a splinter. I hated it. Sure, I had been ignored and even pitied plenty of times when I was floundering through ground combat training. But I had never been a disappointment in the air. It was like Jace was so disgusted with our performance that he wasn't even going to acknowledge how bad it was.

Being disregarded like that lit a raging fire in my chest. I looked at Mavrik. He was bristled and hissing, swishing his tail bitterly. I nodded and clenched my teeth. Next time. We would be better next time. I wasn't going to get shown up like that again.

Jace gave us all a short pep talk about keeping our morale up before he dismissed us. He passed out our new avian uniforms, and gave us our schedule. It was basically the reverse of last year. Instead of starting the day with combat training, we would be attending classes on survival techniques, orienteering, and battle planning until lunch. After the noon break, we would assemble at the gymnasium for combat training that would last for the rest of the day.

I raised my hand to ask, "What about interrogation training? I thought that started this year."

Jace smirked like he found my enthusiasm hilarious and cute. "It's coming. But you're not ready for that, yet."

I was still so angry about the flying at breakfast that I couldn't force myself to eat much. It was a stupid thing to get so upset about. I knew that. I still couldn't help it. I had never had much to be proud of. Our speed had always been our advantage, something about us that was special, and now... it wasn't.

The dormitory was alive with activity as the sun began to rise. We hurried through our morning baths, fighting our way through the other avians who were trying to do the same thing. We got dressed in our new uniforms, grabbed our stacks of maps, and filed down toward the breaking dome with everyone else. The horns on the academy walls began to blare, giving the call to arms. That was our signal to report in for our morning brief.

I can't explain what it was like to stand with all the other dragonriders of Blybrig Academy. But overwhelming would probably be the best place to start. I stood with Felix on one side, and Lyon on the other, lined up according to our rank in the breaking dome. We stood at attention even before the command was called, and we didn't talk to each other. Last year, I hadn't really understood what I was doing there, or what would happen to me. But now, things were different. I was starting to understand my place here. I knew I had an objective, and that was to survive.

Dressed out in our black tunics and pants, with our navy blue cloaks brushing at our heels, and the king's golden eagle pinned around our necks, I knew we looked intimidating to the younger riders. It made me want to stand up a little taller, to put on my fiercest face. I wanted to look capable. I wanted to be a standard that someone could strive for.

Before us, Commander Rayken and the other officers were assembling. They were all dressed out in their formal armor, wearing swords at their hips, and talking in low voices. I recognized many of them. Jace was there, frowning like always. Lieutenant Morrig glanced my way for a second, and then did a double take when he realized who I was. He had been my combat instructor last year.

Even though it wasn't appropriate, I wanted to thank him for putting up with me. Lieutenant Morrig had worked hard to find something I could do when it came to hand-to-hand combat. Not many others would have even bothered, especially considering how I had looked back then. When we locked gazes, I gave him a small nod. I wanted him to know he hadn't wasted his time on me. I wouldn't be a disappointment this year.

Lieutenant Thane's glare caught my attention next. He was standing off to the side, away from the other instructors, with his burly arms bulging like two giant, overstuffed sausages. His dark eyes were narrowed right at me. I could practically taste the cold pressure of his presence. Even after Commander Rayken started calling everyone to attention, he kept glaring at me like he hoped the heat of his wrath might make me burst into flame. Thankfully, it didn't.

"Welcome to Blybrig Academy. For some of you, this is your first time to stand in our midst. For others, you are already a part of our brotherhood and understood the importance of what lies ahead of you this year," Commander Rayken started with basically the same speech as last year. Then he started telling a brief history of dragonriders. It hadn't meant all that much to me as a fledgling, but now the history interested me a lot more. Now I was a part of it.

"There are only a few savage beasts upon this earth that share a bond with man: dogs, horses,... women," he paused. Some of the other instructors snickered and elbowed each other. I guess that was supposed to be a joke. "But greatest amongst these is the dragon. His kind first came to us in our darkest hour, when foreign enemies struck our soil with intent to destroy and enslave us. When we were faced with the greatest foe our kingdom had ever known, one who dared to call himself God Bane. Upon the smoldering field of battle, the first dragon chose a humble infantryman to be his rider. Their strengths and desires were united, bonded for life. They became an image of hope to others, who began to look to the sky as they prayed for victory. More dragons came from their nests far on the eastern coast and followed that example, choosing men of merit and strength as their riders. That was how our mighty brotherhood was formed. We were born from the ashes of devastation, to rise and bring the flames of war upon any enemy who would try to invade our beloved kingdom."

Commander Rayken paused again and looked across our company. No one said a word. "Time has indeed changed us. The ways of old have become a distant memory. But you are all here for that same purpose. The reason for our existence has not changed. We fight and die as one, as brothers, as dragonriders." He saluted, clasping a fist over his breastplate. "For his majesty's honor!"

We all responded without hesitation, snapping a fist over our chests and mimicking that gesture with a shout. That's when I realized my pulse was racing. The sense of purpose that surged through my veins was overwhelming. When I glanced beside me, I saw that Felix looked flushed, too. His face was the picture of fierce determination.

After we were dismissed, we split up according to our classes and started making our way out of the dome. Felix, Lyon, and I were assigned to a survival class first. I was already excited when we hit the door. The huge, sloping room had seats all the way around it like an amphitheatre. We sat together, listening as the instructor stood at the center of the room and explained what we would be learning.

"If you are shot down in Luntharda, or find yourself a prisoner of the Gray elves, you will most likely die," the instructor said sharply. A few students shifted uncomfortably in their seats. "If you do survive, it won't be because of your sword or fighting techniques. It will be because of what you learn here, in this classroom. Survivors pay attention. Survivors listen, learn, and remember. My name is Lieutenant Haprick. Welcome."

I swallowed hard. I didn't feel very welcome. Panicked was more like it. I quickly made a mental note never to zone out during this class. It wasn't hard, though, because most of what he talked about was interesting.

After his introduction, Lieutenant Haprick launched right into listing off exactly what we would be given in our saddlebags to help us survive a worst-case scenario. He had a table set up in the center of the room with a bag exactly like the one we would all be issued. He called it a "go-bag" because in the event of an emergency, we had to grab it and go. We all scrambled to take notes as he took each item out, one by one, and quickly demonstrated how to use it.

The first item was a thick candle made from beef fat. He explained that it would provide light, but it could also be eaten if you were ever in a situation where you were starving. Next was a piece of flint, which he intended to teach us to use in order to light a fire. There was a small sewing kit for treating wounds or mending clothes, several spools of gauze, and a small round tin of an herbal salve that would keep open wounds from getting infected. He went on to list a lot of other things like rope, a knife, a canteen, and snare wire. I lost count, and it took all my focus to keep up with him while taking notes. He said he would teach us more about each item, how to use it, and what to do if we lost it. Then and only then would we be getting go-bags of our own.

"These are tools," he insisted. "Not trinkets or toys. Only once you understand their use and respect their value can you be trusted with them."

Our next class was about memorizing maps. This, at least, was very familiar to us. Last year, Felix had struggled some when it came to memorizing maps. He groaned and slouched in his seat when we were given the same assignments as last year. We would have to duplicate a map of the kingdom down to the very last detail. I hadn't struggled with it that much, so I was confident. Sile had shown us how to divide the maps up into quadrants, and memorize them one by one, to make things easier.

A little before lunch, we finally shambled into our last class of the morning. Battle planning sounded boring, but we had only gotten a small taste of it last year. This year, the instructor promised to present us with problems and battles that we had to present calculated plans for. It looked a lot more difficult than I was expecting.

"An effective plan is half the battle, boys." The instructor, Lieutenant Graul, gave a deep, throaty laugh. "Otherwise we'd all be buzzing around randomly, just as liable to kill our own men as the enemy."

When morning classes ended, we were all dismissed to have lunch. We stood in line, got our ration of food, and sat down at our usual place at the end of one of the long dining tables. Felix was staring down at his food with a glazed look in his eyes. Lyon was swirling a fork in his potatoes. I was starving, as usual, but my head felt like it was going to explode. This was only the first day, and already it seemed like there was a mountain of knowledge looming over me.

"I don't know if I can do this," Felix admitted.

The rest of us looked up at him. I was surprised to hear him sound so defeated already.

"It won't be so bad once we get into it." I tried to sound confident. "It seems like a lot because we just started. It'll get better."

He grumbled angrily, and started stuffing food in his mouth. I couldn't understand most of what he said, but I did catch the words, "I hate maps." The rest was probably a string of curses.

After lunch, we had a few spare minutes to shed our formal cloaks and put on our vambraces and sword belts before combat training. I tucked Beckah's handkerchief into its usual place against my arm, and followed Felix and Lyon to the gymnasium.

I assumed Lieutenant Morrig would be instructing us again. After all, he'd done a good job last year. But as we joined the rest of the avians flocking into the building, I heard a voice that made my insides turn to jelly.

Lieutenant Thrane was standing in the center of the gymnasium, his bulging arms crossed, and his huge bald head wrinkled in a scowl. He was looking at the crowd of students filing in like he was searching for someone. I got the immediate sense that the person he was looking for was most likely me.

Thrane wasn't alone. Jace and Morrig were standing there, as well. There were a lot more avian students than fledglings, so Morrig probably needed the extra help. As soon as we were all inside, Morrig called us to attention and began doling out orders. He divided is into three large groups and announced that we would be working in stations. After two hours at one station, the groups would switch until we had all visited each one.

Station one was basic sword dueling with Jace. Station two was for learning dual wielding with two weapons or with a shield with Morrig. And finally, station three—which was bound to be my favorite—was grappling and barehanded combat with Thrane. All three sounded like they were going to be unpleasant. I was determined not to think about it too much.

I had a lot to prove. Last year, things hadn't gone so well in combat training. Being half the size of everyone else in my class hadn't helped. But that wasn't the case anymore. Now, I was one of the tallest. I knew this was my chance. My performance here would decide the fate of my friends and myself when it came time for the battle scenario. So I clenched my teeth, and did my best not to look at Thrane.

Lyon, Felix, and I were grouped together with twenty other avians and sent to station one. After retrieving a wooden practice sword from the armory room, Jace lined us up in a grid, and unfurled his long, leather whip. He stalked back and forth in front of us like a prowling jungle cat, staring down every student he passed.

"What you did last year was child's play. You are not children anymore. You are men. And you will be held accountable for not knowing your maneuvers. Be glad that it is just the taste of a whip that is your punishment, and not the bite of an enemy's blade." Jace spoke so calmly that it made me nervous. His eyes scanned us as though he were looking for weakness. "Now, show me an opening stance!"

The gymnasium filled with the sound of shouts, of grunts, of Jace snapping his bullwhip, and Thrane bellowing out orders like an angry bear. The first time someone slipped up, it was an avian standing right in front of me. I saw it happen. Jace called a parry maneuver, and the student moved into the wrong stance. In an instant, Jace was there, looming right in his face and demanding to know why he couldn't do something so simple. Then came the crack of the whip. The student screamed. None of us dared to move.

"Now, do it again." Jace snarled. His eyes locked with mine, and I felt my stomach do a back flip. "No mistakes."

Jace had threatened us with that whip before. He was good at popping it right in front of our noses if we stumbled, but he'd never actually used it. It made me realize that practice was officially over. This was the real deal now. And the consequences were going to be just as real.

A few other students got to taste of Jace's whip before the two hours were up, but thankfully I wasn't one of them. Someone blew a horn to signal it was time to switch stations, and we moved toward the other side of the room where Morrig was waiting. He didn't have a whip, but that didn't make me feel any safer.

Morrig had us pair up and form two long lines facing each other. First, he demonstrated new maneuvers with two weapons, and then we all began drilling. Once he felt we were getting a good grasp on it, he started teaching us how to fight with a shield on one arm. I was reminded again that even though

I had grown, I still lacked the sheer bulk of most young men my size. The shield was heavy, and I had a hard time lifting it to shoulder-height like I was supposed to.

"It is not only for protection," Morrig said as he strolled down our lines, watching us perform the maneuvers over and over. "A shield can be a weapon of brute force. It can allow you to advance in close enough to your enemy to catch them off guard. Do not treat it as a burden. Treat it as an extension of yourself, just like your sword."

I tried. My arms were already aching, and raising the heavy metal shield was about all I could manage. I could barely lift it, much less whirl it around. But I didn't want my weakness to show. I pushed myself until I had nothing left. Finally, the horn blew. It was time to switch stations again.

With sweat running down my face and dripping off my chin, I looked over at station three. Thrane was staring right at me. I saw him lick the front of his teeth like a hungry wolf. It was like he was waiting and hoping I would snap again so he would have a good excuse to kill me.

I was determined not to give him that satisfaction.

We put our weapons away before we went to his station. My heart was still pounding in my ears as I lined up between Lyon and Felix. The rest of our group did the same, waiting for Thrane to give us orders.

He walked through our group, sizing us up one by one. When he stopped right next to me and stood there, so close that I could smell his breath. It took everything I had not to look up at him. I knew that's what he wanted. We were at attention. We weren't supposed to move. Thrane was trying to provoke me. I could feel the hate and rage rolling off him like bad body odor. So I picked a spot on the wall straight ahead of me and focused on it.

"All right, ladies," Thrane sneered. He was so close that his voice rustled my hair. "I'm supposed to teach you how to fight like men. Some of you have already proven that you can't, even against each other. I've seen you slapping each other around like little girls. It's pathetic. You want to break someone's arm? This is how you do it."

Before anyone could react, he snatched Lyon by the collar of his shirt. Thrane spun him around, twisting him like a ragdoll and giving his arm a sudden, violent jerk. Lyon's arm made a horrible crunching sound. He started screaming in pain.

When Thrane let him go, Lyon fell into a heap on the ground, clutching his arm. He was still crying out in agony, and a few other avians lurched forward like they wanted to help him. But Thrane raised a hand to stop them. His eyes settled back on me with a vicious smile. This wasn't about Lyon. This was about *me*. He wanted a reaction. He wanted to set off my battle fever again.

The sound of Lyon's screams set my blood on fire. As horrible as it might seem, the fact that he had attacked Lyon instead of Felix was probably the only thing that saved me in that moment. If it were Felix lying there, clutching his arm and sobbing, I don't think I could have held it together. But I managed to keep my composure.

I didn't move. I didn't blink. I kept my eyes fixed on Thrane, and neither of us spoke. I poured as much of my anger into my gaze as I could, like a silent promise. One day, I would make him pay for this. I could be patient. I could wait for the right moment. Until then, I would endure anything he threw at me.

The continuing sound of Lyon's cries made the rest of the gymnasium stop their training. They all gathered around us, eager to see what was happening. Even Morrig and Jace came over, pushing their way through the crowd to see what was wrong.

"Couldn't contain yourself for even five minutes?" Jace snapped at Thrane as he pushed past him. "You stupid barbarian."

Thrane shot Jace a glare like he might decide to hit him. It seemed like they already had some bad blood between them. "I don't see how it's any of your business, pretty boy."

"He's my student. That makes it my business. If you can't be professional, then I'll take this to Rayken and have you formally dismissed back to the frontlines, with or without a wing end." Jace crouched down next to Lyon and began inspecting his arm. "You broke it. Looks like a compound fracture. Do you even realize what that means? He's done. He can't fly like this. And he certainly can't train."

"He was useless anyways. Look at him. His face all plastered together like a broken baby doll. A kid like that won't last two seconds on the front lines. I did him a favor." Thrane let out a cold, booming laugh. Nobody laughed with him. "Don't tell me you're worried because his daddy will be upset? This is avian training. Accidents happen."

"Yes. Accidents *do* happen." Jace cut Thrane a promising look that made the big, burly man hesitate for a second. Even though Thrane was easily twice Jace's size, I got the feeling that if it ever did come down to a fight... size wouldn't be much of an advantage for him. Jace could be every bit as brutal and merciless.

I couldn't focus on combat training after that. Jace and Thrane left to take Lyon to the infirmary. An injury like that would mean Lyon couldn't train anymore. But maybe, if he kept up his training on his own, he could try again as an avian next year.

Morrig had no choice but to put us all in a big block formation and run through the same basic sword maneuvers over and over. My mind wandered, and I felt overwhelmed by guilt. Lyon's career might be over just like that. And it was my fault. If I hadn't challenged him to that first fight, he never would have been a target for Thrane.

When training was over for the day, I found a shady spot on the front steps of the dormitory and collapsed. I leaned against the cool stone, and watched the dragons circling overhead like giant, scaly vultures. Everyone else was going in for dinner, but I didn't feel like eating.

I felt the toe of someone's boot nudge me. "Hey," Felix said. "Get up. We need to eat and study."

I cracked an eye open to stare up at him. "How can you eat? Didn't you see what happened?"

Felix's expression was tense. He had his hands in his pockets, and a serious frown on his lips. "I saw it. But that's the way things are now. We're not fledglings anymore, Jae. The instructors are going to knock us around."

I slumped forward to hang my head and rest my elbows on my knees. "That had nothing to do with training, and you know it. It was personal. It was a threat. Thrane is trying to provoke me into attacking him."

"So don't attack him." Felix shrugged. "Seems simple to me."

I gave him as much of a glare as I could muster. "Right. It's simple now. But will it be simple when he does something like that to you?"

We stared at each other for a few minutes without saying anything. At last, Felix sighed loudly and came to sit down next to me. "You think I can't handle getting my arm broken?"

"I'm not sure *I* can't handle it," I told him. "If I have to watch that happen to you, I don't think I'll be able to stop myself. You saw how I was before. If I get battle fever again, I might kill him."

Felix smirked. "Cocky, aren't you? You really think you could kill someone like Thrane?"

I rolled my eyes. His sense of humor was exasperating sometimes. "I don't know."

"Look, I get it, okay? You feel guilty. But it wasn't your fault. It could have just as easily been anyone else. Lyon was in the wrong place at the wrong time, as usual. And if you ask me, he had this coming to him sooner or later." He patted my shoulder roughly. "Don't blame yourself."

"What if Thrane does something like that to me?" I asked him. "Could you handle it? Could you stand there and watch him break my arm?"

Felix's eyes got distant. I saw his demeanor change from his usual happy-go-lucky self, to someone much more serious. It made him look older, and not in a good way. He squeezed my shoulder. "I don't know. Let's hope it doesn't come to that."

17

CHAPTER SEVENTEEN

My intentions started out great. I was going to apologize before it was too late. But as I stepped out into the cool midnight wind, I started to think—and that's usually when things go wrong for me.

I was only holding one last secret back from Felix. He knew about everything else, including my weird nightmares. What he didn't know was that a few weeks ago, I had been able to heal Sile's wife with my bare hands. I wasn't sure how I had done it, or if I could even do it again. Sile had warned me not do it again, and I assumed that was because doing it had almost killed me before. I knew he probably didn't want me to risk my life like that again, or that someone might catch me doing it. But as I walked alone toward the infirmary, I knew I was about to disobey Sile's warning.

I was going to try to heal Lyon.

His injuries were my fault. It was only fair that I should do everything I could to make it right. Sure, it might kill me. Or I might turn into an old man if it triggered another growth spurt. But I couldn't let his career end like this. It wasn't right. And as far as I knew, I was the only one who could do anything about it.

The infirmary was dark when I opened the door. Only a few candles burned in the hallways, casting heavy shadows into empty rooms. Only one medic was still awake. He was sitting at Lyon's bedside reading what looked like a letter.

"Come to pay your friend a visit?" he asked when he noticed me standing in the doorway. "You should come back tomorrow. He's sleeping now. You should be, too."

I started to get nervous. "I-I want to talk to him now, if that's okay. I know it's past curfew, but this is the first chance I've gotten to come by."

The medic was an old, heavy-set man. He looked at me for a minute, scratching his chin through his curly white beard. "Very well," he sighed at last, and pulled a wooden pipe out of his pocket. "I could use a break for a smoke. Try not to get him too worked up. Poor lad had quite a shock."

I slipped into the room as the medic left. I waited until I heard him go outside, then I quietly closed the door to Lyon's room. If I was going to do this, I didn't want anyone else to see it.

The sound of our voices must have woken Lyon up, because before I could turn around I heard him speak. "Why are you here?"

I faced him and tried not to stare. It was hard, though. Lyon was lying on a small bed, covered in a white sheet up to his chin. His arm was splinted and wrapped up in a thick layer of bandaging, and he had fresh dressings on his nose as well. There were dark circles under his eyes, and his cheeks were swollen like he'd been crying. Overall, Lyon looked awful.

"I came to apologize," I finally managed to say.

"For what?" He sounded confused.

"For what happened with Thrane. It's my fault. It should have been me, not you. I'm the one he really wants to hurt." The words came spilling out of my mouth so fast I couldn't stop them. "I never wanted this to happen. If I could take it all back, I would."

Lyon was quiet for a few minutes. The silence was awkward, and I didn't know if I should explain what I wanted to do... or just do it and let him figure it out for himself.

"I don't get you," he muttered. He almost sounded angry. "Why would you apologize to me? Why would you even care what I think?"

His questions caught me off guard. I wasn't sure how to answer. But before I could try, he started talking again.

"You know you'll never really be one of us. You'll always be the odd man out. There's always going to be people like Thrane, doing whatever they can to break you. They're all waiting for you to make a wrong move. And still you don't leave. You just keep trying. It doesn't make any sense. Why? Why are you doing this?"

Usually, that kind of speech from Lyon would have been filled with as much hatred and sarcasm as possible. Now he looked confused instead.

I sat down in the chair at his bedside and stared down at the floor. "I wonder that, too, sometimes. I want to watch Felix's back the way he watches mine. That used to be my reason. Now I'm endangering him and everyone else by being here."

"So are you just trying to prove that you aren't a traitor?" he asked again.

"No." I shook my head. "I don't have anything to prove. I'm here because this is where I'm meant to be. I believe that Mavrik chose me for a reason. Whatever that reason is, I have to stay here and figure it out. Even if that means being a danger to the people I want to protect."

"Yeah, right." He snorted like he didn't believe me. "Like you would ever want to protect *me*. I'm not stupid, you know. We're not friends."

I looked at him right in the eye. "I would protect you. And I will."

Lyon flashed me a skeptical glare. "Why? After everything I've done to you, why would you want to do anything for me?"

"Because I can. And because you need me to, even if you don't like me," I said. "I know you're alone now. Your friends from last year—they don't come around you anymore."

I watched Lyon's eyes get watery and his cheeks got red. He bit his lip and looked away, like he was trying to fight back tears. "It's got nothing to do with you, Jaevid," he managed to mumble. "It's not your problem."

I couldn't help but smile a little. "You can call me Jae, you know."

He shot me another glare. "Only your friends call you that."

"Yeah." I shrugged. "I know."

Lyon fell silent again. We stared at each other in the dim light of the candle burning on the bedside table. Finally, I knew the time had come. It was now or never. I didn't want to lose my nerve or risk that the medic might come back.

I stood up and went to his bedside. "I'm going to do something really, really stupid." It seemed like a good idea to give him a fair warning in case, you know, I died.

Lyon looked nervous. "What?"

I was nervous, too. I couldn't keep myself from shaking as I reached to lay my hands on his broken arm. "I'm going to tell you something, and it's up to you if you want to turn me in to the instructors or not. If you do, I'll probably get shipped off to a prison camp right away. Or Thane will save them the trouble and kill me. No one, not even Jace could do anything to stop it."

I took a deep breath. Lyon was probably the last person in the world I should have been trusting with a secret like this. But if it actually worked, he was going to figure it out anyway. "You already know I can talk to animals."

He nodded a little. "Yeah, I remember. Like with the paludix turtle last year."

"Well. That's not all I can do." I swallowed hard. "I can heal people, too."

Lyon's mouth fell open.

"Felix doesn't know. No one else does. Well, except for Sile. That's the other reason I came." I looked down at his broken arm. "I'm going to fix it."

"W-will it hurt?" He started stammering. His eyes were wide and afraid. "It hurt so much when they set it. I-I can't go through that again."

I shook my head slightly. "I don't think so."

Part of me knew I should warn him that doing this might kill me. But he already looked terrified. So I kept that to myself, and gathered my courage. These strange abilities I had were getting stronger. It was getting easier and easier to talk to animals. I barely even had to concentrate to talk to Mavrik. And now I could even feel Nova's thoughts if I focused hard enough.

It was now or never. I had to try.

With my hands resting on his arm, I knelt down at Lyon's bedside. I closed my eyes, and looked for that warmth in the back of my mind. I felt it there, tingling like a chill that wanted to spread all over my scalp. I felt the pressure settle on my chest, making it harder to breathe.

My ears began ringing. All around me, the room started to slip away. That little bit of warmth in my mind turned into heat, and it spread all over my body. It was creeping over my skin and making my palms feel like they were on fire. I got the sense like time was slowing down, that the room was spinning, and the pressure on my chest became so intense that I could barely breathe at all. I wanted to panic. The room spun faster, and my vision started to blur.

"No." My body jolted suddenly as I heard my mother's voice in my mind. *"Do not lose focus."*

I braced myself. The room's spinning slowed a little. The heat on my palms burned like I was sticking my hands into a roaring fire. I clenched my teeth to keep from screaming.

When I had healed Sile's wife, it had felt like something inside me snapped. This time, it wasn't like that. This felt like a slow, agonizing tearing sensation in my chest. Like someone was slowly ripping my lungs apart. I couldn't breathe, but I didn't give up. Next to me, I heard Lyon whimper. I felt him try to pull away, so I gripped his arm harder.

Then the tearing sensation stopped. I could breathe again.

My body was suddenly so weak I couldn't keep myself from falling backwards. I landed on the floor, and I stared up at the ceiling. My ears were still ringing so loudly I could barely hear Lyon calling my name.

Then he slapped me across the face.

It jarred me. The ringing stopped, and I could hear him more clearly. Lyon was crouched on the floor beside me, shaking my shoulders. "Wake up, you idiot! You better not die over a stupid broken arm!"

I blinked, and looked at him. Every inch of my body was numb and tingly. I felt so exhausted I could barely twitch a finger, but I managed to ask, "Did it work?"

Lyon hesitated. He looked down at his arm, which was still wrapped up in bandages. Then, without warning, he began ripping them off. He tore through all the layers of gauze, and held his bare arm up to the light. I watched him wiggle his fingers, and run his hand over the smooth, unmarked skin on his forearm.

His arm was completely healed. There wasn't even a scar. It didn't look like it had ever been broken.

Lyon's eyes were as big as saucers when he stared down at me. "What are you?" I heard him whisper.

I was too tired to say anything, even though the answer was simple. I had absolutely no idea what I was. But one thing was certain: I was getting stronger.

The last thing I remembered was Lyon pulling one of my arms over his shoulders so he could drag me to my feet. I must have passed out after that because the next thing I knew, I was lying back in my bed in our dorm room. I bolted up right in bed, and it made Felix scream with surprise. He'd been preparing to throw another shoe at me like he did every morning. Apparently, I had startled him.

"Geez!" He started yelling. "Who the heck wakes up like that? What's wrong with you?"

I ducked as a boot went soaring past my head. Before I could yell back at him, the door to our room opened. Jace was standing there, and he was frowning harder than usual. Felix and I exchanged a quick, panicked glance, like we were silently asking one another who he was here for.

"You." Jace pointed right at me. "Come with me."

He waited right outside the door while I cleaned myself up. I was still wearing my clothes from yesterday. They stank from sweat, so I changed quickly and started for the door.

Felix caught me by the arm on my way out. Our eyes met, and he didn't have to say anything to get his point across. He wanted to know what was going on, and if I would be okay. I wasn't sure. I smiled so he wouldn't worry.

Jace didn't speak as I came out into the hall to meet him. He curled a finger at me, and started walking. I followed him out into the early morning air. A thick fog had settled over the academy, and something about it made Jace seem even more dangerous than usual. His long dark cape rolled off his shoulders and licked at his heels. All I could see was the back of his head, but I knew he was probably scowling like an angry wolf.

Jace had a way of looking at everyone that way—like he was a predator about to strike. Anywhere else, that was probably a terrible way to look at people. No one wanted to be friendly with someone who seemed like they might suddenly bite your head off. However, I had a feeling that on the battlefield, men like Jace were exactly the kind of people you wanted fighting on your side.

He didn't slow down until we reached the doors of the infirmary. By then, my stomach was doing nervous flips. Through the gloom, I could see two figures already standing there waiting for us. The old medic had his arms crossed, and he was looking at me with a hard frown. Beside him, Lyon had a stubborn glare on his face. His hands were clenched into fists at his sides, and he made a point never to look me in the eye.

"Is this the one?" Jace asked sharply.

The medic nodded.

Lyon didn't say a word.

Jace turned on me with a look of wrath in his eyes that was downright terrifying. Still, I didn't let him see me shake. I was learning better than to cringe away from him when he glared at me like that. I was a soldier now. Soldiers didn't cringe.

"Tell me what you did," he demanded. "Tell me now."

"I told you already, he didn't do anything!" Lyon tried to interject. Jace didn't pay him any attention.

When I didn't answer right away, Jace took an aggressive step toward me. He met me nose-to-nose, since we were about the same height now. His cold, dark eyes locked onto mine, like he was silently daring me to lie to him. "Tell me," he repeated.

"I don't know," I managed to say, although I knew that answer wasn't going to fly far with him. "I'm not sure how it works. I don't know why I can do it. I just… can."

"Is it because you're a halfbreed?" The old medic was still scowling at me suspiciously. "Because of your elf blood?"

I shook my head. "I don't know. If you're asking me if a Gray elf trained me to do it, then the answer is no. I've never seen anyone else do it."

Jace looked like he sincerely wanted to hit me. Instead, he backed off and turned away from us. I could hear him cursing furiously under his breath.

"Listen, I may not be a dragonrider, but I understand a threat when I see one," the medic said. There was resignation in his voice. "What he did is nothing short of a miracle, but it's not a threat to anyone. Quite the opposite, actually."

Jace didn't answer, and the silence became very tense.

Lyon flashed me an apologetic expression.

I nodded back at him. It wasn't his fault. I should have been more careful with my planning.

"I owed him a favor. I promised him I would look out for you, if anything happened. But Sile never, ever mentioned anything about this." Jace started to rant, muttering under his breath like a madman. "What am I supposed to do with you now?"

I flinched. Deep down I knew the answer. I had to leave. If Thrane found out what I could do, it would be all the excuse he needed to finally have his way. Miracle or not, any form of a Gray elf doing any kind of magic was not going to be okay with the other instructors here. Thrane would finally have a good reason to kill me that no one else would argue with.

"Now hold on a minute, Lieutenant Rordin." The medic stepped forward and put his hand on my shoulder. "So far, we are the only ones who know about this, correct? So it ends with us. We won't speak another word about it."

"Are you being intentionally dense?" Jace growled. "Everyone in that gymnasium saw his arm get broken. Do you expect them to believe it just got better on its own overnight?"

"They saw what they *thought* was my arm getting broken," Lyon piped up suddenly. He had a confident grin on his face.

We all turned to look at him.

I'd never considered lying to be a valuable skill. But the way Lyon did it—well, I don't know how it could be called anything else. It was his craft. Some men made saddles, others painted beautiful artwork. Lyon told superb lies.

"No one except us knows it for sure," he said. "So we say I got better. It was dislocated, not broken like we thought. No one else has to know anything about it."

"Thrane will want an explanation." Jace didn't sound convinced. "You can bet he was sure he broke it. He won't believe otherwise."

"Then he can come to me." The medic patted my shoulder roughly. "As good as he is at breaking bones, he isn't a medic. If he wants to talk specifics, send him to me. I've dealt with him before. Don't give him credit for brains he doesn't have."

I slowly started to realize that these men were rallying around me. They were actually trying to find a way to keep my abilities a secret from everyone else. It made me uneasy, especially since I didn't even know the medic. People didn't usually do kind things for me just because they could. I felt my face get hot with embarrassment.

The medic must have noticed me blushing, because he started to chuckle. "Make sure no one suspects you. In your case, my boy, any attention from Thrane will be negative attention, I'm afraid. Try to keep out of his way."

I nodded. When I looked up again, my eyes met Jace's. He still didn't look happy. I knew I had a lot of explaining to do, and I wasn't sure where to start. But I had to try. "Lieutenant Rordin, I—"

"Are you with us?" Jace interrupted.

His question caught me off guard. "I don't understand, sir."

"Do you understand that you are here to be a part of something greater than yourself? The people of this kingdom assume that we fight for them, for the kingdom, and whoever is wearing the crown. But you will learn quickly that kings and politics don't mean anything when you are faced with the battlefront. You fight for the man next to you. You bleed for your brothers, because they would do the same for you. Our brotherhood, your peers and instructors, they have to be more important to you than your own vendettas." Jace snapped in a bitter voice. "So I'm asking you, are you with us? Or is there something else that is more important to you?"

I swallowed hard. I don't know why, but I immediately looked over at Lyon. If you had asked me last year if I was willing to lay down my life for him, well, I probably would have said no. Now things were changing. I was changing. And as far as I could tell, this was only the beginning. While we struggled together, we were all learning that petty differences didn't matter. What mattered was our loyalty to one another. Protecting each other against any enemy. Trusting each other in times when one slip up could cost everyone dearly.

As I looked back at Jace, I felt a strange sense of calm come over me. I saw the same glare in his eyes, and this time... I understood it. This wasn't just a job to him. He wasn't being harsh, or ill tempered when he glared at everyone. He was giving this mission the best of his dedication because there were lives at stake—our lives and his.

From now on, I knew I had to do the same thing. "I'm with you," I said.

"To the death?" He narrowed his eyes.

"If it comes to that." I gave him a firm nod. "But don't think for a minute that if it comes down to choosing between revealing my abilities to the others and saving someone, that I won't make the obvious choice."

Jace *smiled*.

Okay, so it wasn't actually a smile. More like a challenging smirk. But it was the closest I'd ever seen him come to one. It gave me the creeps.

He glanced me up and down, and made a snorting sound. "Nice of you to finally show up, avian," he quipped. "Fear is useless to me, so maybe you'll finally be of some value."

18

CHAPTER EIGHTEEN

Lyon, Jace, and I left the infirmary together. It was still dark as we went outside the academy walls for our usual morning routine. No one said a word, even when Felix ran up to meet us. He was still sending me questioning looks. I knew I would have to confess to him sooner or later. He'd never let it go otherwise, and patience wasn't exactly one of his better qualities. But for now, I was going to need to tread carefully. The less he knew, the better. Someday, when Thrane was out of the picture—or at least not in a good position to break anyone's arms—I would be able to level with him completely.

As the days began to blur by, I discovered that my talk with Jace had put a new fire in my veins. I muscled through running laps and intervals of strength training exercises, but I didn't feel defeated. Each day, I could tell I was growing stronger. Each day, I felt less and less like a victim, and more like a soldier.

Of course, Jace was as ruthless as ever. He made us do one-handed and knuckle push-ups. A few times, he even had us run laps with bags full of rocks on our backs. He growled out commands as we ran through our new combat moves over and over. He was always armed with that whip in case we messed up. For some reason, the sound of it cracking in the cool air, only inches from my nose, didn't scare me anymore. I could hear his words ringing in my head. *"Fear is useless."* Those words made me push myself even harder.

My confidence always started to fade once we started for the Roost, saddled up our dragons, and strapped on our armor. By the time we took to the air each morning, the sun was finally rising. It turned the horizon pale pink, and like clockwork I could feel my ears start to burn with frustration under my helmet.

Jace always paired us together, and immediately poured on the speed. He went streaking through the sky like a gray comet, and Mavrik and I flailed around while trying to keep up. It was an absolute battle. I couldn't even match anything he did much less outdo him. All the speed and agility I had felt so confident about was basically useless to me now.

Every day, I landed several minutes behind him. I was so angry I could have spit dragon fire myself. Jace ignored me altogether, like I was invisible because my efforts were so pathetic, and I left morning drills ready to punch the first person that crossed my path.

One day, I couldn't take it anymore. As soon as Jace was out of sight, I ripped off my helmet and threw it as hard as I could.

"Feel better now, you big baby?" Felix was smirking at me.

"Just shut up. You try competing with that every day. You haven't had to fly with him even once." I glared at him and stormed away to get my helmet.

Felix crossed his arm and swaggered after me, like he was enjoying watching me throw a tantrum. "That's exactly your problem, dummy. Quit trying to compete with him and try learning for a change. Watch what he does, how he moves. That's the point of all this, you know. He's obviously grooming you."

I picked up my helmet and dusted it off. Thankfully it wasn't scratched. "Grooming me for what? Public humiliation?"

Felix rolled his eyes. "To be his wing end. Don't you know? When young seasoned lieutenants like him come back from the battlefront to teach, it's usually because they lost their old wing end or lead in battle. Look, you already know we always fly in pairs. Seasoned lieutenants have a choice if they lose their partner. They can either pair up with another seasoned lieutenant, if there's one available that they want to work with, or they can pick up a new graduate like one of us to be their wing end. Sile must have told him about your speed. That's why he always flies with you. It's common knowledge that out of all the dragonriders, Jace and Ghost are the fastest pair. Jace is auditioning you because you might be the only other pair that can actually keep up with him. He's waiting to see if you can handle being his wing end or not."

I felt downright stupid for not realizing that myself. I glared down at my helmet, and thought about throwing it again. How had I not seen it? It was so simple. It had been staring me right in the face the whole time. This had to be the reason Jace was ignoring me. I hadn't done anything worth acknowledging yet.

But that was going to change. I slammed my helmet down onto my head and turned around to get back on Mavrik's back.

"What about breakfast?" Felix called after me. "We've still got a day full of training, you know. You should be resting."

I swung my leg over the saddle and started buckling myself in. Mavrik shifted and flexed beneath me, spreading his wings wide. He understood my thoughts; we had work to do.

I gave Felix a thumbs up to let him know I was okay. "I'll rest when I'm dead."

Mavrik and I went over the drills again until I had no choice but to put my gear away and go to class. I barely had enough time to put on a clean shirt and sprint to the auditorium before the instructor began. I threw myself into the seat between Felix and Lyon. They both stared at me while I sat there, gasping for breath.

After a few minutes, Felix leaned over to whisper, "You smell horrible."

I shrugged. "Who cares?"

"I do. I have to sit by you," he muttered.

We settled in to listen to the lecture. Hours passed, and my stomach started to ache. Skipping breakfast was a bad idea. I couldn't pay attention, and my belly was growling so loudly I was sure everyone else could hear it.

Then I felt someone nudge my knee. Lyon glanced my way from where he sat on my other side. He bumped my knee again to get my attention. I watched his eyes track down, gesturing under the table. He passed me something wrapped up in a napkin, making sure no one else saw. It was a big square of cornbread leftover from breakfast.

When I looked back up to thank him, Lyon was staring diligently toward the instructor like nothing had happened. I didn't even want to imagine the punishment I would get if I got caught eating in class, but I was too hungry to care. I snuck bites of the cornbread until it was gone.

That was how my new morning routine started. I flew and trained right up until I barely had enough time to race to class. Felix complained about how bad I smelled. Lyon snuck me scraps so I didn't cave in from hunger. Then at lunch, I wolfed down as much food as possible before it was time for combat training.

The first time Thrane spotted Lyon back in the lineup, I had to fight to keep from smirking. The look on his face was a priceless mixture of shock and total confusion. It didn't take him two seconds to snap an accusing glare in my direction, though. He suspected me right away. I saw him pull Jace aside and the two men argued in hushed voices. Thrane pointed at Lyon and me. I could read the wild rage in his body language easily. Jace waved a hand at Thrane dismissively. He was playing it off like Lyon's injury hadn't been as serious as everyone thought.

Our plan was working. Sure, Thrane suspected something, but no one else did. It helped that he had basically established himself as a barbaric, overly aggressive idiot by breaking Lyon's arm in the first place. Basically everyone thought he was crazy now, even the other instructors.

Crazy or not, Thrane had a new hatred for me. He made each day at his training station a special slice of agony. His favorite teaching technique was what he called a "drill-down." He had us all line up in a big circle with one person standing in the center. The student in the middle sparred with everyone standing around him one-by-one. Win or lose, he stayed in the center of that circle until he'd fought all nineteen of the other avians in our group. It sounds easy, but nineteen fights back-to-back like that is nothing short of torture. Each person fights differently, has different strengths and weaknesses, and exhaustion makes you want to be careless and clumsy. That can be deadly when you're facing a fresh opponent every time.

Of course, I was usually the first one in the middle of the circle, so everyone I fought was *especially* fresh. I lost a lot of fights at first, and Thrane got to call me an assortment of creative racial slurs. But as the weeks passed, I started to get stronger. I didn't lose as many fights. My reflexes became faster. My body was changing and I was actually starting to gain a few pounds of muscle. Thrane's special attention was actually doing me more good than bad. I knew it was purely by accident. He was probably hoping I would break under the pressure, but I was beginning to thrive instead.

I lost all track of time as the months ran together. Our schedule intensified, and I was more and more thankful to have the sleeping remedy Felix offered. I took it every night, and I didn't have any more nightmares. There were no more sleepless nights, no more waking up in cold sweats.

The only reminder of time passing was the change in temperature. As the summer settled in, I was reminded why they called this valley the Devil's Cup. It was a desert, after all. The heat was so intense during the day that it made the horizon look like bubbling liquid. Fortunately, the bulk of our outdoor work happened before the sun ever rose.

The seasons were the least of my worries as I chased Ghost's tail through the twilight skies every morning. Felix's advice was burning in my brain like it had been branded there. I didn't try to compete with Jace anymore. I watched every move he and Ghost made, and tried to copy it. I made a mental note of very twist and turn, every wing beat, and precisely how he responded to the air around us. I memorized his patterns, and soon, I was able to predict them.

Our flights improved almost immediately. All the extra work was paying off. After a few weeks, I could keep him in my sights. Then after a few months, I could keep my position off his left wingtip like I was supposed to.

The first time I landed right beside him in perfect formation, Jace finally acknowledged me. He glanced me up and down, nodded, and told me that one of my first turns wasn't tight enough. That was the first recognition I had ever gotten from him, and my heart soared higher than any dragon could fly. I felt unstoppable, and with that new confidence came a willingness to take risks.

One of those risks was writing a letter to my brother. I wasn't even sure he would ever receive it. I'd heard how rough things were on the battlefronts. I wasn't even sure he was alive, but I still wanted him to know what was happening. I wished him well, let him know I was staying at the house, and told him he would be welcome whenever he wanted to visit. I hesitated to tell him about the scimitar I had taken from his room. I wasn't sure if he would appreciate me going through his things like that, but then, he had given me the house along with everything in it. If he wanted it, surely he would have said something. I decided not to bring it up.

I wrote another letter. This one was to Beckah. It took me a lot longer to come up with things to say to her that didn't sound stupid. I told her a little about training... but mostly I admitted how much I missed her and how I wished I was back at the beach in Saltmarsh with her. I crammed the rest of Sile's leftover money into the envelope, too.

I tried to keep the letter to Beckah a secret from Felix. Apparently he could smell my embarrassment like a bloodhound. He waited until the worst possible moment to tease me about it, though. While we were sitting down at lunch with the rest of our group from combat training class, he cleared his throat and glanced up at me with that scheming twinkle in his eyes. My blood ran cold.

"So, were you asking her to the officer's ball?" Felix asked casually.

The mention of a girl got the attention of everyone at the table. All eyes immediately turned to me, and I glared at him. "No."

"Oh?" I saw that sadistic glint of pleasure in his smile. "So you don't mind if I ask her, then?"

I gripped my fork so tightly it turned my knuckles white. I debated lunging over the table to throttle him. The thought of him asking Beckah to the ball, even out of spite, made me furious.

"Who?" Lyon asked, glancing between us curiously.

Felix was still grinning as he leaned back in his chair, making a big show of this so that it would be as embarrassing as possible for me. "Believe it or not, Jae is in love with an instructor's daughter."

A chorus of excited noises went up from the crowd sitting around us. I wanted to crawl under the table. My face was so hot it made my eyelids tingle.

"You aim high." Lyon snorted and went back to his mashed potatoes. He clearly still had no faith in my ability to have a romantic relationship with anyone.

"Oh it gets better," Felix went on. "She gave him a love token before training. Isn't that right, Jae?"

I didn't answer, and I didn't dare to move. The last thing I wanted was to betray the fact that I was actually carrying it around with me. Felix would have pinned me down to take it from me just so he could parade it around in front of everyone.

"Maybe this will be the year he finally kisses a girl and becomes a man." Felix batted his eyes at me sarcastically and pretended to wipe away a tear. "Kids—they grow up so fast."

Another avian sitting behind me clapped a hand on my shoulder and laughed.

"We'll be rooting for you. But is her dad really an instructor? Better not let him catch you."

"Better make sure you make your move fast. If she's good looking, you know those infantrymen will be all over her," Lyon murmured with a mouthful of food.

"He's right. She's pretty cute." Felix pointed his fork at me. "You might have some competition."

My stomach started to churn and suddenly I lost my appetite. I hadn't considered that someone else might try to compete with me for her. My eyes wandered around at the crowd of older, much more eligible avians sitting around me. They would all be looking for a girl at the ball, too.

"Just make sure you're the first person to ask her to dance." Another avian chuckled and jostled me as he walked by. "That way you have her attention right away."

I shuddered at the thought of dancing. Beckah had tried to teach me some last year, but that was so long ago I barely remembered any of it. Well, except for stepping on her toes several times. "I'm not a very good dancer."

"You can't be as bad at that as you are at sparring," Felix teased.

Everyone else laughed.

I didn't.

"Seriously? You don't know how to dance?" Felix's smile faded. He was starting to look genuinely concerned.

I shook my head. "Who would have taught me something like that?" No way was I going to tell him Beckah had tried. The last thing I wanted to do was give him anything else to tease me about.

"The ball is still a few months away. You've got time to learn." Lyon shrugged like it was nothing.

"When do I have time for that? I'm already training nonstop from the moment my eyes open every morning," I grumbled. The idea of losing Beckah over something stupid like not knowing how to dance made me frustrated and angry.

"Calm down. It isn't the end of the world." Felix was still grinning at me, sitting kicked back in his chair with his arms crossed. He was the picture of confidence, as usual. "You've made a lot of progress with Jace lately, right? You can afford to back off the extra flight training a few times a week. Lyon and I will work on teaching you to dance."

"Don't volunteer me for that!" Lyon's face went red.

Felix glanced at him coolly, "Why not? We need a third person. Who else is going to play the girl?"

Lyon fumed. His eyes were smoldering. "Why not you? You guys act like an old married couple anyway."

"I'm too manly to play a girl. Besides, you're the shortest," Felix retorted quickly. "And you whine like a girl, so it'll be very realistic."

Laughter erupted around us. Lyon looked embarrassed enough to puke. His face was a frightening shade of red, and he was glaring daggers at Felix. I decided if it did come down to a fight, I was going to stand back and watch this time. These two might never get along, but at least their arguments didn't come to blows anymore.

Even though I was still learning about Lyon, it didn't take me very long to figure out that he was a stubborn hothead. Felix was stubborn, too, which was why I knew they would probably never see eye to eye. As long as they didn't kill each other, I decided it was better to stay out of the way and let them duke it out on their own. Playing referee with them only prolonged the inevitable.

I was hoping they were just kidding about teaching me to dance. I was dead wrong about that, though. The next morning, after another perfect landing in formation with Jace, Felix caught me by the arm and gave me that scary, scheming grin.

"Ready?" He looked a little too excited for my comfort.

"We are not doing this, Felix. It isn't a big deal. I don't have to dance with her," I whispered. The whole time, I was watching Lyon glare at us out of the corner of his eye, like he knew what was about to happen. "I didn't even ask her to the ball."

"Idiot! Why not?" Felix slapped me hard on the back. "Write her again and ask her. And yes, this is a big deal. You're a dragonrider. You're expected to know how to dance as well as you fight. It's not all about swords and wearing strings of fallen enemies' ears around your neck, you know."

I stared at him in horror. "Who is wearing ears around their neck?" For some reason, the only person I could envision doing something like that was Thrane. Yeah, he definitely seemed like the type to make jewelry out of his fallen enemies.

He waved off my question. "That's beside the point. Jae, I am going to teach you something that will take you a lot further in life than sword fighting or air combat techniques ever will. Something that has saved men's lives and reputations countless times. Something invaluable. Something more precious than the finest gold or rarest gems. Something that will have duchesses and queens falling at your feet."

"And what is that?"

He smirked at me and winked. "Charm."

"You want to teach Jae to be charming? That'll be the day." Lyon snickered.

I scowled at them. "Shouldn't be very hard, if you two manage to pass for charming. You both eat like hogs and fight like wild animals."

Felix shook his head. "Sure, we can be like that around each other. But being at a ball will be different. You'll see, Jae. There's a code for how you have to act around girls if you want to get anywhere. It's like a game. And believe me, as dragonriders, we are expected to always win."

19

CHAPTER NINETEEN

For the record, I didn't enjoy Lyon playing the girl any more than he did. In fact, Felix was the only one who seemed to be enjoying that arrangement. He kept coming up with new, creative ways to tease us the entire time as I staggered through leading the dances. I was too flustered by the complicated footwork to pay much attention to his taunting, but Lyon's face stayed so red I was afraid he was going to start bleeding from the ears.

Three mornings a week, after our laps and drills were finished, I tolerated being teased while Felix coached me through different line dances and waltzes. Lyon and I refused to make eye contact as I was forced to hold his hand and, even worse, his hip. The first time Felix actually got us to stand in a waltz pose together, he burst into laughter. Lyon snapped. They punched each other for a few minutes, and I considered leaving the room and walking off the nearest cliff. It seemed better than having to hold Lyon like that ever again.

I still had a shred of dignity left, though. I was learning to dance, and Felix insisted I was getting better. It gave me some hope that maybe I wouldn't completely embarrass myself at the ball.

"Lyon dances like a three legged cow," he assured me. "So it'll be easier with a real girl. They're much lighter, and more graceful. And a lot less ugly."

Lyon cursed under his breath. "Oh right, well excuse me for not dancing like a girl." We only had a few weeks left before the ball, and I knew he was probably just as ready as I was for this dance class to end.

"Remember what I said about greetings and introductions. Confidence. Eye contact. Charm. It's a state of mind." Felix snapped his fingers at Lyon like he was summoning a pet dog. "Let's run through it one more time."

Lyon sputtered a few more curses as he stomped toward me. I tried to visualize Beckah standing in his place with her warm smile and deep green eyes. It was nearly impossible, though. Lyon was definitely a boy. And this was definitely the most embarrassing thing I'd ever done in my life.

As soon as we had gone through our awkward bows and stepped into an opening dance pose, the dorm room door to our room burst open. I was holding onto Lyon's waist and hand, as usual, and he was pretending to hold up a dress. We both froze, too stunned to react.

Jace was standing in the doorway. He looked at all of us, his brows raised and his expression completely blank.

My last shred of dignity withered and died.

"When you're finished with... whatever this is, I need to see the lot of you downstairs to be measured for your formal uniforms." Jace managed to say, although he sounded a little hoarse. I could have sworn I saw him suppressing a smile. "Hurry up."

The door shut, and I died a little inside. Lyon shoved away from me. Judging by the shade of red his head was turning, he was too angry and embarrassed to speak. I couldn't say anything, either.

The only person who could make a sound was Felix. He was laughing so hard he was choking. He fell down on the floor, gripping his sides. I had to step over him in order to get out of the room. Lyon followed me, but he kept his distance. I couldn't blame him for that.

"You think he will tell any of the girls at the ball about this?" I heard Lyon mutter from behind me.

I glanced back at him. That hadn't even crossed my mind. "He better not. I know where he sleeps."

Lyon met my gaze and sighed. "You know, I used to envy you. Felix's family is the most powerful in the kingdom, next to the royal family. I thought it must be nice to have friends in such high places."

"And how do you feel about that now?" I couldn't resist smiling.

"I'm wondering how you've managed to survive him this long." Lyon actually laughed. He sped up to walk beside me down the stairs.

Felix caught up with us halfway, still snickering under his breath as he draped his arms over both of our shoulders.

The dining hall was filled with chatter when we arrived. Avians and instructors were rushing around like crazy, taking measurements and placing orders with the tailors who had set up work areas at different ends of the long dining tables. Felix drifted away to talk as soon as we entered the crowd. He disappeared, leaving us to hold a spot in line until it was our turn to get measured.

"Morning classes are canceled today," he announced. He sounded really excited about it. "Some kind of emergency meeting for all the instructors. Some of the guys are planning on taking a joyride. We should go, too."

Lyon shrugged. "As long as the instructors don't mind."

"What's the meeting about?" I had a feeling Felix was holding out information. He loved gossip too much not to find out all the details he could.

"They're keeping it a secret, but rumor is it has something to do with the battle scenario this year." Felix gave me a funny look. "Maybe even something about crazed animals."

My stomach twisted into a knot. I looked away, diving headfirst into worry as I waited to be measured for my uniform. If they were calling meetings about it, did that mean things were getting worse? I cringed at the thought. I was worried about Beckah and the rest of Sile's family. I knew I had to write her another letter as soon as possible. I had to warn them.

After we were measured, the three of us filed out to the Roost and saddled up with a handful of other avians. We took off and spent the rest of the morning goofing around in the air. It was nice to ride for pleasure instead of chasing Jace's tail. But as much fun as it was to swoop through spirals and launch pretend attack runs on Felix and Nova, I couldn't get into it. My head was in a fog because of what Felix had said. I kept looking back at the academy and wondering what was happening in that meeting. Not knowing was killing me. I couldn't shake the sense that I was somehow *entitled* to know.

That feeling didn't go away even after we landed and started toward the gymnasium for combat training. As we started lining up, Felix elbowed me to get my attention. He was staring at me like he was concerned.

"You all right?" He whispered.

I wasn't sure what to say, or how to explain how I felt. I shook my head a little, and we both snapped to attention as the instructors arrived to start the class. Jace and Morrig walked in together, talking quietly until they split off to manage their separate stations.

Thrane was a bigger jerk than usual when we got to his station. He made us do drill-downs, and of course, I was the first one in the middle of the circle. We had progressed to using practice weapons now, and were learning to fight against multiple enemies who were also armed. Sometimes, we even had to start without one and hopefully steal one off someone we sparred by disarming them mid-fight.

I was expecting to get that kind of treatment when Thrane stuck me in the middle of the drill-down circle first. One by one, the other students in my group moved in to attack me. I disarmed my first opponent in a matter of seconds, catching him totally off guard and twisting his arm until he dropped his sword. The pent up frustration about the meeting must have made me space out, because before I knew it, all the fights were over and I had sparred with everyone else in the circle.

I had won every fight, and I wasn't even sweating.

Thrane pushed through the circle, his dark eyes glittering suspiciously as he eyed me up and down. "You must be feeling proud of yourself," he growled.

I stared back at him. He didn't scare me anymore, and I wasn't stupid enough to answer that comment.

Thrane moved in closer, invading my space until I could see the little pink veins on his eyeballs. Standing that close gave me a real appreciation for how big he was. His neck was thicker around than my leg. His breath blasted on my face as he started to laugh. It was like standing nose-to-nose with a fully grown bear.

"Pick someone," he commanded.

I blinked in confusion. I couldn't stop myself from glancing behind him, catching Felix and Lyon's faces in the crowd. They looked worried. This was new to all of us.

"You act like my training is boring to you. You think you're a soldier, now?" A wicked smile spread over Thrane's face, showing off his horrible, crooked teeth. "So let's see it. Pick someone, or I will."

Panic made my throat seize up. I couldn't speak. I didn't know what to do. Once again, I looked past him at the rest of the guys in my group.

Lyon was looking right at me. When our eyes met, I could read the determination in his gaze. He gave me a nod.

I knew I didn't have a choice. If Thrane was going to make me do something terrible to anyone, it had to be Lyon. He was the only one who knew about my healing power. He was the only one I could fix without risking revealing my abilities to everyone. He must have known that, too, because when I hesitated, he glared at me and mouthed two words, *"Hurry up."*

I pointed at Lyon. He stepped out of the crowd and started walking toward us. Suddenly, Thrane spun and grabbed Lyon by the hair. He pushed him down to his knees in front of me, jerking his head back so that we were forced to look at each other.

"Break his arm." Thrane snarled at me like an angry wolf.

I didn't dare to move an inch.

"A soldier does what is necessary. He doesn't feel pain or guilt in combat. So break his arm, or fight me." He rumbled again.

There was no good option. I didn't want to hurt Lyon, but I definitely didn't want to fight Thrane. It wasn't even that I didn't think I could win. Maybe I could win, but I didn't trust myself not to fall victim to battle fever again in order to do it. I knew that was what Thrane really wanted.

"Tick tock, halfbreed." Thrane was giving me another toothy, evil smile. "I'm about to make the choice for you. Don't act like you don't have a killer instinct. We've already seen that you do. So let's see it again. Let's see if you can handle being a soldier."

"We can't keep doing this," Jace said. He was standing over Lyon's bed in our dorm room, checking both of his forearms. They were freshly healed.

I sat, propped up in a chair at his bedside, wiping the cold sweat from my face with a rag. After healing Lyon's arms three days in a row, I was able to do it without losing consciousness anymore. I still got a little nauseous, but it wasn't anything I couldn't handle. That might have made me a little proud, since my abilities were obviously coming more easily to me now, except that keeping this a secret was getting more and more impossible.

People were starting to suspect—people that mattered. Thrane already suspected that I was up to something, but he didn't have any proof. At least, not yet. Now the other avians were talking. Felix was asking questions, and sulking when no one would give him a straight answer. Lyon was spreading the rumor that he and I were faking it every time Thrane called me out and demanded that I prove myself. The others seemed to like that, like it was some kind of elaborate prank we were playing, but I knew we couldn't keep this charade up for much longer. And Thrane was probably counting on that.

"What other choice is there?" I buried my face in the rag. I was starting to blame Jace for not intervening to stop this. "It's that or I fight him, which is exactly what he wants. Just tell him to stop it."

Jace scowled at me. "I'm not his superior, and by healing Lyon, we're taking away any evidence that he's doing anything wrong in the first place."

"Something has to be done," I insisted. "Lyon can't keep doing this."

"Don't talk about me like I'm not here," Lyon muttered. He looked as frustrated as the rest of us. "I can handle it."

Watching Lyon go through this pain every day was beginning to wear me down. I definitely had a new respect for him. He had the best tolerance for pain I'd ever seen. I had broken his arms four days in a row, and he had yet to even second guess stepping up and basically volunteering for it. He was going through a lot just to save my reputation.

"We should be counting ourselves lucky that he is letting you pick Lyon every time." Jace sighed and moved away from the bed, staring at the door like he was deep in thought. "I suspect that isn't by accident, though. He's hoping to attract attention and suspicion."

"Well, he's doing an excellent job of it." I frowned down at my shoes. "Felix knows this has something to do with me. It's only a matter of time before he figures it out."

The silence was awkward as we all stared at one another. The question of what to do hung in the air, but no one had the answer. Even after Jace retired to his own quarters, and Felix came back to the dorm with dinner for us, I couldn't shake off my worries. I wasn't in the mood to eat, so I went ahead and settled into bed. It didn't even dawn on me that I had forgotten to take Felix's sleeping remedy until I felt sleep suck me down into the darkness of another nightmare.

When I opened my eyes, I was back in the old house my mother and I had shared. It stunned me to see it, even in a dream. Just like before, everything looked the same as when I left it. It even smelled the same. But I didn't get to enjoy the nostalgia for very long.

I was sitting in an old chair beside my mother's bed. She was lying there, looking so fragile that I was afraid to touch her. It brought back all the pain of what had definitely been the worst time of my life. When my mother got sick, she lost the light in her eyes. That was something I knew I would never forget, no matter how much I wanted to.

My mother turned her head to smile at me from her pillow. She was so thin, and her lips and eyelids were a strange purplish color. I could see little beads of sweat on her brow from the fever.

"You have to be strong, dulcu." Her voice was weak and soft.

Like in the other dreams, I couldn't make myself move at all. I couldn't touch her, or hold her hand, or wipe the sweat away from her face. It made my heart hurt even more.

"Mom." I started pleading with her. "What's happening to me? I can speak to animals. I can heal people. What's happening to me?"

Her smile started to fade as her eyes became distant. "We always remember our ancestors," she started to whisper. "Always, even after they are gone. It keeps us bonded. It draws our spirits together like reeds in a basket."

"Mom?" Nothing she said made any sense to me.

"Listen to them, dulcu. Listen and be strong." Her eyes widened. Her face twisted up like she was about to start screaming, but she never made a sound. The darkness swallowed me up again, wiping away everything and dropping me back on that muddy, snowbound road.

The dream of the Gray elf warrior murdering the royal family began to play out before me again. I struggled to move. I did everything I could to will it away, and force myself to wake up. Nothing worked. I was trapped in that repeating nightmare, just like before.

I saw the lone Maldobarian guard standing with his sword in hand, facing the murdering Gray elf with no hope of winning. I saw them draw, stepping into combat. This time, thanks to my training, I could appreciate more of the logistics behind their footwork and strikes.

I held my breath as the Gray elf moved in for the kill. Everything he did was so deliberate. It was smooth, calculated, and completely flawless—from the way he gripped his weapons, to the way he measured his steps. Nothing was left to chance. I shuddered to think of what he would do to the guard, who could barely stand because of his wounds.

The dream started to collapse on itself again. The only thing I could think about, the only thing I could hear, was that Gray elf's voice ringing in my head like a tolling bell.

"*What would you do to save your own life?*"

20

CHAPTER TWENTY

The nightmares were back. No matter how much of Felix's sleeping remedy I took, I couldn't get any relief. Every night I woke up drenched in a cold sweat with my heart pounding in my ears. Sometimes the pendant around my neck would burn like it was on fire, and other times I gasped awake alone in the dark feeling cold and terrified. After that, I couldn't go back to sleep at all.

I tried not to let it affect my performance in training, but I knew the lack of sleep was starting to show. Even I could see the baggy circles under my eyes growing darker by the day whenever I saw my reflection. I was always tired, and it was hard to stay awake and pay attention in class.

Whenever we were in front of instructors, I tried not to let my fatigue show. I didn't want anyone, especially Jace, to think I wasn't on top of my game. But Thrane seemed to pick up on it right away. It was almost like he could sense I was closer than ever to finally snapping and giving him the fight he wanted. As much as I tried to put up a tough front, he pushed me harder than ever, just waiting for me to break.

The days dragged on, and the rest of the academy began buzzing about the annual officer's ball. I was looking forward to it, too, but having those nightmares made it hard to think about anything else. When the others started going on about who would be there, or where the ball was going to be held this year, I always seemed to space out. A few of my classmates actually noticed, and asked me if I was okay. I sloughed off their remarks, and tried to make it seem like I was just studying late at night.

I couldn't fool Felix, though. He saw right through it, and he seemed to take it personally that the sleeping remedy wasn't working on me anymore.

"Maybe you've built up a tolerance to it," he suggested.

I shrugged. I was digging through a pile of new uniforms Jace had brought to our room. The tailor had stitched our initials into each of the pieces, so it was easy to arrange them into three piles for Felix, Lyon, and myself.

"Have you talked to the medic? You're pretty chummy with him, right?" he asked, and I could feel the sting of accusation in that question. Whatever was going on between Lyon and me, Felix knew it had something to do with the medic.

I shook my head. "Why would I? It's not a medical problem, Felix." I sighed and rubbed my eyes. They felt itchy and tired. "There's nothing he could do about it anyway."

Felix was quiet again. He was sitting on his bed with his legs crossed and his arms folded behind his head. I could feel his eyes on me, like he was trying to find some clue about what was going on.

"You're chummy with Lyon, too." He baited me. Lyon was still taking a bath, so he wasn't there to back up my story.

I tried to keep my voice steady. I didn't want Felix to know how nervous his questions made me. It was hard enough to watch Lyon lie to him, but it was almost impossible for me to fool him. "Why wouldn't I be? He's part of our team."

Felix snorted. "Team? What team is that?"

"You know, Jace's team." I said.

"We're not a team, Jae. Not yet, anyways. We might not even get sent to the same post after this. You know that, right? We may never see each other again." I knew he was just trying to twist my feelings so I would spill all my secrets. He wanted to make me feel bad—and he was doing an excellent job of it.

"I'm always going to be watching your back, Felix. It doesn't matter if we're posted on opposite ends of the kingdom." I reminded him.

I heard the bed creak as he sat up. "Right. Just like you've got Lyon's back, right?" He snapped at me angrily.

I turned around to frown at him. "Don't tell me you're actually jealous because I'm friends with him now?"

Felix snorted again and glared at the floor. "I don't understand how you can be friends with someone like him. Think of everything he's done. He beat you up multiple times last year. I even had to save you from him once. Don't you remember that? He probably would have killed you if I hadn't shown up. He's said horrible things about you, even this year. He betrayed us and left us to die at the prison camp. How can you trust anything he says? How can you trust him more than me?"

Words didn't come to me right away. It was hard to explain, and I wasn't that great with words to begin with. "Do you think I should hate him?" I finally asked.

Felix raised his eyes up to stare back at me. "I don't see how you can't."

I nodded. "Should I hate everyone who's ever done something bad to me? Even if they were sorry for it later?"

"You know that's not what I mean." His eyes narrowed. "Lyon's proven over and over that he's nothing but a coward. He can't be trusted. You're making a mistake by sharing secrets with him."

"Maybe you're right. Maybe he will betray me, and maybe I'll end up wishing I hadn't given him any more chances." I took a deep, uneasy breath. "I think I'd rather give someone a chance to prove me wrong, than live under the assumption that no one can change."

The door opened suddenly, and Lyon came stumbling into the room. He was struggling to carry three brand new pairs of black uniform boots. "Look!" He announced proudly, dropping two of the boots as he tried to shut the door. "They're already polished and everything!"

While Lyon fumbled around, Felix and I kept glaring at each other in silence. I knew he might never understand. He was stubborn that way. But I needed him to trust me. And more than that, I needed him to respect me enough to let me make this kind of a choice on my own. If I got burned, it wouldn't be his fault.

The academy fell silent as we settled in for the night. I stayed awake long after the others fell asleep, twirling my mother's necklace between my fingers and watching the shadows from the moonlight move across the ceiling. I was afraid of what I would see if I closed my eyes.

By the time dawn finally broke, I had managed to sneak in a few short spurts of sleep. It was enough to keep me from crashing, although it didn't do anything to help the circles under my eyes. The academy started waking up. Noise came from the hallways outside our door as people fought for their turn in the baths.

I sat up on the edge of my bed, staring at the stack of clean new uniforms I had set out the night before. Today was the day. Tonight, I might see Beckah again. My stomach squirmed nervously as I reached to pull her handkerchief out of my pocket. I ran my thumb over the stitching of the two dragons. Seeing it always made me smile, no matter how bad things seemed.

"Rise and shine, kids!" Felix shouted as he bounded out of bed. It almost made me have a heart attack.

Lyon basically fell out of his bed with surprise. He came up cursing and sputtering, looking for something to throw at Felix.

"Tonight is the big night. Tonight, we wine, dine, and dance until dawn!" Felix patted my head roughly as he walked past, gathering up his towel and soap. "So comb your hair. Shave your chin—except for you, Jae. We all know you can't grow a beard. Gray elves can't grow body hair, right? I guess that applies to halfbreeds, too. Such a shame. The ladies love beards."

I glared at him.

"Ooh, watch it. You don't want your face to get stuck that way just in time to scare all the girls away. You look like an angry old buzzard with those circles under your eyes." He laughed. His sunny mood was really grating on my nerves this early in the morning. "Come on, show a little enthusiasm! Tonight, you'll be dining at my house, after all."

"Your family is hosting the ball?" Lyon perked up.

Felix grinned smugly. "That's right. It was supposed to be a surprise. You guys have no idea what you're in for."

"But what about your dad?" I asked. "I thought he was sick?"

"A lesson about nobles, Jae," he said with a smirk. "We are never too sick to throw a party."

Lyon laughed like that was a good joke. "What he means is, when it comes to showing up the other noble families, there's nothing they won't do."

"Absolutely." Felix had a mischievous twinkle in his eyes that was a little scary. "Dad would have thrown this ball from his coffin. Besides, Mom's been writing me and asking for ideas. We've got a guest list two miles long and enough wine and ale to float a ship. My whole estate has been preparing for this night for the past two months. Trust me, this will be a night to remember."

WE LEFT THE DORMITORY WITH OUR SADDLE BAGS CRAMMED FULL AND SLUNG over our shoulders. All our new uniform pieces were packed and ready. Every buckle and button was polished to perfection. I had even taken the time to trim my hair a little, so the ends didn't look as frayed. Felix teased me about it, of course. He kept poking fun at me about not having to shave, like it was a big deal or something.

The sun wasn't even up, but the Roost was already packed with people moving their dragons in and out of stalls when we arrived. A few groups had already taken off, and were catching the first few bursts of chilly morning air. Jace was waiting for us beside Ghost, and he started shouting at us to hurry up the second we got there.

With our armor strapped on, our bags tied down, and our dragons saddled, the four of us took off in formation toward the rising sun. Jace flew in the front, leading the way for the rest of us like a big flock of geese going south for the winter. It took all day to fly across the kingdom, past the royal city of Halfax, to the eastern shores where Felix's family lived.

The estate of Duke Farrow was so big I could see it even from miles away. Except for the royal castle, I had never seen a place that big before. As we swooped down through the clouds, the sunlight caught off the hundreds and hundreds of gothic-styled arched windows. It looked kind of like a massive cathedral made out of pearly white stone, perched high on a rocky cliff overlooking the cold eastern sea below. I counted a dozen spires of different shapes and sizes rising up toward the sky, flying blue and gold banners with the king's eagle stitched on them.

Ahead of me, Felix turned around to give me a thumbs up. Jace even let him take the lead as we started our descent into one of the big grassy courtyards where other dragonriders were taking turns landing and unloading their gear.

The closer we got to the cliffs and the sea, the more excited Mavrik got. I could feel his heart pounding against my legs, even through the thick saddle padding. His big nostrils puffed as he scented the air. His bright yellow eyes darted around, and he chirped at the other dragons. They all chirped back excitedly.

"It must remind them of home," Lyon muttered once we landed. Demos was giving him a hard time, squirming around like he was eager to get back in the air.

"What do you mean?" I asked.

"They come from the highland cliffs further north, up the coast. Didn't you know? It's not that far from here." Lyon pointed toward the ocean. "The land rises and creates these massive, steep cliffs that drop hundreds of feet into the sea. That's where wild dragons nest."

I tried to envision that. It wasn't hard to imagine that many dragons, not when I spent my time around so many of them every day. But as soon as I started trying to picture it in my mind, Mavrik took over. He changed the image, showing me what it was really like. A huge stone cliff face that went on for miles and miles, jutting straight up out of the dark, foaming ocean. Dragons flew, catching the strong winds in their powerful wings, and building their nests on the narrow ledges. They ate fish from the sea, or flew many miles inland for larger game to bring back for their hatchlings. The roaring sound of the waves pounding against the rock was constant, and the rich smell of cold, deep ocean water filled my lungs. It was hard to tell which was just a picture coming from Mavrik's mind, and which was real.

"Beautiful," I murmured.

Mavrik crowed with agreement. I grabbed my bag off his back and stepped out of the way as he took off, filling his wings with air that smelled like home to him. It made me smile.

The closer we got to Felix's house, the bigger it seemed to get. The gates had to be at last twenty feet tall, and were plated with bronze that shone like gold in the light of the setting sun. All the courtyards and pathways were paved with white cobblestones. Felix told us it was limestone straight out of the heart of this kingdom.

"It's the oldest castle in Maldobar," he said. "My family was one of the first to settle here, hundreds of years ago."

The inside of the estate was even grander and more beautiful than the outside. Two massive mahogany doors were opened to welcome guests into a foyer that was at least the size of the breaking dome. The vaulted ceilings were detailed with dark stained wood. Huge iron chandeliers sent candlelight sparkling over white marble floors, and enormous hearths in every room roared with fires. There were paintings and elaborate tapestries hanging on all the walls, depicting all the years of Felix's family history. All the furniture was made of polished wood, silk, and animal furs. It looked expensive, but welcoming and comfortable. The arched windows were adorned in wreaths made from holly, pine needles, and the rugged-looking flowers that grew in this area. It made the castle smell as good as it looked, and put me at ease right away. The whole place managed to be incredibly lavish without seeming untouchable. It felt warm and inviting—well, as far as noble estates go, anyway.

As Felix led the way through the estate, guiding us down long hallways lined with portraits, we passed more servants and maids than I could count. They all wore similar blue and white uniforms with gold aprons and ties. They smiled at us as we passed, but when they spotted Felix, they quickly bowed or curtsied to him and asked him if they could help carry his things. He kept waving them off, telling them that he could manage it on his own.

"I was hoping maybe I had been away long enough they wouldn't recognize me," Felix complained as he opened the door to his chambers. Apparently, we were staying in his wing of the estate tonight.

Jace made a sarcastic sound in his throat. "Good luck with that. You look too much like your mother."

Felix stared at him, looking a little nervous. "How do you know that?"

"Because I tried to get her to elope with me. It was at a ball just like this. She was young and beautiful. I begged her to fly away with me," Jace answered bluntly. He didn't even give Felix a second glance, like it wasn't a big deal.

No one was ready for that, especially not Felix. I don't think any of us realized that was Jace's bizarre attempt at a joke until *he* started laughing. Even then, I was afraid to assume anything.

"It's refreshing to have such gullible students," Jace chuckled as he patted Felix's shoulder roughly.

For a few seconds, Felix looked like he was going to throw up. He managed to suck it up, and crack a smirk as Jace wandered away to explore our housing for the night. As soon as he was out of sight, though, the three of us all shared a horrified moment of silence.

"You think he was serious?" Lyon whispered.

Felix shot him a poisonous look. "Shut up. Don't even say things like that. My mother is a saint."

I couldn't help but laugh, which promptly got me punched in the arm.

Felix's chambers were bigger than my entire house. I understood now why he had insisted it would be fine for me to stay with him during the interlude; he basically had a small city's worth of rooms all to himself. He had his own library, four or five different bedrooms, balconies, parlors, and a washroom that could have comfortably bathed a dozen people at once.

"Make yourselves at home," he said casually as he threw his bags down on a sofa and started for a buffet table in the corner of the room that was stacked with silver platters of desserts. Seeing them reminded me of Beckah, and my stomach squirmed nervously again. I wondered if she was already here, waiting somewhere in this huge castle.

Everyone split up as soon as we got settled, rushing around to get ready as quickly as possible. I wiped the sweat off my neck and face with a warm washcloth, and went to work trying to braid my hair. I knew there was no way I would ever get it to look as good as when Beckah did it, but I wanted to try. After a few minutes of tying it in knots, though, I finally gave it up and brushed it back into a long ponytail.

Felix had given each of us our own room in his chambers. While we were cleaning up, a small army of servants had come in and set out all our belongings for us. I found my uniform, armor, boots, and weaponry laid out perfectly on the bed. It even looked like they had taken the time to polish my breastplate and vambraces again.

Seeing all that fancy stuff made me anxious, but I took my time getting dressed. My formal uniform pants were black and made of more expensive cotton. They had a blue line down each side of the leg that was trimmed in gold. The blue tunic was made to match, with black and gold stripes down the sides of the arms, and a high collar that fastened with a gold button. There were gold plates on the shoulders with special clasps for the thin breastplate that buckled against my chest.

The breastplate wasn't made to be worn in actual battle. The metal was way too thin, and it was plated in silver with intricate gold detailing in the shape of the king's eagle with swords and spears in its claws. The vambraces were made the same way; to be comfortable and light, but beautiful. The servants had polished them all until they shimmered like mirrors.

I laced up my tall black riding boots, and buckled my long black cloak onto the gold plates on my shoulders so that it hung down my back and barely brushed the floor. When I stepped to the mirror to make sure everything was straight, I barely recognized myself. I looked older, more mature, and except for the pointed ears and ash-colored hair... I actually looked like a dragonrider.

"Not bad," Felix called from the doorway. He was already dressed in the same thing I was wearing. "Are you ready for this?"

"Sure," I lied.

He laughed. "I seriously doubt that. Just remember what I taught you. This is a show, Jae. It's all a game. And if you want to win, you have to have two things."

I followed him out of the room. We walked side by side toward the main parlor where we were supposed to meet up with Lyon and Jace. "Oh? Remind me what they are again?"

He smirked at me with that familiar cunning light in his eyes. I had figured out a long time ago what that look meant. He had girls on the brain. He tossed his feathery blond hair out of his eyes and chuckled. "Charm and confidence."

DUKE FARROW HAD OPENED UP THREE OF THE ESTATE'S HUGE BALLROOMS FOR the ball. They sparkled with dazzling décor, and roared with the sound of laughter and music. The air was filled with the smell of pine needles, flowers, and food. Hundreds of men in uniform, infantrymen and dragonriders, gathered to watch the nobles arriving through the front entryway. Carriages were lined up one after another, pulled by horses with ribbons tied in their manes and tails. Each carriage was given an introduction before the doors were opened and a few fledgling students rushed to help the noble ladies and gentlemen out.

Felix was right, it really was a show. The ladies were wearing gowns made out of silk, velvet, or expensively embroidered cotton. They had flowers or ribbons in their hair, and expensive jewelry on their necks and wrists. They laughed, giggled, and waved at some of the other dragonriders as they arrived. A lot of them seemed to recognize Felix.

I'd never seen anything like this up close—I mean, girls like this had never visited the Gray elf ghetto or my father's house. My mother had never owned a dress like that, and she certainly didn't have any jewelry with big gems and crystals like these girls were wearing. At first, I stared at each one that walked past us. I couldn't help it.

Then Felix elbowed me again. "Not charming, Jae. Quit gawking. And close your mouth."

I swallowed hard and tried to remember some of the stuff he had taught me before. I guess I wasn't naturally a very charming person. The best I could manage was a smile that must have looked as disturbing as it felt, because the girls all gave me strange looks as they walked past. Being charming came so naturally to Felix, though. I watched him wave at the girls. He even winked at some of them, and it always made them blush.

As soon as the introductions were finished, and the last of the carriages were emptied, Felix's mother stood up at the front of the room and gave a welcoming speech. I decided Jace must have been joking about Felix looking like his mother, because they didn't favor much at all. Her eyes seemed sad and exhausted. She wished us all a good evening, and offered a toast up to her husband who wouldn't be able to join us because of his illness.

As soon as his mother's speech was over, Felix vanished like a racehorse after the starting gun. He practically vaporized into the crowd, and the next time I caught a glimpse of him, he was standing in the middle of a big group of girls.

Anyone else probably would have been upset about being left behind like that. I guess I was a little shocked he bolted so quickly, but I knew better than to think that Felix was going to coach me through tonight. He had his own agenda, and nothing was going to get in the way of that.

"I'd give my left arm for some of his connections," Lyon murmured next to me. He was watching Felix with envy written all over his face.

"I'd give my right arm for some of his confidence," I added.

Lyon laughed. "He's got plenty of that to go around. So where's your girl? Didn't she come?"

I glanced back at the open doorway that led out the front entrance. There were still carriages arriving, a few guests running late, but no sign of Beckah. I tried to convince myself there was still hope that she might come. I'd never gotten up the nerve to write another letter to her and ask her about coming. I was starting to worry that maybe I should have. Maybe she had been expecting it, or even waiting for it, and I had failed to deliver.

Lyon patted my shoulder. I guess he could tell my hopes were hanging by a thread. "She's probably just running behind. It's a long ride out here."

I nodded, but I didn't feel any better. After all, Beckah probably wasn't going to come by carriage—not when she had a set of wings that would take her wherever she wanted to go.

The ball got underway, and I mixed with the other guests about as well as oil and water. Lyon stuck close by me most of the time, except when he got the nerve up to ask a girl to dance, and I felt bad for holding him back. He didn't have much trouble getting girls to notice him. He wasn't as tall as some of the infantrymen, but he was still a dragonrider with a noble pedigree. Felix had been right about our armor attracting more attention. The girls definitely gravitated toward dragonriders over everyone else, and I got the impression right away that the infantrymen had a big chip on their shoulders about it.

Lyon at least had the good taste to wait his turn, though. Felix on the other hand, treated the infantrymen like they were invisible, or faceless obstacles in his way, whenever there was a girl he wanted to dance with. Several times, I felt my heart starting to pound because I was so sure one of the infantrymen was going to finally lose his self-control and start a fight. That was not something I wanted to deal with tonight, but I was obligated by the bonds of friendship to have Felix's back in a fight... even if he was the one being a jerk.

The armor didn't help me much, though. Any girl that got close to me took one look at my pointed ears, and made an immediate sprint in the opposite direction. It shouldn't have surprised me, let alone gotten under my skin. But after about the fourth time of finally working up the nerve to ask someone to dance, only to have them run away like I was carrying some kind of deadly disease, I was beginning to ask myself why I even bothered.

"Have a drink," Lyon said as he handed me a glass of wine. "You look like you need it."

"Tell me this is almost over," I groaned. I'd never tried wine before, so I didn't think much about it before turning up the glass and drinking it all at once. That was a horrible mistake. The strong drink made my stomach ache immediately.

Lyon snickered as he watched me choke. "You're the only dragonrider I know who hates parties."

"Probably because I'm the only halfbreed you know." I shot him a glare.

He nodded in agreement. "You need to dance at least once, though. Want me to pull a bait and switch for you?"

"And what is that, exactly?" I couldn't help but sound suspicious.

"You know, ask a girl to dance, then come up with an excuse to leave, and suggest you dance with her instead. That way she can't say no, and you get some face time with at least one girl tonight." Lyon shrugged like this was a completely normal tactic.

I frowned as I glanced around the room again. I looked at all the noble girls in their expensive dresses, hanging on the arms of men who were probably better worth their time and effort. Men who had something to offer, and who didn't have to explain why they had pointed ears. As much as I hated feeling sorry for myself, this was getting depressing.

"No, don't worry about it." I sighed. "I think I'll go sit outside and get some air. Have fun."

I smiled at Lyon and punched his arm the way Felix and I always did to one another. He didn't seem to get it, though. I left him standing in one of the ballrooms as I moved through the crowds, looking for the doorway that led out onto a balcony.

When I finally found one that wasn't as crowded, I took a seat on a marble bench and let the cool night air wash over me. The balcony had an impressive view of some of the estate's gardens. There were little pathways leading away into the dark, lit by candles inside glass globes. Beautiful fountains filled the silence with the sound of burbling water.

I leaned forward to let my elbows rest on my knees, and stared down at the floor. Underneath all my fine clothes and polished armor, I was still a halfbreed. I was still a coward, and I felt like an idiot for thinking this might go differently. What had I really been expecting, anyway? I couldn't even answer that question for my own peace of mind.

"It doesn't look like you're having very much fun," someone spoke to me. It startled me because it was a girl's voice, but what I saw when I looked up left me at a loss for words.

Beckah was standing only a few feet away, looking more beautiful than I'd ever dreamed. She was wearing a long black and gold dress with sleeves that dragged the ground. Her hair was fixed up in a gold pin shaped like a bird's wing, and her sea green eyes were outlined with something like charcoal that made them stand out even more. I'd never seen anything like that, even on the other girls.

She must have noticed me staring because she started to blush and look away. "It's called kohl," she said. "Momma says it's all the rage in the eastern courts. She thinks I'll start some kind of fashion craze by wearing it here. What do you think?"

I was still having a hard time remembering how to talk. It was definitely Beckah. It was her voice, her smile, and her mannerisms. But the girl in front of me looked so different. She was a little taller, more slender, and seemed so elegant without even trying. It made me acutely aware of how awkward I was as I stumbled to my feet.

Her brow crinkled slightly, and she looked worried. "You don't like it?"

"I do!" I finally forced out words. They came out way too loud, though, and a few people standing nearby stared at us. I was so embarrassed.

Beckah giggled. "Why are you sitting out here all by yourself? Where's Felix?"

It was hard enough just to look at her when she smiled at me like that. But when she reached out to touch my arm, I almost jerked away from her for fear I'd do something to mess up how great she looked.

"He's... somewhere." I tried to explain. "You know how he is. This is his paradise."

She nodded, and slipped her arm through mine. When she looked up at me again, she was standing so close I could smell her perfume. It made my head spin. "Well, I've found you now. So don't leave me. I'm so nervous I'm going to trip on my stupid dress. I told Momma it was way too flashy, but she never listens."

"Y-you look really pretty," I managed to croak.

She flashed me a disbelieving glance. "What's the matter with you?"

I could have written her a complete textbook full of answers to that question. But the simplest explanation was the truest. "I didn't think you were coming."

"So you sat out here moping by yourself? Don't be ridiculous. This is supposed to be your debut." She arched a brow. "Besides, I promised you last year we would dance together, didn't I? Did you think I forgot?"

I swallowed hard. "I thought a lot of things."

She slid her hand down to grasp mine tightly. "Don't doubt me, silly knight. I hope you haven't promised to dance with anyone else because now you're all mine."

Beckah had held my hand plenty of times before. Usually, it made me feel more courageous. This time wasn't like that at all. My palms were sweaty and clammy. I didn't know what to say to her, or how to look at her, or what I should do next. This time, I realized that I was crazy, insanely, and completely in love with her.

"Let's dance," she said excitedly.

I would have agreed to anything she said at that point. She could have suggested we go walking barefoot over red hot coals, and I would have tripped all over myself to get my boots off. Ballroom dancing wasn't much different, though. Or at least, that's how it seemed to me.

As I led Beckah to the dance floor, I started noticing how the other men were looking at her. Infantrymen and nobles started grinning after they glanced her up and down. I didn't like the glint I saw in their eyes one bit. Other dragonriders, even some of my avian peers, got that same hungry look on their faces, too. It made me squeeze her hand tighter, and pull on her slightly so that we walked close together. I didn't want anyone else getting any ideas about talking to her.

I wanted them all to know that she belonged to me.

The instant the dance started, panic made me forget almost everything I had learned with Felix and Lyon. Fortunately, Beckah was well acquainted with my sad attempts at dancing. She eased me into it, and smiled like she was having the time of her life. The more she grinned, the more confident I got, and the better my dancing became. I forgot about everyone else there. It was just me and her, and no one else mattered. By the end of the dance, I was trying the more daring steps that were a lot more complicated.

"You've been practicing, haven't you? Who else have you been dancing with?" she teased as the song finally ended and we left the dance floor.

I was happy to go to my grave without ever answering that question.

Beckah squeezed my arm a little and leaned in close to whisper, "Look, everyone's staring at us!"

She was right about that, but I knew better than to think any of them were actually looking at me. Well, at least not for the same reason they were looking at her. They were all wondering what we were doing together, a beautiful girl and a halfbreed.

"Let's go for a walk in the gardens," she suggested as we made our way back outside.

I started to suggest I get her something to drink first, since Felix had advised me that this was a charming thing to do, when someone I didn't recognize stepped into our path.

They were infantrymen. I did know that much. Their matching uniforms were telling enough, and they were looking at Beckah with expressions that reminded me of the wolves I had fought in the mountain pass. It was a predatory look that put me on guard immediately.

"If you're finished with her, how about letting someone else take a turn?" The one standing at the front of their group spoke to me without ever looking my way. He seemed older than me, and he had a lot of medals pinned to his uniform that probably meant he had been in combat multiple times.

I was immediately at war with myself. I didn't want to share her with anyone. But Felix had advised me about this kind of situation. The chivalrous thing to do was to step aside, and let it go, even if I outranked them—which I did, since I was a dragonrider. It was good manners.

I cleared my throat so that he was forced to look at me. For the first time, I felt thoroughly pleased that I was a lot taller than someone else. It made me feel more powerful for some reason. "I'll allow it." I kept my tone as dry as possible. "So long as you remember to address me as sir next time, soldier."

That stung him. I could feel it in the air, like a fog of anger rolling off the infantryman's back. I knew it had to be embarrassing for him to be talked down to by a dragonrider in front of his buddies, let alone a halfbreed. For an instant, I saw wrath in his eyes. I wondered if he would actually try to fight me, and I was actually kind of hoping for it.

Thankfully, he didn't. He clenched his teeth, and managed a "Yes, sir" before offering Beckah his arm. She took it, but I could tell she was reluctant about it. She glanced at me with a worried expression, and I tried to reassure her with as much of a smile as I could manage.

"I'll be waiting right here," I promised.

They walked back toward the dance floor together, and it took everything I had to stand there and watch. Felix hadn't mentioned anything about how angry it would make me to see her dancing with someone else. The longer they danced, the more frustrated I got. I had to stop myself from stepping in and stopping it. After the song was half over, I decided I was going to need another glass of wine if I was going to survive the second half without punching anyone. I went to grab one off a servant's tray, and returned to my spot immediately.

But when I got there, I didn't see them anymore. In fact, I didn't see them on the dance floor at all.

They were gone.

My blood started boiling. I was seeing red as I shoved my glass into the hands of the nearest stranger without ever taking a sip. I started combing the crowds, looking through every ballroom for Beckah. The more I looked, the more desperate I got, and the more I started to panic. She was gone. There wasn't any sign of her or that scheming infantryman anywhere.

Lyon caught me by the arm as I flew into the last of the three ballrooms. "Hey, what's going on? Are you okay?"

I didn't know where to begin. There wasn't time to explain it all. All I could do was look at him and growl, "He took her. I can't find her anywhere."

Lyon's eyes widened. "Who?"

I was too angry to speak. I shook my head and stormed off to start searching again. Lyon fell in step beside me, abandoning the group of noble girls he had been talking to. "You need to calm down, Jae." He warned. "You're going to lose it and this is the worst possible place for that. She's got to be here. She didn't just vanish. Have you checked the gardens?"

21

CHAPTER TWENTY-ONE

Lyon was right. As soon as we started searching the candle-lit paths that led into the gardens, I could hear Beckah's voice screaming. The sound of the music and roar of the crowds in the ballrooms had drowned it out while I was inside. But in the quiet of the outside air, I heard her right away. My pulse raced even faster, and I started running and calling her name.

Lyon hesitated to leave the ballroom. He shouted about going to find Felix, but I wasn't going to wait for reinforcements. I knew he was worried I might lose it again and launch headlong into battle fever. At that point, though, I actually wanted to. I wanted to hurt these soldiers for ever thinking they could lay a hand on Beckah. I wanted to do a lot worse than break a few arms.

But I started noticing something strange the closer we got to the sound of her voice. Beckah wasn't screaming in terror or pain. She was screaming in rage. In fact, the only sounds of panic I heard were coming from men.

When I burst through a line of hedges, the last thing I expected to see was Beckah pinning a guy to the ground in a complex choke hold—but that's exactly what was happening. The three other infantrymen who had been following their ringleader when he asked to dance with her were lying nearby, groaning in pain.

"Say it! Say it you piece of filth!" Beckah screamed again, tightening her choke hold on the soldier who was struggling to get free. "You think you can force yourself on any girl you want? Well, you picked the wrong girl this time! Now, say it!"

"U-u-uncle!" He managed to gasp.

She let him go, and he sucked in a desperate breath. He started clawing at the ground, frantically trying to get away from her. I was the last thing he expected to see when he finally got to his feet. He turned to run from her and smacked right into my chest. The infantryman bounced off me, completely stunned, and I took that opportunity to get a little revenge of my own.

I hit him. I punched him across the face as hard as I could. I felt his nose break as it met my knuckles, and he crumpled to the ground to join the rest of his buddies.

For a few seconds, Beckah and I just sat there looking at each other. Her hair was falling out of the gold pin, and there was dirt smudged on her cheek. Her dress was rumpled and her eyes were wild. But in that moment, I had never seen her look more beautiful.

Lyon ruined my moment of awe. He and Felix broke through the hedges behind me, and skidded to a halt to stare in awe at the mess.

"What did you do?" Lyon gasped as he surveyed the damage. "How did you beat them all so fast?"

I didn't know what to say. But before I could think of anything, Beckah interrupted. She got up and ran toward me, throwing her arms around my waist and beginning to make desperate crying noises.

"He saved me! He beat them all!" She sobbed.

I was stunned.

Lyon and Felix were, too, but for a completely different reason. They seemed to actually believe her.

"We need to get out of here before they wake up. Is she all right?" Felix grabbed my shoulder and started pulling me away.

Beckah laid her head against my chest and trembled. "I was so scared," she sniffled. "They ruined my hair. And my dress."

While Felix started checking the infantrymen to make sure I hadn't hurt anyone important, I unclipped my cloak and put it around her shoulders. Our eyes met for a moment, and I knew without a doubt that she was just acting. I could read it in her face, even if she had the others fooled. She might have been upset, but she wasn't really crying. In fact, she looked more embarrassed than anything else.

Lyon left us once we got far enough away from Beckah's unconscious victims to give him peace of mind. He didn't want to be anywhere nearby when someone found them, or they started waking up. I didn't blame him at all for that.

Felix stuck around a little longer, though. He kept apologizing to Beckah like it was his fault she'd been attacked. I guess he felt guilty because it had happened at his house. She told him over and over that she was fine, thanks to me, and promised she didn't blame him for it at all.

"I'm so glad you're okay." Felix sighed, looking relieved. "Well, I'll leave you two alone. Try not to kill anyone, Jae." He gave me a strange little grin as he left us sitting together on a stone bench in the garden.

It was awkward. At first, we couldn't even look at one another. I didn't know what else to do, so I started trying to wipe the dirt off her face with the handkerchief she'd made for me. Her fake crying had made the kohl around her eyes run down her cheeks, too.

As I wiped her face, Beckah sat there and stared at me. She almost looked afraid, like I might get angry at her and start shouting. I wasn't sure if I should be angry or not. She had fought all those trained soldiers by herself, and I was still trying to wrap my mind around that. I was so relieved that she was okay—that was the most important thing.

Finally, I had to ask, "What just happened?"

She dropped her eyes away from mine as though she were embarrassed or ashamed. She pulled the pin out of her hair so that it all fell down over her shoulders. I could see worry on her expression, like she didn't want to tell me.

"It's okay." I took her hand gently and tried to give her a reassuring smile. "I'm not going to tell anyone. You know that."

"Dad's been teaching me to fight," she confessed. "Please, you can't tell a soul. No one can know. Promise me you won't tell. If anyone found out, they would arrest me for impersonating a soldier."

My first reaction was anger, which wasn't what I was expecting. I wasn't angry at her, though. I was angry at Sile. He had acted all high and mighty a few months ago, insisting that Beckah could never be a dragonrider even if she had been chosen by the king drake. But now he was teaching her to fight?

"What do you mean he's been teaching you? Why would he—?" I was furious.

Beckah frowned dangerously. "I have just as much right as you do."

"That's not what I mean." I shook my head. "He was so against this before. He wouldn't listen to me about it. What changed his mind?"

She let out a small sigh, and her frown melted away. My stomach did a nervous backflip as she leaned and put her head against my shoulder. I saw her hands shaking some as she fidgeted with the gold pin she'd been wearing in her hair. I hadn't even noticed it before. Now I could see the thick calluses on her palms and fingers. I had those same marks on my hands. They were marks that could only come from learning swordplay.

"He was against it," she answered quietly. I could hear something different in her voice when she talked about Sile. She had always acted a little childish around him, which I assumed was a father-daughter thing. Now when she mentioned him, she sat up straighter and her face became serious. She wasn't calling him "daddy" anymore.

"I think he still is," she continued. "Things are starting to happen, Jae. Dad said you probably wouldn't know. He said they like to keep students in the academy sheltered so you don't worry about anything but your training."

I got a sick feeling that I knew what this was about a few seconds before she said it.

"There's something wrong with the animals in the kingdom. They're turning on people. More and more of them every day. It's much worse the closer you get to the northern border," she said. "At first it was only predators like wolves or bears. Now people are getting attacked by their own horses, dogs, even flocks of birds. It's like nature is starting to go crazy. Dad can't deny that something is coming, and whether he likes it or not, I'm a part of it now. Icarus chose me to fight with him. It's what I have to do. I can't explain it."

"So you've been training." I had to say it out loud so I could believe it.

"I'm good at it, too," she added. I could hear a smile in her voice. "I'm not as heavy as you big boys, but I move a lot faster. I'm also good with a bow, just like Dad was. I think he's actually impressed."

As much as I wanted to be happy for her, I couldn't be. I didn't want Beckah to fight. I didn't want her to get hurt. That sudden rage when I thought the infantrymen might be hurting her was eye opening to me. It had pushed me right to the brink of my sanity, and the thought of her being in real combat made me downright nauseous.

"Are you okay, Jae?" she asked.

I shook my head. "I don't know how to feel about any of this."

"Because I'm a girl?" Once again, she gave me a meaningful glare. I could hear bitterness in her voice.

"Because you mean more to me than anyone else," I clarified. "If anything happened to you, I don't think I could stand it."

It must have caught her off guard because her mouth opened slightly, but no sound came out. She started fidgeting with that hairpin again. "Nothing's going to happen to me. I'm very careful."

"You just fought a bunch of infantrymen twice your size," I reminded her. "And you did it while wearing a party dress and the biggest ball in the kingdom. There are literally hundreds of people here, Beckah."

"I won, though." She started giggling proudly.

I didn't think it was that funny, though. "You could have been hurt. Or what if someone else had seen you?"

Before I could put my defenses up, Beckah leaned in and batted her eyes at me. If she was trying to charm me so I didn't get angry with her, it worked brilliantly. Her smile was very distracting. I couldn't help but smile back. And when she put one of her hands on my face and started touching my ears, I knew I was probably blushing like crazy.

The urge to kiss her rose up in my chest like a tidal wave. It was impossible to look at her without my eyes wandering down to her lips. She must have noticed because she started blushing, too.

"No one else saw." She mumbled. Her fingertips tickled the point of my ear. "I have to do this, Jae. It's okay. I'm not scared. I bet I could even beat you in a duel now."

I was entranced. I couldn't even move. "P-probably." I stammered without thinking.

It made her laugh and she leaned against my shoulder again. "I missed you a lot. I bet you didn't even miss me at all."

"That's not true! I've thought about you every day!" I was trying to make up my mind about kissing her. I didn't know how to do something like that. I didn't know if I should ask her permission, or do it and hope she didn't hit me for it.

"Is that why you look so tired?"

I knew she was just teasing me. But those words wiped all the thoughts of kissing right out of my mind. I hadn't told her anything about my dreams. Felix was so sure there was nothing strange about them. Thinking about all those sleepless nights spent drenched in sweat and terror gave me chills. I looked away, and tried not to let her see the embarrassment on my face. It didn't work.

"Jae? What's wrong?" She leaned in closer to stare into my eyes.

I shook my head. I didn't trust myself to speak without telling her everything.

She put her hand in mine again and squeezed it tightly. "Come on, tough guy. You can tell me."

As I started describing my nightmares to her, I realized that I actually *wanted* to tell her. It was a relief to tell someone I knew wouldn't slough me off or treat me like a potential traitor. I described all my dreams from the time they started, even the parts with my mother in them. Beckah listened, and she kept holding my hand so tightly it made my hands even sweatier.

"Even the sleeping remedy doesn't work anymore," I finished. "I can't sleep for more than a few hours before the nightmares start, and no matter how hard I fight, I can't stop them."

I leaned over to put my head in my hands so I could rub my forehead. Talking about the nightmares made me feel anxious. I could see them so clearly in my mind, even now. It gave me a headache.

Beckah put a hand on my back and started rubbing my shoulders. It immediately made me feel more relaxed. "You've been trying so hard," she cooed.

"It doesn't matter. I'm barely holding it together." I muttered. "I can't keep fighting them much longer. It's driving me crazy."

Her hand stopped moving on my back. I glanced over at her. She was staring back at me with a serious expression, looking wild and powerful with the wind in her hair.

"So stop fighting them," she suggested suddenly.

"What do you mean?" The idea alone made me nervous. I was afraid of what I might see if I surrendered to those dreams. I hadn't actually witnessed the Gray elf warrior killing that guard yet, but I knew it was coming. It had to be. And for some reason it felt like I might die with him if I actually saw it happen.

"It's just a dream, Jae," she said like she could read my thoughts. "It can't hurt you. You can sense that something is coming, too, can't you? Like the animals can? You're a part of it. We both are. This could be some kind of warning, or a clue to what's going on. You need to pay attention to it. You need to quit fighting it, and try to listen instead."

Moments like that reminded me why I needed her in my life so badly. She was so much smarter than I was. She saw things I couldn't. Fate didn't scare her. She was the bravest person I knew, and the only reason I was still clinging to my sanity. I needed her to be at my side forever—and that realization was as crippling as it was amazing.

I was about to tell her that. I wanted her to know exactly how much she meant to me. I wanted her to know that I loved her more than anyone. Just as soon as I got up the nerve, she spoke first.

"When you see me again on the battlefield, you can't let anyone know who I am. You have to pretend you don't know me." She looked at me firmly.

I choked out loud. "What do you mean 'on the battlefield?' You're not actually thinking of going to war, are you?"

Beckah's expression never changed. "Why else would I be training to fight, Jae? To fend off wild animals? Dad can handle that himself. No, I'm fighting for the same reason you are. I'll do whatever it takes to protect the people I care about."

Anger stirred up in my chest like a storm. I couldn't believe what I was hearing. It was one thing for her to learn to fend off a few infantry thugs, but it was a completely different issue for her to actually show upon a battlefield and fight an enemy that would kill her without a second thought. I didn't want that.

"You can't do this." I glared at her. "You'll be killed. You aren't ready for the battlefront. You have no idea what you're getting into."

She snapped an angry scowl back at me, like I'd just insulted her in the worst possible way. "It's not your decision to make. I'm no less prepared than you are."

"That's what I'm trying to tell you! I've been training for over a year," I tried to reason with her. "And I'm still not ready. You'll be killed! And then what am I supposed to do? How am I supposed to live with that?"

She didn't answer.

Beckah stood up and started walking away into the gardens. Overhead, I heard the familiar sound of huge wing beats booming in the air. I saw a ripple in the night sky as Icarus's black body blotted out the stars.

Before she disappeared into the garden, Beckah stopped and looked back at me. Her long dark hair blew around her face. I couldn't tell if she was angry at me, or really sad.

"My dad wanted me to tell you to prepare yourself. He said the next few months are going to be the hardest you've ever faced," Beckah said. "But I know you'll make it. I believe in you, Jae. I always have."

I was at a loss for words. When our eyes met, I saw that sad look on her face more clearly, and it tore at my heart. I couldn't stay angry at her. I loved her too much.

"I'll see you again." She promised.

I wanted to believe that. I wanted to tell her how I felt, but that moment slipped through my fingers and was gone in an instant. She sent me one more smile, and disappeared into the night. In the distance, I heard Icarus's bellowing roar like a rumble of thunder.

After I pulled myself together, I started back toward the party alone. Things were still lively inside. People were laughing, drinking, and dancing under the light that sparkled off the polished marble floors. Music filled the air. All the guests seemed to be in good spirits. Every now and then, I caught a glimpse of Lyon or Felix roaming through the crowds with girls hanging onto their arms. It looked like they were having a good time, too.

I finally made up my mind to try to rejoin them. Sure, I knew I was probably about to get shot down cold again, but this was as good a time as any to get some revenge on Felix for embarrassing me all the time. I couldn't pass that up.

The sound of someone crying stopped me in my tracks before I ever got back into the ballroom. I could barely hear it over the music, and I almost shrugged it off. But then I was sure; it definitely sounded like a girl was crying somewhere nearby.

I didn't see her right away. She was hiding behind a giant porcelain flower pot right beside the doorway. But when I peeked around to see what the noise was about, she gasped in surprise. She looked as shocked to see me as I was to see her.

I didn't recognize her. At least, not at first. But when she tried to smile at me, I knew it had to be Julianna Lacroix. I remembered Felix saying something about her teeth being big. They were, I guess, but it wasn't like she was ugly. She had coppery colored hair, and warm brown eyes that were red from crying.

"I-I'm okay." She sniffled and kept trying to smile even though there were tears in her eyes. I was not an expert on how the female brain worked, but she definitely did not look okay.

"Are you sure?" I came a little closer to get a better look at her. Part of me was worried maybe she'd been attacked by some infantrymen the same way Beckah had. I glanced around for any possible culprits. There was no one else nearby.

Julianna had squeezed herself into a tiny corner between the outside wall and the flower pot, like she was trying to hide. I squatted down so that I could be eye-level with her. The instant I asked her that question, she started to cry again. It was that real, frantic kind of girl-crying that makes us men spin into a state of panic because we don't know how to fix it.

Remembering Felix's intense training on how to be charming, I took out my handkerchief. It had a little bit of dirt and kohl on it from when I had wiped Beckah's face, but I didn't know what else to do. I couldn't leave her there like that. She was obviously miserable. I felt sorry for her.

"Here, take this." I offered her the handkerchief and tried to smile at her in a non-creepy way. "It's okay. Just try to calm down. Are you hurt?"

"I-I'm okay. I promise." Julianna took my handkerchief and immediately started blowing her nose. I made a mental note not to use it myself until it had been washed.

"Do you want to talk about it?" That seemed like a safe question to me.

She sniffled some more as she dabbed at her eyes. "No one will dance with me. Not even the lowest ranking soldiers. They laugh and give me all these excuses." The more she talked, the more she cried, and soon she was sobbing again. "I know it's because I'm such a horrible dancer. I know I'm terrible. It's useless. I hate parties like this!"

I remembered everything Felix had said about this girl and how she accidentally spat on people all the time when she talked. He had warned all the other avians at our dining table not to dance with her because she was awkward. It had annoyed me at the time, but now it made me feel bad for her. I knew what it was like to be teased and unwanted.

"I'm not a good dancer either," I said as I sat down beside her.

She blinked at me like she was surprised. "But I saw you earlier. You were dancing with that girl in the black dress. You looked so beautiful together."

"Yeah, well, that was only because I had to practice with some of the other guys in my class for weeks," I confessed. "Those were basically all the dance moves I know. Good thing she didn't ask for another one, huh?"

I heard her laugh. It was weird since she still had tears in her eyes, but at least she was smiling now. "You mean... you really danced with other boys to learn?" She started laughing harder, and covering her mouth with her hand. "I-I'm sorry! That's just so funny!"

I smirked and nodded in agreement. It was funny. And I was glad she was laughing now instead of crying her eyes out. I started telling her about how Felix made Lyon and I practice as dance partners, and how Jace had walked in on us once while we were doing a romantic waltz pose. By the end of my story, Julianna was giggling so hard her cheeks were red.

"I guess we're both awkward dancers, then." She sighed and handed my handkerchief back.

I shrugged as I stuck it back in my pocket. "Maybe. But that doesn't mean we can't have fun. Do you want to dance?"

Julianna looked hesitant. "You're sure you want to? Even if I trip or step on your feet?"

"Sure. As long as you don't care that I'm a halfbreed." I chuckled.

She smiled at me brightly, and bobbed her head up and down. "Okay! Let's dance!"

I stood up and helped her crawl out of her hiding place behind the flower pot. She was pretty tall for a girl, probably even taller than most of the men, but there weren't many people around who were taller than I was. I still towered over her, and she seemed to like that because I kept catching her looking up at me with these strange little smiles.

When we stepped into the ballroom, she leaned over to whisper, "You know, I didn't know halfbreeds could be so handsome."

I tried not to blush. Felix had warned me that it wasn't very charming to act like a kid. I had to be cool and confident. "Thanks."

"Are you courting that girl? The one you were dancing with before?" She asked as I led her out onto the dance floor. "It's just, well, you two looked so happy together. Everyone else was making comments because, um, because you're a..."

She didn't have to finish. I knew what she meant. "Because I'm a halfbreed. It's okay. I'm used to it."

"Right." She nibbled at her lip as she stared up at me. We started slowly moving through a few simple dance steps. "So, are you courting her?"

I wasn't sure how to answer that. Technically, I wasn't. The problem was asking Sile if I could. According to Felix, I had to get her father's permission, and somehow I seriously doubted Sile would ever allow that. I distinctly remembered him threatening to rip my ears off if I messed with her.

"No," I finally answered.

"But you want to be. I can tell. It's written all over your face." Julianna let out a sigh as she gave me a weird, misty-eyed smile. "It's forbidden love, right? That's so romantic!"

It took all my brainpower to keep from turning beet red again. "Right. Something like that."

"You should tell her how you feel," she insisted. "It's always better to be honest, even if it's difficult."

I swallowed hard and tripped over my own feet. Thinking about it made me nervous. "It's too late for that. I think I already blew my chance to tell her."

Julianna smiled brightly. "It's never too late to tell someone you love them."

We both tripped and stumbled a lot while we danced through three or four songs together, but it was fun. A lot more fun than dancing with Lyon, anyway. She didn't spit on me at all, even though I probably deserved it since I accidentally stepped on her feet at least ten times. I couldn't figure out what Felix had against her. In my opinion, however little it counted, I thought she was kinda great.

When we finished dancing, she started introducing me to some of her noble friends. They didn't look very interested in getting to know a halfbreed. In fact, most of them looked terrified. But the fact that she was trying meant a lot.

As soon as Julianna started telling them about my forbidden romance with the mysterious beauty in the black dress, all the girls lit up like torches. Suddenly, they were all interested in knowing every single detail, even though none of them had recognized Beckah. They didn't know who she was, and I decided not to tell them. The last thing I needed was Sile showing up in the dead of night to beat me senseless because he'd heard through the grapevine that I was having a secret romance with his daughter.

"Isn't it wonderful?" Julianna giggled with excitement. "It's like a fairy tale! She might even be a princess. Her makeup was pretty exotic, wasn't it?"

The other noble girls ate up that idea like expensive dessert. They gossiped and laughed, whispering things and looking at me out of the corner of their eyes. It made me nervous because of the way they were all blushing and staring. I had no idea what kinds of things they were saying about me, and something told me I didn't want to know.

It didn't take long for that much female excitement in one area to attract Felix, Lyon, and some of the other avian students from my combat training group. They gathered around to join the conversation. Felix was quick to introduce himself as my best friend, and that made the girls even more excited because now I was associated with the resident celebrity.

Now that I had found a niche, the ball was a lot more fun. We took turns dancing, and the girls seemed understanding about how horribly I danced compared to the other men. They told me it was adorable, which I figured was about as much of a compliment as I could hope for. Felix always had a different girl on his arm every time I turned around. He changed partners almost as quickly as he drank glasses of wine. The more he drank, the louder he got, and less he cared about how many infantrymen he insulted on his way around the ballrooms.

It didn't take long for things to deteriorate to a full on drunken mess. Some dancing was still going on, but a lot of couples had broken off and left to find a quiet spot to be alone. Lyon and Felix had teamed up to challenge a few of the other infantrymen to arm-wrestling contests. Well, it started with arm-wrestling, then it quickly devolved to other pointless feats of strength.

The girls seemed to enjoy the show. Those that were left were talking loudly and giggling, hanging on the arms of whichever man had won their loyalty for the evening. For me, that was Julianna. She stuck at my side and held onto my arm, which I didn't mind. I didn't think she was expecting anything from me since she knew about my feelings for Beckah.

But I was wrong about that.

She asked me to walk her to the restroom so she could refresh her makeup. It probably should have seemed strange to me, especially since I had already picked up on the way the other girls always seemed to go together in pairs or groups to do that kind of thing. But I was so distracted by watching Felix arm-wrestle a soldier who was twice his size, I didn't think twice about it.

I led her out of the ballroom and down a hallway, still trying to catch a glimpse of the showdown going on at the arm-wrestling table even as we left. I was expecting Julianna to go on and leave me to wait for her. But she didn't. Instead, she grabbed the collar of my tunic, pulled me down toward her, and kissed me on the mouth.

It only lasted about two seconds before I managed to pry her off me and hold her at arm's length so she couldn't try it again. "What are you doing?"

"I just wanted to see what it was like," she said with a dreamy-eyed smile. "I've never kissed a dragonrider before."

"I-I'm sorry, Julianna." I struggled to keep my voice quiet. "You know I'm in love with someone else."

She eyed me sheepishly. "I know. But she left you here alone, didn't she? Don't you like me? Even a little bit? No one else has to know. I won't tell a soul."

"No. I can't do that." I kept a firm hold on her shoulders. Sure, it was a little tempting. I was a guy, not a saint. The way I felt about Beckah kept me from wanting to do that with anyone else. She was the only girl I wanted to kiss.

We exchanged an awkward moment of silence, staring at one another. She kept smiling like she was waiting for me to surrender to that foggy look in her eyes. I was waiting for her to give it up so I could go back to the ballroom and forget this had ever happened.

"You really do love her, don't you?" Julianna finally sighed and took a step back. "I guess that's a good thing. It isn't fair, though."

I was relieved. "Please don't try that again."

"Fine, I won't." She agreed reluctantly. "But tell me one thing. That was your first kiss, wasn't it?"

"Uh," I started to answer. I didn't want to admit that it had been. Felix acted like that wasn't something I was supposed to be proud of.

She seemed to know just because of my reaction. She smiled a little and patted my arm. "I'm sorry. You were saving it for her, weren't you? Well, don't worry about it. You didn't kiss me back, so it doesn't count."

"It doesn't?" I wasn't so sure Beckah would see it that way.

Julianna nodded. "Oh, of course. Besides, you can blame it all on me. Tell her I forced you."

Technically she had forced me, so that wasn't exactly a lie. Regardless, I decided I was going to take this to my grave. No one needed to know—especially not Beckah.

When we returned to the party, things had gotten even more rowdy. A huge crowd was gathered on the balcony, pushing and shoving to see something going on outside. I held onto Julianna's hand so she didn't get swept away, and muscled my way to the front. I had my suspicions that this had something to do with Felix, and of course, it did.

Felix was in a fight with a much older man. In fact, it looked like the same big burly soldier he was going to arm wrestle when I left. They had taken their disagreement down into the gardens, and were duking it out on a patch of grass right below the balcony. The man was dressed like a high-ranking infantryman, and it looked like he had the upper hand at the moment. Felix was pinned underneath him, taking blow after blow while the older soldier punched his face in.

Julianna gasped and turned away to hide her face against my shoulder. "That's horrible! I can't watch!"

Fury rose up inside me like a roaring fire. Felix was such an idiot, picking a fight with someone like that when he was too drunk to win. I was going to have to clean up this mess before he got beaten up so badly he couldn't go back to training.

I led Julianna to the edge of the balcony and planted her hands on the railing. "Stay here," I commanded.

She nodded frantically. "But what are you going to do?"

I had a crazy thought. It was stupid, really. But no one was ever going to remember me for doing the sensible thing in a moment like this. I pressed out with my thoughts, calling to Mavrik in my mind, as I shoved my way through the crowd. I found a servant with a tray of liquor bottles. I snatched up two of the bottles and started back for the railing.

I heard a few people scream my name, probably Lyon and Julianna, as I jumped up on the stone railing of the balcony overlooking the garden. It was about a ten foot drop to the spot below where Felix was still losing the fight. I waited, listening, and when I felt the buzzing presence of a familiar dragon ringing in my mind, I threw one of the alcohol bottles into the air as hard and far as I could.

Dragon flame erupted into the night sky. Mavrik spat a burst of venom that made the bottle explode into a shower of fire. The fight immediately came to a stop. People screamed and backed away at first. Then, they all started *clapping*. I guess they thought it was some kind of show.

I took that opportunity to throw the second bottle. Mavrik swooped down again, the air humming over his wings, and ignited the second bottle. It sent fire showering down over the dewy grass. While everyone was distracted, I ran down the steps toward the garden.

My plan had worked. The older soldier wasn't hitting Felix anymore. He was too busy trying to put out a fire on his shirt sleeve. He didn't even notice me until I grabbed him by the collar and dragged him off my friend.

When he saw who it was—or rather, when he noticed I was a halfbreed—he started to throw random punches at me. He was too drunk to aim well enough to hit me, though. I dodged his blows easily, and tossed him face-first into a nearby water fountain. Water splashed everywhere, and he came up dripping and gasping for breath.

"Fight's over," I growled at him. "So cool off."

I turned around to find Felix struggling to get his feet. His cheeks were swollen and his nose was bleeding from being punched in the face so many times, but he looked like he was going to be fine. At least, fine enough to take a swim. I grabbed him by the collar, and threw him into the water fountain, too.

"You jerk!" He yelled as he came up for air. "What was that for? I thought you were on my side!"

"Sober up. You're embarrassing us all and acting like an idiot," I snapped as I glared at him.

That shut him up. He stood knee-deep in the water fountain, soaked to the bone, staring at me with his mouth hanging open.

I got a round of applause as I climbed the stairs back to the balcony. Julianna hugged me, which was weird, and it took me a while to pluck her arms off from around my neck. I wasn't used to being accepted by anyone, let alone a court full of noble guests. Normally they would have treated me like a filthy rat. But it was nice to see them all smiling at me. I kind of enjoyed it.

"Nice one!" Lyon laughed as he patted my shoulder roughly. "They'll be talking about this for years!"

"I hope not." I stole a quick glance at Felix as he struggled to climb out of the water fountain. "I don't think his ego could take it."

22

CHAPTER TWENTY-TWO

The party finally ended as the sun began to rise over the ocean. Nobles staggered to their suites in the duke's castle, or were escorted to their carriages to start the long journey home. The ballrooms and gardens were eerily quiet and empty. They were also a complete wreck, and servants were already beginning the long process of getting them cleaned up again.

Lyon and Jace didn't waste any time retreating to their rooms to sleep off the night's excitement. I was exhausted, too, but I couldn't calm down enough to try sleeping just yet. My exchange with Beckah had me contemplating how I should handle my dreams. I was starting to wonder if she was right. Fighting these nightmares wasn't getting me anywhere. Maybe if I listened to them, I would finally get some answers.

I was in a daze as I changed out of my formal uniform and into some casual clothes. I started looking for a quiet place where I could sit and think. That's when I found Felix.

He was standing alone on one of the balconies attached to his wing of the castle. His shoulders were hunched as he leaned against the tall stone railing, staring into the glare of the rising sun. His face was bruised up from his fight with the infantryman., and his formal uniform still looked damp from his swim in the fountain.

When he noticed me staring at him, Felix let out a heavy sigh. "I'm not mad at you, if that's what you're worried about."

I walked over to stand next to him. "I'm sorry about throwing you," I said.

He shrugged. "I deserved it. We're fine. Besides, everyone seemed to like your little fire show."

"Why did you get so drunk?" I dared to ask. "You could have gotten seriously hurt. That guy looked like he wanted to kill you."

Felix's eyes closed slowly. He hung his head, and wouldn't look up. "I got called away from the party for a few minutes last night," he replied. "I guess you were outside beating those infantrymen to a pulp."

I could hear some kind of tension in his voice. It was strange, though. It didn't sound like anger or frustration. It was disturbing, and I wasn't sure how to respond.

"Why? Did something happen?" I dared to ask.

He laughed hoarsely, but it was an eerie, humorless sound. It gave me chills. "I guess you could say that."

We stood there in silence for a few minutes, listening to the distant roar of the waves against the cliffs. The sun was warm on my face, and it made the tops of the waves look like ripples of light. Seagulls made lonely cries as they rode the strong winds. The cold sea air cut right through my clothes and chilled me to the bone. I could only imagine that Felix was freezing since his clothes were wet.

"My dad died last night," he said at last.

I couldn't believe what I was hearing. It didn't seem possible. No one had said anything about anyone dying last night.

Felix didn't look up. "Mom called for me not long after the ball started. She said it had just happened, but not to tell anyone. She didn't want to ruin the party. She wouldn't even let me see him. She made me go back, so no one would suspect anything was wrong."

His voice cracked and I saw his shoulders tense up. His jaw clenched. He was trying to keep it in.

"Can you go see him now? I'll go with you, if you want," I offered.

"What's the point?" He frowned harder. There was a quiet rage in his eyes. "He never liked me, anyway. I was always a disappointment to him."

Without thinking, I put my hand on Felix's shoulder. I could sense his pain and grief. It shocked me how intensely those emotions surged through me, resonating in my mind almost like the way Mavrik used images to speak to me. It made my heart surge with shared grief, and without realizing it, I started squeezing his shoulder really hard.

"That kinda hurts, dummy." Felix was looking at me curiously.

I snatched my hand away. I felt the coldness of the air rush back over me suddenly. "Sorry," I muttered.

Felix looked away again. He stared out toward the sea with the wind blowing in his shaggy hair. "Anyway, now I have to decide if I'm going to stay here and take over the estate, or return to the academy."

I didn't want Felix to stay here, plain and simple. We had started this journey through training together, and I wanted to finish it that way. But I couldn't tell him what to do. It was his life, and I knew I had no right to impose my selfish opinions on him.

"What do you think I should do?" he asked without ever looking away from the horizon. I was surprised, and a little suspicious he could read my thoughts. "I know you well enough by now to be able to tell when you have something on your mind. So just say it and quit making all those weird faces at me."

I joined him in watching the waves. "I can't tell you what to do, Felix. It's your life, and your choice. So do whatever you think is best, and I'll support that."

He didn't reply.

"But if you want my honest opinion," I added. "I think you have to at least ask yourself if you would regret quitting or not."

He nodded a little, although he still didn't say anything. I didn't blame him for that. He had a lot to think about now. As of this morning, he was heir to everything we were looking at. All this land, the castle, and the towns inside the Farrow estate belonged to him. Felix was a duke now, and he was going to have to deal with that eventually.

It was late in the afternoon when we finally got packed up and ready to make the long flight back to the academy. Jace said we could have given it another day, since we would have a short break when we got back, but we were all ready to get back to work. So after lunch, we loaded all our gear, checked our saddles, and took off toward the western coast.

Felix left with us.

We didn't arrive back at Blybrig until well after dark. Other riders were still coming in, taking their time putting their dragons to bed in the Roost, and hanging up their saddles in the tack room. I stuck closer to Felix than usual. He didn't talk much at all, not even to the instructors who kept giving him compliments on how great the ball was. He wasn't his usual smiling self, not that I expected him to be.

I didn't ask him about deciding to come back to training, either. I knew he had his own reasons, and I wasn't going to assume that anything I had said made a difference when it came down to making that choice. I was glad he came back, though. I couldn't imagine returning to the academy without him.

We were given a few days of rest before training started up again, and even then, it seemed unusually calm. Even Thrane had backed off his game a little bit, and didn't torment me as much as usual. All the instructors were acting kind of tense, and even though no one said it, I had a feeling it was because of what was happening with the animals in the kingdom.

As the interlude approached, that tension only got stronger. Rumors started filtering in about more and more attacks. A flock of birds had slaughtered a whole family on an open road near the royal city. Horses were throwing off their riders and trampling them to death for no reason. Wolves, mountain cats, and bears were roaming the cities without fear. Even a farmer outside of Mithangol had been trampled to death by his cows.

"It's like the whole world is going crazy," Felix muttered as we stood outside the dormitory.

We were watching the last of the fledgling students take off. It had taken almost a full week for all of them to clear out of the dormitory. Last year, Felix, Lyon, and I had left with them for a three-month break in training while the avians were put in their battle scenario. This year, all we could do was watch.

"I hear they're worried about the dragons turning on us next," Lyon murmured like he was afraid someone might hear.

"I don't suppose you could talk to any of them and make sure they're not about to go homicidal?" Felix sent me a sarcastic smirk.

So far, no dragons had been effected. At least, not that I could tell. "I think they're just as scared as we are. These animals aren't doing this on purpose. The ones I interacted with couldn't even answer me when I tried to call to them. It was like they were possessed by something."

"Possessed? By what?" Lyon stared at me with wide, haunted eyes.

"I'm not sure," I answered. "It felt like chaos."

Felix made a groaning noise. "Great. Well that's peachy. No wonder the instructors are on edge. If the chaos is spreading, then putting us on the Canrack Islands could be like throwing us in a meat grinder."

I shuddered at the thought. It was almost time. We had two months of intensive interrogation training left, and then the battle scenario. The anxiety was so thick in the air, it literally made me nauseous.

"They won't let us go unless they're sure it's safe, right?" Lyon fidgeted nervously.

No one answered him. I wanted to believe the instructors wouldn't toss us to the wolves like that—literally. Except this was supposed to be the most intense training we ever endured. It would make or break us. So maybe it wouldn't matter. They might send us there regardless.

"We have to be prepared." Felix let out a noisy sigh. "Nothing else we can do but hang on, and brace for whatever comes our way."

Those words rang in my ears like a reminder. Ever since we'd gotten back, I had been trying to follow Beckah's advice about my dreams. I was trying, but it wasn't going well so far. Every night when I got into bed, it felt like I was bracing for impact. Watching that scene play out crippled me with fear, and it always made the dream start to fracture and fall apart. I didn't know how I could overcome that, except that maybe eventually I would get used to seeing people being butchered mercilessly like that. If I saw it enough times, then it wouldn't scare me anymore. I didn't want to get used to something like that, though. I didn't want to end up like Thrane, who actually seemed to enjoy watching other people suffer.

The next morning, the call to arms sounded earlier than usual, and we all gathered in the breaking dome. With all the fledglings gone, our group was smaller, but far more serious than usual. The instructors stood before us as we got into a block formation, and none of them looked pleased. Commander Rayken addressed us the same way he always did, giving a short speech on the glory of the dragonriders and how we should all be proud to be standing in this company. I was eager for him to get to the point.

"By now I'm sure you have all heard the rumors circulating about the mysterious animal attacks happening throughout our kingdom," Rayken said with a grim expression. "No doubt, you are all wondering if this will have any effect on your training. I'm here to tell you that as of now, it doesn't change anything. There have been no reports of attacks in our immediate area, so for the time being, we are going to carry on as normal."

A few of the instructors, including Jace, shifted uncomfortably. They didn't look happy with that decision. It made me nervous to see that they weren't all in agreement about this.

"Some of you already know how things will progress from here, but for those of you who don't, listen up." Rayken continued. He didn't seem eager to dwell on the topic of the animal attacks any longer than was necessary. "As of right now, everything changes. You are being groomed for the frontlines of combat, and we expect a premium level of performance from every single one of you. There will be no more scheduled morning calls. No more scheduled meals. You are guaranteed nothing, and expected to be prepared for everything. As of this moment, you are no longer boys in training. You are men. You are soldiers. Everything you do will decide whether or not you graduate and join your brothers in battle."

Commander Rayken went on like that for almost an hour. He explained that we were going to be issued our go-bags with all our survival gear in them, and we were expected to have them ready to go at a moment's notice. Our combat training would be intensified, and for the first time, we would be learning complex aerial attacks using dragon fire. Very little time would be spent in the classroom, and no day would be the same. That comfortable rhythm of class, food, and rest was officially over.

It was a lot to take in. Everyone looked slightly rattled when we were finally dismissed. We filed toward the dormitory, and lined up in the dining hall to be issued our go-bags. Each bag was exactly the same, and I recognized the tools from our survival training class. There were a few new items, though. There was a thick, coarse brown cloak tied up in a bundle. It was plain and felt like there were several layers of some kind of padding inside, so it was pretty heavy.

"It's waterproof," Felix announced as he unrolled his and tied it around his shoulders to test the fit. "It's for camouflage on the ground, I guess. Or you could use it to make a small shelter."

We spent the rest of the day sorting through our bags, and standing in line for more new gear. We were issued thicker boots with steel toes made into the leather. We were also given our shields, daggers, and a generic-looking sword.

"These are just basic weapons," Jace explained as he showed us how to wear our shields slung over our backs comfortably when we weren't using them. "You'll get to choose something more specific to your style later on. But for now, everyone is given the same thing so there are no unfair advantages during the battle scenario."

As he spoke, Jace and I locked eyes for a few seconds. I had an unfair advantage, and we both knew it. He didn't have to say anything to get his warning across. His glare said it all. I wasn't supposed to use any of my abilities during the battle scenario. Trouble was, I didn't know if I was going to be able to follow those orders in the heat of combat.

When Jace stared at me like that, as though he were expecting some kind of acknowledgement, I had no choice but to look away. I couldn't promise him anything. Especially not when there was a chance things go could wrong. If our dragons started turning on us, I would be forced to act. I wouldn't hesitate, and he was going to have to make his own peace with that.

No one really said much as we ate dinner that night. Felix was staring silently down at his food. Lyon was using his fork to arrange his peas into a pyramid. I was thinking about the animals, my nightmares, and the million other things I had to worry about now.

We were all shocked when the table flinched, and Jace sat down with us with a tray of food. He *never* ate with us. He was an instructor. He always ate at their table at the head of the room, or by himself.

"It's like dining with corpses," he muttered as he started cutting his meat into neat little squares. "You should eat. You'll regret it later, if you don't."

Everyone was staring at him in surprise.

"S-sir." Felix was the first one to get up the nerve to say anything to him. "We're all worried. You know, about the battle scenario."

"Because of the animals?" Jace didn't even look up from his food.

The rest of us exchanged a wide-eyed glance at one another. Our silence was as much of a yes as we could muster.

"Forget about that. It's irrelevant," Jace said with a cheek full of potatoes. "The Canrack Islands are the most hostile territory this side of Luntharda. That's the reason we have the battle scenarios there. The purpose of all this training isn't to beat you senseless or watch you writhe in pain for our own amusement. Our objective is to prepare you to endure and survive what you'll be facing later. The environment on the Canrack Islands is the most comparable to Luntharda. Even some of the trees and animals are the same. It's the best place to test you. And it's extremely dangerous, even if the animals aren't going berserk."

That was not comforting at all. In fact, Lyon looked like he might throw up from anxiety.

Jace looked up at us suddenly, his cold eyes as piercing as sword points. "Does that frighten you?"

No one answered.

"It shouldn't." His voice snapped over us, making me sit up straighter like I was standing at attention. "You are dragonriders, and we are bred to fight things that make other men stand paralyzed in terror. We are the kingdom's last hope. Remember that. No matter what awaits you on any battlefield, you have been prepared to handle it."

His words were inspiring, but I wasn't satisfied. As everyone else finished, or gave up on eating, I sat there across the table from Jace and waited for the room to clear. Finally, we were the last ones left.

Jace was taking his time eating, but he didn't waste any time getting to the point once we were alone. "You need to think long and hard about what you're going to do if things do go wrong."

I clenched my fists. "I have, sir. People have questioned my reasons for fighting on the side of humans from the very beginning, and my answer has always been the same. I fight for my friends. That's it. And there's nothing anyone can do to me that will make me too afraid to do whatever I can to help my brothers."

A strange, disturbing smirk curled up Jace's lips. He looked at me, twirling his fork thoughtfully between his fingers. "Brave to the point of stupidity," he said like he was quoting someone. I had a feeling I knew who it was. "Sile told me I would like you. I didn't expect him to be right, though. You've surprised me at every turn."

His eyes darkened then, and he calmly placed his fork back down on the table. "But I fear that bravery is about to be tested. I pushed for Rayken to postpone this year's battle scenario. There's no need to let you all be butchered for the sake of tradition, not when you may be needed very soon to protect cities and villages from being overrun by their own livestock."

"... But you just said that it shouldn't matter what's going on. You said we are prepared to handle it." I was totally confused, and a little upset to hear him contradicting himself like this. It seemed like he was lying to everyone to keep them calm.

Jace shrugged. "Morale is everything, avian. Wars are won and lost before anyone ever sets foot on the battlefield. Broken spirits lead to broken bones."

"You shouldn't have lied to us," I dared to sound defiant. Sure, his reasoning made sense, but it still didn't sit right with me.

"So it would be better to send them all into the jungle completely terrified?" he countered.

I frowned. "No, I guess not."

"Few of us live to see things get this bad. And those who do can't help but feel hopeless and afraid, even if they are supposed to be the ones standing firm and fearless. But you need great darkness in order to see great light." Jace stared at me from across the table. His expression was hard to read, and his dark eyes burned with something I couldn't understand. "Don't let the darkness shake you. I believe the world is about to witness something incredible. I believe we are all about to watch you shine. The question is, are you ready for it?"

CHAPTER TWENTY-THREE

I wasn't ready. As much as I wanted to believe I was prepared for what was coming, there was no way anyone could have been. The months leading up to the battle scenario were just as terrible as everyone had promised they would be, and then some.

There was no set schedule. That probably doesn't sound like such a bad thing. But after you've lived in a constant state of routine for so long, not having any idea what's coming next is like living in the constant state of drowning. I could barely keep my head above water.

Sometimes the call to arms sounded at the normal time, and we got up, dressed, and started our aerial combat training with our dragons. We still had a lot to learn when it came to attacking targets on the ground and using our flame against the enemy without hurting any of our own forces. Some of the maneuvers were extremely difficult, and we switched up partners daily, so I was never able to get used to anyone else's style.

But then, on other days, the battle horn would blare in the darkness long before the sun ever rose. The eerie, panicked sound of it made me bolt upright in bed. My whole body tingled like there was ice in my veins. We all scrambled to put on our armor, grab our go-bags, and get our dragons saddled as quickly as possible. The instructors gave us a brief mock-scenario of a battle, and we had to fly specific attack patterns to do mock attack runs. It was supposed to simulate how things would be once we were put on the real battlefront.

Sometimes, they would mix the two days. We would be sitting calmly, listening to an instructor give us a lecture about some of the dangerous plants and animals in Luntharda, and then the battle horn would blare. Immediately, everyone bolted into action, rushing to get to the Roost.

I figured out right away that falling behind was not a good idea. The first time I was a little late coming to the Roost, I felt the bite of something across my back. It didn't hurt that badly at first, but then the pain hit me like someone was holding a white-hot branding iron against my skin. Jace had popped me across the shoulders with his whip, and it set my back on fire. The pain brought me to my knees instantly, and I could barely breathe. When I checked under my shirt later, I realized I had a huge black and purple welt where the tail of the whip had snapped over my back. It took days for the swelling to go down enough for me to sleep on my back comfortably.

The closer we came to the battle scenario, the more intense training became... and the more I started to wonder if my nerves were finally going to start snapping. We were called by the battle horn in the dead of night, or even after we had only been asleep for a few hours. The scenarios the instructors gave us were getting more and more difficult. Our attacks had to be precise and synchronized. We barely had time to sleep, much less eat or study. If you didn't know something, forgot some of your gear, or were too slow to respond, you got to taste of an instructor's whip. We were all being pushed to the limit, our noses shoved into the molten gears of war to see if we could handle the fire.

Then the interrogation training started. All my other training at Blybrig Academy had been difficult from the very start. I'd spent days with all my muscles aching, drenched in sweat, and feeling like I was going to drop at any moment. But interrogation training was, by far, the most horrible thing that had ever happened to me. There was no comparison to anything else I had been through so far.

I was already exhausted, starving, and in a constant state of panic because I was terrified I was forgetting something. It was impossible to ever feel relaxed or confident. Lying awake in my bed, I strained to hear the sound of the battle horn. Every second felt like an eternity, and my brain played tricks on me, making me believe I was hearing things that weren't there.

Then the door to our dorm room burst open. Six or seven instructors filed in, all wearing wooden masks that covered their faces. I couldn't tell who any of them were, and I was terrified that one of them might be Thrane. They dragged us out of bed, and tied our hands behind our backs before shoving us out into the hallway. I caught a glimpse of Lyon before they slammed a burlap sack over my head; he looked completely terrified.

They herded us down the stairs and out into the night, and forced us to walk for what felt like an eternity. Then someone kicked me in the back and I went flying forward, landing on my knees and face. Someone else ripped the bag off my head, and grabbed me by my hair.

When my vision cleared, I was finally able to see who was standing over me.

Lieutenant Haprick, from our survival training class, leered down at me through the holes in the wooden mask. I knew it was him. I could tell by the color of his eyes and the shape of his body against the pale starlight. I was so relieved I actually smiled. He probably didn't understand why, or took it as sarcasm, which was also probably why I got another lash from a whip across my back. But honestly, I was just so glad it wasn't Thrane.

They ripped us out of bed like that at random. Sometimes, it happened every night for a week straight. Then other times, they would only do it once every few days. We never knew when it was coming, and we never knew what to expect once we got there. Usually, we were bound up and dragged into the night, only to get beaten or whipped until we were too weak to scream. Instructors wearing those wooden masks would demand to know our names, or where our forces were hiding. We were not supposed to say a single word. That was the whole point of this training. We had to be steady and keep our mouths shut no matter what the enemy did to us. We couldn't betray our brothers, even if we were threatened with death.

We seemed to be holding our own fairly well. That is, until they started singling members out. The first night they only took Felix out of our room, and left Lyon and I to sit there and stare at each other in the dark, I was so stunned I couldn't speak. Neither of us made a single sound until morning. When they finally brought Felix back, he was a little bruised up, but he said they mostly made him walk around all night. Lyon and I were actually the ones being tested. If we had made a scene, we were going to get a meaningful taste of Jace's whip.

"We've got to make a pact," I insisted as we gulped down a quick meal the next morning. "If Thrane comes after one of us—"

"—you mean *when* Thrane comes after one of us," Lyon interrupted.

I nodded grimly. "Right. Well, when he does, we can't let anything he does or says break us down. Even if the others in our group start losing it, we have to stand together. Thrane is going to be looking at us even harder at the battle scenario. There won't be any more reason for the other instructors to stop him from coming after us."

"Are you thinking he's going to use the battle scenario as an excuse to finally attack you?" Felix sounded tense.

"I hope so." My answer made both of them stare at me in surprise. I shrugged and kept eating. "Better me than you. I can take whatever he dishes out. But I don't want either of you to suffer any more because of me, so when he does come for me, don't try to intervene."

"Because you don't think you can stop the battle fever? Even after everything he's done so far?" Lyon asked. It was easy to read the concern in his tone. After all, he had been Thrane's primary target until now.

I hated admitting to that kink in my armor, but there was no avoiding it. "Yeah," I replied, and tried not to look at Felix. He still didn't know about my healing abilities, but I knew it was only a matter of time now. He was already starting to figure out that it had something to do with my other strange powers.

"I think you should practice with your powers," Felix announced suddenly.

Lyon and I swapped an uncomfortable glance.

"Seriously, I do." He pointed his fork at me accusingly. "If something does go wrong on Canrack, and we get into a spot where the only thing standing between us and getting crushed by a bunch of angry forest creatures is you, then I want you to be on top of your game. No more desperate last minute saves. I want the full-force of your weirdness to be ready to go at a moment's notice."

"When am I supposed to practice?" I scowled at him. "The instructors watch our every move. And we never know when they are going to sound the battle horn."

Felix's frown hardened. "I don't know, but you need to figure out something. We're running out of time."

I knew he was right. As uncomfortable as it was to admit I had these abilities, they might be our lifeline in a bad situation. I needed to be ready. There wouldn't be time for foul-ups and second chances.

The only time there was to do that kind of experimentation was during training. It wasn't ideal, but I didn't have much of a choice. Not with Thrane and the other instructors breathing down my neck, beating me senseless in the middle of the night, or shouting commands.

I started out as gently as I could. I held conversations with Mavrik and Nova in my mind while we flew through aerial drills. I gave Nova simple instructions, like getting her to do spirals or breathe flame even when Felix hadn't asked her to, and then I watched to see if she obeyed. When she did, I started to get more confident. I started talking with other dragons, too. Demos was a stubborn, arrogant jerk if I'd ever seen one, but he was also the most experienced out of all the dragons when it came to actual aerial warfare. I took his advice on maneuvers when he showed me how he thought the scenarios were going to play out, and most of the time, he was right.

Having the dragons all whispering in my mind with their endless stream of images and colors was very distracting. Thankfully, the more I did it, the easier it became to balance what I saw in my mind with what was happening around me. It was like having eyes everywhere at once. It gave me an edge, and it was completely undetectable to all the other dragonriders.

I started talking to the birds next. There weren't many wild animals around in the Devil's Cup. That was part of the reason they had put the academy there in the first place; it was remote and there wasn't much you could accidentally burn down except for a few prickly shrubs. But there were birds and small animals. I started calling them to our dorm room window, which bothered Felix a lot. Apparently, he didn't like birds.

My powers were definitely growing. I didn't even have to concentrate at all to talk to Mavrik anymore, and it was starting to become that way with the other dragons, too. Mavrik's presence was always the loudest in my mind, though, and our bond was getting stronger by the day. I asked him repeatedly about what was going on with the animals. His answer was always the same. He showed me the same scene Nova had of a place in the forest, and a moss-covered staircase leading down into the dark. I could sense his anxiety and fear. The other dragons gave off that same sense as well. They knew what was happening. They could feel something bad coming, and they were every bit as helpless to stop it as the other wild animals.

"If it comes down to it," I told Mavrik as I sat in his stall, scratching his head after a day full of training. "If you have to choose between leaving me behind and saving yourself from that chaos, don't sacrifice yourself for me. That wasn't part of our deal."

He growled with discontent, and shot me a dirty look.

"Hey, I don't like it any more than you do, big guy. But I would rather stand and fight alone than watch you turn on me because that chaos had possessed you." I scratched that special place right behind his ear, and he couldn't help but purr. "I know you want to protect me. I want to do the same for you."

Mavrik lifted his head. His big yellow eyes stared down at me. When the moonlight reflected off of them, it almost looked like they were glowing. He pushed his massive snout against my chest and let out a deep sigh. Hues of blue and yellow swirled in my brain.

"I know," I said as I ran my hand over his scaly head. "I'm scared, too."

I COULD FEEL THE INSTRUCTORS' EYES ON ME, BURNING HOLES IN MY BACK with their stares. Across from me, Felix was poised for the attack. I could barely see his eyes over the top of his shield. Sweat ran down the sides of my face, dripping off my chin. All around us, the other avians were shouting, but it just sounded like muffled noise. They cheered us on, trying to distract us or tempt us into making a careless mistake.

This was the last day of training. It was the final test before we packed our things and left for the Canrack Islands. We had spent all day in the battle dome under the glare of firelight from the big bronze braziers burning all the way around the arena floor. Early in the morning we had drawn names to see who we would be dueling for our final sparring match. This match would be judged be all the instructors, and we were encouraged to win...at all costs.

I wasn't stupid enough to believe that I had been paired with Felix by chance. I knew Jace was probably responsible for it. Felix was the only avian who actually posed a challenge to me in the sparring ring anymore. He was consistently perfect in form, and he hit with so much strength it made my teeth rattle every time our blades locked. He was a lot more muscular than I was, with easily twice as much brute strength, but he couldn't match my speed. I had to use that, and the fact that I was taller and my arms were a lot longer than his, to strike from a distance before he could defend.

After nearly an hour, though, I was beginning to get tired. No one else had dueled for this long. What started out as a small crowd of our peers gathering around to watch had now grown into a full-blown mob. I didn't dare stop to check, but it seemed like the whole academy had gathered to watch us.

Felix dove at me again, letting out a roar of frustration as he swung his sword. It hummed through the air, coming down against my blades as I parried. For a brief moment, I regretted not picking a shield instead of two blades. It was way too late to be thinking about that now, though. The force of the impact made my bones creak. I saw him rear back, preparing to use his shield as a weapon while we were so close together.

I quickly dodged, sidestepped, and made a wild strike at his arm. I didn't expect it to work, but Felix must have been getting tired, too. His reactions were becoming more sluggish. That big shield was weighing him down. I felt my blade hit something solid and snap it.

It was one of the straps on his shield that held it onto his arm.

The big sheet of bronze clattered into the dirt, and Felix spun to face me. He bared his teeth, and made another wild dive with his sword swung wide. I spread my stance, and prepared to take him on. Without his shield, he would be a lot easier to deal with.

At least, that's what I was hoping.

Our strikes were furious and fast. We moved through technique after technique, testing each other at every turn for any possible weakness. The roaring of the crowd grew louder.

Then I got the hilt of one of my blades locked perfectly with his. I'd tried that same maneuver at least a dozen times already, and he had evaded it effortlessly. This time, I saw panic in his eyes. I twisted my sword, and jerked his sword out of his hands. It went skidding across the dirt to the other side of the arena, far out of his reach.

The crowd went silent.

Felix stood back, his chest heaving as he panted for breath. He watched me, his eyes narrowed like he was waiting for me to end this. The duel was technically over. Or it should have been, anyway. I had disarmed him. I had won. All I had to do was make that final strike and force him to surrender.

But it seemed too easy. Felix's strength wasn't spent. He still had fight in his eyes. I knew in a real battle, he wouldn't have surrendered just because he didn't have weapon. Felix didn't know when to quit—he was stubborn like that.

"Finish it!" Someone shouted from the crowd.

I snapped a punishing glare to the hundreds of eyes watching us. "Stay out of this!" I shouted so loud it echoed off the dome's ceiling.

Felix was still staring at me. He squinted his eyes a little, canting his head to the side like he was trying to figure out what I was going to do. The expression of pure shock on his face was priceless when I suddenly threw down both of my blades and balled my fists, assuming a fighting stance.

A dark smile spread across Felix's face. "What, all that wasn't enough for you?" He chuckled. "You really think you can beat me hand-to-hand?"

I curled a finger at him slowly, taunting him in to fight me. "I think I can."

Felix didn't need much encouragement when it came to diving into a fistfight. That kind of combat was his specialty. He ran for me at full speed. The crowd exploded into cheering again. We met in the middle of the arena, and Felix stunned me with a barbaric right hook to the stomach.

We fought until our knuckles bled. I still couldn't match his strength, but I still had speed on my side. When he finally managed to knock me down with a leg sweep, I did everything I could to stay out of his grappling hold. I knew if he managed to get an arm or a leg around my neck, it was over. I wouldn't be able to break free.

As I reached the end of my stamina, I started to make stupid, desperate choices. A risky attempt at a complicated pin cost me big time. Felix managed to twist me around and mash my face into the dirt with his elbow.

"You know, I'm kinda used to being surprised by your crazy decisions. But this is especially stupid, even for you." He growled at me, putting his face close to mine so no one else could hear. "You've already won this. What are you trying to prove?"

"That Thrane better be prepared when he comes after me," I answered with a mouthful of dirt. "I want him to know I'm not easy to kill!"

"Well, you picked a dumb way to do it," he snarled as he grabbed a handful of my hair and used it to lift my head far enough to slip an arm around my neck. "You've never beaten me hand-to-hand before. And you never will!"

I didn't know what else to do. Felix was right, it was stupid to challenge him like this. I couldn't afford to lose. In a moment of wild desperation, I threw my head back against his and head-butted him as hard as I could.

It was like my brains were scrambled the instant our skulls hit. His grip on my neck loosened, and I pushed off the ground to flip us over. The crowds were screaming so loudly that it was disorienting. The lights of the braziers seemed to be spinning around me as I tried to crawl away from him.

When I looked back, Felix was on his hands and knees. He was dazed, too. At first, I thought he might get to his feet and use that moment to claim the upper hand. But he didn't. Instead, he slowly raised his head and looked at me. I saw him smirk for the briefest second, wink, and fall over onto his side.

Felix didn't move again. The crowd started to count. When they got to ten, the victory was mine. I had beaten Felix in armed combat and hand-to-hand.

Except, I knew I hadn't. Felix did a pretty good job of acting when Jace went over to see about him. He played it off like my head-butt had knocked him out. But I knew better. That smirk and wink was his way of letting me know he was throwing the match for my sake. He was doing it so I didn't look weak in front of Thrane and the other instructors.

For some reason, that really made me angry. I knew why he'd done it. It made perfect sense. I had gotten in way over my head by challenging him to a fistfight like that. Still, being treated like some helpless little kid was annoying. We were too old for that now. I wasn't a kid anymore, and this wasn't a game.

This was war.

CHAPTER TWENTY-FOUR

The morning of the battle scenario was colder than usual. A thick fog had settled over the academy, making the morning seem darker as we gathered our gear and moved to the Roost. Lyon, Felix, and I walked together with the rest of the avians in our class. No one spoke. The silence was intense, and I knew I wasn't the only one dreading what was waiting for us later that day.

As we filed into the Roost, a few instructors stood waiting at the door. They were handing out folded pieces of paper sealed with wax. They told us to go ahead and get our dragons ready, but we weren't supposed to read what was on the paper until the battle horn sounded. Then we were officially dismissed to move out.

My hands shook with restlessness as I checked my saddle. Mavrik could sense my worry. I knew he was nervous, too. I could feel his strong sides shuddering slightly as he trembled with that anxious energy. According to Jace, the dragons wouldn't be able to help us once we reached the island. They would drop us off, and wouldn't be set loose to pick us up again until the scenario was over.

I was dressed in my full armor, sitting on my saddle, looking down over my dragon's large head through the glass-covered slit in my helmet. Outside the Roost, I could see the skyline beginning to turn purple and orange as the sun rose over the mountain peaks.

Together, Mavrik and I waited. I was clenching my teeth to keep them from chattering. The paper rattled in my hands, and I thought about sneaking a peek at what was on it.

Then the battle horn sounded.

Frantically, I ripped open the wax seal and started reading the paper. Written on it was our scenario, a brief set of instructions, and a map of where we were supposed to land on the Canrack Islands. Our first objective was to land in a small clearing near the center of the island. There was a stone fortress, sort of like an outpost, positioned nearby. That was our destination.

The paper didn't say anything about it, but I had a feeling that was where the interrogation was going to take place. It did say that we would be set loose on the island to find our way to the beach, where our dragons would be picking us up. We were going to have to prove that we could survive the jungle, even after being beaten and tortured.

I heard the thundering roar of the other dragons as they began to take off. It took me a few minutes to finally pry my eyes off the paper. I was second guessing everything. This was going to be horrible, just like Sile had promised. I didn't want to go through it. I wasn't sure I was strong enough, or if I had enough training. I didn't know if Thrane was going to try to kill me, using the battle scenario as an excuse. I didn't know if any of us would even make it out alive.

Mavrik sent me an image. In my mind, I saw Beckah on the night of the ball. She had seemed so sure about her own destiny. I envied that about her. She was strong, wise, and beautiful in a way I only barely understood. Jace had called me brave before, but what little courage I had was nothing next to hers.

Thinking about her made me more aware of the lump under my vambrace where I still had her handkerchief hidden. Felix had reminded me not to take anything with me I couldn't stand to lose. I had left my mother's necklace beside my bed, but I couldn't leave Beckah's token behind. Having it with me gave me strength, and reminded me that there were things still worth fighting for.

Underneath all my fear and doubt, I knew Beckah was right. I was here for a reason—the same reason she was training. Giving up was not an option. Felix and Lyon were going to that island, and they might need me. There was no other choice. I had to protect the people I cared about.

Mavrik let out his own booming cry as he leapt into the sky. We caught the rush of cool morning wind, and turned west toward the sea. As we soared up above the fog, I saw other dragons and riders flying all around us. I started looking for my friends, and when I couldn't find them, I reached out with my thoughts. I called to Nova and Demos, asking them to come closer.

I heard Nova's roar from over my shoulder. When I looked back, Felix was giving me angry hand signals.

Quit steering for me, he gestured.

I smirked under my helmet.

We flew in formation toward the sea. After several hours, the air started to smell more and more like salt. In the distance, I could see big, dark spots rising up on the horizon. The islands were like droplets of green in an endless blue sea.

The largest was where we were supposed to find the clearing and make our way to the fortress.

It was easy to find the clearing. The rest of the island was covered in jungle so dense, it looked like a quilt of rustling leaves. It was so thick you couldn't see anything below the canopy. The clearing obviously had been man-made by cutting down some of the trees, and I could see the sandy-colored stone of the fortress peeking out between some of the branches not far away.

I gestured to Lyon and Felix to hang back and circle while the other avians landed, dismounted, and sent their dragons away. We were the last ones to touch down. I hurried to unload my go-bag, buckle my helmet to the saddle, and clip my sword to my hip. As soon as I was finished, I gave Mavrik a gruff pat on the neck.

He stared down at me. I could sense his worry and fear. He didn't want to leave me and honestly, I didn't want him to go.

"Go on," I pushed against his head. "I'll be fine. If anything happens, I'll call you."

Mavrik growled at me, but he didn't argue. He puffed an angry snort, blasting my face with his hot breath, and then took off to join the other dragons who were returning to the Roost.

Felix dismounted next. I waited for him in the clearing, and then we stood together while Lyon took his turn. Dressed in our brown cloaks and carrying our bags and weapons, we probably looked prepared. But deep down I knew we weren't. We were like lambs being led to the slaughter.

"Remember our deal," I said as soon as Demos took off.

Lyon and Felix stared back at me with wide, worried eyes. They both nodded.

"We can't stay close to one another. They already know we're friends, so they'll probably try to use that against us. But any doubt we can give them would work to our advantage. Once we're let back into the jungle, we need to find each other. We have a better chance of surviving if we work together to get back to the beach." I looked around the clearing and picked a tree nearby. It was taller than the others. "When they let us go, let's meet there. Okay?"

Once again, they nodded. One by one, we broke off and started for the fortress alone. I waited to go last, watching Felix's back as he marched off into the trees. When it was my turn to go, I was so caught up in staring at the jungle around me it wasn't hard to let my thoughts wander for a second. Jace had said this place was a lot like Luntharda, and seeing it gave me strange chills.

There were huge ferns everywhere with fronds as tall as I was. The tree trunks were covered in moss and vines, and the canopy over head was so thick that almost no sunlight made it down to the forest floor. It was almost like the branches of the trees had woven together to make a living basket. Strange sounds came from everywhere, but I didn't see any animals. I tried to press outward with my thoughts to see if I could sense them.

Then something hit me on the back of the head.

Everything went dark.

When I started to wake up, I could feel that my hands were tied behind my back. I also realized that I was completely naked. All my gear and all my clothes were gone. Overall, not a good way to start a day of training.

I forced my eyes open and squinted into the sunlight. Immediately, I saw the familiar sand-colored stone of the fortress. I rolled over onto my side. The back of my head was hurting from where I'd been hit, and I could hear others moving around nearby. There were other avians sitting all around me, stripped down and tied up like I was.

"What's going on?" I rasped as I sat up and started testing my bonds. Whoever had tied my hands had done a great job. I couldn't slip free.

"Shut up," a familiar voice growled at me. It sent anger burning through my veins about a second before I felt him grab a fistful of my hair. I glared into Thrane's eyes as he forced me to look at him. "Welcome to Hell, demon. You should feel right at home."

I didn't answer.

He let me go and slung me back down on the ground. I waited until he had moved away to sit back up again. All around me, the other avians were sitting in a circle. Everyone was tied up the same way while a few instructors, including Thrane, stood guard over us. I saw more instructors stripping down the few remaining students, and taking their gear into the fortress's only building.

The compound wasn't much. The center building was only two storys tall, and it had no windows that I could see. All around us was a stacked stone wall that was at least twenty feet high, with only one gate that led out into the dark jungle. The tree branches spread out and almost completely covered the compound, even though there were no trees inside the walls.

We were sitting in an empty dirt courtyard. The only other thing standing was a tall wooden post that stuck straight up out of the ground. I hadn't seen anything like it before, but it didn't take a genius to figure out what it was. If the old blood splattered around it wasn't evidence enough, then the shackles hanging from the top of it made it pretty clear what that post was used for. It was a whipping post.

When the last of us had been captured, the instructors made us all get up at once. We were marched into the fortress in a line, which was completely humiliating. No one wants to walk around naked like that. Anyone who tried to step out of line or run was immediately punished, usually with a punch to the face.

I really can't go into much detail about what happened in that compound. Some things just shouldn't be said. What I can say is that Sile's warnings about this training didn't come anywhere near how bad it actually was. Not even the interrogation training could compare.

After what must have been several days, I started wondering if I would live to see the sky again. They kept us in the dark as much as possible so that we lost track of time. But worse than that, they kept us alone. The cells they crammed us into were so tiny I couldn't stand up straight. There wasn't enough room to sit with your legs straight, either, so it was impossible to find a way to sleep or even be comfortable. It was a miserable, cold, dark, stone box.

The first time I heard someone break down, I was terrified it was Felix or Lyon, but I couldn't tell because of how the voices echoed off everything. I heard someone crying and screaming hysterically, begging to be let out. I wanted to yell back at them, to remind them to keep quiet. I heard the instructors take him out of his cell. I heard them beat him until he was quiet. Then they threw him back in his cell.

A few others broke down like that. Each time, I covered my ears and tried not to hear it. I was afraid it would be one of my friends or that I'd hear them call out to me for help. But there was no refuge in the silence because when it was quiet, you were reminded of how hungry and thirsty you were. At first, they didn't feed us at all. Then they let us out into the courtyard and threw a few rations out, so that we had to fight for them. I didn't fight very hard, though. Something about the way Thrane was watching us fight, like he was enjoying it way too much, made me suspicious.

In the end, I was glad I hadn't tried to get any of the food. The ones who did were doubly rewarded with a turn at the whipping post. Five lashes in exchange for those few bites of food.

Eventually, they did give us our clothes back. By that time, I was so filthy from scrounging around in the dirt that I hated to put anything on without bathing. There wasn't much choice, though. It was better than being naked.

Once we were all sufficiently weak from hunger, thirst, and the psychological torment of being trapped in a windowless, dark cell for days... the actual interrogation finally began.

They pulled us out into the courtyard one by one. They beat us. They yelled, and demanded information. They even promised food or freedom if we talked.

When it was my turn, I knew Thrane would be there even before I saw his big ugly face leering down at me. My hands were still tied behind my back, and my body was so weak from dehydration I wasn't sure I could survive one of his beatings. But I did.

Afterwards, my face was so bruised it felt like raw meat, but I was alive and I still had all my teeth. I knew that was probably because of Jace. He had been there the whole time, standing off to the side and watching with that cold look in his eyes. He didn't seem to care when Thrane hit me, but I let myself hope that if it went too far—if Thrane actually tried to kill me—then Jace would intervene. I think the fact that I didn't break down and talk actually surprised them. I got a little pleasure out of that as I limped back to my cell.

In the end, we never knew who talked and who didn't. We never saw one another. At least, not until everyone had taken several turns. Then it was time for a different approach.

We were all herded back into the courtyard like cattle and made to stand in lines. As I looked around, I noticed everyone else looked about as bad as I felt. Every one of us had been bruised up badly, although some were worse than others. I searched the faces of the other avians, but I couldn't find Felix or Lyon. I was kind of glad about that. I didn't want to feel anything. It was safer not to feel until this was over.

The instructors started pulling us out one by one to interrogate us in front of everyone. They picked on the weaker students first, trying to see who would react. I was surprised that I didn't get called out... that is, until I realized it was only because Thrane had something *extra* special in store for me.

"That one." Thrane turned his nasty smile in my direction and pointed. "Take him to the post."

My stomach twisted painfully. I couldn't help but look back at the whipping post. It was spattered with fresh blood now. Fear immediately made my legs feel even weaker. I started having radical thoughts about trying to run, or fighting back. I didn't think I could handle a beating like that, not without having a full mental breakdown in front of everyone. I was so tired, so hungry, and in so much pain from the beatings I'd already taken. The thought of the lash of that whip over my skin—it was unbearable.

But I didn't have a choice. I had to go. This was the moment Sile had warned me about; the moment when my strength would truly be tested.

"We don't want him to get lonely up there, do we? Nah, of course not. Send that one, too. They seem real fond of each other already." Thrane laughed hoarsely as he pointed to someone else.

I knew I shouldn't look. I didn't want to see who it was. It was better not to see, to let it all roll off and stare at the ground. But I couldn't help it. As one of the instructors shackled me to the post with my arms above my head, I looked up to see who else they were pulling from the group.

Felix was looking right back at me. His face was so battered I barely recognized him. The instant our eyes met, I knew what was about to happen.

We stared at one another as they shackled him on the other side of the post so that we were forced to look into each other's eyes. I knew he had to be thinking the same thing I was: Thrane knew about us. He had been waiting all this time for the perfect moment to finally break me by using the one person who could push me over the edge. I was not ready for this, and I could already feel my sanity starting to slip through my fingers.

"You seem to like taking the fall for this piece of filth." Thrane walked up to Felix, curling a long, braided leather whip around his arm. "Did you think I wouldn't notice? Maybe the others didn't, but I know a con when I see one. You threw that fight for this demon. I'll admit, I was a little surprised. They say you're a high noble. Well, that may be, but I'm willing to bet your blood is red just like everyone else's. I guess we'll find out, won't we?"

My heart was pounding in my ears so loudly I could barely hear anything else. I clenched my teeth and started to twist my hands in my shackles. Immediately, Felix's expression changed.

He glared at me fiercely and shook his head.

Thrane grabbed my chin suddenly, jerking my eyes away from Felix so that I had to stare back at him. "The beating stops when you talk. You've fooled everyone else here into thinking you're one of us, but you don't fool me. I've seen your kind. I've watched your people butcher my brothers like cattle. It's time you show these people whose side you're really on, demon. Until then, watch him bleed for you."

There was no way to win this situation—not in my eyes. If I kept my mouth shut, I was betraying my whole purpose for being here by letting Felix suffer. If I talked, I was proving that I couldn't be trusted. Thrane had me cornered, and there was no way out. Somehow, I'd walked right into his trap.

I started pulling against my shackles as they cut Felix's shirt off his back. He was still looking straight at me. Even though he didn't seem afraid, I couldn't calm down. I fought the iron chains with all my might.

"Stop it," Felix whispered suddenly. Behind him, I could see Thrane unfurling his whip. "We had a deal."

I stopped struggling long enough to whisper back, "He's going to kill you!"

Felix sent me one of his typical, carefree grins. He opened his mouth to speak, but he never got the words out.

The whip cracked in the air.

It cracked over, and over, and over. Each time, Felix yelled, and his whole body jerked violently against the chains. His blood ran down his legs to drip onto the ground at our feet. His head sagged to his chest, and his knees had buckled so that he was basically dangling by the shackles on his wrists. I could hear him struggling to breathe. I was terrified he'd stop, that any one of those haggard breaths might be his last.

But the lashes kept coming. Even after Felix stopped screaming altogether, as though he didn't even have the strength to make a sound anymore. The metallic smell of his blood hung in the air. It made me sick with rage. Thrane curled that whip again and again, smiling at me the whole time.

I hated myself for not stopping this. I hated Felix for not letting me. I hated Thrane because there was nothing I wanted more than to rip his heart right out of his chest. I hated Jace for not intervening. Didn't he see what was happening? This wasn't training. This was torture.

Another instructor beside Thrane was keeping count of the lashes. It was the only other sound other than the awful sound of that whip cracking in the air.

"Twenty-two. Twenty-three. Twenty-four…"

I squeezed my eyes shut. I let my head sag to my chest. Deep inside me, something was starting to rise up. It was a familiar burning heat, like someone had poured dragon venom into my veins. Before, I had always tried to fight it. I'd been so afraid of it, or of what would happen if I lost control. But now I had no reason to be afraid. I didn't have any reason to resist it.

So I surrendered.

Immediately, my mind snapped into focus. Strength bloomed through my body despite the pain, hunger, and thirst. None of it mattered anymore as I raised my head, and stared past Felix's slumped body to where Thrane was standing.

I wanted to kill him, and nothing was going to stop me.

I didn't even notice the way the post was beginning to sprout branches. At least, not until I felt the ground move under my feet. The post was coming to life. It was sprouting roots that dove into the earth around our feet. It was growing branches and leaves in a matter of seconds.

I heard the others starting to scream, but that sound only stoked the fire in my chest. I could feel the post now. It wasn't just wood anymore. It was a living thing, and it would obey me.

I commanded it to set us free. Immediately, a branch began twisting round the thick iron chains and squeezing them like a boa constrictor.

The chains snapped.

Felix was badly hurt. He couldn't even stand. As soon as his chains were broken, he started to fall. I caught him long enough to make sure he made it to the ground without cracking his head. Then I set my eyes upon Thrane.

Thrane was terrified. Everyone else was, too. They were running, yelling, or standing in awe as the whipping post grew bigger, turning into a large tree in the middle of the courtyard. But none of that mattered to me.

"You will pay with your blood," I snarled at Thrane. I barely recognized my own voice. I sounded like some kind of a growling beast.

Thrane was fumbling around, trying to figure out how to fend me off. He drew back his whip, and lashed it at me.

I caught it in the air and let it wrap around my forearm. Then I pulled on it hard enough to make him loose his footing. Thrane fell to his knees.

He started frantically grasping for his sword. His expression of fear changed to rage and hatred. When he got to his feet, he started toward me, bellowing like a maniac. He raised his sword, ready to cut me in half.

The heat in my chest suddenly swelled. It spread throughout my body, blazing out to every finger and toe like a roaring inferno. It sent such a jolt through me that my legs buckled. I was on my knees, but I wasn't surrendering.

I was just getting started.

Thrane took three steps before the ground beneath him started to rumble and move. Three huge vines erupted out of the soil around him. They wrapped around his arms and legs, snagging him like giant tentacles. He started to scream as they lifted him into the air.

"End it," I heard myself snarl.

A splinter of doubt pierced my chest, but I couldn't stop it. The rage had overtaken me. It was battle fever—the *kulunai*. Thrane was getting what he wanted, a lot more than he bargained for, and precisely what he deserved.

A flex of my hand made the vines all squeeze at once. There was a nasty crunching sound, and Thrane's screams went silent. I felt it as he died, almost like I was crushing a glass ornament in my hands. It was shattered completely, and there was no way to repair it.

Suddenly, something struck me. It hit me hard in the chest, right at my shoulder. I looked down, surprised to see the shaft of an arrow sticking out of my body. It didn't hurt, though. The battle fever prevented me from feeling anything but the boiling fire in my body. I immediately stood up and started looking around for the person who had shot me. They were the next threat that had to be dealt with.

I saw Jace. He was slowly drawing another arrow back. He stood only a few yards away, his expression just as brutally wrathful as though he were facing down someone he truly hated.

I was confused. I knew his face, even through the haze of the battle fever. I didn't understand why he was shooting at me. But when he fired again, hitting me in the side, I felt the fires of my own fury start to rise again. It didn't matter who he was, then. He was a threat that needed to be dealt with, and that was all I cared about.

"No!" Someone yelled. I was sure I had heard that voice before.

Lyon burst from the ranks of panicking avians and threw himself in between us. He was facing me, his eyes wide and desperate. "Jae, you have to stop," he yelled again. "You have to stop this right now! Thrane is dead! It's over!"

The roaring fires in my veins start to fizzle—until I felt the pain of the arrows in my body. That sensation spun me back into the battle fever in a matter of seconds.

"Get out of the way," I growled at him.

Lyon didn't move. He stood between Jace and I, his arms spread wide, staring me down. Behind him, I could still see Jace, and he had another arrow notched and ready to fly.

"No. I won't let you do it." Lyon said. I saw his chin tremble some, like he was trying not to lose his nerve. "Are you with us?"

That question struck a chord. It roused a memory I had almost forgotten. Someone had asked me that before, but I couldn't remember who. The battle fever made everything seem so out of control.

"Answer me! Are you with us?" Lyon shouted louder.

Coolness washed over me so suddenly that actually gave me chills. The fire within me died, reduced to ashes as the battle fever left my body. Before my legs buckled again, I managed to answer.

"Always."

I wasn't expecting any kindness, not after what I'd done. Part of me was okay with whatever they chose to do with me. I wasn't going to beg for my life, not when I was so obviously guilty. I was a murderer, and I couldn't ask for mercy when I hadn't shown any myself. So I let myself slip away, sleeping off the exhaustion from using so much of my power, and hoped that I would never wake up. Maybe they'd just behead me in my sleep. I didn't want to face Felix, Lyon, or Jace again, anyway.

As the haze of fatigue finally cleared from my mind, I woke up in the darkness of a prison cell. The wounds left by Jace's arrows had been bandaged, but they still hurt. Thankfully, it didn't seem like he had been shooting to kill me, because they were nothing more than flesh wounds.

As I started to get my bearings, I realized there were voices speaking loudly nearby. One of them sounded like Lyon.

"He's the only one who can do it. Let him show you!" Lyon was pleading. "He's done it to me dozens of times already!"

"He's telling the truth," Jace insisted. "I've seen it myself."

"That... that *thing* cannot be trusted! He almost turned on you, too!" I heard someone arguing. He was joined by a few other voices, all grumbling in agreement.

"But he didn't," Jace countered. He sounded as calm and collected as ever. "It was my mistake. I struck him first. If I hadn't presented myself as a threat, he wouldn't have even considered me one. You saw how Lyon was able to talk him down. He was rational because he didn't perceive Lyon as a threat."

"Don't be a fool, Lieutenant Rordin," someone else snarled in defiance. "We've all seen these creatures when the battle fever possesses them! We've witnessed firsthand what they are capable of! They are not rational!"

No one spoke for a moment. I didn't move from where I was lying on my back, staring up into the darkness of my prison cell. Then Jace said something that made me go numb.

"I don't think it was battle fever." He sounded very solemn. "I know we suspected that after the first incident with Lyon. It certainly seemed the likely explanation, considering his heritage. But now, having witnessed what else he can do, I think this is something else. You all saw how his eyes glowed. You saw how his teeth turned to fangs, and how he made those plants obey him. I've never seen that before from battle fever—or from any Gray elf, for that matter. Whatever he did—whatever he is—it's something we've never encountered before."

Once again there was silence.

All I could do was lie there and try to comprehend what Jace had said. My eyes had glowed? And my teeth had turned to fangs? I poked at them with my tongue to be sure, but they didn't feel any different from normal now.

"So what exactly are we dealing with?" Another voice asked. It sounded like Lieutenant Haprick. I was too dazed to be sure. "Surely you aren't thinking he could be some sort of pagan Gray elf deity?"

Lyon snorted. "Jae's not a god. He'd tell you that himself if you asked him."

"Regardless of what he is, there's no reason we shouldn't let him save his friend. Everything he did was for that same purpose, and his ability to heal has never provoked a violent attack before," Jace said. "Besides, I don't see any other choice. We can't escape even to send out a distress call. If we don't act soon, Felix will die of infection. I can't let that happen. It's my fault he's in this state. Thrane took things too far, and I didn't stop him in time."

Hearing that got me on my feet in an instant. I walked to the iron bars at the front of my cell. A small group of instructors and avians stood close by, huddling together under the light of a single torch.

"Let me save him," I begged. "Please."

My words made everyone, including Jace and Lyon, jump in surprise. They all turned to face me. I could see the fear in their eyes. It made me realize I was more alone now than I'd ever been before. Now, they all saw me as a potential threat.

"What are you? How do we know we can trust you?" Lieutenant Haprick demanded.

My shoulders sagged. "I don't know. And I don't know how to prove to you that I don't want to hurt anyone else."

"Well, you've done more than that." Jace sighed and took a step toward me. "After your little outburst, it's like the whole island has gone mad. We can't even get out of the compound now. The few of us who have tried were killed in minutes, before they could even reach the wall."

I stared at him, trying to understand everything he said. "The plants?"

"And animals," Lyon added. "It's unbelievable, Jae. Remember how you woke up that ancient turtle everyone thought was extinct? There are monsters outside right now no one has ever seen before. They didn't even know creatures like that lived on this island. They attack anyone who dares to step foot outside the door."

"Because of me?" I swallowed hard.

Jace's expression said it all. It really was my fault. "We can't even send anyone out to call for help. We're trapped here. Our supplies won't last a week. But Felix's wounds will kill him long before hunger and thirst do."

I frowned at them as hard as I could. "Then let me out. I have to heal him. If you let me do that much, then I will call the dragons back here for you. You won't have to send anyone else outside."

Lieutenant Haprick's brows rose in surprise. "Are you bargaining with us?"

I narrowed my eyes at him. "Yes. And as far as I can tell, it's the best option you've got. You don't even have to take me with you when the dragons come. Leave me here to die alone, if it makes you feel better."

"Jae, that's not—" Lyon started to protest.

"They won't trust me again after this, right? Then it's better if I stay." I snapped at him.

"There's no way the dragons can pick us up here." Jace started rubbing his chin thoughtfully. "The forest has completely invaded the compound. The canopy is too thick for them to land. We have to get to the beach."

"Maybe he can talk to the trees?" Lyon suggested. "You know, get them to move or something?"

Lieutenant Haprick scoffed, "Do you even hear yourselves? Talking to trees?! This is ridiculous!"

"No, what's ridiculous is letting everyone here die on principle because you don't understand what I am. You don't have to like me. You don't even have to trust me. You have to let me try. I'm the only chance you've got to escape this place." I growled at them. "So let me out. Now."

CHAPTER TWENTY-FIVE

Felix was in bad shape. When I entered the small, dimly lit room where they had him resting, the smell of infection hit me like a rock to the forehead. It was a disgusting, sickly-sweet smell that made me gag.

Felix was lying on his side facing the door. His back was wrapped in bandages that were soaked with blood. Jace had already warned me about that. They were out of medical supplies, so they were trying to reuse what little they had on hand.

A small audience of instructors and avians were gathered in the doorway, but they didn't follow me into the room as I went to kneel down at Felix's bedside. They all kept a safe distance from me now, as though they were afraid I would snap and go crazy again. I couldn't blame them for that.

"You know, when I said I wanted to see what amazing, unexpected thing you were going to do next, this is definitely not what I had in mind." Felix opened his eyes slowly and stared right at me. His voice sounded weak, but his usual sense of humor was still there.

I had to smile back at him, even if it felt like it might be the last time we ever spoke like this. "Too late to back out on me now, though. Right?"

He smiled faintly. His forehead was dripping with sweat from fever, and I could see the pain in his eyes. He was suffering.

"As if any of your weirdness would scare me off at this point." He grabbed one of my shoulders roughly and squeezed it. "I know you've always kept secrets from me, which I guess was your way of trying to protect me, but I'd rather be remembered as the friend of a weird halfbreed than a duke who only cared about his reputation."

"After this, neither of us will have much of a reputation left to defend," I managed to whisper. "I'm so sorry, Felix."

He smiled again, and punched my arm with a little bit of that strength I'd always envied. "Don't be. We're family, Jae. Maybe not literally, but you're the closest thing to a real brother I've ever had."

"I know." Somehow, I was able to smile back at him. "Which is why no sacrifice I make for you will ever be enough to repay you for everything you've done for me. So shut up and let me heal you. I'm going to do something else amazing after this, and I know you won't want to miss it."

No one said a word as I placed my hands on his back. I could feel how his body was burning up with infection. I could feel his pain, and how the subtle glow of his spirit was growing weaker. It flickered and struggled like a candle slowly smothering without air. Jace was right. If I didn't heal him, he might not last another two days.

I let my power flow. It surged through my body so suddenly that it made me flinch. Never had this ability come so effortlessly to me. It felt more natural and calm than ever before, seeping out of my body and washing over his like a cleansing water.

I heard Felix suck in a sharp breath. I felt him go tense as my power took hold of him. In the doorway, the others were whispering, or gasping in awe. Only Lyon seemed to be able to keep his composure. He just looked on with a firm, confident gaze.

When it was finished, I took my hands away and backed up a few steps. Felix stirred on the bed. He was panting for breath, and staring at me with eyes so wide I thought he might scream in alarm. Instead, he started to sit up. His body was shaking, but I knew that was normal. It would take a few minutes for my power to finally leave his body.

Jace immediately rushed into the room to help him. Lyon followed and started peeling away the old bloody bandages from his back. Underneath was nothing but a few faint scars. The wounds, fever, and infection were all gone. Felix was perfectly healed.

The others rushed in to see, stumbling and climbing all over each other to touch his back like they thought it might be some kind of trick. One by one, they slowly turned to face me. Their faces stared at me with haunted expressions.

I bowed my head in submission. "Now, please let me try to save the rest of you."

"We've only managed to stand out there for a few minutes at most before the animals start to converge," Jace explained as he led me to a small balcony on the backside of the complex. "This is the only way out other than the main entrance."

"A few seconds is all I'll need." I nodded as I walked quickly after him.

After my attempts to call back the dragons from inside the fort had failed, the instructors had given everyone back their armor and sword. But before I went diving out the main gate to try anything radical, I needed to do a test run. I hadn't forgotten about my encounter with the wolves and mountain cat. The chaos that had possessed them had also made them deaf to my voice. If that was the case here, then that might explain why I couldn't get my calls to reach out beyond the canopy. All my power might be useless, which basically meant we were doomed.

"And if it doesn't work?" Jace asked as he stopped at the heavy wooden door that led out onto the balcony. He pulled a big iron key out of his pocket and started to unlock it.

"Then we'll have no choice but to take our chances in the jungle. It's that or die here, right?" I said as I pressed a hand against the wound on my shoulder. It still hurt, but at least it wasn't infected. "You can cover me with your bow, right? Without shooting me this time?"

Jace snorted and shot me a poisonous glare. "Just do whatever it is you do, avian, and leave the rest to me." He grasped the door handle and let out an anxious breath. "Ready?"

"I never am," I muttered as I braced myself. I gave him a countdown with my fingers. On three, Jace opened the door and I stepped out onto the balcony.

The sunlight filtering through the leaves cast everything in a greenish glow. Jace hadn't been exaggerating. The jungle had swallowed the compound completely. Vines and moss covered all the walls. Fully mature trees were growing everywhere, even knocking over portions of the wall to make way for their swelling trunks and branches. Strange flowers bloomed in every color imaginable, and some were so big I could have used one of their petals as a blanket. The air was thick and humid, and it smelled richly of soil.

Being on the second story put me right in the midst of the branches. They were so big I could have walked on them easily, but I stayed on the small balcony with the door right behind me. I wasn't feeling confident enough yet to venture very far away from it.

"All this... is because of me?" I heard myself ask.

"Apparently. Whatever you did before started some kind of chain reaction." Jace grumbled from behind me. "Hurry up. You're pressing our luck here."

I forced myself to focus. Jace was right. Apparently two instructors had already tried this and ended up paying the ultimate price for their bravery. I clenched my teeth and took a few more steps away from the door, stopping to look up through the interlocking limbs of the trees. I reached out to them with my thoughts, gently at first but with growing intensity. I commanded them to recede, to move away from the compound.

All I got was silence.

I shut my eyes and tried to focus harder. I tried to visualize what I wanted them to do. That's when I got my first little taste of something foul and all too familiar.

Chaos stung my mind and scrambled my thoughts. The balcony flinched under my feet. I heard a piercing, screeching sound that sent a cold pang of alarm through my body. I had heard that sound before, but only in my nightmares.

"Jaevid," Jace growled my name like a warning.

When I opened my eyes, I saw it. I knew what it was right away, even though I had never actually seen one in person. Felix had told me about the creatures Gray elves rode on; monsters that were supposed to be the natural archenemy of dragons.

Crouched before me on a thick tree limb, only a dozen yards away, was a shrike. It was as terrifying as it was beautiful. All I could do for a moment was stare at it, completely in awe.

The shrike was about the size of a small horse, though its shape was more like a six-legged cat. It had a long, flowing spine, robust shoulders and haunches, and a slender tail. Its entire body was covered in tiny scales that reflected the jungle like shards of a broken mirror. It was extremely lean, with a bony-looking exterior and a long tapered snout. Its sleek wings were made of nearly transparent feathers that almost looked like they were made of purplish tinted glass. Its eyes glowed like sunlight through leaves, focused right on me.

I immediately understood why Felix and Lyon had seemed so afraid of these creatures. It was difficult to differentiate where the shrike's body began and ended unless it was moving. It blended in so perfectly with the jungle around it. Its bony jaws were lined with teeth like a crocodile's that were about as long as my index finger. There were also claws on each of its toes that were long and curled like an eagle's talons.

I could sense the shrike's strength, speed, and power just by looking at it. It was a wild, brutally vicious creature. But something about it was incredibly beautiful. Even so, its presence in my mind was tossed amidst the chaos. I tried to talk to it anyway. I tried to ask it to acknowledge me, to see if it really was possessed.

It acknowledged me, all right.

The shrike snapped its jaws and let out a blood-curdling snarl. Its body rippled with raw, brutal strength, and the sunlight danced off its mirror-like scales as it sprang at me, jaws open wide for the kill.

An arrow zipped past my head, hitting the shrike in the chest. It screamed with pain and rage, and kept right on coming. It moved so unbelievably fast, I barely had time to think, much less react. At the last second, I frantically dove out of the way. As the shrike barreled past me, one of its razor-sharp claws caught my face. I could feel it tearing through my skin, cutting to the bone.

"Get in here!" Jace yelled.

I scrambled back toward the door and held it shut as he locked it again. While the shrike clawed at the door, we both stood there panting and staring at each other in shock. That had been way too close.

"My power isn't working," I managed to rasp. I could feel the hot, wet sensation of blood running down my face. "I couldn't talk to it at all. I couldn't even get my voice out past the trees. They're acting like a cage, keeping the chaos trapped in."

Jace scowled. "You must not be doing it right. It worked before. And your eyes didn't glow like last time."

"I can't let it go that far again." I glared back at him with fresh blood running down my face. As much as I hated to admit it, I couldn't control my reactions very well in that state. Battle fever or not, it seemed too dangerous. What good would it do to hold the forest at bay if I killed all my friends in the process?

"What other options do you think we have? If you don't do this, we're all dead anyway," he roared back at me so loudly it made me cringe. "We only have enough water left to last us three days at most. If we don't get off this island, we will all die here in this god-forsaken place."

The door rattled again as the shrike clawed at it from the outside. The terrible noises it made sounded like the feral scream of a cat mixed with an eagle's cry. Hearing it made me wonder what other horrors would be waiting for us in the jungle if I did try to lead everyone to the beach.

"Fine," I answered at last. "But swear to me if I start to turn against you again, you won't hesitate to put an arrow in my skull. No more flesh wounds. You might not get a second shot."

Jace's mouth pinched up like he'd tasted something sour, but he agreed. "If it comes to that."

The silence between us was awkward as we returned downstairs to the large open room where everyone else was gathered. The large doorway of the main entrance was barricaded with every piece of furniture in the compound, and all the supplies left were piled in a corner. There wasn't much left. The food was already almost gone, but more importantly, we only had a few barrels of fresh drinking water.

The rest of our group looked up with grim, haunted faces as Jace and I came down the stairs. I was holding a rag against my face to stop the bleeding. The cut was deep, and it had narrowly missed my eye, but Jace insisted it would be fine. His expression told me otherwise, but I knew better than to complain. Thanks to Thrane, and everyone's efforts to save Felix, most of our medical supplies were probably gone.

As we entered the main room, the instructors and avians gathered there stared at me with a mixture of fear and hope. I hated that I didn't have better news for them. All I could do was shake my head.

Immediately, I sensed the morale in the room start to crumble.

"No dragons. No moving the trees. So I guess we try the jungle, then?" Felix spoke up as he came to meet us. "We should leave soon, before everyone's too weak from hunger to make the hike."

"This is suicide," another avian murmured nearby.

I wanted to agree with him, but for the sake of the rest of the group, I tried to sound confident. "If we are fast and silent, we might be able to make it through without causing much of a disturbance. I'll go out first in case we encounter anything. Jace and the instructors should form a barrier with all the other students in the center."

Felix crossed his arms stubbornly, "Yeah, right. Look at you; you've already almost lost your head to one of those monsters. I'm not letting you offer yourself up like some kind of martyr. I'm walking right beside you."

"Me too," Lyon agreed as he came to stand right next to Felix.

I stared at them and wondered if it was even worth trying to argue. I decided against it. Felix was too stubborn and Lyon would ride his coattails to the bitter end. Besides, having them both close by actually made me more confident. It was a stupid thing to hope for, but I was thinking maybe if either of them got into real danger, then my power would grow strong enough to make sure nothing from the jungle would come close.

"All right, let's get everyone up." Jace clapped a hand on my shoulder as he brushed by us.

He started rousing everyone and giving commands, and Felix joined him. I stood back and watched as the instructors advised everyone to have their weapons at the ready. Anyone with even a little skill at archery was encouraged to carry a bow and quiver. They poured what was left of our water into as many canteens as they could find, and started passing out our go-bags.

I was relieved to be reunited with the rest of my belongings. I found Beckah's handkerchief and carefully tucked it back under my vambrace without getting any blood on it. Of course, the only thing missing were my medical supplies, which had most likely been scavenged.

"Here," I heard Felix say right before he started roughly tying something around my head. One of my eyes went dark as he started wrapping cloth over the wound on my face like an eye patch. It was a piece he'd apparently cut off his cloak. "Jace said it was a scratch. Lucky for you it wasn't a bite. No venom in the claws. If it'd bit you, your whole face would start rotting off."

I looked at him with my uncovered eye, but I didn't know what to say except, "Thanks."

He shrugged. "It's better than watching you bleed all over the place. Good thing it missed your eye, huh?"

I wasn't ready to call myself lucky, yet. With my bag slung over one shoulder, I stood in front of the main entrance while a group of instructors moved their makeshift barricade out of the way. My heart was pounding, and I was beginning to question myself again. Willingly surrendering to that power for only a few seconds had weakened me so much before. I wondered if I could last the entire hike to the beach.

"It's seven miles to the beach," Felix announced. "If we don't get lost."

I sighed and drew my sword as the last piece of debris was cleared out of the way. "We won't. Getting lost is the least of our worries, anyway. There's still an angry shrike out there."

Felix chuckled and punched my arm so hard it almost knocked me over because I wasn't ready for it. "There's always something right? Shrike in a jungle full of killer plants, king drake and a prison camp full of angry guards—what's the difference?"

I punched him back as hard as I could. "Right. Just another work day for us."

"Not going to run away this time, are you?" Felix teased Lyon.

I didn't find it that funny, and neither did Lyon. He'd come over to stand with us, and kept staring at the ground while his face turned red. He didn't try to tease Felix back or defend himself. It was an awkward subject for all of us now.

We all fell silent as two instructors started working the crank that opened the big iron-gilded doors enough for us to slip out. The hinges groaned and creaked, and green light poured in. The rich jungle air flowed through the open doors, and I took a deep breath. I let it fill my lungs. Somehow, it made my body seem lighter and stronger. It was more refreshing to me than normal air.

Felix, Lyon, and I went out first. They both stared around with their mouths hanging open in silent awe at how the jungle had reclaimed the compound in only a short time. It was barely even recognizable. The sight made Felix draw his sword.

While the others followed us out, I kept my good eye and both ears alert for a shrike. In the dim light, I knew it would be hard to see until it was much too late because of its scales. But I had another, better way of detecting it. I let my mind reach out, spreading my senses over the area around us. If anything besides plants and trees got too close, I would know about it.

"All right, weirdo," Felix said as he poked me with his elbow and destroyed my concentration. "Do your thing."

I shot him a glare. "I was trying, idiot. Be quiet."

I couldn't risk him messing me up again, so I took a few steps away before I tried again. Slowly bowing my head to my chest, I let my eyes roll closed and my thoughts slowly fade into silence. I searched through my body for that fire. When I couldn't find it, I started to panic. I started to doubt myself again, and wonder if I wouldn't be able to do it at all.

Then I felt a hand rest on my shoulder. It was strong and warm, and it filled me with confidence. It soothed my worries and quieted all my doubts. My mind drifted back to that horrible moment when I thought Felix was going to die right in front of me at the whipping post, and found that fire flickering deep in my memories. It started to burn brighter, blazing outward through my chest and sizzling through my arms and legs.

When I looked to see who had touched me, but there was no one there. Felix and Lyon were still standing a few yards away, helping the others get into a block formation. For a moment, doubt started to leak back into my mind. I was confused and a little afraid.

"*Don't be afraid,*" my mother's voice whispered in my mind.

The heat inside me surged even brighter then, and set my heart ablaze. I wasn't alone. Somehow, she was with me. And whatever I was turning into, she didn't want me to fight it. She didn't want me to be afraid of it. Realizing that gave me courage. It gave me confidence that everything would be okay because this wasn't a mistake—I was supposed to be this way.

My body shuddered with the sudden wave of power. My mind broke into that state of eerie, perfect calm. Everything seemed to move in slow motion around me. I could see it all, the jungle with its many wonders, like it was a disobedient child. And I was here to deliver a well-deserved spanking.

"Let's go." My voice had become that strange, growling tone again. I knew by the way the others were looking at me that the eye they could see must have been glowing again. Tracing my tongue over my teeth, I could feel that my incisors on top and bottom had become long and pointed like animal fangs.

But this wasn't the time to be worried about that. I started into the jungle with Felix and Lyon on either side of me. The others followed a few steps behind, their weapons at the ready.

The foliage swallowed us like a green maze. It was disorienting at first because there was no horizon or sunlight to determine direction. But it didn't confuse me for long. I could feel the sea, or rather, I could sense the point in the distance where the forest ended even though it was a long way off. That was the direction I led everyone.

It didn't take five minutes for the first threat to show itself. The instant I knew something was approaching, I stopped dead in my tracks. The feeling of pressure coming from whatever was headed our way made me shudder, and made my aura of power ripple. Whatever was coming, it was large and strong.

Felix and Lyon stopped on either side of me. I could sense their fear. It wasn't the first time I could remember feeling a person's emotions like that. I remembered the morning after the officer's ball, when I had been able to glimpse a little of Felix's grief over his father. Just a simple touch on the shoulder had allowed me to tap into his feelings. I was doing the same thing now, except I didn't have to touch any of them.

At that moment, though, I was too distracted to think about their feelings much. My bigger concern was coming towards us with booming footsteps that echoed from the dense trees. The sound of them seemed to come from everywhere at once, and I could feel the ground flinching under my boots.

"Look there!" Felix shouted suddenly.

A monster nearly ten feet tall lumbered into our path, bringing with it a stench that reminded me of the paludix turtle. It was the smell of old, rotting leaves, fermented swamp water, and decaying plants. Not something you'd want to run into on purpose. But this creature definitely was *not* a turtle. In fact, it looked more like a giant wolf. Its fur was so matted with leaves, sticks, and mud that it almost seemed to be made out of the jungle itself. Its white eyes flickered like bog fires in the dim light, and it was starting right at us.

As soon as it saw us, the beast stopped. I could hear its deep, growling breaths. Slowly, its snout start to wrinkle, showing us giant yellow fangs. I could sense the chaos rolling off the monster's body like a poisonous smog. It hit my nostrils and made the fire in my body blaze with fury. For whatever reason, feeling this creature turn against me filled me with unspeakable anger. It was like being betrayed by a family member I had trusted. I refused to stand for it.

The beast started hunkering down with intent to strike. I felt my irritation grow in response. Felix tried to stop me as I started walking toward it, but I jerked away from him.

"No," I commanded the monster. My voice sounded bizarre, like a mismatched chorus of different languages all speaking at once.

The beast growled so loudly it made the earth tremble. Its flickering eyes were fixed on me, and I raised a hand toward it, letting it feel the heat of my power like a silent warning. I didn't want to fight. I only wanted the respect I deserved.

"You will regret your disobedience," I promised.

The monster bristled, the matted fur raising along its neck and back. Chaos resonated so deeply inside it, entangling with its free will like a knotted ball of string. I knew it would attack no matter what I said. There was no reasoning with it.

With a twist of my wrist, the earth began to shift. Vines burst from the ground like before, growing to be as thick as a man's arm, and wrapping around the monster's legs and neck. It fought, snarling and biting as it tried to get free. But for every vine it broke, three more grew in its place until the creature was pinned against the ground. It let out a howl of frustration.

The other dragonriders behind me didn't make a sound. They all stared like they weren't sure what to be more afraid of: me or the monster I'd just brought down.

I stepped toward the pinned beast. It stared back at me through the fog of that chaos and the vines that were holding its head to the ground like a hundred giant pythons. I could sense its panic and rage. I knew even though I had established my dominance, if I let that creature go now, it would still try to attack us rather than flee. I couldn't allow that.

So I drove my sword into its skull.

Immediately, the beast's energy began to fade away, taking that sense of mindless fury with it. It drew one last, rasping breath, and finally lay still and soundless.

Behind me, Lyon was whispering, "He just killed a rotwolf with one blow."

I snapped a punishing gaze back at him. The death of this animal was not something to celebrate. Feeling its life slip away gave me the same sense of despair as when I had killed Thrane. Even in my anger, seeing a life be crushed was like watching someone smash a glass sculpture into bits. It wasn't fixable. It wasn't something you could ever duplicate again. It was destroyed forever, and I was to blame.

Suddenly, my legs started to feel weak and numb. I stumbled, and Felix rushed up to catch me. I noticed my nose was bleeding. We still had a long way to go… and I was already beginning to feel the effects of using so much of my power. I wasn't sure I would make it seven minutes, let alone seven miles.

It was time to do something radical again—before I was too weak to do anything at all.

I pushed away from Felix and widened my stance, gripping my sword in both hands and raising it high above my head. I threw my head back, looking to the trees overhead, but pressing all my thoughts and power into the ground under my feet. The vines seemed to be my most obedient tool. I could use them easily. So I would use them as much as I possibly could to save my dragonrider brothers.

I plunged my sword down into the ground with all my might, and at the same time, poured every ounce of my will into the earth with it. The ground began to rumble. The trees groaned. The wind howled around me, and a wave of wild energy spread out through every inch of the island.

Vines burst from the ground again on each side of me. But instead of a few, or a dozen, it was hundreds—maybe even thousands. Some were normal-sized, others were as big as tree trunks. They snaked across the ground, compiling and weaving together to create a living barrier around us. They continued on into the forest, mixing with the trunks and branches of the trees, and forming a protective tunnel that led away into the jungle. It was seven miles long, and would take my brothers all the way to the beach.

My whole body shook with exhaustion as I pulled my blade from the soil. I could barely grip it, and I tried not to let it show. The others stared at my creation. They stared at me, too.

"Go," I said without looking back. "This will take you safely to the beach."

The instructors didn't stop to ask any questions. I guess they had seen enough miracles already to obey me. They herded the rest of my avian peers toward the tunnel, making a wide berth around me as they hurried past.

Felix, Lyon, and Jace didn't follow them. They stood around me, but no one seemed ready to say why. I waited for someone to give me an explanation, searching the faces of my friends one by one. I could sense their apprehension, their awe, and their fear. They were afraid of me, even if none of them were ready to admit that.

"We aren't leaving without you," Lyon finally said.

"Don't be stupid," I snarled at him angrily. Didn't he realize I was doing all of this for them? If they didn't go, then all my efforts were for nothing. "I've served my purpose. Go with them. *Now*!"

"Knock it off," Felix growled back at me. "We've come this far together. We won't let them throw you in some prison camp. You have to trust us."

I laughed darkly, and all the voices mixed with mine laughed, too. "You honestly think there is any prison in the world that can hold me now?"

That made them all look a little pale.

"I am master here. This is where I belong." I turned a wrathful glare to Felix.

"Okay, master, but you're bleeding from the ears now, too. You have to stop. You're killing yourself." Felix took a fearless step toward me.

I touched one of my ears, and saw that he was right. Blood was dripping from both of them. That rattled me. I dropped my sword and staggered back away from them. Through the flames of power burning inside me, I had a moment of clarity. I knew Felix was right. I had to stop.

It was harder to call back the flames this time. They burned so freely through my body, filling me with that intoxicating heat and power. Getting it under control was as much a fight as calling it out had been. The fire didn't want to be contained. It wanted to burn forever, even if it consumed and killed me in the process.

A sudden screeching cry made us all look up at once. I knew that sound just as well as they did, and it stoked that roaring fire in my chest all over again. It was a shrike.

"Time to go," Jace ordered as he drew an arrow from his quiver. "Grab him, and let's go!" His voice was drowned out by another screech, and then another, and another. One shrike was bad enough, but now it sounded like we were facing a whole flock of them.

Felix threw my arm over his shoulder and started dragging me into my tunnel of vines with them. We ran, or in my case staggered, as fast as we could over the ferns, rocks, roots, and fallen trees. Being in the vine tunnel made things darker than usual, and after tripping all over ourselves for a few minutes, Jace finally stopped and tore open his go-bag. He pulled out his candle and lit it. Felix and Lyon did the same. Then we started running again.

"They're following us," I said as lifted my good eye to the ceiling of the vine-tunnel. I could feel them there, beyond the barrier I had created. They moved so quickly, flying through the twisted arms of the trees with more speed and agility than a dragon could ever dream of.

"How many?" Jace demanded.

"Four on the outside." I answered. "They're looking for a way in. Two are already in the tunnel, chasing us. They're too wary of me to come closer, but not for much longer." My body was starting to fail me in more ways than one. My legs were completely numb, and I was beginning to have trouble breathing. It reminded me of that horrible coma-like state I had been put in when I'd healed Sile's wife. That must have come from pushing myself too far.

Jace cursed, and we kept running. I held on for as long as I could, but about a half a mile from the end of the tunnel, I couldn't take another step. I crumpled to the ground, bringing Felix down with me. My ears were ringing so loudly that everything else was muffled. The fire suddenly snuffed out leaving me limp, drained, and completely useless. I couldn't move at all.

Felix hooked his arms around my chest and tried to drag me. It didn't work. The ground wasn't flat and smooth. It was the jungle, after all. The soil was wet and spongy, riddled with all kinds of snags and roots. He only made it a few feet before he tripped and fell, almost landing on top of me.

"I won't leave him!" I heard Felix roar in frustration.

"There's no choice!" Jace bellowed back.

From down the tunnel, I heard the screeching of the shrikes coming closer now. I couldn't defend my friends anymore. Bits of bark and wood started falling from the ceiling of the tunnel, raining down upon us. The shrikes on the outside were using their venom-laced teeth to gnaw through the vine tunnel.

We were out of time. And I was out of miracles.

I was busy making peace with my demise when I felt something prick at my mind. Even in my paralyzed state, something familiar reached me through the numbness and exhaustion. It was a presence I knew all too well, and the last one in the world I thought would ever find me here. It was a presence so great, so old and powerful, not even the canopy of the jungle could keep it from reaching me.

There was an explosion from overhead. Felix, Lyon, and Jace dove for cover. I still couldn't move my body, so I kept lying there, staring up into the dark with my one uncovered eye, and hoping someone would remember to drag me out of the way before I got crushed or eaten.

I needed to make a noise. They were looking for us, and when my power was snuffed out so suddenly, they had lost track of me. But I knew that this was our last hope. They had to find us, or it was all over.

I called upon all the power I had left. Even if it killed me, I knew it might save my friends. It took every ounce of my will to call out with my thoughts, *Here. I'm here.*

His answer was a roar like the eruption of a volcano.

Icarus dropped through the canopy like a boiling inferno, bathing the forest in his dragon fire and smashing the trees with his giant wings. He was big enough to crush his way down, making a path through the foliage and a hole in my vine tunnel. Sunlight poured down over us.

Icarus's show didn't last. He couldn't stay on the ground, and just as violently as he arrived, he started wriggling free of the branches and bursting back up into the air. The shrikes emerged from the forest again, four in all, and started to attack us.

I fought with all my might to get up, but I couldn't even wiggle a finger. A shrike made a vicious lunge at me. I couldn't move to fight, let alone flee. I thought I was dead for sure until an arrow caught it in the head ... right between the eyes.. It dropped dead immediately.

Everyone was still getting up. Felix had his sword in his hand. Jace was scrambling to get his bow ready. Even Lyon was running toward me, sword in hand, shouting my name. He skidded to a stop right beside me, crouching down and taking up a defensive stance like he was going to protect me while the others fought.

But only one person was doing any real fighting.

From up in the trees, arrows rained down with deadly accuracy. Two caught another shrike in the back of the skull, killing it just as instantly as the first. I caught of glimpse of her stepping along the tree branches like a phantom. I couldn't see her face since she was wearing a helmet, but I knew it was her. Beckah was fighting with us.

And she was starting to make us look bad.

When she ran out of arrows, she dropped from the trees into a crouch and drew a pair of long, slender scimitars from a sheath on her back. Her body was completely covered in sleek black battle armor that was painted with six sets of golden angel wings on the helmet, chest, back, forearms, legs, and feet. Her face was completely covered. To look at her, no one ever would have known it was a girl under all that armor. She'd grown so much she really just looked like a small, skinny guy.

Beckah may have looked like a knight, but she fought like a demon. Her strikes were so fast, I knew I wouldn't have been able to keep up with them. She never missed. She never hesitated. And she killed all the shrikes who attacked her in less than five minutes, making it look like child's play.

Everything was quiet except for the crackle of burning dragon venom still smoldering on a few of the trees. Beckah stood over her last kill with her blades dripping with blood. Slowly, she turned to look at us through her helmet's small eye slits.

Jace, Felix, and Lyon were speechless. They hadn't even moved, or tried to help her fight at all. It was over before they could find their weapons and figure out what was going on.

"W-Who are you?" Lyon stammered in awe.

"Seraph," she answered in a deep, hoarse tone. She must have been trying to make her voice sound like a man's.

Just as she was turning away, placing her blades back on the sheath across her back, something rustled behind us. I couldn't move or look to see what it was. But I saw Beckah whip around suddenly, ripping her scimitars back out again.

There was a gory, crunching sound.

Someone let out a garbled scream, and out of the corner of my eye, I saw Lyon crumple to the ground. There was a shrike on him, digging its teeth into the back of his neck.

Beckah sprang back into action before anyone else. She moved out of sight like a black shadow, but I could still hear the sounds of combat and the dying screech of the shrike. It must have been slinking around in the dark, waiting for the perfect time to attack. With my body drained of all its strength and power, I couldn't even sense the shrike let alone warn any of them.

The others started shouting in panic. I couldn't see Lyon. I couldn't tell if he was still alive. All my abilities had completely fizzled out, so I couldn't even try to sense if he was there or not. Pure panic coursed through my body as I lay helpless because of how much of my power I had already used. With all that remained of my physical strength, I was able to turn my head enough to see where Lyon was lying only a few feet away.

They were trying to stop the bleeding. Jace was pumping on his chest and breathing into his mouth. But Lyon already had a distant expression on his face. His eyes were glazed over, and his skin looked pale.

Lyon was dead.

26

CHAPTER TWENTY-SIX

Everyone was complaining about the rain. Sitting in the dining hall, I listened to the chatter of my peers as they enjoyed their dinner. It was our last meal together before graduation. Tomorrow, at first light, we were going to be sent off to the royal city of Halfax to officially be sworn into the king's service. What would follow would be a grand celebration, and then we would learn where our next assignment would take us. But everyone was worried that the rain might slow us down.

Felix sat right beside me. He hadn't left me alone for days except to attend Lyon's funeral. Of course, I hadn't been invited. It was only for nobles and close friends. But I wrote a long letter of apology to Lyon to be burned on his funeral pyre. Felix agreed to take it, even though I still hadn't spoken to him. I hadn't really spoken to anyone, though. There was a lot I needed to sort out before I felt like talking about it.

First of all, it was still sinking in that I wasn't about to be shipped off to a prison camp or locked in a dungeon. The instructors and avians from the battle scenario hadn't spoken a word about anything I had done on the island. They all acted like nothing bizarre had happened at all, apart from things going awry when a few animals went crazy. They had blamed it all—including Thrane's death—on the jungle coming alive and attacking us. Commander Rayken wasn't even suspicious of me.

After a few days of hanging in suspense, waiting for the doors to burst open and elite guards to slap shackles on my wrists, I started to wonder if it had all just been a nightmare. I was thinking that again, hoping that somehow it had been another one of my horrible dreams. Then I glanced to my other side where Lyon usually sat, and that stupid hope came crashing down around my ears. His seat was empty. Lyon was gone, and he wasn't coming back. He was dead because I hadn't been strong enough to keep my own power under control.

I knew Felix would be furious if he knew I was thinking those kinds of things. I couldn't help it. I was the only one who could have healed his injuries. I could have saved him. Instead I made a stupid tunnel out of vines that had nearly put me into another coma. It had taken days for me to be able to move normally again, and in that time, I could only lie there while everyone else grieved and mourned for my friend.

My other worry was about Beckah. I hadn't seen or heard from her since she had appeared to save us on the island. The other riders were talking about her plenty, though. They didn't know it was a girl under that helmet, but everyone was very impressed with a knight who had been able to take control of Icarus and could fight so well without ever setting foot in the academy. Rumors were flying about the mystery knight's real identity, and some people were even suggesting it might be the King of Maldobar himself.

"Nah, the king is way too old for that. You should have seen this guy. He had to be young to be that fast. He called himself Seraph," Felix explained.

He was telling the story again to a table full of our peers. When he glanced my way, our eyes met, and I knew he was keeping the rumor going on purpose. He knew who was really under that armor, thanks to me. I'd already told him about Beckah being chosen as a dragonrider, and I knew he wasn't stupid enough to believe it was anyone except her.

I waited until after dinner to finally ask the question that was driving me crazy. "Why are you keeping her secret?"

Felix closed the door to our dorm room and sat down on the edge of his bed. Behind him, Lyon's bed was still empty and untouched—exactly the way he had left it before the battle scenario.

"Because there may come a time when we need her help again." He sighed and rubbed his forehead. "So you've decided to talk now?"

I sat down on my bed across from him. "I'm trying to understand what happened... and why no one has arrested me yet."

Felix snorted like that was a bad joke. "No one is going to say a word about it, Jae. You saved us. Monster or maniac, those guys don't care what you are as long as you're on our side. And you proved that a hundred times over. No one would have made it off that island if you hadn't intervened. They know that. I know it. You just aren't ready to admit it, yet."

"I'm a halfbreed. They used to care a lot about that," I reminded him coldly.

"Things change. Sometimes even people change, too. Since you came here last year, you've made everyone second guess what they thought about halfbreeds." He sighed and shook his head. "As much as I hate to admit it, you were right about Lyon. He was able to change, and I didn't want to let myself see it. Now it's too late and I'll feel like a jerk forever."

"Not forever," I said.

Felix shook his head. "I wasn't going to tell you about this. I wasn't even close friends with him like you were, but hearing it made me sick. When I went to his funeral, I saw his father and grandfather standing in their old dragonrider armor. I went up to talk to them, since they were both pretty famous before they retired, and as soon as I got close enough to hear them talking... it all started to make sense."

"What made sense?" I stared at him.

"Why Lyon ran that night at the prison camp. Why he was so mean to you, and why he seemed to hate me so much before. His dad and grandfather were talking about how Lyon was such a disappointment to them. I couldn't believe it," he said, and as he spoke, his voice started to shake with emotion. I saw rage filling his eyes. "At first, I thought I was imagining it, or that maybe they were talking about someone else. But they were standing there, over his funeral pyre, talking about how he'd never been cut out to be a dragonrider. They said they never understood before why he didn't want to go to the academy in the first place. Now, they said they saw it was because he couldn't handle it. They called him weak for not trying harder, and said it was better that he never stepped foot on the battle field."

Felix had to stop and calm down. He was so furious he was clenching his fists so hard that his knuckles turned white. "For me it was the opposite, you know. I wanted this so badly, even though my parents didn't approve. Lyon didn't want to be a dragonrider. He must've been terrified the whole time. I'm sure knocking you around when you were little probably made him feel like he actually belonged here. It probably made him feel braver and stronger."

"Probably," I agreed.

"I wanted to punch them both in the neck for talking about him like that," Felix snarled. He was clenching his teeth. "But I stood there and realized I was just as guilty as they were. I hated him, Jae. I wanted an excuse to beat him up all the time. And I'm not saying what he did to you was right, but..."

"It's okay. I understand." I started rubbing at my face. My fingers traced over the stitches on my forehead and cheek. The medic had done the best he could fixing my face from where the shrike had scratched me, but he said it would definitely leave a scar. A memory etched into my skin.

"Where do we go from here?" Felix asked. When I looked at him again, he was staring at me with the most haunted expression on his face.

"I'm going wherever they send me," I told him. "I guess you have to decide again whether or not you're going to stay with the dragonriders or go be a duke."

He pressed his lips together into a frown. "That's not what I meant. I'm already a duke. My mom signed the estate over to me, and I gave her permission to act in my place when I'm not there. I'm going with you to war, Jae."

"Then what do you mean?"

"I mean, Lyon is dead, the animals and plants are conspiring to kill us all, and you're turning into some kind of vine-wielding forest deity. What do we do now?" He asked again. "What's happening to the world?"

I stopped to think about that. While I decided how to answer, I reached under the mattress of my bed and took out the scimitar Bren had restored for me. I ran my thumb over the elven crest on the pommel, the head of a stag engraved in the shimmering metal.

Felix stared down at it with wide eyes, and I could see his reflection in the side of the polished sheath. "Where did you get that?"

"I think I was supposed to find this." I sat the blade down on the bed beside me, and started digging under my mattress again. I pulled out the bone-carved necklace my mother had given me and put it back around my neck. It felt good to have the familiar weight of that talisman against my chest again. "I think I've been missing a lot of things I was supposed to find. Answers that have been staring me in the face all this time."

"Answers? To what?"

I started unlacing my boots and unbuckling my belt, changing into my night clothes. "To the same questions we've all been asking ourselves since the first time I called to Mavrik. What am I? Why do I have these powers? What am I meant to do with them?"

Felix shifted uncomfortably, and eyed me skeptically. "And you think you know how to figure all that out now?"

"Maybe not all of it, but I think I know where to start." I crawled into bed and held the scimitar against my chest. "Goodnight, Felix."

I could sense him scowling at me. It was like a familiar stink in the air. He didn't like vague answers, but I wanted to wait until I was sure before I shared it with him. Beckah had suggested I listen to my dreams, and now I was beginning to believe she was right. I needed answers. And so far, my dreams held the only person in the world who could give them to me.

I STOOD ON THE MUDDY ROAD. AROUND ME WAS THE SNOWY VALLEY, WHITE-crested mountains, and the looming wall of trees I knew was Luntharda. The air was so cold it made me gasp, and the sunlight sparkled over the snowdrifts. Before, when I saw this place in my dreams, it had always filled me with fear because I knew what was coming. I clenched my teeth and tried to control my emotions.

I wasn't going to be afraid. I was determined to see it all, to the bitter end.

"It's just a dream," I reminded myself out loud.

"No, not a dream," a familiar voice spoke softly. "A memory."

I looked, surprised to see a new figure standing right next to me. It was my mother.

She was much shorter than I was, giving me a real appreciation for how petite her people usually were, and how different I was by comparison. Her silver hair was flowing down her back, and her strange eyes reflected the blue sky, making them shine like aquamarines. Her clothes were strange and exotic. She was draped in one long ivory sheet of silk dotted with stitching of green vines and purple flowers. It was wrapped around her like some kind of ancient goddess, and there was a golden band in her hair made to look like rose vines twisted together. She looked ageless and powerful, and it surprised me. I'd never seen my mother look like that.

"But I don't remember any of this," I argued with her.

She smiled without ever looking back at me. "I never said they were *your* memories, dulcu. Now hush. I cannot stay with you much longer. My presence draws his attention."

I obeyed and turned my gaze to the road again. I stood beside my mother in the muddy road, prepared to face what was going to happen next. Neither of us said a word as we waited. In the distance, I heard a horse whinny. Anxiety started to swirl through my brain as the carriage and company of guards approached. Knowing what was about to happen made dread turn my stomach sour.

The Gray elf warrior appeared, just like before. When he spoke, I noticed my mother's expression was hardening. Her eyes seemed to darken with frustration and disapproval, and when he drew his blade and started to slaughter the guards, she turned her face away. There were tears in her eyes.

I couldn't comfort her. I couldn't even move except to turn my head around some, so I watched the battle again. Emotion swelled in my chest with every passing second. Overhead, I heard the familiar screech of a shrike. I could see its shadow blur over the ground as it flew around us. Each swing of the Gray elf's blade made my heart pound painfully. He dragged the king out of the carriage like before, and murdered him first. Nothing about the scene seemed different this time, though. I had seen it play out so many times, after all. I wanted it to be over.

But then something caught my eye.

The glimmer of sunlight off metal made me look at the king again. He lay on his stomach in the mud, motionless and dead, but there was something sticking out from under his cloak. It was the hilt of a blade.

My heart hit the back of my throat so hard I couldn't catch my breath.

I knew that blade. I knew it because *I* was the one carrying it now. It was my scimitar, the one with the elven crest on the pommel. It had belonged to the King of Maldobar!

Beckah's words resonated in my mind like an echo, reminding me why I had to pay attention. All my anxiety melted away. She was right, I had been missing things because I was too afraid to watch. Emotion had clouded my sight, and my own fear had pulled the dream apart.

I braced myself, setting my eyes upon the Gray elf warrior. He moved like a predator over the bodies of the people he had murdered. His sneer was ruthless, and he cut his eyes right past me to look as the wounded guard, the only survivor, stood up shakily with his sword in hand.

The guard could barely keep a grip on his own weapon. Blood made his hands slick, and there was a deep gash on his leg that would definitely be deadly if it were left untreated. But I could see him fix his eyes upon the Gray elf through the slit in his helmet. Something about him was so familiar, and I studied him over and over trying to figure out why. I still couldn't see enough of his face to recognize him, though.

"Aren't you brave?" The Gray elf warrior taunted, spinning his strange white blade like it was weightless. "Tell me, little soldier, just how brave are you? What would you do to save your own life?"

I saw the guard brace for the attack, squaring his stance and preparing to stand and fight. My heart was beating out of control, and every fiber of my being cried out to let me step in and stop this. But I knew better now. It wasn't real. I had to watch. I had to see and understand.

The Gray elf lunged like a panther, crossing the distance between them as the guard raised his sword and prepared to defend. They collided in combat, locking blades and pressing in to test each other's strength.

"You are made of tougher stuff than the rest of these fools," the Gray elf purred with approval, grinning from ear to ear. "You might be very useful indeed." He twisted his stance in the blink of an eye, easily dropping the guard to the ground by kicking his already wounded leg.

The guard scrambled to get away. It was no good. The Gray elf planted a foot on his chest to pin him down, and lowered the tip of his sword until it barely touched the guard's throat. He was caught with no choice but to lie there, staring death in the eye.

"Perhaps destroying such bravery and strength would be a waste, even if you are only a human. Why don't we make a bargain, you and I? You want to live, and I need an errand boy. You see, there's something that belongs to me hidden away in that forest. An artifact my people call the god stone," the Gray elf said as he pressed his blade a little harder against the guard's throat. "Bring it to me, and not only will I spare your life, but I will reward you handsomely. Betray me, and I will hunt you down to the ends of the earth, along with everyone you have ever cared for. You will watch your entire family, your friends and loved ones, all pay the price for your disloyalty."

I waited in horrified silence. I couldn't imagine the Gray elf would ever keep his word, or that the guard would even agree to help this murderer. Everything about this was wrong.

"Swear to me," the guard rasped from under his helmet. "Swear that you will not lay a hand on my family, if I agree."

The Gray elf's grin widened. His eyes glittered maliciously, like a spider eyeing a fly caught in its web. "I swear it on the god stone."

A hot, buzzing sensation pricked at the back of my mind. It made me shiver at those words.

"Then I agree." The guard reached for the point of the blade at his throat and pushed it away. He started to get up, limping on his wounded leg and meeting the Gray elf's gaze with a bitter, defiant glare.

I recognized that glare an instant before he started taking off his helmet. It fell from his hand, and my heart fell with it. The helmet made a sound like an empty metal bucket when it hit the ground and rolled away.

The guard brushed a hand through his hair, and turned so that he was looking right in my direction. I could see his face. He was scowling toward me with the same harrowing look in his eyes I had seen a thousand times before.

I knew exactly who he was.

27

CHAPTER TWENTY-SEVEN

I couldn't eat breakfast. The sight of food made me even sicker, as though all my insides were rotting away. I sat with my eyes squeezed shut, trying to see anything but the image that was burned into my mind like it had been branded there. It was the face of someone I knew, someone I had thought I understood. Now I knew I was only beginning to truly understand the truth—the ugly, despicable, awful truth.

Felix elbowed me as he got up, letting me know it was time to go. We had to leave for the graduation ceremony soon. My mind was hazy as we gathered up our bags again, put on our armor, and saddled our dragons. Only the graduating avians were allowed to leave, which amounted to about twenty of us in all. The rest were either too wounded, or hadn't performed well enough to pass. They would have to wear another stripe and try again next year. I should have been proud to be one of the students who had been given the honor of graduating, but all I felt was complete disgust with myself. I had been so blind for so long, and the truth had been staring me right in the face.

A few instructors, including Jace, had volunteered to go with us as chaperones. I was surprised to see him standing in Mavrik's stall when I came in. My former instructor was standing there, already dressed in his armor, casually chewing a piece of straw. He glanced at me, and frowned down at the scimitar hanging off my belt.

"Interesting choice of weapon," he mumbled. "Some would call that heresy, or even treason."

"Are you going to ask me whose side I'm on again?" I snapped with as much defiance as I dared. I walked past him and started buckling my bags onto Mavrik's back.

Jace snorted. "No. I came here to ask if you wanted to be my wing end."

I froze. Slowly, I turned around to make sure I wasn't hallucinating. "You still want to fight with me? Even after what you've seen me do?"

"Actually, I'm surprised I'm the only one who's asked you. I guess the others are waiting until after you graduate. Lucky me for getting to you first." He smirked and nodded toward Mavrik. "You two are the only ones to ever be able to keep up with Ghost and me. My last partner couldn't keep in formation. That's why he got killed. You think you can handle being my wing end?"

I debated pinching myself to make sure this was really happening. But I didn't want to run the risk of looking like an idiot, so I nodded. "Only if you think you can handle my occasional weirdness."

Jace's smirk widened, and it was starting to freak me out. Smiling came about as naturally to him as it did to a hungry wolf. "I'm counting on it. After all, we're the only ones who stand any chance in an aerial skirmish with shrikes. Being able to talk to Ghost and anticipate his moves makes you my number one choice."

Thinking about shrikes made me sick all over again. I went back to buckling down my gear and put my helmet on. "So, I guess that will put us on the frontlines?"

"To the worst parts of them, in fact. We'll be going to Northwatch. We deploy from here in five days. That should give you time to get things squared away at home—that is, unless you planned on getting married before you leave." Jace stopped on his way out the door and gave me an expectant look. "Were you?"

I was so glad I already had my helmet on so he couldn't see me blush. "No, sir."

He made a grunting sound, like he approved. "Good. Then don't be late. And quit calling me sir; I'm not your instructor anymore."

THE CLOSER WE GOT TO HALFAX, THE HEAVIER THE SECRET I WAS CARRYING became. It threatened to break me, to send me spiraling into a reckless rage that would more than likely get me killed. I struggled to keep it together and remain calm. There was still so much uncertainty. My mother had told me I was watching a memory instead of a dream, but wasn't she merely a dream, too? She had died a long time ago, and I was certain about that. How could I trust what I saw in my dreams wasn't a trick of my own mind? Felix had seemed so sure that the real king wasn't dead. I knew he would never lie to me, especially not about something like that.

We started our final descent to the royal city, and I could hear music even several hundred feet in the air. I could see the streets around the castle were filled with people coming to welcome us. As we got closer, Jace took the lead and brought us to a wide, open courtyard in the middle of a beautiful garden right in the middle of the city. There was enough room for all of us to land together, and people cheered as we arrived. They threw so many flowers and petals that it looked like colorful snow.

"Keep your helmets on," Jace warned us as we all dismounted.

Dressed in our finest armor, with sweeping black capes buckled over our shoulders, we followed him as he led the way down a white stone path that wound through the city. The path led all the way up to the front gates of the castle. Everywhere we went, people were clambering to see us. Girls threw handkerchiefs. Kids waved flags with the king's eagle on them. I saw lots of them with their faces painted to look like dragons. It was a huge celebration, but I was almost too anxious to enjoy it.

"Why can't we take our helmets off?" I whispered to Felix. He was walking right next to me, waving to the crowd and drinking in all the adoring looks the girls were giving us.

"For you, idiot." He winked at me through the eye slit in his helmet.

I frowned. Right away I knew Jace was trying to shield me from any more discrimination. He didn't want the crowds to see I was a halfbreed, probably because he was concerned they wouldn't accept me. But I was not in the mood to be coddled like some child who might get his feelings hurt. I did have some pride left.

I ripped my helmet off and stuck it under my arm. A few people standing nearby gasped so loud I could actually hear them over the noise. They stared at me in complete horror. A young girl screamed.

Jace whipped around and glared like he might actually punch me. "What are you doing?"

I glared back at him. "They'll find out sooner or later. I can't change what I am, so either they will learn to accept me, or they won't. Either way, it isn't my problem."

Felix took off his helmet, too. He was grinning and laughing when he draped an arm over my shoulder. That made even more people gasp in horror. "He's right. Let's have a good time."

When he took off his helmet, I could see Jace's nostrils were flared like an angry dragon about to breathe fire. But he didn't say anything else about it. He kept walking toward the castle gates, and we followed while we waved to the crowd.

People were definitely staring at me. Most of them didn't look happy. They probably had never seen a halfbreed before, and definitely not one wearing a dragonrider's armor. But nothing they said could touch me now, though.

I looked through all the unfamiliar faces, and didn't see a single person I knew. There were no Gray elves in the audience, either. They were all locked away in the poor ghetto where I had lived with my mother, only a few blocks away from where I was standing at that moment. Thinking about it made my insides twist painfully.

The king was waiting for us at the front steps of the castle. The huge gates were open wide to let everyone inside the perfectly manicured courtyard. People poured in by the hundreds. Banners hung off every roof and gable, and garlands of roses adorned either side of the walkway leading up to the front steps. Guards in gleaming armor stood at attention, their swords drawn in a parade stance as we passed.

But I couldn't look at anyone, or anything, except the king. He was at the top of the staircase that swept up from the courtyard to the front doors. There were six elite guards on either side of him, all wearing those white masks I remembered all too well. The sight of them made my chest burn dangerously again, and I clenched my fists to keep from lashing out. I reminded myself over and over that I had no proof. There was no evidence except for a dream and a coincidence. That wasn't nearly enough for me to do or say anything.

Felix had been telling the truth when he said the king looked pitiful. He was small, bent over like an old man, and every inch of his body was covered—even his face. He wore a porcelain mask painted in blue, red, and gold. It looked regal, and was supposedly hiding the gruesome scars of his battle with a shrike.

One by one, we each went up the stairs alone to meet the king. Felix went ahead of me. He knelt at the king's feet, kissed the royal signet ring on his hand, and swore an oath to be obedient until death. Then they took off his old black cloak, and put a new blue and gold one in its place.

Suddenly, it was my turn.

As I walked past Jace, he muttered, "Don't look him in the eye. Keep your head down. And for kingdom's sake, don't do anything stupid."

I didn't answer. I was wondering what, exactly, he meant by "stupid." Tripping, maybe? Or drawing my sword and ramming it through the so-called king's chest before his elite guards could save him? Both were definitely stupid, and entirely possible for me at that point.

At the top of the staircase, I decided to follow Jace's advice. I kept my head bowed, and my eyes on my boots as I knelt before the king. Being close to him made my heart beat loudly in my ears. Over and over, I reminded myself that there was no proof. It was a dream. I couldn't do anything based on a dream.

The king's hand appeared in front of my face. It was covered in a white glove, and there was a big golden signet ring on his middle finger with the shape of an eagle engraved on it. My soul burned as I kissed it. The metal tasted bitter.

"This is the first time a halfbreed has ever knelt at my feet." The king spoke in a hoarse, gravelly voice that made his words hard to understand. "How did you become a dragonrider?"

I couldn't help myself. Slowly, I looked up and met the king's eyes through the holes in his mask. They were bloodshot, and their color reminded me of cracked amber glass.

"I was chosen," I said.

The king didn't reply. He stood there, staring back at me until I lowered my eyes again. Then he went on with the ceremony like nothing had happened. He spoke the oath, and the words passed over my ears like white-hot flames. "Do you swear yourself to the service of the kingdom of Maldobar? To protect it and its people with every bit of your strength, even unto your dying breath? And do you swear yourself to the service of its king, to honor and obey him in all things without hesitation?"

I hesitated. I was thinking about doing one of those stupid things Jace had warned me about. Then I bit my tongue, and squeezed my eyes shut. "I swear."

The elite guards removed my old black cloak, and clasped the blue and gold one onto my shoulder armor. It was made of expensive silk, and the neck was trimmed with white fox fur. When I stood, there as a reluctant round of applause, and I went back down the steps feeling like I had just sold my soul to a demon.

I didn't smile. I didn't wave. This wasn't something to be happy about, much less proud of.

When everyone in our group, except the two instructors, had gone up to take their oath, the crowds erupted in cheering and applause. Music and laughter filled the air. People rushed in upon us, eager to meet the newest dragonriders to join the ranks.

Not many people came close to me. Only a few brave souls dared to smile and bow, or offer me a handshake. But I could sense their apprehension and disapproval when they did. The only ones who didn't give me that kind of greeting were the children. They didn't seem to care what I looked like, and a few of them rushed up to stare at me and ask me weird questions, like how heavy my shield was, before darting away.

The sunset drove the people out of the streets, but it didn't put a stop to the festivities. The castle wasn't open to us, but every single shop and home in Halfax was. Felix was set on going from tavern to tavern until he was too drunk to stand up. The others seemed to like that idea, but I had other plans for the evening. I followed them to the first few taverns, watching as they laughed and eager citizens bought drinks for them and thanked them for their service.

"We'll be getting our first lieutenant's pay soon!" Felix chuckled. He had that mischievous glint in his eyes. "Better drink up while it's free, and before some woman comes along and gets her hands on your money!"

I smiled at him. It was good to see him in high spirits again. I was beginning to realize he hid a lot under that cunning, dangerously charming smile—all the things he didn't want anyone else to see. I didn't know how to put up that kind of a barrier, not when all of my emotions smoldered so near the surface.

I waited until it was very late. We were on our fifth tavern, and I knew everyone was too distracted to realize I wasn't drinking. When I saw a good chance, I ducked out the back door of the tavern and walked the dark alleyways with my helmet still under my arm. I let my feet guide me, taking me on familiar secret paths I hadn't taken in years.

There was a hole in the wooden wall that separated the elven ghetto from the rest of the city. When I was little, I had used it to sneak in and out so I could run errands for my mom. But now I was way too big to fit through it anymore. That wasn't about to stop me, though. I pried the boards apart with my bare hands, and managed to squirm through the gap even with my armor on.

Beyond that fence, it was like stepping into another world. There was no light except for the moon and stars because it was well past curfew. The narrow dirt streets were empty. Trash was scattered everywhere. The wooden shacks leaned in all directions, looking more like piles of debris that had been raked together than something anyone would want to live in.

I passed several city guards on night patrol as I walked the dark, filthy streets of the ghetto. They stared at me, but as soon as they saw my armor, they hurried on their way and never said a word. Halfbreed or not, I was out of their reach now.

I walked past the old shack my mother and I had shared for so many years. Seeing how little it had changed put a pain in my chest like I'd been stabbed. I wanted to go inside and touch the things that had once been my entire world. But there was light coming from inside, and shadows were moving past the windows. Another family was living there now. So I stared at it for a moment before continuing on.

My feet carried me to a place I had almost forgotten. On the far edge of the ghetto, closest to the castle, there was a skinny, three-story building that backed right up against the perimeter fence. The old Gray elf woman who had lived in the shack beside it had made herself a lattice out of scrap wood, and she always grew flower vines on it in the springtime. I had used that lattice as a way to climb up to the roof of the building a few times, when I was feeling especially brave. You couldn't beat the view from up there.

The climb might have been easier because of my height, but my armor definitely made up for that. I clambered up to the flat stone roof, and sat on the edge like I had when I was little. I could see all the lights of the city stretching out around me. I could see the castle bathed in the light of a thousand torches. Overhead, the stars glittered beyond my ability to count.

This place still made me feel as small and forgotten as it had years ago. Once, that feeling had been so frustrating to me. Now, it was a nice change of pace. It felt good to be out of the spotlight for once.

"You're missing your own party, you know."

I jumped to my feet, turning around at the sound of a soft, feminine voice coming from behind me. Beckah was standing with her long dark hair spilling over her shoulders. In the glow of the city lights, I could see her smiling at me. It was more beautiful to me than all the stars hanging over our heads. It made my world move, and pulled toward her like an ocean tide.

"Sorry, I should have said something sooner. But I saw you sneaking away, and I wanted to see where you'd go." She started nibbling on her bottom lip.

I couldn't speak. I just ran to her and hugged her as hard as I could.

Beckah hugged me back. She put her arms around my waist, and buried her face against my breastplate.

For a long time, we stood there holding each other without ever saying a word. Finally, she pulled back so she could trace her fingers over the scar on my face. I saw her expression change, as though seeing it made her feel guilty.

"Does it hurt?" she whispered. "I'm so sorry. I should have gotten there sooner."

I took her hands and squeezed them firmly. "I can live with a few scars. You saved our lives, Beckah. That's the only thing that matters."

"I saw you lying there like you were dead. I was afraid I was too late. You were so pale, and you weren't moving, and—" She choked on her words. I saw her eyes welling up with tears, even though she was trying to smile at me. "I'm so glad I wasn't too late. I love you, Jae. I can't lose you."

I had been resisting doing stupid things all evening. Eventually, I was bound to slip up. When she told me that, I didn't even think about it. I grabbed her face and kissed her as hard as I could.

She gasped, and at first she was stiff. I was beginning to think this might be a mistake. I might be about to get punched in the face by a girl half my size. But then I felt her put her arms around my neck.

She kissed me back.

We sat together as the first light of dawn started to turn the skyline pink, slowly melting away the stars. I had an arm around her, and she was leaning against my side while holding my hand. It was the best feeling in the world.

"I'll be going to Northwatch," I told her. "Jace asked me to be his wing end."

She smiled strangely as she wriggled her hand down into my vambrace and pulled out the handkerchief she had stitched for me. Seeing it made her cheeks turn pink. "You carry it with you?"

I laughed. "You told me to!"

Beckah stuck her tongue out at me. "Do you always do what girls tell you? I heard you already kissed someone else before me."

Panic hit me right in the chest so hard I literally wheezed out loud. I stared at her and tried to think of how to explain. But when I tried, no sound would come out.

Then she started giggling. "Look at your face! You look like a fish gasping for air!"

"H-how did you know about that?" I managed to ask. "I-It's not what you think! Julianna practically attacked me!"

Beckah smirked and pinched my nose playfully. "Oh stop it, I know that already. Gossip travels fast, especially about a noble girl tackling a halfbreed like that. I wish I could have seen your face. But I bet you looked just like you do now." She started laughing again.

I still wasn't sure if it was safe to laugh with her or not. I gave a few careful chuckles and tried to remember how to breathe normally. "I thought you would be upset about that."

"Upset because some other girl kissed you?" She rolled her eyes. "Oh please. If I were going to be upset with anyone, it would be her not you. She's gone around telling everyone how you rejected her and broke her heart because you're in love with some mystery girl. But it was my fault, anyway. I shouldn't have left you alone at the ball. If I had stayed, it never would have happened."

I put a hand over my face to cover my embarrassment. "She promised she wouldn't tell anyone…"

"Only a man would believe something like that," Beckah quipped. "Women tell each other everything, Jae."

I filed that crucial information away for future reference. "Well, I'm sorry. I should've realized what she was up to."

Beckah smiled and planted a kiss on my cheek. "Don't worry about it. You're so naïve when it comes to girls, but it's really cute. And you're all mine now."

We sat in silence again, watching the sunrise. I was trying to figure out if being called cute was a good thing or not. She seemed happy and content. The morning light shining in her eyes made them sparkle. I could see all the freckles on her cheeks.

I hated to ruin the moment. I wanted this to last forever. But there was something I had to tell her, and I was running out of time. Soon, Felix and the others would come looking for me. Then I'd have to head back to the academy and prepare to deploy to Northwatch.

"Beckah." I squeezed her hand to get her attention.

She looked at me with that blissful smile still on her lips.

"I took your advice. I paid more attention to my dreams," I started to explain. Anxiety and bitterness made my hands shake, and I watched her smile start to fade away.

"What did you see?" she asked quietly.

I didn't know where to begin. So I told her everything I could think of as quickly as I could. I told her every detail of my dream, from beginning right up until the guard had taken off his helmet. I showed her the scimitar with the elven royal crest on the pommel, and explained how I had found it hidden in my half-brother's room. I told her how the dream, the Gray elf warrior had made a deal with the guard to let him live, but in exchange he had to take something from the forest. But not just anything. No, he only wanted the god stone.

Beckah listened. She studied me and the scimitar, and waited for me to give her that last piece of the puzzle. "The guard," she pressed when I didn't offer it up quickly enough. "You said he seemed familiar somehow. Do you have any idea who he is?"

"Yes," I answered through clenched teeth. "Before the dream ended, I saw his face."

"Who?" She was staring up at me with wide eyes and gripping my hand so hard it cut off my circulation. "Who is it?"

I hated the answer because if it was actually true, then I was just as responsible as he was. I hated seeing his face whenever I closed my eyes. It took all my self-control to keep from shouting as I glared at the royal castle.

"The guard in my dream, the traitor who made a deal with that murderer and stole the god stone from Luntharda," I growled furiously, "... is my father."

TRAITOR

The Dragonrider Chronicles Book Three

CHAPTER ONE

The world had changed.

And so had I. Nothing was simple anymore. Nothing was as it seemed—or as I thought it would be. I always lived my life with one little shred of confidence. Even though I had no idea where I was going, be it to a prison camp or to the dragonrider academy, I at least knew exactly where I'd come from. My mother was a beautiful, gentle Gray elf woman. My father was a cold, abusive, tyrannical human who made saddles for dragonriders. Those were facts I'd known I could rely on.

But as it turned out, not even that was true. Every passing night brought more dreams and more strangeness. Secrets were mocking me from the shadows of my past. I couldn't shut out the noise anymore. And it was beginning to wear away what little bit of sanity I had left.

When I had first set foot into Blybrig Academy for Dragonriders as a terrified child, I was the very last person you'd ever want to stick into a dragon saddle and send off into combat. But now, as I leaned into Mavrik's speed, feeling the strength of my dragon's wings as if they were my own ... I knew I wasn't that child anymore. I couldn't be.

I was a dragonrider—not only because I had been chosen, but also because Blybrig had made me one.

I'd fought through hell and back, been baptized in the inferno of combat and survival training to prove that I belonged here. Now I could stand and be counted among the men who called themselves the Dragonriders of Maldobar. I'd worked until I bled for every single step of progress. Was I terrified? Absolutely. Fear was a constant, but it paled in comparison to the sense of duty that burned in my gut now.

I wouldn't fail. I wouldn't falter. I would fight until my very last breath. Not for myself, or my own glory—I was fighting for the people I loved.

The battlefront was beckoning, and I couldn't ignore that call. No dragonrider could. But I'd seen what it had done to others of my kind, and that impending reality was frightening.

You see, the battlefield changes everyone. You can't get back what it takes from you, and you can't erase the marks it leaves behind. I could look at my instructors and tell that much. Not all of them had gruesome physical scars, but they all had the same dead look in their eyes. It was the look of a soldier—the somber sense that they had seen things they couldn't tell anyone about. They were living ghosts, mere specters of their former selves haunted by the things they'd done all for the sake of a blue banner bearing the king's seal.

I poured my thoughts into my dragon's mind. Our minds were melded together as one, so we exchanged wordless conversations as we darted through the steep, rocky canyons and soared over the sprawling, bowl-shaped desert valley. Blybrig was the only spot of civilization in sight. That stony fortress had been our home for so long now, and I couldn't imagine being anywhere else.

But our time was almost up. We had to join my new squadron at Northwatch soon. I was supposed to be partnered up with my former instructor, Seasoned Lieutenant Jace Rordin, and act as his wing end. Together with our dragons, we would fly in combat until the war ended, we retired, or one of us got killed. That was the dragonrider way.

Jace had already left to rejoin the forces at the citadel. He'd given me a few days to gather my stuff and say goodbye to my family—which would have been nice if I'd had any worth speaking of. I hadn't heard a word from my father, Ulric, since I'd started training. My half-brother, Roland, was the only one of my family members who had ever reached out to me. He was stationed with the infantry at Northwatch, too, and part of me was hoping I'd get to see him again.

As Mavrik and I reached the edge of the mountains that surrounded the valley, we soared higher and gazed out across the desert. The dark silhouettes of other dragons flickered against the blazing glare from the setting sun. The heat made the air ripple like water, and yet the mountains around us were crowned with snow. It was a beautiful contrast.

We flew until it was nearly dark, bolting through drills and running through every test of speed and aerial acrobatics we could. I pushed the limits of what I knew my body could take. It left us both exhausted when we landed back at the Roost. As I unbuckled from the saddle, Mavrik shook himself. He seemed glad to finally be free of my weight.

"Dinner?" I asked him as I took off my helmet.

He snorted in agreement.

I brought him up a bucket of cut meat scraps and refilled his water trough before I started taking off his saddle or my armor. It was a lot of work, and I had to make sure to check over every buckle and strap for possible damage. I stacked all our gear in the corner of his stall and sat down on the open ledge that overlooked the academy. My body ached from riding. My hands were sore and my palms were raw from gripping the saddle handles—even through my thick riding gauntlets. I was tired, filthy, and hungry. But this was my last time to watch the sun set over the academy. I didn't want to miss it.

When Mavrik finished eating, he strolled over to flop down beside me. He curled his tail around his body and tucked his wings in close to his sides, resting his huge snout right next to me. I heard him puff a loud, deep sigh.

"I know what you mean." I sighed, too. "I'll miss this place."

Mavrik's catlike yellow eyes looked up at me, and an image of Felix and his dragon, Nova, popped into my mind.

Felix Farrow had been my best friend basically since we first met, which had been in our fledgling year of training. We'd been through a lot together since then, and still didn't seem at all bothered by any of the bizarre things that were happening in my life. For that reason alone, I was determined to do everything I could to be as loyal to him as he had been to me.

"Yeah. We can't let them go alone. Somebody's got to keep that idiot from getting himself killed." I smirked as I scratched his snout. It made Mavrik purr and his eyes closed. "Besides, there's nothing left for us here."

Once he was calm and settled in his stall, I carried all our gear downstairs to the tack room and stored it. It was dark when I started for the dormitories, so I didn't think much of it when I passed people on my way. There were still plenty of students and instructors milling around, running last minute errands before they retired for the night. The few craftsmen that had come to make saddles and armor this year were already closing down their shops and dousing their forges.

I was looking forward to a hot meal and some sleep, maybe even a bath to soothe my aching shoulders, but someone suddenly grabbed my arm. I stopped, turning back to squint through the darkness.

At first, I barely recognized him.

It had been a year since I'd spoken to Bren, and he didn't look at all like he had the last time we'd parted ways. Last I had seen him, he had been smitten with my former childhood friend, Katalina Crookin. They had both been in an apprenticeship to become blacksmiths, and Bren had demonstrated a lot of talent when he fixed my scimitar. He was kind of a simpleton, but I had to give him some credit. He had a good heart, and a sunny disposition that sometimes made me want to choke him. Despite that, and Katty's fiery disapproval, we'd become friends after I had saved him from being mauled to death by a pack of wolves.

Seeing him now was sort of bittersweet, though. He still wasn't even close to being as tall as I was—not that many people were—but he looked older. Much, much older. He had the beginnings of a short beard on his chin and there were heavy, dark circles under his eyes. His hair was longer, and he looked a little thinner. When he smiled, it put crow's feet in the corners of his eyes.

"Jaevid Broadfeather? My, the Fates are kind. I was hoping I would see you. It's been a long time, dragonrider." He put out a hand toward me.

I smiled back at him and shook it firmly. "I'd say so. Glad to see you made it here without me this year."

He laughed at that, but it was a hollow, forced sound. "Barely, I'm afraid." I could see worry in his eyes as he turned away, nodding toward his forge. It was unsettling. "Could I get a hand?"

"Of course." I followed him to his temporary shop. I half expected to see Katty there, unloading the wagon or closing down the forge for the night. After all, they were supposed to be partners. But there was no one else with him.

"I just need to get these last few crates stacked up," he explained as he climbed up into the back of his wagon.

I joined him and started helping move the heavy wooden crates, one by one, into his work area. It brought back memories of helping my father when he'd brought me here to be his apprentice.

"Are you alone this year?" I dared to ask.

He swallowed stiffly. "Yes. It couldn't be helped. Mr. Crookin retired. I guess last year's run-in with the wolves and mountain cat was all he could take. And it's too dangerous to bring Katty through the mountain pass right now. I left her at home with the baby."

Through the gloom, I spotted the metallic glint of a wedding band on his left hand. It gave me a weird feeling. Not jealousy, though. Definitely not. I was actually wondering if he really was happy with Katty. He'd aged a good ten years in such a short time. Did that usually happen to newlyweds? "Congratulations. If I'd known I would have sent you a gift or something."

Bren just shook his head dismissively. "There wasn't really a ceremony to speak of. And Katty was calling all the shots. I tried to talk her down, but she insisted she didn't want you to know about any of it."

"It's okay. I understand." I hefted the last crate out of the wagon myself, carrying it over one shoulder and stacking it up with the others. "Maybe it's not my place to ask, but is everything okay? You look ... tired." I tried to phrase it gently.

With the last crate out of the wagon, Bren started unhitching his team of horses. He hadn't asked for my help with that, but I decided to give it anyway. He looked like he might drop from exhaustion at any moment.

"I wasn't counting on being the sole provider this soon," he admitted quietly. "I'm barely out of my apprenticeship, I've no funds built up, and I'm already here working the spring orders alone. Katty didn't want to stay behind. The baby, well, that wasn't exactly planned. We rushed the marriage because of it. As much as I need her here to help, I couldn't risk hauling them both over the mountains right now. Not with the way things are."

I nodded. "I've heard the animals are getting worse."

"That's putting it mildly. This madness—it's spreading like a sickness all over the kingdom. There's too many animals infected for it just to be a coincidence now. Every day we hear new stories of villages and cities being overrun. Creatures no one has seen in hundreds of years are suddenly stirring. It's like the whole world is going mad." Bren glanced sideways at me, like he wasn't sure how I would take this. "People are saying it's coming from the elven forest. That it's something they sent to be a plague among us."

"I hope so."

His eyes got wide.

"Because if it is, then there might be a way to stop it," I clarified.

"I suppose that makes sense," he agreed. "Mithangol hasn't been hit hard yet. Just a few cases of cattle and dogs. We've been waiting and hoping for orders to come down from the king, that soldiers or dragonriders would come to help us. But the king doesn't seem to care about any of this. He only has eyes for Luntharda. Crushing the elven armies is all that matters to him. Meanwhile his own people are being stamped out like cockroaches."

I put a hand on Bren's shoulder. I understood now why he looked the way he did. I could sympathize—but only to a degree. I'd never been married, and I'd never been a father. The weight of being both, and then being forced to leave them behind so he could provide, regardless of what was happening in the world, must have been incredibly hard on him. No wonder he'd aged so much.

"Don't give up." I tried to sound reassuring. "As long as there's even one dragonrider left to fight, then there's still hope."

Bren gave me another tired smile. "I know," he said. "That's why I came."

I LEFT BREN TO FINISH HIS WORK AND STARTED BACK FOR THE DORMITORY. The stars were out and the air was so clear I could make out the dusty, milky smear of dust painted through the night sky. It mixed with the glittering of the stars, like they were swimming in a thin cloud of white ash. The breeze felt cool on my skin, like a breath of relief from the hot desert daylight.

As I made my way through the compound, I heard voices whispering near the large, dome-shaped building where morning briefs were held. I could barely see a group of students huddled near the doorway, talking like they didn't want to get caught. I knew they were fledglings because of their uniforms. They were wearing those trademark blue tunics with the golden eagle of the king stitched across the chest.

They all went silent as I walked past, staring at me like they hoped I hadn't noticed them. It was strange to be looked at like that, not because I was a half-breed—because I was the same age as they were. Most dragonriders were seventeen or eighteen when they started training. But I was a sworn-in lieutenant already. I had started my training when I was only fifteen, and now I was almost eighteen ... even if I didn't look it. We were the same age, but I outranked them.

Of course, they probably couldn't tell that. Felix still teased me about looking like I was in my twenties. That was part of the reason I didn't raise as many brows now when the older riders saw me standing in the lineup. At least I looked old enough to be there.

Wearing my fur-collared cloak, given to me when I took my oath as an official dragonrider for king and country, and sporting a scar from a shrike's claw across my cheek, I probably looked like a seasoned rider. Especially to a bunch of fledgling students who didn't know any better. I guess that was why they all went stiff when I stopped and faced them.

"Get back to your dorms," I growled, trying my best to sound like Sile or Jace whenever they barked orders at me. "It's past curfew."

They scattered at the sound of my voice. Some even apologized as they scrambled back to their dormitory. Something about it made me smile. Sure, it was a little fun to order them around, but that wasn't the main reason I liked it. I remembered being like that, scared to death of anyone who even looked like an instructor, and seeing it from the other side made me nostalgic.

The dining hall was lit and filled with the sounds of voices. Students sat at the long tables that stretched the length of the room, while instructors shared a table at the head of the room. That was where I sat down. A few of the other newly sworn lieutenants from my class sat around me, and we struck up a conversation. We started reminiscing, telling stories and recalling good memories about our own training.

I had my face down in a mug of spiced ale to take a few sips when I felt someone grab my long ponytail and yank it. It made me choke and sputter. I didn't even have to look to see who had done it—he muscled his way into our group and slumped down into the seat beside me.

"What are you girls clucking about? You sound like a bunch of old hens over here." Felix Farrow chuckled as he leaned his elbows on the table. He had been my best friend since the beginning of training, despite the fact that he was now a duke. Normally, his social standing would have forbidden us to be acquaintances, let alone friends. But apparently no amount of wealth or social prestige prevented him from teasing me like a ruthless big brother every chance he got.

I rolled my eyes at him and wiped the ale off my face. "Where have you been?"

"Finding out who my partner is. My orders are official now. I'm headed for Northwatch, with you, Jaevid." It didn't take him two minutes to start stealing food off my plate. He swiped a few slices of bread and stuffed them into his cheek.

Hearing that we'd be stationed at the same citadel made me exhale deeply. I was relieved. We'd assumed that's where he would go, after all, top graduates were usually sent to the hottest points of conflict on the battlefront, and Northwatch was by far the most dangerous since it sat on the border with the enemy kingdom of the Gray elves, but nothing was guaranteed.

"So who is it? Your partner?" I was dying to know. Everyone else was already paired up with a senior rider; someone they would shadow in combat until they achieved enough experience to be called a Seasoned Lieutenant. It was called being a "wing end" and while it sounded like an easy gig, it came with its own share of challenges.

Everyone else at the table leaned in closer to hear his answer. I could tell by the smug grin on his face that we were about to get an overly embellished version of the truth. He loved the attention.

"I got four bids from Seasoned Lieutenants to ride with me as their wing end. But there's only so much of my greatness to go around." He sat back in his chair and gave me a sarcastic wink. "I took one from a rider named Prax. They say he's been at this since the war began. He's refused dozens of promotions just so he could stay active on the battlefield. He's supposed to be a real war dog. More importantly, he's in Northwatch—where all the action is. And I mean, someone has to make sure this guy doesn't get shot down on his first day." Felix reached out like he was going to yank on one of my pointed ears.

I managed to deflect him with my fork before he could. "So do you know which flight you're in, yet?"

"Nope," he said with a sigh. "And you'll find out before me, probably. I've already been cleared to run a few errands before I head north."

"Getting married before you go?" I teased. He always bragged about how good he was with girls, but I'd never actually seen him get serious with one. I doubted marriage was actually on his agenda.

Felix grinned. "No way. I need to stop over at my estate and see my mom first. I'm leaving her with a lot of responsibilities that should have been mine. She doesn't even argue about me leaving anymore, though. I think she's accepted that I'm going regardless of what she says. I did promise her that once I'm promoted off the frontlines, I'd go back home and be the boring old duke she's always wanted me to be."

That surprised me. "You must be feeling really guilty about leaving her, then."

"I actually thought about going back now that training is over. I guess I do feel kind of guilty," he admitted with a shrug. "But when I heard there was a chance for me to go to Northwatch, I figured this was fate's way of telling me my favorite halfbreed sidekick might need my help again."

I narrowed my eyes at him dangerously, even though I was secretly overjoyed that he was coming to Northwatch with me. I couldn't let that show. I had a reputation to uphold. "You're calling *me* the sidekick?"

"Don't look so happy about it," he chuckled. "I may not always be around to watch your back, you know. Sooner or later, you're going to have to learn how to be awesome by yourself."

"Yeah. Right. Whatever you say." I rolled my eyes and took another drink from my mug.

The dinner conversation rolled on casually. Everyone was excited and nervous, eager to talk about what was to come. Not all of us were going to Northwatch, but those who were definitely had a lot to think about. We were going into the very teeth of the war; to face the closest battlefront to the elven forest and all its horrors. We would see the brunt of what our enemy had to offer. Shrikes, evil magic, and poisoned weapons were waiting for us in the coming days.

My stomach began swimming with nerves when I thought about all that. It had been so long since I had even seen Gray elves—well, apart from the dreams about my mother, but I tried desperately to push those thoughts from my mind whenever they arose. The prospect was daunting, and I wasn't sure how I would react the first time one drew on me with intent to kill.

One by one, the others at our table started breaking off to go to bed. Tomorrow it would all be over. We had to go our separate ways, and for many of us, this would be the last time we ever saw each other. Some of us would die in combat. Others would be wounded badly enough to be honorably discharged and allowed to go back home. A few would go on to have long, distinguished careers. But one way or another, this was the end.

Finally, it was only Felix and myself left at the table. We sat side by side, staring at the nearly empty dining hall. Something about it made me even more anxious.

"You know, we first met in here." Felix broke the awkward silence.

I remembered that day, which had coincidentally been my first day as a student. He had sat down with me at a table just across the room from where we were sitting now. He'd stolen some of my food and then sauntered off without ever introducing himself. That was how our friendship had started.

"Someone should have warned me about you then." I smirked at him.

He laughed and elbowed me in the ribs, then he tried to steal my last bite of roasted potatoes. "Don't be like that. You know you'd be lost without me."

I tried to stab his hand with my fork, but I wasn't fast enough. I could out maneuver him with a sword any day, but when it came to stealing food—it was like Felix had some kind of divine superpower.

"I'd definitely be a lot less hungry without you," I said.

"It seems like it was yesterday." Felix's eyes got distant as he chewed the last bite of my dinner. "And now who knows what we'll be up against."

I sighed and pushed my empty plate away so I could lean against the table. "Can't be anything worse than usual, right?"

He grinned at that. "Yeah. One thing I know I can always count on is that when I'm with you, there's always a chance I'm going to get kidnapped, killed, eaten alive, or maimed."

I smiled. "Never a dull moment, right?"

"Never," he agreed.

We sat in silence again, watching as the last few students got up to leave the dining hall. The room was empty now, except for us. It was unbearably quiet, and my thoughts were drawn to the dark possibilities of what really was waiting for us at Northwatch.

"I heard a wild rumor that someone spotted Icarus in the royal city during the graduation ceremony," Felix murmured like it was a question, even if it wasn't one.

I shot him a look. "If you're asking whether or not I saw Beckah, the answer is yes."

His grin was so wide it was almost disturbing. "And? Did you guys, you know ... ?" He let his voice trail off suggestively.

"I don't see how that's any of your business." I knew it was futile to defend myself now, he'd believe whatever he wanted, regardless of what I said.

"That's a yes," he announced proudly, like we still had an audience. "Well, congratulations. It's about time. So, do I get a wedding invitation, or what?"

"It's not that simple and you know it. You're the one who said I shouldn't mess with her in the first place. Sile would never let me marry her. He'd probably kill me if he knew I had even kissed her." I turned my face away so he couldn't see how badly I was blushing.

Felix gave me a sympathetic pat on the back. "True. You picked one heck of a challenge. Not to mention, she fights better than most of us do."

There was a suggestive edge to his words. It made me immediately suspicious that there was something he wasn't telling me—something about Beckah.

"What?" I looked at him squarely.

His expression became reluctant, like he wasn't sure he should tell me. "Well, it's just something I heard. I don't know how true it actually is."

I squeezed my hands into fists on the table. "What?" I repeated.

"Some of the Seasoned Lieutenants were talking about it. Icarus has made a few appearances at Northwatch, too. He and his mysterious rider, who calls *himself* Seraph, have intervened in a few skirmishes. Beckah's been busy, and apparently, she's becoming some kind of hero to the dragonriders there. They're talking about Seraph like *he's* some great savior who has stepped forward to end the war," he explained, adding emphasis where we both knew the details had been skewed.

I sank back in my seat. Beckah was still passing herself off as a man in order to fight. Women were explicitly forbidden to be soldiers, even dragonriders, and I wondered how long she could hide herself and her secret behind that helmet. I was terrified of what would happen if anyone ever found out who she was. She was playing an incredibly dangerous game.

"Don't worry, dummy. She'll be fine." Felix tried to reassure me.

All I could do was nod in reply. I was worried about her. I loved her. And as much as I knew she wanted to fulfill her destiny, the fact that I might hear about her being killed in combat through some kind of rumor like this was almost more than I could stand.

But there was nothing I could do. When she got her mind made up about something, Beckah was like a force of nature. Nothing could stop her now.

Nightmares weren't anything new for me. I'd been suffering with bizarre and terrifying dreams for years now. I'd nearly forgotten what it felt like to sleep and wake up actually feeling rested and calm. That never happened anymore.

So I wasn't thrilled to leave Felix in the dining hall and trudge to the temporary room I'd been given in the instructor's wing of the dormitory. The unfamiliar surroundings didn't help. It was a small, cramped room with only one tiny bed and no windows. The sleeping remedy Felix had been slipping to me didn't help anymore, either. No matter how much of it I took, it didn't make a bit of difference. The instant I closed my eyes, my dreams came alive.

They usually revolved around my father being the traitorous coward who had stolen the god stone from Luntharda for some conniving, murdering Gray elf warrior. The details had begun to get hazier, though, and I still didn't understand why the god stone was so important. I'd only seen it once, completely by mistake, in a prison camp outside of the royal city of Halfax. At the time, nothing about it had seemed all that special to me. It was just a big, round, green rock—not anything worth killing kings over. There had to be something else I was missing. The god stone had to be important, I just didn't know how or why yet.

I packed up all my things and took a bath before I tried settling in for the night. As I lay awake, staring into the darkness overhead, I thought about my upcoming journey. Tomorrow I would leave for Northwatch. Felix was going to his own estate, so we wouldn't be traveling together. And Beckah was somewhere out there in the void of war; so far away I could barely picture her face.

I was restless even before I closed my eyes, already dreading what my dreams would show me. But as I drifted off, I saw something I hadn't seen in a very long time ...

The maw of a deep pit opened up before me. All around was the jungle, dense, deep, and filled with bizarre sounds. As I stood on the edge of that cavernous hole, I could feel something welling up from inside it. It felt like energy, something ancient that made the hairs on the back of my neck stand on end. Cold, earthy-smelling air wafted past my nose, and my eyes were drawn to the moss-covered staircase that spiraled around and around, down into the depths of that pit.

"*It's time*," a voice whispered right beside my ear. It sounded like a woman speaking in the Gray elf language, but it wasn't my mother's this time.

I turned around to see who it was.

My breath caught in my throat. I froze where I stood—nose to nose with a shrike. Its lean, powerful body rippled like water as a thousand mirror-like scales on its hide reflected the beauty of the jungle. Its wild eyes were the color of amethysts, sharp and predatory. I felt its hot breath on my face.

I was absolutely terrified. Without thinking, I took a step backward. My first instinct was to run. I had to get away. I had no weapon, not that it would have helped me much anyway. You couldn't kill a shrike that easily.

Suddenly, I felt my feet begin to slip, I was teetering on the edge of that pit. I flailed my arms wildly to try to regain my balance, but it was no good.

I started falling into the darkness.

CHAPTER TWO

As usual, I bolted upright in my bed with a cold sweat making my clothes feel damp and clingy. My heart was pounding, and I was scrambling to catch my breath. I squeezed my hand around the bone-carved necklace my mother had given to me when I was a child. I never took it off. It was all I had to remember her by.

Just like all the other times I'd had weird dreams, the pendant felt warm to the touch. I could feel it pulsing with a radiant heat in my palm. It didn't make any sense. It was just a piece of bone strung onto a resin cord. To be honest, I didn't even remember my mother ever wearing it herself.

It took me a few minutes to collect myself and get moving. I changed into my uniform and gathered up the saddlebag that contained all the possessions I owned in the world—well, except for my old family home. I did own that, courtesy of my older half-brother. But frankly it could have burned to the ground and neither of us would have cared too much.

It was barely sunrise when I stepped out of the dormitory and started for the Roost. Jace was expecting me by the end of the day, so I needed to get an early start. He wasn't my instructor anymore, so he couldn't order me around like he had before, but I wasn't dumb enough to think there weren't plenty of other ways he could make my life miserable if he wanted to. So being late probably wasn't in my best interest.

Felix was already gone. I knew it because when I walked into the tack room to get Mavrik's saddle, all his gear had already been cleaned out. It upset me a little. I'd missed saying goodbye. And he hadn't bothered to throw a boot at my head to wake me up one last time. Things were different now. We couldn't act like kids. He had a lot of responsibility to deal with, and part of me wished I could have gone with him to his family estate. Felix's relationship with his parents hadn't been very good, from what I had learned. He was an only child, and his father had passed away suddenly last year due to an illness. And I knew he had to be worried about leaving his mother alone while he went off to war. Sure, he put up a tough front. He laughed everything off most of the time. But I knew Felix had been struggling with a rocky relationship with his mother for years now. He'd talked to me about it a little, and apparently she hadn't wanted him to become a dragonrider in the first place. Now that he was the duke of the family estate, he was supposed to be taking care of her as part of his duties. He wouldn't be able to do that very well from the frontlines, though.

I tried not to think about it too much. It was his business, not mine. I wasn't going to try to tell him what to do. I wouldn't have known what to do in his situation anyway. Besides, Felix was made of tougher stuff than I was. He could handle it.

Heaving Mavrik's saddle and all my gear over my shoulders, I started up the stairs to his stall. He was being strangely silent this morning. Usually he was already filling my head with excited questions and swirls of curious color. I just assumed he was still asleep. After all, I had pushed him pretty hard yesterday. And we had a long way to go today; a little extra rest for him was probably a good idea.

But as I came to the door of his stall, he started sending me waves of worried blue-green hues. I could sense his uneasiness. He was nervous about something. With my thoughts, I asked him what was wrong even as I opened the door to go into his stall.

Then I got my answer.

My former instructor from my fledgling year of training, Sile Derrick, was standing in Mavrik's stall. It looked like he'd been waiting for me. Immediately, my temper caught like a wildfire. Anger made my teeth clench and my vision go hazy.

I stopped in the doorway and stared at him, waiting for some kind of explanation. He'd obviously come here to talk. I wasn't exactly opposed to that. There was plenty I wanted to say to him, too.

"I see you managed to survive," he said coldly. He didn't smile.

I didn't smile, either. "No thanks to you."

"That's a bold thing for you to say to your instructor, boy," he growled.

"You're not my instructor anymore," I reminded him. "In fact, I'm not sure what you are ... except a liar."

Sile's face started to turn a furious shade of red. Even though it had only been a little over a year since I'd last seen him, he looked much older now. More of his hair had turned gray, and there were wrinkles on his forehead and in the corners of his eyes. He was thinner, and there was something disturbing about the wide-eyed way he glared at me. It was as though he half-expected someone to jump out from behind me and kill him.

"I never lied to you," he snapped bitterly.

My temper stared to flare up. "You never told me the whole truth, either. Keeping the truth from me while acting like you don't know anything about what's going on is the same thing as lying. You've known about me all along. You knew what I was capable of—that's how you knew I could heal your wife."

He didn't reply. I saw his hands curling up into fists.

"Don't worry, I don't expect you to start telling me anything useful now. You'll probably leave me to flap in the wind with no idea what's going on, as usual." I turned away to put down all my equipment.

When he spoke again, his voice was strangely calm. "It's not my place to tell you these things. My understanding of what you are is limited. Anything I told you would be a poorly educated guess."

"Right. Well, whose place is it, then?" I narrowed my eyes back at him challengingly.

Sile stiffened. He glared at me with his mouth pinched up into an uncomfortable grimace. "You don't understand," he said quietly. "I made a promise. I swore on my honor I wouldn't tell you anything unless there was no other choice. We agreed that the less you knew, the safer you would be."

With my arms now empty of my gear and saddle, I stood up and faced him. I flexed my hands, curling my fingers as I summoned some of that strange power that made the air around me hum with wild energy. The heat of it tingled through my chest.

From where he was curled in the back of his stall, Mavrik hissed in disapproval. It made him nervous. But I didn't stop.

The wooden floorboards under Sile's boots began to groan, sprouting branches and leaves, which started to entwine around his legs.

"I'm not giving you a choice this time," I threatened. "Tell me what you know."

Sile watched the floorboards coming to life like it wasn't a surprise at all. He didn't even look scared. "Don't try to intimidate me, boy. I've seen better tricks than this."

"I know," I snarled and flexed a bit more of my power. The dragons outside the Roost all sent up a chorus of roars at exactly the same time, answering my silent call like a clap of thunder. "Because you've been to Luntharda, haven't you? Don't try to lie your way out of it this time, Sile. I know all about it. You went in by yourself, and came out completely unharmed. Everyone says that should have been impossible—that the jungle should have eaten you alive. But now I know there's only one way an outsider could have made it out without a single scratch."

I took a bold step toward him so that we met face-to-face. If he was going to lie to me again, I wanted him to be looking at me squarely as he did it. I wanted to see the lie in his eyes. "You knew someone else with power like this. Someone who could make things grow. Someone who could control the jungle and protect you from it."

Sile's lip twitched.

"You knew my mother," I growled through clenched teeth.

Sile's mouth opened slightly like he was going to argue, but he didn't. He never said a single word. He didn't have to. I saw the answer as plainly as I could see the guilt and frustration on his face. I was right.

"Why did you go into Luntharda?" I demanded. "Did you go looking for my mother? Was it about the god stone?"

Mentioning the stone made Sile's expression harden again. He looked away. "It's not time yet for you to know that."

"Why not?" I yelled as I lost my temper.

Sile, on the other hand, was still calm and collected. He didn't even raise his voice. "Because you haven't seen it yet. You haven't seen what this war has done. The citizens of Maldobar are suffering. The poor starve to pay for a war that has turned the very balance of nature on its head. They live in anguish and ruin. But so do your mother's people. And in many ways, they've lost much more than we have. You won't understand until you see it for yourself."

I was stunned. Sile was the last person in the world I would have thought might sympathize with the enemy. He was a retired, highly decorated dragonrider. He had fought and probably killed plenty of Gray elves before. Hearing those words leave his lips, and seeing the devastated bitterness blazing in his eyes, made me forget how to speak.

Sile took a step toward me, kicking free of the floorboards that had begun to climb his legs. His expression was earnest as he put a hand on my shoulder and squeezed it firmly. "If you value your life or those of your friends, then don't speak of the god stone again. Not to anyone," he warned. "There are ears everywhere just waiting to hear those words leave your lips. All they need is one excuse to put an axe to your neck."

"That's why you've been hiding all this time, isn't it?" I dared to ask as I finally found my voice again. That truth had been staring me in the face all this time, but I had only just now been able to make sense of it. "That's why someone tried to sabotage your saddle, and why the Lord General was going to execute you. It wasn't some kind of ritual."

Sile's grip on my shoulder slackened some. Once again, his expression told me everything.

As long as I was on the right track, I decided to take it a step further. "You know something about the god stone, don't you? Something worth killing over ... "

He didn't speak. As his hand fell away from my shoulder, I saw him nod slightly—just once. He did know something. And whatever he knew was putting his life in danger. He was living in constant fear for himself and for his family. He probably felt like he couldn't trust anyone after what had happened here at the academy, and now he was worried that anything he told me would definitely put me in that same danger. Why else would he still be trying to protect me?

My anger started to dissipate. I felt sorry for him. I didn't understand why he was involved, or what had happened to cause all of this, but it was obviously affecting him. He had the same weary, dark circles under his eyes Bren had.

"We don't have much time. You need to leave soon." Sile turned away to look at Mavrik. "Don't tell anyone you saw me here."

I doubted anyone would believe me if I did. I wasn't even sure how he'd gotten here in the first place. But as he started to walk away, I just had one more question.

"What about Beckah?"

Sile stopped mid-stride. He shot me a glare that probably would have singed my eyebrows right off my face if I'd been standing a little closer. "What about her?"

"I just wondered what made you change your mind about her. You trained her to fight. You sent her into battle without a wing end. You did everything you said shouldn't be done for a girl." I tried to at least keep my tone neutral, even if my questions were somewhat accusing.

I knew I had no place to interrogate him about his parenting choices. After all, he'd threatened to rip my ears off if he ever found me messing with his lovely young daughter. Unfortunately, that ship had sailed. I was in love with her. And now I wanted to know why he had gone from being adamantly against her being a dragonrider to training her for it himself.

"I did what had to be done." He didn't sound happy about it at all. "There's a reason she was chosen. I may not agree with it, or understand it, but at this point those choices are no longer mine to make. All I can do is try to prepare her for the worst."

"She could get hurt," I reminded him. "Or killed."

Sile snorted and cast me a dark, almost mocking smirk. "You won't let that happen." It sort of sounded like a threat.

"There may not be anything I can do about it, Sile. No matter how much I love her, I can't bring people back from the dead. And at the rate she's going—"

He was on me before I could finish getting the words out. He lunged so suddenly, I barely had time to react. He took a swing at my face, and I blocked. He tried to grab one of my arms and force me down into a grappling hold, but I knew these tricks already. I hadn't just spent a year in absolute hell for nothing.

I twisted myself around, wrenching free of his grasp. Before I could catch myself or even think about it, my body reacted. I punched him hard across the cheek, twice.

I could have stopped there. I probably should have. Those hits had only been instinct, after all, and he was the one who'd started it in the first place. But it felt *so* good to get a little vengeance for all the frustration and lies. So I hit him again, one more time, right in the gut. That one was just for spite.

We broke apart and staggered back, glaring at one another. I was poised, ready to dive right back into the fight again if he sprang at me. My face was burning with rage as I waited to see what he would do.

I had a pretty good idea why he had jumped me in the first place. Now he knew how I felt about his daughter. Considering her current situation, it was probably a bad time to bring that up. Regardless, I had my own reasons for wanting to punch his nose in. I hadn't completely forgiven him for holding out on me—keeping valuable information out of my grasp. Not knowing that stuff had almost gotten me killed several times now.

But Sile wasn't going to budge. I knew him well enough to guess that much. He wouldn't tell me anything, no matter how many times I hit him. He'd never tell me what he really knew about my past, my mother, or what my father stealing the god stone had to do with any of this.

"Not bad." Sile laughed dryly as he wiped blood from the corner of his mouth onto the back of his hand. "Looks like you did learn something after all."

"Why did you even come here?" I tried to sound intimidating. "Was there a reason? Or were you just checking to see if I was still alive?"

Sile let his arms drop. He stood, frowning at me like I was still a big disappointment to him. Before, that look had always hurt my pride and my feelings. Now it just pissed me off.

"No," he said coldly. "I came here for two reasons. First, I heard about what happened on the island during the battle scenario. Is it true that your power didn't affect any of the animals possessed by the sickness?"

I swallowed uncomfortably. I didn't exactly have happy memories of the battle scenario. What happened on the Canrack Islands was supposed to have been our final test to see if we were fit for the battlefront. But it had ended up a complete disaster. The madness that was now spreading through the animals in Maldobar like a disease had already infected the whole island. We had barely made it out of there alive. Well ... most of us, anyway.

"Yes," I answered at last, letting my gaze fall to the floor.

Sile's brow furrowed deeply, like this wasn't part of his grand master scheme. "Then my second reason for being here will be much more difficult than we anticipated."

"Why? What are you talking about?"

"You have to go into Luntharda." He looked at me squarely, like he was daring me to refuse. "Knowing the jungle won't obey you is going to make that very complicated."

I practically had to scrape my jaw off the floor of Mavrik's stall. "Are you insane? I can't go in there! I barely made it off that island, and that was only because Felix dragged me out!"

"You don't have choice." Sile rolled his eyes like I was the one being unreasonable. "Your power hasn't fully manifested yet. And you're going to need it—all of it—very soon. So a ritual must be performed, you must be chosen publically, and we're running out of time for that to happen. The longer we wait the further the sickness will spread. More and more people will die."

"What ritual? How do you even know all of this?" I tried to ask.

He acted like he hadn't heard my question. "The abilities you're using now are child's play compared to what you are truly capable of. You have to perform the ritual, otherwise you'll keep collapsing every time you try to use too much power. That's part of the balance."

I was struggling to keep up with what he was saying. Actually wrapping my mind around it was something I'd have to work on later. I spent a lot of my spare time trying to figure out the things Sile told me, so it's not like this was anything new.

"Are you even listening?" He swatted the back of my head to get my attention again. "Quit standing there gaping like a beached fish and remember what I'm telling you."

"Sile, I can't go in there," I argued. "If the jungle doesn't kill me, the Gray elves definitely will. They hate me every bit as much as humans do. And they'll hate me even more when they see me dressed like a dragonrider. They'll cut my head off before I even get a word out."

He gave me another weird, sadistic grin. It was probably the most disturbing thing I had ever seen. "You should be so lucky. Your mother's people aren't as forgiving as humans. And they don't offer quick, painless deaths to their enemies."

I swallowed hard.

"But you'll be fine, more or less." He didn't sound worried at all, even as he grabbed the front of my tunic and yanked me closer. He stuck his hand down the front of it and started feeling around. I was about to take another swing at him when he pulled out my mother's necklace.

I tried to snatch it back from him. "Hey!"

"Good. You still have it," he said with a sigh of relief. "Keep it on you at all times. Never take it off. Understood?"

I shot him a glare. "It's just a necklace. It doesn't mean anything."

As much as I wanted to believe that, my heart wasn't convinced. A haunting memory from two years ago, when I was a fledgling, came back to me as soon as he brought it up. A Gray elf had recognized it, and even asked where I'd gotten it. I had almost forgotten about that.

At the time, it hadn't mattered. There had been other things I was way more worried about—like rescuing Sile and keeping my friends safe. Now, as I watched him examine the bone-carved pendant carefully, I started to get anxious. I was beginning to wonder how much I had been overlooking. All this time, everyone had been telling me to focus on my training, not to let myself get distracted, and to put all my other worries out of my mind. Had keeping my eyes fixed on that one goal made me blind to the hand of fate moving around me?

I was starting to think so.

"Sile," I started to speak. My tone must have caught him off guard, because he dropped my necklace back against my chest and stared at me with concern. "I found a scimitar at my father's house. It had the mark of a stag on the hilt. Someone told me it was the royal crest of the Gray elves."

He pressed his lips together uncomfortably, glancing down to my belt where I had the scimitar clipped against my hip. "I know. I gave it to your brother for safekeeping. I'm glad to see he kept his word."

Closing my hand around the newly refurbished hilt, I drew the blade from its sheath so he could see how it had been restored. "I saw it in a dream, too. I've seen a lot in my dreams. Horrible things; things everyone else says can't possibly be true."

Sile took the scimitar from my hands and held it up to the light. The expression on his face was distant, maybe even a little sad. It was as though he was remembering something—something that had happened a long time ago. "The first time I saw this blade, the person who gave it to me asked me to destroy it," he said in a quiet, somber voice. "I couldn't do it. Even then, it just felt wrong."

"Was it my father?" I guessed.

He didn't answer right away. He just ran his thumb over the stag head engraved upon the pommel. "Until that moment, I wouldn't have refused him any favor he asked of me. Your father and I were like brothers. We both served in the infantry as common foot soldiers. We went through training together. We were both newly married with young wives waiting for us at home, and neither of us had an extra dime to spare. We weren't fighting for glory or because we even believed in the king's campaigns. We fought to put food on the table. It was our struggles that brought us together."

I watched Sile carefully as he turned the blade over, inspecting the runic marks engraved down the length. When our eyes met at last, he handed the scimitar back to me. "Your father was a different man back then. Much different than the one you know now. He was a lot like you, actually. I always admired his bravery—brave to the point of stupidity. Surrender just wasn't in his vocabulary."

I remembered Sile saying something to me like that before. Still, it was hard to imagine that he and my father had been close friends. It was even harder to imagine my father being brave or even friendly. I'd never seen that side of him. The Ulric I had known growing up was cruel, intolerant, and harsh. He hated me. He'd beaten me more times than I dared to count, and had basically abandoned me once I started my training to become a dragonrider.

Needless to say, I wasn't in a hurry to start feeling sorry for him.

"Then it is true," I replied, "what I'm seeing in my dreams; the Gray elf warrior and the death of the king. It all happened, didn't it?"

Sile wouldn't meet my gaze again. "It's not time to talk about that yet."

I started to get frustrated. He was clamming up, right when I was about to get some good answers. "What about my father, then? He stole the god stone from Luntharda, didn't he?"

That one answer would have been enough to satisfy me. But Sile wouldn't give me anything. He just put his hand on my shoulder, like he was trying to reassure me. "Have some patience, Jaevid. I know it doesn't seem fair. But you, of all people, should understand that there is no fairness in this world anymore."

What more could I say? None of my questions were going to be answered—that much was clear to me now. Standing there arguing with him was pointless.

I turned my back to Sile long enough to pick up all my gear again, grumbling angry words under my breath the whole time. By the time I turned back around ... he was gone. Sile had vanished like a ghost without a trace, and I was left standing there gaping at the patch of empty floor where he'd been only a few seconds ago.

My mind felt like someone had taken a jar full of moths and shaken it just to watch them panic. Thoughts and worries fluttered through my brain, frantic and directionless with no hope in sight. I was so confused about what he had asked me to do. It sounded impossible, not to mention suicidal. I was angry with him for even suggesting it, especially when he still wouldn't tell me what was going on in the first place. I couldn't see how going into Luntharda and getting disemboweled by Gray elves or eaten by some monster would make things better for anyone, least of all me. Besides, it had taken me years to win the trust of my dragonrider brothers. Marching into Luntharda out of the blue would completely destroy that.

I wasn't going to do it. My mind was made up even before I finished putting on all my layers of weatherproofed padding and battle armor. The work was a welcomed distraction, and I took my time fixing Mavrik's saddle snuggly against his scaly hide. I buckled down my bag of possessions, checked every belt and buckle over again, and then took one last look at the view of the academy from inside Mavrik's stall.

Sitting in the saddle with my legs fitted down into the sheaths on either side of his body, I was looking down Mavrik's neck and snout at the steep drop to the ground below. The morning sun made the sky burn brilliant red and it cast a pink glow over the snow-crested mountains. My heart was beating with wild, anxious energy.

This was it—the turning point. The minute we left this place behind, my days as a student were over forever. There was no going back.

I gave Mavrik's neck a pat. He chirped in response, and I felt the muscles in his shoulders grow tense under his hard, plated scales. He flexed, letting out a thunderous roar as we leapt into the air. He spread his wings wide, catching the wind and immediately surging upward toward the breaking dawn.

CHAPTER THREE

Northwatch was so close to the border of Luntharda it made me restless just to look at it. Less than ten miles away, the ominous wild jungle of Luntharda loomed with nothing to separate it from Maldobar except a big, man-made wall of stacked stone. I could imagine the soldiers inside the citadel always kept one eye trained on that wall, dreading the day they saw something nightmarish coming over it.

Over the top of the wall, I could see the dark, massive trunks of trees that stood like giant columns. They grew so close together, they seemed to make a wall of their own, and the interwoven canopy of their branches squeezed every drop of light from the air.

The tower of Northwatch itself was much more impressive, though. It was an enormous structure with many skinny slot-shaped windows and different tiered levels going up at least fifty stories into the air. It stuck out of the center of a city like a great black spike, visible from miles and miles away. In fact, it was the first thing I had spotted on the horizon that let me know I was getting close. The king's gold and blue banners hung like frayed old rags, fluttering tiredly against a dull gray sky.

A snowbound city lay just outside the tower's main gate. Three circular walls surrounded the base of the tower, each one with tall ramparts lined with what looked like giant crossbows made of wood and steel. I'd read about those kinds of weapons during my training. They were used to launch javelins at enemies on the ground or in the air, but it took at least two men to fire them. From the air, I could see infantry soldiers dressed in armor walking the ramparts, manning their posts, and operating the heavy gates leading in and out of the tower.

The lower levels looked plain enough from the outside, but the upper levels all had broad, open platforms where dragons could land. Huge arched doorways led from the platforms into the tower, and iron gates closed off all the entryways to keep enemy forces from slipping inside. It truly was a fortress—a structure made of dark stone and iron—and nothing about it was beautiful at all. Jace had jokingly called it the "spearhead of the war" once, and now I understood why.

It was growing dark when Mavrik and I made our final descent and circled the tower, looking for a good place to land. Fortunately, the platforms were lit with braziers, and I quickly spotted a few soldiers gathering on the end of one. They were waving green flags and giving me hand signals to land. After spending all day in the saddle, crossing most of the kingdom without stopping, I was happy to oblige. My rear end was sore and my back was aching from straddling Mavrik for so long. I was ready to pry all the heavy armor off my body as soon as possible.

As we prepared to land, Mavrik flared his powerful wings and stretched out his hind legs like an eagle. The floor of the platforms had been coated with something like tar mixed with gravel. It gave the dragons something to grip onto with their claws when they touched down. As soon as we landed, the iron gate at the end of the platform was cranked open, and a few more soldiers came out to greet us.

I let out a sigh of relief. When I pulled my helmet off, I got a deep breath of the bitterly cold air. We were farther north than I'd ever been before, and the air was so cold it almost hurt to breathe it in. It made my long, sweaty hair feel cold against my neck and back.

After unbuckling myself from the saddle, I climbed down and started to unfasten my bag. Being so far up in the air, near the top of the tower, meant the wind was howling. It made it difficult to hear anything.

But I did hear a voice shout at me, "Toss it here!"

I glanced back to see who it was.

Jace was standing right behind me, his steely eyes as piercing as ever. It was like staring a wolf in the eye, and when I was his student, it had been terrifying to try to meet his gaze. But I was used to it now.

I wasn't surprised he had come out to meet me. He'd been expecting me to arrive all day, after all. I was a little shocked he was offering to help with my gear, though. He wasn't usually so ... friendly.

Until recently, he'd been my instructor at the academy; one of the men responsible for making sure I was ready for battle. Now he was my partner, so I started wondering if that meant things would be different between us.

"Hurry it up; we can't have the gate open for more than a few minutes. Safety procedures." Jace held out a hand expectantly, so I tossed my go-bag with all my equipment and possessions to him.

I carried my helmet under my arm as I followed Jace into the tower. Mavrik crawled along behind us, chirping curiously at the unfamiliar surroundings. As soon as we had all passed into the entryway tunnel, a pair of infantrymen turned a huge crank that dropped the heavy iron gate back into place. I have to admit, having that metal partition made me feel a little safer—but only a little.

Jace gave me a quick tour of the upper levels of the tower. All the dragonriders posted here were housed in the top ten floors. Even our dragons had their own floor that had been designed like a large stable. It could accommodate several hundred of our scaly companions but there wasn't much room to spare. They each had a stall that felt cramped. It was just big enough for a dragon to squeeze in, curl up, and sleep. The floors were covered with old hay and there were water troughs that Jace said were refilled daily.

Everything in the tower seemed dark because of how few windows there were. It was like we were all living on top of one another, with barely enough room to breathe. Because of that, the air had a twinge of salty sweatiness to it that reminded me of the gymnasium at the academy where we had combat training. Man-smell.

I got Mavrik settled into his stall, which wasn't easy. He didn't like the close quarters. Lucky for me, he was too exhausted to give me much trouble about it. After I fed him, filled his water trough, and rubbed down his back where my saddle had probably made him sore, his big yellow eyes started to get droopy. He yawned widely, showing me all his jagged fangs and the back of his throat, before he flopped down and put his snout on his tail. As I left his stall, he sent cozy, satisfied colors swirling through my brain.

I didn't dare have any expectations about what my room was going to look like. Turns out that was a good thing. I probably would have been disappointed otherwise.

It wasn't much better than Mavrik's stall, to be honest. Granted, we were on the most dangerous and active battlefront in the kingdom. Things were bound to be rugged. When Jace let me in and tossed my bag onto the floor, he gestured to the cramped little space that we would be sharing. There wasn't much to it: one small, skinny window, two rickety single beds on opposite sides of the room, and one washstand with a cracked mirror.

"Just be glad you aren't on the infantry floors," Jace said with a smirk. "There are four of them in a room this size."

"Oh." Frankly, I was just relieved to see a bed with my name on it. I went over to sit on it. The mattress sank horribly, and it smelled like it had been used—a lot. But I was too tired to care. "So do we get to go out into the city at all?"

Jace shrugged. "Occasionally, when we aren't on waiting shift. There are about two hundred riders here. We all answer to Colonel Bragg. He runs this tower and every rider in it. He's your new boss. Chances are, you won't meet him—and that's a good thing. You don't want to meet him. Meeting him means you did something stupid and he's about to hang you by your toenails for it."

I made a mental note of that as I started unbuckling my cloak and taking off all the layers of my riding armor and weatherproofed padding beneath. I dressed down to my plain uniform, kidney belt, vambraces, and boots. Since that's all Jace was wearing, I reasoned it was probably okay for me, too.

"Like I said," Jace continued, "we're all in one of two shifts. We call them squadrons. There's Blue Squadron and Gold Squadron. We rotate duties to keep everything running as smoothly as possible. Waiting shift means you are on standby, ready to deploy immediately when the battle horn sounds. You can't leave the tower during that time, and you're expected to devote your spare time to resting and keeping up with your training. Then there's working shift, which means you've recently come back from battle. You'll be responsible for helping maintain your area of the tower, mucking dragon stalls, repairing gear, that kind of thing. When one squadron does deploy, we do what we can to make sure all the work gets done. We all do our part to keep this place livable. When you're on working shift, you can leave the tower for short periods of time, but never without your wing end. Just because you're on working shift doesn't mean you can't be called up for duty if there's a dire need."

"So which squadron are we in?" I stood up as Jace waved for me to follow him back out into the hall.

I tried to ignore the wide-eyed stares I got from all the other riders who were hanging out in the halls. It had been a while since I had gotten stared at like that; it bothered me a lot more than I expected it to. It was almost as though I could sense their emotions—which ranged from shock and awe to outright rage and disgust. None of them looked excited to see a halfbreed wandering around in a dragonrider's uniform.

"Blue Squadron. We're on working shift, so you and I have been assigned cargo duty. We'll be moving crates of supplies into the tower." Jace glanced back and gave me a sarcastic look I'd only seen him give one other time—when he was teasing Felix about his mother. "Try to contain your excitement."

I rolled my eyes. "Sounds better than mucking stalls."

Jace finished up the rest of his tour without any more of his weird jokes. He showed me the dining hall, the saddle rooms, the armory, the battle planning rooms, the community washroom, and the infirmary. Everything was clean. Well, as clean as you can imagine with that many men living in close quarters. Jace emphasized again and again that I was going to have to carry my own weight, clean up after myself, and not create work for anyone else.

"Places like this can be a hive for disease, so we try to keep things regulated. No outsiders are allowed in, human or otherwise," he warned. "No visitors. No lady friends. We can't run the risk of any incidents. It's as much for our protection as it is for theirs. So you'll have to save your girl-handling for when we go out."

I couldn't tell if this was another one of his jokes or not.

"Any questions?" He finally stopped when we were standing back outside our room.

I thought for a moment. "Just one."

Jace arched a brow expectantly.

"How many of the other riders here know I'm a halfbreed?"

That question made him frown. His brows furrowed, and he moved his jaw around like he was chewing on the inside of his cheek. "None that didn't need to know. I told the other members of Blue Squadron. That's it."

"That explains the staring, then." I sighed and shook my head.

Jace frowned harder. "Don't worry about it. You've already proven yourself. Word travels fast here. After what happened on the island, you'll be fine."

It was my turn to give him a sarcastic look. "Do me a favor, then. Eventually, someone is going to have a problem with me. They always do. I'm not dumb enough to think a rumor is going to change that. And when it does happen, let me handle it. I can defend my own honor."

His frown wavered. He looked confused. Then he returned my smirk and gave a snort. "No problem."

Turns out, there were a lot of traditions when it came to new lieutenants arriving on the battlefront. Jace informed me that I had a lot to do. I tried to be enthusiastic because from the sound of it, he had been the one responsible for planning everything. But I was so tired from flying all day; I wasn't sure I was up to it.

"I already paid off a few guys to cover our shift unloading crates," Jace said as he stepped into our room long enough to grab our cloaks. He shoved mine into my hands on his way toward the large staircase that led down and out of the tower. "We're going out with the rest of the riders in our flight."

"Flight?" I asked as I followed, trying to buckle my cloak over my shoulders without tripping down the stairs.

"The two squadrons are split into two legions, and then again into two flights. There's sixteen riders per flight, and we always fly and operate as a group in battle," he explained. "The flights tend to be competitive between one another, so watch your back."

I wasn't sure how to take that. "Why? What'll they do?"

"Usually just pranks. Nothing serious. It's mostly just a distraction. After you've spent some time knee deep in blood, you'll welcome any distraction you can come by. Trust me."

The stairs seemed to go on for an eternity. It took forever to get to the base of the tower, and by then, my calves were practically screaming. The thought of going back up all those steps to get to our room made me want to throw up.

There was a group of thirteen other riders waiting for us by the large open gateway that led out of the tower into the city beyond. They were all dressed in their casual uniforms, and most of them looked a lot older than I was—which wasn't exactly shocking. I doubted many teenagers got to walk through these halls as sworn-in lieutenants.

When the other riders saw Jace, they started calling out to him, laughing and taunting him for making them wait so long. Their smiles looked friendly enough. But when they saw me, their smiles all begin to fade one by one. They stared. No one said a word, and the silence got tense.

I glanced at Jace's back. I thought he had told them about me already. That's what he'd said, wasn't it?

He kept right on walking in their direction, but their tense expressions made me stop short. I couldn't decide if they were glaring, or just looking at me like a mutant at a freak show. I did know that if this devolved into a fight, I was vastly outnumbered.

"What's wrong with you?" Jace demanded suddenly. He was looking at me like he was afraid I was about to do something embarrassing.

I bowed my head a bit, unable to hide my apprehension as I trudged toward him again.

Behind Jace, one of the other riders let out a deep, booming laugh. It caught me completely off guard. He was an impressively huge man who loomed over everyone else, including me. He was bulky to boot, and looked like he could have cracked me in half with his bare hands if he wanted to.

The big man walked right up to me and planted one of his monstrous hands on my shoulder. He shook me a little, and my life flashed before my eyes. It wasn't very often I had to look up to anyone else these days. But this man loomed over me like a giant. He had to be almost seven feet tall.

But that wasn't what struck me the most about him.

"I hope you don't scare this easy in battle, rookie," he chuckled and patted the top of my head roughly like he was comforting a puppy. He had a broad, cunning smirk and a twinkle of mischief in his eyes. It made my throat swell shut immediately so I couldn't make a sound.

This man—his build, the sound of his voice, his smile, even the dark golden color of his hair—he looked *just* like Felix! Granted, Felix wasn't nearly this tall. He was shorter than me, in fact. But the resemblance was downright creepy.

I started to get a sick feeling in the pit of my stomach. I may not have been all that experienced when it came to matters of love and relationship, but I could put two and two together. Immediately, I glanced over at Jace because he was the only other person around who I thought might notice the resemblance, too.

Jace met my gaze with a knowing expression. He winced, nodded, and looked away quickly.

Great.

"I'm Lieutenant Darion Prax," the big man announced.

My bad feeling got even worse. It was like there were snakes swimming around in my gut. I could barely look him in the eye as he offered to shake my hand. Felix was going to be flying with this guy. This wasn't good.

Prax practically shoved me toward the rest of the riders. They probably mistook my lingering shock and horror as nervousness, because they all gave me that same gruff, warm greeting. They teased me about being a rookie, but meeting them didn't scare me nearly as much as the idea of Felix meeting Lieutenant Prax. That was going to be a horrible, awkward, and destructive moment for sure.

We left the citadel as a group and crossed through the gates and under the ramparts on our way to the city. All the way, I got harassed for being the new "baby" lieutenant. Jace told them every embarrassing thing he could remember about me, and they all got a real kick out of hearing I had been caught ballroom dancing with another student. I was beginning to realize that moment of utter humiliation was likely going to haunt me until the day I died. I also realized that being the newest lieutenant meant you were doomed to be everyone's favorite joke.

As we made our way into the city of Northwatch, the topic of conversation gradually shifted to arguing over where they were going to take me for my first drink. They bickered about bars and taverns, and Jace gave me a nudge to get my attention. He handed me a small cotton drawstring bag with the letters "LT" stamped on the front. I could feel coins rattling around inside it as I tucked it into my pocket.

"Your first pay," he said quietly. "You get to buy us all a round of ale with it. Congratulations."

I laughed. "Right. Lucky me."

The consensus was reached that we were going to a tavern near the citadel—one that was apparently a dragonrider favorite. They called it the Laughing Fox, and insisted that place had the best-looking barmaids in the city.

From the outside, it didn't look like much. The battered wooden sign hanging over the door had a picture of a smiling fox painted on it, and the roof was slumped like the buildings on either side were squishing it. But one look through the windows gave me hope. Warm light came from inside, and when Prax opened the door, the smell of spiced ale and roasted meat made me dizzy with hunger.

We claimed a table at the back of the room, close to the fire that roared in a big stone hearth. Everyone unbuckled their swords and cloaks as they settled in, making a lot of racket that didn't seem to bother any of the other patrons. In fact, none of them even looked up. They must have been used to hearing dragonriders and soldiers carry on. We were undoubtedly the loudest group in the room.

Two young barmaids brought us a round of warm ale, which I paid for, and several platters of roasted pork and potatoes, fresh bread, and soft cheese. I got ribbed a few times about the pretty girls, but I didn't notice if they were human or not. I was too interested in the food. I hadn't eaten all day, so judging anyone's looks was not topping my list of priorities.

I started piling food onto my plate and gulping it down while Jace told them about my little show at the officer's ball when Felix got into a fistfight with an infantryman. I wasn't embarrassed by that story, though. I'd broken up the fight, spared Felix from getting his face bashed in, and managed not to look like an idiot in the process. That didn't happen often for me.

"So, this Felix," Lieutenant Prax chimed in, "I hear that's the boy who took my bid to be my new wing end. Tell me about him. I only got a few stories from the instructors. Jace is keeping a tight lip about him. I guess he only likes bragging on his students with pointy ears."

I grimaced. Out of the corner of my eye, I saw Jace's mouth twitch. Thankfully, I had a mouth full of food so I didn't have to answer.

A passing barmaid stopped to giggle. She had a tray of empty mugs in one hand, shapely hips, a low cut blouse, and a coy smirk on her lips. She grabbed the tip of one of my ears and tugged at it playfully. "He's cute, even with the ears."

I caught her giving me a wink. It made me blush and choke on my food. Women *never* looked at me like that.

"Gods, woman! Don't you know men don't want to be called cute? Puppies are cute. Babies are cute. But never tell a man he's cute!" Prax started teasing her, and I saw yet another disturbing similarity between him and Felix. They both liked to flirt it up with girls.

"Oh, forgive me! I'm sure he's very rugged, too," the barmaid teased. She gave my ear one more tug before she walked away.

Jace snorted like he wasn't impressed. "Don't get too excited, Jae. These barmaids will flirt with anyone who might give them a big tip. They know new lieutenants are good for that. They'll sucker you right out of every cent you have, so keep your coins in your pocket."

"Ah yes," Prax agreed with another booming laugh. "But it's good fun to watch them try. Now, tell me about that boy I'm supposed to ride with. Felix Farrow, right? Isn't he the duke's son?"

Once again, I was really glad to have a mouthful of food. I had a legitimate excuse to look at Jace expectantly along with everyone else.

I guess he didn't appreciate that, though, because he shot me a scathing glare before he answered, "Yes. Word is that now he's taken charge of his family's estate. His father passed away last year, so he's the new duke of Farrow Manor."

"Hah! A duke before he's even set foot on the battlefield? That'll be a good show," one of the other riders in our group muttered. He sounded sarcastic and annoyed at the idea. "Those noble types always think they can order you around even if they've never held a blade in combat before."

The others grumbled in agreement.

"Felix isn't like that." I sat up a little straighter as all eyes turned to me. I didn't get many chances to speak up in Felix's defense, but I certainly wasn't going to sit here and let anyone badmouth my best friend. "His family has pressured him not to be a dragonrider from the start. He chose this because he wants it, and he's dedicated to the cause. He's a good fighter, and a loyal friend."

"Is that so?" Prax was smirking at me tauntingly. "You act like you know him well."

It was almost impossible to look at Prax when he was grinning at me like that. It was like seeing a much older Felix sitting across from me, giving me that same grin he always did when he was about to try to steal something off my plate.

"I do know him well. Better than anyone. We've been in training together since we were fledglings. I'm proud to know him." I tried to sound confident.

Prax elbowed Jace a few times, nearly making him spill his mug of ale. "You hear that? A noble who's befriended a halfbreed! Forgive me if I sound condescending, but I've never heard of such a thing. This Felix must be an interesting fellow indeed. I look forward to meeting him."

One glance at Jace's uncomfortable scowl, and I was pretty sure I wasn't the only one who was dreading that meeting.

"Y-yeah," I stammered nervously. "It'll be great. I'm sure you two will get along ... really well."

Thankfully, the subject changed quickly after that. We drank and ate for several hours while the rest of the riders in Emerald Flight introduced themselves. Most of them were seasoned lieutenants who had seen more than their fair share of battle. But there were a couple of other riders who hadn't been out of the academy for very long. Even though they all made an effort to be friendly, I could tell they were being cautious. No one wanted to be the first to ask about my mixed racial heritage.

Finally, Prax was the one who couldn't hold in his curiosity anymore. "Jace warned us about, well, you know." He leaned in toward me and lowered his voice. "The ears 'n whatnot."

I smiled at him. "I'm glad he did. I'm guessing you wouldn't have been this nice about it otherwise."

Prax nodded in agreement. "I'll be first to admit it, we were all pretty put off by the idea, at first. I mean, no one likes for the lines of loyalty to be blurred. But he said you were a fine rider—finest he's seen in a while. He told us about what happened during your battle scenario. You've got guts for a rider who hasn't even seen battle yet."

I tried not to blush because that definitely wasn't manly. The amount of ale I'd been drinking didn't help me much, though. "I'm glad you approve. Honestly, I was surprised Jace asked me to be his wing end in the first place."

"If you're as fast as he says, then we'll be glad to have you and that wild dragon of yours running point for us," another rider from down the table chimed in and raised his mug. "A toast, to the newest blood in Emerald Flight!"

We all raised our mugs together.

"May the enemies of Maldobar hear legend of the mighty dragonriders. May they shake in terror! May they twist with dread! And may they all remember this battle cry—for it brings a fiery death!" Prax's voice boomed so loudly everyone else in the tavern started staring.

"*Thunder!*" All the dragonriders at our table shouted in unison. We clanged our mugs together and took a drink.

I couldn't keep from grinning as I joined in. It was the first time in my life I'd ever felt truly accepted by this brotherhood. I'd been a student, which did count for something. But this was entirely different. This was where I belonged. I was now and forevermore one of them. These men were my brothers, and we would fight and die together.

I HAD ASSUMED THAT THE GOAL OF THE EVENING WAS FOR ME TO GET TO KNOW all the other riders in my flight. I'd expected the eating, the drinking, and the voluminous debates over pretty girls and battle scars. But that, I thought, was where it would end.

I was wrong.

The goal, which I only became aware of after it was *far* too late, was to get me as drunk as possible without killing me—and that last part was iffy. It was another rookie tradition, evidently. And the riders in my flight must have been having a blast watching me because they laughed and cracked jokes the whole time.

I barely made it back up all those stairs to our room. Jace walked behind me the whole way with a hand on my back to keep me from falling to my death. It was a good thing, too, because it felt like the whole world was spinning. Or maybe I was spinning. I couldn't tell the difference. My head lulled beyond my control. My face felt hot. When we got to our room, I couldn't even figure out how to open the door.

"You're not much of a drinker," Jace observed under his breath as he pushed me out of the way. He herded me farther down the hall to a different door.

I guess I was at the wrong one.

Once we were in our room, I staggered to my bed and fell face-forward onto it. "This hurts," I managed to groan. "I feel sick."

"You better not throw up on your bed," he warned. "It'll reek in here for days. Here, use this."

A bucket hit me in the back of the head as I tried to sit up.

The room was still spinning all around me as I turned around to sit on the edge of the bed and position the bucket between my feet. "Jace, did you notice Lieutenant Prax—"

He cut me off immediately, "We are not talking about that right now."

"But they look exactly alike—and, and I would know!" My stomach was swimming and churning dangerously.

All three of the Jaces standing across the room from me rolled their eyes. "Just hurry up and puke so I can get some sleep."

I obliged.

My stomach rolled painfully and the next thing I knew, I was lying on my back with a cold, wet rag draped over my face. All I could do was groan. My head was throbbing, but at least I didn't feel quite as sick anymore.

"You need to drink some water." Jace appeared over me with a cup.

I sat up slowly, gritting my teeth against the painful knots that twisted in my gut. Sipping the water did make me feel a little better, although it still looked like the room was sloshing back and forth whenever I tried to look around. It made me nauseous all over again, and I was fully expecting to reunite with that bucket at any moment.

"Felix is going to be so upset when he finds out." I could only imagine how that moment would play out. It was bound to be world-shattering for him. "Do you think maybe they won't notice?"

Jace gave me an exasperated stare. "Only if they're both blind, deaf, and brain damaged. Look, it's best to just stay out of it. Family matters are for family members. Let them take care of it. As far as I can tell, Prax isn't even aware he has a child. He never married. For all we know, they could be cousins. And Felix's mother is a high noble. Slandering her name in any way is a punishable offense, even for a dragonrider."

"You did it before," I reminded him. "At the officer's ball. You said you courted her."

His mouth scrunched up like he'd tasted something sour. "That was supposed to be a joke, and the lot of you were too stupid to know any better."

I couldn't answer. I was too busy throwing up into the bucket again.

"Just drink the rest of that water and go to sleep," he said with a heavy sigh. "You'll have a ripping headache tomorrow, but you'll live."

"It doesn't feel like it." I groaned again.

He chuckled on his way back across the room to his bed. I watched him sit down and start unlacing his boots, trying to focus through the way everything still seemed to be swirling and twirling around me. I managed a bit of clarity just in time to see him taking off his tunic while he changed into his bedclothes.

I immediately wished I hadn't.

Jace had scars all over his body. His skin was literally an anthology of violence, and it told a long, gruesome story. The worst by far were the ones around his wrists and neck. I wasn't sure, after all things were still hazy, but those marks almost looked like they had been made by shackles.

I tried not to stare, but it was impossible. I had seen wounds before. I even had a few scars of my own. But judging from the size of some of those marks, Jace was lucky to be alive. It was a sobering thing to see.

"You know, I don't know anything about you." I tried to sound casual as I looked away. "We're going to be partners from now on, so maybe we should get to know each other better. Do you have a family somewhere?"

"No," he answered sharply.

"You mean you're not married?" I tried again.

"No." His unwelcoming tone didn't change.

"So how did you become a dragonrider?"

"I was given a dragon." His answer was sarcastic, and I couldn't understand why. He said it like it was some kind of bad joke. He wouldn't even look my way as he pulled a clean shirt over his head and settled into his bed.

He was putting up walls faster than I could come up with ways around them. But I wasn't giving up that quickly. If I was going to be fighting side-by-side with him, I wanted to know something about him. "What did you do before you were a dragonrider?"

Jace made a noisy, annoyed, growling sound. "Jaevid, let it alone. What I was or what I did before this doesn't matter. It's irrelevant."

"We're supposed to be a team. We're supposed to watch each other's backs," I countered. "So it's relevant to me."

He was silent. After a few uncomfortable minutes, I decided he wasn't going to say anything at all.

"I just want to know if I can trust you," I added.

That must have made him angry because his tone became venomous. "I will do my job, rookie. Don't insult me by doubting that."

"What happened to your last wing end?" It was a bad time to ask about that. I knew it even as the words left my lips. But I still tore open that old wound shamelessly. I wanted to make my case. I knew his last partner had been killed in combat—that was the whole reason he'd gone to Blybrig to be an instructor in the first place. He had been scouting for a new wing end.

"He fell behind." I couldn't see Jace's face, but I could hear the tension in his voice. It sounded like he was clenching his teeth. "I told you that already. He couldn't keep up."

"So you just let him die?" I pressed. I don't know why. Maybe I was too drunk to be sensitive. Or maybe I was hoping he'd get caught up in his emotions and tell me something useful about himself on accident.

"No," Jace snarled furiously. He turned over to give me a smoldering glare. "Are you always this obnoxious? Shut up. Go to sleep."

I saw what looked a lot like grief cross his face. Whatever had happened with his last partner, it had damaged him somehow. And he wasn't over it yet.

I didn't ask any more questions. Even though I couldn't fall asleep right away, I stayed quiet and listened to the sounds of the tower. Men walked past our room with their armor clinking. Unfamiliar voices echoed down the hallways. The faint roar of dragons lulled me to sleep, and for an instant, I almost forgot where I was.

Then the battle horn sounded.

4

CHAPTER FOUR

Fear shot through my body like a bolt of cold lightning. At first, I thought it was real. And then I noticed that I wasn't in my bed. I wasn't even in the tower anymore.

I was clinging to the back of a shrike, sitting in a saddle made from layers of soft animal hide.

Even in a dream, riding on a shrike felt completely different from riding on a dragon. They were much smaller, and so fast it was downright terrifying. The saddle fit down the length of the shrike's back, and flexed with its spine as it zipped through the air on translucent feathered wings. I could feel every movement the creature made, and I had to press my body down against its back so we could fly together without becoming unbalanced. I had to move as it moved, as though we were one with our balance and weight in perfect synchronization. It was a lot more difficult than sitting in a dragon's saddle.

All around me, the Kingdom of Maldobar spread out like a carpet of familiar landscape features. I'd spent so much time as a fledgling memorizing all the different parts of Maldobar, right down to the last mountain peak and river bend because it was part of my training as a dragonrider. I wasn't going to be very effective or useful if I got lost. Judging by the landmarks, I knew we were on the northern battlefront—somewhere very close to Northwatch.

It was hard to pinpoint my location exactly because of what I saw right in front of me. There was a lot on my horizon. The rolling hills of the valley rushed up to meet the ominous boundary where our two kingdoms met. The dark forest of Luntharda, the land of my mother's people, looked like a sea of rippling green leaves and white snow that stretched on forever. Even from a distance, I could sense the power of that place. It was like a wild, untamable beast crouching on the edge of Maldobar. Seeing it like this made my body shudder with anxiety.

I clung to the bone-carved handles on the shrike's saddle as we skimmed the clouds. We were flying high, using our speed and the shrike's mirror-like scales to camouflage ourselves. I didn't know why, but I was terrified. It was as though I was fleeing from something, although every time I looked back, I couldn't see anyone chasing us.

Pain struck me suddenly, hitting me right in the chest. I winced, looking down at what appeared to be the broken-off shaft of an arrow. How long had that been there? I didn't remember being shot. Just by the look of it, it had been a few minutes because there was already a lot of blood running down the front of my clothes.

I was beginning to feel faint. I gripped the saddle as my head spun. Underneath me, the shrike let out a whine of concern. It turned its head to the side, gazing back at me like it was worried—or maybe just making sure I was still alive.

"Hurry," I heard myself say.

But the voice wasn't mine. It sounded like someone else; someone who spoke the elven language far better than I did. Not to mention, it sounded like a *girl*.

The shrike poured on more speed. We passed dozens of plumes of black smoke that rose above the clouds. I didn't pay much attention to them at first. There were so many, and most were far away in the distance. I just assumed they came from cities, mines, or recent battles where dragon fire had been used to turn the tide. After all, large amounts of dragon venom could smolder on its own fuel for days.

Then I got close enough to actually smell the smoke.

The awful stench made me choke. My shrike sneezed and growled bitterly. Down below, I couldn't make out exactly where it came from. We were so far up, and there was so much of it. But that putrid black smoke made my eyes water and my throat want to close up.

The shrike didn't want to get any closer, but I wanted to see where that smell was coming from. I already had a good idea what it was. I'd smelled something sort of like it before in a prison camp outside of the royal city of Halfax. This was much worse, though.

As we broke down through the clouds, dipping quickly into view, I got my first good look.

Suddenly, it all made sense. All the training. All the preparation. All the yelling, beatings, and hours spent learning to hide my emotion behind the steel visor of my helmet. It was because of this.

The silence was haunting. Miles of carnage and ash spread out below me as far as I dared to look. The bodies of Gray elves and human men were twisted together like a flame-scorched briar patch. I saw their milky, glazed eyes staring up at me. Their gazes seemed to follow me as we zipped past.

Dragons lay with their scaly hides pierced by so many arrows they looked like porcupine quills. Shrikes were torn apart like children's toys. They all lay together in the stillness of the cold spring air.

The smell of it all stung my eyes and burned my throat. It made my insides turn sour. I urged the shrike to pull away, and he beat his wings harder to surge back above the clouds.

I thought I had gotten away from it. I just wanted that horrible image out of my mind. But as soon as we pierced the clouds again, I looked out over the horizon and saw other plumes of black smoke.

There were more than I could ever count.

My mother's pendant was burning against my chest like a red-hot coal. The pain of it pressed against my skin made me bolt awake. I yanked it off as fast as I could.

My hands felt tired, like I really had been clinging to the saddle of that shrike. My body was damp with cold sweat, and my heart was still pounding as I looked around the small, dark room to steady myself. Everything was calm and quiet. Jace was sleeping with his back to me, and the bucket was still sitting on the floor beside my bed in case I got sick again.

I certainly felt sick, but it wasn't from drinking too much ale now. I was shivering as I pulled back the blankets and sat up on the edge of my bed, letting my feet rest against the cool floor. I was trying to sort it all out in my mind. I'd never dreamed about riding a shrike like that. Until recently, I'd never dreamed about them at all. The tone of my nightmares had definitely changed. I could feel it—like the weight of impending doom on my chest. Something was coming.

The longer I sat, the cooler the pendant became, until at last I was able to put it back on and tuck it under my shirt. I pressed my hand over where it hung against my chest. Sile had warned me not to take it off. He acted like it was very important.

Now I was beginning to question why my mother had given it to me in the first place.

I was lost in thought, remembering my encounter with Sile. I sat that way for hours before I eventually decided to get up. It was early, but I knew I wasn't going to be able to get any more sleep.

My commotion while I was gathering my things for a bath must have woken up Jace because he rolled over to glare at me like an angry dragon. "Do you ever sleep?"

"Not as often as I'd like."

He didn't say anything else as I left for the community washroom. But when I came back, he was wide-awake. In fact, he was doing pushups upside down in a handstand against the wall.

I just stood in the doorway for a moment and watched because I'd never seen anyone do pushups like that before. It looked like something I might break my neck trying to do.

"You need to keep up the habit of training every day," he warned as he finished his last set. He did a fancy backflip and landed on his feet. "You'd be surprised how much you'll backslide in just a week or two. Too much ale and sleep will make you go soft in the waist."

"Right," I answered as I shuffled over to my bed and started getting out my uniform for the day.

"Hurry up and get ready. Our work shift starts in an hour." Jace wiped the sweat off his face and neck onto one of his tunic. Then he put it on—which I found a little disgusting.

I didn't dare say anything about it, though. I put on clean clothes, buckled my kidney belt around my waist, and kept my opinions to myself. If Jace wanted to stink all day, then that was his business.

"After our shift, we hit the training rooms and spar until dinner," he said as he laced his vambraces around his forearms.

I was busy doing the same thing. "Jace, there's something I've been meaning to ask you."

He shot me a dangerous look, like he suspected I was about to ask him more personal questions about himself. "What is it?"

"My older brother is stationed here, too. Well, he's actually my half-brother. He joined the infantry and left home. I haven't seen him since I started training as a fledgling. I was wondering if I could to try to find him."

I was fully expecting Jace to refuse. Dragonriders and infantry didn't mix. I knew that. But I couldn't come here and not try to find him. Roland had been looking out for me when he gave me the house my father had left behind. He'd even written me a letter, which I still had crammed into my stash of personal belongings. If there was even a chance I could see him and thank him, I wanted to take it.

Jace looked curious. He perked an eyebrow like this was news to him. "You have a brother?"

"Roland Broadfeather," I answered. "I just want to see if he's okay. It wouldn't take long."

He made an unhappy, grumbling sound as he sat down to put on his tall black riding boots. Finally, he rubbed his forehead and let out a noisy groan. "Fine. But we'll have to make it fast. We're not supposed to be down there in infantry territory."

He kept on muttering under his breath the whole way down a dozen or more flights of stairs, winding a path through the tower I knew I wouldn't be able to duplicate on my own. The inside of the tower was like a labyrinth of narrow passages lit by torches, and all the intersections and hallways looked exactly the same to me.

But Jace seemed to know precisely where we were going. He led us to a place where one of the halls opened up wider in front of a pair of large, iron doors. There were a few infantrymen dressed in their battle armor standing outside to guard the entrance, keeping track of who came and went. They stared at me as Jace and I approached. I saw one of them rest his hand on the pommel of his sword, like he wanted me to know he didn't trust me.

We stopped a few yards away from the soldiers. I was so busy watching for one of them to draw a blade, I forgot why we'd even come until Jace gave me a nudge that nearly made me trip over my own feet.

"Go on," he huffed. "We've got things to do."

I had to swallow my dread. I didn't want to talk to these guys; they were practically snarling at me. But there wasn't any other choice, and I couldn't back out now.

I started toward the soldiers. As I approached, one of them rolled up a scroll of paper. It must have been a roster of names because I could see lines and lines of writing on both sides of it.

In the interest of survival, I got straight to the point. I explained who I was, and that I was looking for my brother. When I asked if I could see him, the soldiers exchanged a dubious glance.

"We don't have any halfbreeds here," one of them snapped. He'd apparently taken that suggestion as an insult.

"He isn't one," I clarified. "He's human. His name is Roland Broadfeather. I just want to talk to him."

They were silent for a moment. The one holding the scroll examined me up and down like he was trying to decide if he could take me in a fight or not. I knew he couldn't, but now wasn't the time to start that kind of nonsense.

"I know him," the other soldier said at last. "But he's never mentioned you before."

"Would you have?" I asked him bluntly.

He grinned dangerously. "No, I suppose not. But you're out of luck anyway. Broadfeather mobilized with the rest of his battalion a few days ago. They were sent to retake Barrowton."

That was not at all what I wanted to hear. Roland was fighting. And I wasn't there to make sure he made it back alive. "Do you know when they might come back?"

The soldiers glanced at one another again and exchanged a shrug. "Depends on if they can take the city quickly or not," one of them guessed. "Barrowton was overrun. It's a regular beehive of those silver-headed demons. I wouldn't expect to see anyone come back for another month, at least."

I thanked them and went back to where Jace was waiting, tapping his foot impatiently. He met me with another serious but curious frown. "Well?"

I saved my explanation until we had rounded a corner and put some distance between the infantrymen and ourselves. As I told him everything they had said, Jace's expression darkened. I caught a glint of dark suspicion in his eyes as he glanced sideways at me.

"That brother of yours, can he do any of the magical stuff you can?" he asked.

I frowned back at him challengingly. "I don't know. We've never really been close."

Jace had always been a difficult person for me to read. He didn't say anything else about it as we made our way back to our section of the tower. But I wondered what he was thinking. I wondered why he wouldn't tell me anything about himself. Surely a man his age, somewhere in his late thirties, had a family, even if he wasn't married. He had to have parents, or siblings, or cousins.

We'd used up all our breakfast time indulging my curiosity, so when we got back to the dragonriders' level of the tower, we went straight to work. Our job was simple—painfully simple. We were moving crates of supplies off the pulley-operated elevator system that ran from the ground level to the top floor of the tower.

I couldn't help but be amazed; I'd never seen anything like it. A huge shaft went straight down the center of the tower, plunging into darkness, with several stops on a few floors along the way. A wooden platform suspended on thick ropes could be raised and lowered by operating a huge crank on the ground level. Jace said they had a team of draft horses hitched to it that operated the crank and moved the elevator up and down.

"A lot better than carrying these crates up fifty stories," he pointed out as we worked. Together, we were moving the crates from the platform onto two rickshaw carts that we were supposed to use to get them from the elevator to the storage rooms.

I leaned over the edge to peek down into the dark shaft that plummeted straight down below us, marveling at how the ropes had all be strung together so that they were synchronized perfectly.

"Why can't we use this?" I asked. "You know, instead of walking up the stairs every time?"

Jace grabbed the back of my tunic suddenly, jerking me back into the elevator. "First, because of stupid people like you who decide to lean over the edge and fall to their deaths. Quit that. Don't you have any sense at all?" he growled as he got back to work loading the rickshaw. "Second, because the stairs serve as a deterrent to keep people from leaving the tower any more than necessary. It's better to keep everyone in one place in case we're needed on short notice."

Walking up all those stairs was definitely a good reason for me not to leave unless I absolutely had to. Doing it sober was bad enough. Trying to climb them after the members of my flight had coaxed me into drinking too much ale was absolute torture. I wasn't eager to repeat that scenario anytime soon.

It took eight trips and most of the day to move all the crates from the elevator to the storage room. We only stopped once for a quick bite of lunch. By the time we unloaded the last crate, my clothes and hair were soaked with sweat. Now I understood why Jace hadn't cared too much about how dirty he was this morning.

When we were finished, we didn't stop to rest. As soon as our shift was over, Jace led the way to the sparring room so we could train together. It was a decent sized room with skinny windows on three sides to let the cold, fresh air blow in —which felt amazing after working for so long. The ceiling was a lot higher, too, and there were an assortment of different training weapons hanging on the far wall.

A few other men were already practicing. Some were sparring with swords, and others were grappling on the floor. Jace must have had something more intense in mind because he plucked a wooden scimitar that was a similar size and weight to mine off the wall and tossed it to me. Then he took two swords for himself and nodded toward one of the big sparring circles painted on the floor.

I'll admit, I was nervous. I had sparred against Felix and all the other avian students in my graduating class more times than I could count. I'd even sparred against Sile a time or two. But I had never once locked blades with Jace—not like this, anyway.

He had a reputation for being especially brutal. I wasn't sure what to expect from him when it came to style and technique. I'd never seen him *really* fight anyone.

Our eyes met from across the sparring mat as the atmosphere between us changed abruptly. My instincts came alive, and all my senses snapped into focus. I forgot about how tired I was and I couldn't feel how my back and arms were aching from working all morning.

"You've learned to fight human enemies," Jace said as he paced the outside of the circle, spinning both of the swords over his hands with effortless speed. "Fighting against Gray elves is completely different. Like our dragons, we hope to never fight on the ground. But if that becomes necessary, you need to know what you'll be up against."

I stepped into the sparring circle with my mind quiet and my breathing calm and steady. I never took my eyes off him. "And what is that, exactly?"

"They're smaller, faster, with reflexes that border on the supernatural. Their bones are as hard as metal, and their strength is impressive for their stature. They will hit you hard. And they will hit you often. Their strategy is to overwhelm you, to put you on the defensive immediately." He stared me down like a wolf, powerful and likely to strike at any given moment. I could see that dead soldier's look in his eyes. "But their weakness is their independence. For whatever reason, they don't fight together as a unit."

I narrowed my own eyes and tightened my grip on my scimitar. "Shouldn't we have learned this at the academy?"

Jace stopped his pacing and he turned to face me with a humorless smirk on his lips. "Probably. But the ruling powers decided that the role of the academy is to produce as many effective riders as quickly as possible. Some things had to be cut from the curriculum in order to meet the demand of riders to replenish the ranks. And let's face it, not all of you are cut out to put your sword and flame against a Gray elf."

I sank slowly into a defensive stance and raised my scimitar as a signal; I was ready. "Let's get on with it, then."

His dark eyes glittered with feral energy as he snapped his arms out wide, a sword in each hand. That was all the warning I got. Jace rushed me like a hurricane, striking with speed and precision I'd never experienced from anyone. Sure, Felix hit with incredible force, but his blows were slower and easier to predict. Sile was fast, but his aggression made him reckless and careless when it came to defensive maneuvers.

Jace was as close to flawless as I imagined a fighter could be.

We blurred through our best combat moves, testing each other at every potential weak point. It didn't take Jace more than a minute to find one of mine. He feigned a strike, which I fell for like a complete dummy. In a blur, he disarmed me and my scimitar went clattering across the floor as Jace planted a kick squarely in my chest and sent me flying.

I hit the ground hard, gasping for breath. There was a boot print on the front of my shirt and I could see stars winking in my vision as I got back to my feet and picked up my weapon again.

"Don't be stupid," he snarled. "On the battle field, you're always one stupid mistake away from having a blade hilt-deep in your gut."

I watched as he stepped back and assumed a defensive stance. It was my turn to strike first. There was a flicker of a smirk on his lips—which I could only imagine was his way of taunting me.

"You have some of that Gray elf speed in you. I've seen it before," he said. "So use it."

My blood was boiling. I was making rookie mistakes. I couldn't afford to be this sloppy. It wasn't just my life on the line now; I had the rest of my brothers in Emerald Flight to think about.

"You want me to use a Gray elf skill on you? That's new." I glared at him with renewed energy.

"I want you to do whatever you have to in order to stay alive." He curled a finger at me, taunting me further by inviting me to attack him. "Now shut up and hit me ... if you can."

CHAPTER FIVE

The weather turned foul on the day Felix was supposed to arrive. Powerful storms weren't uncommon here, and the already dismal skies were growing even darker. Thunder growled over the mountains, and the temperatures plummeted below freezing. From the safety of the tower, I watched the king's banners whipping in the violent winds. Snow mixed with frozen rain made the platforms miserable to land on. Soldiers were frantically spreading salt over them to keep them from freezing over.

I'd only been in the tower for a few days myself, but I already felt like a caged animal trapped behind these stone walls. The howling wind was like music to my ears, and the cold made me feel alive again. I breathed it all in as I watched the sky.

I saw her an instant before I heard the sound of her roar. Felix's dragon, Nova, came in with her wings flared and her legs outstretched for landing. I winced when she finally touched down. Her feet slipped and slid dangerously on the icy platform, but she managed to stick the landing.

Right away, the soldiers working the platform cranked open the iron gate. Several of them rushed out to help guide Nova into the tower, and I followed to meet Felix as he came in out of the storm.

Prax hadn't been able to trade his shift in the armory, so he'd asked me to come and meet Felix for him. I was more than happy to stand in and spare my best friend from that moment of personal horror for as long as possible. Just seeing Nova lumbering into the tower, shaking ice and snow from her wings, made me grin. She was making irritated chirping sounds and twitching the end of her tail like angry cat. I guess she didn't like the cold any more than Mavrik did.

I felt Mavrik's emotions swell in my mind. He could glimpse into my thoughts, and I guess seeing Nova got him all worked up. He started sending me excited swirls of pink and orange. Apparently they had some sort of dragon-romance brewing—or so Mavrik thought. I couldn't tell that she was willing to give him the time of day.

He chattered at her musically when she crawled past his stall on the way to her own bed. Then he stuck out his chest, raised the black spines along his back, and tried to puff himself out to impress her. It didn't work. She just stopped and sniffed him a few times before moving on.

I gave him a sympathetic pat on the snout. "Sorry, buddy. Looks like she's playing hard to get this time."

Mavrik grumbled his agreement and curled up in his stall again, snorting an irritated breath over the end of his tail.

Suddenly, someone punched me in the arm. I swung back immediately without looking. There was only one person in the world who did that to me.

"Miss me?" Felix laughed as he took off his helmet. His lengthy, dark golden hair was a tangled mess from being crammed under it for so long.

Despite the inevitable chaos he was most likely about to endure when he met his partner, I was still glad to see him. Of course, I couldn't tell him that. The laws of masculinity forbade it. "Nah, not really."

"You never were a very good liar." He gave me one of his usual smirks, but I noticed right away that something was off. He wouldn't look me in the eye for very long, almost like he was trying to hide something.

I followed him to Nova's stall, and stood by the door while he got her settled in and took off her gear. I was silently wondering what was going on, or if something had gone wrong with his mother. He looked tired—which was completely understandable. Flying in weather like that was like being sloshed around in a bucket full of icy water.

Once Nova was settled, I picked up Felix's bag and nodded down the corridor that led into the tower. "Quite a place, huh?"

He nodded, but still wouldn't look my way. "No kidding. I couldn't see much, though. This storm is pretty bad. My visibility was lousy."

We walked together in silence almost the entire way to the room he was going to be sharing with Prax. With each step, I realized more and more just how awkward and quiet he was being. I started to get afraid that maybe his mother had already told him about Prax. Did he know? Was he upset? Should I even say anything about it until he brought it up on his own? Jace was right; it was a personal family matter. It wasn't any of my business. I shouldn't be sticking my nose in it unless I was invited to.

When we got to the door, Felix hesitated. He was chewing on the inside of his cheek vigorously and his brow was furrowed. We stood there for a few seconds while he just stared at the door like that. Eventually, he seemed to snap out of it. He flicked me a glance, forced a smile, and reached out to take his bag.

I hesitated to give it to him. "Is everything all right?"

Our eyes locked, and I saw it plainly; there was worry and absolute sadness written all over his face. I'd never seen him like this before. But he acted like he was ashamed of it; like he'd done something really horrible and he didn't want me to know about it.

So I dropped his bag on the ground between us, put my boot on it, and crossed my arms. I wasn't moving until I got some answers. "What's this about?"

I was expecting him to scowl or maybe even fight back a little. But his shoulders dropped and he looked away dejectedly. "Fine. But I'm not talking about it here. Is there somewhere we can go?"

I knew of a place that was sure to be deserted at this time of day. After we threw his bag onto his bed and took off his outer layer of armor and padding, I led the way up to the sparring room. I knew everyone was bound to still be working their shift jobs, so we had the room to ourselves.

Felix glanced around for a moment like he was taking it all in. Then he strolled over to one of the windows that lined the two exterior walls, staring out at the raging spring storm that was wailing against the glass. He had that strained expression on his face again, and I noticed he was clenching his hands into fists so hard his knuckles were white.

Standing behind him, I decided to wait until he felt like talking. It didn't take long. After a few minutes, he turned back around and leaned against the wall.

"The king issued a decree demanding that all Gray elf refugees in Maldobar be immediately deported from their residences and taken to Halfax." He didn't mince words or dance around the topic, but he couldn't hold my gaze while he spoke. "The prison camp at Halfax has been rebuilt. It's much bigger than it was before. I passed over it on my way to my family's estate. I could see the smoke for miles and miles. When I got back home, I heard about the decree. The Gray elves are being taken there by the thousands every day from all corners of the kingdom—men, women, and children. And judging by the smoke rising out of that cesspool, it's not a big mystery what is happening to them there."

My heart was beating so loudly, and the silence between us was so heavy, I knew he would be able to hear it.

"It isn't right. Those people came here for shelter." Felix looked up at me at last. I saw bitter wrath blazing in his eyes. "The king isn't interested in winning this war—he's interested in exterminating their entire race."

I was so stunned by what I'd just heard my reactions were delayed. Panic made my blood run as cold as the freezing rain outside. I was angry. I was speechless and utterly horrified. All I could say was, "Why?"

Felix shook his head. "Does he need a reason? He's the king. His word is law. No one can refute it."

My legs were beginning to get weak. I turned around to lean against the wall. A few seconds later, my knees buckled and I found myself sitting on the floor next to him.

"I gave word to every servant in my household to give secret refuge to any Gray elf they found on my family's grounds," he said very quietly as he sat down next to me. "I signed up to be a soldier, to fight in defense of Maldobar. But I won't be anyone's executioner. It's one thing to fight their warriors on the battlefield. It's another to butcher innocent civilians."

Doubt crept into my mind. What was I doing here? It was only a matter of time until I was sent to fight. In a few days, or maybe even hours, I could be facing this same choice—to kill my mother's people or not. And what would I do then?

"As far as I know, halfbreeds are exempt from the decree. Technically, people like you aren't even supposed to exist, right?" Felix gave me a nudge like he was trying to cheer me up. "I'm sorry, Jae."

"I saw Sile before I left Blybrig," I blurted suddenly. I don't know why I told him. Sile had warned me not to tell anyone. But Felix was one of the only people in my life I knew I could always trust.

His brows went up in surprise. "He came back? Why?"

I bowed my head slightly and buried my face in one of my hands. "He told me to go to Luntharda. He said he wanted me to see what my mother's people were going through. He said there was some sort of ritual that I had to perform in order to tap into my full power."

Now Felix was the one being quiet. When I looked at him again, I could almost see the wheels turning in his eyes. He was busy thinking about something. "So I guess this means your power does have something to do with the Gray elves," he whispered.

I cringed. "I guess so."

"Do you think he knew this was coming? This mass genocide?"

"I don't know," I admitted. "He didn't say anything about it. But then again, he probably wouldn't have told me even if he did know."

We sat there without saying a word for what felt like a long while. In that time, my fears and worries ran rampant through my brain. I was confused. I didn't know what part I had to play in all this, or what my power, the god stone, or my dreams had to do with it all—but there was no escaping it now.

"So that just leaves one question," Felix said as he let out a deep sigh.

I was really curious how he had narrowed everything down to one question. I couldn't even wrap my mind around most of what was happening now. I sent him a dubious look and waited to hear what that one question was.

He laughed humorlessly, like this whole situation was cruelly ironic to him. "What amazing, unexpected thing are we going to do next?"

Hearing such awful news from Felix had effectively distracted me from what was sure to come next. He was a new lieutenant, which meant he had a night full of brotherly bonding and excessive drinking ahead of him. Not to mention, he was about to meet his partner—the man I also suspected was his real father.

I should have warned him.

As soon as I heard the sparring room door open, I regretted having talked myself out of it. There definitely wasn't time bring it up now. Jace, Prax, and a few of the other riders in our flight were coming our way.

"Thick as thieves aren't they?" Prax chuckled as they gathered around us, laughing and peering curiously at their newest rookie.

Felix and I got up right away. I kept my mouth shut while my best friend started introducing himself around the group. He shook hands with the other men, smiled, and carried on like nothing was the matter.

That is, until he got to Prax.

"I'm Lieutenant Darion Prax," he said in his cheerful, booming voice. "I take it you took the bid to act as my wing end?"

Felix hesitated when the big rider extended one of his hands to shake. Seeing them standing together, face to face, was downright eerie. Felix wasn't nearly as tall as Prax was, but his brawny build was practically the same. They definitely had the same wavy, dark gold hair, although Prax's was beginning to turn gray. They had the same face-shape, the same casual demeanor, and the same cunning twinkle in their dark eyes. There was no way they couldn't be related. They just had to be.

The longer I stood there comparing all their similarities, the harder it was for me to keep my expression neutral. Anxious tension put a hard knot in the back of my throat. I started noticing the way everyone else in our group was looking at them, too. Jace and I weren't the only ones who were seeing it now. The question was ... would Felix and Prax notice it, too?

Prax's hand hung out there, waiting to shake Felix's, for what felt like an eternity. I sucked in a sharp breath.

Then Felix smiled. He laughed. And he shook Prax's hand like nothing was wrong. "Yes, sir. You came very highly recommended. I look forward to riding with you."

That was it.

They went on talking like nothing was wrong. In fact, they seemed to really be hitting it off. They were laughing and talking, already acting like they had known each other for years. I didn't see any hint of recognition in either of their faces.

As we all started to leave the sparring room, I stepped in closer to Jace wanting to ask him about it. Before I could get a word out, Jace punched me in the side hard enough to make me stagger and wheeze. He shot me a scorching glare of warning and growled, "Stay out of it. It's none of our business."

I wheezed again and nodded.

Once everyone had gotten off their daytime work shifts and met down at the bottom of the tower, we set out into the city for another welcoming party. Everyone started bickering like a bunch of angry hens about which bar was best, and yet we ended right back at the Laughing Fox again. I was starting to suspect this was a typical routine for them. No wonder it was known as a "dragonrider bar."

Knowing the evening was going to be geared toward getting Felix as drunk as humanly possible, I was extra cautious about how much I was drinking. Felix unfortunately had no idea what was going on. I sort of doubted he would have put up much of a fight, though, even if he had known. Four mugs of ale in, he was starting to slur and was having a hard time sitting upright. But I'd seen Felix drink a lot more than that, so I knew we still had a long night ahead of us.

I sat next to Jace and nursed my one mug all night. Thankfully, no one noticed. Or if they did, they didn't care. Felix was their victim tonight, so I was left alone for the most part.

That is, until one of the barmaids started getting a little more friendly than usual with me. I still remembered what Jace had told me about them—how they were just after tips and being a new lieutenant made me an easy target. So the first time she ran a hand through my hair teasingly, I didn't think much of it. Granted, I wasn't exactly used to being petted like that, but it didn't really mean anything.

Or so I thought.

She was pretty, I guess. That was this bar's claim to fame, after all. But I tried not to make too much eye contact with her. She had ginger-colored hair tied up in ribbons with a few curly pieces framing her face. She batted her eyes at me, and always made a point to touch me somehow whenever she came around the table to bring us another round of ale or food. The other riders in my flight noticed, and the heckling inevitably started.

"Guess she'd like to take a nibble of those pointy ears, eh?" Prax laughed.

"You should have seen him juggling the girls at last year's ball," Felix chimed in. "It's like they didn't even notice he was a halfbreed. Totally not fair."

Beside me, Jace snickered in agreement. "It's the cheekbones. Women go stupid for that kind of thing."

Despite my best efforts to keep it in, my face was burning with embarrassment. I couldn't even think of anything to say in my own defense. Not that it would have done me any good if I'd tried.

Thankfully, I got a good excuse to leave the bar for a few minutes when Felix started to get sick. After six mugs of ale, I knew he was bound to pass out or throw up—maybe even both. So when he started weaving dangerously in his seat and complaining that his stomach hurt, I knew it was time to go outside for some air.

"Come on. Let's take a breather," I said while trying to coax him out of his chair. I let him lean on me as I hauled him out the back door of the bar.

Felix didn't put up much of a fight. But he did insist, amidst his slurred words, that we were coming back for more. The rest of the riders in our flight, Jace and Prax included, cheered him on as we went. I guess they approved of his determination to jump right back into a fresh mug of ale as soon as he was finished.

No one could ever accuse Felix of being a lightweight. He could drink with the best of them. But those men in our flight were really putting him through the ringer tonight. We barely made it out the back door before Felix was on his knees, throwing up in the alleyway. I couldn't do much for him except make sure he didn't choke or pass out.

"You should probably take a break," I suggested as I watched him heave. "Have some water or at least eat something before you drink anything else, yeah?"

I couldn't understand his reply. It was garbled as he started throwing up again. He definitely needed to drink something other than ale or liquor if he was going to make it through tonight with his dignity intact.

The weather outside was still miserable. Where we stood in the dark, narrow alley behind the bar, there was snowy slush gathered along the sides of the cobblestone street. The wind was still blowing fiercely, and without my cloak, I was feeling every puff of frigid air against my body.

Felix was standing up again, wiping his chin on his sleeve, and squinting at me like he was too drunk to remember who I was. I started to loop one of his arms over my shoulder when a sound made us both stop cold in our tracks. It wasn't anything either of us had ever heard before—at least, not like this. But as soon as we heard it, both our gazes snapped upward to the tower that loomed over us.

The battle horn was blaring.

We hurried back inside where Jace and the others were putting on their cloaks and getting ready to leave. No one was smiling or laughing anymore. We only waited long enough for Felix to pound a glass of water before we left the bar in a hurry, the horn still blaring in the cold night wind. Torches were being lit along the ramparts, and I could see the dark silhouettes of soldiers running to and fro. People were trickling out of their houses and shops, holding candles and wearing heavy coats, to peer curiously up at the tower.

No one in our group spoke as we jogged all the way back through the gates into the tower. We ran up the stairs, and everyone was thoroughly winded and sweaty by the time we made it to the dragonriders' levels. Inside, the halls were packed with men and gear. It didn't take us long to figure out that Gold Squadron was being deployed to Barrowton.

Memories of my training in the academy, of many sleepless nights spent dreading the mournful wail of the battle horn, came rushing back as I stood against the wall with Jace and the other riders of Blue Squadron. We watched as those being mobilized rushed to prepare. They came out of their rooms fully dressed, their helms under their arms and go-bags over their shoulders.

As the riders of Gold Squadron filed down to the stable, we followed in complete silence. My nerves were drawn tight. I was on edge watching all these steel-eyed men gather in full battle dress to hear Colonel Bragg give them a quick brief of their situation. It wasn't something the rest of us were required to hear, but it wasn't something I would have dared miss.

The atmosphere was tense and so quiet you could have heard a pin drop as he explained they would be departing immediately, keeping tight formation because of the storm. They would be making for Barrowton for a dawn surprise assault. Things weren't going well in the effort to retake the city, apparently. The infantry on the ground had called for aid.

And the Dragonriders of Northwatch would answer.

All I could think about was my brother. Roland was at Barrowton. He was one of those infantrymen calling for help. I couldn't even consider that he might already be dead. Roland was strong. He would survive—or so I prayed.

There were about fifty riders in Gold Squadron, and watching them all mount up with their armor gleaming was a beautiful sight. Something about it made emotion stir in my chest. I was proud to be counted among them, but I was also terrified of when my own day came to be standing where they were.

The heavy gates of the tower were rolled open. One by one, the riders filed out into the howling spring storm. It was like watching bats exiting a cave as they all spiraled and swarmed at the top of the tower, waiting until everyone was out to assume their formations. They vanished like phantoms into the gloom of the cold night, leaving us all in a state of numb silence.

Then came the boom of a familiar roar.

I knew it right away—even before I saw the shape of a monstrous, winged black beast sailing past the tower. Icarus let out a second, bellowing roar that shook the very foundations of the tower. He spat a plume of flame that lit up the dark, illuminating the black-armored rider sitting on his back.

All the dragonriders standing around me inside the tower cheered in triumph. They chanted the name "Seraph" over and over like it was some sort of battle cry. Just the sight of Icarus was absolutely terrifying. I couldn't blame them for being inspired by it. But knowing it was the woman I loved sitting on his back, riding toward blood and doom, made it impossible for me to join in.

"They've lost almost ten thousand men trying to retake that city,"

Jace said quietly as we all sat around a table in the dining hall. We'd gone there with the intention of finishing up Felix's welcoming party, but no one seemed to feel much like drinking anymore.

"It's idiocy," another rider muttered in agreement. "Barrowton is overrun. We cannot take it back. Not without burning it to the ground."

Prax shook his head. "Colonel Bragg would never support such a decision. There are still too many civilians trapped inside. The Gray elves are wise to keep them alive. It's the only thing that prevents us from raining dragon fire upon their heads."

Without thinking much about it, I had started fidgeting with my necklace. I twisted it in my fingers thoughtfully, listening and trying to process it all. I didn't offer my opinion. I didn't have much of one yet, anyway. After the news Felix had dumped on me earlier, seeing the other riders deploy, and catching a glimpse of Beckah as she followed them into battle ... I had a lot on my mind.

"That she-elf harpy must be leading the forces out of their jungle again," I heard someone else growl bitterly. "She's the only one who has been able to rally their forces in the past."

Jace snorted with disgust. "It should have been us. We should have been sent to retake the city."

"You just want another crack at her, eh?" Prax chuckled softly, like he was trying to ease some of the tension in the room. "She slips through your fingers like hair through a comb. Face it, Rordin. You've met your match in that witch."

Hearing something even remotely personal about Jace made me snap out of my trance. "What are you talking about? What witch?"

"The princess of the Gray elves. She's the only one to ever outmaneuver him in the air." Prax was grinning knowingly at Jace, who was scowling down into his mug like he wished we would change the subject. "He takes it rather personally."

Even Felix was acting curious now. "How do you know she's a princess?"

"The Gray elves dress their royalty in a long war headdress. It's easy to spot; you can't miss it. It has the white horns of a deer on it," Prax explained. "Jace has brought down all three of the princes before her in an effort to demoralize our enemy into surrender. They may not be fond of fighting together as an organized unit, but they won't fight at all without someone to lead them. But now he's met his match in that crafty little she-demon."

"I wounded her last time, and you know it," Jace snapped in angry defiance. "She went limping back to her forest before I could catch up to her. It won't happen again. She won't escape me twice."

Memories of my last dream flickered through my mind in an instant. I still remembered vividly what it had felt like to be clinging to the back of a shrike, wounded, and fleeing toward Luntharda. I'd never had a dream quite like that before. That is, I'd never been someone else in my dreams. I'd always been myself, usually invisible and irrelevant to whatever was happening around me.

But that time, I'd been a wounded Gray elf—a wounded *female* Gray elf. Surely that was just a coincidence, wasn't it?

The sick, swirling sense of dread in the pit of my stomach begged to differ.

Prax leaned over to me, interrupting my moment of private panic, and murmured, "She lost him in the clouds. Their speed and the camouflaging scales of a shrike make it near impossible to track them when they hide like that."

"I'm not deaf, you know." Jace slammed his mug down on the table, making all the dishes rattle. "Mark my words. I will have her head on a pike the next time we meet."

A few of the other riders sitting around us laughed and rolled their eyes. They started going on about how embarrassed they would be if a woman had shown them up like that. I wondered how they would feel if they knew their so-called hero, Seraph, was a woman, too. I doubted they would find that very funny.

"So, what are the chances of us actually getting called up to Barrowton?" Felix piped up. I suspected he was changing the subject on purpose. He was the only other person besides Sile and myself who knew who Seraph really was.

Thankfully, it worked.

"The only reason we would be called is if they need reinforcements or if there's another battle elsewhere that requires our attention," Jace answered. "We're immediately put on waiting shift. The next horn that sounds is meant for us."

"And so we wait," Prax agreed.

6

CHAPTER SIX

I noticed there was something strange in the pocket of my pants—something I definitely hadn't put in there—when we got back to our room later that night. Jace was busy grabbing up things to take to the washroom, so he didn't notice when I pulled a small square of folded paper from my pocket. I was baffled. How had that gotten in there?

Then I remembered the barmaid at the Laughing Fox. She'd been awfully touchy feely with me, which was beyond strange. Human girls weren't usually so eager to be friendly with me. She must have slipped it into my pocket when I wasn't paying attention.

At the risk of being teased in case it was something embarrassing, I waited until Jace had left to take his bath before I read it. It was just a small slip of paper with a few plain words scribbled on it. But the sight of them made my adrenaline surge:

On the roof. —B.D.

I quickly grabbed my cloak and sword, just in case, and started out the door. The tower was fairly quiet this late at night. Only a few people were still milling around in the halls, and none of them gave me a second look as I slipped to the staircase and started to climb.

It wasn't far up to the top level of the tower, just four or five flights. But the roof was barred by a large iron-reinforced door, made like a hatch, which was held closed with two bars of solid iron. Each one of those bars weighed nearly a hundred pounds, so it took me a moment to move them so that I could open the door. As soon as I did, fierce cold wind came howling into the small, dark corridor. Another narrow staircase led up to the very top of the tower, which was open to the stormy night sky.

Against the roaring winds and frozen rain, I saw the shape of someone standing at the top of that staircase. At first glimpse, it looked like a knight; a petite man clad in armor that shimmered like obsidian glass and adorned in painted golden wings, even on the gauntlets and helmet, giving the wearer an angelic appearance.

I stretched out my hand toward the black armored knight, who had started descending the steps. Once we were both inside, we began working together to push the door closed again to keep out the cold.

Then she took off her helmet.

Beckah's long dark hair fell down over her shoulder in a braid. Some of her bangs were sticking to the moisture on her forehead and the sides of her face, and her lightly freckled cheeks were flushed from the cold wind. When her bright green eyes looked up at me in the darkness, I felt like I couldn't breathe.

I kissed her. It was a much deeper, more passionate kiss than any we'd ever had before. She put her arms around my waist and hugged me close, and for a long time we just stood like that. I couldn't believe how much I'd missed her in such a short amount of time. Under all that armor, she was still the simple, beautiful girl I'd eaten peaches with on the beach in Saltmarsh. She was still the Beckah I loved.

"I'm so glad you're here," she whispered as she laid her head against my chest. "I've missed you so much."

I ran my fingers through her soft hair and wished I could have said the same to her. But I couldn't. I didn't want her to be here, on the battlefront, risking her life like this. I wanted her somewhere safe. Unfortunately, the world seemed to be running out of safe places to be.

"How did you know I'd be at that bar?" I asked.

She pulled back some—just enough to give me a coy little grin. "I saw Felix and Nova arrive this morning. Lucky for me, dragonriders gossip worse than old ladies in a knitting circle. I had heard you both wound up in the same flight, so I knew you'd be coming out tonight. I followed you all to the bar, then I paid off that barmaid to slip my note to the naïve-looking halfbreed in a dragonrider uniform," she explained.

She sounded rather proud of herself, and I have to admit, she was much sneakier than I had given her credit. I already knew she was smarter than I was, which could be scary at times. It was a good thing, though. She probably wouldn't have lasted this long, disguising herself as a man and fighting in battle alongside dragonriders, if she hadn't been so clever.

"I thought you were going to Barrowton," I said. "I saw you leaving with them."

Beckah put her head back against my chest and sighed. "I am going, but not yet. I had to see you first. Besides, I can't fly with them in their formations; it would be much too risky. It's better for me to arrive fashionably late to see where I'm most needed once the battle is underway. Icarus's presence alone makes the enemy forces scatter and panic. He takes good care of me, you know."

I held her tighter. Once again, I didn't trust myself to say anything because I might slip up and tell her how I really felt. I didn't want her involved in this. I didn't like that she was fighting. But I knew better than to start that conversation. This was where she was meant to be, and how I felt about it didn't matter. Arguing about it wasn't going to make any difference.

"There's something else, Jae. Something I have to tell you." Her voice grew softer so that she was nearly whispering. "I've thought every day about what you told me in Halfax, about your father and the god stone. But it wasn't until I came here that I started to understand what the stone might mean in all this."

Now I was the one pulling back so I could look her in the eyes. "What are you talking about?"

"The god stone," she stared up at me earnestly, as though she were afraid I wouldn't believe her, "it's precious to the Gray elves somehow. I'm not sure why, but they're desperate to get it back. So desperate that they are willing to send their soldiers on suicide mission after suicide mission just to find it."

"How do you know this?"

Her expression faltered. She looked down and didn't say anything at first. Then she spoke in a quiet voice, "You've heard of the city called Dayrise? It was once a place much like Barrowton—a flourishing trade stop near the border of Luntharda. It's nothing but ashes now. Icarus and I hid out there for a while when I first began to fight."

Beckah's voice became unsteady. She put her hands on my chest, although I couldn't feel any of her warmth because she was still wearing her riding gauntlets. "I couldn't bear to stay there for long. It's essentially a mass grave. But I found one building still standing. Inside it were the remains of a dozen or so Gray elves. They weren't much more than charred bones gripping rusted swords, but one of them had used the point of a dagger to etch something into the walls. Two words …"

"Return it," I finished for her.

Her eyes grew wide. For an instant, she almost seemed afraid of me. "H-how did you know that?"

"Those words have been echoing in my mind for years now," I explained. "Until now, I didn't understand why. Beckah, what if I'm the one who is supposed to return the god stone to Luntharda? What if that's why I'm having all these dreams?"

"Jae, you can't be serious." Beckah was shaking her head in protest. "Regardless of what your father did, that doesn't mean you have to be the one making amends for all his mistakes. Going into that jungle is suicide, even for someone like you. You saw what happened on the Canrack Islands. Your power was essentially useless there. How do you know it will be any different in Luntharda? And even if you made it to one of the Gray elf cities, the likelihood that they would even listen to—"

"I know that!" The words came out much more harshly than I intended. I was so frustrated by it all, but I tried to soften my tone when I spoke to her again. "You told me once, when Icarus first chose you, that you felt like there was something you were supposed to be doing. That's how I feel now—like every force in the universe is pointing me toward something that I'm supposed to be doing. I don't know what's waiting for me at the end of all this, and frankly thinking about it terrifies me. But I may not have a choice."

She didn't look convinced. Her eyes narrowed dangerously, and she took a step away from me.

I wasn't letting her get away that easily. I knew she could be stubborn, just like her father. So I put my arms around her again and dragged her toward me. She resisted a little, at first. Then I kissed her again. And the second our lips touched, I felt her begin to relax.

"You know just as well as I do that feelings like these are impossible to ignore. I can't outrun them. I can't push them away. I've been trying to do that for years, and it's driving me insane," I said once I was sure she would hear me out. "I'm not interested in dying, either, just for the record."

"Please don't do anything stupid," she muttered angrily.

I smiled and put one of my hands against her cheek, brushing a bit of her hair away from her eyes. "I'll try. At least, no stupider than usual. I don't have any plans to go tromping through that jungle, believe me. Felix and the others need me here."

There were tears in the corners of her beautiful green eyes as she looked up at me again. Her lip was trembling as she spoke. "So do I, Jae. I can't lose you. I should have listened to Mom. I should never have fallen in love with a dragonrider."

"That's not fair." I wiped away one of the tears that was sliding down her cheek. "You became one, too. I'd call that a double standard."

I managed to solicit a weak smile from her. "It doesn't count if I'm not official."

"Oh it definitely counts." I laughed and tugged on her cheek playfully. "Besides, now you know how I feel every time I see you flying off without me."

We both became quiet as we stood in the dark, with nothing but the sound of the wind howling outside the tower to fill the silence. I let my forehead rest against hers. She always made me feel braver than I knew I was. Her strength gave me strength. I prayed I made her feel the same way.

Because we were both going to need it.

I couldn't sleep once I got back to my room. Everything was pitch black. Jace was sound asleep in his bed. Except for him stirring and wheezing every now and then, everything was completely silent. But my mind was restless with the possibility that my suspicions were correct. Was the god stone really the cause of this war? Was it so important to the Gray elves that they were willing to risk all out war for two decades just to get it back? I didn't see how it could possibly be worth all that trouble. There were just too many unanswered questions.

It took forever for me to finally drift off. And when I did, I only got a few short hours of sleep before it was time to get up and start working again. We all had to work extra hard to carry the load of Gold Squadron while they were away. That meant longer shifts for everyone, and even some different jobs just to pick up the slack.

Jace and I wound up working a second shift mucking out dragon stalls, which is gross anyway but even worse when you're cooped up in a tiny room with not much ventilation. We worked all day, taking breaks only long enough to grab a gulp of water or a bite to eat. There wasn't even much time to talk, not that anyone seemed to feel much like talking. The atmosphere was still just as tense as it had been when Gold Squadron departed. It was like we were all holding our breath and straining to listen in case the battle horn sounded again.

Two days later, at the end of yet another long workday, the tension had begun to ease off a little. Everyone in Emerald Flight was settling down at one of the long tables in the dining hall. Strong ale and hot food always got the men talking, so I settled in to listen and enjoy my meal. Sitting between Felix and Jace, I had a front row seat to the antics of my comrades. Fortunately, tonight I wasn't the focus of their abuse.

One of the riders was busy teasing Felix mercilessly. I guess him being the newest between the two of us made him the target of choice. "So Long-Hair-And-Pointy-Ears tells us you're a duke already. The duke of Farrow Estate, no less! A bit young for that, eh? Can you even lace your boots up by yourself?"

"Isn't that what servants are for?" Felix just laughed, like he was taking it all in stride. That's how he handled all their teasing—even when the subject was about how similar he and Prax looked. He just sloughed it off like it was nonsense.

It was a good thing, too, because that was becoming one of their favorite topics to taunt him over.

"I hear your lovely mother had quite an eye for dragonriders back in the day," another rider chimed in. He was one of the younger lieutenants who had graduated only a year or two ahead of me.

That was a step over the line. We all knew it. It was one thing to compare them or tease them about having the same awful taste in liquor, and a completely different thing to bring a guy's mother into it.

Those of us who could get away with it snuck him a punishing glare for even going there. He flinched and cursed, so someone must have kicked him under the table. I wished I were sitting closer so I could have kicked him, too.

Now it was a salvage mission. Everyone tried to keep laughing, but it was painful and obviously forced. We were all sitting stiffly, bracing for what had the potential to be explosive, unpleasant, and maybe even deadly.

Felix just rolled his eyes. "Yeah, yeah. I've heard that one before. Jace beat you to it last year."

"Bah! Jace isn't old enough to remember it." Prax's booming voice was so loud it filled the whole dining hall. "Those were grander days, when the war had just begun. And I was a much younger, much better looking man."

"It's hard to imagine you ever being good looking," Jace sneered, carefully trying to steer the subject away from Felix's mother.

It worked, thank the gods. Prax started trying to defend his masculine beauty, whatever that was, and Jace baited him on. I let out a breath of relief and glanced sideways at Felix, who still looked blissfully unaware of what we all suspected was more than just a long string of bad jokes at his expense. I couldn't believe he hadn't noticed just how much he and Prax favored one another. Maybe he really was brain damaged.

Despite Jace's repeated warnings that I should keep my nose out of it, I wondered once again if I should tell him. On the one hand, Jace was absolutely right—it wasn't any of my business. But then again, Felix was my best friend. Not telling him felt cruel somehow, almost as though I were betraying him.

I was at war with myself over it by the time we finished dinner and retired to our rooms. Since my life had fallen back into a comfortable, fairly predictable routine, I could move around and function without giving it much thought. Jace noticed I was distracted, though, and he called me on it while I was packing up a few things to take to the washroom.

"I know what you're thinking," he said as he planted himself firmly in front of the door. "You need to let it go. A man's personal life is his own business. Felix is more than capable of handling this without anyone else meddling in it."

I frowned. "How did you know I was—?"

"Because you've had that same stupid scowl on your face this whole time," he interrupted.

I didn't like being chastened like I was still some sort of kid, especially not when it came to stupid scowls. Jace had no room to talk. "Well, you would know, I guess. I'm supposed to be partnered with you until death and I still don't know anything about you."

"It doesn't matter," Jace snapped. "Whatever or whoever I was before this is irrelevant."

"It's relevant to me," I snapped back just as fiercely. "This isn't just a job for me. It's not just a payday, and I'm not here to be a tourist. Being this—becoming a dragonrider—is all that saved me from ending up in a mountain of charred corpses in some prison camp. I don't expect you to understand that at all. But it does matter to me who I'm partnered with. The heart of the man standing next to me in battle always matters."

When he didn't retort, I picked up my stuff and stormed past him toward the door. I was muttering under my breath, wondering out loud why he had even chosen me to be his wing end in the first place. Just because I could do a few nifty magic tricks? So what. Big deal. My power had barely been enough to get us through the battle scenario. I doubted it would do much for me in a real battle.

Jace grabbed my arm in a vice-like grip to stop me before I could get out of the room. His eyes met mine, and there was an eerie stillness in his gaze. "I do understand that. We have a lot more in common than you realize. But unlike you, I choose not to wear it on my sleeve. Some things are better left in the past."

I didn't know how to take that. At least, not at first. But the words came to me suddenly, and I felt bolder in that moment. "There's a difference, between wearing it on my sleeve ... and not being ashamed of it."

He let me go, and we stared each other down in silence. I could never tell what he was thinking. His gaze was as unreadable as the stars in daylight. But whoever he was, or whatever he had been before he became a dragonrider, he was apparently determined never to let that history surface. He'd buried it deep. I just wondered if he had done it out of necessity, or out of shame.

Once we had both settled in for the night and the tower had gotten quiet again, I found myself toying with my necklace as I lay awake. I started thinking about things I hadn't in a long time—like the paludix turtle and how the Gray elves had treated us after we had helped set them free. They had been kind enough to share their food, though I suspected that was only because we had stuck our necks out to save them from the slavers.

That had been my last face-to-face encounter with my mother's people. It had been years ago, and yet the memories were still fresh in my mind. I remembered the way that young Gray elf man, Kiran, had looked at my necklace. He'd acted like he recognized it, though I couldn't imagine why. In all my years living with my mother in the Gray elf ghetto, I had never seen anyone else wearing one before. To my recollection, my mother hadn't even worn it. That's why I'd never thought much of it in the first place. If it had been truly precious to her, wouldn't she have worn it herself?

I was so caught up in my thoughts and memories that the sudden blare of a horn made me bolt upright. Across the room, Jace did the same. Through the darkness, we exchanged a meaningful look.

It was the battle horn blaring again.

CHAPTER SEVEN

I wish I could say that I was cool, calm, and collected as I gathered my armor and dressed for my first battle. But I wasn't. My heart felt as though it had quit beating. I couldn't keep my hands from shaking. Cold sweat poured down my back as I quickly dressed in the layers of weatherproofed padding. I had to clench my teeth to keep them from chattering as I buckled on each piece of my armor. I'd done this a thousand times or more, and yet now it was a struggle just to remember which piece went where.

When I thought Jace wasn't looking, I checked to make sure Beckah's good luck token was still in its usual place tucked under one of my vambraces. I always kept it with me now. Seeing it gave me courage. It was just a handkerchief—one she had embroidered with a blue and black dragon—but it meant the world to me. Especially right then.

I went to grab my helmet, but my hands were still trembling so badly that I dropped it. It went clanging across the room and I cursed out loud. The noise must have alerted Jace to what a wreck I was because he turned around and examined me up and down. Without saying a word, he walked over and began adjusting the straps to my shoulder pauldrons.

"T-thanks," I stammered.

He made a disapproving sound and gruffly lifted one of my arms up to check the buckles on each side of my breastplate before he was satisfied. Then he picked up my helmet from where it had rolled partway under the bed.

"Stop thinking," he said as he handed it back to me. "You'll make yourself sick and now is not the time. Follow your training first. And if that doesn't work, follow your instincts. Every ounce of sweat you spilt in the academy was in preparation for this moment."

I took a deep breath to steady myself and nodded.

"You're a dragonrider. And we are called to be bold when no one else dares to be." Jace took a step back to pick up his weapons from where they always hung off the footboard of his bed. He carried a pair of short swords in a cross-shaped dual sheath that buckled onto his back.

I fastened my own weapon to my hip, letting my fingers graze over the pommel of the scimitar for a moment. Jace was right, as usual. Now wasn't the time to start losing it. I had to pull myself together. I had a job to do.

We started for the door. But before we could leave, Jace paused. He turned to me with a strange expression. "You want to know something about me?"

I was too shocked to respond right away.

"My last wing end died because of me. I assumed he could keep up. I took a bid with him based only on what everyone else had told me about what he was capable of. They said he was fast enough. They said he could handle flying point. When he died, I vowed never to make that mistake again. I vowed that my next wing end would be someone I knew could match me in every way. It would be someone I had personally scouted and trained with. There would be no room for doubt about his ability. I wouldn't leave anything to chance, and I wouldn't take anyone's word for it—not like last time." His gaze was fierce, almost like he was thinking about punching me. But maybe that was just because talking about himself, his past, and his feelings made him really uncomfortable. "So now I live with the knowledge that his death was my fault. I have to carry that to my grave."

Words failed me. What could I say to something like that? I felt pity for him. But I also felt a touch of pride that he thought I was worthy. That's when I realized why he had told me this; he was trying to reassure me. I could handle this. He wouldn't have brought me here, to fight by his side, if he hadn't been absolutely sure that I could handle it.

"Let's do it, then." I extended a hand toward him.

He grasped it firmly. "Just don't do anything stupid. War heroes often die too young."

Jace and I left our room dressed from head to toe in gleaming battle armor with our fur-collared blue cloaks sweeping the ground at our heels. My heart was still hammering in my chest, but I refused to let my thoughts waver back toward the fear churning in my gut. I let one hand rest on the hilt of my blade, my helmet tucked under my other arm.

As we strode down the hall, other riders fully outfitted for war began emerging to join us in our final march to the dragon stables. I spotted Felix through the crowd once, though only for a moment. He and Prax were standing together, looking like a mirrored reflection of the same person in their armor. It was a bittersweet sight.

I stepped into Mavrik's stall and immediately got to work preparing his saddle. He craned his huge head to watch as I checked over all the buckles and straps, the same way I had since the beginning of training. It wasn't anything new to me. I probably could have done it blindfolded. But right then I was still a nervous wreck.

Mavrik chirped at me anxiously, stirring in his bed of hay as I slung the saddle over his back.

"We knew this day was coming, right?" I muttered to him as he craned his neck and started sniffing at my hair. "Are you ready?"

He snorted, sending a blast of his hot breath across my face. That usually meant, "yes."

With his saddle in place and all my gear strapped down and set, I stood outside the stall to wait. I knew what was coming next only because I'd seen it already a few days prior. All around me stood my dragonrider brothers, the proud warriors of Blue Squadron. No one spoke. No one looked around. Straight ahead and several stalls down, I could see Jace's back. He was standing at the ready, too. Once we were airborne, I knew I had to find him again so we could keep to our formation.

Colonel Bragg came out to give us his briefing. When he began to speak, the atmosphere in the room grew heavy and intense. This wasn't going to be good news, and I think we all knew that. If we were getting called up in addition to Gold Squadron, then something must have gone horribly wrong.

"By now you all know about the situation in Barrowton. The city is occupied by a large number of enemy forces. They are keeping the villagers there as hostages, but have not welcomed any form of negotiation." Bragg's voice carried down the corridor. "Two legions of infantry have been lost trying to retake the city without any further civilian casualties. Those campaigns have failed. Your brothers in Gold Squadron were deployed to coax a response, to hopefully force our enemy into a new course of action. News arrived earlier today that half the squadron has already fallen. They encountered resistance unlike anything we have ever faced before. We are the cavalry, gentleman. Our enemy is fierce and desperate. Do not hold back. We cannot lose this city."

I was starting to get a bad feeling. I remembered what Beckah had said about Dayrise, and how it had fallen just like this. It was nothing but ruins now. There hadn't been any survivors in that situation. That meant my chances of ever seeing Roland again were slim to none. In all likelihood, he was already dead.

And I was about to join him.

"We have been given permission straight from the throne that if the citizens cannot be evacuated, and if the enemy cannot be overthrown by any other means, then we are to raze the city with fire until there is nothing left," Bragg continued. It was clear in the way he looked at us and by the tone of his voice that he sincerely didn't want that. Who would?

"If that order comes down, I expect you all to respond accordingly. I pray whatever gods may be watching this will have pity on us." Colonel Bragg bowed his head. We were dismissed, and we all filed back into our dragons' stalls to mount up.

I hoisted myself into Mavrik's saddle, fitting my boots down into the sheaths on either side and double-checking my safety straps. I put on my helmet and riding gauntlets, then leaned down to pat Mavrik's neck a few times. I'm sure he could tell I was nervous. Likewise, I could feel his unease. His big nostrils were puffing as he breathed in deeply, and his muscles were flexed and taut under his scaly hide. The pupils of his eyes narrowed to hair-thin slits as he crawled out of his stall, snapping anxiously at any of the other dragons that got too close.

In a noisy stir, we all lined up in the narrow corridor that led out onto the platform. The gates were rolled open, and one by one the dragonriders of Blue Squadron took to the air. The line moved slowly, at first. It gave me far too much time to begin thinking again. My stomach was tangled up in horrible knots, and I couldn't keep myself from gasping for breath. My thoughts were a swirling torrent of pure panic. Terror welled up in me like I was drowning.

And then it was my turn.

Mavrik crawled through the gates and out onto the platform. The air was cold, but the storm had long passed. It was still very dark outside, and yet a thick fog had settled over the city. Far below, I could barely see its lights winking in the night. A drop of fifty stories made my stomach churn and my head feel dizzy. But Mavrik didn't give me long to contemplate it.

We leapt into the air as one, wings stretched out to catch the northern winds. I felt weightless for a second or two, and then Mavrik's powerful wing beats carried us higher and higher. As we spiraled around the tower, I saw the host of other dragonriders circling overhead like a column of roaring black bats.

I let my eyes fall closed and reached out with my thoughts. I could feel the other dragons, their voices like whispers scurrying across my brain. It was strangely comforting, giving me a sense of control.

Mavrik and I joined up with Jace and his dragon, Ghost, as soon as we found them. I hung close at his side, flying in tight formation as we circled the tower and waited for all the dragonriders to take flight. When we saw the gates roll closed and the torches go out, I knew it was time to go.

Barrowton was waiting.

Jace began relaying our battle plan to me as soon as we were on our way. Using our complex code of hand signals, he advised me to hang back with him near the rear of the group. Our speed was our greatest strength, so we had to conserve as much strength and energy as we could until we arrived on scene at the battle.

"*We should hit Barrowton at dawn,*" Jace signaled. "*We'll go high, use the light of the rising sun to hide our approach, and make our first sweep toward the greatest threat point. Stay close.*"

I gave him an affirmative gesture and followed as he ducked under the immense formation of dragonriders, slowing his pace and falling toward the back of the group. We stayed back there, biding our time and conserving our speed, until Barrowton was finally in sight.

I was busy going over battle tactics in my head, things I had learned through all my time training at Blybrig, when I first saw it. An all-too-familiar plume of black smoke was rising out of a charred mass of buildings. The city sat uncomfortably close to Luntharda, which had probably been a good thing when our kingdoms weren't at war and the city was used as a trade stop. Now, it just put the inhabitants of Barrowton on the enemy's doorstep.

From a distance, it looked like someone had kicked open a hornet nest. The glistening shapes of shrikes zipped through the air faster than I could count, battling dragonriders. Columns of dragon flame burst into the air spontaneously. On the ground, infantry forces were trying to breach the city from all sides, but had been outflanked by Gray elf legions who rained down heavy fire with bows and arrows.

As we got closer, I was able to see more and more detail. And what I saw made me absolutely sick with fear.

The Gray elves were using beasts from their jungle home as war beasts. Creatures I had no names for roamed the battlefield, charging like mad into the Maldobarian lines. Some looked like giant boars with long barbed tusks, and others like big reptilian monsters with scaly hides and long, lashing tails.

The war beasts were cutting through the infantry lines over and over, and it looked like the soldiers weren't able to do anything to stop them. Even the cavalry horses bucked and panicked when threatened by a boar's jagged tusks or the bellowing charge of those apelike creatures.

"*What the hell are those things?*" Jace was signing frantically.

I had no idea. But it looked like they were most likely the reason we were about to lose the battle for Barrowton.

I watched as the ranks struggled to scramble fast enough to reassemble formation before they were charged again. They couldn't do it. Each pass from one of those creatures sent bodies flying in all directions. Some men just dropped their weapons and fled. Meanwhile, the Gray elves were firing volley after volley of their poison-tipped arrows.

A blind fury boiled in my veins and I leaned down against Mavrik's back. Roland might still be down there. And somewhere else in this fray, the woman I loved and my best friend were fighting, too.

I wanted a crack at some of those monsters.

If I could get close enough, then maybe I could use my power to drive them away. Or at least I might be able to confuse them long enough for someone else to kill them. Either way, Jace had said we were going for the greatest threat point. So I waited for him to choose our first target and set my focus there.

Jace led our aerial assault at blitzing speed. His dragon, Ghost, snapped his wings in close and dropped into a steep dive while Mavrik and I hung close at his side. Shrikes blurred past us like tongues of mirrored lightning. When Gray elves began training their bows upon us, we spiraled to avoid the shots. I felt the air humming off the arrows that zipped past my helmet.

I tried to reach out with my thoughts, to reach the creatures that were running amuck through the infantry lines, but it was a mess. The battle raging all around us formed a confusing chorus of whispers in my mind. It made it nearly impossible to focus. Shrikes, dragons, and horses were all familiar sounds to my mind's ear. The Gray elves had their own war mounts and monsters, and their voices were all foreign to me. I couldn't make sense of them.

My brain seemed to swell with the overload of battle. I heard the cries of the wounded; dying pleas resounded all around me. Desperately, I tried to push it all away and focus on our first target. Jace was zeroing in on one of the giant boars, and he gave me the signal to strike with him. I stretched my thoughts toward the beast, calling for it to acknowledge me.

It wasn't clear to me if whatever madness was infecting the wild things of the world was also afflicting these creatures, but when I got no response I began to suspect that might be the case. I tried calling to it again, all of them this time, asking for them to depart and leave us in peace.

The creatures answered me with a reply like a tolling bell in my thoughts. It was so loud it made my teeth rattle—there could be no peace. Their rage for having been summoned from their jungle was wholly justified, and not so easily appeased.

We were seconds from contact.

I felt Mavrik's sides swell as he took in a breath, preparing to shower his burning venom upon our enemy. I tried one more time to will the beasts away from our infantry. I poured as much will into my command as I could, which seemed like a great idea at the time.

I guess I had forgotten what happened when I let myself go like that.

Burning heat surged through me, roaring through my body like an inferno. The noise of the war suddenly seemed to grow faint. I heard only the voices I chose to hear. My vision sharpened. My instincts came alive.

I was losing control again.

My body moved without my permission. I couldn't stop it. I was guided by those primal urges that welled up from deep within. I steered Mavrik with my thoughts and brought myself closer to the ground, skimming over the battlefield.

Jace started giving me angry hand signals to get back in formation. I wanted to obey. But I couldn't. He couldn't see what was happening to me—that my eyes were glowing and my canine teeth had become pointed fangs—because I had my helmet on. He'd witnessed me go into this state more than once now, and I think he understood that there wasn't anything I could do to control it.

A sense of authority swept over me. I felt like a king among commoners. I could sense the aura of power that rolled off my body like a rippling heat. Standing up in the saddle, I walked down the length of Mavrik's back while he glided over the battlefield, just out of reach of sword or spear. I bade him duck lower at the first opening he saw, and when he did, I leapt into the air.

My feet hit the ground and I kicked instantly into a roll to absorb the force of the impact. As I stood, I pulled my scimitar from its resting place. It was all one fluid motion, perfect and effortless. Around me, infantrymen looked at me with awe. They probably couldn't believe I had just willingly dismounted my dragon. The Gray elves looked equally confused, like they weren't sure what my angle was.

I quickly answered their puzzled glares when I ripped off my helmet and dropped it at my feet.

When the Gray elf warriors saw my face, the way my eyes were glowing like lanterns, they immediately began backing away. Some of them even threw away their weapons and dropped to their knees. They spoke to me in their native tongue, crying out desperately and calling me by a name I'd never heard before —Lapiloque.

I hadn't come for them, though.

I stepped through their ranks, which parted for me like a sea of sword and shield. One of the monstrous boars was charging straight for me. I could feel the earth trembling with its thundering steps. It was huge, nearly ten feet tall, with wickedly barbed tusks jutting from its lower jaw and a mane of quill-like spines down its back.

This beast had ignored my command. It had defied me. I wouldn't tolerate that kind of insubordination.

I raised my blade toward the boar, daring it one more time to disobey. But it just kept coming, barreling toward me and snorting with rage.

"So be it," I murmured.

My body moved, seeming to know just exactly what to do next. I snapped into a wider stance and swung my blade wide, slicing the air and leaving behind a rift of power that burst forth with brilliant green light, emitting waves of raw energy.

The boar slammed right into it, and immediately began squealing in panic.

The rift swallowed it like a gaping maw, leaving nothing but echoing shrieks of fear and a radiant white-green light that began to grow smaller and smaller until at last it died away.

A single seed, about the size of a pumpkin seed, fell to the ground where the boar had been.

All around me was silence.

I could feel the anxiety and quiet horror in the air as the eyes of soldiers, both human and elf, stared at me. I made a point not to look at any of them as I bent down to pick up the seed, slipping it calmly into my belt and looking skyward.

Mavrik answered my unspoken command to return. I could easily pick out the sound of his roar even in the midst of battle. Slipping my blade back into its sheath, I reached skyward and caught one of the handles of my dragon's saddle as he swooped low. I was pulled skyward by the force of his wings, ripped off the earth and carried back into the churning, war-lit sky.

I began looking for another target—another rebellious child to punish. But something cut through my mind like a cold splinter. It wasn't something physical. It was a sound; a sound I knew.

I heard a dragon's agonized bellow. It wasn't just any dragon, though. Over the swell of noise, the cries and clashing of blades, and the roaring drone of combat, I knew it was Ghost.

It pierced me to the very core and snapped me out of my trance.

I looked around frantically, searching the sky for Ghost and Jace. I spotted them in the distance, darting in frantic evasive maneuvers as a pair of shrikes chased after them viciously. They were flying directly over Luntharda, skimming dangerously close to the tops of the trees. I could see arrows flying, and the shapes of riders on the shrikes' backs. One of them was wearing an elaborate, colorful headdress with white horns.

It was the Gray elf princess.

I snarled and bared my teeth. Mavrik did the same. We turned and swept higher, beginning our pursuit.

Ghost had already been hit multiple times. Arrows were sticking out of his scaly hide, and yet he refused to go down. He was in pain. I could feel it. The poison from the arrows was coursing through his body, making each breath and wing beat a struggle. But he was fighting desperately to stay airborne—fighting because he knew if he fell, his rider would die.

"Hold on," I growled. "Just hold on."

I saw the Gray elf princess draw back another arrow. It was as though it all happened in slow motion.

The arrow left her bow, blurring toward its mark, hitting Ghost right in the back of the skull.

The dragon lurched. His wing beats stopped abruptly. In my mind, his voice went silent.

That sudden silence jarred me violently.

Ghost's limp body plummeted from the sky with Jace hanging onto him for dear life. It was a horrible moment of déjà vu. I had seen another mentor of mine, Sile, fall from the sky like this, but I had managed to save him.

I didn't know if I would be able to duplicate that miracle now, though. We were still so far away. I urged Mavrik to go faster, and he poured every ounce of his speed into our pursuit.

The green canopy of Luntharda swallowed Ghost and Jace. They disappeared, and I frantically began trying to detect whether or not Jace was still alive. I was already weakened from the amount of power I had used to deal with the boar. I could barely grip the saddle handles as Mavrik stormed forward, swerving past other dragons and shrikes that passed us in the air. My head was swimming, and my extremities were becoming numb. Pressing through all the noise and the growing exhaustion that made my senses sluggish, I focused only on Jace.

I could still feel the presence of his life force. It was faint. But it was there.

I knew what I had to do.

"Get as close as you can. Then put me down," I panted.

Mavrik growled in reluctance. He cocked his head to the side so that I could see one of his big yellow eyes. He didn't approve of this plan.

"It's okay, buddy." I patted his neck. "I have to do this. It's my fault he got pinned down in the first place. We abandoned him. I can't do it a second time. He's still alive. That means he survived the crash. I can get him out of there. I'm the only one who can."

Mavrik sent me worried hues of blue and orange and flashes of memories from the battle scenario. He was worried I wouldn't be able to make it out alive by myself, let alone with Jace. I couldn't really argue his logic. There was no guarantee.

And there also wasn't any other choice.

"As soon as I'm off, I want you to go find Felix. Do whatever you can to back him up. Understand?" My voice got tight. Emotion made my chest feel heavy. "And when this is over, if you can't feel my presence anymore ... then you are free to go back home. That was our deal. Remember?"

Mavrik made a sorrowful series of chirping sounds as he acknowledged my last request. He spread his wings wide, ducking down under another dragon, weaving out of the way of a shrike or two. Ahead of us, the jungle grew closer and closer by the moment.

When we were close enough, he dropped even lower and started a steep turn. I pulled my legs out of the boot sheaths again, and kicked away from the saddle. In a matter of seconds, I was on the ground, watching my dragon disappear into the battle-ridden tangled sky.

I didn't have time to reflect. My legs were already getting wobbly. I'd used so much power, and whatever I still had left in me was going to serve one final purpose. I was going to heal Jace and get him out of that jungle alive, even if it killed me.

I owed him that much, at least.

8

CHAPTER EIGHT

I staggered over the boundary that separated our kingdoms, passing between the trunks of the giant trees of Luntharda. They loomed all around me like moss-covered columns, their interwoven branches blotting out the light of the sun and the cold wind of the springtime. It was an entirely different world; slathered in varying shades of green, and filled with alien sounds that came from all directions. The air was thick and humid, and it smelled of rich, moist earth. Behind me, the sound of the battle was distant and easily forgotten.

I had nothing to guide me except my power, which allowed me to pinpoint Jace's location amidst a riot of whispering voices. I didn't see any animals, so at first, I wasn't sure what was making all the racket in my brain. Then I realized—it was the trees.

I stumbled into the crash site so suddenly it caught me completely off guard. Ghost's body had broken through the canopy and lay still, tangled up in branches and vines that had snagged on him as he fell.

Only a few yards away, I found Jace.

He was dying. I knew it right away. Lying on his back with his legs bent in the wrong directions, there was blood coming from his mouth and ears. He couldn't move, and based off what I could sense, most of the bones in his body were broken.

I fell to my knees beside him, pushing away limbs and leaves that had fallen on top of his body. "Jace! I'm here!"

He blinked at me confusedly, like he wasn't sure who I was at first. "You came back."

"I'm so sorry, Jace." I tried to apologize. I shouldn't have left him. I'd broken all the rules of my training and let myself get carried away. "I can fix it. I can get you out."

"It's all right," he said in a strangely calm, quiet voice. "It doesn't hurt. I don't feel it. Just let me go."

"I can't—" I started to argue.

"I've waited a long time for this." He wouldn't let me finish. "I've paid back my debt."

Whatever debt he was talking about, it would have to wait or be paid back with something other than his life. I wasn't about to let him down again. I could save him. I could heal his broken body. It might cost me my own, but that was the price I would have to pay for leaving him in the first place.

I put my hands on his chest, letting my eyes roll closed as I called forth whatever remained of my power. It was going to be costly. I probably would pass out, which was essentially a death sentence in Luntharda based on everything I'd heard and studied. But I was okay with that. He would live. That's all that mattered.

"When this is done, I want you leave this place," I told him. "Run. Don't look back. And don't waste your efforts trying to carry me out. You won't have that much time to spare."

The drain was immediate. His failing body gobbled up my power greedily, drinking it in and beginning to repair all that had been so badly broken. I felt bones knitting back together, flesh mending, and the surge of energy flowing through every muscle.

Jace took in a shocked, violent breath. He gripped my arms suddenly like he wanted to push me away. But my work was nearly done.

As the last drop of power left my body, the darkness began closing in. All strength left me. I was numb and paralyzed as I fell sideways onto the soft jungle floor.

That was when I saw him.

He was standing between two enormous ferns, peeking out at me with those eerie, color-changing eyes. He wore intricate, colorful battle attire, carried a longbow in one hand, and had red war symbols painted on his body. His long white hair had been woven into hundreds of braids and was pulled back away from his face. As our eyes met, I wondered if this was good luck ... or an extremely bad coincidence.

"Kiran," I managed to rasp his name.

His eyes widened with recognition.

I knew he had seen me heal Jace. There was no question about it. He had that same, awe-struck and slightly mortified expression the other Gray elves had when I revealed myself on the battlefield.

Jace was beginning to sit up. He was panting for breath, feeling over his freshly healed body with amazement written all over his face. He obviously hadn't noticed we were being watched.

That didn't last long.

With a flash of light glinting off hundreds of mirror-like scales, a shrike landed between Kiran and us. It let out a piercing shriek, regarding Jace with its peculiar gleaming green eyes. There was primal intelligence behind them, and I could feel its presence faintly bleeding into my overexerted brain. It was curious about me, not sure what to make of my mixed scent, and trying to decide if I was a threat or not.

Jace, on the other hand, it definitely didn't like. When he scrambled to his feet, drawing both of his swords, the shrike hissed and flared its translucent feathered wings. Its long tail lashed slowly to and fro, and the muscular shoulders of all six of its legs rolled like a cat waiting to pounce. They were in a standoff, each waiting for the other to make a wrong move.

Then I saw her. Or rather, I caught a hint of movement out of the corner of my eye. I couldn't move my body, but I saw a bit of sunlight gleam off the point of a blade that was poised right behind Jace's neck.

He was absolutely clueless about it, though, until she spoke.

"Drop your weapons, pig." a young woman's voice snapped bitterly. Her speech was rough, like she wasn't used to the human language, but she seemed to have a fairly good handle on it.

Jace let out a curse when he realized he'd been ambushed. He dropped both his swords.

"Hands behind your head. On your knees," the she elf commanded. She began pacing a circle around Jace as he obeyed. At last, she stepped directly into my view.

I couldn't see her face—not at first—because she still wore the royal battle headdress Prax had told me about. It looked like a mask with an attached mane of brilliant colored feathers, leaves, and shrike scales that hung all the way down her back. It had a pair of slender white deer horns that swept back from over the ears. Those, I understood, were the true mark of Gray elf royalty.

Her clothes were equally bizarre. I'd never seen Gray elves dressed in their traditional style before. All the elves that had lived in the ghetto where I grew up wore human-looking clothes. But these were more exotic, more beautiful, and *far* more revealing.

She sported a pair of baggy, dark blue silk pants low over her broad hips. They ballooned out a bit and were gathered at her feet. She wore a short tunic of the same fabric and style, cut low across her chest and gathered at her ribs and wrists—leaving her entire abdomen bare. A long, banner-like belt was strung around her waist on golden cords. It was so long in the back that it dragged the ground like a train on a gown, and it boasted an intricate embroidered design in the shape of a stag's head. The front was just as ornate, but it was set with jewels.

There was no doubt she was royalty. She walked with poised, predatory grace. I could see her multicolored eyes studying Jace carefully through the holes in her mask. She glanced at me quickly, and then leveled her blade back at Jace's throat.

"You should be dead," she insisted. "I saw you fall."

Kiran suddenly emerged from his hiding place. He kept his head low as he went slinking up to the princess, cowering like a submissive puppy. He pointed at me and began speaking in the elven language.

My mind was so hazy I could barely piece together what was being said. It didn't sound good, though. Kiran used the word "*caenu*" several times, which generally didn't bode well for me. It was the word they used for all halfbreeds, and it basically meant the same thing as "filth" in their language.

The princess set her harrowing gaze upon me again. Jace flinched as she began to walk toward me, but she left no room for him to try anything funny. She ordered Kiran to draw on him and make sure he didn't move. With a poison-tipped arrow aimed squarely at his nose, Jace didn't move again.

The Gray elf princess crouched over me. She pulled back her battle headdress, sliding it up onto the top of her head, to get a better look. I couldn't move enough to look back at her, though. All I could do was stare at the tops of her black leather boots.

She grabbed my chin, turning my head to look directly into my eyes. Her face was devastatingly beautiful ... and yet eerily familiar. It was as though I should have known her, though I couldn't imagine how.

I watched her nose wrinkle in disgust as she regarded my dragonrider armor, my pointed ears, and my long ash-gray hair. She dropped me back onto the ground and actually wiped her hand off on her pants like I might have some kind of disease.

Then Kiran spoke, and I actually caught what he said this time. "No, no. He wore it. It must be under his clothes."

The princess sneered down at me again. Curling her lip, she grabbed the front of my breastplate and stuck her arm down the front of my shirt. She went groping around under my clothes and armor until at last I felt her hand close around my mother's necklace. She pulled it out, and with one quick jerk, broke the resin string.

I wanted to scream in protest. That was *mine*. She had no right to take it. But I couldn't do much more than give a disapproving groan as she held it up to the light.

Her expression cleared like storm clouds breaking on a calm morning. Her eyes shimmered with mystification. Her lips parted, and I saw a hint of lovely color flush across her elegant cheeks. When she looked down at me again, her expression was much different. She seemed puzzled and slightly horrified at the sight of me now.

"Where did you get this?" Her voice held quiet suspicion as she spoke to me in the human language again. "Speak, demon!"

It took all I had, the very last of my strength and will, to get the word out. One word was all I could manage, so I chose it wisely and spoke it in her native language.

"Mother."

When I opened my eyes to nothing but darkness, I just assumed I was already dead. I was delirious, and it seemed very likely that I'd probably been killed either by the Gray elf princess or some horrible monster that had stumbled across me lying unconscious on the jungle floor.

Then I heard a sound like something or someone breathing next to me.

"H-hello?" My voice was hoarse, and for some reason, my throat was absolutely killing me.

"Keep it down," a familiar tone answered. It was Jace.

I didn't understand. But as my delirium began to clear, I became more and more aware of our situation.

It was bad. Incredibly bad—even by my standards.

I was sitting on what felt like a stone floor. It was cold to the touch, and the fact that I could feel it rather obviously let me know that I was completely naked. The Gray elves had taken my armor and my clothes. When I tried to move, I realized I was tied up. My wrists and neck were tightly bound to what felt like a metal pole. No wonder my neck was sore. I couldn't move my head or do anything about the blindfold that had been pulled over my eyes.

"Where are we?" I whispered. "What happened?"

"I don't know. Somewhere in the jungle. You were unconscious for a long time," he answered. His voice echoed all around, making it impossible to tell how far apart we were.

"Are you tied up, too?" I asked.

"Yes. They took all our gear, clothes, and anything we had on us." He paused a moment, as though he were thinking. Then he said, "Jaevid, they're going to torture us. You need to prepare yourself."

My insides wrenched up with frantic anxiety. I couldn't breathe. Memories like nightmares of the battle scenario ran through my mind. I did my best to calm myself, to keep my head clear. Panic was the enemy. I knew that. Somehow, I had to keep my head on straight.

"This is my fault," I realized aloud. "If I hadn't let things get out of control—"

"Don't even start with that." Jace's tone was serious. "It doesn't matter now."

My guts were writhing around like I'd swallowed a live snake. "There's something I have to tell you. I should have told you before."

He was quiet while I gathered my nerve.

I was going to tell him about my father. He deserved to know that our torture might be worse than expected because of that. If any of these Gray elves remembered the horrible sin my father had committed, then they might also recognize that I favored him. We might be made to suffer even more.

I didn't get the chance, though. No sooner had I opened my mouth to speak than I heard the sound of footsteps and angry voices coming toward us. I sat perfectly still and didn't make a sound. Neither did Jace. Inwardly, I was paralyzed with fear. I didn't know what was going to happen. All I could do was strain to listen and try to piece together the elven words to figure out what was being said.

It had been so long since I had even tried to speak my mother's native tongue that my comprehension of it was poor. I caught only every other word. But from that, I could draw a few conclusions.

One of the voices I recognized right away. It sounded like the princess from before. "The halfbreed wore it. Some of the survivors from the cavalry claim to have seen him working miracles on the battlefield," she insisted.

The man she was bickering with sounded much older, and apparently he was resolute against believing her claims about me. "Did you see any of these so-called miracles?" he demanded.

"No," she admitted. "But surely you see the possibility. If he truly is the Lapiloque, then—"

"Silence, Araxie! Do not dare speak that blasphemy to me," the man shouted suddenly. "That lineage died long ago. Any member of that bloodline is a traitor."

"Let him be tested, then!" the princess yelled right back. "What harm is there in being sure?"

The man didn't answer her. Or rather, it seemed like he was ignoring her outright. Their voices had come so close now that I knew they must have been standing close by, maybe even looking at me.

I tried to stay calm and to keep my breathing even. Of course, I was humiliated. I was completely naked while two strangers stood over me, deciding my fate. But there was nothing I could do except wait and see what fate had planned for me next.

"Show me his face," the man ordered.

All of a sudden, the blindfold was ripped from my eyes. Light from two bronze braziers burning in a cavernous room blinded me for a moment. I looked up to face my accusers as I blinked away the spots in my vision.

I had been right. The female arguing with such spirit was indeed the princess. She looked down at me with a tense, unreadable expression. Her arms were folded under her chest and her muscular hips were cocked to the side in a defiant stance.

Next to her was a much older Gray elf man. I didn't recognize him at all, and yet I was sure he must be their king if only by the way he was dressed. He wore flowing robes of dark blue silk, and a waist wrap of gold that, even when tied, dragged the ground at his feet. The big bell cuffs of his gold-trimmed tunic touched the floor as well, and there was an intricate crown made of gold on his head. His silver hair was long and had been combed out to be perfectly straight, like a curtain of platinum that hung down his back.

The dark, weary circles and wrinkles around his eyes belied the ferocity in the way he was glaring at me. I got the impression right away that he wasn't pleased to have me in his kingdom—not that I was necessarily thrilled about it either. Sile had told me to come here, but I sort of doubted this is what he'd had in mind.

To my right, I could see Jace was tied up right beside me, though I didn't dare look at or draw any attention to him. Instead, I kept my eyes trained on the two royals standing before me.

The king leaned down to have a closer look at me, his multicolored eyes shining with severity and bitterness. I watched his expression sharpen. His eyes narrowed and his eyebrows furrowed deeply.

"Kill him," the king snarled suddenly. "He is the spitting image of that demon pig—the one who started this!"

The princess, Araxie, didn't seem convinced. "Perhaps it's just a coincidence. After a while, they all look similar."

"No! I know those eyes; they looked at me on that day. This is his progeny, and likely something foul Hovrid has sent to deceive and destroy us!" The king backed away from me, but his eyes never left mine.

I knew the rules. The memories of my interrogation training demanded I sit in total silence. I shouldn't speak a word to these people. But emotion ran away with me before I could stop myself.

"I don't know anyone named Hovrid," I declared in the human language. I didn't trust that my elven was good enough to sound anything but ridiculous to them. "I'm the son of Alowin."

They both froze and exchanged a wide-eyed look. Then the princess began to grin smugly. "See? Just as I told you."

Her father's glare returned and was more dangerous than ever. I knew he probably spoke the human language, too. Or at the very least, he understood it. But he refused to speak it and kept snapping angrily in elven. "Don't be a fool, child. We underestimated Hovrid once. I won't make that same mistake again. Who knows what power he has amassed in this time? This creature cannot be allowed to live. Kill him immediately."

Araxie scowled rebelliously. "And if you're wrong? If he truly is her child—our blood—then what?"

The king glanced at me as he turned and began to walk away. His expression was different, though, at that suggestion. Rather than fury, I saw plainly a look of hurt, like betrayal, etched into his features. "Then I've expunged the last of the traitors from our line. Nothing more."

With only the princess left standing before me, regarding Jace and me with a look of distaste, I thought it was over. I would be killed for association with someone named Hovrid. There was nothing I could do about that. But I decided quickly that if I was going to die, then I wanted to at least try and get a few answers first.

Araxie had just begun to walk away when I called out to her as best I could in her own language. "Did you really knew my mother? Alowin, I mean."

She paused.

Without turning around I heard her answer, "Yes."

"Why is he calling her a traitor?" I pleaded.

Araxie glanced back at me over her shoulder, and once again I couldn't interpret her expression. She seemed sad, angry, and terribly afraid all at the same time. "Because she abandoned us when we needed her most."

That vague, cryptic answer was all I got.

The princess left without another word, and Jace and I were left alone again. I couldn't wrap my mind around what she could possibly mean by that. My mother had abandoned them? How? By becoming a refugee in Maldobar, maybe? None of it made any sense.

"I take it that didn't go well." There was a sarcastic flavor to Jace's voice.

"No, not really," I admitted. "But on the bright side, so far they only seem interested in killing me."

Jace scoffed. "Oh, don't worry. I'm sure I won't be left out. I've killed three of their princes."

He was probably right about that. They may not have brought it up because it was a given that he would die—but the jury was still out on what to do with me. Or at least, it had been. Now things were looking pretty grim in that department, too.

"Can't you use any of that magic to get us out of this?" he pointed out.

I thought it over. "It depends, I guess, on how far we are from Maldobar. Remember before? I don't last very long once I go into that state. And you can't very well carry me out."

Jace grunted in agreement. "Then we'll have to bide our time and come up with a better plan. How long do you think we have?"

"I don't know. Not long, probably." I didn't want to give him any false hope. The king obviously had a special sort of hatred for me. I doubted he would allow me any extra time to plead my case.

Now that my eyes were uncovered, I could see a bit more about our situation. We were tied up in what appeared to be some kind of stone chamber. If I stretched out with my thoughts, which was slightly painful after having recently used so much power, I could sense that we were underground. The voices of the jungle were distant and faint, and I could feel the presence of earth above and around us.

A swirl of color fluttering through my brain surprised me, but only until I realized who it was. I could feel Mavrik's presence, his relief that I was alive, and his concern for me. He was looking for me.

I sent him my thoughts and told him what was happening ... and what I suspected was to come. I wished I could have severed our mental bond so that he didn't have to experience it right along with me. I asked him if Felix and Beckah were alive, and he confirmed that they were.

But the battle was over. Barrowton had been burned to the ground.

"Whatever happens," I murmured aloud without thinking, "it was an honor to have flown with you."

"And you as well," Jace answered quietly.

I decided not to tell him I hadn't been talking to him.

9

CHAPTER NINE

I wish I could tell you the Gray elf king had a sudden change of heart. That Princess Araxie was able to reason with him, and Jace and I were set free. But when it came to luck, I'd never had much of any.

The king did change his mind about killing us right away, though. Instead, he decided to interrogate us. Day after day we were dragged away to another dark room and beaten, whipped, or flogged. Many times, I blacked out during it only to wake up and find myself tied to that metal pole again.

At first, they didn't demand information. They just beat us. When they finally did start asking questions, though, it wasn't at all what I expected. They demanded to know who I really was and for me to tell them anything I knew about this Hovrid person. Most of all, they wanted to know where the god stone was.

Needless to say, my answers were never satisfactory. I told them over and over that I was the son of Alowin, that I didn't know anyone named Hovrid, and that I had no idea where the god stone was. Those replies never earned me anything but a more severe beating.

I honestly had no idea how much time passed, although it felt like an eternity. We never saw the sunlight or breathed the fresh air. They rarely brought us food, and when they did, it was mostly rotten scraps that left me feeling sicker than before. I was always weak from hunger and the beatings, and my throat was raw for want of even a few drops of water.

When they caught Jace and I talking, they gagged us, then there was nothing to ease the suffering. Sometimes, Mavrik would muscle his way into my thoughts and try to comfort me—but I quickly drove him out. I didn't want him to go through this with me. I didn't want him to have to feel me suffering.

The beatings began to get worse.

After they broke several of my ribs, I couldn't even take a breath without white-hot agony stinging through my body. The first time they broke one of my arms, I begged for them to just kill me and be done with it.

Of course, they didn't.

It was bad, yes. But listening to Jace take his beatings was much worse. I could hear his screams echoing off the walls from somewhere in the distance, hear him cursing them, crying, and pleading for death just as I had. Knowing there was nothing I could do made my mind go to dark places. It made me wish there was some way I could kill him, just to end his suffering so he didn't have to go through this anymore.

It became such that the sound of footsteps or voices immediately made me go into shock. I panicked. My body trembled beyond my control, and I immediately started screaming through the gag they had tied over my mouth. I never knew which of us they were going to take.

This time, however, something was different.

Usually our torturers came in groups. I never saw exactly how many because I was usually blindfolded. But there was only one set of footsteps coming toward me, and no voices.

Still, I couldn't keep myself from reacting with terror. I pitched against my bonds. I cried out for someone, anyone, to help me.

"Be quiet, *caenu*," someone whispered to me harshly. Then he took the blindfold off my eyes and pulled the gag out of my mouth.

It was Kiran.

Crouching beside me in the dark, he was staring at me with a constrained look of horror from under the hood of a long dark cloak. I must have looked as awful as I felt. I couldn't see clearly out of one eye because it had swollen shut, and I could feel the crusty sensation of dried blood around my nose and mouth.

He didn't waste any time. From under the cloak, he took out a water skin and uncorked it. "The princess continues to plead for your life," he said as he held it to my lips.

Fresh water filled my mouth, cool and delicious. I gulped it down as greedily as he would allow. I could taste that it was tinged with something herbal, but I didn't bother asking what it was. Whether it would kill me or make me feel even the slightest bit better, I didn't care.

"W-why do they keep asking me about Hovrid?" I managed to rasp. "Who is that?"

He must have believed me, because he flashed me a slightly sympathetic glance as he pulled a small bundle of rough cloth from his clothes. It was bread—

coarse, dark bread. He began pinching bits of it off and feeding it to me slowly. It hurt to swallow.

"His name is spoken like a curse among our people," Kiran whispered. "He was an infamous traitor, the eldest son of Alowin, the last Lapiloque. He started this war."

That new information settled over me like a foul stench and left me reeling. Could this Alowin—Hovrid's mother—possibly be the same woman who was also my mother? Surely not. My mother would have told me if I'd had any Gray elf siblings.

Right?

After letting me take a few more gulps of water, Kiran shuffled over and began administering the same care to Jace. He was a lot less responsive, though. His face was swollen and battered such that I barely recognized him. He didn't speak or make a noise. The only way I could tell he was even alive at all was because I could see his chest rising and falling as he breathed.

"I came because the end is coming soon, *caenu*," Kiran said as he cradled Jace's head and poured water down his throat. "King Erandur is out of patience. Princess Araxie still argues with him, but he has decreed that you both will be executed at dawn. There isn't much time."

I wasn't as upset about that news as I probably should have been. It actually came as a relief. "T-thank you, Kiran," I said.

He stood up and hastily gathered his belongings. "I have not forgotten what you did for me."

Smiling hurt, thanks to my battered face, but I made myself do it anyway. After all, he might be the last person I got to smile at. And I was glad he had survived and made it back to his people.

Kiran came back over to put the blindfold on my eyes, but before he could put the gag in my mouth, I felt him hesitate. "If you truly are Lapiloque," he whispered so quietly I could barely hear him, "then you must put an end to this war."

"I d-don't even know what that is," I told him.

"Lapiloque. It is the name we use for the one who speaks for the will of nature. The shepherd of all wild things. The stonespeaker."

In the distance, I could hear voices echoing off the walls. Our time was up. They were coming closer. Kiran swiftly put the gag back in my mouth. I heard his steps retreat into the distance and then vanish altogether.

I knew the Gray elves were coming for us. They were going to carry out the king's command. I should have been terrified, but I was too distracted to think much about how my life might be about to come to a violent end.

I was turning Kiran's words over and over in my head, hoping for a revelation. I wondered why the princess was so adamant about sparing me. I wondered if I truly was this Lapiloque—this stonespeaker—everyone kept talking about. If I was, then what did that mean? Was my fate tied to the god stone?

Most of all, I wondered if my mother had been keeping a lot more secrets from me than I'd ever suspected. Actually, I couldn't afford to think otherwise now. My time with her had been brief, but sweet. She'd loved me and yet she'd hidden everything about herself from me. I didn't understand why. Maybe it was to protect me. But now I needed to know the truth.

Sile had told me to come here, that some ritual had to be performed, and that the power I would wield would make the tricks I could do now look like dumb parlor tricks. If that was true, if I was capable of much more, then I might actually be able to grant Kiran's request. I might be able to tip the scales and end this war somehow.

The problem was, I didn't have much time left.

I could tell by the number of voices filling the room that at least three Gray elves had come to fetch us. They cut our bonds just long enough to yank Jace and me to our feet. Then they promptly tied our hands again, tighter than ever, before herding us out of the chamber. It was the first time we had left that room together.

We began climbing stairs. Even with the bit of food and water Kiran had given me, my body was still weak and battered. I didn't last long before my legs buckled. When they did, the Gray elves dragged me my by arms.

We went up stairs for what seemed like an eternity, then we began turning corners and weaving a path I knew was leading us out of the underground. I could sense it. And I could smell it. Until now, the air had always been cold and damp, as though we were in some sort of cave. Now I caught puffs of fresh, warm air flowing from the surface.

In the distance, I could hear the booming sound of drums. Then there was light. Even through the blindfold, I could see it and feel it on my skin. There was the smell of the jungle, of the plants and trees, and the rich soil.

When the drums abruptly went silent, I could hear the voices of other people —many of them. I wasn't sure exactly how many until the blindfold was ripped from my eyes. The light blinded me at first. It stung my eyes and confused me. But as my vision cleared, I started to realize the situation we were in.

Jace and I stood on the front steps of an ancient temple. If not for the fact that we were both about to die, I would have been distracted by how incredibly beautiful it was. Giant, moss-covered trees towered all around us. They were so big that the Gray elves had cut away some of the bark and carved spiraling staircases into their trunks.

The temple itself looked like it was in the process of being devoured by the jungle. Enormous roots had grown over it, cracking through stone as though it were as brittle as chalk. Moss grew all over walls and flowering vines were choking out ancient stone statues in the courtyard before us.

There must have been nearly a thousand people gathered to watch whatever horrible thing was about to happen to us. Gray elves of all shapes and sizes, men, women, and even children looked on with mixed expressions of hatred and disgust. They cursed at us—at me particularly—and spat in our direction. Thankfully, I think Jace was too delirious to appreciate anything anyone said. He was weaving on his feet, looking like he might collapse at any moment.

I heard Princess Araxie before I saw her. She was standing with her father, hissing furious words at him. "This is blasphemy! We will be cursed for it. It is forbidden to carry out such a sentence on this sacred ground," she insisted.

If the king was listening to her, it didn't show. He wouldn't even look at her. His gaze was focused squarely upon me with a mixture of controlled rage and sorrow churning in his eyes.

He didn't waste any time. The second he raised a hand to the mob gathered before us, they all went silent. You could actually hear the wind rattling the leaves and the alien, melodic calls of birds.

"This one has murdered three of my sons. He would have done the same to my daughter, if not for the mercy of the gods that brought her home to us," the king began proclaiming. He spoke in their native language, so I knew Jace didn't comprehend any of it—not that it mattered. He was so out of it, he probably wouldn't have understood anyway.

"And this one claims to be the heir of Alowin." The king turned his scathing glare back to me. For a moment, I caught another glimpse of that strange sorrow wrinkling across his brow, as though I'd hurt him somehow. "He carries the totem of the Lapiloque, and works miracles. But I say to you, that lineage died with my sister when she betrayed us and fled to the human kingdom! She bore no heir. The line of the Lapiloque is dead. This abomination has been sent to mock us. He has the face of the one who defiled this temple and stole the god stone. He is an instrument sent from Hovrid to destroy what remains of our people!"

As badly as it hurt, I couldn't keep my eyes from growing wide as I stared at the king. Alowin—my mother—was his *sister*? If that were the case, then that would mean I was related to the king of the Gray elves. I was ... royalty.

I took a panicked breath and flexed against my restraints. I wanted to know if it was really true. But before I could get a word out, the guards watching me noticed I was perking up. They immediately kicked out my legs, forcing me to my knees before the king.

"He has tried to make himself look like us." The king curled his lip in disgust as he glared down at me. "And yet he wears their mark and fights with those demons."

A few people in the crowd began spitting and cursing at me again.

The king grabbed a fistful of my hair. I'd always worn it long because of my mother. She'd insisted on it, saying that it was a matter of pride to Gray elf people that they never cut their hair.

The king took a long, curled knife from inside his robes. I thought this was the end. Maybe he would slit my throat. Maybe he would ram it into the side of my head. Either way, I was going to die.

I felt the cold of the metal touch the back of my neck, then a violent jerking, tearing sensation. The king tossed my severed, ash-gray ponytail down before me. The crowd cheered.

"You are not one of us," he growled as he gave a motion to the guards still holding my arms.

They began dragging me up to my feet.

Once I was able to look him in the eye again, I studied the king's face. I searched for any similarity between him and my mother—any tiny detail or feature that might mark them as siblings. But I couldn't find anything.

So I asked him, "Are you really my uncle?"

He didn't answer. His expression cracked for a moment, breaking into something stricken and tragic. Then he turned away as though he couldn't bear to look at me for another second.

"Take him to the pit and be done with it," the king ordered. "Then do the same with the demon pig. Their bodies will be offerings to Paligno."

Araxie began cursing loudly in elven. The drums began thrumming. As the guards took me down the temple steps and out into the courtyard, the crowd parted for us. They yelled curses and profanities I'd never heard before.

Then I saw it.

Before me was something I had already seen over and over, without ever understanding what it was. A huge open pit delved down deep into the darkness of the earth. A staircase overgrown with roots went around and around until it disappeared down into the cold gloom. My heart lurched, remembering the dreams I'd had of this place—a place I'd never seen in person until now.

The guards brought me to the edge and forced me to my knees again. Looking down, I could imagine if I fell in, I might find myself falling forever. But that wasn't what scared me. No, it was the cold steel of a sword's blade on the back of my neck again.

I knew what was coming next. I shut my eyes tightly. I heard the nearly musical humming of a blade being swung through the air. I waited to feel pain, or release, or anything at all.

But there was nothing.

In fact, there was no sound at all. The drums stopped. The crowd was completely quiet. Even the wind and the birds seemed to have gone silent. I could only hear my own heart pounding in my ears, reminding me that I was still alive.

I opened my eyes. At the same time, the hold the guards had on my arms began to slacken. The one brandishing the sword suddenly dropped it. Then they both began backing away from me.

I dared to look up, to try and see what was happening. Her eyes, shining with cold light like two stars, met mine. I sucked in a sharp breath.

She looked just like my mother. But it couldn't be her. My mother was dead. And this being, whatever it was, was hovering over the expanse of the bottomless pit before me. With her body draped in billowing robes of purest white, her bare feet stood on nothing but air and the outline of her body rippled like a reflection on water.

"M-mom," I managed to rasp.

She smiled and reached an alabaster hand out toward me. "*It's time, dulcu.*" Her voice echoed through every corner of my brain, but I never saw her lips move.

I was about to ask what she was talking about. Then a commotion behind me made me glance back. All the Gray elves gathered at the temple were kneeling. One by one, they all dropped to the ground and prostrated themselves. Even Araxie and the king bowed in reverence, hiding their faces in shame.

"*Only the blood of the traitor and the hands of the speaker can restore the balance,*" another voice spoke to me firmly, sending chills over my body. "*You must return it.*"

I immediately looked back and found my mother was gone. In her place was something else—a being I had no name for. And yet it felt as though I knew it, or had known it, for a very long time.

It hovered over the expanse of the pit, exactly where my mother's image had been. It was about the size of a small horse. Its lean, graceful body was covered in a mottled mixture of shimmering white fur and pearlescent white scales. At first glance, I would have mistaken it for a stag if only for its size, shape, and the large pair of sweeping white horns that grew from its head. But it wasn't a deer, even if it did have cloven hooves. Its muzzle was tapered and much shorter, and a pair of long fangs dripped below its jaw line. A flowing mane of pure white hair grew from its head all the way to the end of its lion-like tail.

The creature began walking toward me on nothing but thin air. Two piercing, glowing green eyes blazed with ancient power as they gazed at me steadily. At that same moment, I felt the bonds on my wrists vanish. My hands were free, so I started to get up.

Everyone else was trembling with fear. Some of them were even praying and wailing in sorrow. But I didn't feel afraid or intimidated by this creature. I actually felt calm, peaceful, like someone had wrapped me in a warm blanket.

The animal walked until it was hovering just in front of me. Then it lowered its head. I reached out my hand, and the strange beast rested its nose against my palm. I could feel the strength of its breath like a storm front's mighty gust. My heartbeat thrilled at the contact. All the pain in my body seemed to melt away. I felt stronger. My mind was sharper. My senses were honed. Heat and power rolled through my body, and yet I didn't feel like I was losing control.

"*You are my chosen servant,*" the creature spoke in my mind again like a harmony of voices, male and female. "*You will carry the banner of my will unto the world.*"

All the whispers from my dreams, the subtle words spoken to me through the years that I thought had foreshadowed my inevitable destiny, seemed to bubble up from my subconscious. It all came down to this one moment, this single touch, and a choice. To accept this fate, or to continue to struggle against it like I had for so long in my ignorance.

I didn't have to speak out loud for the creature to understand me. Just like with Mavrik, our thoughts and desires were melded. We were one in our innermost minds. So when I accepted, the creature simply began to fade. It dissolved into the air, becoming a fine glittering mist that was carried away into the jungle without another sound.

When I opened my eyes again, I knew something was different. There was a peace in my soul that had never existed there before. I had been sleeping, but there were no more nightmares. There was no more fear. I didn't feel stretched thin or strained, like I was trying to cram myself into a mold that didn't fit. I wasn't soaked with sweat or filled with panic. I could take deep, calm breaths and enjoy the fact that my mind was relaxed and quiet.

Lying on a soft pallet made of animal furs, I could tell that I was inside a hut of some kind. Sunlight winked through the thatched roof and the smell of freshly cut wood and burning incense floated in the air. As I sat up, I realized I was wearing new clothes—Gray elf clothes. There was a long, bell-sleeved tunic of dark blue draped over my shoulders and a dark green pair of baggy pants tied around my waist. I had to admit, they were pretty comfortable compared to the heavy wool clothes I usually wore. Most importantly, my mother's necklace was hanging around my neck again. I immediately wrapped my hand around it, giving it a grateful squeeze.

"How are you feeling?" I recognized Araxie's voice right away—even when she was speaking the human language. She was sitting in the corner of the small room, watching me with a guarded expression, like she wasn't quite sure what to make of me yet.

"Good." I had to laugh because it had been so long since I had actually felt *good* when I woke up. "What happened? Where am I?"

"Not far from the temple grounds." I could see Araxie's color-changing eyes sparkling as she watched me. "You passed out after Paligno gave you his blessing."

"Paligno?" I had a feeling I knew what she was talking about. I just wanted to be sure.

"The god who first seeded this earth," she said. "Do you really not know the ancient stories? Alowin never told you?"

I bowed my head slightly. "We didn't have a lot of time to discuss things like that before she died."

Araxie's expression was sympathetic. "What is your name?"

"Jaevid," I answered. "But you can call me Jae, if you like." I ran a hand through my now chin-length hair. It surprised me a little. I'd almost forgotten the king had cut it so short.

The silence between us was awkward and tense. I could tell just by the way she was chewing on the inside of her cheek that there must have been a lot she wanted to say.

"Thank you," I offered at last.

That must have jarred her. She frowned and sat up straighter. "Why would you thank me?"

"You tried to save me. It didn't work, but you did try." I smiled at her. "I'm grateful."

Her eyes narrowed a bit, like she wasn't sure if I was being serious or not. "Ever since I was a little girl, I have prayed that Lapiloque would return to us somehow and end this war. You aren't what I expected, but who am I to question the will of the gods?"

"I don't think this is what any of us expected," I agreed.

Araxie sat quietly for a moment or two, twirling a lock of her silver hair around one of her fingers. Finally, she spoke in a quiet voice, "My father is in mourning. He is filled with shame for almost killing the one who speaks for the god stone. He should be here to greet you but he won't leave his private chambers."

I was disappointed to hear that. He was my uncle, and even if we'd gotten off to a horrendously bad start, I still wanted to talk to him. I wanted to get to know him, and try to understand what had happened that made my mother leave her people for Maldobar. For now, I decided not to press the issue, though.

"And my friend?" I asked. "The human who came here with me, where is he?"

Her expression tightened and she looked away uneasily. I knew she had some history with Jace. A lot of bad blood ran between them. "Alive, but only barely. We have done all we can, but his injuries are great. He fell under a fever two nights ago and our healers cannot break it."

"I need to see him." I tried to sound firm, but gentle in my request. After my encounter with Paligno, I was only beginning to understand my place in this world. But I did know enough now to suspect they probably wouldn't refuse me anything I asked. I wasn't going to use that as a license to be a jerk. After all, she was my first cousin. For me, friendly family members had always been hard to come by.

Araxie tucked some of her long hair behind one of her pointed ears and huffed unhappily. "Why do you favor him? He is a murderer."

"We're all murderers now," I reminded her. "War tends to do that to people."

She didn't like that answer. I could tell, even if she didn't argue. "Very well, then. Come with me."

I started to stand, but my knees nearly buckled underneath me. Before I could fall, Araxie seemed to appear out of nowhere and helped me steady myself. She was petite, a full foot shorter than I was actually, and yet I could feel strength in her that probably surpassed my own.

"S-sorry," I stammered with embarrassment. "I feel strange. Like I've been asleep for a long time. How long was I out?"

"Three days." Once I was confident enough to walk on my own, she stood back and took a long length of black silk from a hook. She began to roughly wrap it around my waist several times before tying off the ends and tucking them in. "The power of Lapiloque has been sleeping inside you for a very long time, but it can only be awakened when you accept Paligno's blessing. Things will be different now. Now that the ritual has been completed, you will embody his power and be able to control the things of nature."

I realized that this must have been the same ritual Sile had told me about. "And if I had refused?"

"Your power would have faded away and been given to another," she replied matter-of-factly. "There must always be a Lapiloque. It is the balance, you see. So long as the stone endures, so too must the speaker endure with it."

Her vibrant eyes caught mine under the dim light. She held out two more things for me to take, both of which I had given up as lost forever. One was the scimitar—the one with the stag's head on the pommel that had been robbed from the King of Maldobar years ago. I took it and slid it into my waist wrap. The other was the handkerchief Beckah had given to me before my avian year of training. It was stained with sweat and blood now, and some of the edges were getting ragged, but the sight of it made me smile.

"I know this beast," Araxie muttered as she pointed to the image of Icarus, the black king drake, embroidered onto the fabric. "I have seen it in battle. This is a woman's token, is it not?"

I blushed. "Yes. It was a gift."

"From the one who rides the black dragon." She sent me a satisfied grin. "I knew it must be a woman when first we fought."

"How?" I was curious how Araxie had figured that out. Granted, Beckah was definitely a woman, but I thought she'd done a pretty decent job of obscuring that fact so she could fight.

"Because I've never met a man, human or elf, who could match me in battle. When she bested me, I knew it must be a woman." She twirled a hand in the air like it was obvious as she swaggered away.

When she opened the door of the hut, the sounds and smells of the jungle rushed in at me like a warm tidal wave. For whatever reason, I'd just assumed we were on the ground. We definitely weren't. We were at least a hundred feet in the air, inside a hut that hung off the side of a giant tree. Gazing out, I could see the endless expanse of the forest all around us. Other huts like ours clung to the sides of the trees, connected by the spiraling staircases engraved into the bark. There were swinging bridges and intricate terraces that formed a network—a whole village far above the jungle floor. Its beauty was staggering, and I was immediately transfixed by it.

Araxie had been exactly right—things were different now. There wasn't any stress or strain on my body to feel the world around me. I didn't have to focus or force myself to listen to the voices of the jungle. It didn't cause me any discomfort. They were a part of me, every bit as constant as Mavrik's presence in my mind.

Araxie stood beside me in the doorway. I noticed she didn't look nearly as mesmerized by this place as I was. If anything, she looked deeply worried. Something was still bothering her. I certainly wasn't any kind of genius when it came to women and the way their minds worked, but even I could tell that much. She was frowning and chewing on the inside of her cheek again, looking around like she was expecting something bad to happen at any moment.

"Come along, if you still insist on seeing that murderous friend of yours," she said and gave me a nudge out the door.

"Jace," I corrected her. "His name is Jace."

She just wafted a hand in the air like it didn't matter what anyone called him.

We left the hut and began making our way down the elaborately carved staircases and across the swinging bridges that led to the ground in a zigzag pattern. On the way, I realized Araxie wasn't the only one acting tense around me. The villagers we passed wouldn't even look me in the eye. They bowed their heads or turned their faces as though they didn't want to have anything to do with me.

Eventually, I got up the nerve to ask Araxie what was going on.

"They are ashamed, too." She glanced back at me with a small, reassuring smile. "Because of what happened they fear you will refuse to help us now."

Directly in front of us, I saw a young woman with a pair of toddlers, trying to herd them out of our path. She appeared flustered and afraid, and she kept casting panicked glances in my direction. Suddenly, one of her children broke free of her grasp and came running toward me. She cried out in alarm, calling for him to come back.

The little boy, who couldn't have been more than two, didn't pay her any attention. Instead, he wrapped himself around one of my legs. He gazed up at me with big, curious eyes sparkling in all different hues. When he grinned at me, I bent down and picked him up. His poor mother was pale with fear. She stood by, clinging to her other child while she glanced between Araxie and me like she wasn't sure what to do.

"Funny thing about being a halfbreed—if I didn't know how to survive a little abuse, then I wouldn't have any friends at all," I said and smiled as I handed the child back to his awestruck mother. "Don't worry about it. You're not the first ones to beat me within an inch of my life. I doubt you'll be the last."

I almost ran into Araxie when I turned back around to keep following her. She had stopped to watch and was gazing up at me curiously. "You don't look anything like her," she said quietly. "But when you speak, I hear her spirit."

"My mother?"

She nodded. "I was just a little girl when she walked among us. But she taught me so much. We all loved her, Jaevid. That's why no one understood it when she left. I think it hurt my father most of all because she had always been something of a mentor to him, even if she was the younger of the two. He trusted her above all others. Without her, he ... seemed to think his fate was sealed to fail."

"She never mentioned any of this to me. I didn't know I had any family here." It was a little painful to admit that. I didn't understand why my mother had kept this all from me.

"There must have been a reason," Araxie decided. "She always had reasons for everything she did."

I wanted to believe that was true. And yet when it came down to it, I was forced to acknowledge the hard truth that I hadn't really known my mother at all. I'd known her smiles, her love, and her gentle words. Those things were important. But now I was wishing she had told me more about herself, her family, and what my future might be like.

Araxie gave me another nudge, pushing her shoulder against mine to get my attention. She offered a tentative, comforting smile. It made her already pretty face glow with otherworldly beauty. And once again, I got the eerie sensation that I'd seen that smile somewhere before.

"It seems like you've had an interesting journey," she said. "You should tell us about it. It might help everyone feel more at ease if they knew where you came from and how you got here."

She was probably right about that. And telling them about my past might actually help me start to piece together some of the mysteries in my life. I also had a faint hope that it might help guide my steps in the future.

Our eyes met again, and that's when it hit me. All of a sudden, I realized who she reminded me of. She favored my mother. They had the same face shape and that familiar glittering energy in their eyes. When Araxie smiled, it was even more obvious. The family resemblance was strong.

And for whatever reason, that put a twinge of jealousy in my gut. I looked so much like my human father. Now that I'd met her, I started wishing I looked a little more like my mother's side of the family.

I kept those thoughts to myself and followed her down to the ground toward the ancient temple. There was so much to take in—villagers going about their daily lives all around me—I didn't realize where we were going until I was standing on the stone front steps.

We entered the temple through a pair of massive double doors. Inside, a long atrium boasted a domed ceiling that was open to the jungle above. All manner of plant life was spilling down into it, growing down the walls and filling the spacious room with the smell of flowers and earth. The floor was adorned in a beautiful mosaic of Paligno, the stag-like creature who was supposed to be a god, standing amidst a sea of stars.

"Seems like an odd place to torture your prisoners," I pointed out.

Araxie didn't look back as she led the way deeper into the temple. "Believe me; I have no preconceived notions that Paligno won't punish us somehow for this sacrilege. But if there's any excuse for it, it's only that we have nowhere else to go. Sometimes I think the only reason we haven't suffered any divine wrath is because we are already living in hell."

"What do you mean?"

"First, see to your friend. We'll discuss the rest after," she whispered quietly as we came to a stop at an open doorway. Beyond it, a few oil lamps created heavy shadows in a small, windowless room. I could smell incense burning, and the familiar sickly sweet scent of infection.

Jace was lying on a pallet on the floor with a few old women, who must have been healers, seated around him. They were burning medicinal herbs that filled the air with fragrant smoke and making poultices to help cleanse his wounds of infection.

When I entered, however, they all bowed their heads and began to clear the room. They didn't go far. In fact, there was quite an audience of people gathered in the doorway, pushing and shoving to watch. It was bizarre, and I could sense their hopeful apprehension at what I was going to do.

Even though it had been a few days since our last beating, Jace didn't look good at all. He looked worse, actually. His face was more ashen. There were dark circles around his eyes. His body was covered in a sheen of sweat and his breathing was shallow and labored. He was in pain. I could sense it. I could taste it like a coppery flavor in my mouth.

I knelt down and put my hand against his forehead. "Jace?"

He didn't respond.

Through that small amount of contact, I could tell he was fading. He wouldn't live much longer. Not unless I intervened. I wasn't sure what to expect from my power now. Things were definitely different, and I honestly wasn't sure what I might be capable of, be it good or bad.

But for his sake, I had to try.

Before, whenever I healed someone, it always caused a stretching, straining sensation that drained me to the point of near exhaustion. Now, it was as simple as reaching out to hug someone, and it gave me a warm feeling very similar to that. It was comfortable.

I simply took some of the power that now flowed freely through my veins and used it like a thread to stitch his broken body back together in my mind's eye. I saw the palm of my hand beginning to glow with radiant green light. I felt Jace's heartbeat quicken. His body grew tense. I flushed the fever from his system—the infection, the suffering, the broken bones—I took it all and washed his body clean of every ailment.

And at the end, when my work was done, I was completely at peace. That is, until I got a glimpse of something I hadn't intended to.

It only lasted a second or two, but it left me reeling: the image of a young boy standing barefoot in the ashes of a burning city, his clothes tattered and his tears making clean streaks down his face. He looked terrified. And he looked quite a bit like Jace. There were chains around his neck and wrists, binding him to the saddle of a black horse. I saw the reflections of flames in his eyes, burning brightly against a dreary sky.

And then it was gone. I took in a sharp breath. I'd been able to meld my mind with animals before. That wasn't difficult. But for as many times as I'd healed people, I'd never gotten anything in return except violently ill. I'd never been able to glimpse into their minds.

Until now.

I looked down to find that Jace's physical appearance had changed. He looked like himself again. The swelling, bruises, and fever were all gone. His skin had a natural, healthy glow to it and his breathing was calm, deep, and even. He didn't appear to be aware of what I had seen in his mind. A nightmare or a memory ... or perhaps both.

From the doorway, I heard whispers of amazement from my captive audience. Some of them had started chanting what I suspected were most likely prayers. It was weird, and it made me pretty uncomfortable. I wanted to leave.

I glanced over at Araxie, who was quietly stepping into the room. She squatted beside me and studied Jace with a steely expression. "Will he live?"

"Yes." I was confident about that much, at least. "He just needs to rest now."

Without needing to look up, I could feel the pressure of her intense gaze upon me. "You've done this before, haven't you?"

I had to laugh. "Yeah. A few times."

10

CHAPTER TEN

There wasn't any time to celebrate my ability to heal people without almost killing myself in the process. From outside the temple, the sound of horns blaring echoed through the halls all around us. I looked at Araxie. The color was draining from her face.

She cursed in the elven language and jumped to her feet, stealing out of the room without an explanation. I followed her as she walked briskly back out onto the temple's front steps, right into the face of absolute chaos. Gray elves were running everywhere, screaming as they frantically tried to gather up their belongings and family members. They were coming straight for us, fleeing into the temple.

Araxie didn't run. She stood firm, her eyes narrowed, and her silver hair flying. I heard her make a sound, like the shrill call of a bird, and from overhead there was an answering, shrieking sound that I knew all too well.

Her shrike landed before us, snapping its jaws eagerly as she stepped lightly to the saddle and unhooked her blades, bow, and quiver. Her sharp eyes tracked to me, and at once I understood. I'd seen that look before—though not on her face.

Something was coming.

As villagers ran past us, packing themselves into the temple for shelter, I shrugged out of the long, bell sleeves of my tunic and tied them around my waist. I couldn't afford to have them getting in the way. I drew the scimitar from my hip and took a place beside Araxie. The heavy temple doors shut behind us, sealing off the temple, but we weren't alone. Other Gray elf warriors dropped from the trees armed with their bows, spears, and swords.

Kiran was among them. He came over immediately and stood beside me, glancing me up and down swiftly as though he were surprised to see me out here with them. "Those clothes don't suit you," he muttered as he pulled an arrow from his quiver and strung it along his bowstring.

"I agree." I smirked.

"Hush!" Araxie hissed, raising a hand and calling her warriors to attention.

We stood frozen, listening to the forest around us. At first, everything seemed normal. I started to wonder if it had been a false alarm, although I didn't know what we were looking for to begin with. Then I felt it.

Weight settled over my chest, squeezing at my mind uncomfortably. It was a burning, stinging sort of pressure, and it offended that part of my soul that was now fused with Paligno. The balance was compromised. The wild was turning on itself.

The jungle at the far edge of the temple grounds began to move, shuddering violently a few seconds before the monsters burst through it. Two primate-like beasts with stumpy hind legs, huge muscular front arms, and wooly hides mottled with crystalline-looking growths and moss stormed the clearing. Each one was at least fifteen feet to the shoulder, and I could sense the raw brute force of their strength.

Whatever they were, they were possessed by the sickness—the rage that was also infecting animals in Maldobar. Their gaping, toothy maws foamed. Their eyes were so bloodshot that they seemed to glow red. They wouldn't be deterred. They had come for blood.

Araxie never flinched. She tilted her chin down toward her chest, her eyes never leaving her enemy, and gave the command to open fire. Arrows hummed through the air, but even I could tell that wasn't going to do much besides make these animals angrier than ever. Their hides were bound to be too thick for an arrow or a sword to pierce.

I was trying figure what to do, or if there was some way I could help. Without my dragon, I wasn't sure what use I would be. All of a sudden, I felt something—something new. It was like a tugging on the back of my mind, like someone was poking me repeatedly to get my attention. It wasn't Mavrik or any other presence I was familiar with.

I turned my focus to it. Tingling heat swept over my skin, and thoughts started whirling through my brain almost faster than I could comprehend. They were a flurry of pictures, of scenes like from my dreams. I saw someone else fighting a creature like this, wielding power over the jungle. Then I remembered something my mother had said to me before. My dreams weren't dreams. They were memories.

I knew what I had to do. I sheathed my blade and glanced at Kiran. "Watch my back."

He nodded.

While Araxie led her warriors in an assault on the monsters, I let my mind retreat to the fountain of power bubbling up from inside me. I flexed my will, calling on the jungle to observe my place as Paligno's chosen one—just like the figure from my vision.

And this time, it obeyed without question.

The ground rumbled. The trees groaned. Before me, the earth split and a fissure opened up. It spouted roots and vines by the hundreds. They surged skyward like a living tied, twisting together and taking on a humanoid shape.

My golem lumbered forward at my command, bigger than both the simian creatures that bellowed at it in fury. They charged, and I braced for impact.

The golem moved when I moved, driven by my gestures, and I managed to grab the first of the creatures by its scraggly neck. It pounded its giant fists into my golem's head, snapping vines and roots with each blow. It was much stronger than I anticipated. But I felt no pain, and neither did my elemental creation.

I grappled with it, flinging the beast to the ground just as the second one mauled me. My golem stumbled under its weight, and I pitched to try to fling it off.

But I wasn't in this fight alone.

Araxie was incredibly fast. And her aim with the bow was flawless. She fired a shot straight into a weak spot under the primate's arm, piercing softer skin and making the beast howl in pain. It fell off my golem, giving me a chance to wheel around and pin it.

The first monster was getting up, dazed but undeterred. It began thundering toward the fight again, slinging foam as it roared. One golem wasn't going to do it.

I needed to try something else. Something new. I tapped into those memories again, searching for something more powerful to try.

I drew my scimitar again and raised it skyward, pressing power into the metal until it glowed with energy. Then I plunged it into the ground. A shockwave went out around me, spreading like a ripple on a pond. It made a low, concussive sound and for a few seconds, there was silence.

Suddenly, a chorus of screeches went up from the trees around us. Shrikes descended like a flock of ravenous crows, blurring through the air and attacking the first monster mid-charge. Maybe it could have handled one or two shrikes without a problem, but the primate wasn't able to deal with thirty or so. Jaws laced with venom bit at the creature from all sides, overwhelming it and bearing it to the ground. It pitched and flailed, trying to beat them off. But there was no escape.

Without my will to drive it, the second beast was ripping my golem apart like a scarecrow. At least it was distracted. I turned just in time to see Araxie pouncing fearlessly from an overhanging limb, her bow drawn taut with three arrows notched. She fired all three at once, finding yet another soft spot on the back of the simian's skull—just like she had with Ghost.

The creature froze instantly. Its bulky arms drooped. It made a sad, gurgling sound and fell face-forward onto the ground ... and it didn't move again.

Standing over her kill, the Gray elf princess looked wild. Her formal dress was tattered some, and her hair was falling out of its intricate braided design. She looked at me, and I understood why Jace had had such a hard time fighting her. She was truly a force to be reckoned with.

The Gray elf warriors rallied quickly, falling back to the front of the temple and forming a line in front of me. Araxie strutted proudly in front of them, her shoulders back and her chin tilted up with pride. She wasted no time putting them to work. Injuries had been minimal, so there were plenty of hands at her disposal.

I watched them split off. One group formed a scouting party who left to secure the perimeter of the village and make sure there weren't any more surprise monsters coming to visit. The rest began cutting the dead animals apart.

"Nothing will be wasted. Meat is too hard to come by not to harvest everything we possibly can." Araxie glanced me up and down as she sauntered over to stand with her arms crossed, an authoritative scowl on her face. "I suppose I owe you my gratitude. This is the first encounter in years where we haven't had to bury any of our own."

I wished I could have felt happier or more proud about that. "So this sickness isn't just affecting the animals in Maldobar," I realized aloud. "How long has it been here?"

Araxie and Kiran exchanged a glance like they suspected I might be out of my mind.

"Jaevid, it began here." Araxie cleared her throat. "It seems there is much more you don't know."

Araxie tried insisting that I should stay in my own hut. I guess it was strange for the stonespeaker not to be staying with the royal family, and the hut in question had been cleared out especially for me. But I couldn't accept that. I wanted to stay near Jace. I knew when he finally woke up he was probably going to be confused and afraid of our hosts. That was totally understandable. And I definitely had a lot of explaining to do. Poor Jace knew basically nothing about my past or anything I'd been through before he became my instructor.

Boy was he in for a surprise.

The Gray elves brought back all our armor and gear, fixing up the stuffy little room in the temple as comfortably as they could with another bed and soft fur pelts on the floor. The villagers still wouldn't meet my eyes for more than a second or two, though. I wondered how long that would last. It was beginning to make me uneasy.

The morning after those simian beasts had attacked, I stepped out of the room Jace and I were sharing to find a heap of stuff piled all around the doorway. I almost tripped over it. There were pots, bits of jewelry, weapons, and portions of food wrapped up like presents.

"Gifts from the villagers."

Kiran was standing off to the side, just out of sight. The sudden sound of his voice about scared me to death.

"Gifts? Why?" I squatted to pick up a dagger made of strange white material. It wasn't bone. In fact, it almost felt like some sort of wood.

Kiran smirked. "Word has spread of what you did—singlehandedly bringing down two graulers. You saved many lives."

I rolled my eyes. "Technically, Araxie killed the second one."

"It seems she's willing to give you the credit if it will help smooth things over." He shrugged. "So now everyone is thankful to have Paligno's blessed one among us again. It is the first time in a decade they've had anything to celebrate. A small victory."

"I'm still waiting for someone to explain that to me," I reminded him.

"Soon, *caenu*. King Erandur has emerged from his mourning to announce there will be a great feast tonight. I suspect you'll get all the answers you can stand there."

I studied him carefully. "So why won't you call me by my name? By now I'm sure you know what it is."

"Does it matter what I call you?" He arched one of his eyebrows.

"Calling me a piece of filth isn't exactly a pet name," I pointed out.

Kiran grinned devilishly, almost like he was hoping I would want to fight about it. "You misunderstand. Gray elf men must never be too friendly unless they are family."

"Oh really? Why is that?"

"Because we compete for the same thing," he said as he made a curvy outline of a feminine shape in the air with his fingers. "We are rivals until one of us takes a mate."

I chuckled. "I've already chosen mine. And I doubt very much she'd be someone you would want, unless you're interested in human women."

He furrowed his brow, but didn't look quite as disgusted as I'd expected he might. "Oh."

"So call me Jae." I started moving some of the gifts around to make a path so I could at least get out the door.

Kiran wandered over to help me. I noticed he was also examining every gift, like he was trying to decide if it was something he might want or not. He picked up the dagger I had been examining earlier, testing the point by pricking his own finger. It was definitely sharp.

"See anything you like?" I decided to give him that invitation, since I didn't see myself trying to haul all of this stuff out of Luntharda anytime soon.

He flicked me a disbelieving look. "You don't know what this is, do you?"

I could only make a pathetic guess. "A nice knife?"

"A greevwood blade," he corrected me. "Very rare. Very difficult to harvest. Greevwood trees only grow deep in Luntharda. Once you cut away their flesh, you only have a few hours to shape it before it hardens. Then it can never be cracked or broken. Blades made from it will never go dull."

I studied the blade with a new appreciation. "I see."

"No, you don't." He twirled the blade over his hand as though he were testing its balance. "That is not what makes them so rare. Greevwood trees are flesh-eaters."

That struck a chord. All of a sudden, I remembered reading about these in my studies as a fledgling rider. There were trees in Luntharda known to be carnivorous, and they were considered highly dangerous.

"The roots grow out over the ground like a spider's web," he continued. "They are covered in many tiny hairs. When touched, they release a dust in the air. I forget the human word for it."

"Spores?"

He nodded. "Yes. When you breathe it in, it makes your body go numb. You become paralyzed and very easy to digest by those hungry roots."

I shuddered and looked at the blade more carefully as he offered it to me. The idea of a tree eating anything was downright creepy. I didn't like the visual at all.

Kiran smirked. "You see? This is not a trinket. It is a valuable gift."

"Understood." I took it from him and slipped it into my belt.

He finished helping me sort through the gifts, moving as many of them into my small room as we could fit. The commotion must have been louder than I realized because it woke up Jace, who started groaning and rolling over. He appeared delirious at first, like maybe he thought we were still at the tower in Northwatch.

Then he bolted upright and his eyes shot to me with utter terror. He spotted Kiran and scrambled off his sleeping pallet, snatching up the nearest thing he could use as a weapon—which wound up being one of his own boots.

"It's all right, Jace." I tried to sound comforting. "Relax. Everything is fine."

He clearly didn't believe me, not that I blamed him. He snarled at Kiran, brandishing that boot threateningly as he backed himself into a corner. His hands were clenched until his knuckles were white and his chest was heaving in frantic breaths.

"Kiran, can you give us a few minutes?" I decided it was probably better to do this without a Gray elf looming in the room. Once he was gone, I shut the door, which wasn't much more than a curtain strung over the entrance, and started to explain.

It took a long time, even though Jace knew I wasn't exactly normal to start with. After all, he'd seen me heal people before. But there was still a lot to tell. Starting from the beginning, with my encounter with the slavers, my nightmares and visions, my discovery about my father, how Sile was involved in everything, and the fact that I was apparently the chosen servant of an ancient forest deity ... it would have been a lot for anyone to take in.

Jace took it better than I expected, though. He only cussed at me a few times. Sitting on his pallet again, angrily lacing his boots and vambraces up, he shot me several scathing glares. "Why the hell didn't you tell me any of this before?"

"I didn't tell many people," I admitted. "I was afraid of what would happen, or that I'd be accused of being a traitor for something that isn't my fault. I can't help what I am, or what I can do. The dreams I had were terrifying to me. And I had no way of knowing what they were supposed to mean."

He didn't look sympathetic. He shot me another punishing look and stood up to buckle his kidney belt around his waist. "And now we're stuck here with the savages, being held captive until they decide to butcher us again."

"I don't think that'll happen," I said. "We're not captives anymore."

"You aren't," he corrected me and put an accusing finger in my face. "I'm still the one who murdered three of the king's sons. The magical elf rock didn't choose me, idiot."

I scowled back. "You think I'd just toss you to the wolves? I've already stuck my neck out for you. Araxie wanted to let you die. I wouldn't allow it."

He snorted. "Maybe you should have."

"My sentiments exactly," a sarcastic female voice chimed in. Araxie was standing in the doorway, her hips cocked arrogantly. She was looking at Jace appraisingly, like she was sizing him up in case she found a good excuse to kill him later.

He started to glare bitterly back at her, his lip curled into a challenging sneer. But for whatever reason, he seemed to have a hard time keeping that expression up for very long. Maybe it had something to do with the way the light of our oil lamps made her darkly tanned skin gleam like bronze. Or maybe it was the way her long, platinum colored hair flowed over her chest all the way to her narrow, bare midriff.

Whatever it was—the longer Jace stared, the less angry he looked. I saw him swallow stiffly.

Araxie obviously wasn't as impressed with him. She just made a dismissive *pfft* sound and looked right back at me. "My father desires that you come and join us tonight for a feast in your honor. You and your human pet."

Jace growled a few profane words under his breath that I couldn't quite make out. He turned around and started angrily fidgeting with his sheath and twin swords.

"We'll be there," I told her.

The princess flicked a quick, spiteful smirk at Jace's back. "Excellent. I hope you'll both enjoy our hospitality."

"I've had about all of their hospitality I can stand," Jace muttered after she had gone. "That little witch is just waiting for a chance to put a blade through my neck. You just wait. They'll find some excuse to do it. I'll be roasting on a rotisserie with a big fat apple in my mouth by nightfall."

I smirked and shook my head. "On the contrary, Jace. I think you like her."

11

CHAPTER ELEVEN

The whole village had worked tirelessly all day to prepare for this feast, and they wouldn't let me lift a finger to help. A bonfire was built in the middle of the courtyard, stacked high with the pieces of my golem that couldn't be used for anything else. By the time it began to grow dark, things were beginning to get lively. Lanterns were lit throughout the tree-born huts and walkways, making the jungle around us sparkle like a sea of warm yellow stars. Slabs of meat from the graulers had been marinated in fruit juices and herbs and now sizzled over red-hot coals. Barrels of wine and strange smelling breads were passed around.

A group of older men and women were playing bizarre pipe instruments and beating on drums. They filled the clearing with music, which in turn got the young women dancing. Children ran to and fro, chasing each other and laughing. Young men and warriors sat together in small groups, talking and eyeing me from afar. I couldn't tell if they were just curious or trying to decide if I was a rival or not.

Jace must have been incredibly nervous. I couldn't think of any other reason he'd stick so close to my side as we approached the festivities. I'd managed to talk him out of carrying his weapons, since that would definitely send the wrong message. He wasn't happy about it. Not one teensy bit. And I had a sneaking suspicion that he was sticking so close to me not because I made him feel any safer—but because he planned on using me as a living shield if things went badly.

Blankets and furs had been spread out on the ground for everyone to get comfortable on. I found a place next to Araxie to sit down, but I still didn't see her father anywhere. She smiled at me, and passed another quick, unenthusiastic look at Jace who sat down on my other side and began to sulk.

Araxie was dressed in fancier, more intricate clothes than usual. Although, they still showed way more female skin than I was used to seeing. There were colorful feathers and beads woven into her hair, and a bit of red paint dabbed onto her lips and in a pretty flower design on her forehead. Long dangling earrings made of hammered copper hung from her pointed ears, and there was a string of crudely cut precious stones around her neck. Most of the young women were dressed up sort of like that, but her attire was decidedly more extravagant. It marked her as a notch above the rest on the social ladder.

"Father should be here soon," she said as she passed me a goblet of what smelled like some sort of sweet, fruity wine. "Does your pet want anything?"

Jace's jaw clenched as though he were gritting his teeth. He scowled, crossed his arms, and looked away. Thankfully, he didn't retort. Since I wasn't interested in repeating my last experience with alcohol, I passed the goblet of wine to him. He sniffed it, curled his lip, but took a drink anyway.

When King Erandur finally made an appearance, the music fell silent. No one spoke or moved, apart from leaning so they could get a glimpse of him. I thought at first it was only because he hadn't come out of his chambers in several days.

I was wrong, though.

The king had cut his hair. All those flowing locks of silvery white were gone. His hair was as short as mine now, lopped off right at his chin.

"Why did he do that?" I gave Araxie an uncomfortable glance because I had a feeling it had something to do with me.

"To express his shame and sorrow for what was done to you," she whispered.

The king didn't look happy at all about being here as he made his way to where we were sitting. Araxie scooted away from me, offering him the seat of honor between us. But before he could sit down, I decided I needed to do something to smooth things over.

I stood up swiftly and stepped toward the king. He regarded me with a wide-eyed, cautious expression and hesitated, as though he wasn't sure what to expect from me. Granted, I probably did look much more intimidating now that I wasn't beaten to a pulp. I was younger, a lot taller, and far more muscular than he was.

Sitting on the ground behind me, Araxie was watching me like a hawk. In fact, everyone in the whole village seemed to be holding their breath to see what I was going to do.

"Lapiloque—" the elven king began to address me.

I hugged him.

Sure, I was well within my right to be furious for what he had put me through. He'd nearly killed me. No amount of chopped off hair was going to fix that. And yet I wanted to get past this somehow. I wanted to get to know him. He was family.

King Erandur was completely stiff. It was like embracing a corpse. So I didn't force-hug him for long. I squeezed him once, just for good measure, and stood back to smile.

"I'm glad to officially meet you, Uncle," I said.

Erandur's mouth was hanging wide open. It was awkward. I could tell he was struggling to regain some of his composure. At last, he extended a hand toward me with uncertainty written all over his face. "I am ... pleased to have the honored Lapiloque amongst my people again."

Araxie giggled. She was smiling from one pointed ear to the other. I guess from where she was sitting, it looked like things were going well. That was reassuring.

I wasn't so sure, though. The king wouldn't acknowledge me as a blood relative. I didn't know if that was because I was expected to act as Lapiloque first, and as family second—or if it was because he still harbored a lot of resentment toward my mother.

I hoped to get to the bottom of that as we all sat down again. The music resumed, and the villagers began passing around big platters and bowls of food. It was a different way of eating a meal than I'd experienced before. They didn't make themselves a plate—they just ate a few bites off the platters as they were passed around over and over.

The food was delicious, though, and even Jace seemed to be enjoying it. He never said that out loud, of course, but I noticed he was eating a lot. He also apparently liked their sweet wine, too, because he refilled his cup four times before I lost count.

The feast also brought out a side of the Gray elves I'd never seen before. Young women in their flashy, revealing clothes danced together before the light of the roaring fire. They smiled and swayed their hips in teasing ways, stopping only long enough to pull other people up to join in. It didn't take long for the men to take them up on that offer. They approached me, too. Thankfully, I was able to respectfully bow out of every invitation. I had a good excuse. Despite lots of practice and coaching, I was a horrible dancer, and the way the Gray elves did it was even more bizarre than what I'd attempted before.

Araxie had been sitting quietly beside her father while we ate and drank, but her eyes never left the dancers who were frolicking in the firelight. When another pretty elf woman came over to invite us to join in, she jumped up and linked arms with her. The two women giggled and wandered back toward the bonfire, disappearing into the crowds.

Now I was alone with Jace and the king—neither of which were making for very good company so far. Jace was scowling at the dancers, although I noticed his eyes were scanning the crowds like he was watching someone in particular.

The king, on the other hand, had produced a long wooden pipe and was puffing smoke rings over the rim of his wine glass.

Great. Lucky me.

After what felt like an eternity of sitting next to each other and awkwardly avoiding eye contact, King Erandur finally spoke up, "My daughter speaks very highly of you."

I spotted Araxie through the moving crowds. She was smiling and moving with the music. The firelight gleamed off her silk clothes and jewelry. "I feel as though I haven't done anything to deserve that kind of loyalty from her. But I'm thankful. I owe her a lot already."

"She is a good judge of character," he said as he puffed another smoke ring. "Far better than I am, it would seem."

As long as he was talking, I decided this was as good a time as any to start trying to get some answers. Too bad there wasn't a smooth way to broach that topic. "I'm sure I don't have to tell you that there's a lot we need to talk about."

"Yes. I know." His reply was hushed and somber. When I turned to meet his gaze, I was surprised to catch him staring at me with that mournful look in his eyes again.

"I hate to spoil the party, but there's a lot of people losing their lives in a war that—as best I can tell—my father is responsible for. I'd like to do what I can to put an end to it." I wasn't going to try to justify what Ulric had done. He didn't deserve that.

"Answer me this first." Erandur began studying me intensely. "How did my sister die?"

I let my gaze wander back toward the bonfire. Talking about my mom was still difficult. And it was even harder to do it with someone like Erandur, even if he was her brother. "Of a sickness. I honestly don't remember much beyond that. I was young, and losing her meant I had to go live with my human father, who had nothing but hatred for me."

The king sat quietly, as though he were reflecting on those words.

When he didn't speak up, I kept talking. I realized this was my chance to argue my mother's case and heal some old wounds. "We lived in a refugee ghetto in the royal city. Our house was tiny, but she could make anywhere feel like home. She grew things all the time. Our house was always filled with all sorts of flowers and vegetables. She never told me anything about you, or Araxie, or that she was the Lapiloque. When she gave me this necklace, I had no idea it meant anything at all."

"That is the totem of the Lapiloque," Erandur explained. "It is passed on to whoever inherits the gift. Legend says that it is carved from the bone of Paligno."

I instinctively ran my hand over the smooth, white bone pendant. "It's the only piece of my mother I have left."

"And the human man? Your father? Did she marry him?" His voice was stiff.

I frowned. "No."

"Did she love him?"

That was a difficult question for me to think about. As a child, I'd never paid much attention to which men my mother seemed to prefer, so I had to think it over. "Ulric had another family. He had a human wife and children. Whatever relationship he had with my mother began and ended with me—at least, that was the impression I was always given. I already told you how he felt about me. I never saw any evidence that he felt any differently about my mother. He never talked about her at all. And she never told me that she cared for him, either."

Erandur let out a deep sigh. He bowed his head slightly as though in resignation. "Then I am the biggest fool of all. I assumed that when she left us, she simply betrayed us. I thought she had run off with that human man who came here to plead for forgiveness for the sins of the traitor who took the stone."

"Sile Derrick?"

He shot me a suspicious look. "You know him?"

"Yes," I admitted. "He and my mother were definitely conspiring about something, and I believe that something was me. But I don't think there was ever anything romantic between them. Sile has his own family, and it's always been clear to me that he loves them deeply."

"When she left with him, it tore my people apart. They lost faith in my ability to protect them. Lapiloque symbolizes the blessing of the gods upon us. It is an immense responsibility and one that we have always taken very seriously." Erandur's tone was still cold. His expression had become hard and fierce as he glared straight ahead. "What you see before you is all that remains of my once proud nation. Two thousand men, women, and children where once I governed hundreds of thousands throughout this land."

I found myself at a loss for words. Looking around at the people who were dancing, laughing, and enjoying their meal ... it put guilt like a heavy weight in my chest. I'd assumed that this was only one small settlement—a tiny piece of a much larger population. Hearing that this was all that remained of them was nothing short of horrifying.

"Because of the war?" I asked.

He snorted as though he wished that were the case. "Some, yes. But the jungle has devoured more than the human ranks ever could. When Paligno's curse began to spread, many fled to your human kingdom. I assumed they had found refuge there."

I was starting to feel sick. Refuge? No. They'd found a new form of hell. They'd been forced to live in squalor, starving and constantly abused by city guards. They'd been rounded up and driven to prison camps or sold as slaves. And now they were being murdered.

"The curse will only grow worse. Like with the graulers," Araxie's voice chimed in suddenly. She had come up behind us to eavesdrop without either of us noticing. "When the god stone is removed from its sacred resting place within the tomb, the balance is thrown off. All of nature turns upon itself violently in order to find it and restore it. That is what we call Paligno's curse."

"You mean like the madness? The same one that's spreading through Maldobar now?" Jace surprised us all when he spoke up. I hadn't even realized he was listening in.

Araxie nodded. I saw their eyes meet briefly. "Most likely. It begins with the animals. First the lesser, stupider ones go mad. Then more and more dangerous creatures will be wakened to ravage the earth until the stone is found and brought back to the tomb."

"And where is this tomb?" I demanded.

Erandur stretched out a finger, pointing to the cavernous pit where Paligno had appeared to me. "Down the stairs into the dark, that is where you'll find the tomb of a god's mortal body. Paligno once walked the earth along with the other ancient gods, seeding it with all manner of life. When he died, his physical body was entombed there, although his spirit endures eternally through the god stone. It acts as a host to his essence. Lapiloque is his fleshly servant chosen to carry out his will. The two must always exist."

It was time. Hearing that and understanding now the true purpose of my birthright, I knew I had to tell them everything. And just like with Jace, it took a long time. There was a lot to tell.

I was nervous about how this news would be received. Even so, I didn't spare any details. I told them all about the details of my dreams and nightmares, the visions of my mother, and the Gray elf warrior murdering the King of Maldobar. I told them about my encounter with the paludix turtle, and how my powers had grown steadily over the years. When it came to Sile, I tried to be as forthcoming as possible without painting him in a negative light. He obviously knew a lot about what was going on, and he'd gone to great lengths to keep me ignorant of it. But he had insisted that I come here so I could see the suffering of my mother's people—and I made sure they knew that.

Of course, they had a few questions. Well, more than a few actually. Araxie didn't know much about human culture, so I had to explain a few things to her—like who the king's elite guards were. They seemed to be taking everything well, nodding and listening, until I mentioned the king's recent decree that moved all Gray elves to the prison camps. I think they understood right away that was the same thing as a death sentence.

Araxie sat back. Her face was pasty white with horror. I could see her chest rising and falling with furious breaths. At last, I guess she couldn't take it anymore. She stood up and stormed away from us without saying a word.

I didn't blame her at all for being upset. I wasn't exactly happy about it, either. The King of Maldobar was committing mass genocide against people who had come to him for peaceful refuge. It was inexcusable.

But where Araxie expressed brazen rage, her father simply bowed his head and closed his eyes. "Please forgive her. She is young."

"There's nothing to forgive," I replied. "If anything, I should be apologizing to you all. I was given this responsibility to help you, and I haven't done anything. I'm sorry that it's come to this. And I will do whatever I can to set things right."

Erandur looked at me squarely—without frowning or glaring this time. For the first time, I got the impression he was actually *seeing* me. "Are you sure about that?"

I nodded firmly, although I felt he still knew something I didn't.

"I think I can answer your questions about your dreams, Nephew." He put his pipe back in his mouth and began puffing on it again. "I believe it's time you learned a bit more about your relatives."

MY HEAD WAS SPINNING, AND IT WASN'T FROM ALE OR WINE THIS TIME—although I did feel like I needed to throw up. I left the feast early and started back toward the temple. I wanted to lie down and think things over for a while. I didn't know what I should do, or even what I could do.

One thing was certain, however: I had to do something ... because this infamous traitor they all called Hovrid was my brother.

According to Erandur, my mother had been married before, but her husband had passed away. She'd had another son, much older than I was, named Hovrid. He hadn't been born blessed with Paligno's power like I had. The way Erandur explained it, that wasn't altogether abnormal. Sometimes that blessing even skipped generations. It was rare, and it wasn't something my mother or anyone else got to choose. Only Paligno could pick the one who would be Lapiloque.

But for Hovrid, being passed over had been difficult for him to swallow. He'd harbored a lot of resentment toward my mother, who he blamed for having not been chosen. He hated her for it. He'd tried many times to reach the stone, to touch it or get a glimpse of it despite my mother's warnings about what might happen. Touching it would drive a person to insanity. Glimpsing it, for those weaker in mind, might even have the same effect. Even I would have felt those effects if I had touched the stone before the ritual had been performed where Paligno had openly proclaimed me as his servant. No one was immune.

In the end, Hovrid driven himself mad, either from contact with the stone or from hatred and jealousy toward anyone else he deemed to be somehow superior to him.

He was sick in a way that couldn't be cured. There's no remedy for a wicked heart.

Erandur said that Hovrid had vanished a long time ago. They never knew where he went. And while they had tried to find him, scouring the jungle in hopes of bringing him back, other events had eclipsed the importance of his disappearance.

Namely, the theft of the god stone.

At last, the last few pieces of the puzzle were in place. The Gray elf warrior from my dreams—the one who had butchered the King of Maldobar and his family—was Hovrid. He was the one who had urged my father to steal the god stone. And now, Erandur suspected he was the one ruling from Maldobar's throne as a so-called king.

"Hovrid's hatred for us is second only to his need to possess the god stone. If he cannot wield it, he will make sure no one else can," Erandur had explained quietly. "We have all been deceived. We have spilt blood and destroyed countless lives warring against a false enemy."

Those words were still ringing in my ears as I entered the atrium of the temple. Moonlight was spilling down through the opening in the ceiling. It made the large mosaic of Paligno sparkle under my feet.

"Tell me you can stop this." A weak voice pleaded from the darkness.

It made me stop short. I turned around to see Araxie standing in a darkened corner, tears on her cheeks shining in the pale light, her expression wrathful.

"I've already lost a mother and three brothers to this war, Jaevid." She started walking toward me slowly. "Likewise, I'm sure I have murdered just as many fathers, sons, and brothers from your homeland. I can't justify it, though I want to. It has to stop. You have to return the god stone."

That's not all I had to do. She'd left too soon to hear her father telling me about Hovrid, but I figured she was probably already aware of who he was and that he was likely the culprit behind all this. I also suspected that she understood I would have to kill him in order to get the stone back. I doubted he would give it up easily. He'd spilt so much blood over it already, what were a few more drops?

"I will," I promised, although I let my tone carry an edge. "But there's something I need you to do for me."

She didn't hesitate. "Anything."

"Teach me to fight like the Gray elves do. I've seen how my enemy fights in my dreams. I'm no match for him right now. You said no man has ever beaten you in combat. So if I'm going to stand any chance against Hovrid, I'm going to need your skills."

Araxie started to grin—but it wasn't a friendly, warm, and fuzzy kind of expression. Her eyes burned like two cold stars in the darkness. I could see eagerness brimming in every corner of her face. "That, I can do."

"And while you're at it, you can teach me, too." A heavy hand fell onto my shoulder. Beside me, Jace was wearing a determined glare.

"Teach a human dog the ways of my people?" she said like it was a deeply offensive, ridiculous idea.

"He can't do it alone. There's going to be an army of elite guards and dragonriders between the throne room and him." Jace shook my shoulder gruffly. "We'll have one shot at this. We need to even up the odds."

I hadn't expected him to be so comfortable with a plan to assassinate a king—even if it was Hovrid in disguise. But I guess hearing that he'd spent his life in sworn servitude to an imposter was enough to turn his loyalties. Or perhaps his loyalties were shifty to begin with.

"Human men are too weak." Araxie flashed him a dismissive glance from head to foot. "You lack predatory instincts. Many generations of drinking too much liquor have made you fat and lazy. You won't last a day."

Jace narrowed his eyes challengingly. "Try me."

12

CHAPTER TWELVE

Dragonriders don't generally use bows in the air. Our weapon of choice is always our dragon's flame. Bows can be clumsy in flight, and it's difficult to aim while accounting for wind and constantly changing direction. At least, that's what I'd always been taught. Now some riders had an uncanny amount of skill with it—like Sile and Beckah. But I'd only handled a bow maybe ten times during my training—just enough to establish that I definitely wasn't some kind of rare, bow-wielding prodigy.

Big surprise there.

But the next morning, Araxie started her own brutal form of training, and teaching us to work with an elven bow was the first thing on her list. There were no more flowing, showy robes in my wardrobe. Jace and I were given the same sort of garb that Gray elf warriors wore under their armor. It amounted to a pair of dark pants, a sleeveless silk tunic, and a pair of vambraces that were made with wrist stabilizers.

Araxie was also wearing something similar, though her pants were split up the sides to show off her legs and her shirt was shorter and much more fitted to reveal most of her midriff. She shoved a bow and quiver into our hands first thing in the morning and began leading the way out of the village.

Jace eyed the bow like he wasn't impressed. "Never in a million years did I think I would be learning archery this way," he muttered.

"From a Gray elf?" I guessed.

He snorted and rolled his eyes. "No. From a woman."

We weren't alone as we began our dangerous trek away from the temple grounds. A few other curious warriors were following us—including Kiran. It was obvious they had a much easier time keeping up with the princess as she climbed over the railing of a high terrace and began running along the mossy, broad limbs of the trees. She moved like a jungle cat. She was sleek, quiet, and quick as a shadow as she stepped lightly through the trees with her weapons strung across her back. There was something dangerously beautiful about it.

I heard Jace cursing wildly under his breath as he eased out onto each limb, his legs wobbling at first. "Had to be heights," he grumbled through clenched teeth.

That sounded weird to me, coming from Jace. He didn't strike me as the kind of guy to be afraid of anything. "You're afraid of heights?"

He shot me a dirty look. "Shut up. Usually there's a dragon between the ground and me."

I snickered and looked away. I was trying my best to keep up with the rest of the warriors. Amidst the sea of vibrant jungle all around us, the brightly colored clothes the Gray elves wore made more sense. They blended in with the wild colors of the foliage, and the silk was light enough that the humidity and heat didn't make me feel stifled as we moved.

We passed through the trees, going from bough to bough like a bunch of squirrels until Araxie froze. She called the rest of us to a halt with a raised hand. Everyone stopped and immediately dropped into a low crouch against the limb where we stood. Jace and I did the same.

Far below, I saw the reason we'd all stopped.

There was a herd of creatures moving through the tall ferns. They were peaceful, I suppose, because no one drew on them. They seemed content to move slowly through the underbrush, nibbling on the green ends of fronds. We all just kept quiet and observed.

The creatures below looked like some species of elk or deer, although each of them was roughly the size of an eight hundred -pound bull. They were muscular, more so than a horse, and yet somehow graceful looking with their long legs and thick necks. Their pelts were a ghostly white color, mottled with gray stripes. The males had long white antlers sweeping back from their heads. I counted about ten sharp points on each horn.

As the herd moved on, Kiran shuffled closer to me. "Faundra," he whispered. "They are very strong and swift, and can jump a great distance even with a rider. Once we could tame them. Now they are the most likely to turn on us. It is too dangerous to go near them."

I watched the last of the faundra disappear into the jungle. I could imagine how much damage even one of those beasts could do if it were possessed by Paligno's curse. A whole herd would be deadly. It gave me a new appreciation for them.

Once the herd had moved on, Araxie gave a whistle and we all got back to our feet. She led the way through the trees to a place where we could climb down and there was a wide, open area between the trunks. The undergrowth wasn't so dense there, thanks to the thickness of the canopy that blotted out most of the sunlight.

We waited while she descended first and paced the clearing like a cautious doe. She was scanning for any potential threat, and she checked the ground thoroughly before she signaled up to the rest of us.

Climbing down was harder than going up—especially without a staircase. I wasn't sure Jace was going to make it. The other warriors were trying to help him some, but it didn't make much difference. He was cursing wildly until I heard a cracking sound, which I supposed was his boot breaking off a ledge of bark he'd been standing on.

He beat us all to the ground because he fell the last few feet.

When the rest of us got down to meet her, Araxie was already busy setting up targets. She squashed a few red berries between her fingers and painted circles on big leaves before hanging them on the tree trunks. I didn't have to ask what those were for.

Araxie wasted no time getting down to business. She instructed us to get ready, so Jace and I took off our bows and quivers. Elven bows were different from the human ones I had dealt with before. The string was made of some kind of thick resin, and the draw was incredibly difficult. The bow itself was almost as tall as I was, and had been painted to blend in with the jungle.

I had a difficult time drawing back the string until Kiran came over to show me a trick. "You start facing down. Use the strength of your legs, stomach, and shoulders." He demonstrated the motion for me as he explained, "Chest out. Shoulders back. Now, twist up as you draw."

I nodded and tried it. He was right. Using my whole body to draw the arrow was much easier. However, once I had the string drawn, my arms started to tremble under the strain. I clumsily fired an arrow toward one of the targets, but it just sailed away into the jungle. I didn't even hit the tree.

Kiran laughed. "A good try. Now, do it again."

Lucky for me, Jace wasn't doing any better. Some of the other warriors were trying to show him the same drawing technique Kiran had taught me. Unfortunately, Jace didn't have the same advantage of size that I had. I was several inches taller than he was, and he didn't have the benefit of a Gray elf's unnatural strength.

It took all morning for us to get a beginner's grasp on Gray elf archery. By noon, we were both able to at least draw and hit the target—albeit not in the center. When we stopped to rest, my arms had gone from aching to being entirely numb.

But I was determined. I had to get the hang of this.

It took hundreds of shots and several days before I was able to get anywhere near the center of the target. Once he figured out how to draw, Jace actually did better at it than I did. He was too stubborn to give up, and I had to give him credit for that.

The Gray elf warriors teased him in their native language while he struggled to fire shot after shot. They taunted him when they thought he wasn't looking. And still he never gave up. He clenched his teeth and narrowed his eyes. The muscles in his arms and shoulders went solid, and the veins in his neck stood out against his skin as he drew back each arrow.

He was the first to hit the bullseye.

After that, the warriors quit teasing him.

Araxie wasn't so easily impressed, though. She paced back and forth between us while we practiced, barking out orders and corrections. When Jace made that shot, she walked right up to him and commanded him to draw another arrow. I stopped to watch.

He obeyed, and she immediately began tweaking his position with a scrutinizing glint in her eyes. "Arms like this. String always at your cheek." She talked in a quiet, sharp voice as she moved his body into the proper form. "Feet apart. Don't flinch when you fire. Take a breath as you draw. Hold it until you release. Keep your eyes open."

Jace gave a slight nod and stood firm, holding his position and his breath until he fired again.

It was another bullseye.

"Good." Araxie gave him a satisfied smile. "Now do it again."

They were standing awfully close. Even I noticed it. She didn't seem quite as disgusted by him now. Or at least, she was so preoccupied with our training that touching him apparently didn't disgust her anymore. Either way, it made me grin to myself...

...mostly because I could have sworn Jace was blushing.

Every morning Araxie took us out into the jungle to train. And each time, I saw more of my mother's homeland for the wild, beautiful, and dangerous place it truly was. Being immersed in it was sharpening my senses. It quickened a part of my soul that had been lying dormant my entire life.

My power was growing stronger by the day, although I was hesitant to show it to anyone. The villagers were already wary around me, and I wasn't sure how Jace would respond if I showed him some of the new things I was capable of. It wasn't just the plants and birds that responded to my will, now. Tapping into those memories was awakening new abilities almost daily.

Moreover, I could sense the spread of Paligno's curse throughout the jungle. It was all around us, looming like an oppressive heat in my mind that made me nervous. I was beginning to question if simply putting a stone back into its resting place was going to fix all this. It seemed a little too easy.

That's why I felt compelled to seek out Paligno's counsel every night. I'd been trying it for almost a week. After Jace and everyone else went to sleep and the village was quiet, I found a place in the atrium of the temple where I could sit and meditate. I was hoping that the usually silent god would somehow give me a helpful hint about how I was going to fix all of this. But I never got any answers.

And then I got another reckless and potentially life threatening idea.

The temple compound was pitch black as I slipped out into the night. Everyone except for a few warriors who were watching the perimeter was sound asleep. Overhead, oil lamps burned in the huts strung about the tree trunks. They glowed with a warm orange light through the slats in woven grass blinds or on the swinging rope bridges. Frogs and insects sang an eerie melody in the foliage, and the ground was wet with dew.

I walked to the edge of the pit where I had seen Paligno for the first time— the pit that had haunted me in my nightmares. It looked even more daunting in the dead of night. I could see the staircase winding around the edge, carved into the earth and overgrown with moss and vines. It delved so deep into the dark I couldn't see the bottom. The air rising up from inside the pit was bitter cold and it smelled of rich, moist earth.

I took a deep breath and started down the spiraling staircase. The deeper I went, the less I could see. It was like being swallowed by the earth. I had to keep a hand on the wall just to make sure I didn't accidentally wander too far to the side and fall to my death somewhere far below.

Once I reached the bottom of the pit, I could barely see the opening overhead anymore. All around me was pitch black. I decided to try using some of my newfound power.

Pulling a large, walnut-sized seed from my belt, I cupped a hand to my lips and blew gently onto it. The seed began to glow brightly, piercing the dark with radiant green light. Holding it out before me, I got my first good look at the cavern.

Directly ahead was an opening leading farther into the gloom like a tunnel. It was tall and circular, and by the look of it, no one had come down here in a very long time. The walls and ceiling were nothing but hard-packed dirt. Roots from trees and plant life hung down like spider webs and brushed against me as I started forward. Looking down, I saw only one other set of footprints in the soft soil apart from my own. But even they appeared to be old because dust had settled into them so that they were nearly unnoticeable.

When the tunnel came to an end, it opened into a massive circular chamber. I willed the seed to glow brighter. It filled the open air with more and more light, revealing something I'd only heard rumors about: Paligno's tomb.

The ceiling itself must have been forty or fifty feet high, but there was no manmade grandeur about this place. There were no gilded adornments, gifts, burning incense, or indications that this really was a tomb. All I saw was a single slab of white stone about four feet high standing in the very center of the chamber. On it were the skeletal remains of something that looked like an animal. The bones were clean and pale like alabaster. The sight of it made me suck in a sharp breath.

I walked toward the makeshift grave, wary of the bones that lay there. The way the skull seemed to be staring at me through its eyeless holes was unsettling. My pulse was pounding in my ears as I dared to go a few steps closer to it.

As I drew nearer, I could see more clearly what it was. Or at least, what it sort of looked like. The skull had sweeping, elegant white horns on it, exactly like the vision of Paligno I had seen when I received his blessing. Before it was a small, bowl-shaped indentation in the white stone. It was empty now, but instinct told me this was the place where the god stone had once rested.

I let my fingers brush over that empty space, wondering at the irony of finding myself standing here. Years ago, my father had stood in this very spot to steal the stone. Thinking about that filled me with bitterness and anger. How could he be so foolish? Had he really thought there wouldn't be consequences for taking it?

"*Do not judge him so harshly, dulcu,*" my mother's voice spoke to me.

I turned around to see her ghostly image flickering before me again. Her eyes were shining like stars and her robes and hair flowed around her as though they were blowing in the wind. But there was no wind down here.

I can't explain why I wasn't surprised to see her this time. Maybe part of me had been expecting to find her here, waiting for me where this had all begun. The sight of her was no less difficult for me, though. It still brought back all those distant childhood memories, and it made me miss her terribly.

"Is this really you?" I asked suspiciously. "Or are you Paligno wearing this form so you don't frighten me?"

She smiled. "*He didn't frighten you before, did he?*"

"Well, no. I suppose not."

"*Those who are chosen to be Lapiloque are bound to him eternally. Their spirits are joined with his in life and in death. As long as he endures within the stone, I too endure. Our spirits are marked by him, and so they are bound together. So it is for all who are chosen by him.*" She moved closer to me, although I noticed her feet weren't touching the ground. She reached out a hand to touch my cheek, but I didn't feel anything more than a strange cold chill on my skin. "*And so it will be for you, too, dulcu.*"

I tried not to let the sad expression on her face distract me from the reason I had come here. I needed help. I needed answers. And as far as I knew, this was the only place left where I might find them. "I understand what I have to do. I have to reclaim the god stone and bring it here to restore the balance and appease Paligno's curse."

Her hand fell away from me and she closed her eyes. "Yes."

"And that means I will probably have to kill Hovrid," I continued. "And I'm guessing he won't give it up without a fight."

My mother's expression became tragic. She lowered her chin, looking away as though she were ashamed. "*No. He certainly won't. He is not unlike your father, who was a much different person when he stood where you are now. Ulric's desires were not selfish when he took the stone. He wanted only to protect those he loved. The man he became afterward was the result of his sin. As you know, touching the god stone is dangerous for one without Paligno's blessing. The single brush of a finger can drive a person into madness. Even now your father's mind is still being poisoned by that contact. Hovrid is no different. His obsession cannot be quenched until he feels he possesses it entirely, both physically and spiritually. He won't stop. He won't be reasoned with.*"

"I want to know what happened. I want to know why you left Luntharda, what kind of secret dealings you had with Sile Derrick, and why—" I hesitated on the most difficult question I'd ever asked anyone. "—why you decided to have a halfbreed child with Ulric."

"*Only the blood of the traitor and the hands of the speaker can restore the balance. That is the law set forth by Paligno when life was first seeded upon this world. None can overrule it. I knew this the moment the stone was first taken. Only the blood of the traitor, the one who had taken it, could absolve that sin. And only the hands of Lapiloque could touch the stone in order to put it back without being driven insane by it.*" Her words rang clear and firm in the darkness of the chamber. "*I left because there was no other choice. It was by the blessing of fate alone that Sile Derrick came to plead for Ulric's sin. I could sense the goodness in his soul. I knew he could be trusted. And I knew I would need his help in order to set things right. I'm sure by now you realize that there is nothing Lapiloque can do to heal those afflicted by Paligno's curse. They are beyond our reach. So in order to stop it from spreading, I had to leave. I had to find Ulric. I needed his blood, and Sile helped me claim it.*"

It was a lot to take in. The more she explained, the more I began to feel the storm of confusion finally calming in my mind. Years of what I had thought to be random luck suddenly didn't seem quite so random anymore. At last, I could breathe easier. I could shake off the feelings of uncertainty and frustration that clouded my thoughts.

"*I intended to take you and the stone back to Luntharda to restore the balance. After all, you have your father's blood. But when you were born with Paligno's blessing, I realized that the simple plan I had concocted was not what destiny had in store for you. You were meant to be more than I had ever dreamed.*" My mother smiled again with that parental adoration shining in her ghostly eyes. "*I knew my work as Lapiloque was complete. You were the one born to bring peace and balance. You had to survive. So I sought out the help of the only human I knew I could trust to watch over you and guide you until it was time for you to know these things. Sile agreed wholeheartedly. He agreed that he would watch over you from a distance, and then when the time was right, he would prepare you for that moment when your destiny would be realized."*

"Why didn't you tell me any of this? Why didn't you tell me what I was?" I pressed.

Her smile faded a bit. *"Because Hovrid knows there is only one threat to his plan to claim the stone's power for himself. And that threat is you, dulcu. The one chosen to speak for the stone is the only one who could possibly take it from him and end this war once and for all. It was safest for you to know nothing so that his attention would never be drawn to you before you were old enough to stand against him."*

I stood in silence for a little while, thinking it all over. My questions were answered. I had everything I needed now—except for one last thing. "When you say that my blood will atone for that traitorous sin, what exactly do you mean? Am I going to die?"

My mother's expression was unreadable. *"I cannot speak for what Paligno will require of you."*

That wasn't comforting at all.

I guess she could tell that her answer had made me uneasy, because she reached out to comb her fingers through my short, hacked up hair. Once again, I couldn't truly feel her touch. To me, it only felt like a cold puff of wind.

"If you trust nothing else, trust that Paligno chose you deliberately for this task. You are capable just as you are to do what is necessary. Do not fear what you can do, for these gifts were given specifically to you for a purpose. And when the time comes, dulcu, you will be able to face this destiny without regret." She smiled affectionately and planted a kiss against my forehead. It made my skin prickle. *"I love you, my son. I am so very proud of the man you have become."*

Words failed me as I watched her image begin to fade. In a matter of seconds, I was left standing alone again, with nothing but the bones of a dead god to comfort me. I looked back at the skull, fearing it less than before now.

"I will do this. I will end this war and take back what was lost. But in return I want some assurance," I said to it. I wasn't sure if Paligno was listening, or if I even had the right to start making demands. Probably not. But he could smite me for my insolence if he wanted to—I was still going to ask. "Enough blood has been spilt. I want your assurance that the lives of my friends, of the people I love, will be spared. Will you grant me that?"

Of course, I got no answer.

13

CHAPTER THIRTEEN

"Araxie will lead you on the safest path back to the boundary of your kingdom." King Erandur gestured to the map of Luntharda that was embroidered onto a large silk tapestry. He'd spread it out on the floor so that Jace and I could get a better look while we put together our plans.

Until then, I hadn't realized how many cities the Gray elves actually had in this jungle. It just seemed so wild and untamed when we went exploring every morning. The jungle itself was vast, and there were no clear-cut roads or paths anywhere—well, unless you were as good at finding your way through the trees as Araxie was. But scattered across the map, marked by different symbols, were the positions of a dozen or more large cities throughout the vast woodland.

We were sitting in the makeshift royal wing of the temple where Erandur and Araxie lived. They had made it as nice as possible, furnishing it in the Gray elf style with furs and colorful woven rugs on the floor. We were leaning against silk, feather-stuffed cushions as we studied the map by the light of oil lamps.

"Where will you go once you are back in your own territory?" the king asked.

"Not directly to Halfax." I glanced sideways at Jace to make sure he was listening. "We're going to need some help, and I know where to get it. We'll make for Barrowton. My dragon tells me the city is all but abandoned now, and I can reunite with him there. Then we will head straight for Mithangol to regroup and finalize our plan. During that time, you'll need to muster what forces you can and prepare for our return. It'll be a quick turnaround. Do you think you can manage it?"

The king nodded. He seemed confident, if not a little anxious about this whole idea. Granted, he wasn't used to my level of crazy when it came to wild rescues.

Jace sat beside me, rubbing his chin thoughtfully. We'd been here close to three months now, and he had definitely taken on a different attitude about the Gray elves—especially when it came to Araxie. Of course, I could tell he was trying not to show it, but I caught him looking at her often. When he did, his usually fierce wolf-like gaze softened and there was something almost desperate in his eyes.

Unfortunately for him, she didn't appear to be on the same page. Or if she was, she was a lot better at hiding it. Her comments to him were still derisive and sarcastic for the most part. She still looked at him coldly, even if she did act a slightly more tolerant of his presence. I still hadn't heard her say his name once, though.

I didn't really blame her. He had killed three of her family members, after all. A few months of training and sizing each other up didn't even come close to making up for that. But I still couldn't ignore the change in Jace. He'd begun wearing Gray elf clothes rather than his Maldobarian ones. He was hungry to learn their ways and had even started trying to speak their language fairly well—almost as well as I could.

"It will take three days to reach the boundary nearest to Barrowton," Araxie said grimly. "It would be much faster to climb to the top of the canopy and hail your dragon from there to pick you up."

I shook my head. "I can't risk being seen. Mavrik tells me the dragonriders at Northwatch are running frequent patrols along the border. I'm sure by now most everyone thinks Jace and I are dead, so they must be anticipating a retaliation attack. We need to use that to our advantage, keep their eye focused here, so we can keep a low profile and do our work within Maldobar. At least if we make it to Barrowton, we can fly along the mountains and stay hidden."

"We can't spare any warriors to help escort us. It will have to be the three of us." She frowned harder at the map. "All the other forces will have to rally here and prepare for your return."

"Four, if you'll permit," Kiran spoke suddenly. He was standing in the doorway watching us with a determined look on his face.

Erandur was grinning like he found the warrior's courage amusing. "You're awfully young to be asking for such a thing. Have you even taken a mate yet?"

Kiran stiffened and I saw him clench his teeth slightly. "No. But I have already been to the human lands once. I know the way."

"I suppose if you are volunteering, I see no reason why you shouldn't be allowed to go. But I will let Araxie have final say," the king said as he glanced at his daughter.

She never looked up from the map. "If that's what he wants."

"It is." Kiran sounded more determined than ever.

"Then I'll permit it, so long as you don't slow us down."

We went back to plotting our course out of the jungle. It was going to be a hard trek. We would have to pass through a grove of the greevwood trees and the ruins of the elves' royal city. Neither were places Araxie seemed thrilled about going, but she advised that this would be the safest course.

"How did you make it here so quickly before? When you first captured us?" Jace piped up as we all took one last look at the map.

The princess scoffed at his question like it was a dumb thing to ask. "How fast do you think we got here?"

"It didn't feel like three days," he countered.

She rolled her eyes at him. "It was two. We are able to move faster when there are more warriors to guard the formation. We carried you in shifts. But human legs are slower and more easily fatigued."

"Why don't we use shrikes?" I was getting curious now.

"It is too dangerous. Paligno's curse has spread further here than in your kingdom. Many of our mounts have already been infected, that's why we cannot allow them to dwell among us in the village anymore. In battle it is less of a concern." She hesitated and gave a sudden, bitter glance in Jace's direction. "We all assume we are going to our deaths, anyway."

Erandur began folding up the tapestry, sliding it to the side as if to end the subject there. I was grateful for that. "You should leave first thing in the morning," he suggested. "I will have supplies readied for you."

"When I have the stone and begin heading your way, I will send word. Even if Hovrid is dead, it's likely some of the men who are still loyal to his guise as the King of Maldobar will be chasing us." I reached out a hand across the space between us to shake his.

He grasped it firmly and smiled. "We will be waiting for you at the boundary, Lapiloque. Araxie and I will rally as many to our cause as possible."

A strange silence settled over us as we sat together, feeling the weight of what was about to transpire. Erandur seemed to be the most optimistic out of all of us. Araxie, Jace, and Kiran all wore similar expressions of focused concern.

I was worried, too. I didn't know what would be waiting for us when we returned to Maldobar. I didn't know if Felix, Beckah, or my brother were still alive. I didn't know if my plan would work, or what would happen if it were discovered that Jace and I were trying to slip back into the kingdom. We might very well be arrested as traitors—and rightfully so. We were about to commit the greatest act of treason possible against our so-called king.

After an uncomfortably quiet dinner, Jace and I got up to return to our room. As usual, there were more gifts piled outside our doorway. I had to rake a path clear so we could get inside.

"How does it feel to be a demigod?" There was a flavor of sarcasm to Jace's question.

"I'm not sure," I fired back. "How does it feel to be in love with the enemy?" That shut him up.

He gave me a dirty look but didn't say another word as we both settled in for the night. I guess I hit the nail on the head more squarely than I'd anticipated. It was a cheap shot to take, which made me feel a little guilty as I stretched out on my pallet and stared up at the ceiling.

I let my mind go quiet, sifting through the whispering voices in my brain that had become commonplace to me now. I looked for the one that was most familiar—the one I had pushed far away until now. Before, I hadn't been ready to reunite with him, but things were different now. And it was time to get my partner up to speed.

Mavrik's consciousness leapt out to greet me with excited swirls of color. I could feel him trolling through my memories, investigating me thoroughly like a dog sniffing over its master. I didn't hide anything from him. When he was satisfied, I started relaying our plan to him. I asked him to meet me in Barrowton.

He reminded me of what I had wanted to forget. Barrowton was nothing but ash and cinders now. It was abandoned, which suited my plan but simultaneously filled me with sorrow and anger. More lives had been lost, swallowed up by the blazing forge of Hovrid's war. He was trying to drive his own species into extinction ... and he was succeeding.

AT DAYBREAK JACE AND I WERE BOTH STANDING ON THE FRONT STEPS OF THE temple, waiting for Araxie and Kiran to emerge. The jungle was filled with the peaceful sounds of early morning. Birds sang high in the trees. The air was cool but comfortable, rich with the smell of plant life. I breathed it in deeply, realizing how much I was going to miss that smell.

I'd given up my comfortable Gray elven robes for my dragonrider's uniform and armor again. My scimitar was buckled to my hip, and my helmet and cloak were packed away into a bag I wore slung over my shoulder. I'd stocked it full of rations and a few useful tools I had found amidst the piles of offerings the villagers left me every day. I couldn't take everything they'd given me, obviously, but the greevwood dagger was stuck down in the side of my boot, hidden and ready if I needed it. My mother's pendant hung proudly around my neck. I wasn't going to hide it under my clothes anymore.

Jace hadn't been able to put on all of his old dragonrider clothes. They had been ripped and damaged during his fall, so he wore a hybrid of Maldobarian and Gray elf attire that looked strange. His pants were more or less intact, but they were spattered with blood. So were his uniform boots, kidney belt, and cross-styled sheath for his swords. His tunic had been essentially destroyed, so he wore a dark green elven one in its place. The rest of his gear and armor were packed away in a bag like the one I was carrying.

He was shifting his weight anxiously from one foot to another while we waited in silence. I couldn't tell if he was still annoyed with me for calling him on the obvious crush he had on my cousin or not. No guy likes having that kind of thing shoved in their face—especially when the girl in question hates your guts.

Kiran was the first to join us. He came out of the trees dressed in his warrior's attire and carrying a spear, bow, and quiver. His long white hair was tied back in a long braid, and there were two red lines of war paint smeared down his cheeks.

"You really think your plan will work, *caenu?*" He gave me a teasing grin as he came to stand next to me.

"That depends, *brevad.*" I smirked back. I knew he was just calling me that to get on my nerves, so I'd taken to calling him the Gray elven word for "short" just to even things up a little.

Kiran's little taunting smile quickly turned into a scowl. He did *not* like his new pet name. "Depends on what?"

"On whether or not we make it to the border in one piece." I laughed and gave him a rough pat on the shoulder, which only made him scowl harder.

"I take it you are all ready to go?" a female voice called out in a chastising tone.

All three of us turned around to see Araxie striding out of the temple. As usual, her clothes were exotic, revealing, and undeniably beautiful. It had to be painful for someone in Jace's position to look at. Her baggy sirwal pants rode low on her hips and her midriff was bare thanks to the short, tight-fitted top she wore. She was carrying her own set of weapons, scimitars with a bow and quiver, and her shimmering hair was left to flow loosely all the way to the base of her back. She had purple and green war paint on her skin as well, outlining the curves of her muscular frame with ornate, swirling symbols. She also wore a small head-dress with two short, white horns on them. That, I assumed, was to mark her as royalty. No one else wore white horns like that.

I noticed Jace's eyes following her as she walked right through our midst and began leading the way into the forest. He didn't say a word, but his mouth was hanging open like there was something he might have wanted to say.

Then he caught me staring at him.

I grinned knowingly. I just couldn't help myself.

Jace's face turned a disturbing shade of red and he let out a string of curses as he stormed away to follow her. Kiran and I casually followed, too. As bad as I felt about giving him a hard time, now I could better appreciate why Felix enjoyed teasing me about every girl he thought I liked. It was fun. And honestly, I was just glad I wasn't the victim of the teasing for once.

We crossed over the boundary of the temple grounds and into the wild heart of Luntharda again. We didn't usually go in this direction whenever Araxie led us on her educational sprints through the trees, so this was unchartered territory for me. We moved quickly and quietly, the way she had taught us, making as little a disturbance as possible as we slipped through the trees. I doubted I looked as graceful as Araxie and Kiran did while lightly stepping from one large tree branch to another. For them, it looked natural.

As I leapt from branch to branch, rolling and ducking while keeping up the rigorous pace, I felt more confident than I had when we'd started our training. I didn't look at the ground. I wasn't afraid of falling or tripping. I was focused on what lay ahead, on the next obstacle, and on keeping as quiet as possible.

Jace had improved some, as well, though he still muttered curses whenever we got a good glimpse of how far we were off the forest floor.

We moved fast. Araxie had led us ten miles away from the village before she allowed for a break. We all took a seat on an especially large limb and passed our water skins around so everyone got a few gulps. Far below, the jungle was calm. I couldn't detect any glaring threats from Paligno's curse for miles in any direction. So far, we hadn't seen anything beyond a few herds of faundra, brightly colored birds, and a snake or two.

When we started up again, Araxie let our pace slack off a bit. We took our time, moving more carefully. I could tell she was growing more and more tense as night drew in. I wasn't sure why until I finally glimpsed the haunting dark shapes of what appeared to be buildings through the trees. We had arrived at the Gray elves' royal city.

Or at least, what was left of it.

Just as with the fort compound during the battle scenario, the jungle had all but reclaimed the area. Paligno's curse made the plants go wild. They were eating away at every trace of civilization, smothering buildings and covering the ground. From where we stood, high in the boughs of the giant trees, I could see the ruins of the city stretched out for miles.

The buildings were squared, made mostly from carved rock. Through the gloom of the evening, I could see a few sparkling remains of gleaming mosaics in the city squares and the sparkling of gold set into the domed roofs of temples. This place had once been grand and beautiful—an ancient civilization blossoming with power and luxury.

But now it was overgrown and eerily quiet. Roots had invaded the foundations of most of the buildings, cracking them in half like eggshells. There were no lights to be seen anywhere, and not a single soul in sight.

The expression on Araxie's face was tragic. Her shimmering, multicolored eyes panned the horizon slowly. It was as though she were trying to keep her emotions contained—as though she didn't want anyone to see how this place made her feel. I could imagine she had a lot of memories tied up in this place. It had been her home, once. And now it was more or less a mass grave for those who hadn't been able to flee the city in time.

There were old bones in the streets. I didn't notice them at first because many of them were covered with plant life. But I realized it after I accidentally stepped on a rib bone and crushed it. I was more careful then.

Darkness was falling when we came to the front steps of what must have been the royal palace. Sweeping stone steps led up to a broad open passage lined with massive, pear-shaped alabaster columns. Each one had been painted with flowers and creatures from the jungle—although that paint had now almost entirely been chipped away. I noticed the bases were plated in gold, though, and the floors were adorned with huge, magnificent mosaics made from chips of colorful rock and precious stones.

"What is this place?" Jace asked in a quiet voice.

Araxie's reply was just as soft. She was walking close to one of those large columns, letting her fingers brush against it as she passed. "It was ... my home."

Jace studied her up and down, as though he wasn't sure what to make of that answer. Or maybe he just wasn't used to her talking to him without her tone dripping with disdain. "What happened?"

"It began here just as it did in your own kingdom. The animals, livestock, and birds all turned on us. We thought we could manage. We thought we could survive and defend our city. But it was a foolish hope. In the end, we had no choice but to leave. So many died, and we could not even return to bury them. Paligno's curse spares no one. Its wrath will burn eternally if the stone is not restored."

I put a hand on her shoulder, coaxing her to look at me. When she did, I could see the moisture of tears making her eyes seem glossy. She quickly turned her gaze away.

"Will we be safe here for the night?" Kiran sounded doubtful.

Araxie let out an uneasy sigh. "We should be, yes. So long as we are quiet and we do not make our presence obvious. Come, I know a place where we can build a fire."

She led us deeper into the palace, our footsteps echoing off the high stone walls and vaulted ceilings. There were large bronze braziers lying knocked over on the floor. Empty porcelain vases as tall as I was were overflowing with the plants that had been put in them. The mosaics on the floors had been mostly covered by moss, and shallow reflecting pools contained nothing but still, algae-filled waters. Much of the palace was still fairly well preserved, if only because it was cut off from the natural light needed for the plants to invade. But there was still evidence everywhere of the struggle—weapons on the floor. Arrows and spears mingled with the bones of animals left to rot where they'd fallen.

It became too dark to see much of where we were going. That didn't stop Araxie, though. She seemed to remember her way around this place as though she'd never left it. When we came to a hallway lined with old tapestries, some of them having rotted off their hanging rods and fallen into heaps on the floor. She stopped. At the end of the corridor were a pair of double doors. One was cracked open slightly.

"My old chambers," she whispered as she pointed.

Beyond was a set of lavish chambers that looked nearly untouched by the jungle's creeping grasp. It had been well sealed off. All other passages leading in and out were barred with metal beams. The windows had also been closed off. Nothing could come or go except through those double doors. Perhaps that was why the room looked as though it had only been abandoned months ago, rather than years.

Araxie went into her quarters and we followed her without hesitation. Inside, the air held a musky, stagnant odor like stale perfumes. There were plush, soft rugs stretched out along the floor, and intricately carved low couches all positioned around a shallow marble fire pit. Cushions were strewn everywhere, and it was obvious that in their final days living in this city, this was the only room the princess had been able to inhabit. Everything was covered with years' worth of dust. Our presence had stirred some of it off the floor, making Kiran cough and sneeze as he slipped around to investigate.

Araxie's dejected expression kept us all from saying or touching anything. It felt wrong. This stuff was hers, even if it had been abandoned when she and her family had fled the city.

She picked up a gold-plated hand mirror and dusted it off, briefly glancing at her reflection before putting it back down. "Bring in anything you think we can burn. Then we'll bar the doors for the night. We should be safe here. My attendants and myself managed to take refuge here for two weeks before we fled. It's well barricaded."

Once we were settled in, sitting around the small fire we had built, a strange silence settled over us. Jace was just staring at the flames with his brow furrowed. Kiran was doing the same, but while spinning a dagger through his fingers over and over. I was sitting between them, nibbling on the last of my day's rations.

Araxie was the only one who had seemed interested at all in sleeping. She unfurled a small sleeping pallet from her pack to curl up on, pulled down one of the old blankets that was left draped over a sofa, and turned her back to us.

"Someone should keep watch," Jace murmured suddenly.

I agreed. "I'll take the first one."

No one argued me for it.

Kiran stretched out on one of the sofas and was asleep in minutes. Jace, on the other hand, sat up a while longer still gazing at the fire. I wondered what he was thinking so hard about. It was obvious that something was bothering him, or whom he might be thinking about. At last, he let out a heavy, defeated sigh. He laid back on one of the plush wool rugs, using his travel pack as a pillow. I knew he was asleep when he started to snore and wheeze.

Hours passed like centuries. I kept the fire burning low, adding a few chips of wood from a smashed up chair every now and then. The embers glowed and filled the room with a warm orange light.

When everything was quiet, I heard Araxie begin to stir. She rolled over, facing both the fire and me. It didn't look like she'd slept at all. She had a thoughtful frown on her face similar to the one Jace had been wearing earlier.

"Something bothering you?" I asked.

Her eyes shimmered strangely in the light of the fire, changing colors to match the movement of the flames. "There's somewhere I want to go," she answered quietly. "But I'm terrified to go there."

"Why?"

"Because I was just a child the last time I went." She looked at me squarely. "And I'm not sure if I would be welcomed back."

I thought about that for a moment. "Is it close by?"

Araxie nodded.

"Then let's go." I stood up and dusted off the back of my pants.

Her eyes went wide and she sat up. "N-now? But what about them?"

I glanced at Kiran and Jace. They were both sound asleep and showing no signs of stirring anytime soon. "They'll be fine. It's close by, right? We'll make it fast. They won't even know we're gone."

She didn't act quite as eager to get up and join me. More than once she flicked an uneasy, calculating glance between the rest of our group and me, as though she were still trying to make up her mind.

"If you don't go, will you regret it later?" I asked again.

"Yes," she answered in a faint voice. That was all the motivation she needed, apparently. She stood up and walked past me, her bare feet not making a sound on the marble floor as she brought me to a place in the corner of the room where one of the wooden panels on the walls could be pushed away to reveal a hidden door in the wall. It led into a small tunnel—so small that I barely fit. Fortunately, it was only a few feet long.

She opened another hidden door that emptied into a dark, disheveled library. The walls were covered in grid-like cubbies that were stuffed full of scrolls from floor to ceiling. Many of them had been torn from their resting places and scattered all about the floor. They were yellowed and curled with age and exposure to the moist air. I picked one up only to realize it was written in a language I couldn't understand. It certainly wasn't the human or Gray elf language.

Araxie must have noticed my puzzlement. "We stored many texts here, records of times past from kingdoms long forgotten. Chronicles of an ancient past."

I let the scroll slip from my fingers. It fell back to its resting place on the floor at my feet. "Seems a waste to abandon them here."

"Perhaps one day we can return and restore them." Her words were hopeful, but her tone betrayed how she really felt. She didn't have much faith in our plan. Or at least, she didn't believe she would ever get to live here again.

We continued on through the palace, slipping as quickly and quietly as possible through abandoned halls and ransacked chambers until at last we came to a grand but strangely cold staircase. It led downward into a darker part of the palace where the faint light of the moon could not reach. I hesitated to go down it because that dreary, ominous descent reminded me a lot of Paligno's tomb.

Araxie didn't seem too concerned with it though. She went on ahead and left me no choice but to follow. When the darkness became so thick that we couldn't see anymore, I pulled another large seed from my belt and willed it to light the way. As soon as the air filled with its radiant green glow, I caught a glimpse of her face. She was staring at me with a mixture of awe and fear.

I just smiled at her. "Turns out those voices in my head are good for a few things."

"So you really can hear them? The memories of your ancestors?" She stared at the glowing seed curiously. "My father told me that the Lapiloque can recall all the powers and memories of his past manifestations. Because you are joined with Paligno, you are also connected with those who came before you."

I could tell she wanted to ask something—something I suppose she was afraid would offend me. It wasn't hard to follow her logic. So I asked it for her. "Can I hear my mother's memories?"

Her expression became timid.

"Yes," I answered her with a smile. "But it isn't just the memories of Paligno's chosen ones. Sometimes, he lets me glimpse his memories, too. I think that's how I was shown what Hovrid had done to the real King of Maldobar."

Araxie took a step back, looking away as though speaking about this made her somehow uncomfortable. "I've never heard of such a thing. Perhaps Paligno is vesting more power and energy in you than the others."

I understood why she was reluctant. Hope was a dangerous thing. And if she placed too much hope and faith in me, then by failing ... I would be confirming that she had nothing else to hope for at all. If the chosen servant of a god couldn't help them, no one could.

Neither of us spoke again as she continued walking, eventually bringing us to an arched stone doorway. It was beautifully engraved to resemble an arbor with the shapes of two women standing amidst the flowers. Beyond the doorway, I saw at last where we had come.

It was indeed another tomb. But this one wasn't for a god.

Placed on a raised stone platform was a sarcophagus that appeared to be engraved from solid alabaster and adorned in golden details. On the top was the beautiful effigy of a woman lying on her back with her flowing hair spilling over the sides of the engraved structure. The statue had been made so that it looked like she was lying on a bed of ivy, and though her eyes were closed, her expression was peaceful and content.

Araxie stopped dead in her tracks when she saw the sarcophagus. Her expression tightened, and for a few seconds, she looked a lot like a frightened child. Her eyes were big and vulnerable and her brow was drawn up like she might start to cry.

I went past her to get a better look at the tomb and the statue of the woman carved into it. She was obviously a Gray elf. Her ears were long and elegantly pointed. There was also a crown of flowers on her head. Her slender arms were crossed over her chest, and I could see that whoever had made this had paid special attention to every detail. They had even taken the time to paint golden details onto the flowers.

"Your mother?" I guessed as I glanced back at Araxie.

She didn't have to answer out loud. I could tell just by the way her expression fell to anguish that I was right. Slowly and cautiously, she began to make her way closer to where I stood. Her eyes, however, never left the sarcophagus.

"Why did you think you wouldn't be welcomed here?"

Araxie's lips scrunched up like she was biting back emotion. "Because I am not the woman she was. This war has required me to become something she never would have approved of."

"And what is that?"

"Cold," she replied.

I felt her grasp the sleeve of my tunic as though she needed comfort, so I put an arm around her and drew her closer to my side. She laid her head against my shoulder.

"I was under the impression Gray elf women could be warriors if they chose to be."

"Yes," she said. "But I am a princess. There are different expectations. Or at least, there were. When my brothers were killed, their responsibilities were passed to me. I am expected now to exemplify my people's bravery. I can't falter. I can't show any weakness. I must be the knife's edge of my father's army."

We stood in silence, showing a few minutes of quiet reflection and respect for the dead queen before either of us dared to speak again. I was thinking about her brothers, which inevitably brought Jace to mind. He'd been the one to kill all three of them in battle. Likely they hadn't had a burial at all, let alone one like this.

"You know, I think Jace feels pretty bad about what happened with your brothers. I mean, now that he's been here amongst your people, it does seem like he's changed a lot."

Araxie stared up at me like I'd suddenly grown a third eyeball.

"All I'm saying is that I've noticed he's acting differently," I amended quickly. "And to me, as an onlooker, I can tell he admires you."

She snorted disbelievingly. "Probably because he's not used to having his rear end handed back to him by a woman."

I couldn't exactly refute that. Jace was an extremely good fighter. He probably hadn't lost many fights before meeting her.

"Do you think I should forgive him?"

Her question caught me completely off guard and it took a few seconds for me to mull that over. Forgiving someone for murdering your siblings was a tall order for anyone. I couldn't imagine the grief she'd endured. And for her, losing them had changed the course of her entire life. It had left her with only her father to support her and it had also dumped a lot of responsibility squarely upon her shoulders.

"I think everyone deserves a second chance," I decided at last. "Especially if they are willing to change. But I don't think that kind of forgiveness can happen instantaneously. It takes time. You also have to look at intent. Until recently, you were enemies at war. The rules of war suspend normality. Under any other circumstances, I doubt he would have gone out of his way to hurt them—just as I'm sure you wouldn't have hurt anyone if you were still just a princess and not also a warrior."

She was studying me carefully, as though trying to assess if I had some ulterior motive. Finally, she turned her gaze back to her mother's grave. "I suppose I hadn't considered it that way."

"I have a human half-brother, too. And I don't know for sure, but there is a good chance he died in the battle for Barrowton. A Gray elf more than likely killed him. Should I blame the warrior for doing that? Should I hate him for it? Every soldier that falls, elf or human, is someone's father, brother, son, or husband. If we can't forgive those deaths, then peace means nothing and Hovrid has already won."

14

CHAPTER FOURTEEN

There was a tug in the back of my mind as we turned to leave the burial chamber. It made me pause. I listened to the whispers of those memories for a moment, and then decided to leave behind a token for the late Queen of Luntharda. It only seemed right for me to offer something to honor her memory. The queen had been my aunt, after all.

The power was new to me, something I hadn't tried. I had manipulated life, things preexisting. But I'd never created anything before. With gentleness in my thoughts, I bade the ground open up just enough for two living rose vines to emerge and cover her effigy. The blossoms were each as big as a man's hand and pure white. I had to take special care in crafting them, since there was no sunlight this far underground. But these wouldn't require any, and their blossoms would never wither or fade. They would be as eternal as her memory.

Araxie appeared to be in much better spirits as we retraced our steps back to her chambers. She had a calm smile on her face and a more confident spring in her step. That blissful expression reminded me somewhat of my own mother. It made me miss her fiercely.

We had almost made it back to the library. The night sounds of the jungle still echoed through the cavernous stone halls of the palace. Without being able to see what might be lurking behind the next corner, I kept my senses on alert for anything that might be a threat.

But something else reached out and grabbed at my brain, instead. I stopped and stood perfectly still so I could be sure.

When Araxie went to walk on ahead of me, I reflexively grabbed her arm to stop her. She looked at me with a puzzled grin, at first. Maybe she thought I was playing around. My expression must have tipped her off that this wasn't a game because her smile faded and her eyes grew wide.

I only had seconds. I dragged her behind me and planted myself between her ... and *him*.

I spotted his silver eyes gleaming through the darkness. He was coming toward us slowly. Each of his paws was big enough to crush my skull without even trying. He moved toward us like a phantom, a soundless vapor with dripping fangs and curled talons as long as my finger.

He emerged from the library where I could only assume he had first picked up our scent. When Araxie saw him, she sucked in a sharp breath and grasped onto my shoulder. The intensity of her grip betrayed her fear.

The beast before me was different, however. I could sense his curiosity even from a distance, but I detected no fear. He was a predator, one of many in Luntharda, but he was a very clever one—even for a feline. At roughly six feet to the head, he could have easily ripped us both apart while we floundered around in the dark, trying to get away from him.

It was my presence that stopped him.

He wasn't possessed by Paligno's curse. He recognized me for who I was. I, on the other hand, didn't know what he was exactly. If anything, he favored some species of tiger. He was sleek and powerful, with a long body and small, rounded ears.

When he stepped into the soft green light of my seed-spell, I could better appreciate his size. Dense muscles rolled in his shoulders. His fur was an exotic shade of smoky blue and it was adorned with black stripes and swirling patterns. There was a ridge of longer, spiky black hair that ran from his neck all the way to the end of his tail. His snout was longer and more tapered than a normal cat's and I could see his black nose twitching as he smelled us.

"No!" Araxie hissed in warning as I started to move away from her.

I handed her the glowing seed and tried my best to reassure her with a smile. "Don't you trust the Lapiloque?"

She recoiled. But when I started to move away again, she didn't stop me. Instead, she kept her eyes focused squarely on me.

The enormous cat was nearly able to look at me eye-to-eye as I approached him. I was only a few inches taller than he was, after all. I reached out with my thoughts, not with humility as I always had before. It wasn't my place to be humble anymore. I knew what I was now. Predator or not, king or not—I had authority here.

Paligno had given me that authority.

I asked him to acknowledge me, to show his respect for Lapiloque, the one who spoke for Paligno's spirit.

His rounded ears perked and his wild silver eyes searched mine. He opened his maw to gape at my scent when I extended my hand. I could sense his strength just as clearly as I could sense how intelligent he was. He was mulling it over, sizing me up and trying to decide what to make of me. Araxie had said that the curse took the minds of dumber creatures first, that must have been why he was able to resist it. He had a proud soul, but a good and wise one.

I heard Araxie gasp when he closed his eyes and bowed his head, pressing his cheek against my hand. It was a gesture of affection. I smiled and let my fingers roam over his silky blue fur. I even gave him a good scratch behind the ears, just for good measure. That had always worked with Mavrik.

He made a deep, purring sound.

"I'm going to have to ask that you don't eat any my companions," I told him.

The cat made an annoyed grumbling sound in his throat. His bright eyes drifted toward Araxie. He licked his lips.

"Especially not her." I laughed and gave his neck another scratch before returning to where the princess of the Gray elves was still paralyzed with fear.

"He'll be nice," I assured her.

"H-how ...?" she started to ask, but she must have thought better of it. After all, she'd probably seen my mother do similar things years ago.

We started back into the library and slipped quietly through her secret passage into her private chambers. The cat followed us and stood watching curiously as we disappeared through the hidden door in the wall. Thankfully, Kiran and Jace were still sleeping soundly right where we'd left them.

I let out a sigh of relief and tossed a few more pieces of wood onto our small campfire. Then I went over to wake Jace up for his shift at keeping watch. I decided not to mention the enormous jungle cat that was still lurking just on the other side of the wall. I could sense him there. He was waiting for us to come back.

Jace didn't need to know that. He didn't strike me as a cat person, so it probably would have just freaked him out.

By the time the sun had risen, we were already packed up and ready to move again. There was no time to waste. The sooner we made it to the border of Luntharda and Maldobar, the better.

We pushed open the doors of Araxie's private chambers. Suddenly, Kiran let out a snarling battle cry. In the blink of an eye, he leapt forward with his bow in hand, ready to fire. Jace acted quickly, too. He drew his blades and immediately stepped defensively in front of Araxie.

Our blue-toned cat friend just looked baffled at first. But the sight of weapons put him on edge. He snarled, bearing his impressive teeth and bristling the black mane of hair that ran down his back. He snapped at Jace, although it was basically just a warning.

If he'd wanted to hurt us, he certainly could have.

"All right, everyone just calm down. He's not going to hurt us."

"That is a tigrex!" Kiran protested.

"And he is Lapiloque," Araxie retorted. "Or have you forgotten? All creatures of nature must bow to him."

Kiran shot her an exasperated look, but managed to keep his mouth shut.

I approached the cat and pressed my hand against his side, urging him to be calm. He obeyed, although he was still growling and eyeing Jace hungrily. It took me a few minutes to finally talk him into trusting us.

I was worried it might take me longer to convince Jace of the same. And petting him probably wouldn't help, either. But after a few minutes of sizing one another up from a distance as we walked out of the palace, Jace actually took to it better than I thought he would.

The giant striped cat followed us, sometimes falling behind to sniff the air and twitch the end of his tail. His eyes were always moving, always watching. He was on guard, and I was glad to see it. I wasn't about to complain about having another set of keen senses patrolling our surroundings for potential threats.

"Still full of surprises, I see," Jace muttered with a strange smirk on his lips. He reached over and ruffled my hair.

I smirked. "You have no idea."

He really didn't. None of them did. The whispers in my mind, rippling echoes of battles past, promised powers I'd never even toyed with before. I was eager to try them out, to test myself against those who had come before me. But it wasn't quite time yet for anyone else to know what I was really capable of.

The ruins of the Gray elf city weren't quite so daunting in the daylight. I'd always assumed the Gray elves to be barbaric. As I walked past the crumbling remnants of marketplaces, temples, and intricate archways, I could see how the way they were being forced to live now clearly didn't reflect the grandeur of their former lives. I was blown away by just how beautiful it was.

All around us, hidden under the overgrowth of foliage or peeking out of the rubble, were hints of what had been. Majestic statues of past kings gilded in gold and silver stood watch over the streets. Beautiful fountains that had long gone dry boasted glittering tile mosaics in vibrant colors. A small river snaked through the middle of the city, and there were many gracefully carved bridges crossing it. Flowering water plants grew near its banks and stones engraved with the faces of deities stared up from where they rested in the river's depths.

Seeing it all brought up a strange mixture of awe, delight, and sorrow within my heart. I'd never been here before, and yet it felt like this place was somehow a part of me.

Jace was walking close behind Araxie as we crossed one of the bridges to the far side of the river. He stopped at the center to look down at the shimmering pebbles under the water's crystalline surface.

"I always envisioned your people living in stick huts. You know, sleeping on the dirt, eating your enemies, and painting your faces with blood," he said quietly.

Araxie paused. Her color-changing eyes reflected the movement of the water.

"That was just what we were told," he went on. "That you were nothing but soulless savages squatting in the mud. Now I'm wondering if anything they told us was true."

I didn't dare say a word as I saw Araxie's expression soften. She took a few careful steps toward him. Then she caught me staring at her. She stopped, frowned, and turned away to keep walking.

I cursed myself for being so obvious. If they were going to make any progress at all, I was going to have to give them some space. I just hoped I hadn't blown their only chance to finally clear the air.

Araxie put us back on a rigorous pace through the treetops. Once again, we found ourselves being swallowed by the immense jungle as we left the Gray elf royal city behind. Jace was busy making friends with the tigrex as we traveled. He'd been sharing bites of his rations, so the cat had really warmed up to him.

The only person who seemed to mind our new companion was Kiran, who still acted tense around the beast. I didn't necessarily blame him for that. He'd probably grown up being terrified of superior predators like the tigrex. It was hard to shake that kind of thing off. He made a point to keep a wide berth between himself and the cat, and usually made sure I was standing between them.

The landscape had begun to change when we stopped for a quick meal. The jungle wasn't quite so thick around us, so the air felt a bit cooler and freer. The trees were larger than ever, and their canopy was so dense that it choked out all sunlight. Only a faint greenish glow lit our path. Far below, the jungle floor was barren of the dense plant life that seemed to grow everywhere else.

As we all sat together on a branch, surveying the path ahead and the ground below, we passed our water skins back and forth. I noticed that there were a few places scattered in the distance where the canopy had been broken just enough for beams of glittering sunlight to filter through. The heavy humidity sparkled when it passed through the light, and the effect was as mystical as it was pretty.

I was sitting between Kiran and the tigrex—which Jace had now officially named Blue. I guess creativity wasn't his strong suit.

Without the dense layer of jungle foliage beneath us, things were much quieter here. There were no birds or small animals to make shrill noises. Only the sounds of our voices echoed off the tree trunks. It was strangely calming.

That is, until Blue started to perk up. He stood and sniffed the air, his long tail swishing and his ears swiveling back and forth as though he heard something.

Whatever he was responding to, I didn't see it. I couldn't sense it yet, either, which was much more troubling.

I glanced at Araxie, who had already put her food and water skin away. She didn't look afraid, though. In fact, there was a curious, almost excited glint to her eyes as she stood.

"What is it?" I whispered.

"The curse?" Jace echoed my concern. He already had his hand resting on the pommel of one of his blades.

She grasped his arm to stop him, but her eyes never left the forest floor. She was acting weird. The rest of us were watching her as she stood up on her tiptoes, leaning this way and that as though she were looking for something.

Kiran suddenly pointed to something in the distance. "Look there!"

"Sshh!" She squatted down. Her eyes were as big as moons and brimming with excitement as she whispered, "Not a sound. Do not move. They are coming closer."

I still couldn't tell what *they* were. It was as though my eyes were playing tricks on me. Now and again, I'd see what appeared to be movement, or something shimmering in the light, but I could never tell what it was.

And then all at once, I did see.

If they were some sort of animal, I had no name for them and nothing at all to compare them to. They were tall and lean, their bodies as transparent and fragile as wisps of smoke. They walked upright on two legs, with long narrow arms and hunched backs. They were enormous, so tall they could barely pass under the limbs of the giant trees without stooping, and yet they didn't make a single sound as they moved. No crunching of footsteps. No panting breaths. Nothing but calm, eerily perfect silence.

It was completely surreal. There must have been a dozen of them slowly lumbering toward us through the tree trunks. They left trails of glittering white mist in their wake as their bodies rippled and wavered. Whenever one of them passed through a beam of sunlight, their form would glisten and sparkle like a riot of floating diamonds. It would seem to disappear completely, only to rematerialize once it was back under the cover of the canopy again.

"Mistherders." Kiran breathed the word as though it were something sacred. "I thought they were just a myth."

Araxie looked like she might cry. There was a childish, dreamlike sense of wonder on her face. "So did I."

One of the beings was passing particularly close, and I had to resist the urge to reach out to touch it. I got no feeling from them, no sense of their presence beyond a strange chilling tickle in the back of my mind. Whatever these creatures were, they weren't your usual jungle animals.

They were something more.

"I'VE ONLY HEARD STORIES ABOUT THEM," ARAXIE FINALLY EXPLAINED ONCE we had set up camp for the night on the forest floor. Her expression was still dazed and dreamy, as though she were still looking at one of those ethereal beings. "My mother used to tell me that long ago, when Paligno first seeded the earth with life, he brought with him many great spirits to guard his precious creations and nurture them. Mistherders tended to the green places, the flowers and the fragile things. They were beings of peace, pure spirits of clean energy and gentleness that left the ground kissed with dew every morning."

Jace had an equally entranced expression on his face as he listened to her. He was sitting hunched by the fireside with his chin resting on his hand. I had to admit, listening to her talk about them made me feel sort of pleasantly drowsy, too. It was like hearing a bedtime story.

We'd picked a relatively safe, hidden place amidst some large rock formations to set up our little camp. Here, the canopy was thinner. There was moonlight spilling through the tree limbs, casting long shadows over the boulders around us. You could even see a few stars peeking through.

Blue was curled up close by, warming himself by the light of our fire and purring loudly. Kiran was still nibbling at his dinner rations. And I'd unbundled my sleeping pallet and stretched out to rest my aching feet. All in all, we were as comfortable as we could be.

We'd been especially lucky. There'd been no trouble, no injuries, and no near-death experiences—which was a first for me when it came to carrying out one of my plans. Typically, any journey I went on was bound to be riddled with misfortune. But tomorrow, we would reach the boundary of our kingdoms, and I knew things would change after that. There, we would part ways. Araxie and Kiran would return to the temple and make preparations to receive the stone. Jace and I would return to Maldobar, making a straight path for Mithangol.

I still had some preparations to do on my end. I intended to get them done once everyone was asleep, though. I didn't want an audience breathing down my neck while I was trying out some of my new abilities. Besides, the prospect of sending out messages to my friends, asking them to meet me at my old family home was daunting for me. I'd been gone a long time. By now, everyone I knew in Maldobar was probably assuming I had been killed in combat along with Jace. I wasn't sure how they would respond to an invitation like this ... or if they'd even get it to begin with.

"I'm going to refill our water skins. There's a fresh spring only a short hike from here," Araxie announced suddenly. She got up and started collecting them from all of our travel bags.

"You shouldn't go alone," Kiran protested. He still had a cheek full of food.

She gave him a scolding glare. "Actually, I'm the only one qualified to go alone."

I wasn't about to try to argue that with her and I guess Jace knew better, too, because he just shrugged and began poking at the fire with a long stick.

"I'll keep first watch, then," he volunteered. He sounded tired, like he didn't exactly want to take the first shift. I was about to offer to take it for him when he shot me a dangerous glare out of the corner of his eye, like he was daring me to mess this up for him.

I didn't get it. Not at first. Why would he care so much about taking first watch? What was the big deal? Whoever did it was going to have to keep an extra eye to make sure Araxie ...

Then it hit me.

He wanted some alone time with her. I tried scrunching up my mouth and biting my tongue to keep from smirking. It didn't work too well.

My message sending would just have to wait until later. I'd let Jace have his moment, if that's what he wanted. But that didn't mean I was going to sleep, either. I'd never thought there could possibly be anyone else in the world that was worse with girls than I was. Jace, however, was giving me a run for my money in that department. I wasn't about to miss this.

After Araxie left with the water skins, I lay on my side with my arms folded. It was hard to be perfectly still for so long. I pretended to sleep for a good hour until at last I started to wonder the same thing that was apparently going through Jace's mind, too.

"What the hell is keeping her?" he grumbled. I heard him as he got up and picked up his bow and quiver.

When he started to leave the campsite, I immediately got to my feet to follow him. I had to be sneaky about it, of course. So keeping a distance, I watched as Jace tracked her footprints through the boulders and ferns. It was easy enough. The soil here was soft and moist, and I could smell fresh water in the air. As we got closer, I could hear it burbling somewhere nearby.

When I peeked around a large rock face to make sure I was all clear, I almost got caught. Jace was only standing a few feet away from me, although he had his back turned. I scrambled back behind the boulder and waited a few seconds before I dared to peer around it again.

Jace was still standing there. He hadn't moved an inch and he was staring straight ahead as though he were frozen in place.

Then all of a sudden, I saw why.

Araxie wasn't naked. Not completely, anyway. She was wearing simple undergarments to cover all her private areas as she stood, thigh-deep in the moonlight water of a small lagoon. But that was as close to a naked woman as I'd ever seen —not that *I* enjoyed it. She was my first cousin, which made seeing her like that sort of ... awkward and weird. Recoiling to my hiding spot behind the rock, I wondered if I should go back to the campsite right now or wait and see how this played out.

A female scream and a few curses in the elven language answered that question for me. No way was I going to miss this.

I dared to glance back around just in time to watch her hurl a rock at Jace. It missed him and went sailing right past my head. I practically felt the wind off it as it buzzed past me.

"Pervert!" Araxie was snarling like an angry shrike. She stomped out of the water and right up to Jace, who still looked like he was having a hard time remembering how to breathe and blink at the same time.

She slapped him, *hard*.

That woke him up from his trance. "What's wrong with you?" he yelled back at her. "It's your fault! I only came because you'd been gone too long! You never said anything about taking a bath!"

"My fault? Why you insolent pig! What else would I be doing?" She'd gone wild with anger. I cringed as she reared back to hit him again.

Her hand never made contact, though. He caught her by the wrist just in time and scowled at her dangerously. "Stop that," he warned. "Obviously you're fine. So I'm going."

Araxie snatched her hand away from him with her cheeks glowing bright red. I wasn't sure if it was from fury or embarrassment. "Am I to believe you came out here because you were concerned about me? Hah! I don't understand you, dragonrider. You've brought my family nothing but grief and yet you can't wait to throw yourself between me and anything you perceive to be a threat. Whose side are you on, anyway? Have you no loyalty to your own kind?"

Jace had begun to walk away. Her little rant put a stop to that, though. He paused mid-stride and turned around slowly. His dark eyes were colder than I'd ever seen them before.

"No. I don't." His voice was disturbingly calm.

Araxie was obviously stunned. She stood with her mouth open for a few seconds before she finally spoke again. "Then ... then why? Why fight for them? Why kill for them? Was it for money?"

"Something like that."

"You killed my brothers for money?" Her voice wavered, as though she could barely contain her emotion. I saw her wince as though the idea made her physically sick.

He rolled his eyes. "All dragonriders are paid, princess. Even Jaevid has received payment for his service to our so-called king."

There was a look of quiet horror on her face that actually made me nervous. This wasn't going well. In fact, we were well on track to this being a complete disaster. I had almost convinced myself that maybe I should intervene when Jace spoke up again.

"What? Your warriors aren't paid?" he asked challengingly.

"No! No, of course not! To fight for our people is an honor, not some menial job. To accept payment is to be no better than a common mercenary!" She snatched her skirt off the ground and made a halfhearted attempt to cover herself. Before she did, though, I spotted something on her torso that made my stomach turn. It was a scar—a new one by the look of it—that appeared to have been made by some sort of puncture. My thoughts immediately snapped back to that bizarre dream I'd had about a wounded Gray elf riding a shrike.

Jace grinned, interrupting my epiphany. It was a disturbing, satirical expression. "Oh trust me, mercenary work pays much better."

"So that's it, then? I have wondered since the first time I saw the scars on your body where you'd gotten them. I had my suspicions you earned them killing for sport." Araxie glanced him up and down before curling her lip. "You disgust me."

His confident smirk vanished instantly, and I prepared myself to break up what had the potential to be a very ugly fistfight—one that I doubted Jace could actually win.

"You think you know me, woman?" Jace growled as he took a threatening step toward her.

Of course, Araxie didn't back down an inch. Instead, she stood up straight and met him eye-to-eye. Well, maybe not exactly eye-to-eye. She was almost a foot shorter than he was.

"I've dealt with enough monsters in my lifetime to know one when I see it," she snapped fearlessly.

For whatever reason, Jace seemed almost pleased by that answer. "And what about slaves? How many of those have you seen, princess?"

Her expression faltered, skewing for an instant into what appeared to be confusion.

"In a palace like that, sitting on silk cushions, eating off gold and silver platters—I'm willing bet you've known a lot more slaves than monsters," he went on. "But their lives don't matter, right? They're property, not people. You can crush them under your heel and get them to do just about anything for their next meal. Just tools. Cheap. Disposable. Replaceable. I know your breed just as well as you think you know mine. Royals and nobles, every one of you is exactly the same. You're all too eager to prop your feet up on the living footstool of slavery, so don't talk like you have any moral ground to stand on."

Araxie narrowed her color-changing eyes, canting her head to the side as though she were trying to understand. "We never had ... " Her voice trailed away little by little.

I watched her look back to the thick, gnarled scars on his wrists and neck. I knew there were a great many more scars on his skin than what could be seen under the dim light of the moon. Most of them appeared to be old, although time hadn't done much to fade them. His body was absolutely riddled with marks like that, although I didn't know where he'd gotten them. Jace had outright refused to talk about his past with me.

When Araxie met his gaze again, all the rage in her expression had been replaced by something else—something that looked a great deal like sympathy. "You were a slave?"

He stiffened. His jaw clenched. "For a while. Then I became something worse."

The mood was changing. It was subtle, but I could feel the boiling heat of resentment and anger between them beginning to calm.

I could only imagine that Jace didn't want to look weak, so he didn't move an inch when she reached out a hand to lightly touch the ring of scars around one of his wrists. He was awkwardly still, tensed up as though it took all his self-control not to tear away from her.

"From shackles?" she asked quietly.

Jace gave a single nod. He seemed to be having trouble just looking at her now. His eyes darted this way and that when she moved in closer. It was like watching someone pet a feral dog that cringed away, distrusting of even the slightest touch.

She held his arm up to the moonlight, observing all the marks there that the fabric of his elven-styled tunic didn't hide. "How long did you live that way?"

"Ten years."

"Ten years in chains?"

His frown deepened. "In one way or another. Not all chains are made of iron."

Immediately, I thought of the vision I'd seen when I'd last healed him. It had been of a little boy in chains standing in the ashes of a ravaged village. I hadn't thought much of it until now. I knew Jace wasn't the sharing sort, so it would have been pointless for me to even ask. Now, however, I was beginning to understand what that image had actually been. That vision was of him. It was a glimpse into his past.

"And how does one go from being a slave to a dragonrider?"

"Not easily," he admitted in a reluctant tone. "And not without losing any semblance of a soul. I suppose in that respect, I am some breed of monster."

Araxie was gazing up at him with that look of sympathy still shining in her eyes. She didn't speak for a while, and soon the silence became uncomfortable. Either something was going to happen, or they'd just have to stand that way forever.

Okay, I'll admit I was rooting for Jace. I'd never seen him so open and willing to talk about himself. And more than that, I wanted to see that twenty years of hatred and war could be healed between our kingdoms.

"Do you hate me?" Jace suddenly broke the silence with a question that made Araxie frown.

She took a step back. "Sometimes. Yes."

"Good." Jace appeared to be satisfied with that answer. He bent to pick up the refilled water skins off the bank and slung them on his shoulder before he started walking away.

That made absolutely no sense to me. Apparently, Araxie felt the same way because she narrowed her eyes at his back. "Why is that good?"

"Because if you didn't, then I'd want to stay here—regardless of whether or not Jaevid needs my help."

He didn't stop to look back. He was coming right toward me, making his way back to our campsite. I had to scramble to hide behind some ferns when he passed.

Once I was sure he was gone, I was beginning to feel pretty good about getting away with spying on them, that is right up until Araxie turned directly toward where I was hiding and let out an exaggerated sigh. "Come out of there, please. It's disgraceful."

I blushed beet red. My ears were burning as I stepped out of the ferns to face my cousin. I half expected her to be angry, but she just seemed deflated, even a little disappointed.

"I'm sorry for eavesdropping." I kept my eyes trained on the ground since she still hadn't put her clothes back on.

It didn't seem to bother her if she was dressed or not, though. She took her sweet time wringing the water out of her hair and stepping carefully back into her silken robes.

"S-should I give you some privacy?" I stammered as I instinctively covered my eyes.

"Why?" She sounded confused at first. Then she laughed. "Ah. Forgive me. Sometimes I forget that you aren't familiar with our ways. Baths are not private things to our people. It is not seen as sensual to bathe. In fact, we rather like bathing together in groups. It's a time to be social and exchange gossip."

I dared to glance up at her. Thank Paligno she had finished dressing by then. My nerves couldn't take much more of this. "So then why did you scream at Jace for walking in on you?"

There was a conniving, almost smug little grin on her lips as she quickly wound her long silver hair into a braid. "Because I knew it would embarrass him," she said. "And I think he's rather cute when he's embarrassed."

"Embarrassed?" I hadn't gotten that at all from the way he'd acted. I'd been worried about it actually coming to blows. "Are you sure he wasn't angry? It sort of looked like—"

"Jaevid, how long have you trained with him? He was the one who taught you to be a dragonrider, wasn't he? So don't you know him at all? When he's angry, he says nothing. He pouts like a big child. And when he's embarrassed, he won't shut up."

I swallowed stiffly. "And you think he's cute?"

She shrugged, and I could have sworn I saw a touch of blushing color her cheeks. "When he isn't complaining or acting like a baby, maybe. Just a little."

I PROBABLY COULD HAVE SPENT ALL NIGHT TRYING TO FIGURE OUT THE WEIRD relationship that was brewing between my war dog of a former instructor and my warrior princess of a first cousin. But that would have been pointless. Women still confounded me for the most part. Without Felix there to spell it out for me, there wasn't much hope for me sorting it out on my own.

Fortunately, I had greater concerns to worry myself with. Once Araxie and I arrived back at the camp, and I'd spun up a pathetic excuse about getting lost on my way back from using the bathroom, I volunteered to take my turn keeping watch. It was time to send out messages and rally what allies I could to my cause.

I had more than a few concerns. First of all, I didn't know how many of my friends were still alive. It had been long enough that anything could have happened; more battles, the spread of the curse, or something else. Second, I didn't know where they were. Third, I wasn't sure if they would agree to help me once I explained what I intended to do. And honestly, I didn't know if this would even work at all.

But I had to try.

When things became quiet and I was sure everyone else was sound asleep, I went around the campsite and plucked a few fresh leaves off various plants. I found the perfect spot and sat down on the ground, spreading them all out before me.

I was still learning the method tapping into Paligno's power. Those whispering memories served as guides, feeding me instincts and memories that made the process easier. I couldn't create something from nothing, that much they had made clear. All things came from something else—that was the very nature of life itself. So to fashion my messengers, I had to start with some kind of raw material.

Leaves would be perfect—or so I hoped.

I let my thoughts become quiet and focused as I sat cross-legged on the ground. I let those soft voices and flurrying memories fill my thoughts, whirling around me like flakes in a snowstorm. I saw what I had to do and allowed the instinctual responses wash over me. Stretching my hands out over them, I pressed my will into the fibers and tiniest parts of the leaves. They all began to glow with brilliant green light, slowly rising into the air and hovering around me. The air hummed with energy. It sounded like music, like rushing wind through the arms of the trees.

The tips of my fingers tingled as I bade them take form, and the leaves obeyed. Enveloped in light, I could see their shapes slowly changing. They began to look less like leaves and more like birds—beautiful birds with feathers as green and bright as emeralds.

I whispered my message to them, storing it inside their very essence. And then, one by one, I sent them away. One to Felix. One to Beckah. One to Roland. And lastly, one to Sile. I asked them all to come to Mithangol and meet me at my family home. I would come to them there.

With each message sent, one of the gleaming leaf-birds vanished into a puff of glittering mist and disappeared. Soon, I was left alone in the darkness of Luntharda again. Overhead, the moon had begun to sink beyond the trees. I found myself calling out to Paligno again, hoping that he would answer me somehow. I wanted assurance that I was doing the right thing and that this really was going to work. I wanted to be confident and fearless because that's what this task was going to require.

Of course, just like all the other times, I got no response. No comfort. No voice from the heavens or the earth. There was only me and the music of the frogs and crickets.

It made me miss Beckah.

I was about to give up and go back to the fire so I could sulk and feel sorry for myself until my shift was over, but a new, curious, and familiar presence trickled into my mind. Immediately, I remembered that I wasn't alone. I hadn't been alone in years. Mavrik's colors swirled in my mind's eye and I found myself smiling at their customary patterns. He was checking up on me, as usual.

"Show me again," I whispered as I sent my thoughts to him. "I want to see the place where you came from."

Mavrik eagerly obliged. He was excited that I wasn't pushing him away anymore. I guess he had missed me.

Even as I sat back down beside the fire, my mind raced on the wings of a dragon. I soared through his memories, along the steep cliffs where his kind nested on narrow ledges and in ancient sea caves. They rode the powerful winds that blasted the gray, jagged rocks. The air smelled richly of sea foam, and the waves crashed along the coastline like the pummeling fists of the gods, sending salty spray hundreds of feet into the air.

It was soothing. Every one of my senses was entranced. And when it was time for Kiran to take over the next watch shift, I let those visions lull me to sleep.

15

CHAPTER FIFTEEN

We were up and moving again by daybreak. With Araxie in the lead, we had expectations of making it to the edge of the jungle by dusk —which suited me perfectly. I'd rather get to Barrowton after nightfall when there was less chance of anyone spotting us.

High in the trees, we stayed clear of the marshy, swampy portion of Luntharda that lay below us. I picked up the pungent odor of the silt mud. It reminded me of an unfortunate incident in my fledgling year of training that had involved Gray elves and a huge, angry turtle. I was more than happy to stay out of the mud this time.

Blue was still following us, although he stuck by Jace's side most of the time. Apparently they had worked out some kind of truce that had evolved into a friendship. I feared that it was doomed to end once we left for Maldobar. Blue would never be welcomed there.

Jace had already lost his dragon in battle. He hadn't brought it up, of course. It wasn't his style to let anyone see him grieve ... or feel much of anything, for that matter. But I had difficulty imagining that he wasn't at least a little upset over it. Ghost may not have been bonded to him the way Mavrik was with me, but they had still fought together in many battles. It was depressing to think Jace was about lose another animal friend.

I kept my eyes trained on Araxie as we pressed on, leaving the swamps and smelly marshlands behind. My body was sore. My boots were making my feet raw from all the unnatural movements. Dragonrider boots weren't made for this kind of maneuvering. My stomach was growling and aching, as though it were scraping the back of my spine.

I was hanging by a thread, watching every move Araxie made in anticipation of a rest. Just one swig of water, or a small bite to eat, and I felt like I would have been a little less clumsy and chaotic. Maybe then I could have at least stood without my knuckles dragging the ground.

When she finally raised a hand, signaling for the rest of us to stop, I collapsed into a sitting position on the edge of the branch, letting my legs dangle over the steep drop to the jungle floor. My armor had me smothering in the miserable heat and humidity, and I could feel that my clothes under my breastplate were drenched with sweat.

As soon as Araxie gave the go-ahead for everyone to relax, I took off my pack and unbuckled my breastplate so I could breathe and cool off a little. Then I went fishing through my belongings, desperate to find what was left of my food rations. It wasn't much. We were all getting low on food now. I doubted we could afford to go another day without reaching the boundary.

"How much farther is it?" Jace asked as he looked despairingly at his own rations of dried meat and nuts. It was only a few handfuls—about the same as what was left in my bag, too. It was barely enough to keep someone from passing out from hunger and not nearly enough to satisfy a hungry soldier.

Araxie was sitting with her legs crossed, munching away. "Five, maybe six miles. We should reach it before dark if we do not stop or slow down."

"In that case, I'm going to take care of some business before we get moving again." Jace crammed what was left of his food in his mouth and got up. He stretched, groaning and rubbing his back as he wandered away into the cover of the leaves and branches.

I didn't think anything about it. None of us seemed to, in fact. Kiran, Araxie, and I just went on eating without saying a word. I guess we were all too tired to make small talk.

My thoughts were wandering toward how I would have loved a cold bath. Even Blue was lounging comfortably nearby, licking his paws and yawning like he was wishing for a mid-afternoon nap. We'd gotten complacent.

And that was our first mistake.

Jace came back a few minutes later with his arms full of something that looked like fruit. Each one was about the size a man's fist and was bright pink with yellow spikes all over them. I gathered by the way he was squishing one in his hand that they were softer than they looked.

He was grinning triumphantly as he showed off what he'd found. "These are fruit, right? Can we eat them?"

I would be the first in line to try one.

Then I saw Araxie's expression.

She was sitting perfectly still. Her eyes as wide as saucers and brimming with horror. The look on Kiran's face was eerily similar. Neither one of them made a sound.

"What?" Jace frowned down at the fruit in his arms. He'd picked about a dozen or so of the bright, prickly things.

Slowly and carefully, Araxie got to her feet. "Do not move," she warned. I could see her breathing heavily. There was a fresh sheen of sweat on her skin as she slowly stepped toward him.

He obeyed, although he appeared just as confused as I was.

I could see the fear in Araxie's color-changing eyes as she stood in front of him, carefully reaching out to take the piece of fruit from his hand. She held it like it might bite her. "Where did you find this?"

"Just over there. There were a bunch of them. These are just the ones I could reach." Jace was staring her down as though he were searching for some clue about what was going on.

Meanwhile, Kiran was quickly and carefully gathering our belongings. His eyes never left Jace, and he did an excellent job not making a single sound as he worked. He didn't so much as rustle a leaf.

I decided to do the same. I slowly buckled my breastplate back over my body and stood.

"What are they?" I whispered as I slung my bag back over my shoulder.

"The fruit of the greevwood trees," she answered breathlessly. She'd begun taking the fruit from him piece by piece and carefully placing them on the branch a few feet away from our group.

I instantly remembered that name. Those were the carnivorous trees Kiran had warned me about. I'd even read about them some during my dragonrider training. No one had ever mentioned them having fruit, though.

"And exactly what the hell does that mean?" Jace sounded nervous.

Araxie flashed him a glance, as though she were silently trying to assure him that it would be all right. "They are very deadly. And their fruit is no different."

"Is it poisonous?" I asked.

"No." She shook her head. "But it will explode if you handle it too roughly."

Jace swallowed hard. "Explode?"

Kiran came over to grab my shoulder and pull me back farther away from them. "Yes," he answered. "Quite forcefully. One is enough to blow a man's head clean off."

"Great." Jace sucked in a slow, tense breath. "And I picked a bouquet of them."

"It's all right," Araxie insisted in a firm tone. "Stay calm. Don't make any sudden movements. You made it this far with them. They must not be very ripe. The ones you find on the ground that didn't explode on impact are far more dangerous."

"Or I'm just cashing in on every bit of dumb luck I've got left," he muttered.

She smiled, although I could tell it was forced and probably just for his benefit. She gently took the last two pieces of fruit from him and went to place them with the others that she'd neatly stacked well out of our path.

I let myself relax. Next to me, I heard Kiran let out a sigh of relief. Crisis averted.

"I don't think I've ever had to take fruit so seriously—" I started to joke.

Araxie tripped.

She must have been too focused on the fruit to mind her footing. Her toes snagged on a vine, and she started to fall forward. In an instant, Jace snapped a hand out and grabbed her to keep her from falling. She didn't hit the ground. But we all watched in quiet terror as the two pieces of fruit she'd been holding in her hands went flying through the air. They sailed past me, over Kiran's head, and straight off the limb.

There wasn't time to run. We only had seconds. The fruit fell, and Kiran grabbed the back of my neck and forced me to hit the deck. Araxie tried to do the same for Jace, but it was too late.

Explosions rocked the jungle around us as one piece of fruit set off another … and another … and another. The tree we were in shuddered dangerously. I caught a glimpse of Jace as he threw his arms around Araxie like he was trying to protect her.

I could hear wood splitting and limbs groaning and cracking in two. The branch we were standing on began to buckle under our feet. At first, I thought it was just breaking off, but then I saw the trunk splitting right up the middle. Not good.

Chaos erupted around me. A riot of branches, leaves, and explosions that made my ears ring. There was nowhere to run. My stomach lurched with the sensation of falling.

And all of a sudden, everything went dark.

When I woke up, I was lying on my back on the jungle floor staring up into the glare of fresh sunlight. Dust and debris hung in the air like smoke. Splinters of wood and leaves were piled on top of me. I couldn't hear anything for the ringing in my ears, although it seemed like the explosions had finally stopped.

I was completely disoriented. I didn't know what had happened. One look around answered that question, though. The enormous tree trunk lying on the forest floor, crushed and splintered from the explosive fruit, was a pretty good clue. Huge branches and leaves lay everywhere, and the new opening in the canopy overhead sent bright sunlight showering down over the jungle floor.

I could still feel everything, which was a relief. Sitting up, I dusted off my clothes and did a quick once-over to make sure everything was still intact—arms, fingers, legs, toes. I was bleeding from a few fresh cuts, but nothing serious.

"Jaevid!"

I looked up when I heard Kiran's voice. He was running full speed toward me over the debris, leaping from one fallen branch to another.

"I'm all right," I called out to him.

Apart from a deep gash on his arm that was bleeding out onto his clothes, it looked like Kiran had made it safely through the collapse of the tree, too.

I was still trying to get my ears to stop ringing as he grabbed the front of my chest plate and roughly started tying a strip of fabric over my nose and mouth. He ripped another strip off the end of his robes and did the same thing to himself, then began dragging me after him. "The air is filled with spores. We must find the princess!"

I didn't need any more encouragement than that. We fanned out across the rubble, looking for Araxie and Jace. We called out to them over and over, but got no reply. There was nothing but eerie silence.

My panic turned to dread when I found Blue lying halfway under a huge limb. Most of his body was crushed. I could sense that his spirit was gone. There was nothing I could do for him now.

When Kiran saw what I had found, the color drained from his face. He started calling out even louder, scaling the fallen tree trunk like a squirrel while he searched for Araxie.

I could only assume he was thinking the same thing I was—that our friends had met a similar fate. They could have been buried so deeply under all this rubble we might never find their remains.

A new surge of adrenaline made my senses clear. I dipped into my subconscious, summoning a bit of Paligno's power to try and feel for the spirits of my friends. It worked. I could feel them, their energy, resonating from the wreckage.

They were alive.

I found them together, tangled up amidst branches and vines that had shattered all around them. I yelled for Kiran, but didn't wait for him as I started digging them out. There wasn't time.

The energy coming off Jace was very weak.

When I moved the last few branches, I saw why. He'd been impaled through his chest and abdomen several times. The crude, bloody ends of splintered limbs were sticking out of his chest. Araxie was lying on top of him, shielded from the worst of it thanks to his efforts.

As I pulled her off him and rolled her over, I was relieved to find that the blood on her clothes wasn't hers. She'd taken a pretty stiff blow to the back of the head and was barely conscious, but her injury wasn't anything life threatening. Gray elves were a little more durable, after all.

I could see her eyelids fluttering and hear her groaning softly. She'd probably just have a nasty headache.

Jace was in worse shape. His eyes stared up at me, glazed and distant. I'd seen him look at me like that before. There was blood running out of the corners of his mouth and out of his nose. I could sense the severity of his wounds as if they were my own. Each second, each heartbeat, brought him closer to death. He'd punctured a lung and several crucial organs. He'd also broken his back in several places. I knew he wouldn't last much longer unless I intervened.

"Help me pull him off," I commanded as Kiran sprang over to observe. Together, we heaved Jace off the branches that had impaled him. It was hard, gory work that left us both spattered in blood. Thankfully, Jace was too far gone to even cry out. I doubted he could feel much at all because of how his back had been broken.

When we laid him out on the ground, I got to work right away. Healing was second nature to me now, so I didn't even have to think about it. It came more easily than any of my other abilities, even now that I'd received Paligno's blessing. I placed my hands upon his head and willed my power into him, mending his broken body piece by piece.

Familiar, soothing warmth spread through my mind, over my skin, and out through my palms. It must have hit him with greater force than ever before because I felt his body flinch and heard him make a hissing, gasping sound. His chest rose with a deep breath and he grabbed one of my wrists almost like he wanted to stop me, but I didn't let up.

I knew my work was done when I heard Jace's gruff voice mutter, "I'm gettin' really tired of almost dying whenever I'm around you. No wonder you don't have any friends."

"I have friends." I scowled as I sat back. He was obviously all right if he felt good enough to make wise cracks.

"What about her?" I noticed that his voice took on a much gentler, concerned tone as he gazed at Araxie. Even his demeanor changed as he moved closer to where she was lying nearby, still unconscious, but very much alive. "Is she ...?"

"She'll be fine. Might have a headache when she wakes up," I assured him. "Looks like you get to live to be the hero this time, after all. You're welcome."

Jace just snorted. He was getting to his feet, feeling his chest and torso as though he were making sure I'd actually healed him. Maybe it was still a little hard for him to believe I could do that. He didn't seem to dwell on it long, though. He bent down, slipped his arms under Araxie's limp body, and picked her up. There was a worried furrow to his brow when her head lulled against his shoulder. She was totally out of it.

"Can't you just heal her now?" He gave me a forceful look.

"There's no time. We must go," Kiran urged. "The trees will release more of their spores."

With Jace still carrying the princess, we ran away from the scene of the carnage as quickly as we could. Kiran took the lead, although I had to wonder if he actually knew where we were going—especially when I began to notice the trees all around us looked eerily familiar. It was hard to tell which ones were greevwood unless you looked at the ground. It was riddled with a network of roots that played out like a spider's web, looking to ensnare and devour anything that didn't move fast enough over them. It made running difficult and tripping was not an option. Tripping meant being crushed to death by the roots and sucked dry of your fluids.

I did what I could to clear the way for us. I could reason with some of the trees, commanding them to let us pass without interference. That only worked for the trees that hadn't been infected with Paligno's curse, of course. The ones who resisted my authority released their spores anyway, which were invisible and basically undetectable. Every breath was a gamble.

Jace hadn't stopped to protect himself from inhaling the spores. I noticed his steps were starting to slow. He stumbled and staggered, almost dropping Araxie several times.

Suddenly, his knees buckled. I caught him as he toppled backward. Beneath our feet, the roots began to writhe hungrily.

"My legs feel strange," he slurred. "I can't feel them."

Kiran gave us both a violent shove forward. "Do not stop! Keep running!"

But Jace wasn't going to last much longer. So I decided to try one of those crazy, amazing things again. Too bad Felix wasn't there to see it.

I cut my eyes toward one of the trees nearby, stretching my will out to it and summoning forth a familiar ally. The vines that hung off its trunk all began to groan and shift. They twisted together, morphing into the shape of a staircase that led up into the tree.

"Go!" I shouted at my friends, who were just standing there watching in amazement.

I ran with them toward the staircase, continuing to weave it as we climbed higher and higher. The vines grew, forming new steps right in front of us, until at last we could step out onto one of the tree's large branches. I was hoping that as long as we were up higher, the spores wouldn't be as much of a threat anymore. We could pass through without falling victim to their paralyzing effects.

Unfortunately, Jace had already breathed in too many of them. His legs buckled again as soon as we started out onto the limb. He dropped Araxie and then fell on top of her.

Kiran and I didn't have to speak. One glance and we both knew. If we were all going to make it through this, then we were going to have to work together. He was smaller than I was, so he grabbed Araxie and flung her over his shoulder. I picked up Jace and did the same.

Together, we walked the crooked branches carefully. It was risky when we had to cross from one tree or limb to another. Fortunately, I could manipulate the branches enough to make it possible, though they were a great deal slower to respond than the vines. Trees don't typically do a lot of moving on their own accord. It made our progress frustratingly slow.

We didn't dare stop until nightfall. We made a pitiful excuse for a camp and sat down to rest. It was too risky to go down to the ground again or start a fire since either would make us an easy target for a hungry predator. So instead, we found another broad, flat spot on a branch that was a good ten yards across. It was mossy and there wasn't any exploding fruit in sight, so we agreed it would have to do.

Lucky for Jace, the effect of the spores didn't last long. He was already coming out of it while we were unpacking what remained of our supplies and unfurling the bedrolls. He could already sit up, talk, and move his legs again. Kiran kept insisting that he drink lots of water to help flush the rest of the spores from his system.

Araxie was waking up, too. She'd been even luckier. Well, at Jace's expense, anyway. She only had a good-sized knot on the back of her head and a fierce headache to show for all our near-death adventures.

I offered to heal her, but she cast me a scathing glare of warning. "I'm fine," she hissed. I guess being hurt and carried around like a damsel was all her pride would allow for one day.

I let Kiran fill her in on what had happened ... and explain to her that we weren't sure where we were now. We were away from the greevwood trees—which was the most important thing.

She wasn't happy. But considering that we were all alive and more or less intact, she didn't complain. It could have been much worse.

Normally, not having a fire would have left us sitting in the darkness cringing at every sound. But we were high enough in the trees that a little moonlight managed to trickle down to where we were all sitting. Lying on her sleeping pallet, I could see the faint glimmer off Araxie's multicolored eyes. She was staring at Jace—who was sitting dutifully beside her with a somber expression. He looked like some kind of guard dog, keeping watch over her without saying anything.

Kiran had told her, in a very abbreviated and unflattering way, how Jace had shielded her from what likely would have been her death. Of course Kiran wasn't going to pass out any extra credit to someone he viewed as a rival. But credit had to go where it was due, and Jace had definitely earned it.

My stomach was growling angrily. There was no food left, no fire to keep us warm, and only another day's worth of water. We had no idea where we were now or how far off course we'd wandered. Somehow, we'd have to make up all that ground tomorrow on empty stomachs. I wasn't looking forward to that at all.

Kiran was busy tending to the deep cut on his arm. Despite my offer to heal it for him, he insisted he could do it himself and told me flat out, "Scars are to be worn with honor." I assumed that was just another example of Gray elf stubbornness and pride. I didn't try to argue it with him.

Instead, I sat by and watched him make a poultice out of dried medicinal herbs from his bag. He smeared the paste over the wound and then wrapped it tightly with a strip of bandaging. When he was finished, he curled up on his pallet and immediately went to sleep.

Since Blue was gone, and my ability to sense presences in the jungle around us was now our only line of warning in case something came after us, I volunteered to take first round of watch over the camp. Jace wouldn't have it, though. He was determined to take it, and I had my suspicions as to why. His motives were getting a lot easier for me to read now. Especially since his eyes scarcely left Araxie. The only time he wasn't looking at her is if he was right beside her.

So I let him have first watch in the hopes that he'd do more than sit there and look stern. No sooner had I stretched out on my side to "sleep" than I heard him begin speaking quietly to her. I kept one eye cracked just a tiny bit so that I could watch.

"I've wanted to tell you for some time now—and trust me, I know this won't change anything or make any difference at all," Jace murmured without ever looking her way, "but I am sorry about your brothers."

Araxie didn't answer. Her brow was furrowed apprehensively, like she wasn't sure how to respond to that.

"You were right about me, you know. I was, and am still, very much a monster. I was promised absolution from my past if I did my job well. It was presented to me like some kind of redemption. Like I was proving my loyalty. The more of your people I killed, the more assured my freedom would be. I let that justify the things I did," he continued. "I suppose that's why the idea of dying has never frightened me. I realized too late that I'd only traded one form of slavery for another, so death in any form would be the only real freedom I could ever hope for. I found myself almost wishing for it, hoping that each battle would be my last. I thought it would always be that way ... until today."

"I don't understand." She began to sit up. The movement must have hurt that swollen, angry knot on the back of her head, though, because she winced and almost fell back again.

Jace caught her by the shoulders and held her upright.

They sat frozen like that for a few awkward moments, just staring at one another.

"I didn't want to die," he said stiffly, as though he were forcing the words out past all his internal fortifications. "I didn't want to leave you behind."

Araxie's lips parted slightly. Her eyes widened, and I saw her begin searching his gaze desperately like she was hoping for something else.

I knew that look right away because Beckah had looked at me that exact same way many times before I'd eventually wised up and realized what it meant.

I guess Jace was a little more experienced than I'd given him credit for when it came to women. He got the message right away.

Without hesitating, he pulled her in close enough to press his mouth against hers.

I hadn't quite made up my mind as to whether or not I would help him out if she started to lash out at him for it. She was fast enough that she might be able to snap his neck and both his arms before I even got to my feet.

Well, that and I suspected that if the situation had been reversed and *I* was the one going out on a limb with the girl I liked, Jace probably would have just sat back and laughed if I got beat up for trying to make a move.

Then Araxie grasped the sides of his face and kissed him back, and I decided that was a good time to roll over and give them some privacy.

After all, it's not every day a guy gets to kiss a princess.

AFTER A DAY LIKE THAT, I WAS HOPING FOR SOME GOOD, MEANINGFUL SLEEP. Of course, it just wasn't in the cards for me. As soon as I was settled in and my eyes rolled closed, I was yanked under the grip of another dream that refused to let my weary brain rest.

I found myself in a familiar place, which was a rare thing when it came to my usual nightmares. But that wasn't a comfort to me at all. Standing in the middle of a muddy, trash-strewn street—I knew exactly where I was. I'd walked down this same street many times as a child. I stared up at the front door of the lopsided little hut where my mother and I had lived in the Gray elf ghetto of Halfax. The last time I had seen it, there had been lights in the windows—evidence that a new family was living there. Now, however, I saw nothing but pitch black. The door had been kicked in, and the thin, grass-woven blinds on the windows had been torn away.

Up and down the street, the other huts looked much the same. There were no lights and no signs of life anywhere. I saw footprints—hundreds of them—leading from the empty doorways out into the street. They formed a rut in the middle of the road that led out of the ghetto.

So I followed them.

The trail led out of the city, through the gates, and out onto the open road for almost a mile. All along the way, personal items had been dropped and left behind. Bits of clothing. Shoes. I even saw a child's doll made out of rags trampled into the grime.

I walked for what felt like hours. All the while, I noticed a bright red glow on the horizon. It was in the dead of night, and I was familiar enough with Halfax to know it couldn't have come from any other city. But there was something else—something I was all too familiar with—that I knew had once been nearby.

A feeling of dread began digging deeply at my gut as I drew nearer and nearer to that place. Cresting a grassy hill, I looked down across the valley to where an ominous structure belched fire into the night sky.

Felix was right. The prison camp had been rebuilt.

From where I was standing, I could see the trail of footprints I'd been following led away across the grassy open fields directly toward the black iron gate of the prison camp and disappeared inside. I could see guards dressed in armor walking the perimeter and manning the ramparts.

A column of black smoke belched out of the center of the fortress, churning upward to blot out the light of the stars. I could smell it. I was now intimately familiar with that putrid scent and where it came from. I'd stood over the place in the center of the prison camp where they burned the bodies of the deceased captives once before.

I couldn't breathe. I couldn't move. Horror froze me in place, staring at the prison camp without any doubts about what was happening there. Genocide. Mass, cruel, and unwarranted.

Suddenly, I felt every little hair on my body prickle. A strange warmth spread over me.

"Why are you showing me this?" I dared to ask.

The being standing beside me looked exactly like my mother, but I knew better. It wasn't her. Her eyes had never been green and they certainly hadn't glowed.

This was Paligno.

"*So that nothing will sway you from what must be done to end it.*" The god's words hung in the air like a chorus of whispers. Among them, I could hear my mother's voice.

"You think I won't go through with my plan to kill Hovrid?" I tried not to take that too personally, although it definitely felt like a shot at my resolve.

Paligno turned slowly and focused an ancient gaze upon me. It was enough to make anyone feel two inches tall. "*It is not in our nature to enjoy taking the life of another under any circumstance. But sometimes it must be done, as you have learned. The sacrifice of one life can ensure the freedom of an entire generation.*"

I had to think about that. I'd never stopped or even thought to question myself about whether or not I would be able to kill Hovrid when the time came. He was my brother. Well, half-brother. Despite what he'd done, and was still doing, that was a fact that wouldn't change. The question was would I let it change me? If he begged me for mercy, would I offer it? Was I going to let that family tie trip me up when everything else demanded that he pay for his crimes?

If someone didn't stop him—if I didn't take a stand—then he would continue butchering my mother's people until they were gone. He would continue trying to defile and control the god stone, and Paligno's curse would ravage all of nature until the balance was restored. I couldn't let any of that happen. Brother or not, it made no difference.

"When I became a dragonrider, I swore an oath to obey the commands of the King of Maldobar." I looked back at the prison camp and clenched my fists. "But he is *not* a king. I owe him no allegiance."

Paligno just kept staring at me with those unfathomable, gleaming eyes. It was like stealing a glimpse of eternity—something my feeble brain could barely understand. It was as terrifying as it was comforting, though I couldn't wrap my mind around that, either.

"*Hovrid swore an oath as well. He sealed it with my essence,*" the god said. "*Before the end comes, I will hold him to it. I do not forget. Nor do I compromise.*"

An uneasy silence settled over us as we stood side by side, watching the prison camp scorch the horizon. My mind was racing like wind over a dragon's wings. I was thinking over the scenario that now lay ahead of me. Nothing about it was going to be pleasant. I knew that. And despite my best efforts to grit my teeth and bear it, it filled me with dread.

"*Your father's people will not understand,*" Paligno said solemnly, as though the god could read my thoughts. I didn't doubt that he—she—whatever *it* was—probably could. "*Long have they lived and faithfully served an imposter, and are now caught up in his treachery. Their hands are stained with blood spilt to satisfy his rage. And when you reveal yourself to them, they will indeed call you a traitor. They will curse your name. They will scorn and despise you. They will even try to take your life. The truth you will offer will appear to them as the highest treason because they dwell in a kingdom built upon his deception.*"

"It doesn't matter what happens to me," I replied. "I'd rather die a traitor than live as an indifferent accomplice and watch everyone else suffer."

"*Then when the time comes, you must not doubt me.*" The god smiled knowingly, but it wasn't a comforting smile at all. Something about it chilled me right to the marrow. It reminded me that although I'd seen Paligno's true form and felt the peaceful warmth that came from his presence, I'd yet to witness his wrath.

In that cold, all-knowing sneer, I got my first real glimpse of it.

I WAS ALREADY AWAKE WHEN THE SUNRISE GRADUALLY BROKE THROUGH THE jungle canopy. It filled the air with a faint greenish glow as the light streamed through all the layers of leaves. The birds awoke to pour out their morning songs. Some of them sounded downright prehistoric, although I'd gotten used to all their bizarre calls since I'd been here. I was going to miss that.

A few of the more curious birds, with brightly colored feathers as vibrant as jewels, came close and even landed on my shoulders. I suppose they could sense who I was and knew they had nothing to fear from me. They appeared content to sit there, preening and making conversational chirping sounds.

Sitting a few yards away from where the rest of my companions still slept, I meditated on what my dreams had revealed to me. I was beginning to realize that the path that lay ahead wouldn't be as clear-cut as I had originally thought. When it came time to finally lay out my plans for dethroning Hovrid to all my friends, my loyalty was going to be questioned. Every person I'd ever trusted or cared about might turn against me. But I had already chosen this course. I couldn't turn back now. And for the first time, I felt sure and comfortable with the task that lay before me.

The longer I sat, the more my mind began to wander. Thinking of my friends in Maldobar made my chest feel tight with unease. Thanks to my mental bond with Mavrik, I knew Felix and Beckah had survived the battle in Barrowton. But I had no way of knowing what had happened to my half-brother, Roland. I could only pray and hope that he had survived and that he would be waiting for me at Mithangol with the others.

"You're awfully cheery this morning. Something on your mind?" Jace was joking sarcastically as he sat down next to me. The sudden sound of his voice made me jump and all the birds around me scattered and disappeared into the trees.

Jace was still staring at me expectantly, waiting on my answer, but I just shook my head. I didn't feel like sharing my thoughts just yet. Anything I said to him now was bound to ruin his unusually happy mood.

His whole demeanor had changed practically overnight and it was a side of him I'd never witnessed before. He was in love and it was painfully obvious. He now looked at Araxie like a blind man who was seeing a rainbow for the first time.

It made me miss Beckah terribly. Just the thought of her put a pain in my chest that took my breath away. I couldn't stand still.

"Hey." He caught me by the arm before I could slip away. For an instant, I saw that fierce, instructor-ish glare return to his eyes. "I'm serious. If there's something—"

I cut him off before he could finish. "How do you think the other members of Blue Squadron are going to react to what we're about to do? What about the rest of our dragonrider brothers? Do you think they'll understand? Or join with us?"

Jace's steely expression hardened. I could practically see his mind racing over those questions.

"It's been long enough. By now, everyone most likely assumes that we're both dead," I continued. "If you go back, you're going be associated with me as an accomplice, for better or worse. Those still serving Hovrid are going to use your past to defame you and make you out to be a criminal. Even if we do put the stone back and restore the balance, you will have to live with that stigma forever."

"I've already been a criminal once, Jaevid," he murmured darkly. "So that doesn't exactly frighten me."

"Then are you sure you want to go back to being one again?"

He hesitated. It was only a second or two, but it was enough to let me know that I had hit a nerve. Of course he didn't want to go back to that. Who would?

And now he was in love with Araxie. He had found a place here, in Luntharda where he could start over. What was there for him to go back to in Maldobar? He had no family—he'd told me that himself. He had no dragon, so it wasn't as though he could go back to being a dragonrider. He had nothing there.

"Don't talk circles around me like I'm some kind of idiot. Just say whatever it is you want to say," he growled.

I leveled my gaze on him. "I want you stay here."

Once again Jace fell silent.

"Stay here with Araxie. Start over. Let the past die with your memory in Luntharda."

He slowly let go of my arm. "And what about you? You can't fight Hovrid alone."

"I won't be alone."

"You said it yourself—how do you know any of the other riders are going to side with you? Let's say you do managed to kill Hovrid. When you do, all hell is going to break loose right over your head. Every rider and soldier in Maldobar will be coming straight for you. There won't be anywhere to hide. You may not even make it back to the border with the stone. They will hunt you down like a dog and they will kill you." His voice got louder as he started to get angry. It was attracting attention. Behind him, I could see Araxie and Kiran watching us suspiciously.

I straightened, squared my shoulders, and looked *down* at him—after all, I did have a few inches on him. "They will try. But I'm not that easy to kill."

I met Araxie's worried gaze. I wasn't sure how I would ever explain this to her —at least not in a way that she would understand.

"I don't have much family left in the world that would ever want to claim me, let alone care about me," I said quietly so that only Jace could hear. "Those I do have are precious to me. By asking you to stay here, I'm entrusting you with one of those people. Do you understand how important that is?"

Jace scowled down at the ground silently.

I took that as a yes.

"Good." I patted him on the shoulder to try and reassure him. "Try not to let her down."

"No, you try not to let us down. Got it?" He returned the gesture and gave my shoulder a firm squeeze. "Fly hard. Fly fast. Don't look back."

CHAPTER SIXTEEN

I was back.

Standing on the boundary between Maldobar and Luntharda, I looked up and finally saw the starlit sky stretching out over a landscape I knew well. It was broad and beautiful, glittering with clean silver light that made the dew-covered grass sparkle across the grassy valley before me. It had been months since I had seen anything but trees and branches for as far as the eye could see.

I was standing on an all-too-familiar muddy road—one I'd never actually visited in person before. Not physically anyway. My dreams, however, had brought me here many, many times. This was the place where Hovrid had murdered the true King of Maldobar and duped my father into stealing the god stone for him.

This was the place where the course of history had changed.

Looking at the place where I knew the king had taken his last breath put a strange chill down my spine. It was the worst sensation of déjà vu I could imagine, although there were no lingering remnants of that incident now. No bones. No blood. No tracks in the mud. That had been more than twenty years ago, after all.

"This road will take you to the human city you call Barrowton." Araxie spoke softly as she stood beside me, staring at me as though she were trying to read my thoughts. She hadn't questioned my decision to go on alone. I suppose she trusted my judgment more than I had ever realized.

"I will send a sign when I'm drawing close with the stone," I told her. "Be ready. Muster what warriors you can and anticipate a fight—I'll likely have all the forces of Maldobar on my heels."

She sighed uneasily. Out of the corner of my eye, I could see her chewing on the inside of her cheek. "The people—our people—who are still in the prison camp ... "

"They will be set free," I assured her.

Her expression darkened. "How can you be sure? What if the king who takes the throne in succession to Hovrid has the same hatred for us?"

I couldn't help but smile. "He won't. He doesn't now."

Jace was shooting me a puzzled look. I guess he hadn't put together who would be in line for the throne. With the true king and all his progeny dead thanks to Hovrid, the next king would have to come from the most powerful noble family in Maldobar.

"There will be peace, one way or another," I promised. "So wait for my sign."

Araxie nodded quietly. I could sense her apprehension. She was anxious about what was to come. I was, too, in a way. I knew what had to be done, I knew I could do it; I just wasn't sure what the cost was going to be, not only for me, but also for my friends and loved ones.

"Oh, and see that Jace doesn't get himself killed." I winked at her playfully. "That is, if you don't mind babysitting my human pet."

She managed a small smile in return.

I kept my farewells brief and set out down the muddy road under the cover of night. There was no one in sight for miles, no farms or houses. No one dared to live this close to the jungle of Luntharda.

It took me well into dawn to finally reach the remains of Barrowton. As the rising sun burned the horizon deep scarlet, I saw the charred remains of the city rise up before me. The smell of death was strong on the wind. Smoke still drifted out from behind the battle scarred walls.

I did my very best not to look into the empty eyeholes of the dead that still lay, unburied and forgotten, all around the city. Dragons, men, and elves all lay together in that mass grave, rotting away to nothing but bone under the summer sun. The faces were unrecognizable now, but I was still afraid to look—afraid of seeing the armor of someone I knew.

Normally, there would have been soldiers inside. Infantrymen who were supposed to be holding the city to ensure the elves didn't try to retake it. Maybe even a few dragonriders flying patrol patterns. But the place was deserted. It must have been uninhabitable on the inside with no place left for anyone to hide out. That, or Hovrid had passed an order to have poisoned salts poured into all the city wells. Tainting the water supply like that was a sure fire way to make sure no one could ever live in that city again. It was a common war practice in Maldobar.

All of a sudden, an explosion of color erupted into my mind. Pinks, orange, greens, and blues swirled through my brain an instant before I felt the ground flinch under my boots.

Turning around, I was greeted by a blast of hot, smelly dragon breath on my face.

Mavrik pushed his snout against my chest and sniffed me vigorously. He chirped and growled, rubbing his head so hard against me that it nearly knocked me over. Meanwhile, he was sending me a storm of images—questions about where I had been.

"Easy, there. It's good to see you again, too." I was trying to keep my composure. I couldn't, though. Not for long. I was so glad to see him. I wrapped my arms around his neck as far as they would reach and put my forehead against his scaly hide. "I've missed you, my friend."

He made a deep grumbling, purring sound.

"We've got a lot of work to do." I knew I didn't have to explain. He could see the thoughts and worries that raced through my brain. He knew what I planned to do and exactly how dangerous I suspected it would be. "But once this is over, maybe we can both retire for a while."

A sticky, prickly dragon tongue swiped my cheek. I gagged. Dragon spit is about as smelly as it gets. It's a stink that lingers. And their tongues are a lot like a cat's; covered in little prickly barbs that feel like sandpaper. Put that together and dragon "kisses" are not a great experience.

That is, unless that dragon happens to be yours and you have been separated him for a few months.

"Really? Come on." I laughed and scratched that special place behind his ears that made him purr even more loudly.

He was content to crouch down while I fixed my bag to his saddle and checked things over. I was glad to find everything was exactly as I'd left it. Some of the leather had been roughed up and scuffed, but apart from that everything was in good shape. I could ride to Mithangol without having to make any resupply stops. It would take a day and a half, maybe two if the weather was bad.

Something behind me clattered noisily—almost as though someone had tripped over something.

Immediately, I froze in place. Mavrik's lips curled back into a snarl. He began hissing and letting the black spines down his back bristle up. I put a hand against his neck to keep him steady. Then I slowly turned around.

Kiran was standing only a short distance away, his eyes wide with horror at the death and carnage all around us. He looked even more terrified when Mavrik flared his wings and snapped his jaws threateningly. The color drained out of his face until his skin and hair were almost the same shade of washed out silver.

"What are you doing here?" I demanded.

He suddenly seemed to remember that he wasn't supposed to be following me. He dropped his gaze as though he were ashamed—or maybe just embarrassed that he'd been caught. "My loyalty lies with you," he muttered through clenched teeth. "Please do not send me back. I want to help."

"Does Araxie know you left?"

He shifted his weight uncomfortably. "By now I'm sure she does. I took my leave while they were ... well, you know."

"Ah." He didn't have to finish. I got the picture. "This isn't a guided tour, Kiran. You know what Hovrid is doing to the Gray elves in this kingdom. He'll do the same to you if you're caught."

Kiran looked back up at me with a determined scowl. "I have to be here, Jaevid. I made someone a promise. I am not afraid."

I was about to remind him that fear had nothing to do with it, but then I realized what he'd called me. He'd never used my name before.

"If you take your plans to your human allies without a gesture of good faith from the Gray elves, they might not believe that we truly do want peace. Am I right? I will go with you as validation—so they will know we are in agreement."

I had to give him some credit. He made a good argument. I couldn't exactly disagree with that. "So be it. But you know, you'll have to fly with me."

His multicolored eyes went wide. "O-on your dragon?"

I glanced back at Mavrik, who was still growling and swishing his tail like an angry housecat. His yellow eyes were narrowed suspiciously in Kiran's direction.

"If he'll allow it."

Mavrik snorted. He sent me a mental image of himself chewing on what looked a lot like one of Kiran's dismembered legs.

I tried to reason with my cranky dragon. "Don't be like that. He's on our side. It's just until we get to Mithangol."

"He doesn't like Gray elves?" Kiran asked uneasily.

I gave Mavrik's ears another scratch just to calm him down. "No. He's just not happy about what your people did to me. You know, the whole torturing and trying to behead me business."

"Oh." He glanced between Mavrik and me like he wasn't sure what to say.

I laughed. "Relax. It'll be fine. Here, hand over your bag and let's get going. We're wasting time."

Kiran reluctantly surrendered his belongings—all except for his bow and quiver, which he kept slung over his shoulder. He cautiously hedged toward Mavrik and waited while I buckled down his things to the saddle.

"I've never been so close to a dragon before," I heard him mutter as I slipped my hands into my riding gauntlets and climbed into the saddle.

"Well, now you get to ride on one."

He wrinkled his nose when I offered to help him up as though I'd insulted his ego somehow. In the end, though, he needed it in order to get up into the saddle.

I quickly showed him where to sit and hold on. The whole time, I noticed his hands were shaking. He still looked flushed and nervous. It made me smirk. I remembered the first time I had been in a dragon saddle. I'd been a nervous wreck, too.

Too bad the worst part was yet to come.

"Don't lean against the pull of his speed," I warned as I buckled myself in. I checked one more time to make sure Kiran was hanging on tight.

We took off into the early morning sky like a streak of blue lightning. Mavrik poured on the speed and broke the low-lying cloud cover until we soared above the clouds. Overhead, the twilight sky was still dark purple and dotted with glittering stars. Below, the clouds looked like milky cotton for as far as I could see in every direction.

I planned for us to stay above the clouds, hidden from anyone on the ground below, until we reached the Stonegap Mountains. There, we could keep close to the rock faces and mountain peaks, winding our way down to Mithangol. Hopefully no one would see us. We could stop somewhere high on the cliffs and make a camp just long enough to let Mavrik rest. It was too far for him to fly it all in one stretch, especially with two passengers.

All during our trip, I couldn't keep my gaze from wandering to the east, toward the rising of the sun and the royal city of Halfax. There, all the way across the kingdom, was my enemy. He was enthroned behind halls of stone, protected by the same brothers in arms I had trained with. Just the thought of my graduation ceremony when I had knelt at his feet and swore an oath to him made my blood boil. It made me feel absolutely sick. I'd been right there, standing within arm's reach of him. I could have ended it then. I could have set things right.

I wouldn't let that chance slip by me again.

A new day was dawning.

MITHANGOL APPEARED LIKE A CLUSTER OF WARM LIGHTS TUCKED INTO THE steep canyons between the mountains. It was late in the afternoon the next day when I finally spotted it. The sight filled me with anxiety and adrenaline.

I'd always been careful when approaching my hometown. I didn't want to advertise my coming and going, or the fact that I had a dragon. Now more than ever, I took care to approach from the rural side of the city and circle at a high altitude until it was dark enough to land without being spotted.

As we wheeled in broad patterns over the city, I sensed the presence of someone else following us—two someones, actually. Nova and Icarus joined us in formation, flying off our wing and roaring in greeting. They were a welcome sight, even though both their saddles were empty. Mavrik sent me mental images of my family home as explanation. The windows were lit and there was smoke rising from the chimney. I had company.

My messages had worked.

I sent both dragons away so they wouldn't interfere with our landing. Then I let Mavrik make his descent. I was trying to stay calm. I didn't want to seem unsteady or like I was second-guessing myself. But my heart was pounding and my hands were sweating. As much as I wanted to be reunited with my friends, namely with Beckah and Felix, the fear of how I would be received almost made me want to turn around and run.

Would they be happy to see me? Relieved? Angry?

Mavrik flared his wings and touched down gracefully on the front lawn of my home. He let out a rumbling growl, which I interpreted as a complaint about flying so long with Kiran's extra weight.

I patted his neck roughly. "Good work, buddy. You've definitely earned some dinner, but try to stay close by in case we have to leave suddenly."

He chirped in agreement.

I helped Kiran dismount first. He'd taken his first dragon ride pretty well. Better than I'd expected he would, anyway. He hadn't thrown up—which was good. He just looked a bit pasty in the face as he wobbled away from Mavrik and waited to catch the bags I tossed down to him.

No sooner had my feet hit the ground than the front door of my house opened. Light spilled out of the doorway, and I could see the silhouettes of people crowding to look out at us.

All of a sudden, one of them broke loose and began running straight toward me.

Beckah was barefoot, wearing only a thin white nightgown and a robe, both of which were falling off her shoulders as she sprinted over the grass. Her long dark hair blew around her wildly in the night air. As she came closer, I could see the tears streaming down her cheeks.

I dropped everything to rip off my gauntlets.

"Jaevid!" She screamed my name a few seconds before I caught her in my arms. Without all her armor on, she felt much softer. She felt fragile.

I squeezed her tightly and kissed her. It didn't matter that anyone saw. I was so glad just to see her.

The others were coming outside now. The sight of so many familiar faces standing around me was overwhelming.

Then I saw Felix. He had stopped short, looking at me as though he couldn't decide if he wanted to hit me or hug me. Beside him, I noticed his wing end, Lieutenant Prax, had come along as well. Sile and his wife were lingering on the front porch, watching with somber expressions. Next to them were a few other members of Emerald Flight—my comrades from Northwatch. They all stood by in silence, staring at me with mixed expressions of awe and suspicion.

Then I noticed the shape of someone else still standing in the doorway. It made me hesitate and pull away from Beckah slightly. I just had to be sure my eyes weren't fooling me.

They weren't.

Roland looked so different. The last glimpse I'd had of him had been years ago now, before I'd started my training to be a dragonrider. We'd both been children. Now we were both soldiers. And the war had changed us both.

He was bigger than I remembered. Granted, we were about the same height now, but he was far more muscular than I was. He had a short, dark beard and one of his arms was bandaged all the way to the shoulder and fixed against his chest in a sling. He was still wearing his casual infantry uniform and there was a sword belted to his hip.

When our eyes met, he nodded to me slightly. He'd never been one to say anything unless it was absolutely necessary.

"We all had the same dream." Beckah's voice was hushed. I felt her reach down to take my hand and squeeze it tightly. "We dreamt of you. You said you were coming here and that we should come to meet you. Please, tell us what's going on. We all thought you were dead. That was three months ago. Where on earth have you been?"

I turned slightly and directed my gaze to where Kiran was standing beside Mavrik, holding both of our bags, and eyeing my crowd of friends warily. Everyone else looked with me. I knew Felix and Beckah might recognize him. They had met briefly before, a long time ago, during the scuffle with some slavers during my fledgling year.

The others, however, were strangers to Kiran. And not all of them were going to be thrilled to see a Gray elf standing in the front yard.

"I guess you could say I got sidetracked." I wasn't sure where to begin. There was so much to tell, I needed to collect my thoughts before I started explaining things.

Beckah squeezed my hand again as if to get my attention. Looking down into her soft green eyes, I felt guilt rush over my body like a cold tide. She seemed restless and her face was thinner, like she hadn't been eating enough. That one look from her could bring me to my knees. I knew that I'd hurt her. She'd been living with the assumption that I was dead. Now I was back and she had no way of knowing what I'd been through just to be standing there.

"I'm sorry, Beckah." I tried to keep my voice low enough that only she would hear.

Felix apparently did, though.

Before I knew what was happening, he punched me across the mouth. It knocked the breath right out of me. Beckah screamed and immediately put herself between us. I stumbled back and rubbed my throbbing jaw.

"No! Sorry doesn't cut it! Not this time," he shouted and just kept coming, fists balled up for another attack.

"What are you doing? Have you lost your mind?" Beckah stormed up to him and shoved him back.

Felix had a crazed look in his eyes. "You don't get to do this to me—to any of us. I buried you, you selfish idiot. Buried you on my family's estate grounds. I've had to walk past that headstone for three months! And now you just show up like nothing ever happened?"

I didn't know what to say. From where I was standing, I could see that he was biting back tears. His face was bright red and he looked like he wanted to take another swing at me just to get the point across.

I almost wanted him to. He was right. I'd never really stopped to consider what all of this must be doing to him, or what he'd been forced to deal with when I was presumed dead.

"Felix, you have to let me explain," I tried to reason with him. "I never meant for any of this to happen. But it had to. I know it doesn't make any sense to you right now. Please just hear me out."

He was panting and his eyes were blazing with anger. Even so, I kept walking toward him. He could hit me again if he wanted. If that's what it took for him to forgive me, I was willing to take it.

I gently coaxed Beckah out of my way so we could meet face-to-face, eye-to-eye. "For a while, I was worried you hadn't survived the battle, either."

"I'm a much better rider than you are, idiot," he growled sulkily. "Of course I wouldn't die."

I chanced a smirk and stretched out a hand to him. "And you really think a little stroll through Luntharda would be enough to kill me?"

His eyes narrowed for a moment, like he was still making up his mind about whether or not to forgive me for disappearing. At last, he grasped my hand and yanked me into a gruff, brotherly hug. "I didn't know what to think. I still don't. Where on earth did you find *him*?"

All eyes were on Kiran again.

He'd dared to inch a bit closer to us, still holding all our luggage and dressed like a traditional Gray elf warrior. His presence obviously had my dragonrider brothers from Emerald Flight on edge. They were glaring at him relentlessly.

"And what about Jace?" Prax spoke up in a hopeful tone. I suppose he was thinking that if I had survived, then maybe Jace had, too.

"It's a long story, too long to tell while standing in the front yard." I took Beckah's hand again and nodded toward the house. "Let's go in."

Everyone started shifting toward the front door—everyone including Kiran. He was about to cross the threshold into my living room when a few of my dragonrider comrades stepped into his path. I could sense the tension in the air. This was about to turn into a fight.

"What is this creature doing here?" one of them demanded. He had his hand resting on the pommel of his sword.

Kiran didn't respond. To his credit, he didn't even look intimidated. Maybe he knew better than to do anything to instigate a brawl on my front porch.

The members of Emerald Flight, however, didn't seem to have that same respect for my house.

"Stand down," I snarled at them. I flexed a bit of my power, just enough to make every wooden board and beam in the house shudder.

Everyone stopped. They stared at me, and most of them looked shocked and unnerved. Even Sile was regarding me with a much more apprehensive expression. He was sticking awfully close to his wife and baby, as though he didn't quite trust me anymore.

"This is my home. You'll respect my wishes in it. Now move aside and let him enter." I slowly panned my gaze over them, silently daring them to challenge me on this.

Not one of them did.

They stepped aside and let Kiran in without another word.

"So when do you tell us what this is all about?" Felix asked impatiently.

"Yes," Prax agreed. "You've brought us all here, plus that pointy-eared friend, what is it you want from us?"

Slowly, I let my gaze travel around the room once again. I met the eyes of my comrades, of Sile and his wife, of my half-brother Roland, of Felix and Beckah, and of Kiran. One by one, I studied them and found myself silently begging Paligno for strength and wisdom.

The time had come.

"I've asked you all here because something must be done; something that on the surface will be extremely difficult to understand. Many of you will find it heinous. You won't want any part of it. But if you'll listen, maybe I can explain to you why there is no other choice."

Felix was already shaking his head. "No other choice? Jaevid, what are you talking about?"

I looked at him squarely. I was still praying he would trust me now like he always had. I needed him on my side. "I'm talking about high treason."

Cold, heavy silence swallowed every sound in the room. No one said a word. No one moved.

I closed my eyes.

"I've come to make traitors of you all."

IMMORTAL

The Dragonrider Chronicles Book Four

PART ONE: FELIX

CHAPTER ONE

I lost Jaevid and Mavrik in the fray almost immediately.

In front of me, my partner, Lieutenant Darion Prax, was leaning into his dragon's speed as we made our final approach. Behind me, a dozen more riders were following us in. Below me, the city of Barrowton boiled with the fury of battle. Our lines of infantry were broken, but trying to reform. The Gray elves fought like savages, wielding spears, bows, and scimitars. Some of them rode on the backs of jungle monsters, others were zipping around us through the sky on creatures called shrikes—our natural enemies.

Prax gave me a few brisk hand signals, instructing me to move into place and get ready. I twisted my saddle handles slightly, applying a bit of pressure under the saddle. With a few heavy beats of her wings, my dragon caught up with him and flew right underneath him. Nova was a big girl, bigger than most male dragons twice her age. But what she lacked in speed she made up for in other ways—something the Gray elves were about to figure out first hand.

We dropped down lower. Arrows sailed past my helmet. One bounced off my breastplate and gave me a scare. I leaned down closer to Nova's body for shelter from the hail of fire coming from below. Unlike most of the other dragons, Gray elf arrows couldn't pierce her thick hide.

I checked Prax out of the corner of my eye. He was giving me one finger and a closed fist. First target. Time to hit hard. I clenched my teeth and twisted the saddle handles, giving Nova the signal.

Prax and I dove as one, our dragons spiraling in unison towards the ground. We pulled out of the dive flying side-by-side, barely a hundred feet off the ground behind the enemy lines. I squeezed Nova's sides with my boot heels, and I felt her take in a deep breath.

Together, our dragons showered the ground with a storm of their burning venom.

Gray elf warriors screamed. They fired at us with everything they had. But our rain of fire didn't end until Nova had to stop for another breath.

We broke skyward and began preparing to make another coordinated pass.

But the second time wouldn't be so easy. The trail of flames and burning corpses we'd left behind had gotten the attention of a few warriors on shrikes. I spotted four of them heading straight for us.

I gave Prax the news—we had company.

He quickly replied with a plan.

I was slower, so I was bound to be their first target. But that was fine; I was ready.

When his volley of arrows failed, the first Gray elf rider had his shrike attack us outright. The bizarre creature was like a furious mirage of mirrored glass scales. It wrapped around Nova's neck and started clawing at her eyes. Nova roared and slung her head back and forth. The shrike's rider was twisting in his saddle, drawing another arrow that was aimed right at me.

"Better make that shot count," I yelled and drew my sword.

Suddenly, Prax blurred past us.

There was a crunching sound and a shrike's yelp of pain as his dragon got a tasty mouthful of the monster. I saw the Gray elf rider fall from the saddle and begin to plummet toward the ground. A very small part of me felt bad for him. The rest of me still remembered he'd just tried to kill me.

Another shrike hit Nova. Then another. One was wrapped around her head again while the other hit much closer to the saddle—closer to me—right at the base of her tail. I twisted the one saddle handle I was still hanging onto and Nova pitched into a violent roll. She spun, getting faster and faster.

The shrike on her head lost his grip. He flew backwards, bouncing along her body and whooshing past me. One well aimed thrust of my sword made sure he wouldn't be coming back around for a second try.

The last shrike and rider were a problem, though. She was trying to cut my saddle straps. Clever. Effective, too, if she managed it.

But I wasn't about to give her that chance.

I sheathed my sword and twisted the handles again, hanging on for dear life. Nova snapped her wings in tight against her body and dropped from the sky like a giant, scaly stone. The further we fell, the faster we went. The wind howled past my helmet. The ground was getting closer and closer.

I bit back a curse and looked back. It was working. The shrike was losing his grip, sliding further away from me down Nova's tail.

I squeezed my heels against her ribs.

Nova spat a burst of flame directly in front of us, and I hunkered down against her as she wrapped her wings around herself. Everything went dark. I could smell the acrid venom in the air. It made my eyes sting. I could feel the heat of the flames as I panted for breath.

Dragon venom is funny stuff. It's sticky like sap and highly acidic. It'll burn through just about anything—except a dragon's own hide.

Nova flew through her own burst of flames, shielding me with her wings. When we came out the other side, she flared her wings wide and caught the air like a kite. Below us, a shrike-shaped fireball crashed into the ground.

Prax appeared next to us, giving me hand signals again. *You okay?*

I gave him a thumbs up.

Good. Time for another pass.

THE BATTLE WAS OVER.

The shouting voices and clashing blades had gone quiet. Now, there was only the crackling of the flames still smoldering in what was left of Barrowton. It was a wasteland – barely more than a charred crater littered with the bodies of the fallen.

Yet another ugly scar on Maldobar's landscape.

We'd only just gotten back to the citadel at Northwatch—our little slice of paradise where the forces assigned to protecting the northern border were housed. Group after group of dragons and their riders continued to land on the platform and file into the tower. One hundred proud warriors had left to retake the city only a few days before. Less than forty of us returned.

Still, I was only looking for one.

"Where is he? Does anyone see him?!" I shouted at the top of my lungs and shoved my way through the other dragonriders. I called his name over and over, hoping to spot him or his blue dragon making their way down the corridor ahead of me. They must have fallen behind.

I searched every bloodied, war-beaten face that came walking in from the rain. Before I knew it, I was standing back at the open gateway that led out onto the platform.

Jaevid Broadfeather was nowhere to be found.

Someone grabbed my shoulder. A bolt of hope shot through me as I spun around, hoping to see him standing there.

It wasn't him.

It was my riding partner, Lieutenant Prax, standing over me like a giant in blood-spattered battle armor. He was much older than I was and a far more seasoned rider. That's why the look on his face absolutely terrified me.

"No one saw him or Jace depart with us."

I was instantly sick. I couldn't accept that. Jaevid wouldn't just roll over and die—not this easily. We'd made it this far, gone through all of our dragonrider training together from beginning to end – so I knew he could fight. Sure, I'd teased him plenty about sucking at hand-to-hand combat, but I'd never met anyone faster or better with a blade. He was half Gray elf, for crying out loud. Granted, he hid it well, but I knew he had that elven killer instinct buried down deep in his soul. I'd seen it surface once or twice before when someone pushed him too far.

I had to believe he was here somewhere. I just hadn't found him yet.

I turned around with every intention of standing out on the platform in the driving rain until I saw him land. Boy, was he in for it. That little jerk should have known better than to pull a stunt like this after our first battle, the one time I hadn't been standing right next to him while we did something ridiculously dangerous to make sure he didn't get killed.

Prax grabbed my arm to stop me. There was no shaking off his grip. "We can't go out there. They want the platform clear for the riders still landing. We'll have to wait in the stable."

I stole another glance out of the gateway. The skies were choked with rumbling black storm clouds and the rain was falling hard enough to obscure the city below. Every couple of minutes, the ominous, dark shape of a dragon appeared through the gloom, wings spread wide and legs outstretched to stick the landing. As they landed, infantrymen rushed out to help the riders dismount and escort them inside. Some of them had to be carried because of their injuries. Their cries of pain were drowned out by the sound of the thunder.

"Come on." Prax shook me a little to break my trance. "You need to look after your lady. Then I'll wait with you back at his stall."

I didn't like it. I wanted to be standing right here when Jae finally dared to show his face after making me stress out like this. But Prax was right. My dragon, Nova, was still dressed in her saddle and I needed to get her settled in before I did anything else.

The work was distracting. It kept me from staring at the gateway every single second while I unbuckled her saddle strap-by-strap and checked her over for injuries. Thankfully, she was unharmed. Her scales really were as strong as iron plates. And judging by a few nicks and scrapes I found around her chest and neck, that trait had saved her life more than once.

Once she was fed and nestled into a bed of hay for the night, I closed the door to her stall and immediately made a break for the platform. I had every intention of waiting there again. I didn't make it there, though.

Everyone was waiting on me. The other surviving riders in Emerald Flight had gathered outside Nova's stall.

"They still haven't come back yet?" I looked at Prax, expecting an answer.

He didn't have to give a verbal one. Once again, his expression said it all. Jaevid and his senior partner, Lieutenant Jace Rordin, still hadn't returned.

So we waited.

Sitting outside Jaevid's empty dragon stall, we watched the rest of our dragonrider brothers tending to their mounts like I had. It wasn't looking good. The elves had made an impressive stand at Barrowton and our ranks had taken a beating. Less than half of us had returned and many of those were wounded or grounded because their mount had been injured. The riders landing now were barely able to limp in out of the rain. Some of them even had to be carried.

I watched one rider who had to be dragged off the platform by the infantrymen. He was shouting like a madman, still crazed from battle. I couldn't figure out what he was saying or why he was so upset until a big group of soldiers rushed past us to help restrain him. Then I heard why.

His dragon had managed to carry him back safely to the tower, but the creature had died on the platform shortly after.

The rider's grief-stricken screams mingled with the constant rush of the rain. It was a sound I'd never forget.

I couldn't watch anymore after that. I leaned against the stall door with my eyes closed, trying not to think about or imagine anything. Then, infantrymen rolled the iron grate down over the passage that led out onto the platform. It made an awful clanging sound.

That was it. The last of us who survived the battle had landed.

It was over. We all knew it, and yet none of us wanted to be the first to get up and leave.

It didn't feel real. I didn't want to believe it was. There had to be some kind of mistake. He was going to pull off another miracle, come wandering in with that weird, self-conscious smile on his face and start apologizing—he *had* to. It wasn't supposed to end this way.

"Jace was set on going head-to-head with that Gray elf princess again." Someone finally spoke up and broke the heavy silence. "He must've dragged Jaevid into it, too. Poor kid wouldn't stand a chance in a skirmish like that."

I pushed away from the door and started walking away. I didn't want to hear this. I didn't care how he died. He was gone. The *how* didn't matter.

I thought I managed to get away without any of them following me. But I should've known better than to think Prax would let me go. I heard his heavy footsteps and the clinking of his armor as he fell in right behind me.

He waited until we were well away from the others, standing just inside the stairwell that spanned the full height of the fifty-story tower, to catch me by the shoulder. "I'm sorry, boy."

"Sorry won't bring my best friend back from the dead. Sorry never did anyone any good. It's a waste of everyone's time," I snapped.

He let me go. I could see sympathy in his eyes as he stared down at me. It pissed me off. For a few seconds, neither of us said a word. Then he shook his head. "We've all lost someone today, Felix. Every last one of us. So go do whatever you have to do. Work it out. Then clean up your armor and get ready again. You and I are some of the few who are still battle-ready."

I already felt like a total failure for letting my best friend down. I'd let him die alone in battle. And now I felt worse knowing I'd offended Prax, although there wasn't a lot I wanted to do about it right now. All I knew was that my insides hurt. I couldn't think beyond the rage that was burning in my body like hellfire. I could practically taste the flames crackling over my tongue. I needed a way to let it out.

THREE DAYS. THAT'S HOW LONG IT TOOK PRAX TO RESURFACE AND TRY talking to me again.

I knew he'd be coming. I was already on borrowed time. At any given moment, orders could come down and I'd be sent back to the battlefront somewhere to kill more elves in the name of peace and justice. A bunch of crap, really. Neither existed in my world.

My knuckles were bleeding through the strips of bandages I'd wrapped them in. It probably had something to do with me facing off with a sparring bag every day at dawn, pounding at it with all my strength until I was too weak to stand. I didn't stop to eat and sleeping was totally out of the question so I didn't even bother trying.

Honestly, I didn't know what else to do. I was asking myself a lot of hard questions while whaling against the sand-filled training bag, and most of those questions I no longer had an answer for.

Why was I here? Punch. *What was this all for?* Punch. *Could I even justify not being at my estate now?* Punch.

"Felix." Prax's voice interrupted the rhythm of my internal interrogation.

I stopped and let my arms drop. They were so numb I couldn't even feel my fingers anymore. I turned around, wiping away the sweat that was dripping into my eyes.

I expected to see Prax there, giving me one of those cautious, sympathetic gazes. But I hadn't expected to see the guy next to him. I didn't know him. Rather, I'd never laid eyes on him before. But I knew right away who he must be.

Jae had never been all that chatty when it came to his family. I could sympathize. My own family life hadn't been great, but it didn't hold a candle to what I suspected Jae had put up with.

When we'd first met, he looked like a pulverized, half-starved puppy. Some of the other guys training with us liked to pick on him because he was one heck of an easy target—but they weren't the cause of all those bruises. Some of those marks had been older. Much older. He'd gotten them long before he'd darkened the door of the dragonrider academy. So I went out of my way to ask Sile about them. Needless to say, the answer had been unsavory.

My father had never beaten me, even when I probably deserved it. He didn't have the strength or the audacity. He popped me across the cheek a few times for mouthing off, sure, but that was more embarrassing than anything else.

Jae, though? He probably weighed eighty pounds soaking wet when we first met. And that father of his had been beating him mercilessly for years, according to Sile.

Now I was looking at the one person who should have stuck up for the little guy whenever his dad decided to use him like a doormat. I knew this had to be his older brother. The family resemblance was strong, even if this guy wasn't a half elf like Jae. Same piercing eyes. Same strong jawline.

"Roland, I presume?" I glanced him up and down. He was taller than me, unsurprisingly. Chalk that up to yet another Broadfeather family trait. "You look like hell."

It wasn't an insult. He really did look awful. His right arm was sealed in a crude plaster cast all the way up to his shoulder and he had bloody bandages wrapped around a wound on his head. He was obviously one of the lucky infantrymen who made it back to the citadel from Barrowton—the uniform tipped me off. Except for the stubble on his chin, he looked so much like Jae it would make anyone stop and take a second look. Granted, this guy had a lot more muscle to throw around, but he had the same squared jaw and high cheekbones.

"I don't believe we've met." He was looking at me cautiously. I suspected being in the dragonrider quarters was making him uneasy. Infantrymen weren't supposed to be up here.

"We haven't," I replied. I left it at that, hoping Prax would take the hint that I wasn't really up for a heart-to-heart discussion with this guy.

I walked past them to a corner of the sparring room where I'd stashed a few of my things, including a towel to wipe myself off with. I could hear them both following me.

"Colonel Bragg has issued his official statement. Medics swept the battlefield at Barrowton looking for any remaining survivors and taking record of the dead," Prax spoke up.

I stopped. All the little prickly hairs on the back of my neck stood on end. "And?"

"They never found his body—or Jace's for that matter. But his dragon was sighted in the area with an empty saddle," he answered quietly. "Some of the other riders report having seen them engaging the Gray elf princess in aerial combat. They saw her shoot Jace's mount down. Jaevid was right on his tail, so ... we can only assume ..."

"—That he's dead. Yep. Thanks. Figured that much out on my own, you know, when he didn't come back." I scowled at them both, hoping it would be enough to stop this conversation from going any further.

It wasn't.

Prax turned his attention to the silent infantryman standing next to him. "We cleaned out their room. There wasn't much left behind, but Jae's brother here insisted you should have it."

That's when I noticed Roland was holding something. It was a mostly empty burlap sack. He held it out to me with a tense expression. "They tell me you two were close."

I didn't want to take it. Just the thought of seeing what was in there made me start to feel nauseated all over again. "Shouldn't this be given to his family?"

"That's why I'm giving it to you." Roland fixed his gaze right on me. "I know how you must feel about me. And you're right to despise me. I can only imagine the things Jaevid told you about me let alone the rest of our family. I won't deny any of it. But I never laid a hand on him. Not even once."

I snatched the bag away from him. "Some might argue that joining in and just standing by and watching it happen are basically the same thing."

Roland hesitated. Slowly, his eyes moved down until he was staring at the floor. "We were both trapped in that house, both suffering at the hands of the same man. Jaevid never knew how many beatings I took for him, how many nights I would sleep by my bedroom door so I'd hear if Ulric went outside after him. My every waking thought was about how I could get out of there. But I couldn't just run away and leave Jaevid there alone. I would have never done that to him. So I waited until Ulric came back from Blybrig and told us he'd been adopted by the dragonriders. Then I left."

An uncomfortable silence settled over us. I'm sure Prax was learning a lot more about the Broadfeather family than he ever cared to. After a few seconds I cleared my throat, crammed the bag of Jae's belongings under the rest of my gear, and nodded. "Actually, he didn't talk about his family life much."

"I suppose that shouldn't surprise me," Roland sighed. "I just thought, since you were closest with him, you ought to have what was left of his things. He'd probably want it that way. And considering the circumstances, I wanted to thank you in person."

"Thank me?"

"Yes. I'm not trying to be condescending. But I am grateful that you were willing to step in and befriend him. Someone of your social standing—"

I stopped him right there. "That never had anything to do with it. It wasn't charity."

He nodded. "I understand. I'm just saying that there aren't many others who would be willing to jeopardize their reputation. You're a better man than most. And I want you to know I appreciate that."

"Ah." This was beginning to make me really uncomfortable. I began picking up my stuff and planning a quick exit.

"I also wanted to ask if there was anyone else we should inform," Roland added, as I slung my bag of gear over my shoulder. "Did he ever mention having a lover?"

Once again, my body locked up involuntarily. I hadn't even thought about *her*. Did she know? Who was I kidding ... of course she didn't know. I cursed under my breath and flashed Prax a telling glance. Someone was going to have to tell Beckah Derrick what had happened.

"I'm willing to do it," Roland offered. I guess he could read my expressions well enough to tell what I was thinking.

I clenched my teeth. "No. I'll do it. She should hear it from me. I'm the one she'll blame."

The trouble was, I didn't know how I was going to find her. Beckah lurked on the edge of every battlefield, haunting our blind spots like some kind of avenging angel. To my knowledge, she'd been keeping her distance from the riders otherwise, which was smart since she was playing a dangerous game. Being the only female dragonrider wasn't something to be proud of. It might earn her the hangman's noose or the business end of a sword if anyone found out her real identity.

If anyone could actually catch her, that is. Being paired up with a king drake, the biggest and baddest of all the dragons in Maldobar, put her at a big advantage over the rest of us.

I had my work cut out for me. As soon as I managed to shake off the pity brigade, I headed straight for my room and started thinking of ways to get in contact with her. I didn't know where she was hiding out between battles, though. Jae might have known, but if they had a secret lovey-dovey rendezvous spot, he'd never spoken a word about it to me. That sneaky devil.

I decided to look for clues when I got back to my room. I dumped out the burlap sack of his belongings onto my bed and began to look through them. There wasn't much. It was mostly spare uniform pieces and a few bundles of letters tied together with twine. I hesitated to go through those because that kind of stuff was probably pretty personal. What right did I have to go digging around in his private life?

Then again, what did it matter now? And one of those letters might contain a clue about how to get in touch with Beckah.

Hesitantly, I untied one of the bundles and opened up a few of the letters. None of them were helpful, really, and going through them gave me an eerie feeling. It just felt wrong.

Finally, I came to one that looked like it hadn't been opened in a while. The address scribbled across the front said it was from Saltmarsh, a town down on the southern coast. I'd never been there, never had a reason to. It was a port city, home to mostly fisherman and hired hands looking for shifts on the merchant ships that came and went from the harbor.

Seeing that address struck a chord in my memory. Jae had mentioned to me before that Beckah and the rest of her family lived there. He'd visited them before the start of our avian year. When I opened up the letter, I found only one line scribbled inside. There wasn't a signature, either. Just two initials:

— B. D.

They had to be Beckah's.

I knew she wouldn't be there. It was a long flight between Saltmarsh and Northwatch, too long for her to be going back and forth every time there was a battle. Heck, I couldn't even be sure her family still lived at that address, either. Sile struck me as kind of a shady character, like he had something to hide. He might just pick up and leave without saying anything. But this was the best lead I had. I was going to have to start there and hope for the best.

I lit a candle and took out a few sheets of fresh paper. I wrote three letters. The first one was to Sile Derrick, letting him know what happened and where he could find me. The second one was to my commanding officer, Colonel Bragg, who was in charge of all the dragonriders here at the citadel.

And the last one ... was to my mom.

2

CHAPTER TWO

"Is this what you nobles do? Tuck your tail and run every time something doesn't go your way?" Prax was looming over me, yelling loudly enough to get the attention of everyone in the dining hall.

I'd just told him and the rest of Emerald Flight what I intended to do. I'd thought it over. After sleeping on it for a few nights, I was sure. I was turning in my formal resignation to Colonel Bragg first thing in the morning. It was time to go home.

Obviously Prax didn't agree with my decision. I guess he thought yelling and embarrassing me in front of everyone would make me change my mind. Heh, yeah right. My dad had tried that too, when he was alive. It didn't work.

"I'm not running." I kept my cool. I knew Prax could crush my neck like an overripe banana if he wanted to, but I was willing to chance that he wouldn't actually hit me. "I'm just done, that's all. I don't have to justify myself to you or anyone else."

His glare was smoldering. "You're making a big mistake, boy."

"Probably. I've made a lot of those recently."

"These are your brothers. You're abandoning them," he fumed, gesturing to the rest of our flight.

I have to admit—that sort of got to me. I had to bite my tongue to keep from flying off the handle and giving him the all-out brawl he was probably hoping for. "No. My brother is dead. The rest of you will be fine without me."

I looked around at the rest of the riders in my flight. There weren't many of us left. Six, counting Jaevid and Jace, were gone now. Those of us left behind would never be the same. I guess that was why I didn't get the same resentful sense from the rest of them that I was getting from Prax. I hoped they understood, but told myself it wouldn't matter if they didn't.

Either way, I was as good as gone.

And why not? The war was more or less over. Barrowton had been the last outpost of enemy forces on our soil. That's why the elves fought so fiercely to keep it, and why we'd been so determined to take it back. Driving them out meant sending what was left of their army fleeing back into the god-forsaken jungle they'd come out of. Not even their legendary battle princess could turn the tide now. I didn't know what the king's next move would be, if he'd pursue them any further or not, and I had no intention of sticking around to find out. My work here was done.

"I appreciate everything you've done for me," I told him. Then I offered to shake his hand. Prax didn't respond except to narrow his eyes at me threateningly.

As I walked away, I could still feel the heat of his glare on my back. I'm sure there was a lot more he wanted to yell at me, a lot left unsaid, but I wasn't sticking around for that. With Jae gone, my last good excuse for not going back home was spent. I was pushing my luck by staying away this long in the first place. I'd risked making a mockery of my family's good name, an offense my mom would never let me live down.

It didn't take me long to pack up my stuff. Like most dragonriders, I traveled light. Necessities only, for the most part. I didn't have a lot of sentimental crap to lug around with me. The only people who wrote me letters were extended relatives and old girlfriends trying to suck up and get on my good side. That tends to happen when you're destined for any seat of power—everyone wants a slice of the pie. So I didn't hang onto any of those letters.

Sure, maybe some of them had actually liked me—girlfriends, not relatives. The rules are different for nobles of my standing, though. Heck, the whole game is different. You have to keep one eye on your pocket at all times because you never know who's going to try sticking their greedy paws in and swiping whatever they can. I'd already learned that once, the hard way, and I wasn't about to be the moron who fell for the same trick twice.

Don't get me wrong; girls were good fun—especially drunk, pretty ones. But I didn't trust them. I didn't even trust my own family members. The only person I had ever really trusted was dead now. Jae had never gone after my money or anything else I might have been able to give him. Money and social standing had never mattered to him. He always acted like he didn't understand any of it, and every time I'd ever bought him anything, it seemed to embarrass him.

I stuffed what was left of his belongings into my bag. I still wasn't sure what to do with all that stuff. I'd think of something later. For now, I just wanted to get out of here as fast as humanly possible.

With everything else ready to go, I left my gear stacked by my bed and made my way to the highest level of the tower, where the dragons were stabled. I wasn't leaving until the next morning, but I didn't want to chance running into anyone who might want to lecture me or try to change my mind again.

The stables were quiet and dim, with only a few torches lighting the corridor that ran down the center of the long, circular level. On either side, dragons were snoozing away inside their stalls. It was late and I was confident no one else would be up here at this time of night.

I rolled open the door to my dragon's stable. Nova raised her head, blinking at me sleepily with her bright, sea-green eyes. She yawned, showing off all her teeth.

She must have been able to tell that I was not all right because when I came over to check her tack, I felt a blast of hot breath on the back of my head. And when I turned around, she was right there—inches from my nose—looking at me inquisitively.

"You ready to get outta here, baby doll?" I rubbed her snout and scratched under her chin.

She just puffed another hot, smelly breath in my face.

I didn't know if she could understand me the same way she seemed to have understood Jae. I didn't have the freaky powers he did. But just having her there was a comfort. As of now, she was the only real friend I had left.

I dragged all our saddlery to the middle of the stall and began polishing and checking over every inch of it. It was habit, I guess. Habit and frustration.

Meanwhile, Nova curled around me like a huge wall of bronze, brown, and black scales. I'd always liked her coloring, even though it probably seemed drab to everyone else. Her patterning reminded me of a snake, or the striping on a cat. It was unique.

She plopped her big head down on the floor next to me and watched me work for a long time. I listened to the rhythmic sound of her breathing and tried not to wonder where Jae's dragon was. Mavrik had been caught in the wild, not bred and hatched like Nova. I hoped, for his sake, that he could find his way back to the cliffs he'd come from. I had a feeling that's what Jae would have wanted—for him to go back home and be with the rest of his kind again.

Nova and I both looked up when the stall door creaked. Someone was rolling it open again.

I wasn't expecting any visitors. I didn't want any. And Prax was probably one of the last people I wanted to see right now.

He stepped into my stall and shut the door behind him. He didn't look as angry as before, although I could detect some lingering frustration in the way his brow was furrowed. Some of the other riders in our flight had started teasing us about how much they thought we looked alike. I didn't see it. Sure, we both had dark blonde hair. And maybe we did favor each other a little, but they were blowing it out of proportion. That's the way it is with dragonriders. They're going to find something to tease you about, even if they have to make it up. It only had to be ten percent true. That was the rule.

"I guess you're all packed, then?" he asked as he ambled over and leaned against the wall nearby.

"Yep."

"I'm sure Duchess Farrow will be glad to hand the reins back over to you, eh?" He'd yet to make eye contact with me, which made me wonder what he'd actually come here to say.

"I'm sure she will." I kept my answers brief, hoping an uncomfortable silence would get him to cut to the chase.

Prax cleared his throat. Then he finally looked right at me. "I came here to say that I understand. Maybe you think I'm being hard or callous about this. Or maybe you just think I'm an ignorant old man with a bird's nest for brains."

I smirked. "Getting warmer."

That made him grin too, but it didn't last long. He rubbed the graying beard on his chin and sighed. He was acting fidgety, like there was something important he wanted to say.

"You know, I lost someone too. A long time ago. So I know it hurts. And you don't just get over it or forget. Time doesn't heal that kind of wound, you just learn to cope with it. Losing someone you love is a pain the heart never forgets."

"Careful. Don't get too mushy on me there, old man."

He gave a dismissive shrug. "I can't change your mind. I know that. Just be sure you're doing this for the right reasons, otherwise you'll regret it. And I'd hate to see another kid grow up to be an old man filled with regret."

It was hard to pop an attitude or even be sarcastic when I could plainly see that he was baring a little bit of his soul to me. I wondered what he regretted, whom he had lost. I knew better than to ask, though. Some things were better left alone.

"So what's the plan? You gonna hang around this dump and be a lieutenant forever?" I changed the subject.

"Unless someone kills me first," he replied. "I'm an old dog and we don't do so well with change. This is the only thing I know. And unlike the rest of you lot, I don't have anything or anyone waiting for me behind friendly lines."

"So there's no Mrs. Prax?" I don't know why that surprised me, but it did. I guess I figured an old guy like that, who had even one ounce of charm, would have a lady waiting on him back home, sitting by a window knitting him ugly scarves or something.

He just laughed. "No. Definitely not."

"And no kids?"

Prax shook his head. "Not a one."

I felt bad for him. Must be hard to be alone at his age with nothing to look forward to but the next battle. "It's not too late, you know. Maybe you could find some lady with a thing for old war dogs. Or, you know, a blind girl and we'll all just lie and tell her you're good looking. Either way."

He laughed again and came over to sit down across from me. Grabbing up a piece of my riding tack, he started to help me work. "Nah, I'm afraid it is too late. Especially for stubborn old soldiers who don't care to settle."

I ADMIT, I WAS A LITTLE NERVOUS WHEN I PRESENTED MYSELF TO COLONEL Bragg early the next morning and handed him my letter of resignation. He didn't seem all that surprised by it, though. I wondered if someone had tipped him off, or if he was getting a lot of these kinds of letters from the noblemen in his forces now that the war was essentially over.

"I wish there was some way to change your mind about this," were his only words, as he put his signature and seal at the bottom of my letter and handed it back to me.

I folded the letter and put it back in my pocket. "Sorry, sir. With greatest respect, I'm needed much more at home than I am here."

He nodded as though he understood and dismissed me.

That was it. With a signature and a few drops of red wax, I wasn't a dragonrider anymore. At least, not in the military sense. Now I was just Duke Farrow, like my mom had always wanted.

I'd expected to feel relieved. Instead, I was anxious and uncertain as I left Colonel Bragg's office. Prax's words were getting to me, pricking at my brain like a splinter. I wondered if I really was making a mistake.

I decided not to give myself the chance to go down that road. I hurried to get my bags and made a break for the dragon stables. It was barely after daybreak, and there were already a few men at work mucking out the dragon stalls. I was looking to make a clean escape, to get out without having to make any awkward farewells. Of course, that didn't happen.

I rounded the corner, headed for Nova's stall, and came face-to-face with everyone that was left of Emerald Flight—the guys I'd been fighting alongside. Prax was with them, and at first I was half-expecting to get jumped and beaten within an inch of my life for committing what they most likely saw as desertion.

There were no traces of malice in any of their eyes, however. I prided myself on being fairly intuitive about that kinda thing. As far as I could tell, these guys hadn't come here looking for a fight.

I hesitated and looked around, waiting for someone to explain what was going on.

"We know you're anxious to put this place behind you," Prax announced. "But we were hoping to convince you to come out with us one last time so we can give you a proper farewell."

A few of the others were nodding in agreement.

"To the Laughing Fox?" I asked.

Prax began to smile. "It is a tradition to give a toast to our retirees and drink to our dead."

I wasn't sure how to say no to something like that. I knew better than to try. "Sure."

Prax helped me put my gear down inside Nova's stall before we all began the downward trek out of the fifty-storey tower. The streets beyond were just barely waking. It was late spring, although that didn't mean much here. It was always chilly at night in Northwatch.

We walked together through the mostly deserted city streets, most of the guys laughing and heckling each other as usual. As for Prax and myself, well, I guess neither one of us was in a joking mood. The atmosphere was still heavy. By the time we arrived at the front door of the tavern, I was wondering if he would try to talk me out of leaving again.

He didn't, though.

He didn't say much of anything until we were all settled at our usual table, gripping mugs of warm ale, and reminiscing about the friends we had lost. That's something I'd venture to say all dragonriders love—telling stories, the more outrageous or hilarious, the better. And if your story was good enough, it might even earn you a nickname, but not necessarily one you're proud of.

"Tell us one about Jaevid," Prax insisted suddenly.

That caught me totally off guard. I dared to stare him down from across the table. His expression was steely and impossible to read. I couldn't tell if he was putting me on the spot out of sheer curiosity or if he had an ulterior motive. Was this supposed to expedite the healing process or something?

"Yes," someone else chimed in. "One we haven't already heard."

It wasn't totally justified, but something about being pinned down like this set me off. I put my mug down, crossed my arms, and let my elbows rest on the table.

They wanted to know a story about my dead best friend? Fine. I'd tell them one, all right.

All of a sudden, I had everyone's undivided attention.

"When we were fledgling students, you wouldn't have given him a second glance. He wasn't dragonrider material, and I think we all knew that. A stiff wind could've about snapped him in half. I spent a good portion of my spare time making sure he didn't get the life beat out of him. I wondered how he was ever going to survive in our world, let alone make it to graduation," I recalled. "But then I saw him work magic. I saw him speak to animals. I saw him heal people with his bare hands and bend the elements of nature to his will."

Total silence. I didn't look up to see anyone's expression. I wasn't interested in whether or not any of them believed me.

"Jace saw it, too. So did several others when we were nearly killed during our avian training on the Canrack Islands. They all witnessed what he could do. I should have died there, along with everyone else. But he saved my life. He saved all of us."

"I heard a rumor about this—that there was some sort of elven witchery about him," Prax murmured.

I flashed him a heated glare. "Not witchery. Power. The likes of which I never knew could exist in this world outside of legends and myths."

"Could he really be dead, then? Perhaps he swapped sides."

I didn't see who said it, but the mere suggestion infuriated me. I slammed my fists down on the tabletop. "Jae was many things, but don't you dare smear his name by calling him a traitor. He was a dragonrider—through and through. He never would have forsaken his oath."

"Relax, boy," Prax said gruffly. "No one's slandering your friend. I agree; I didn't take him to be a traitor. And I doubt he would have abandoned his dragon unless death itself pried him from the saddle."

I swallowed hard. I didn't want to sit here for another second. I was already behind on my own schedule.

Prax must have been able to sense that I was on the verge of losing it because he picked up his mug again and raised it to make a toast. "Let us remember him for who he was, for the good he did, for his loyalty and service, and his honorable sacrifice. We honor him and the rest of our dead, good men all. May they find peace on the white shores of paradise."

It was a good change of subject and everyone joined in. I raised my glass, too. But my heart wasn't in it. I was angry. There was a bitter taste in my mouth that the ale couldn't wash away.

The others seemed content to waste the day there, drinking and eating while they told more stories. If my head had been clearer, I might've enjoyed it. It might have been a relief to voice some of the memories haunting my mind.

After only an hour, I got up and put on my cloak again.

"It's not even midday," Prax pointed out. "You could stay a bit longer."

I shook my head. It wasn't open for debate. I was finished here. I knew what he was trying to do, anyway. I wouldn't be persuaded to stay. If anything, I wanted to leave now more than ever.

I kept my goodbyes brief and made a clean break for the door. Pulling the hood of my cloak over my head, I took a breath and stepped out into the pale, hazy light of Northwatch's dreary sky. The air was heavy and it smelled like it was going to rain again soon.

I'd only just left the Laughing Fox behind me. I was headed straight for the citadel, making my way through the streets alone. That's when I started to get the weird feeling that I was being watched—watched and followed.

Whoever it was, they were good. Better than most. I'd only catch a glimpse of a familiar combination of colors and clothing out of the corner of my eye, but just as soon as I'd turn to look they were gone, as quick as a shadow. It had my heart pounding away in my ears.

I decided to alter my route. I took the long way, crossing through the tangled alleyways behind some of the old shops. I thought I might lose them that way.

All I did was make myself an easier target. After all, I didn't know anyone who would have been a match for *her* speed.

I rounded a corner quickly and walked right into the point of a slender dagger. Just like that, she could have run me through. Thankfully, she didn't. Beckah was on our side.

Her big green eyes were wide and desperate as she stared up at me, her hand gripping the dagger with white knuckles

Slowly, I raised my hands up in surrender.

"Why isn't Jae with you?" she rasped. "Where is he?"

I could see she was at her wit's end. Her voice was hoarse and thick and her chin was trembling. Tears were beginning to pool in her eyes.

After staying up all night sorting through my thoughts and writing a letter to her family explaining what had happened, I had hoped I would know what to say when I finally came face-to-face with her. But I didn't. I couldn't remember anything I'd written.

"Gone," I managed. "Dead."

"No!" She pushed the point of that dagger against my neck until it started to hurt. "I saw the roster they posted on the fort gates. I read every name. His wasn't there!"

"Because they never found his body. They only post the names of the ones with a body left to bury, so the families can come retrieve it if they wish."

She took a few deep, frantic breaths. Her eyes widened and her chin trembled. "No ... no, you're lying!"

"I'm not."

"He talked about going to Luntharda. He said he felt that—"

"He talked to me about that too, Beckah. But do you honestly think he'd go without telling us? And during the middle of a battle when he was supposed to be watching someone else's back? I think we both know ... Jae wouldn't have done anything like that."

"Then it's your fault!" She started to scream. "You were supposed to protect him!"

The look of betrayal and raw agony on her face was more than I could take. I let my arms drop to my sides. If she was going to lash out and ram that dagger through my neck, I wasn't going to try to stop her.

"Tell me the truth, Felix Farrow," she railed. "Where is he?"

I couldn't look at her. It hurt, like nothing else ever had. I was a man. I wasn't supposed to show emotion. I had to swallow it, bite it, do anything to keep it from surfacing. But I nearly broke down when she slapped me across the face.

"I hate you. I'll never forgive you. Ever." Her voice was broken by sobs. "You abandoned him. You let my Jae die. You selfish, miserable coward!"

I didn't say anything. She wasn't telling me anything I didn't already know.

Beckah slapped me again, harder this time. "I hope you rot in that castle of yours."

Those words hung in the air, beating down on my head, long after she'd stormed away. I lost track of time as I stood there, staring at the tops of my boots. I was jealous of her. She could let it out. She could say what I was too afraid to admit to myself—that I had let him down. That my best friend was dead because of me.

CHAPTER THREE

Once I made my way back to the citadel, I found I couldn't get out of there fast enough. I didn't want to see or talk to anyone else. I'd had enough with the stalling games, the painful farewells, and the horrible way this place made me feel. After my dragon was outfitted and loaded down with all my gear, I strapped on my armor and clipped my sword on my belt. I pulled my helmet down over my face and climbed onto Nova's back.

The infantrymen manning the platform waved me out as they rolled the gate open so we could pass. Outside, the sky looked heavy. Dull gray clouds were gathering. It was bound to start raining any second.

Nova spread her wings wide, embracing the stormy winds and diving into the air. My stomach fluttered at the sensation of falling. Then we were up, soaring higher, shooting through the clouds, and breaking free to the clear skies beyond. We left Northwatch behind, and I never looked back.

It took well into the night to make it to my family's estate on the eastern coast. As we started our final approach, I could see the winking lights of Solhelm —the city that my family was responsible for as part of our estate's duties. We were the local authoritative figures, answering only to the king himself.

Solhelm was nestled in a shallow valley, between a few small mountain peaks. I'd probably spent more time there as a kid, getting into varying amounts of trouble, than I had at my own house. My family's ancestral house was lit up like a beacon. Mom had really outdone herself this time. There was a candelabra burning in every window, and the paved courtyard for dragon-traffic to land was blazing like she was afraid I'd miss it or something. How embarrassing.

Servants were waiting on me when we finally touched down. They bowed or curtsied as they came to help me bring in my gear. Normally, I would've insisted on carrying it myself. But I wasn't in the mood to argue with anyone else right now.

I handed Nova's care off to one of the stable hands that'd also come to meet us. They would take good care of her; I had no doubt about that. She was in for a good meal of fresh meat, a soft bed of clean hay, and space enough to stretch out if she felt like it. After all, any lady of mine was going to get pampered. And as it happened, she was my queen.

"Welcome home, sir." One of the white-gloved butlers manning the front door addressed me with a stiff bow as he let me inside.

I didn't answer, mostly because of who was standing on the other side waiting for me.

My mom looked older every time I saw her—and not in a good way. It was as though she was withering away, drying up under the searing heat of her own scowl. Her eyes had once only regarded me with apathetic coldness were now brimming with what I could only guess was subdued fear. Why she'd ever be afraid of me, I didn't know. I'd never raised a hand to her, and neither had dad. But she looked thin and timid standing there, looking me over like she wasn't sure it was really me.

I couldn't remember her ever looking at me for that long before. It was unnerving. "Something wrong?"

Mom opened her mouth, but closed it again just as quickly. She shook her head, making the light catch in her jewel-encrusted earrings and hairpins. Her hair was slowly turning gray and her skin was beginning to wrinkle. She still dressed like she was going to a party all the time, decked out from head-to-toe in the finest adornments our estate could afford. It was like a barrier she'd built up around herself, although I wasn't sure what or who she was trying to keep out. Poor people, maybe?

"Send word to the groundskeeper. I want to see him in my study first thing in the morning," I told her as I walked past.

"Whatever for?" She sounded suspicious.

I didn't stop to explain. Did it matter? It's not like she cared. "Don't worry over it, mom. I'm not doing anything to your precious tea garden."

I heard her puff an annoyed sigh as I walked away.

And that was it—my welcome home. That was about as warm as things had ever been between my mother and I. It hadn't ended in a shouting match, which was actually some form of progress for us. When I was growing up, we never agreed on anything.

Actually, I'd never gotten on well with either of my parents. I was an enormous disappointment to them, which they both let me know several times. I was reckless, foolish, wasteful, and unappreciative. I didn't take my role as duke seriously enough to suit them.

Well, that much was about to change. I was lord of this manor now, and I already had my first task in mind. Boy, was she going to be furious when she found out what it was—even if it didn't involve her stupid tea garden.

After they took away all the pieces of my armor and drew up a bath, I dismissed all the servants from my quarters. There was a spread of food set out for me, since I was way too late for dinner, but I wasn't hungry. Instead, I poured myself a tall glass of the strongest liquor I could find in my wine cabinet and went to sit in the bath. I sat, sipping in silence and going over plans in my head, until the water had grown cold. Then I got to work.

I sat hunched over the writing desk in my private parlor, scribbling on sheets of paper until dawn broke. My nightshirt and hands were dotted with ink and there was a stack of completed order forms spread out all around me. It was finished. Or at least, it was ready to begin.

The chimes outside my private quarters sounded, warning me that servants were coming in. They brought in breakfast on shining silver platters, clearing away the meal left from the night before. The housekeeper, Miss Harriet, was the only one bold enough to ask about it, though. She'd been in charge of running the household for as long as I could remember. She was a plump, elderly woman with a blunt way about her, which I'd always liked. She took her job seriously, too. She managed all the other servants and made sure everything ran smoothly, just the way my parents wanted.

Only now, things were going to be done the way *I* wanted, for a change.

"It's not like you to turn down a meal, Master Felix," she pointed out as she poured a cup of tea and sat it down on the desk before me. "Was it not to your liking?"

"I'm sure it was fine. I'm just not in the mood."

I could hear disapproval in her tone. "Not in the mood for poached eggs and bacon over toast? That's not the man I know."

I shrugged as I stacked up all my papers. "Is the groundskeeper in to see me?"

She nodded. "Aye. Waiting in your study. I told him you'd be in shortly, once you'd had breakfast."

"Tell him I'm coming now," I commanded as I stood up and went to get dressed.

"Master Felix?" She called after me. "May I ask what's going on? Are you all right?"

"Fine," I answered curtly. "Planning a funeral just doesn't leave me with much of an appetite."

I guess she got the message—I was not in the mood to be interrogated by the hired help. She left me alone with a few other servants who helped me dress. It was stupid. I knew how to put on my own clothes. But I figured this was one of those "duke-ish" things my mom had always nagged about. When I was ready, I took my papers and headed for my study.

The groundskeeper was waiting, wringing his cap and looking uneasy as I entered. He bowed low and eyed the papers in my hands like he was afraid to know what I was up to.

"Have a seat." I gestured to the chair across from the broad, mahogany desk that stood in the middle of the room. "We have a lot to discuss."

"Sir?" he asked with a tremor of anxiety. "Can I ask what this is about?"

I sat the stack of papers down in front of him. "Absolutely. There's going to be a funeral held here in a month. I'm commissioning a headstone be made and I want everything to be perfect, down to the last detail."

He looked confused. "A funeral, sir?"

"Yes," I clarified. "For a friend of mine. A dragonrider named Jaevid Broadfeather."

Big surprise, mom was furious. Well, furious was putting it mildly. She wasn't exactly enamored with the idea of having someone who wasn't family buried on our estate grounds in the first place. And when she found out he was a halfbreed? I'd never seen her face turn that shade of red before. She started gripping her dinner fork like she might use it as a weapon.

"Is it your intention to scandalize what's left of our good reputation?" she hissed. "To bring this family and all its proud history to the very brink of social disaster?"

I swirled my fifth glass of wine and admired how the liquid shone like liquid rubies in the light. "It's my intention to make sure a close friend of mine receives the honorable burial he deserves. Why is that so hard for you to grasp?"

"They tell me he was out of Mithangol, the product of a scandalous affair," she continued in a hushed voice, like she was afraid someone might overhear.

"His parentage doesn't matter to me."

She balked and made a frantic choking sound. "You don't even have his body! What are you planning on putting in the coffin?"

"Does it really matter?" I polished off my glass with one long swig and sat it back on the dinner table. "This is happening whether you approve or not. So put on a few more gaudy necklaces and get over it."

My mom sat up stiffly, pressing her lips together like she'd bitten into something sour. Her eyes flashed with wrath and I could tell she was choosing her next words carefully. This was going to be a well-aimed threat.

"Your father would be ashamed," she said at last.

I rolled my eyes. Like I hadn't heard that line before.

Getting up from my seat, I pressed my palms down against the table and looked her squarely in the eye. "Yep. I'm sure he would. But he's dead and I'm in charge, so things are going to be done my way. Am I clear? You are no longer in a position to be giving me orders."

Her mouth fell open. I could read the silent horror on her face as she gaped up at me.

I should have stopped there. I'd won. She had no more leverage over me; that should have been the end of it. But I couldn't stop myself. Words just started boiling out of me—words I'd never dared to say before. "Who are you to tell me what's best for this family? Who are you to tell me anything at all? You don't know me. I might as well be a stranger for all the time we've spent together. The only times you ever seemed aware I was alive was when I did something to piss you off. But you see me now, don't you? I am Felix Farrow, Duke and lord of this estate, just like you always wanted."

I didn't know what was happening to me. I'd coexisted with my mother for years, and I'd never spoken to her like that before. I'd been a lot of things—rebellious, defiant, sarcastic, and even rude at times. But I'd never been … cruel.

My hands shook and I felt flushed as I stormed out of the dining room. What I felt was as confusing as it was overwhelming. Rage, guilt, shame, fear—all of it rushed over me like a boiling tidal wave. All I wanted was to get away from everyone and everything.

What was I thinking? Was I totally losing my mind? Prax had been right all along. Of course coming back here was an awful idea. The only time I ever felt free or at all like myself was when I was in a dragon saddle. Being here was like being in a prison- trapped with all my memories of a miserable childhood spent alone- and shoved onto a pedestal I'd never wanted in the first place.

But where else could I go? Staying at Northwatch hadn't felt much different. There, I was haunted by a different set of memories. There was nowhere for me to go and no one I could turn to. I was alone, spiraling into a hell I didn't know how to escape from.

I was out of breath when I made it back to my chambers. A few servants were there, cleaning and preparing the bath and my bed for tonight. I yelled at them to get out, and they quickly obeyed.

Save for one.

Miss Harriet hesitated when she passed me.

I buried my face in my hands so I didn't have to see the look on her face. I knew she was worried. I'd never raised my voice to the staff before.

"This came for you this afternoon, Master Felix," she said softly, taking a letter out of her apron and handing it to me discreetly. "I took care to make sure no one else saw it."

I glanced down at an envelope made of crisp, gold parchment. There was no address. No name. But I recognized the seal stamped onto the back right away. Just the sight of it made my raging thoughts go quiet for a moment. It was like a break in the storm.

"It's been quite some time, hasn't it? Since she last wrote to you?" Miss Harriet kept her voice hushed.

It had. We didn't speak like this anymore. That was a rule of my own making, and one I swore never to break.

I wondered what had possessed her to write to me after all this time.

I tossed the letter onto the writing desk in my private parlor and immediately forgot about it. It's not like I was going to answer it. Nothing written in there was anything I wanted joining the rat's nest of thoughts tangled up in my brain. I poured another glass of strong liquor and went out onto the balcony. My room overlooked the sea, so the wind that blew in always smelled richly of salt. Once, I'd found that comforting. Now it just made my chest ache to be somewhere—anywhere—else.

"Master Felix?" Harriet's voice startled me. I'd forgotten she was even there. When I turned around, I was even more surprised to find her standing right behind me, anxiously wringing her hands in her apron.

"Yes?"

She cleared her throat. "I know you're having a difficult time right now. I just wanted to tell you something, something my grandmother used to tell me when I was a girl."

I kept quiet while she seemed to gather her courage.

"She used to tell me that souls were funny things. We think we own them, but they aren't altogether ours. Everyone we love gets a tiny piece of our soul and we get a bit of theirs, too. Those bits stay with us even after we part ways or pass on. So in that way, we get the smallest taste of eternity," she explained. "Through those tiny pieces of our soul, we are all immortal. If that's true, and I believe it is, then no one who dies is ever really gone. We carry them with us always."

CHAPTER FOUR

I broke through the doors of my private chambers with servants hovering all around me like gulls following a fishing boat. Some were arranging my clothes and doing last minute tweaks to my hair. Another was waving a few sheets of paper in my face, which I gathered were the notes for my speech. About five seconds before I completely lost my cool, Miss Harriet appeared and chased them all away.

"Are you ready?" she asked, as she folded the notes up and tucked them into my breast pocket.

I didn't have an answer for that. Not a good one, anyway. So I just took a breath and nodded.

"Everyone's come. Even the king himself just arrived. His masked guards are making the staff terribly nervous. They insisted on checking the perimeter of the house themselves." She sounded concerned. "The last time I saw such attendance to a funeral was when the king's dear family passed. It's unbelievable."

"And my mom?" I already knew the answer to that question. I just wanted to hear it validated out loud.

Miss Harriet cast me a sympathetic glance. "She refuses to leave her bedroom."

"Good," I snapped. "I don't want her ruining this for me."

She didn't respond to that. Instead, she followed behind me quietly as I descended to the grand foyer that led out to the back portion of the manor. That was where I'd arranged for the reception to be held, so everything was decorated with white lilies—a flower associated with grief in Maldobar. A month of preparing for an event of this magnitude had stretched everyone thin. I'd been colder to and harder on the staff than any noble at Farrow Estate ever was. But I was determined that no one was going to screw this up.

The headstone I'd commissioned had cost a small fortune all on its own. It was made of solid jade, stood over eight feet, and was carved into the shape of a knight standing at the feet of his dragon, with his hand across his breastplate in formal salute. My mom had been horrified to see it being placed in such close proximity to her favorite tea garden, but I wasn't about to move it.

Today, it would be adorned in wreaths of lilies and olive branches. So would the coffin, which I commissioned to be every bit as fine and ornate as the one I would be buried in someday. Of course, I didn't have a body to put in it. I'd settled with burying what I had of his belongings and letters, along with a rolled-up scroll of parchment sealed with my family's crest. That was what had really set my mom off. She'd lost it when she got wind of what was written on that scroll. She immediately locked herself in her room and refused to come out again.

Not that I cared. If she wanted to act a fool in front of everyone, so be it. I wasn't going to coddle her.

At last, I stood before the closed double doors that led out into the garden. Beyond them, I could hear the murmur of the crowd that had gathered. They were here to pay their respects, to watch me make my speech, and then join me in lowering the coffin into the ground. My heart was pounding frantically. I felt flushed and panicked. I locked up, paralyzed with fear.

A hand touched my shoulder. Beside me, Miss Harriet smiled gently. "It's going to be all right."

I desperately wanted to believe that. Regardless, I had to pull myself together. I had to get this done. I owed Jaevid that much. Brushing off her hand, I opened the doors and entered the garden.

It was a bleak day. The dark sky seemed threaten rain at any moment. The wind blowing in off the sea was colder than usual, so most everyone was wearing a cloak and the ladies hadn't removed their gloves or scarves.

The crowd was gathered around the headstone. As I approached, I noticed that a few new items had appeared in the coffin. It looked like mostly letters, flowers, and a few ladies' handkerchiefs. I recognized a few faces—fellow dragonriders from Northwatch, peers and instructors from our days training at Blybrig Academy, Jaevid's older brother Roland, and some of my extended relatives who had probably just turned up to see what kind of spectacle this was going to end up being.

I spotted Sile and his wife standing close together, but Beckah wasn't with them. Sile's face looked ashen and haunted. There were dark circles under his eyes, like he hadn't slept in weeks. When he met my gaze it put a hard knot in my gut, like someone had punched me square in the stomach.

Everyone else was staring at me, too. I could feel their eyes on me, intensifying my anxiety. But I couldn't bring myself to look back at any of them as I stood in front of the headstone and fumbled my speech notes out of my pocket. I almost dropped them because my hands were shaking. When I tried reading them, my eyes crossed. I couldn't focus.

A gust of wind caught them suddenly, sending all the pieces of paper scattering across the courtyard. I didn't even try to catch them. They hadn't been doing me much good, anyway.

Instead, I just started to talk.

"When someone you care about dies, the first thing you think about is all the stuff you should've done or said when you had the chance. You wonder if it would have made any difference. There was a lot I should have told Jaevid. And even though people keep telling me his death wasn't my fault, I'll always feel like there was something I could have done. That I let him down." My voice caught and I let my gaze fall to the empty, open coffin in front of me.

I took a deep breath. "I have parents. I have aunts, uncles, and cousins. But Jaevid was the closest thing to family I've ever had. And it's strange, because I always kinda thought I was the one letting him use me as a surrogate big brother, to keep him from getting beaten to a pulp. As it turns out ... I guess I was the one who was using him. He accepted me regardless of what I had, who I was, or what my social rank or wealth could have done for him. I don't have to tell most of you what that kind of friendship means to someone who always has to take every relationship with the expectation that anyone trying to be close just wants something from me. But Jaevid never asked me for anything. And the only thing he ever expected was that I'd show him the same loyalty he showed me."

It was getting harder and harder to talk. My throat was growing thick. My vision was becoming blurry and I couldn't stop my eyes from watering. I took a second or two to clench my teeth, swallow, and collect myself. Then I stepped forward and took the scroll out of the coffin. I raised it for the rest of the crowd to see.

"That's why by my order as Duke of Farrow Estate, High Noble under the Crown of Maldobar and successor to the royal line, I hereby decree that Jaevid Broadfeather is my adopted brother. He shall henceforth be known as a member of my family, protected and marked by all the power that such a rank entitles him. May you all bear witness."

There was a collective gasp—mostly from my relatives.

I placed the scroll back in the coffin and closed it. I stood back with the others and watched as the king's own guards stepped in to lower it into the ground. Then I turned to Miss Harriet. "See that the burial is completed according to my instructions."

She nodded worriedly. "Aren't you staying for the reception?"

"No."

I couldn't bear being there for one more second. As I turned and made a break for the doors, I heard the sky open up. Thunder bellowed deeply and the pouring rain made a hissing sound over the cobblestone pathways. It chased everyone else out of the courtyard right behind me.

Well—all except for one.

I caught a glimpse of a man still standing over the deep burial plot while the elite royal guards stacked white alabaster stones over it. Through the rain and people clambering to get inside, I couldn't identify who it was at first. Then he looked at me.

Sile looked at me square in the eye with a look of terror, like the world was going to come to an end.

I sat behind my desk, my drenched clothes dripping rainwater onto my office floor. I'd bypassed the reception. I didn't care to talk to anyone down there right now. Rage and shame boiled up in me until I couldn't take it any more. I picked up a glass paperweight off my desk and hurled it at the wall. It shattered into a million pieces onto the floor.

Miss Harriet immediately rushed inside. "Master Felix? What happened?"

I was doubled over my desk with my face buried in my hands. "Nothing! Get out!"

"But Master—" she tried to continue.

"I said GET OUT!" I roared and swung my arm across my whole desk, clearing everything off it onto the floor with one sweep.

She shied back against the door as though she were afraid of me. "S-sir. The King of Maldobar is right outside. He's asked for a private audience. You cannot refuse him."

It took a few moments for me to understand what she'd said. I had to close my eyes and breathe. When I felt like I could think clearly again, I answered, "Fine. Let him in. But I don't want to speak to anyone else. Am I clear?"

Miss Harriet curtsied. "Yes, Master Felix."

She hurried out the door and I could hear some commotion in the hallway outside. Voices murmured quietly until at last the door to my office opened again. This time four of the king's elite guards entered, all dressed in sleek, black leather armor, save for the white, expressionless masks over their faces. Two remained by the doorway while the other two stood behind me. I didn't like having them out of eyesight. Something about them looming right at my back felt like a subtle threat.

The King of Maldobar stepped into my office. I'd seen him before, and he didn't look any different now than he had then—a small-framed, downright pitiful looking old man. His dark crimson robes hung off his bones like wet laundry on a drying rack. He was bent at the back and walked with a gimp to his step. As always, a fur-lined hood was pulled over his head and his face was covered with a gilded mask. I could just barely see his eyes peering out at me as he shuffled over to sit down in the chair across from my desk.

I should have stood, saluted him, or showed him some gesture of respect. But if he'd already spoken with Miss Harriet, then he must have known I was in no mood for this. I was only entertaining him because I couldn't send him away. He outranked me.

That was the only thing that kept my butt in my chair, watching him take his sweet time examining every inch of the room. He glanced down at all the stuff I'd raked onto the floor in my fit of rage, at the decent-sized dent I'd put in the wall, and at all the shattered glass on the floor. Then he let out a deep sigh.

"I know what you must be feeling." His thin voice rasped. "Rage. Regret. Pain. I could feel it all in your words. It reminded me of that day."

I sat back in my chair and waited for him to explain.

"The day my family was murdered before my eyes," he added. Then he stared straight at me with those eerie bloodshot eyes peeking through the holes in his mask. "I know there are those who have begun to question my motives. They wonder if I have lost myself to my need for vengeance. I'm curious to hear what you think. So tell me, Duke Farrow. What do you think of your king?"

"I haven't much, to be honest. As a dragonrider, you were my supreme commanding officer. As a duke, the situation isn't much different. In either case, thinking is generally not in my job description."

The sound of his laughter made me downright uncomfortable. It was a hacking, dry sound. "Well, I see you haven't lost your frankness. My sources tell me you're quite the big-talker. Apparently you were able to make yourself something of a ring-leader amongst your dragonrider peers, regardless of your social rank. They respect you. Some of them might even be more loyal to you than to me."

"Is that so? Checking up on me then?"

I could hear a smile in his voice, even if I couldn't see it past that creepy mask. "You could say that. And I was very surprised to hear that you were so closely associated with a halfbreed."

"You wouldn't be the first." I was beginning to wonder when he would get to the point. He'd obviously come here for a reason. He never tried to make small talk with me like this before. As far as I knew, he seldom said much to anyone at all. So there had to be a motive for him to be singling me out.

"I despise rumors. They're so inconsistent. As king, I want to be sure I always hear the truth." He straightened in his seat, leaning forward with his gloved hands clasped and resting on the edge of my desk. "My sources told me something else—something I wanted to come and hear validated in person."

I frowned. "And what is that?"

"This halfbreed dragonrider, Lieutenant Jaevid Broadfeather, is it true that you witnessed him heal people with some sort of magic?"

I hesitated. This was obviously the question he'd come here to ask. I didn't see how it mattered now, though. Jae was dead. What difference did it make what he had done before?

"Yes," I answered.

"And what else do you know of him? His parentage? Did he ever mention anything about his mother? Her name, perhaps?" The king's voice took on a much more serious tone. It was unsettling. This was beginning to feel a lot like an interrogation.

I didn't like it one bit.

"You think he was a traitor? Or a spy?" I countered. "Is there some lowlife out there slandering my brother?"

He didn't reply.

"Because if that's the case I can assure you that Jaevid was never anything but dedicated to our cause. He gave his life for it. And I won't stand for anyone coming into my home and defaming his name." I stood up suddenly. Behind me, I could hear the elite guards move like they might try to restrain me.

The king sighed heavily.

I'd overstepped my boundaries. I knew it. He undoubtedly knew it, too. So now the question was: how would he respond? Duke or not, I'd just mouthed off to the King of Maldobar. People had been killed for lesser crimes against the crown. But honestly, he could have sent me straight to the hangman's noose and I wouldn't have cared.

"I suppose it was insensitive of me to ask such a thing on this particular day," he said calmly, as he stood up as well. From across my desk, he offered one of his gloved hands to shake. "Perhaps we can discuss it further some other time. I wish you well, Duke Farrow."

I could feel the bones of his hand through the satin glove he wore. More importantly, however, I could feel a surprising amount of strength in his grip. It made me wonder if maybe he wasn't as feeble as he wanted everyone to believe.

CHAPTER FIVE

Things started to become hazy after the funeral was over. Well, I suppose you could say that they took a quick downhill slide. That's a little more accurate. I was losing myself, but I didn't have the energy or the desire to do anything about it. I could see him in my reflection, a ghost of what was staring back at me. But beyond that, I couldn't see much in myself that was still worth saving.

The days were muddied, each passing without any marked significance. At first, I avoided leaving my family's manor at all costs. I hated the way the citizens living in Solhelm looked at me. They stared like they suspected I was going mad —as though any sudden move from me might send them all scattering like rabbits.

Then, I couldn't even bring myself to go outside at all anymore. Every time I did, I inevitably found myself standing before Jae's gravesite, staring up at the headstone. I never knew how long I'd stood there, waiting for some miracle to happen, before Miss Harriet or another one of the servants would eventually come out and ask me if I was all right.

It was a stupid question.

I quit leaving my own quarters altogether. I kept all the drapes drawn to block out the sun during the day. But at night, I would sit out on the balcony sipping the strongest liquor I could find until I fell asleep or the sun began to rise —whichever came first.

Sleeping became its own version of torture. Whenever I tried, my dreams were invaded by visions of battlefields and the mutilated bodies of my comrades. And then there was Jae. A dream of him haunted me just about every night.

Usually, it involved me finding him, wounded and dying, amidst the broken bodies of our dragonrider brothers. I'd reach out to help him, to try to take him away from there, but I was never able to reach him in time. I could only watch while his eyes grew distant and cold, his spirit slipping away right in front of me.

"Perhaps you'd rest easier in your own bed again, Master Felix?" Miss Harriet suggested, as she took away yet another platter of uneaten dinner from the night before.

I was propped up on the sofa in my private parlor, watching the flames crackle in the hearth. "No. I don't like being in there anymore."

She didn't push the issue. She'd already made that mistake a few times now. There were a few more dings in my walls to show for it. I'd yet to actually hit her or anyone else, but I'd come close enough times to get my point across.

"What is that smell?" She wrinkled up her nose as she walked past, pausing and glancing at me.

I shot her a scalding glare. We both knew what it was. I stank. I hadn't bathed or changed out of my bedclothes in a week or longer.

"Your mother has asked about having dinner with you," she rambled on. "I think she misses you."

"If you're going to lie, do a better job." I grumbled and pulled my wool blanket up around my head. I stretched out on my side facing the back of the sofa, so I didn't have to see any more of the pitying looks she kept giving me.

"Sir, how much longer are you going to torture yourself this way? Is this what your friend would have wanted? For you to waste away to nothing in this room?"

I clenched my teeth.

"Come now, at least eat something," she pleaded.

I was about to shout at her again. I wasn't in the mood for any more of this insistent, pointless nagging.

Then I heard my chamber doors open. Another servant called to us from the doorway. "A Lieutenant Darion Prax has arrived. He requests an audience."

I sat up immediately.

Prax was here?

"What does he want?" I demanded.

The servant girl shook her head nervously. "H-he didn't say, sir. He only asked to speak with you."

"Where is he?"

"Downstairs. Waiting in the front foyer," she answered shakily. She kept looking at Miss Harriet, as though she hoped the head housekeeper would save her in the event I lost my cool again.

I threw off the blanket and stood up. It made both of them jump. "Tell him I'll be down in a minute."

Miss Harriet was obviously stunned. She followed me into my bedroom while I pulled on a housecoat. I didn't bother with anything else.

Leaving the familiar dreariness of my room behind, I squinted into the sunlight pouring through the windows of the manor. It was early morning, so everything looked bright and pleasant outside my chamber doors.

I found Prax lounging on a sofa in the downstairs study, dressed from head-to-toe in his dragonrider's battle armor. Apparently, he'd asked for somewhere private that we could talk. The servants had brought in trays of breakfast with tea, coffee, and sweet-smelling pastries. Prax was helping himself. Typical. I'd never seen him pass up a meal.

He stood and gave a formal salute when I entered, which really caught me off guard. It made me feel awkward. Then I remembered that not only was I no longer a dragonrider—I was a high noble. Social custom required him to salute me.

"Knock that off, please." I waved a hand dismissively and went to sit down in a chair across from him.

Tension rose in the air as I watched him study me from head to toe, soaking in every detail. I knew I probably looked like death warmed-over. I definitely smelled like it. So I was just waiting for another one of those infuriating, pitying looks like all the servants and staff gave me.

I didn't get that from him, though. More like the opposite. As Prax looked me over, his eyes grew colder and colder. His brow hardened and he frowned disapprovingly, like he was repulsed by what he saw.

"Are you sick?" he asked.

"No."

"Dying?"

I frowned back at him. "What kind of a question is that?"

"Well I was going to give you the benefit of the doubt, rather than just assuming you're lying around this place, moping in your own filth by choice."

I smirked darkly. "Sorry to disappoint you yet again."

He gave an annoyed sigh and started pouring himself a cup of coffee. My eyes were instinctively drawn to his riding gauntlets and helmet sitting on the table. Just the sight of them brought back memories, stirring a part of me that had been lying dormant. It was like gravity, a pull on my soul I couldn't control.

I missed being in the saddle.

"I didn't come here to squabble over your lifestyle choices," he said sharply, after taking a long swig of coffee. "I came to invite you to come back."

His words hit me like a swift kick to the gut. "Come back?"

Prax nodded. "Mind you, I didn't come here to beg for it. Consider it a modest, hopeful invitation from your former brother-at-arms."

"But ... why? Why now?" I was confused.

He drained his coffee cup and took his time refilling it again before he answered, "Because something is coming. Orders have just come down from the throne—orders that are going to change the face of this world. And the rest of

Emerald Flight and I want you with us. We'd all feel a lot better with you watching our wing."

I could tell he was being intentionally cryptic. He was trying to make me curious. It was annoying—but also effective. Now I was interested. "What are you talking about? What's coming?"

Prax carefully put his cup down on the table between us. "The end."

The force of those words made my insides wrench up painfully. I wasn't even sure what he meant, exactly. But it terrified me.

"The king has ordered a final strike. All the remaining forces of Maldobar are mustering, moving towards the northern border. He means to burn every last trace of the Gray elves from the earth, down to the last infant," he explained. "This will end the war, once and for all. His vengeance will be complete."

Horror choked the breath out of my lungs. "That's insanity," I managed to rasp.

Prax gave a small shrug. "Call it what you will. We are all tired, Felix. Tired of fighting. Tired of blood and flames. We're ready for this to be over, and if this will finally appease the king's wrath, then so be it."

"You can't be serious!" I stood up and shook a fist at him. "It's madness! He's completely lost his mind; surely you can see that? What right do we have to wipe out an entire race of people? What about their women? Their children? Their elderly? You'd burn them to ash, too?"

Prax looked up at me as though he were on the brink of losing his temper. His eyes were smoldering and his teeth were clenched. "I follow orders, just as you once did. I didn't choose my king. But I swore to obey his commands—even the ones I despise. This is war."

"No, this is genocide," I shouted back at him. "The people you'd be butchering are innocent civilians. You should have known better than to come here and ask me to take part in that. I won't. I refuse."

"Then what will you do?" Prax shouted back. He snapped up out of his seat with his eyes ablaze with anger. If not for the coffee table between us, it might have come to blows. "Keep cowering in your castle like a frightened child? You think hiding here, doing nothing, makes you any less guilty than the ones who will burn those elven cities to the ground? No. Your soul will be marked with the same blame as if you'd murdered them all yourself, because you sat here on your rear and did nothing."

I froze. "What are you saying? You're not going to join the fight?"

Prax's expression became ominous. "I said I would fight. But I never said whose side I'd be fighting for."

"Then why make it sound like—"

He cut me off, "I had to be sure you that you'd agree; this is indeed madness. It's not war. It's murder. But I don't have to tell you what could happen to someone plotting conspiracy against a king willing to commit an act like this. So will you help us? Things are progressing quickly and there isn't much time. Our hope is to give the elves some measure of warning. Perhaps buy them some time so they can at least evacuate their women and children before the hammer falls."

I was seething. I didn't like being toyed with like some bratty kid. "You don't need my help."

"But we'd like to have it, regardless," he insisted.

I shook my head. "No, Prax. I'm done. I've already spelled this out for you. Do I have to do it again?"

Prax scowled darkly. "Then you're right."

"Right about what?"

"You have disappointed me." He bent down and picked up his gauntlets and helmet. He wouldn't even look me in the eye as he saluted me again, probably just to piss me off, and started to leave the parlor.

He'd almost made it to the door when it suddenly burst open in front of him. I heard my mom's voice calling my name from outside. I could tell by her tone that she was already worked up—upset or angry about something that was more than likely my fault.

The very second she flung the parlor door open and saw Prax standing on the other side of it, neither of them moved an inch. They stood stock-still, like they were frozen in time, staring at one another with the strangest expressions on their faces. Mom started to get pale. Her eyes widened and she seemed to shrink, drawing back as though in fear.

She knew him.

And judging by Prax's strained, almost wounded expression, he knew her, too.

"Hello again, Maria," he said quietly. He gave her the same formal salute he'd given to me, clasping a fist across his chest and bowing slightly.

My mom didn't reciprocate. She didn't even speak. Her face was pasty and her mouth hung open as though she might scream at any moment.

When he stood up straight again, he shot me one last meaningful glance. "I suppose I understand now, although I'm not sure I can ever forgive you for denying me that right to which I was undoubtedly entitled. You robbed me. You robbed both of us."

Was he talking to me? I thought so. He was looking right at me, after all. But what he said didn't make any sense. Not right then, anyways.

SEEING PRAX DIDN'T PUT MY MOM IN A VERY SHARING MOOD, NOT THAT either of us had ever been very good at communicating our feelings to one another. But there was definitely something wrong with her now. Something had brought emotions to the surface of her usually apathetic face I'd never witnessed before. I'd seen her get angry—usually with me—plenty of times.

But she was absolutely hysterical now.

I followed her out of the parlor as she practically ran back to her wing of the manor, shoving servants out of her way as she went. I finally caught up to her right before her chamber doors. By then, she was gasping back frantic sobs.

"Mom! Stop! What the heck is going on?" I demanded. "How do you know him?"

"Leave me alone! Just go away," she screamed, and tried to slam the door.

I stuck my foot in the way to stop her. "Not until you tell me what's going on."

Mom glared at me through her tears. Makeup was running all down her face and she kept trying desperately to shut the door. "Get away from me!"

"What was he talking about?" I started pushing the door open further and further, muscling my way into the room. "I'm serious, Mom. What did you take from him?"

Until that moment, I assumed it was literal robbery. Maybe she'd actually stolen something from him. Or maybe she'd been party to some kind of embezzlement that had left him out to dry. I wasn't considering anything like ...

Then it hit me.

All the teasing from my peers at the citadel, the weird looks Prax had given me sometimes when he thought I wasn't paying attention, and the uncomfortable knot that formed in my gut every time he gave me that disapproving glare. Man, I really hated it when he did that.

I felt like a total idiot.

Stepping into her private chambers, I shut the door behind us and locked it to keep anyone else from interrupting. "It's true, isn't it? What everyone's been saying about him. They weren't just teasing me."

Mom was sobbing frenziedly. She backed away from me with her hands raised like she thought I was going to attack her. "F-Felix! Please!"

"Just answer the question," I ordered. "Is Prax my father?"

She stood before me with her lips trembling, streaks of mascara running down her cheeks, looking more small and fragile than I'd ever seen her before. She didn't have to answer out loud. I could read the truth in her eyes. But that wasn't enough, not for me. I wanted to hear the truth finally leave her lying, deceitful lips.

"Say it!" I roared.

She cringed away. "Yes!"

I didn't expect hearing it to hurt so much, but it did. It hurt like hell. It made my eyes water like I'd been smacked upside the head.

"Darion Prax is your father."

All the wind was sucked out me. I took an unsteady step backwards and leaned against the door. It was too much to process. I wasn't sure how I felt, or even what I should be feeling to begin with. Was I supposed to be happy? Relieved? Angry? Sad?

All I knew was that my father—my *real* father—wasn't a duke. He was a dragonrider. He wasn't anyone famous. He certainly wasn't a noble. He was just a commoner. He didn't even have a profession outside of being a dragonrider, as far as I knew. Come to think of it, I knew next to nothing about him.

And myself?

I was a bastard child. My entire claim to the birthright of being Duke Farrow was a total fraud. All of a sudden, I was an imposter in my own home.

6

CHAPTER SIX

I wish I could say we shared a mother-son moment of reconciliation, hugged it out, and moved on with our lives having learned from our rocky past. But we'd never been a hugging family. And after that, nothing was the same.

I didn't know whom I could trust, or who knew the truth about me. And my mom ... well, if we'd had a bad relationship before, now we were like two feral wolves trapped in the same house.

She refused to see me and wouldn't even leave her private chambers. She shut me out completely and no matter what I did, I couldn't get her to look me in the eyes, let alone tell me what the heck had happened between her and Prax. I tried reasoning with her. I tried shouting. I tried begging. Nothing worked. I might as well have been a piece of lint on the carpet in her eyes. She'd never made me feel so insignificant.

And it was really starting to piss me off.

Finally, something inside me snapped. It was only a matter of time, I suppose. You could say I'm not the kind of guy who handles loss well. And now I'd lost everything—right down to my own identity.

I threw mom out. Well, not literally; I didn't actually touch her. But I invited her to leave without the option of saying no. If she wasn't going to see me and come clean about her relationship with Prax, then she wasn't welcome in my world anymore. So I sent her packing and didn't bother telling her goodbye. I didn't know where she went. I didn't care. She was good at deception and manipulation, obviously. She'd survive. Otherwise, I wouldn't have ended up the duke of an estate I had no legitimate claim to.

The staff, including Miss Harriet, were understandably distressed. They walked on eggshells around me, which was exactly what I wanted. It made them obedient and cautious. And I had an agenda now, so there was plenty to be done.

My days of moping in my room were over. I shook off the chains of guilt and grief. Was Jaevid's death my fault? Yes, definitely. But was there anything I could do about it now? Nope. So I had to do whatever it took to make those feelings go away, to forget about him and everything that was happening around me. I was going to bury myself so deeply in all the rot and ruin nobles loved wallowing in, that no one would be able to find me.

I would be beyond saving. I'd be every ounce the whopping disappointment all my parental figures took me for.

I did what I'd always done best. I threw parties. At first it was just one every weekend with a few local nobles from the surrounding area. Then, it was two a week. Then three. At some point, it was as though no one ever left. People were coming from all over the kingdom—people I didn't even know. The party never stopped and I always had more than enough guests willing to revel in whatever riches I decided to toss around that day.

The kitchens worked overtime to turn out course after course of extravagant morsels for my guests. Wine and ale flowed like ocean currents. I spared nothing on unceasing music, entertainment and extravagance. Naturally, it didn't take long for things to start getting sloppy. With hundreds of people filing through my family's estate daily, the staff couldn't keep up with the mess.

But my already intoxicated guests didn't seem to mind the smashed wine bottles and goblets on the floor, or vomit in the hallways.

So neither did I.

"You should have quit being a dragonrider a long time ago." A girl I didn't recognize was leaning against my shoulder. She'd been there a while, and she'd had so much wine she couldn't even keep both eyes open at the same time. "You're a lot more fun now."

"I'm just getting started, sweetie." I smirked and looked across the ballroom from where we were sitting on a long silk sofa—one of the ones my mother had picked out. She'd always had an expensive appetite whenever it came to spending other people's money.

It was early in the morning, barely dawn, and the guests were beginning to tire. The dancing had stopped, although the musicians were still sawing away at some jolly waltz. Some of the men were crowded around a pair of infantrymen who were attempting to brawl. They were so drunk that neither of them could get a good punch in, though it was hilarious to watch them try. Some of the guests had even passed out on the floor. Others were draped over various pieces of furniture taken in from the adjoining rooms. I wasn't interested in napping in the filth either, so I had my servants drag a sofa in from a parlor.

"What's next, hm?" The girl started playing with my ear.

I glanced sideways at her, sizing her up. Judging by her tacky dress, she was the daughter of some low-ranking noble who had come here fishing, hoping to snag herself a husband. She was young, a lot younger than I was, maybe sixteen at the most. Pretty, I guess. It was hard to tell with her makeup smeared all down her face. And she was drunk out of her mind.

"Want to go upstairs?" I suggested.

She licked her lips and nodded.

I stood up, surprised to find myself a little woozier than I'd anticipated, and dragged her up with me. She nearly fainted right then, but erupted into slurred laughter instead. She couldn't put one foot in front of the other, so I basically had to carry her out of the room.

Out in the hallway, the girl slumped against me suddenly. I had to catch her to keep her from collapsing into a heap on the marble floor. She was passed out cold.

It wasn't surprising, really. I'd watched her drink more than anyone her size should have been able to handle in one sitting. Young girls like her always thought they had to put on a show, doing anything they could to get me to notice them and hopefully score the spot right next to me as my duchess. Watching them get so drunk they couldn't keep their drool in was supposed to impress me somehow. It was entertaining, I'd grant them that.

That is, until they passed out or threw up everywhere.

I was looking for a convenient place to put her down so she could sleep it off and sober up, when a familiar voice stopped me dead in my tracks.

"Felix Farrow."

I stiffened. Turning around slowly, I narrowed my eyes at the last person in the world I wanted to see here.

She was standing in the front doorway to my estate, just down the hall. The doorman who had let her in knew he'd screwed up. He stared at the floor, the ceiling, and anything to avoid the blazing wrath of my glare. I'd deal with him later. Every member of the staff knew how I felt about *her*.

"Get out," I snarled.

She didn't obey. Instead, she took a step inside and brushed back the hood of her long, gray traveling cloak. Crap. She was even prettier than the last time I saw her. Why did that piss me off so much? It wasn't fair.

She was quiet while her eyes traced around the room at all the damage and garbage lying everywhere. When she looked back at me, it was like she didn't even see the girl I was holding in my arms. She only saw me—just like always.

"She told me it was bad," she spoke quietly. "But I didn't realize it was this bad. I would have come sooner."

"Who?" I demanded. "Who told you?"

"Your mother."

My temper caught fire with explosive force, blazing right through the haze of every drink I'd had that night. "You're not welcome here! I want you out! NOW!"

"That isn't your decision to make." She began taking off her cloak and handing it to the doorman, smiling at him graciously as though this was completely normal.

"Not my decision? Are you insane? This is my house! I'm duke!"

She glanced at me again. Her light brown eyes shimmered like amber glass in the dim glow of morning light. She had her ginger-colored hair wound into a long, intricate braid over one shoulder. Her skin caught the light like porcelain. It just wasn't fair at all.

"And I'm your fiancée. Unbeknownst to you, your father had it added to his dying will that so long as our engagement remains intact, I have shared ownership of this estate. Your mother was the only one who knew about it, and she kept it to herself in case something just like this were to happen." She calmly took her velvet gloves off one-by-one. "So you're wrong. This is *our* house. And I'm here to tell everyone that the party is over."

She called over one of the servant girls and began giving quick instructions for the staff to stop serving everyone, begin calling around carriages, and dismissing my guests.

"You may start with that young lady there." She pointed to the girl who was still sagging, totally unconscious, in my arms. "It seems the party is long past over for her. See to it that she's taken back to her family's home safely."

"I won't stand for this," I started to yell, but neither she nor any of my staff was listening anymore.

She smiled so graciously at everyone, using her presence like a soothing balm on the staff's nerves while giving them careful instructions about how to begin shutting down my party. I might as well have been invisible. Servants and footmen shuffled by without so much as a glance in my direction.

My blood pressure skyrocketed so high it felt like my eyeballs might pop out of their sockets.

"You're all doing a wonderful job. See to it that the kitchen has plenty of help restocking and cleaning up. It's a lot to manage, I know. But we'll get through this together." She patted the doorman reassuringly and sent him on his way. "And would someone call for Miss Harriet? Please tell her that Julianna Lacroix has arrived."

BY MORNING EVERYONE WAS GONE. EVEN THE HIRED MUSICIANS HAD LEFT AND the house was finally quiet. My servants were still toiling away, cleaning up the mess that had built up over the past several weeks. It was going to take them a while. But the atmosphere was calm—too calm—as though the whole estate was breathing a sigh of relief.

It was driving me mad.

Sitting in my study, I pondered the best way to destroy it while swirling my half-empty glass of wine.

The door opened without any knock of warning. Julianna came in with Miss Harriet right on her heels. Neither one of them looked happy to see me. Big surprise there.

"I suppose I should greet you properly." Julianna eyed the hole in my wall leftover from when I'd thrown the paperweight. "After all, it has been quite a while since we met like this."

I made a point not to look up at her.

"Hello again, Felix."

Those words stung. I licked the front of my teeth behind my lips, savoring all the angry things I wanted to say.

"I've asked Miss Harriet to open the guest room next door for me. I'll be staying here until things are put back in order," she continued, without missing a beat.

"Back in order?" I shouted. "What is that supposed to mean?"

Julianna didn't flinch. I couldn't scare her with my temper—I already knew that. She knew me well enough to be confident I wouldn't actually lay a hand on her. "I understand that you're grieving. I can't imagine how much pain you must be feeling right now. But this is no way to honor Jaevid's memory."

"What do you think you know about Jaevid?" I growled, slamming my wine glass down onto the desktop.

"Not as much as you do, I'm sure. I don't claim to have known him well at all. But I do know how much he meant to you. And I don't believe he would approve of the way you've been handling things."

I cut a threatening glare at Miss Harriet. That was her cue to go. She took the hint right away and left us, closing the door behind her without a word.

"And how is it any of your business?" I growled again, once we were alone. "Since when is any aspect of my life your business?"

She crossed her arms stubbornly. "You're drunk, and judging by the way you reek of soured vomit, I'd guess you've been that way for quite some time. You evicted your own mother and are now wrecking your family home."

"Right," I fired back immediately. "This is my family home. Mine. It has nothing to do with you. I don't know what screwed-up dream world you think you're living in, but just because our parents signed away my right to choose my bride doesn't give you any authority over me or anything I own. You really think you deserve to be my wife? I didn't choose you. I'll never choose you."

Julianna's expression skewed. I saw anger flash in her eyes. She snatched up my wine glass and emptied the contents over my head before I could get out of the way.

"I didn't choose you either, you selfish idiot," she muttered bitterly. "And I can't think of anyone who deserves a fate like being your bride. Such a thing would be the worst kind of torture."

I hadn't expected that. In all our years of knowing one another, I'd never seen her get this upset. Before I could come up with a good retort, she stormed out of the room and slammed the door so hard it actually made me cringe.

I was immediately confused—confused and furious. Hadn't she been the one who insisted on our marriage? Hadn't she begged her parents to make the arrangements?

We'd only been children when they'd announced it, and yet I remembered that day so clearly that it made me sick to my stomach. My parents and hers had sent out a public decree and announced it before a ballroom full of friends and family; she and I were to be wed as soon as I took my official post as duke. Julianna Lacroix would be my wife, whether I liked it or not. I had been completely humiliated and emasculated, which was pretty traumatic for a kid just beginning to come into manhood. My parents had decided without even asking me how I felt about it. I was already fighting tooth and nail to convince them to let me have a dragon of my own. And now they weren't even going to let me choose my own bride.

I guess I never considered that she hadn't wanted it, either. After all, that was usually what other girls wanted whenever they came around me. It wasn't exactly a mystery why. I was the highest-ranking noble in Maldobar. The most eligible bachelor in the kingdom. My family bloodline was shared with princes and kings going back generations. Marrying me would bring power, prestige, wealth, and security—everything a woman wanted.

Every woman except for Julianna, apparently.

I didn't know what game she was playing at, but I didn't want any part of it. I'd spent years driving as big a wedge as I possibly could between the two of us, hoping she would take the hint and get out of my life. According to the contract, she was the only one who could break off the engagement. Those were the terms. And I'd tried everything. I'd sabotaged her social standing amongst the other nobles, disgraced her at parties, and pretended not to know her at all. Nothing worked. She wouldn't call off the marriage.

Was it cruel? Yes. But the fact that she grew up to be beautiful, and smart, and ... unfortunately, one of the nicest people I'd ever known didn't matter. She had betrayed our friendship in the worst way. I'd trusted her more than anyone, even my own parents. Going behind my back to plot this forced marriage to me was not something I could just forgive.

Maybe she'd been able to chain me down as her fiancée, but Julianna wasn't going to win this time. This was my last shot at freedom. She thought she could just swagger in here and run my life?

She was in for a rude awakening.

CHAPTER SEVEN

"Give it to me now!" I yelled at the top of my lungs, flinging a tray of dishes leftover from my uneaten dinner across the room. Plates and cups shattered, raining porcelain splinters all over the carpet.

Miss Harriet had to duck to get out of the way. "Master Felix, the mistress has forbidden it. She had all the alcohol in the estate poured out. Even the wine!"

"Are you deaf or just stupid? How many times do I have to repeat myself? This is not her house. You don't follow her instructions. I am the master of this estate!"

I was so out of breath that I had to catch myself against the back of the sofa. My skin felt clammy and my head was swimming. I could barely put one foot in front of the other. All I wanted was a drink. It had been two days since my last one. Just one strong glass of wine and I knew I'd feel better.

"Sir, I can't—" Miss Harriet started to protest again. I picked up another object, which happened to be a sterling silver water pitcher, and reared back to throw it.

My chamber doors opened.

"That'll be all, Miss Harriet. I'll handle it from here." Julianna came striding in with her sleeves rolled up and an apron tied around her waist, looking as cool and collected as ever. She carried a tray full of supplies.

My housekeeper didn't argue. No doubt she'd been looking for an excuse to leave this whole time. She was the only member of my staff who was still brave enough to try coming in to bring me food. Everyone else was too scared of me, I guess.

As soon as she was gone, Julianna gave me a scolding glare. "You shouldn't be so unkind to her. That woman loves you like her own son."

"Hah!" I tried to steady myself. My hands shook so badly I couldn't grip the pitcher any longer. It clattered noisily to the floor and sent water splashing everywhere. "Come to watch me suffer?"

She frowned. "I came to help, since you've driven away everyone else. You've been drinking too much for too long. You're going through withdrawal sickness."

"I'm acutely aware of that, genius." I glared at both blurry images of her, since I couldn't tell which one was real. My vision wasn't so good and my head was pounding.

"Go lie down." She bent down and started picking up the debris I'd smashed on the floor.

I stood over her and watched for a few minutes. I was trying to understand why she was here to begin with. Because my mother had asked her to come? To fix the damage I'd done to the estate? Neither were good enough reasons, in my opinion. They both sounded made up. She hadn't come clean with me yet.

I grumbled a few more curses under my breath as I shuffled away back to my bedroom. My bed was a mess of wrinkled, sweaty blankets that I'd been tossing and turning in for two nights now. I couldn't get comfortable, no matter how hard I tried. Every part of my body felt sore, like I'd been run over by a horse.

I stretched out on my back and draped an arm over my face, trying to block out the light. Even with the drapes closed and the entire room basically pitch black, my head was still throbbing. Any hint of light made it feel that much worse. My insides felt like they were on fire. My throat burned. My body shook. And one drop of liquor, any kind at all, was all I could think about.

Julianna came in carrying her tray. I immediately sat up in bed. I was geared up for another argument, waiting to see what she was up to this time. But Julianna didn't look at me. She placed the tray on the nightstand and lit a candle.

The light stung my eyes. I cursed at her again.

"Hush," she said softly, as she pulled up a chair and sat down beside my bed. I heard liquid sloshing, but I didn't dare open my eyes to see. The light only made my head hurt worse.

I flinched away as she touched my face with something cold and wet—a rag, I guessed.

"I don't like you," I reminded her.

"I know," she answered, wiping the sweat from my face and finally placing the rag over my forehead. "You need to eat something. I brought some rice pudding. It's very bland, so it shouldn't upset your stomach."

I laughed hoarsely. "I already threw up everything I tried to eat before. It's pointless. Just bring me some wine."

Julianna stayed silent.

I cracked open an eye to steal a glance at her.

The warm candlelight made her already beautiful face shine like a star in the dark. My vision was hazy, especially with the bright light making my head pound, but I could see that she looked tired. Two days of this had to be wearing her down. Two days and two nights of me yelling and cursing at her, throwing things, and vomiting every time I tried to eat. Yet here she was, avoiding eye contact with me as she stirred a bowl of what must be the rice pudding.

"Why are you doing this?" she asked suddenly.

I scowled because I had been wondering the exact same thing at that moment. "You think I like throwing up?"

Our eyes met. Her expression was firm, even if there were sleepy circles under her eyes.

"You know that wasn't what I meant, Felix."

I stayed quiet.

"Is it because you want to die, too? Because there are easier ways than drinking yourself to death," she said. "Or is it because you don't know what to do with your grief?"

I had to clench my teeth to keep from yelling at her again. "Blow out the stupid candle and I'll tell you."

"What? Why?"

"The light ... it's killing me. It's making my head hurt even worse," I answered.

With a puff of breath the room went dark again.

I breathed a sigh of relief.

"Are you really going to tell me why you've been acting this way?" I couldn't see her anymore, but I could hear the suspicion in her tone.

"Why does this matter to you so much?" I countered.

She didn't answer, and for several awkward minutes we just sat in darkness without saying anything.

I caved first, probably because I was in pain from the withdrawals. Or it might have been because the truth had been rotting away inside me for so long that I couldn't stand it anymore.

"You have no idea what it's like ... to have no one you can trust. That's who he was for me. Jaevid was someone I knew I could trust. Without him, I have no one. I'm alone. And I'll always be alone." Dang, that had sounded a lot more whiny and melodramatic coming out than it had in my head. It was embarrassing to admit it.

"That's not a very good reason to be acting this way, you know."

I glared in her direction since I couldn't see her anymore.

"And you're wrong." Her voice became so quiet and small that I barely heard her.

"What?"

"You're wrong—I do know what it's like," she repeated. "You were my closest friend before, Felix. I thought I could trust you. You were always so kind to me, and always so understanding. We were only children, but I sincerely thought I would always be able to confide in you."

"Yeah, well, that was before you decided to plant your marital hooks in my back," I sneered.

I heard a scraping sound, like metal on metal. There was a spark, and the candle blazed back to life just in time for me to see the harrowing glare she was giving me. She was holding a flint striker like it was a weapon.

"I'm so sick of hearing you say that," she fumed. "That had nothing to do with me! I was just as surprised as you were when our parents announced their decision. They never mentioned it to me or asked how I felt. They just did it. And before I could explain that you shut me out."

"Well you certainly didn't protest it, did you?" I tried to sound snarky and clever, but actually ... she'd just cut the legs out from under me. I always assumed that she was the instigator behind our arranged marriage.

"Of course I didn't." She began angrily stirring the rice pudding again. I wasn't sure because of how blurry my vision was, but it almost looked like she was trying not to cry.

"So? Why didn't you?" I pressed. "If you didn't want it, then why haven't you said anything all this time? Why didn't you try to stop it?"

She stopped stirring. Her chin was trembling and she wouldn't look at me. I watched her put the bowl down on the tray and stand.

"I think Miss Harriet should be the one to feed you tonight," she said stiffly, as she turned and started to leave.

"Julianna!" I yelled after her, trying to get her to come back so we could clear the air.

But she didn't stop. Instead, she started running. She darted out of my bedroom without ever answering.

THINGS WERE GOING TO GET WORSE BEFORE THEY GOT BETTER. I KNEW THAT. I just didn't know how much worse. I was paying dearly for every drink I'd taken and, believe me, it wasn't even close to worth it.

The next day I started to get sick—beyond sick, really. I thought I was dying. From that point on, each day was worse than the one before it.

I didn't sleep. Even when I tried to sleep, I couldn't because I was hurting so much. My mind raced and my body ached like someone poured hot sand into all my joints. I was sweating like crazy, and even though I'd puked up everything in my stomach, my insides still constricted like I might vomit again.

It hurt. I was exhausted and for the next several days all I could do was lie in my bed and groan. Julianna and Miss Harriet took turns force-feeding me mild soups and water, not that anything ever stayed down for long. They tried to help me bathe, but had to revisit that plan when I collapsed halfway to the washroom and fell on top of Julianna, basically crushing her into the carpet.

I did feel bad about that.

But even when my strength was spent and my stomach was empty of everything including bile, the worst was yet to come.

It was bedtime, or so Julianna had ordered. She was keeping me on a strict schedule. The only time she really left my side was to look after her own needs or to give me some privacy while the servants helped me bathe. She'd forfeited that job after being squished.

I was actually starting to turn a corner—or so I thought. I wasn't feeling quite as awful. My head wasn't pounding as horribly and I could even walk to the bed myself. I'd just reached the bed and was preparing to put a clean nightshirt on when it happened. I started to feel strange. My body began trembling again. My tongue felt chill and I tasted copper. My fingers tingled and began to feel numb.

I barely had time to sit down on the edge of the bed when it hit. It was like being struck by lightning. Every muscle in my body went rigid. I couldn't think. I couldn't breathe. There was only pain and a sense of impending doom as my body shook violently out of my control.

Darkness started to close in around me and I knew I must be dying. But through the haze, I caught glimpses of what was happening around me. Julianna rushed in at the sound of the servants' distress. She held my head in her lap and forced something into my mouth. It was a leather belt.

"Open your mouth, Felix! You have to work with me or you'll bite off your own tongue," she pleaded. I could see tears streaming down her face.

It took everything I had, but I managed to do it.

"You stay with me now. Just keep looking in my eyes. We'll get through this." I could vaguely feel her taking my hand and squeezing it firmly. "You hear me? I'm right here. I'm not going anywhere. I'll always be right here ..."

Then everything went dark.

I DIDN'T KNOW WHAT HAD HAPPENED WHEN I FINALLY WOKE UP. MY BODY still felt strange and tingly, like my arms and legs had gone to sleep. I tried to sit up, but every muscle protested. I couldn't do it. It hurt too much.

"Just rest," a familiar voice whispered.

Julianna sat at my bedside, wearing nothing but a dainty, pale blue nightgown and a long white robe. Her hair was loosely braided over her shoulder with a few stray locks falling perfectly over her cheeks. I didn't have to wonder how long she'd been watching over me. The weary lines on her face and circles under her eyes told that story plainly enough.

She was still holding my hand just as tightly as before, like she hadn't let go of it since I passed out. "How do you feel?"

I tried to speak, but my throat was so dry I couldn't even swallow.

"Here, drink this." She pulled her hand away and poured the contents of a small porcelain teapot into a cup. It smelled good and tasted faintly of honey.

"W-what happened?" I finally managed to ask.

She refilled the cup again and insisted I drink more. "You had a seizure. For a moment there, we weren't sure if you were going to make it or not."

"I wasn't sure, either," I admitted.

Things started to get awkward as we both fell silent. My hand—the one she'd been holding—was still warm from her touch. It stirred things in my mind, emotions I'd tried my best to bury or destroy. For the first time in a long while, I felt clear. I could hear myself think. And all I thought about was her.

"Julianna," I started to talk.

"You need to rest." She cut me off. It was as though she sensed that I wanted to have a serious talk about how I had been a humongous jerk to her for the past ten or so years.

"I can't. Not until I know why." I was the one reaching for her hand this time. "Please tell me. If you didn't agree with the engagement our parents agreed on, then why didn't you say something sooner?"

I saw her stiffen. She looked right at me, like a doe caught out in the open. Her eyes widened and her face started to flush. For a second or two, I thought she might actually tell me.

Carefully, Julianna withdrew her hand and stood. She dragged the blankets up over me and tucked me in, all while doing an excellent job of not making eye contact. Then she started to leave, just like before.

"I'm glad you're all right," she said, as she hesitated in the doorway. "I think things might start to get better for you now. Tomorrow you should try going for a walk."

"Wait! Please. Just talk to me about this." I was beginning to get desperate.

"Just rest. This doesn't have to happen now."

"What doesn't have to happen? Why won't you talk to me?" I didn't know what she meant by that, but it didn't sound good. For whatever reason, it felt like she was slipping away—like she was frantically putting up walls to keep me at a distance. I was losing her. And it scared the heck out of me.

I watched her smile sadly back at me. "Goodnight, Felix."

The door closed and I was left alone. That's when things started to click into place in my brain. Without the booze and misdirected hatred blurring my thoughts, I could see what was happening now was completely my fault.

After everything I'd done to her, I really was an idiot for thinking she'd ever want to be friends with me again. Things couldn't be the way they had been when we were children. I'd destroyed our relationship in every way I possibly could, in the hopes that it would drive her to break up our engagement.

But all I'd done was hurt her over and over. I'd used everything I knew about her from when we were friends, every secret insecurity and fear she'd ever confided in me, to do as much damage as possible. I'd used every bit of my social influence and power to make her suffer.

And now she'd never trust me again.

8

CHAPTER EIGHT

I would have to start over. Julianna didn't trust me anymore. I'd intentionally killed our friendship and every good opinion of me she'd ever had. So if I wanted her back, I was going to have to start from scratch and prove that I wasn't the evil son-of-a-dog she probably thought I was now.

I decided this while sitting next to her on a marble bench, tucked away in one of my mom's favorite tea gardens. It was peaceful there; I could see why mom liked it so much. She'd gone through a lot of trouble to have this place be as private and tranquil as possible. There were flowering fruit trees and perfectly manicured pathways winding off through tall hedges. Bubbling fountains hid amidst the foliage like secret paradises you'd only find by pure accident. The backdrop of deep green ivy and brightly colored flowers made Julianna seem even more beautiful than usual.

She sat next to me, close by but definitely not touching me, flipping through the pages of a book. She insisted I take these walks every day, to breathe in the fresh air and meditate. It was supposed to help calm my grief and give me time to reflect. I guess it did, to a degree, but I couldn't do much reflecting when all I could think about was how cruel I'd been to her.

"You know, I think I've about got my strength back now," I tried to start a conversation, yet again.

She didn't look up from her book. "Just don't overdo it."

I wasn't about to give up that easily. I'd been trying for days to get her to open up, to get a smile or a laugh or anything from her. But she was using that stupid book like a shield, pretending to be too distracted to notice me. Time to bring out my secret weapon.

"I was thinking of going for a ride this afternoon." I tried to sound indifferent, as I stood up and stretched my arms over my head. "Maybe you'd want to go with me? It'd be nice to get out for a while."

She took the bait hook, line, and sinker. Her eyes flicked up, peeking at me over the top of her book. "Through the countryside?"

I shrugged. "Sure. It's a nice day. Might as well make the most of it, right?"

Julianna raised the book higher to block her face from my view. "Okay. That sounds fine."

I smirked. Score one for me. This was my chance—I wasn't going to blow it this time. "All right. Meet me at the stables later then?"

I saw the top of her head move as she nodded. She was still determined to hide behind her book for now, but that wasn't going to work so well for her later. I had a plan.

THE EXPRESSION ON HER FACE WAS PRICELESS AS SHE WALKED UP TO THE FRONT of the stables where my estate's horses were housed. Only—we weren't riding on horses.

Julianna stared at Nova like she was seeing something straight out of a dream. Or maybe a nightmare, I couldn't quite tell. She might have been terrified. Her eyes were wide and her mouth hung open like a fish gasping for air.

Nova was restless. I hadn't ridden her in a couple of months now, so she was itching for a ride. She nipped at me, giving me dragon love-bites while I fixed her saddle straps and checked all the buckles. When she spotted Julianna, though, she started to get even more anxious. I'd never let anyone else ride Nova with me before.

"I-I thought we were going horseback riding!" Julianna stopped about twenty feet away from us and wouldn't come any closer.

I grinned at her. "Where's the fun in that?"

"Felix, I can't do thi—"

"Don't even say it, Jules. You really think I would ask you to do this if I thought it was the least bit dangerous?" I arched a brow at her.

She didn't trust me, or so I'd thought. But as she started to take tiny, cautious steps to me, my hopes grew by leaps and bounds. Maybe, somewhere deep down, she still believed that I wouldn't let anything happen to her.

I held a hand out to coax her in. "Come on."

She gripped my hand like she wanted to pop it off my wrist. "I'm not dressed properly for this," she whimpered.

Nova swung her huge, horned head around and put her big snout mere inches from Julianna's face.

I thought Julianna was going to pop right out of her skin. She bounded behind me and clung to the back of my shirt. "I-is she friendly?"

"Sometimes." I laughed. "She's not gonna hurt you, I promise."

Julianna didn't appear convinced. She was chewing fiercely on her bottom lip as I basically shoved her back in front of me. I took one of her hands and brought it to Nova's snout, showing her that it really was all right.

The more she touched, exploring Nova's scaly hide, the more I saw Julianna's apprehension and fear become excitement. She started to smile, a smile that grew wider and wider by the second. Nova closed her big green eyes and made a deep, purring sound.

"She's incredible," Julianna whispered. She giggled when Nova started sniffing her over, blasting her with hot dragon breaths.

I was smiling now, too. "Ready to ride?"

When she looked back at me again, I saw nothing but pure exhilaration. She was finally seeing me again, without remembering all the terrible things I'd done to her.

She hadn't looked at me like that since we were children.

I had some casual riding gear leftover from my youth—before my training at Blybrig Academy—that I was able to loan her. It was huge on her, of course. But it would do for now. I helped her strap the helmet down over her head and pull the gauntlets up over her arms. She was light, so it was nothing for me to pick her up and get her situated in the saddle. I gave her a quick walkthrough about where on the saddle she could hang on, even though I knew she would probably freak out once we actually started flying. First-timers always did.

Then I put on my own equipment and climbed into the saddle behind her.

It was weird being so close to her. Her back was pressed up against my chest as I reached around her to grip the saddle handles on either side of Nova's neck. I gave Julianna a warning pat on the shoulder.

We took off in a whirlwind. Nova was eager to leave the ground behind, so she wasted no time climbing skyward. Over the rush of air, I could hear Julianna screaming her head off.

Once we leveled off and started soaring, dipping through the clouds like we were skating over fields of white cotton, her screaming stopped. Though I couldn't see her face, I could feel her body beginning to relax. The landscape below us slipped by sluggishly—rolling hills of green that stretched all the way to the eastern cliffs. Then, there was nothing but ocean as far as the eye could see.

I sat back in the saddle, relaxing to take everything in, and I was shocked when Julianna did the same. She actually let go of the saddle and spread her arms wide, her long red braid and frilly ends of her skirts whipping around in the cold air. It made me smile again because I knew what she was feeling.

There really is no comparison to the rush of freedom you get when you're sitting in a dragon's saddle.

We flew for hours until I finally had Nova land in one of the grassy, rolling meadows north of my estate. There, amidst the soft grass, I unpacked phase two of my plan in the form of a picnic. I had a blanket and a few snacks stowed away in my saddlebags.

Julianna wobbled around like a newborn fawn when she got her feet back on the ground again. I guess the rush and excitement still had her shaking. She didn't say anything as she helped me spread out the blanket and unpack the food. We sat together while Nova rolled in the grass, basking in the warm afternoon sunshine like a fat housecat.

"I remember you promising to do this when we were little." Julianna spoke up in a quiet voice as she fidgeted with the strap on my water canteen. "Riding dragons was all you ever talked about."

I remembered that, too. "I guess not much has changed in that regard."

She gave a small, guarded smile. "No. But everything else has."

The atmosphere between us was starting to get awkward again. Only this time, she didn't have a book to hide behind. Now was my chance.

"You're never going to tell me, are you?" I asked.

She glanced at me warily.

"I wish you would. I want to understand. I've turned it over and over in my mind, and it just doesn't make sense. If I'd known—"

"It wouldn't have mattered, Felix. I didn't say anything or try to stop the engagement because ..."

She hesitated to continue. I held my breath and hoped she would.

"Because I was already in love with you. But everything you did, everything you said, made me believe that you definitely didn't feel the same way. And like a fool I kept hoping you'd eventually calm down, think about things, remember how close we'd been before. I hoped that maybe you would change your mind. You were my first love, and I wanted you to be my last."

I swallowed hard.

"I clung to those memories of our childhood for so long. You were my best friend, and I wanted that Felix back. Without him ... I had no one." She turned away so that I couldn't see the expression on her face.

"Julianna, I—"

"It's okay. You don't have to say anything. I understand now how you must have felt. You'd always expressed to me how your parents didn't try to see things from your perspective. They didn't consider any of your opinions or wishes when they made decisions about your life. When they announced our engagement, you must have thought I was trying to do the same thing."

"That doesn't make it right," I said. "I shouldn't have treated you that way. And I'll spend a lifetime regretting it. You have to know how sorry I am."

She looked at me then, and I saw everything I'd been afraid I would see. The betrayal and pain on her face, the tears in her eyes, and the overwhelming sense that I'd succeeded in driving her away.

"I lied to you, Felix," she admitted.

"About what?"

She took a trembling breath. "I didn't come here because your mother asked me to. She did write to me to tell me what was happening, apologizing for your behavior, but I was already planning to come to the estate long before that. I wanted to make it official in person."

I didn't know what she was talking about. "Make what official?"

"I'm terminating our engagement," she said in a quiet voice. "Actually, I already did several months ago. I should apologize for that, too. I never had the authority to take over your estate, but I suppose you weren't aware of that. You never opened the letter I sent, did you?"

The letter in the golden envelope. I'd completely forgotten about it. It was probably still sitting unopened on my desk at home.

Now I was the one who was afraid. I was losing her—no, I'd already lost her. I just hadn't been aware of it until now.

"I wasn't even sure if I could help you or not, but I would have never been able to forgive myself if I didn't at least try. And now you're free of me, just like you always wanted." She smiled at me but it wasn't sincere. I saw the sadness in her eyes. It was like someone was driving a red-hot spike into my soul.

"That isn't what I want anymore," I tried to protest. "I was just being stupid, Jules. I was acting like a dumb kid. And I'm sorry—I really am. If I could take it all back, I would."

She shook her head and started to withdraw. "Please don't say that now. I can't bear it. I've worked so hard to put my feelings aside. It's time for me to let go of those childish things and move on."

"But—"

"No!" She shouted suddenly and got up.

Julianna started to walk away, although I wasn't sure where she thought she was going. It was miles back to my estate—too far for her to walk by herself. Besides, it's not like I couldn't catch up to her. I wasn't the fastest guy in the world on foot, but I wouldn't have been much of a dragonrider if I couldn't outrun her.

I caught up to her and grabbed her arm to make her stop and face me again. She was crying and she wouldn't look me in the eyes. But that didn't matter. I just needed her to hear me.

"I love you, Julianna."

She squirmed in my grip, trying to pry herself away from me.

"I love you, and I'll never deserve you," I repeated it because it was true. Every word.

At last, her teary eyes raised to stare back at me. It didn't look like she believed me at all. She seemed angry, like maybe she wanted to hit me.

So I kissed her.

She fought me. She beat her hands on my chest and tried to shove away. I didn't let her. If this was goodbye, then I was going to savor this one little taste for as long as I could. She could hate me for it if she wanted; just add it to the stack of awful things I'd done to her already.

Then I felt her stop struggling.

All of a sudden, she wrapped her arms around my neck and squeezed me so tightly I could barely breathe. She kissed me back, and I'd never felt anything so sublime.

"Marry me," I begged, when I felt her start to pull her lips away from mine.

"Have you lost your mind?" She eyed me like she suspected I might be drunk again.

I dropped to my knees in front of her. I didn't know what else to do. "Please, Julianna. I know I don't deserve it. But I'll try every day to be worthy of you—to be the man you'd always hoped I would be."

She was hesitating. I could see her eyes darting back and forth like she was scrambling to think it over.

Then she smiled. "Even though you think I have big teeth?"

"I'll pull all my teeth out and gum my food for the rest of my life," I promised.

"And even if I'm a terrible dancer?"

"If I can teach Jaevid to dance, then I can teach you."

Julianna laughed. She put her soft hands on both sides of my face and bent down to kiss me again. "All right then, Felix. I'll marry you, if that's really what you want."

I couldn't hold back my relief. "It's the only thing I want."

9

CHAPTER NINE

And then I lived happily ever after, right?

Yeah. I wish. But there was still a problem I had to take care of—one last demon to face, if you will.

I felt better about talking to mom this time, though, because I wasn't doing it alone. Julianna was with me, holding my hand as tightly as ever, as I climbed the steps of the small summer home where she'd taken up residence since I evicted her. And by small, I mean it had only fifty bedrooms rather than two hundred and fifty.

Mom was sitting on a balcony overlooking the sea, sipping tea like she was alone in her own private universe. When we entered, she didn't even look up at us.

"Mom?" I tried to get her attention, which was basically the story of my entire relationship with her.

She just went on sipping her tea.

Julianna leaned in to whisper in my ear, "Maybe I should just let you two have some time alone?"

"No, it's okay. You're going to be my wife. I don't want to go another step into our relationship without being honest with you." I tried to show her a reassuring smile, but I just couldn't quite get there. Julianna didn't know about me—that I was an illegitimate child. I was nervous and a little afraid she might change her mind about marrying me once she found out.

"That's quite a change you've made." My mom spoke up so suddenly it made me jump. Her tone had a strong flavor of sarcasm to it. Typical. "I suppose you've come to ask about Darion again, is that so?"

"Yes. But I also didn't come here to fight with you. Either you're ready to tell me what happened or you're not. Regardless, we can't go on like this, mom." I pulled up a chair for Julianna and then for myself. "So what's it gonna be?"

Mom put down her teacup and looked at me, then at Julianna, then back to me again. "You really want to discuss this in front of her?"

I nodded. "She might as well find out straight from the source."

"Very well, then." Mom sat up straight and folded her hands in her lap. "You were right. Duke Farrow was not your father. Darion Prax is."

I already knew that. She was just saying it again for Julianna's benefit, maybe even in an attempt to scare her. A hard knot of emotion formed in my throat. I didn't dare look at Julianna because I was honestly afraid to see her expression. Shock? Horror? Disgust? When I finally got the nerve to look, I didn't see any of those. She looked upset.

"You had an affair?" she asked, before I could say anything.

My mom smiled at her scornfully. "No. I was already pregnant when the Duke and I were married. Now tell me, is that better than an affair? Or worse?"

Julianna's expression tightened, as did her grip on my hand. "If the duke didn't know about it, then about the same."

"Darion and I had been lovers in secret for quite some time. He was just a merchant's son. No money that amounted to anything, and no prospects of improvement. At the time, that didn't matter to me. I was just a stupid, lovesick child. He'd been saving up what he could of his earnings working on the docks, I believed, so that we could be married and live on our own. But then he went off and spent it all on a dragon hatchling. I didn't even find out about it until the next solstice holiday when I had hoped he would propose. That was when he told me of his intentions to join the king's ranks as a dragonrider."

Mom's tone was venomous, as though the memories still burned in her heart. I could hear anger and resentment in every word. "Darion had never intended on marrying me. I was just something for him to toy with. And it was only after he'd left for training and we had severed all contact that I realized I was pregnant with you, Felix. In an effort to save my reputation, I took the first offer for marriage I received—which happened to be from the duke. My parents were elated at the news. No one questioned my acceptance because a marriage to the duke would mean a comfortable life for me indefinitely. Only a fool would have refused a proposal like that."

"And you were able to cover up the pregnancy," I finished for her.

Mom shrugged like it was nothing. "Not so much cover up, as replace the one responsible for it. We were married quickly and I announced my pregnancy shortly after. You were born a few weeks late, which only wound up strengthening my story about your parentage. No one else ever had to know. That is, until you started to grow."

I shifted in my seat because I had a bad feeling I knew where this was going.

"You didn't look anything like me or the duke. You've always favored him. And every day since your birth I've been forced to look at the reminder of how Darion abandoned me. He treated me like dirt—as though I were disposable. Soon I found it was easier to simply not look at you at all." She managed to say that, too, without ever glancing my way. "So there you have it. Are you satisfied?"

Sitting back in my chair, I tried to decide whether I was or not. I had my answer. I just didn't feel like I had any closure.

"Don't you love him at all?" Julianna spoke up again, and this time she sounded really annoyed. "He's your son. He can't help whom he looks like or who his father is. How can you treat him this way?"

Mom didn't reply.

Julianna didn't back down. "Do you hate him?"

"Yes. Sometimes, I think I do." My mom's answer hung in the air like a foul stench. "Does that surprise you?"

Julianna did seem shocked; I'm sure we both did. I hadn't expected my mom to be so forthcoming. And while hearing that hurt me like you wouldn't believe, it also made me feel strangely calm. It gave me the closure I wanted, even if it sucked. She was a scorned woman. And she was determined to stay scorned and angry. I couldn't change that.

"No, it doesn't surprise me," I answered as I stood up. Julianna stood with me and clung to my arm as though she were afraid my mom might attack her. "I'll let you continue living here. Consider this house and everything in it yours. But I don't think your presence at our family estate is a good idea. You're not the sort of grandmother figure I'd want to subject my future children to. I trust you understand."

Honestly, I didn't care if she did. If she ever had a change of heart, maybe we could revisit the idea of letting her come back. But until then, she could stay here and stew in her bitterness.

"Goodbye, mom." I bowed formally, and then I took my fiancée's hand and left.

That was it. It was done. As I walked out of the chateau, I felt renewed. It was as though a weight had been lifted off my shoulders and I could breathe easily for the first time in my life.

Julianna, however, was still visibly tense. Her brow was furrowed and her eyes were fixed on the ground ahead of us as we walked hand in hand. I didn't know what she was thinking, and it made me nervous about how she was going to react to all this. I waited for her to speak first, though.

She stayed silent until we were alone inside our carriage, headed back to my family estate. "Are you all right?"

I grinned at her. "Never been better, actually."

Julianna's eyes widened. She probably thought I was off my rocker. "But Felix, she just said—"

"She told me the truth. For us, that's a first." I shrugged. "I guess I've always known she didn't love me. I just needed to hear her say it."

"Well, I'd still like to smack her. Someone should." I felt her squeeze my hand. "What if she tells everyone else?"

I squeezed hers back gently. "She won't. And even if she does, it doesn't matter now."

"What do you mean? If you aren't the duke's real son, then couldn't someone try to take away your title and inheritance?"

I smirked and waggled an eyebrow at her. "Why? Worried you're about to marry a regular old poor guy?"

Julianna shot me a dirty look. "That's an awful thing to say. You know I don't care about your money. I just don't want to see you get hurt again. What if she tries to publically humiliate you? I don't think I could refrain from wringing her neck."

I laughed. I couldn't imagine Julianna wringing anyone's neck. Except for mine, maybe. "Don't worry, Jules. Everything will be fine. When Duke Farrow signed over the estate to me, I became his chosen, rightful heir the second he put his seal on it. Who my father is doesn't have any effect on that. For better or worse, Farrow Estate is stuck with me."

She still didn't seem altogether satisfied. "And what about your real father, Darion Prax? Are you going to speak with him? Does he know who you are or even that you exist?"

Leaning over, I planted a kiss on her cheek. It made her blush. "Yeah, he does. We didn't exactly part on good terms the last time we spoke, though. I suppose I'll have to find him and apologize."

"Please do. I'd like for you to have a decent relationship with at least one of your parents. Otherwise holidays are going to be so lonely." Julianna put her head on my shoulder and out a small sigh. "Is it true what she said? Are you really a lot like him?"

"I'm not sure. I don't know him that well personally. People say we look alike, though."

I could hear a smile in her voice. "I can't wait to meet him."

THE KING STILL HADN'T MOBILIZED HIS GRAND ATTACK ON LUNTHARDA. Word in the court was that he was having a hard time gathering enough of his forces to accomplish it. So I wasn't concerned about finding Prax. As far as I knew, he had no life outside of being a dragonrider. Actually getting up the nerve to talk to him? That was going to be a lot harder.

I must have looked just as nervous as I felt, because while I checked over my saddle, Julianna hovered right over me. When I kissed her goodbye, she squeezed me extra hard.

"Are you sure you don't want me to go with you?" she asked, as she fretfully straightened the buckle of my cloak.

"I'll be fine," I assured her. "It's just for a day. I'll be back tomorrow night."

She put on an unconvincing smile and stood on her toes to kiss my cheek. "All right, then. Just please be safe."

I had plenty of time in the air to think about what I was going to say. And yet when I touched down in Northwatch and set my eyes upon the citadel, everything got scrambled around in my brain. I didn't know how Prax would receive me or if he'd even want to talk to me at all. Our last meeting hadn't gone well—and that was putting it mildly. His last words to me still burned in my mind.

"You have disappointed me."

That hurt. It hurt a lot more now that I knew he was my dad. I'd never made anyone proud in my life—although it was sort of an intentional effort on my part. The duke, who'd raised me like his own because he didn't know better, had been unhappy with my behavior as a child, and the way I fought him tooth and nail over every little thing. I hadn't done much to deserve his good opinion. And my mother ...

I put Nova up in the stable of one of the higher-end inns on the outskirts of the city, and then started for the citadel. On my way, I bumped into another member of Emerald Flight, standing on the corner just outside the Laughing Fox Tavern. He waved at me, and I strolled over to shake his hand.

"You look good," he said with a laugh. "Not at all how Prax described you. He made it sound like you were determined to drink yourself to death."

I tried not to let that faze me. "What can I say? I gave it my best shot. Speaking of Prax, do you know where he is?"

My former comrade pointed a thumb back in the direction of the Laughing Fox. "We all took the week off while we're waiting for rally orders. Most of the men went home for a few days. But you know Prax—he's got no one to go home to."

Well, that was about to change.

I thanked him and left, heading straight for the tavern. I hadn't been there in months. It felt strange to walk through those doors again. I spotted a few familiar faces around the dimly lit room.

And there, sitting by himself at the end of a long table, I saw my dad.

Prax was hunched over with his elbows resting on the tabletop. The light from the hearth put heavy shadows over his face, outlining every wrinkle and crease. It made him seem older and much more somber, as though he were lost in miserable memories.

I walked across the dining room, weaving around the tables until I was standing right beside him. "Hey, Dad."

He looked up in surprise. I saw him search me, examining every detail of my clothes and demeanor as though he were looking for evidence that I was still a wreck. Then he gave a small, almost bemused smile.

"I take it this means I was right," he said. "Maria finally admitted it?"

I spread my hands out wide and shrugged. "Yep. It's a boy. Sorry I didn't bring you any flowers."

Prax chuckled and nodded to the chair across from him, gesturing for me to take a seat. Things got awkward the second I settled in, though.

Neither of us seemed to be able to find a good place to start. We weren't even making eye contact, though whenever he wasn't looking at me, I took the opportunity to study his face. The face of my father—a face I supposedly shared.

By the time I came up with something semi-intelligent to say, Prax spoke up first. "I want you to know that I'm sorry, Felix."

I tensed. "Yeah. Me too. For a lot of stuff."

"You're not a disappointment to me," he continued like he hadn't even heard me. "And I should have been there for you when you were a child. As soon as I heard Maria had given birth, I was suspicious that you might be mine. The timing was too convenient to ignore. But you had a family and a father figure who I reasoned was much more stable than I would ever be. I had no evidence that you really were mine, and no desire to upset your life ... or Maria's. Now I see I was wrong. I should have gone to Maria right away and insisted she tell me the truth. I'll never forgive myself for that. I've missed a lot. Now you're a grown adult and we might as well be perfect strangers."

He reached across the table and grabbed my hand. He gripped it hard as he stared directly into my eyes. "But I want you to know I am proud of you and the man you've become. You are my son. And I love you."

Suddenly, it was painful to swallow. I couldn't shrug this off or act like it wasn't a big deal to hear him say that. It meant absolutely everything to me.

"It's not all your fault." My voice was hoarse and broken. "I need to apologize, too, for everything I said before. For acting like a moron. And for leaving the ranks like that."

He let go of my hand and waved off my apology like he was dismissing the whole issue. "Don't worry about it. You have an estate to look after. And a young bride, too, I hear. I would never fault you for putting those priorities first."

If only my motives in leaving had been that pure. "We both want you to come to the wedding. Do you think you can manage it?"

He laughed that loud, booming laugh that filled the entire room. "You really think I'd miss my only son getting married?"

"Well, I told her I wasn't sure since we won't be serving any alcohol." I smirked. "I'm trying to keep this new leaf turned over."

Prax nodded like he understood. "Change is never easy, boy. If it were, most people wouldn't be so terrified of it. But the beautiful thing about it is that once the uncomfortable part is over, we get a chance to start again—fresh and unbound by the mistakes we made before."

"I've made a lot of them lately," I admitted. "And it almost cost me everything I've ever loved."

"Well, you seem to be better off now. At least you've bathed. That's an improvement over the last time I saw you." He winked, and we both had another good laugh.

Things got easier and much less awkward then. We talked for hours about absolutely nothing, but I needed that nothing more than anything. He wanted to hear about my life, and I wanted to know about his, as well. After telling him about my childhood, I asked how he'd wound up in a dragonrider's saddle. I saw his demeanor begin to change.

"I did it for Maria," he said quietly.

That was the exact opposite story I'd gotten from my mom, who insisted he'd abandoned her for the dragonriders' ranks. "What do you mean?"

"I asked her father for her hand, but he turned me away. He said I didn't make a good enough living to deserve her. We could have eloped, I suppose. She probably would have jumped at the idea. But your mother was a respectable girl from a good family. I didn't want to disgrace her like that, and I didn't want our life together to start out by driving a wedge between her and her family. So I had to find some other means of employment—some way to make myself worthy of her." He rested his chin in his palm and stared down at the table. "I was too proud to tell her that her father wouldn't give me his blessing. I was embarrassed. And I suppose that's how she got the impression I didn't want to marry her at all."

I sat back in my chair. I was completely blown away by how the whole situation had gotten misconstrued. Mom had taken it entirely the wrong way. She was bitter and filled with hatred over nothing.

"She said she hates me." I blurted without thinking. I guess I just needed him to know that.

Prax's expression was pained, but sympathetic. "It's not you she hates, son. It's me. Don't let her deceive you. I'm not there to face her anger, so she's directing it all at you instead."

"Regardless, I can't have her in my life when she's like this. It upsets Julianna. And frankly, it pisses me off."

"She's going to have to come to terms with what happened," he agreed. "But maybe I can lend a hand with that. It's long past time for her and I to have a talk."

I wasn't so sure. "You really think she'll sit and talk to you?"

"No, not willingly. But I don't intend on giving her a choice. Maria's always tended to be overly dramatic when she doesn't get her way. She was like that even when we were young. Now she's spent all these years taking out her hatred for me on her only child. It's time for both of us to move on with our lives. She can't go on blaming you for my mistakes, and I can't go on hiding here rather than returning to Solhelm and facing her."

I didn't think it would matter to Mom if he tried to reason with her or not. She was basically insane, as far as I could tell. Sitting around and stewing in hate tended to do that to people. But if he wanted to try, that was his business. I wasn't going to try to stop him.

"The wedding is next month. I suppose I can mark you down as attending?" I tried to change the subject. "We set the date for the engagement ball in a few days. I know it's short notice, but do you think you could make it to that, too?"

He smiled. "I'll be there with bells on. Awful quick though, isn't it?"

"Well, it's not like we're strangers. I've known Julianna since we were kids. She used to chase me with strawberries when we were little."

Prax cocked an eyebrow. He clearly didn't get it.

"I'm allergic to them," I clarified. "Anyway, we've technically been engaged for a long time already. I love her and I don't intend on changing my mind. And she's had a good, long while to reconsider it herself."

I decided not to tell him that I had almost lost her. I'd been downright awful to her. Luckily, Jules had a strength and resilience to her that any soldier would admire, even if she happened to be soft and delicate on the outside. It was one of the things I'd always found most beautiful about her.

"It'll be time to have a few tots of your own then, eh?" Prax teased.

I blushed. "L-let's not rush that."

He went on making playful jabs, questioning when he would be made a grandfather, passing the time while the tavern emptied of patrons and the barmaids began wiping down the tables and chairs. They'd be closing soon, but I didn't want this to end.

Prax had gone silent, and appeared lost in the same painful thoughts he'd been stewing in when I found him. His eyes were fixed on the mug of cider in front of him. He'd elected not to drink alcohol either, out of courtesy for me.

"They found the blue dragon," he said suddenly.

All the wind rushed out of me, like someone had punched me in the gut. He didn't have to explain which blue dragon he was talking about—I knew. He meant Jaevid's dragon, Mavrik.

"He never goes far from the edge of that forest. A few men tried to chase him down, but he's too quick. Only Jace's dragon could ever match pace with him. And as far as they could tell, he's still wearing all his saddle and gear. One even told me they saw him on the ground, roaring into the trees like he was calling for someone. Odd behavior for a dragon. Never heard of one acting like that before, even with a bonded rider."

I began to feel nauseous, and yet I hung on his every word. "So what does that mean?"

Prax met my eyes from across the table. I saw the intensity smoldering there. He had a theory, all right. "They never found his body on the battlefield. I, for one, don't believe they ever will because I don't think it's there at all. You told us before you'd seen him do things—strange works of power the likes of which this world had never seen. If that's true, then who's to say he isn't in Luntharda?"

I narrowed my eyes. "Are you calling him a traitor?"

"I never said that," he replied quickly. "But if something happened to Jace, if he was shot down, then you of all people should be able to tell me whether or not you think Jaevid would have gone down after him."

I had to stop and think about that. Yes, I'd been Jae's closest friend. I knew him well enough to make a guess about what he might do ... and Prax was right. If Jae had seen Jace go down into the forest, he probably would have headed in after him. He'd done something similar for Sile when he was only a fledgling rider.

Not only that, Jae had mentioned to me once, not long before the battle, that Sile wanted him to go into Luntharda. It had something to do with a ritual—I couldn't quite remember the details. But maybe it was possible ...

"So then you're suggesting he's still alive?" I demanded. I was beginning to get my hopes up.

Prax sat back from the table and gave a heavy sigh. "No, of course not. I'm not suggesting anything. Personally, I don't think he's still alive because if there was any way for him to come back to us, with or without Jace, I believe he would have done so by now. I'm saying that if he is as powerful as you believe, as you claim to have seen, then we have to accept that we may never know what really happened to him. There's been a lot of strangeness in the air lately—apart from the animals going madder than ever. Seraph has vanished, which many are taking to be either a sign that the war is finally over ... or that something terrible is going to happen."

We were silent again for several minutes. I listened to the sound of the barmaids scratching at the stone floor with their brooms as they swept away the day's dirt and crumbs. My heart was aching. It was as though a heavy weight was settling over my shoulders.

"I miss him," I admitted.

Prax patted my shoulder from across the table. "I wish I could tell you that feeling goes away, son. But it doesn't. The important thing is to try to turn your focus to the living, to the ones who need your love and attention right now. That bride of yours, for instance. She needs you—all of you—and that is what should matter most. Take it from an old, lonely man who's spent a lifetime in the saddle and has nothing to show for it; family should always come first."

10

CHAPTER TEN

I was dreaming.

I had to be; I'd never been in a place like this before in my life. It was cold and dark. The air smelled of a heavy musk, like damp soil. I walked forward slowly with my arms outstretched, feeling around for something. My fingertips brushed against what felt like the cold, moist walls of a cave.

Groping forward through the dark, I couldn't tell which way led up or down. I couldn't see anything and couldn't hear anything, except for my own frantic breathing. Then suddenly, there was a light in the distance. It was only a pale flicker, but it gave me hope and a direction to move in.

The nearer I got to the light, the more I could see of my surroundings. I was standing inside some sort of cavern with a ceiling so high you could have flown a dragon around inside it. It was bizarre. Soft, sterling light seemed to hang in the air without coming from any place in particular. It gave me the creeps.

I didn't feel any better when I noticed what stood in the very center of the chamber. It looked like some sort of altar made of a single slab of white stone. There were bones arranged on top of it, like someone had left an animal there to rot away, alone in the chilly silence.

When I reached the altar, I stretched out a hand to touch the antlers of the skull. They were long, sloping, and beautifully pointed, like they belonged to some species of elk. But the tips must have been sharp as razors, because as soon as I let my hand slide across them, I pricked my finger. It stung. Droplets of my blood peppered the altar and pooled in a place where the stone had a bowl-shaped indentation.

In the blink of an eye, everything went dark. It was as though something had sucked all the light out of the air in one breath. Noises began echoing all around me—the sound of footsteps, snorts of breath, chirps, screeches, and whispers.

I spun around. I could see spots of light winking in the darkness, a thousand eyes, all blinking and watching me. They were everywhere, slithering down from the ceiling and prowling just out of my reach.

A hot blast of breath rustled my hair.

I whirled around again and reached for my sword, but it wasn't there. Too late, I remembered that I'd stopped carrying it. I wasn't a dragonrider anymore.

"Something is coming." A soft voice spoke over the noise of the creatures lurking in the dark. Over my shoulder, I saw a pair of eyes that stood out from the rest. They were shining as brightly as stars.

"W-who's there?" I demanded.

He stepped forward, seeming to part the darkness around him like a curtain. Jaevid stood right in front of me, draped in a long, black cloak that covered everything except his face. His stare was piercing. It cut through me like he was inside my head, searching through my thoughts.

"Jaevid?" I rasped his name, hoping to see some semblance of my friend in that harrowing gaze.

But his expression never changed. "I have to return it," he said. "Everything depends on it."

"Return what? You're not making any sense."

"The stone. The balance must be restored. Otherwise Paligno's curse will ravage this world. All of nature will turn on itself. Everything we know and love will be destroyed."

My view of him was suddenly eclipsed, as something monstrous and scaly crawled by between us. When he reappeared, he was standing much closer. It startled me and I cringed away.

"Go to Mithangol, to my family home. Bring with you only those you can trust completely—those who are willing to fix what has been broken. I will be waiting for you there." He tilted his head back, raising his gaze up to the ceiling.

I looked up, too. Overhead, the ceiling had opened up—or dissolved away, I really wasn't sure—to reveal the night sky. The moon hung above like a giant, lidless, silver eye.

"Meet me there on the night of the next full moon," he said.

I stared up into the sky, wondering what the heck was going on. And when I looked down again, Jaevid was gone. So were all the creepy shadow animals. I was completely alone, except for those gleaming white bones.

"Jae?" I called for him, turning in circles to search the whole chamber. But he wasn't anywhere to be found.

And then the ground fell out beneath me.

It gave way with a rumbling crack and I fell, down, away from the light, until I landed on the flat of my back on top of a huge pile of round, smooth stones. I shambled back to my feet, squinting up into the single shaft of light that filtered down from above.

That's when I realized they weren't stones under my feet—they were skulls. Human skulls crunched under my boots with every frantic step I took to try and get away. I sank down, and no matter how I fought I couldn't get free.

"*The balance must be restored,*" a whispering voice hissed in my mind, just as the sea of skulls swallowed me completely.

I wasn't sure how to tell Julianna what I had seen in my dream, or even if I should. I didn't know what to make of it, myself. Was it real? Had Jaevid actually been trying to contact me? Or was I just riding the emotional backslide from talking about him with Prax?

Sitting at the breakfast table across from her, I couldn't follow a word she said to me. She was going on about something wedding related. Colors of flowers, maybe. All I did was stare down into my teacup and twirl my spoon across my knuckles over and over again. My other hand was fidgeting underneath the table.

"Felix?"

I glanced up quickly when I heard my name. "Yes?"

"Is everything okay?" She was obviously concerned. Her soft eyes were brimming with worry.

I could lie to a lot of people and get away with it, but Jules knew me better than my own parents. I couldn't slip anything past her, so I didn't even bother trying. "I'm not sure."

She immediately shut the thick book where she'd been jotting down all our wedding plans and pushed it away. "Talk to me, then."

So I did. I told her about what Prax had said about Mavrik and that Jaevid's body still hadn't been recovered. Then I described my dream. When I was finished, I fixed my gaze back down into my teacup and chewed on the inside of my cheek.

"The next full moon is only a few days away, Felix." Her voice was quiet and thoughtful. "It's the night after our engagement ball. Remember? We moved the date so the two wouldn't coincide. It's bad luck."

I nodded. "I know."

Julianna sat quietly for a moment. I didn't dare look up to see the expression on her face. How could I go? No, I shouldn't. It was just a dream, nonsense, nothing more.

A small paper swan appeared next to my teacup along with Julianna's hand. The sight of it made me smile involuntarily.

"You have to go," she said suddenly.

"What?"

She was sitting up straight with a gentle, but stern look fixed on me. "If you don't, you'll always wonder. You need to go. It's the only way to be sure it wasn't anything more than a nightmare."

I picked up her paper swan and marveled at its clean creases. She'd made them all the time when we were kids. It was her favorite prank to leave them hidden around the estate in our favorite playtime places for me to find.

"What about our wedding plans?" I asked.

Julianna shook her head. "They can wait. Besides, you'll just keep agreeing to anything I choose, right?"

"I don't want you to think I'm putting this ahead of you," I muttered uncomfortably. "Our wedding is more important."

She smiled as she put her hand on top of mine to stop me from fidgeting with the swan. "You're a sweet man, you know, but sometimes you say really stupid things. You don't have to lie just to make me feel better. I know how much Jaevid meant to you. And I know you won't be satisfied until you know the truth. So go, please?"

I felt guilty because she was right. I wanted to go. I wasn't going to be able to think about anything else until I knew what that dream meant—if it even meant anything at all. Taking her hand, I felt myself begin to relax as she wound her fingers gently through mine.

"You sure you'll be okay here without me?"

Julianna rolled her eyes and gave me a teasing smirk. "Come on, Felix. How long have I gone without you before now? Besides, I've still got to pay a visit to my parents and explain what's happened. The last I spoke to them, I had just told them I was planning on breaking our engagement."

I groaned and slumped in my chair. "I should be the one telling them that. I'm sure they've wondered what the heck was wrong with me all these years."

She giggled, and made that cute expression where she nibbled on her bottom lip. I loved it when she did that. I think she must have known, because when our eyes met, she winked at me. "They're just going to be happy that everything is better now. So don't worry about a thing."

"Pfft. Right."

"You mentioned Jaevid told you to bring only people you could trust," she said, obviously trying to change the subject. "Who will you ask?"

The thought hadn't even crossed my mind. I'd been so caught up in trying to decide whether or not to go, I hadn't even considered taking anyone with me.

"Prax, I guess," I answered. "He's the only one who might actually believe I'm not out of my mind. I suppose I should write to him about it. Maybe he can convince a few of the others from Emerald Flight to come with him."

"And you trust those men?" Jules didn't seem so sure that was a good idea.

"They all knew Jaevid. The blood we shed in battle made us brothers. I trusted them with my life then, I see no reason not to now. There might even be a few other riders from our little excursion during our avian year who haven't forgotten what Jae did on that island."

"But do you trust them now?" she repeated earnestly.

I couldn't answer. It was a difficult question—one I was going to have to think about.

Julianna seemed unsettled as she sat across the table from me, still holding my hand. It looked like there was something else she wanted to say—something she wasn't sure she should.

"What is it?" I probed.

She dodged my stare. "What do you suppose he really was? Or still is, if that's the case."

"Who?"

"Jaevid. I mean, after everything you've told me about him ... do you really think he's just a normal person?"

I didn't know what to think about Jae. I never had. Every time I thought I'd seen his last trick, he came out with some new, magical secret that saved our butts just in time. That was why I couldn't discount this dream as just a fiction of my twisted, stressed out imagination.

"He was my friend and that's really all that matters to me," I decided.

Julianna nodded. "Just be careful. My mother used to tell me stories. Old tales about the ancient gods who could shake the foundations of the earth until the mountains coughed fire, spin storms in the skies, and make oceans swell until they swallowed up the dry land. Those stories used to make me feel so terribly small and helpless. And when I hear you talk about what Jaevid could do, I get that same feeling."

I gave her hand a reassuring squeeze. "Trust me, Jules. Jae may have some strange powers, but he is definitely not some ancient god. I've never heard of a god who sucked at hand-to-hand combat as badly as he did."

"Someone told me he beat you once," she countered.

"That is such a load of crock. I let him win that match! Who told you about that? Was it Fredrick? That soft-handed little weasel always had it in for me. Next time I see him I'll ..."

Julianna started laughing. I realized she'd just been baiting me into getting riled up over nothing. Crap. She'd really gotten me good that time.

I blushed and tried unsuccessfully to sulk.

Then she spoke again. "Just promise me one thing." Her voice became quiet and she sounded worried. "One way or another, swear you'll come back home."

I didn't know where all this insecurity was coming from. Maybe because I'd mentioned the skulls in my dream? "Jules, nothing's going to happen to—"

"You don't know that," she said. "So just promise me. I know better than to ask you not to do something dangerous. So instead, I'm just asking that you survive it. Please."

I guess I already knew that whatever might be waiting for me in Mithangol was probably dangerous. It usually was with Jae. But what could I say to that? If I was required to make the ultimate sacrifice, would I go through with it? It would mean leaving her alone, burdened with my family estate and—worst of all—my mother.

I shuddered. No, I couldn't do that to the woman I loved. Prax was right; I had to start thinking about more than just myself. Julianna depended on me now. After such a long time of being the biggest disappointment a fiancée could ever be, I wasn't about to repeat my mistakes as her husband.

I nodded and agreed, "I promise, Jules. I'll come back."

11

CHAPTER ELEVEN

"I'm not asking you to do anything," I said, after I finished explaining everything to Prax. He'd come in a day early for our engagement party, at my request, just so I could have this little chat with him.

And in all honesty, I had absolutely no idea how he was going to react.

My story was bizarre. It sounded insane even to me. Dreams about ancient caverns and mountains of skulls? Just thinking of it made me shudder.

Sitting across from me in the privacy of my office, I could practically see the wheels turning behind his eyes as he studied me for several long, uncomfortable seconds. At last, he let out a heavy sigh and scratched anxiously at his chin.

"And you believe this was his way of trying to contact you?" He didn't sound convinced.

"I don't know what to believe. That's exactly why I'm going."

"Felix, I understand wanting to believe your friend is still alive. Truly, I do. And please hear me when I say that it was never my intention to give you any form of false hope about Jaevid's fate," he began to explain.

I cut him off, standing up from behind my desk. "No offense, but this had nothing to do with you. I've never understood why Jae could do the things he did. I may never understand. But I believe in him and if he needs me, I'm going to be there, sword in hand, ready to fight at his side until the bitter end. We are dragonriders—that's what we do."

Prax's expression was complex, a mix of confusion and concern. I guessed he was thinking I'd finally lost whatever marbles I still had rattling around between my ears.

And then he laughed. He laughed himself to the verge of tears and sat back, slapping his knee and trying to collect himself enough to speak.

I assumed he was making fun of me.

"I'm sorry, boy," he managed to rasp. "It's just that—Gods and Fates—I wish I could claim that courage and determination came from my side of your blood. But that was a speech straight out of your mother's mouth. When she was younger, she had that same fire in her blood. Seems there's more of her in you than she'd ever let anyone believe."

I stood a little straighter when he got to his feet.

"You're mad, of course. But it's good. Very good." He gave me a proud smile. "So give me the order."

"The order?"

His eyes glinted with mischief. "I can't just up and leave Northwatch of my own accord without being marked a deserter. You asked me to come here for your engagement ball, Your Grace, and of course I'm pleased to oblige. So if you'd like anything else from me, you're going to have to give me a direct order."

I hesitated, then stumbled over the words. "R-right. Lieutenant Prax, I request that you, and as many men from Emerald Flight as you deem worthy, accompany me to Mithangol."

"As you wish, Duke Farrow." Prax smirked and nodded approvingly. He stepped closer and began roughly adjusting the collar of my tunic and straightening the buckle on my formal cloak. "And let's just be clear—am I to tell them what you told me?"

"No," I answered quickly. "Just tell them to come and be ready. I hope I'm wrong, but we may be in for a fight."

He opened his mouth to add something, but Miss Harriet came flying into the office. She was flushed and her hair was wild.

"Master Felix, the king has just arrived!" She came at me armed with a golden collar that she draped over my shoulders before she started fussing with my hair.

"What?" I was stunned. Of course I'd sent him an invitation. It was a social obligation for someone of my standing, but I'd never expected him to show up.

"Yes! His carriage just pulled onto the drive. He brought his elite guard, thirty soldiers, and four dragonriders. No one has ever seen such a procession. They say he's brought an entire wagon filled with gifts."

I couldn't have cared less about the gifts. As if I didn't have enough stuff already. But I was having trouble understanding why he'd come and brought so many guards with him. It was beyond excessive. This wasn't a dangerous place. I had my own guards stationed around the house, watching the perimeter, and I knew every one of them was capable.

"Very good. You're dismissed." I shooed her away from trying to wipe smudges off my face with her thumb. She looked like she might faint with nervous excitement. I hoped Julianna was faring better.

As soon as she was gone, Prax and I exchanged a meaningful look. I knew we both had to be thinking the same thing.

"Sounds like he's brought a small army," Prax observed with a careful tone. He knew better than to speak out of turn—not that I would have cared.

I was already making a break for the door. "And to my doorstep, no less. How much you want to bet they aren't here just to dance and eat the free food?"

Prax fell in step beside me as I left my private chambers. His hand rested anxiously on the pommel of his sword. "I'm not a betting man, but even I like those odds."

We almost made it to the foyer when Miss Harriet caught up to me again. She seized me by the arm and practically dragged me into a parlor near the ballroom where all my guests were gathering. She went on about how it was nearly time and that I had to stay out of sight until the right moment. Julianna had gone to a lot of trouble planning everything. Blah, blah blah.

Prax just laughed and swaggered away to join the rest of the party. He didn't look very sorry for me at all. The big jerk.

I sat alone in the darkened parlor, listening to the noise of the gathering crowd and the swell of beautiful music. My mind was racing over everything—the wedding, the king and all his guards camping out on my lawn, and Jaevid. Things were getting more complicated by the second. And if there's anything I'd learned about myself it was that I don't handle complicated very well.

"Master Felix?" Miss Harriet appeared in the doorway, speaking softly as if she were afraid of disturbing me. "Are you ready?"

I snapped to my feet. "Always."

She led me back out into the hall. The sound of the crowd was louder, echoing off the ceilings. Two of my servants in their finest uniforms stood ready to open the doors to the largest ballroom.

And then I saw her.

Julianna was waiting for me. The soft light of the chandeliers made her hair shine and her fair skin glow. Her smile stopped me dead in my tracks. I'd seen her wear fancy ball gowns before, in all styles and colors, but I had never seen her look this beautiful.

I tried to tell her that when I finally got the courage to approach her. But like a total moron, I choked on everything I tried to say.

She smiled wider and threw her arms around my neck. I hugged her tightly, picked her up, and twirled her around. Girls like that kind of thing.

Behind us, I heard Miss Harriet sniffling.

"Are you sure about this?" Julianna whispered. "This is your last chance to escape, you know."

I slipped one of her gloved hands around my arm. "Tempting. But I think I'll pass."

One of the servants waiting to open the doors cleared his throat, so I gave him the signal. It was time. The doors opened before us and golden light spilled out. Julianna squeezed my arm nervously.

Good. At least I wasn't the only one.

AFTER MIDNIGHT, THE PARTY WAS IN FULL SWING AND THERE WERE NO SIGNS of it slowing anytime soon. Couples continued twirling away on the dance floor, filling the ballroom with laughter and conversation. There was still plenty of food, and even though we weren't serving any wine or ale, everyone seemed to be in good spirits. I couldn't remember the last time I'd felt so relaxed and comfortable in a setting like this. It was a much different feel than the parties I'd thrown myself. This had Julianna's delicate fingerprints all over it. It was formal, refined, but comfortable—just like her. She looked happy, too. Happier than I'd seen her in a long time. That alone was enough for me to have a good time.

Besides the king, nobles and gentry had come from all over the kingdom. Everyone, of course, except my mother. I have to admit, I did look for her. I sort of expected she might show up, sour-faced, and skulk around like an old crow ready to badmouth me to anyone who might listen. But she didn't. For whatever reason, that disappointed me. I suppose as much as I wanted to believe I was completely done with her and it didn't matter what she said or how she treated me—none of that was true. I'd never be able to break the emotional tether that bound us together. Like it or not, she'd always be my mother. I'd always want her affection and approval.

The nobles that had come to wish us well on our marriage brought stories and rumors with them, some that I wished I hadn't heard. As much as Julianna tried diligently to change the subject, steering it away from those grim details, it just couldn't be done.

"Six hundred head of my finest cattle had to be butchered," Count Davron complained. "All because a few of them started showing symptoms of the madness. Such a waste."

"Well, didn't you hear? Baron Wingate's own hounds turned on his youngest boy. The poor dear is doomed to lose his arm, they say," another gentlewoman said in a hushed voice.

Julianna's face began to look pasty. "And they still can't find what's causing all this?"

"It must be the work of the elves. That's what everyone believes. How else can it be explained? It smacks of dark magic and witchery." The Count's wife muttered from behind her feathered fan. "The king himself has declared it a national emergency. Just think of what would happen if the dragons took ill."

I saw Julianna take a deep breath, as though trying to steady herself. Definitely time for a distraction.

I slipped a hand around her waist and pulled her away towards the dance floor. "Come on. I haven't had enough of you just yet." My diversion didn't seem to convince her, though. She knew me too well.

As soon as we were alone, dancing to a slow waltz, she hit me with the full force of those worried, but lovely eyes. "Is that true? Could the dragons turn, too?"

"Dragons are smarter than cows and dogs, Jules," I assured her. "You really think Nova would try to hurt me?"

She didn't answer, but the troubled furrow in her brow told me she wasn't so sure.

Frankly, neither was I. I couldn't shake the feeling that something was about to happen—maybe something to do with the dream Jaevid had ...

I stopped myself there. I couldn't let myself get caught up in that, not yet, not until I had some facts. I didn't know if my dream was real or not, but most importantly, I didn't know if Jae was alive.

"What is it?" Julianna was staring up at me pleadingly.

I almost didn't tell her, but then I thought better of it. "There was this time, when we were in training as dragonriders, I asked Jae to talk to Nova. When he did, he said that she was afraid; that she and the other dragons could tell something was coming—something bad. I just wonder if this is what he meant."

She squeezed my hand tightly. "Felix, if the dragons turn ... if they catch this madness."

"I know," I said. "There won't be anything we can do to stop them."

We finished our dance without saying another word, both of us imagining the horrors of what might be coming. The waltz ended and I escorted her to get a drink.

We never made it to the punch bowl.

One of the king's elite guards, wearing that eerie, expressionless, white mask over his face, stepped into our path. He bowed and gestured to the open doorway that led out into the candlelit gardens behind my estate.

"His majesty requests a private audience with you, my lord." His voice sounded young, but it was muffled behind the mask's thin mouth hole. Something about it was strangely familiar. "May I offer myself as a substitute escort for the lady until you return?"

Julianna was looking him over like she was trying to decide if she should run or not. The masks freaked her out—or so she'd told me. I had to agree with her. And after that encounter with the Lord General, I didn't trust any of them as far as I could throw them.

But what choice did I have? You didn't say no to the king.

"Right," I answered stiffly, and passed Julianna's hand over to him. "See that you take good care of her."

The guard bowed again, much lower this time, and Jules shot me a dirty look over her shoulder. Crap. I was definitely gonna hear about this later. I'd just have to make it quick.

I found the king standing alone before the burial site I'd erected for Jae. He looked small and fragile, hunched over a bejeweled cane as he eyed the large statue through the holes in his golden mask. He'd come dressed for the party, although I'd yet to see him talk to anyone. Come to think of it, I hadn't even seen him come inside.

"I hear you brought quite the entourage with you." I spoke loudly, giving away my approach as I went to stand next to him. "I didn't realize engagement parties warranted that kind of security."

"One can never be too careful," he rasped, not taking his gaze away from the statue.

"Were you expecting to meet an enemy here?" I decided to press my luck by not letting the subject drop without an answer.

He wobbled some as he turned to face me. "I wasn't sure who I would meet, based on what I've heard about your recent struggles. They say you went mad."

I stiffened. "Never mad enough to try assaulting a king."

He chuckled, which was an uncomfortably thin, dry sound. "Fair enough."

"You'll have to pardon my rudeness, but I have a bride waiting on my return. I was told there was something you wanted to talk to me about?"

He wasn't in a hurry to get on with it, which was beyond frustrating. I watched him sigh, nod his head a few times, and turn back to face the statue of Jae and Mavrik looming before us. "Do you know why no one speaks my name anymore?"

"No, your majesty."

"It was at my own request. All those years ago, as I buried what remained of my family—my progeny—I asked that no one in the kingdom ever speak my name again, because I buried myself with them that day. I had to, you see, in order to become someone terrible enough to carry out the vengeance they deserved."

I swallowed uncomfortably. "I see."

"I believe we must all do that, in some form, in order to be reborn. Names have unimaginable power—not just for the person bearing them. Just think of what power your own name, Duke Farrow, possesses now. It garners respect, fear, and admiration from your subordinates." He stopped there and peered at me through the holes in his golden mask. "What does the name Lord General mean to you?"

My heart took a swan dive into the pit of my stomach. Gods ... did he know about what happened fledgling year? My mind raced, and in a matter of seconds I decided to play as dumb as I could. "I know you've yet to name a successor to the one that met with an unfortunate death a few years ago."

"Yes. I take the name of Lord General especially seriously. Such a person would be my right hand. It would have to be someone I felt I could trust unconditionally to be faithful to my every command. Someone who has sworn himself to me completely. Only then would they be granted all the power that name warrants," he said. "Surely you can see why it would take me some time to find an appropriate replacement."

"Of course." I dared to take a breath and let myself relax again.

"To be my right hand would give you power you cannot imagine. There would not be a single door in this kingdom that would not open for you. Nothing would be beyond your reach. Command of every dragonrider in my service would be yours."

"The way you're talking," I interrupted. "It almost sounds as though you're offering me the job."

"And if I was?"

His words hung in the air between us. Me become the next Lord General? The offer was tempting. Beyond tempting, really. Even if I hadn't given up the saddle, thinking of what it would be like to lead—to achieve the highest rank a dragonrider could ever have in his lifetime ... It had me star-struck for a moment.

"Of course, this would only be possible if you were to swear yourself to me eternally," he added. "It would be an oath far more significant than the one that put you in my service previously. But the rewards would be great. You would be privy to the ancient secrets of magic known only to royalty—knowledge I've never entrusted to anyone else."

"And that's all I have to do? Promise myself to you?" It sounded too good to be true.

"Yes. There would be a certain ritual, of course, to make sure that you kept your word. But since I have no doubt that a man like you would stand by his word until death, it would be purely a formality." His voice sounded different, as if he were smiling behind that mask. "What do you say, Duke Farrow? Are you the dragonrider destined for the title of Lord General?"

PART TWO: JAEVID

CHAPTER TWELVE

It's not an easy thing to do—asking people to betray their kingdom, put their lives and the safety of their families at stake, and murder the man they call king. So I wasn't surprised when I didn't get a standing ovation at the end of my long explanation as to why we had to do it. Everyone was gathered around me, mute and wide-eyed, in the light from the kitchen hearth in my home in Mithangol. One-by-one, they began drifting away without a word. At last, the only people left sitting beside me at the kitchen table were Kiran, Beckah, her father Sile, and Felix.

It was going to take some time for this news to sink in. It's not every day you learn that your king is actually a traitorous, murdering imposter who's been waging a genocidal war based on nothing but jealousy and bitterness. Unfortunately, time was not something we had a lot of.

"So that's why he always wears a mask," Beckah whispered, thinking aloud. "To hide the fact that he isn't human at all."

"It's to hide much more than that," I replied. "But yes, I suppose that's true as well."

"None of this makes any sense, Jae." Felix was shaking his head. "I want to believe you. I really do. But do you seriously want us to believe you're the embodiment of this pagan elf god?"

I sat back in my chair and let my hands drop into my lap. If only it was that simple. "I never said that. Paligno chose me to act in his place. That's the reason I have these abilities—the only reason I've ever been able to do these things. He's given me power and authority over the creatures of the earth with the understanding that I am to carry out his will."

"And now he's commanded you to kill the King of Maldobar?" Felix sounded more skeptical with each passing minute.

I frowned down at the tabletop. "He's asked me to restore the balance to nature—to put the stone back in its proper resting place. If you think you know a way to get Hovrid to surrender it peacefully, then by all means share it."

"There is no other way," Sile said suddenly.

Everyone looked at him. Even I was surprised.

"He can't be reasoned or bargained with. Either we do this, or we stand by and watch him wipe out all that remains of the Gray elf race while Paligno's curse continues to spread and ravage this world and destroy everyone else left in it." Sile fixed me with a grim stare. "I've spent a lot of time looking for some other means to put an end to this. Hovrid himself has tried to appease and manipulate the stone by using blood sacrifices. There is no alternative, either Hovrid dies or we all do. It's that simple."

A stifling silence settled over us. I didn't know what else to say to them. I couldn't do this without their help, and yet nearly everyone had wandered off without any indication as to whether or not they believed a word I'd said. Not even my half-brother, Roland, had hung around to ask any follow-up questions.

"You look tired. You know, some of us came a very long way to see you. I'm sure we could all do with a night's sleep to clear our thoughts." Under the table, Beckah took my hand. She must have been able to tell I was fighting that sinking feeling of failure. If she'd only known it was so much more than that.

I nodded. Next to me, Felix puffed a loud, exhausted sigh. Sile still looked deeply aggravated as he got up, rubbing the back of his neck, and headed for the stairs.

I watched him go and silently marveled at everything he'd seen and done. I believed I knew the majority of it now. He'd spent a large portion of his life trying to clean up the mess my father had made when he stole the god stone from the Gray elves. So much of his sweat, blood, and time that could have been spent with his family had been invested in one thing—one chance at atonement for Ulric's mistake.

And I was that chance.

In some respects, I imagined that had been fairly disappointing for him. Especially when we first met, before I'd hit the Gray elf version of puberty and started looking less like a sickly, child-sized skeleton. I wondered if he'd questioned his own sanity when he volunteered to take me on as my sponsor and instructor. Any other sane person would have.

It wasn't until that moment that I realized there was a lot more furniture in my house than there had been when I left. Rather, I'd left it nearly bare because Ulric and my stepmother had all but pried up the floorboards and took them along with them when they moved out. Now there were pictures on the freshly painted walls, parlor chairs perched near the fire, wool rugs on the floor, and new curtains on the windows.

Beckah had a knowing grin on her lips, like she'd been waiting for me to notice. "Well, you did say my parents could move in here if things got complicated. After your funeral, when we all thought you'd died, we moved here in secret."

"It looks good with a woman's touch," I said. "I'm not much of a decorator."

"My mother said it was the cleanest house she'd ever been in." Beckah giggled and nudged my shoulder with hers. "I told her about all the furniture you made. Now she's determined to pay you to make a crib for the baby."

I smiled. "I suppose when this is all over I could give it a try. I won't have her paying me for it, though."

"Well, you know, after this is over, you might find occasion to make lots of cribs," she mumbled and avoided my eyes. I could have sworn her cheeks looked a little red.

I started blushing, too.

"I think I might puke." Across the table, Felix smirked from ear to ear. "A whole flock of pointy-eared lady dragonriders running around. Just what we need."

I blushed harder. I'd forgotten he was still sitting there.

"Oh shut up. You're the one getting married in a month. To the girl you've been bullying all your life, no less. I'm tempted to ask if you held her down and threatened to spit in her eye if she didn't say yes." Beckah fired right back without hesitation.

"Wait, you're getting married?" I couldn't believe it. It had to be a joke. "To who?"

Beckah batted her eyes sarcastically in Felix's direction. "Julianna Lacroix."

My jaw dropped. "Wait—*that* Julianna? From the officer's ball?"

Felix's ears were beginning to turn red. "Yeah, yeah. Let's not make a big deal of it, okay?"

A big deal? Last time I'd checked, he absolutely hated Julianna. She was the only girl he'd ever taken special care to warn everyone away from. He'd almost single-handedly made sure no one would dance with her at any ball.

"You really think I'm just going to drop it after everything you—"

Beckah cut me off, "Oh, Jae, he's been holding out on you. He's been engaged to her for years. Since they were children, even."

Now Felix's whole head was red. He looked like a beet wearing a shaggy blonde wig. "I'm going to bed," he grumbled as he stormed away from the table.

"Humans," Kiran muttered under his breath. He didn't look amused.

"I should go help get the beds ready," Beckah announced, as she stood up as well. "It's going to be close quarters, housing so many. We'll have to put pallets out on the floor. My parents want you to have your room back, though."

I tugged at her wrist to stop her. "No, please tell them to keep it."

"Are you sure?"

"Yes. I don't sleep much these days, anyway."

Kiran cast me a meaningful look. "Paligno has a lot to say?"

"Always. Seems like my loyalty is in question—as though he's afraid I'll lose my nerve." It was strange to talk about my dreams so openly. I'd never been able to do that before. Not without worrying that people would think I was out of my mind.

Beckah brushed her fingers over my cheek. "You'll do what's right. You always do. Even when the courage of everyone around you is failing."

Across the table, Kiran cleared his throat noisily. Now he was the one grinning tauntingly at me. But before he could make a snide comment of his own, Beckah seized one of his pointed ears and pulled him to his feet.

"You best keep your thoughts to yourself," she warned him, wagging a finger in his face. "I am not a woman to be crossed. Human or elf—it makes no difference to me. Now come, we need help making the beds."

Kiran dragged his feet as he followed her, grumbling complaints in the elven language under his breath. It made me smile. That is, until I realized I was now alone at the table.

I sat for a long time, listening to the strange, new sounds in my house. The fire in the kitchen and living room hearths crackled. Roland had disappeared upstairs, and I could hear Sile's wife barking orders on the proper way to make the pallets on the floor for everyone to sleep on. She was giving Sile and my older half-brother a hard time if they didn't make them to her satisfaction. Now and again I heard her baby let out an excited shriek or coo. Beckah laughed. Kiran argued in elvish. Quarters were going to be cramped, and I got the impression there weren't enough blankets.

But these were happy, warm, comforting sounds—sounds that hadn't echoed through this house maybe ever. Certainly not when I'd lived here with Ulric and his family.

For some reason, I just couldn't bear to listen. I felt bitter, frustrated, and estranged as I walked to the front door. My heart was heavy in my chest. I needed some space and a little time to sort things out before I tried to sleep myself.

Prax, Felix, and the other members of Emerald Flight were gathered on the porch, talking amongst themselves in low voices. A few of them were smoking long pipes, blowing smoke rings into the chilly night air. They all went silent and began watching me anxiously when I walked past.

"Everything all right?" Felix called out as I started out across the lawn. He sounded concerned.

"Fine. I just need to think." I tried to sound casual.

He still looked uncertain when I turned away, leaving him standing amidst our dragonrider comrades. But he didn't follow.

I walked without realizing where I was going. It wasn't until I found myself climbing the ladder to my old room in the loft above Ulric's abandoned workshop, that I even bothered to notice my surroundings. Up there, in that drafty place, I blew the dust off my childhood memories. Everything was just as I'd left it. Moonlight filtered through the gaps in the warped boards, casting strangely-shaped shadows on the floor.

I sat down beneath the window where I'd peeked out at Sile when I was just a kid. That same year, I was chosen by Mavrik. I became a fledgling dragonrider, and my life took a drastic turn in a direction I never would have expected.

It felt so far away now, a distant memory. I'd cowered here in this room, filled with so much fear and uncertainty. Now I sat in the same spot, as a man, warrior, and dragonrider, with those same feelings turning my insides to knots.

And yet, part of me felt like that frightened little boy again.

"So this is where you're hiding." Beckah's head popped up through the door in the loft floor, startling me. She carried a candle and wore her nightgown and robe. She shuffled over to plop down right beside me.

I couldn't think of a single thing to say to her. Rather, there was so much I wanted to say that I had no idea where to begin.

"Everyone's asleep." She placed the candle down on the floor in front of us. "Except for Felix. He's still sitting on the porch. Waiting for you to come back, I expect. He was a mess after you—well—after we all thought you'd been killed at Barrowton. I think he's worried you'll run off and leave him again."

I listened and watched the candle's flame dance before us.

"I was so awful to him." Her voice got quieter. "I want to tell him I'm sorry. I'm just not sure how."

"I'm sure he knows you didn't mean it."

"Even so, he was suffering, too. I was selfish— cruel even. But the thought of losing you ..." Her voice faded into silence. She turned to look at me, and I could see the pain in her eyes. "We don't have to teach ourselves how to fall in love, you know. We just do it without even trying. But no one ever warns us about how, if that love is damaged or destroyed, we have to teach ourselves how to go on without it. It just doesn't seem right, does it?"

"There's not much right in the world anymore," I replied. "At least, that's how it seems from where I'm sitting. This was my room, you know. When I was younger, before I became a dragonrider, this is where I slept every night. Ulric and his wife didn't want me in the house. To them it must have seemed like a punishment to put me out here. But ... I liked it. I liked being far away from them. It was the only time I wasn't afraid."

Beckah's touch was gentle as she took my hand. She gave me a small, hopeful smile. The warm candlelight bathing her face made her eyes shine like evergreen-colored stars.

"I slept right over there, and every day I looked out this window. That's where I got my first good look at your father. He came to get a saddle. Maybe that was just an excuse to spy on me." I laughed because the memory seemed so ridiculous now considering how far I'd come. "I was different, back then. I know I've changed a lot. I'm just not sure it's all been for the better."

I could feel her thumb rubbing against the back of my hand in a comforting way. "I don't think that's something we get to decide for ourselves, Jae," she said quietly. "We change because of what's around us. Little by little, the events of our lives chisel away at us until we're someone altogether different at the end."

I managed to smile back at her. I was determined to at least look like I had it all together, even if my heart felt so heavy. I suspected it was the weight of reality sinking in—the reality of the terrible thing I was about to do. It was going to change the world. It was going to make things better for everyone else. Or so I hoped.

But I wasn't stupid enough to think that change like that wouldn't come at a price.

She smiled and began tracing her fingertips lightly along the scar that ran from my brow down over my cheek. Then she brushed some of my hair away from my eyes and let her forehead rest against mine. "What happened to your hair?"

"It's a long story," I murmured as I stared at her, hypnotized by how close she was.

"I can't believe you're back," she said softly. "It's like I'm too afraid to let myself feel it. Did you miss me?"

Reaching under the leather vambrace strapped to my forearm, I took out a small, stained, tattered piece of cloth. It had once been a handkerchief—one she'd embroidered especially for me with the image of two dragons. I'd carried it with me into battle, into Luntharda, and now it was looking a little worse for wear.

Her eyes widened with amazement as she took it carefully and held it up to the candlelight.

"Sorry it doesn't look as nice as it did before," I started to apologize.

"Oh Jae," she whispered as she ran her fingers over the stitching. "I can't believe you still have it."

"I'm never giving it up," I assured her. "It was like carrying a piece of you with me."

Without saying a word, she folded the handkerchief up and placed it next to the candle.

Then she doused the light.

The sudden darkness blurred my vision and I was confused until I felt her hands on my neck and her warm lips press against mine.

FELIX WAS STILL WAITING ON US WHEN WE RETURNED TO THE HOUSE. HE SAT on the front step, hunched over with his elbows on his knees and a dejected expression pointed out into the darkness. He perked up a bit when he spotted us making our way back.

"I had a nice long chat with the others," he announced proudly as he got to his feet. "They're all in agreement. We're with you, Jae, to the bitter end."

Beckah gasped. "How did you manage that?"

He grinned and combed his fingers through his hair proudly. "Charm, of course."

"Right. Because that nonsense works on war-hardened soldiers." I rolled my eyes. I wasn't about to show it, but I was impressed. Felix had a way with people that I clearly lacked. It made me grateful that he didn't hate my guts for disappearing and making him believe I was dead. I was going to need him in order to pull this off.

For a few awkward seconds, none of us spoke. Felix was giving me a meaningful look out of the corner of his eye, and I got the feeling he still hadn't forgiven me for letting him think I was dead.

"Don't be too long, it's getting late. I can only imagine how interesting tomorrow is going to be," Beckah whispered. She gave me a wink before disappearing into the house.

And I was left alone, staring my best friend in the eye. The atmosphere between us was still tense and awkward. My face hurt where he'd punched me for not letting him know I was alive. I'd probably have a nice bruise there by morning.

"Figures," I heard him mutter under his breath as he sat back down on the steps.

I sat down next to him. "What does?"

"That you'd still be alive. That I went through all that hell for nothing." He made a point not to look my way. "I adopted you, you know. Signed the documents and everything."

"Adopted?"

"Yeah. So technically now you're my brother. That makes you a marquess, if you're interested. Also, it would be appropriate to change your last name to Farrow, you know, as a gesture of gratitude."

I gaped at him. "Why did you do that?"

"It's always the way I've felt. I just decided it was time to make it official. And since you were dead, you couldn't argue with me or give me that dumb look you're giving me right now."

"Sorry." I closed my mouth and tried to compose myself. "Thank you. That ... well, it means a lot."

I was stunned. I'd almost shaken that heaviness in my chest, that feeling of anxiety and pain. But knowing he'd done something like that for me brought it all back with a crushing vengeance. I couldn't look him in the eye.

He shrugged. "I'm still pissed at you, for the record."

"I know. You have every right to be."

"See, that pisses me off even more. You could at least act like you were justified or something. Be a little self-righteous about it." He reared back and punched my arm hard. Bruise number two.

I winced. "Fine. I was doing what I thought was right. I couldn't allow myself to reflect on what was going on here because every time I did, it clouded my judgment."

"That's better." Felix smirked as though satisfied. "Now you're sounding more like a Farrow."

More time passed and we sat together without saying a word. I had a lot of questions for him—particularly about how he was apparently marrying a girl I had assumed he hated. I had a hard enough time imagining him getting married at all. He didn't strike me as the "till death do us part" sort. But what did I know? Besides, now didn't seem like the right time to get into all that. I had a bigger question in mind, one that had nagged at my brain for years.

"Why did you befriend me in the first place?"

His eyebrows went up and his mouth scrunched uncomfortably.

"When we were fledglings at the academy, you went out of your way to sit with me and get to know me. I've always wondered why."

"I'd heard about the halfbreed student who was joining our ranks. Everyone was talking about how puny you were and that they didn't expect you to last one day in real training," he recalled. "I suppose I just wanted to see for myself what you were really like—if you were actually that brave, or just dumb."

"And? What was the verdict?"

Felix grinned again. "I dunno. The jury's still out."

That wasn't exactly the answer I'd been hoping for.

Before I could come up with a good comeback, he draped an arm over my shoulders and gave an over-embellished sigh. "We really are going to die this time, aren't we?"

I couldn't tell if he was serious or just being sarcastic by his tone. Knowing him, I decided to bet on sarcastic. "Probably."

"Well, it was bound to happen sooner or later," he chuckled. "You know, they'll write songs or tell tales about us. We'll be remembered as heroes."

"More likely, villains," I retorted. "Evil or not, you don't kill a king and expect to walk away with a clean reputation."

Felix shook his head. "Nah. I'm too good-looking to be a villain. Besides, anyone who's actually met you knows you're basically an overgrown fluff ball with pointy ears and a bleeding heart. Definitely not villain material."

"Gee, thanks."

My guard was down. I wasn't even thinking about how he'd positioned himself to put me in a perfect headlock. Before I could react, he squeezed my neck with his arm so hard I could barely breathe. I flailed and tried to get an elbow into his ribs without success.

"Seriously though," he growled threateningly. "If you ever do that to me again, I will kill you myself. And your headstone will say something like 'I was a total jerk and I really am dead this time.' Got it?"

I made a choking sound I hoped he would take as a yes.

"Good," he said as he let me go.

"That hurt, you know." I shot him a glare. Bruise number three.

He scowled back. "So did thinking you died in battle. We're even."

I cursed at him as I rubbed my neck.

"And now you just act like it's nothing," he rumbled.

"What's that supposed to mean?"

He looked frustrated as he kicked the toe of his boot into the dirt. "You're always like this. You keep everything inside, hiding it from everybody including me. You've always kept things from me because you think I can't handle it. And that really sucks, because it feels like no matter what we've been through, you've never really trusted me unless you had no other choice. You are my family. And I buried you. Do you have any idea what that was like?"

I didn't. And all I could do was hang my head in shame. "I should have let you know somehow that I wasn't dead. I realize that now. I'm sorry, Felix."

"Like I said, sorry doesn't cut it."

"Then how can I make it right?" I was beginning to wonder if he'd ever forgive me. "Tell me. Whatever it is, I'll do it."

"Don't let it happen again, for starters. The rest ... I'll just have to think about." He was muttering under his breath. "From here on out, whatever happens—regardless of how weird or dangerous you think it is—you better tell me what's going on. I can't stand by you if I don't know where you are. That's what we do, you know. It's what we've always done. There's nothing you can do or say that's going to scare me bad enough that I won't be there, ready to fight to the death right beside you."

"Felix," I started. I wanted to tell him. Gods and Fates, I *needed* to.

He just looked at me and waited.

"I think I'm going to die. I think at the end of this, Paligno is going to take my life as compensation for what my father did. There's nothing I can do. I can't barter for it. It has to be Ulric's bloodline who pays the price and it has to be the lapiloque who puts the stone back—it has to be me."

Felix didn't reply.

I tried to hold it in. I tried swallowing, looking away, rubbing my forehead, and anything else that might help. Men weren't supposed to cry—dragonriders least of all—and definitely never in front of other men. It was an unspoken law of manhood. No one liked to see a man that way, vulnerable and broken. But suddenly the weight, the stress, the lies, the years of pain and fear bore down on me all at once. I couldn't take it. Something snapped.

I turned away so he wouldn't see.

Felix put a hand on my shoulder.

I bit down hard on my words, and yet I still couldn't keep from stammering. "D-don't tell Beckah. P-please."

"Not a word."

After a few deep breaths, I found I could talk without choking and stuttering. But despite my best efforts, my voice still sounded as broken as I felt. "I know I can't afford to second-guess myself. This has to be done," I confessed. "But I'm terrified. I'm angry. I want the assurance that this really will put an end to the war, that it's all going to be worth it. But whenever I ask Paligno for an answer or a sign, all I get is silence."

"We don't get to know that kind of stuff, dummy. Even if you are this god's 'chosen one,' we just have to go on faith." He shook my shoulder roughly. "Faith in the cause. Faith in the people we love. Faith that however this ends, we'll have done everything we possibly could to make things right."

I wiped my face on the sleeve of my shirt. "Are you still going to feel that way if we fail and Hovrid puts us all to death? Or if the curse spreads and devours every living thing on the earth?"

Felix wore that cocky, crooked, know-it-all smirk. "Sure. And now that we have that settled, let's go over this plan of yours. How do you intend to overthrow the King of Maldobar in his own throne room?"

13

CHAPTER THIRTEEN

As much as I needed—and wanted—to sleep, it just wasn't in the cards for me. My brain was a tangled rat's nest of worries that I tried desperately to unravel as I lay on the floor in front of the living room hearth. I was stretched out on a woven wool rug that Mrs. Derrick had put down. I used a rolled-up blanket as a pillow and watched the dancing flames cast flickering shadows over the walls until dawn.

Beckah, Felix, and Kiran were the first to wake, bounding down the stairs like rowdy children. They made a lot of racket, enough to wake everyone else up, as they began clanging pots and pans together. Beckah handed out orders as efficiently as her mother, instructing them on how to properly light the kitchen fire, crack the eggs, and cut the vegetables for breakfast. Kiran was much better at taking her directions than Felix.

I lay still with my eyes closed, hoping that anyone who peered in at me would just assume I was asleep and let me have a few more minutes alone with my thoughts. Besides, it was interesting to hear them squabble back and forth. Beckah was in rare form.

"Congratulations on your wedding, by the way." She heckled Felix mercilessly. "It was good of you to finally make an honest woman out of Julianna."

"Yeah, yeah," Felix mumbled. He sounded embarrassed. "She had to make an honest man out of me first, though. Which wasn't so easily done, unfortunately. If there's one thing I do best, it's making a fool out of myself."

"No argument there." Beckah giggled. "Still, we were all glad to hear you two had resolved your differences. Especially since no one was even sure you were still engaged. And then when she kissed Jae at the officers' ball—"

Someone—probably Felix—dropped one of the metal pots on the floor. It made an awful racket. "She what?"

"Or maybe he kissed her. I don't remember which it was." I could tell Beckah was baiting him on with her dismissive tone. It was working beautifully.

Felix was practically beside himself. "Gods and Fates, woman. How could you not remember which?"

"What difference does it make?" Kiran grumbled as though the whole conversation were annoying to him. "A kiss is a kiss."

"What difference does it make?" Felix repeated his question in a mocking tone. "Well, either my fiancée kissed my best friend, or he kissed her. Makes a pretty big difference, if you ask me."

Beckah was laughing again. "Oh come on, Felix. We all know she just did it to make you jealous. And can you blame her? The way you fawned over every girl in the room right in front of her. Honestly, it was as disgusting as it was pathetic."

"So she kissed him?" Felix didn't even seem to notice that he'd been insulted.

"You really think Jae would force himself on a girl he just met?" Beckah countered.

"No. I suppose not."

Beckah huffed. "Of course he wouldn't. Like I said, I'm sure she only did it to get your attention."

"Yeah, well, it didn't work," Felix was the one grumbling now.

I could hear the smirk in Beckah's voice. "Seems like it's working now."

"I hear a lot more talking than I do breakfast-making," Sile barked from the top of the stairs. His heavy footsteps descended into the kitchen, which was a relief. I needed time to scramble and come up with a good excuse for not telling Felix that Julianna had kissed me. Of course, I hadn't known she was his fiancée. I hadn't told him because I thought he hated her and letting him know I'd locked lips with her would be the perfect invitation for more of his teasing.

And for the record—she was definitely the one who kissed me.

I listened to them banter and continue to taunt each other, as the house filled with the lively sounds of my friends and the smell of a delicious breakfast. The smell lured the rest of our guests down from upstairs and eventually I went to join them in the kitchen as well.

Leaning in the doorway, I watched everyone muscling around to get a bite to eat. Beckah had made biscuits from scratch, fried up two-dozen eggs, and roasted more links of sausage than I'd ever seen in my life. There was plenty to go around, which was good since the majority of our group were full-grown men with big appetites, but I couldn't bring myself to join in.

"Strange, isn't it?" Roland appeared next to me, seemingly out of nowhere. It startled me a little.

I glanced over him again, now from a much closer angle. He'd changed so much I barely recognized him, especially with a beard. It made him look older and less like our father. Too bad I couldn't grow one myself, if only for that reason.

Roland still had his arm bandaged up and cradled against his chest in a sling. I wondered if he would refuse if I offered to heal it for him.

"What is?" I finally remembered to ask.

"Seeing this many people here all smiling. Hearing laughter instead of screaming, crying, and cursing. I didn't think I would live to see the day when I witnessed this happening in this house."

"I've been thinking the same thing since I got here," I answered.

"If you're wondering whether or not I'll follow you into this insanity, the answer is yes." He still spoke in that same somber, serious tone I remembered from my childhood. He'd never been keen on self-expression or drawing unnecessary attention to himself.

"I'm glad to hear it."

Then he cut to the chase. "That girl with the long, dark hair. She's yours, isn't she?"

I tensed because I had no idea where he was going with this. "She might argue the reverse—that I'm hers, that is."

For a brief second, it almost looked like he cracked a smile. "I thought as much."

"Why do you ask?"

Roland was in no hurry to let me in on whatever it was he was thinking. And when he finally did explain, I wasn't sure how to respond. "I was afraid after the sampling of family life you'd had with us, you wouldn't want it for yourself. That you might never want to marry or have children of your own."

His tone, much quieter and reluctant than usual, made me wonder. "Is that how you feel?"

He gave a noncommittal shrug. "Sometimes I worry that one day I'll wake up and realize I've become someone I hate, someone like Ulric. I don't think I could stand that. And even worse, I don't think I could forgive myself for putting anyone else through it. I've never courted anyone for that reason. I'm not sure I ever will."

"I know what you mean," I replied. "But I don't think that would be the case, if you did decide to take a wife. We're not like that—we're not like him."

He didn't reply. He watched everyone as they went on eating and talking, oblivious to the irony of their company in this house.

My eyes were drawn to Beckah, as though by gravity. That's when a new, harrowing realization reared its ugly head in my already frazzled brain. I made a radical decision.

"Can you promise me something, Roland?"

He stared straight at me with piercing eyes. "Yes."

"If anything should happen ... to me. Something unfortunate. Look after her, would you? I don't want her to be alone. Felix already has someone. You'll be the only family I have left who could do it. She's a special person. She deserves to be happy. She won't like it. She might even try to scare you away. But promise me you won't give up on her."

The noise from the kitchen filled the silence between us until, at last, he gave a small nod. "Very well, Jaevid. If that's what you want."

I hoped it wouldn't come to that. I was still clinging to a fleeting hope that Paligno had a greater plan, and that whatever happened next would mean an end to the war that everyone in this room got to witness—including me. But I didn't know that for sure. All I knew was that for the stone to be replaced and the balance restored, the blood of the traitor who had stolen it would have to be spilt.

I had to be prepared for the worst.

After breakfast had been cleaned up and the kitchen scrubbed to Beckah's satisfaction, we gathered at the table again. Only Mrs. Derrick and her baby were absent, banished upstairs until we were finished. Sile didn't want either of them involved.

I sat at the head of the table, looking around into the eyes of the only people in Maldobar I knew that I could trust. It was time to settle things. Felix and Beckah sat on either side of me wearing stoic expressions. Only Felix knew the details of what I intended to do. Maybe that was why he was sweating so much.

"Before we go any further, I need to know who is with me. I need to hear it from your own lips because what comes next will be dangerous. It will be treason, and it will very likely kill every last one of us. But if we are successful, then we may see the end of a war that has gone on for far too long." I chose my words more carefully than I ever had. "No one will blame you or think badly of you for walking away now. And I won't mince words; I want to be very clear. I have every intention of killing Hovrid—the man you've known as the King of Maldobar. So speak now, if you intend to stay and fight with me. If you choose to go, now is the time."

No one spoke at first.

Then Felix clasped a fist over his chest, giving the dragonrider salute. "I'm with you."

"So am I." On my other side, Beckah repeated his gesture. A few riders from Emerald Flight looked at one another as though confused. It seemed they still didn't know who she was.

"If Felix goes, then so do I," Prax chimed in.

"And if you go, then so do the rest of us," declared one of the dragonriders from my old flight, and the rest of them muttered their agreement. That put a decent number of strong, skilled swordsmen on my side.

From the corner of the room where he was lurking and watching, Roland raised two fingers. "I'll go."

"With that bum arm, you won't be much good in a fight," Prax reminded him.

I smiled down at the tabletop. "Never mind that. I'll take care of it. He'll be fit to fight."

From across the table, Kiran gave me one of his finest, cunning, Gray elf grins. "I look forward to dying at your side, lapiloque."

Dying—his brand of a joke. Very funny.

"That just leaves you, then. Seems you've had quite a hand in all this. So are you going to see it to the end?" Prax pointed an interrogating stare in Sile's direction.

Normally, I would have jumped to his defense. But Sile could handle himself, and this was his choice to make. I wasn't going to add any pressure in either direction.

"Guard your tongue, Prax. I've raised more dragonriders than you." Sile's words were venomous, but somehow he managed to sound complacent. "I didn't come this far just to abandon my mission now."

Right. For him, this wasn't about me. It wasn't even about Hovrid or the war. It was about setting things right—about undoing the damage Ulric had done under his watch. It was about keeping his word to my mother.

"It's settled then." I closed my eyes and collected my thoughts. Then I began laying out my plan, detail by excruciating detail. Hours ticked past. They had a lot of questions, and I did my best to answer them. It wasn't going to be simple.

But we did have one factor that I thought might tilt things in our favor, and that was the element of surprise. Hovrid wouldn't be expecting any of this. His eyes were fixed on Luntharda, anticipating an attack from there and pouring all his efforts in that direction. His rage and desire for vengeance would be like blinders on a carriage horse. We were going to hit him from within his own borders with a weapon he didn't even know existed—me. He didn't know the stone had chosen a new lapiloque, and he certainly didn't know what I was planning. I felt confident about that much.

That is, until Felix sheepishly raised his hand. "Actually, that's not ... completely accurate."

You could have heard a pin drop.

"What do you mean?" Sile's face had gone a pasty white.

Felix shrank back in his chair as though he knew this was going to be bad. "I may have let it slip to him that Jaevid could do things."

In an instant, Sile was in his face. He practically dove across the table and grabbed the front of his tunic to jerk him out of his chair. "What did you say? What exactly did you tell him?"

Felix stammered out the specifics, and when he'd finished, Sile basically threw him back into his chair. "You're a fool. A useless moron! Do you have any idea what this means?" He snarled as he thrust a finger directly at me. "If Hovrid knows he's coming, none of this is going to work. He'll put every dragonrider in Maldobar in our path!"

"Not every dragonrider," Prax countered.

Sile's eyes bulged and his nostrils flared. I sensed a fight was about to break out if I didn't do something to resolve it.

"Stop it, all of you." I stood up and shouted loudly enough to get their attention again. "This doesn't change anything except our timing. We'll have to act now, immediately, before Hovrid can call together any more of his forces. Our plan will still work."

"And if it doesn't?" Sile still had a challenging growl in his voice.

I narrowed my eyes at him, letting him feel a bit of pressure from my power, and making the floorboards and beams of the house groan. "Hovrid isn't the only one with reinforcements at his disposal."

For the first time, Sile backed down. He dropped his gaze, shoulders drawing in somewhat. I wasn't the shy, scrawny little boy he'd trained. I wasn't even a dragonrider anymore. I was something else—something even a battle-seasoned rider like him might fear.

"Very well, then." Beckah stood up and started whipping her hair into a braid. "Shake the lead out of it, boys. We've got work to do."

14

CHAPTER FOURTEEN

Time was against us. Our key element was gone. And while I didn't necessarily blame Felix for it, he'd hardly said a word as he followed me around with his head down—literally.

As much as I wanted to console him, there wasn't time for it. We could only reasonably allow one day to prepare. Every hour could mean Hovrid gathering more and more soldiers to himself to defend the stone. That meant more swords, armor, and dragonflame would be standing between us and our goal. Felix was going to have to pull himself together on his own.

There was a lot to go over. Our gear had to be prepped, saddles checked, and swords sharpened. We reviewed the specifics of our plan over and over again, leaving no room for confusion.

That is, until it came to Beckah.

As far as I knew, the rest of the dragonriders from Emerald Flight, including Lieutenant Prax, still had absolutely no idea who she really was. I became certain of it when she marched out the front door of my house, down the steps, and straight towards us with her battle armor on and her helmet under her arm. Every bit of her gear had been polished until it shone like obsidian glass, and the golden wings painted onto the various pieces looked like they had been touched up as well. She walked with her head held high, confidence in every step. When she wore that armor, she wasn't Beckah anymore—she was Seraph.

Every one of the dragonriders around us, except for Felix who already knew who she was, stared at her like she'd spontaneously grown a second head.

"What's this? Some sort of joke?" One of the riders began to protest.

Prax eyed her up and down like he was experiencing a bad case of déjà vu. "That armor ... it resembles ..."

"A dragonrider's?" Beckah interrupted him. "Or Seraph's? In either case, you'd be right."

"But you're a woman." Prax scowled at her disapprovingly. "And a very small one at that. I doubt you can even heft a sword."

"You've seen Seraph do it plenty of times, haven't you?" Beckah scowled back at him fearlessly. "Or perhaps you'd rather draw your own sword and test me?"

It didn't take long for another rider to chime in. "You honestly expect us to believe this little girl is Seraph? The rider chosen by Icarus? The one we've witnessed turn the tide of battle after battle?"

The rest of Emerald Flight muttered their agreement. A few of them were even laughing at her, as though the idea were totally ridiculous. To them, it must have seemed that way. No woman, big or small, had ever been a dragonrider. It was absolutely forbidden.

I was going to intervene, to speak up in her defense, but I never got the chance. Icarus put an end to the debate when he landed behind us with a thunderous boom. The monstrous black dragon flared his wings and spines, baring all his jagged teeth as he crawled closer and put his huge head right beside Beckah. She rewarded him with a scratch on the chin. "You'll have to excuse him. Since he chose me, he doesn't like it when it seems like someone's threatening me."

No one was laughing now.

A dragon had chosen Beckah, the same way I was chosen. By the most fundamental law of the dragonrider brotherhood, that meant she was one of them—regardless of who she was.

"Good. Now that we've got that settled, I'm sure none of you will argue with her leading the second group?" I couldn't resist a proud smirk as I waited for someone to dare to object.

Of course, no one did.

Prax chuckled suddenly. He slapped a hand on Felix's shoulder so hard it almost made him fall over. "Don't tell me you knew about this the whole time, son?"

Felix was wearing a coy little smirk, too.

It only made Prax laugh harder. "Sly devil. Got it from my side, I'd wager."

I'd missed it at first, but when Prax said that and looped an arm around Felix's neck to wrestle him into an aggressive, headlock-enforced hug ... it hit me. He'd used the word "son," and not as a joke.

I stared at Felix, hoping for some kind of clue as to when this had come out.

Felix didn't give me one. He was grinning at Prax, seeming proud of himself, and looking disturbingly like a much younger version of the elder dragonrider. I'd been right all along, then. Prax really was his father.

Boy, did Felix owe me an explanation about that later. He had no idea how I'd wrestled with asking him about it. I was relieved, though, and glad I'd listened to Jace and kept my nose out of it.

"We should practice formations. None of us have ever fought against another dragonrider in anything but training. We've trained to kill shrikes, but never our own kind. It's my intention to get through this without ever having to take the life of another dragonrider, but in the event that you have to choose between your own life and someone else's, you'll need to be prepared. Even more challenging will be that some of you will have extra passengers," I said. "So let's use the time we've got left. Tonight at midnight, we decide the fate of this kingdom."

I sent up a request for the rest of the dragons to gather. At my command, our fleet of dragons dropped below the clouds and began landing, one-by-one, in a circle around us. They shook their heads, snorted, snapped, and growled with anticipation. Next to me, Kiran seemed very anxious.

"Beckah, you'll have to double-up so Roland can ride with you. Prax, you'll take Sile. Kiran, you'll have to ride piggyback with Felix. He'll probably need your archery skills to give him some defensive cover since he won't be able to match my speed. Remember, no one goes it alone. This only works if we stay together."

Together, all my comrades gave me the dragonrider salute—even Roland. Then we took to the air, keeping above the cloud cover as much as possible to avoid being spotted by anyone in the city below.

When it began to get dark, we landed and let the dragons loose to feed and rest before battle. The rest of us took the time to fix anything we'd found wrong with our gear, eat a last meal together, and sit down to rest. It probably would have helped to sleep, but everyone else was just as anxious and fidgety as I was. No one was sleeping tonight.

I SET ABOUT HEALING ROLAND'S ARM, AND EVERYONE GATHERED AROUND TO watch curiously as I unwrapped it from the bandages and assessed the damage. His arm was broken in two places because it had been wrenched backwards while still buckled to his shield. It was already healing on its own, so all I had to do was finish the job. I brushed my fingers over his skin, leaving behind a faint, glowing trail of soft, green light. The pieces of bone knitted together. The irritated muscles relaxed. I took his pain and stiffness, and when I was finished, his arm was bound to feel as though it had never been broken.

"Told you," Felix said smugly to the rest of my captivated audience, who were stooping over to watch with wide eyes. "And this is nothing. You should see what he can do with vines."

Sile swatted him on the back of the head.

The crowd gathered around us began to disperse after that. With every passing hour, the atmosphere grew more tense. Some of the riders were pacing nervously. Felix spun a dagger over his hand, over and over, while he talked quietly with his father. Beckah was sticking close to her mother, holding her baby sister on her hip, and doing a great job of acting like nothing was wrong.

Everyone waited, doing whatever they could to keep themselves sane while the time ran down. Well, everyone except for me. I still had work to do.

The whispers of my predecessors, their memories and wisdom, buzzed around in my head like a swarm of bees. I'd learned how to use those memories in Luntharda. By channeling them and listening to them, I was able to tap into more of my abilities than ever before. I had powers that even I wasn't aware of yet, but the whispers were very good at guiding me.

Knowing Hovrid might be expecting our attack had me worried—worried that our meager forces wouldn't be enough. We needed more people on our side. We needed assurance we could reach the temple where the stone was meant to rest.

Basically, we needed a miracle.

Roland and Sile were right on my heels as I left the house, following from a cautious distance as though afraid I might tell them to go back. It was dark, but instead of carrying a lantern or candle, I opened my palm and called my power into an acorn I picked up off the ground. It glowed brightly, filling the night air with a green aura. I walked into the forest almost half a mile, a safe distance from the house, and found a small clearing where the ground was open and flat. There, I started to prepare.

Roland cleared his throat to get my attention. "Can we help?"

"I need a small pile of brush just there, in the center. Use only green, freshly picked branches and leaves," I instructed.

"Green stuff won't burn," Sile was quick to point out.

I smiled. "I never said I was going to burn it."

While I cleared away the dry, dead brush from the clearing, Roland and Sile worked. They came back with their arms full of broken-off branches and leaves from all sorts of different trees. I picked the ones that were most perfect, and began arranging them on the ground in a circle.

I took a deep breath as I stepped into the center of the circle and sat down. I crossed my legs and let my palms rest on my knees. "All right. Stand back."

"Where did you learn to do this?" Roland asked.

"I didn't. Others learned it for me."

He arched a brow, looking unsure of what that meant.

"It's hard to explain. I'm not the first person Paligno has chosen, and the spirits of the others still exist within him. So they exist within me, too. It's like bits and pieces of their memories run over into mine. It used to only happen when I was asleep, through dreams, and I had no control over it. But now I can access those memories at will." I struggled to find the least insane-sounding way to describe it to him. "It's sort of like animal migration, I guess. The instincts of one generation are passed on to the next. I can hear them sometimes."

"So ... you hear voices?"

"Yes."

He nodded like he understood and as if it didn't make me sound absolutely insane.

"I take it this is about those reinforcements you mentioned?" Sile had a challenging tone to his voice, like he was still waiting to be impressed.

"Yes." I closed my eyes and let my mind become still. "When they get here, don't move, don't speak, and don't look any of them in the eye. I can't control them like I can other animals."

"They?" Sile asked.

I didn't answer. I had pushed out all other sounds, voices, and thoughts from my mind. I was alone in the dark, feeling the thrumming energy of the world around me—the trees muttering to one another like shy children, the roots of the earth squirming far below my feet, and the spirits of the animals still untouched by Paligno's curse. Those spirits shone like stars to my mind's eye—pure and quietly powerful. But there were others, the ones the curse had touched. Though they weren't close to me, I could feel the heat of their presence like a foul breath on my neck. It was offensive and infuriating not only to me, but also to the other generations of lapiloque that had gone before me.

My eyes were closed, but I could sense the movement of the green branches and leaves around me. I felt them rise and fuse together, twisting and changing until they hung around me like a halo of brilliant, green light. Then, with one push of my will, the light burst and spread out in every direction like a ripple on still water.

It took a few minutes. After all, waking the ancient spirits of the earth isn't done every day. Many of them, like the paludix turtle, hadn't been roused for a great many centuries. I honestly wasn't sure how they would respond, or if they'd even come at all.

But they did.

I knew it when I heard Sile and Roland gasp and their footsteps retreated backwards a ways. Opening my eyes, I found myself face-to-face with a host of creatures I had no name for. Each one was stranger than the last, and they all seemed to materialize out of the dark forest around me, gathering to look at me with glowing eyes that flickered like bog fires.

"*Why have you have summoned us, my lord?*" one of them spoke. It resembled an enormous fox with black and silver fur. On its back were wings like a raven's, and its fur was covered in curling, swirling markings that shimmered in the moonlight. The creature loomed over me, bigger than a dragon, and with a presence that reminded me of a cold, dark winter's night.

Around him, the other spirits waited, gazing at me expectantly.

I laid out my request.

"Such a thing will cost us dearly, for even we cannot break the laws of our god that forbid us from murdering our children," the foxlike creature hissed. "What you ask must be bought at a high price, lapiloque."

"I understand."

There was a tense silence. Though I couldn't hear them, I sensed the spirits communicating with one another. They had some sort of link, as though their minds were able to commune instantly without uttering a sound. Unfortunately, I wasn't invited to the debate.

"We know the price Paligno has demanded to be paid for the sins of your father," the creature said at last. "The blood of the traitor must be repaid. So we will ask for something else. Something far more precious than blood."

I was starting to get nervous. This wasn't something I'd anticipated, but it was far too late to turn back now. We needed their help. Without it, even if we had the stone, we might never make it back to the temple. I had no other choice.

"Name it," I said as I stood up. I offered a hand to the creature, pulling back the sleeve of my tunic to reveal the bare skin of my forearm.

In the blink of an eye, the ancient foxlike spirit dissolved into a cloud of black mist that swallowed me whole until I couldn't see anything around me.

"The wisdom of the ages, the secrets of Paligno known only to lapiloque—all are contained within the memories of your ancestors. We will have it all." The spirit's voice cut through my mind like a cold wind ripping over a hillside.

"So be it," I agreed. "But only after you've held up your end of the bargain. No one touches them. If one life is lost, the deal is void."

I felt a sharp, scalding pain on my arm that made me double over. And just as quickly as they had appeared, the ancient spirits dissolved into their own curling clouds of mist and vanished—leaving me alone in the middle of the clearing.

My head spun and I could barely stand. Through the haze of my pain, I saw the black mark left on my arm. It was burned into my skin as though branded there. I could feel the power resonating from it; it was as wild and ageless as the spirits who had given me the mark.

Just as I felt my knees buckle, someone caught me and held me on my feet. Roland pulled my arm over his shoulder on one side and Sile did the same on the other. Together, they helped me stagger out of the forest.

"You want to tell us what just happened? We couldn't make out a word of it. All just snarls and hissing—sounded like a foreign language," Sile growled. He sounded frustrated and maybe even a little worried. I doubted it was about my welfare, though.

"I made a deal," I rasped. "They're going to help us."

Roland was as pale as if he'd seen a ghost. I could feel him shaking. "What did they do to you?"

I didn't want to tell him. I was used to keeping that sort of thing private because my friends couldn't handle it. Felix would have freaked out. Beckah would have been furious. But these two were possibly the only people who might understand.

"Everything has a price," I replied.

I felt better once they helped me back to the house. I sat down at the kitchen table and leaned over to let my arm rest where the mark wasn't touching anything. Touching it just made it worse.

"Yeah." Sile muttered as he turned away. "Too bad you're the only one footing the bill."

I watched him go, wondering if that fact really bothered him or not. He seemed fine enough to let me do it, although I was technically the only one who could. He knew about the god stone and what it would take to put it back. Not just anyone could do it. It had to be someone with the blood of the traitor—my father's blood—who put it back ...

I froze. Across from me, Roland had sat down with a bowl of clean water, a rag, and some bandaging for my arm. I realized I wasn't the only one who could pay the blood price for Ulric's sin.

Roland had the traitor's blood, too.

I vowed to myself right then that he would never—*ever*—know that.

I couldn't risk that he might try to intervene and offer himself as an alternative. Whatever the past had been between us, I couldn't allow that to happen. Roland was my brother, my closest blood relation besides Hovrid. I loved him and I wouldn't let him take my place.

This rite was mine and mine alone. It was bad enough to have come here and asked my friends, the people I loved and cherished most in the world, to join me in this potentially suicidal endeavor.

"*So you finally see,*" Paligno's whispering voice trickled through my brain. It gave me chills.

I didn't dare answer out loud—not with Roland sitting there.

"*That love, the love of a family, is not so easily dissolved. It is a bond that is nearly impossible to destroy,*" Paligno continued. "*It transcends all other bonds of love and loyalty. Blood is the tie that binds beyond the grave.*"

I bowed my head slightly. So this was why the god questioned my ability to see it through to the end. Hovrid was my half-brother as well. I had the same familial bond with him that I had with Roland, only we shared a mother instead of a father. That bond might make me weak, might cause me to stumble or question the task that had been charged to me.

Paligno's whisper became louder and more insistent, "*You must not fail.*"

I clenched my teeth. Across the table, Roland was quietly tending to the wound on my arm. He mistook my reaction as pain and cast me an apologetic glance.

"Jaevid! Where have you been? What happened?" Beckah's voice interrupted my conversation with Paligno. The god fell silent and my focus was broken as she came flying down the stairs and across the kitchen to see what had happened to my arm.

"It's nothing. I'm fine. Just a little training accident. We were, uh, letting me practice using my power in combat," I tried to wave her off, but of course she wasn't having that.

Roland quickly covered the mark with a bandage before she could see it. I gave him a grateful nod and he went on wrapping my arm like nothing was wrong.

"Can't you heal it?" she asked worriedly, as she brought a chair up to sit beside me.

"I can't heal myself," I admitted. "But Roland's doing a pretty good job."

Beckah clearly wasn't buying what I was selling. She narrowed her eyes at me like she knew something was up. She didn't push the issue, though.

All of a sudden, Kiran came striding into the kitchen fully dressed in his gear. He'd had to improvise with a few human weapons, like a short sword and a collection of daggers, but he still brandished his elven bow and quiver proudly. "It's nearly time," he announced.

Roland tied off the bandage and jerked my sleeve back down over my arm just as everyone else began to gather around the table. Not everyone was completely dressed and ready to leave yet. We had a few minutes left, after all. Just a little time left to stand around before the coming storm and consider our fate together.

I took a deep breath.

"All right," I heard myself say. I was so numb, it was like an out of body experience. "Let's go."

15

CHAPTER FIFTEEN

At midnight, our carefully organized plan was set into motion.
I stepped off my front porch and into the darkness. There was no turning back. I knew that from now on, my name would either inspire hope or hatred in every heart across the kingdom. It was very likely I was going to be the most hated person in Maldobar's history. I might even be tortured or killed. But the slim chance of success, of ending this war, was more than worth it.

Gathered around me in the chilly night air, I looked across at the faces of my friends, comrades, and family. No one else knew what we knew—that the king was not really the king, or that the god stone was the reason all of nature was going mad. Not to mention that it was my own half-brother who had kept this genocidal war going for over twenty years, and unless we did something to stop it, the curse that was ravaging this land would spread and destroy the entire world. The stone had to be returned to its proper place in Luntharda, and the price of blood had to be paid for the sacrilege of removing it.

I called down our dragons, and they began descending one after the other through the moonlit clouds to land nearby. No one smiled or spoke. I saw their eyes fixed upon me, looking to me for guidance and assurance that this was the right thing to do.

I gave them a nod. It was time.

We split off into our groups to do our preflight check on all our gear. From across the lawn, I watched Beckah expertly examining her saddle while her huge king drake, Icarus, nuzzled at her shoulder. She was beautiful, strong, and confident in a way I only wished I could be. She always accused me of being the brave one—though she couldn't see herself and how her presence inspired things in the other dragonriders. She was the brave one, the real hero.

I just couldn't take it anymore.

Crossing the yard, I grabbed her in my arms, armor and all, and kissed her. It felt like the night had frozen, like time paused long enough for me to hold her close. I forgot anyone else was there, or that her father was one of the people watching us.

Slowly, I let her go.

Out of the corner of my eye, I saw Felix grinning like an idiot.

Sile's eyes narrowed and his jaw tightened. I saw him stiffen as his scorching gaze went from me, to Beckah, and back again.

Beckah wasn't paying them any attention, though. She seized my hand and brought it up to her face. Under all that armor, her skin felt so soft and fragile. "Please be safe."

"You, too."

"When this is over, let's go back to the beach." When she smiled, I could see tears gathering in her eyes.

"We'll do anything you want." I kissed her again. Somehow, I was able to smile back. I prayed she wouldn't see the pain in my eyes or suspect the secret I was carrying. Even if I survived, I might not remember her. I already bargained away my ancestors' memories for a chance at saving her and the others. While I didn't know for sure how much those ancient spirits might take from me, or what they might leave intact, I had to accept the possibility that they might take everything—including my memories of her.

Guilt made my insides sour as I walked back to my dragon, Mavrik, and attempted to focus on checking my gear. That secret burned in my mind like a smoldering ember. It was going to hurt her. She might never forgive me, but someday, she might understand it.

There wasn't a price I wasn't willing to pay for her to live.

Next to him, Prax gave Sile a taunting jab in the ribs with his elbow. "Don't look so sulky. Surely the chosen servant of a god is good enough for your daughter?"

Sile kept on glaring daggers at me like he might throttle me the first chance he got. "No one is good enough for her." Somehow, he made that sound like a threat.

As soon as Beckah was in her saddle, Roland clinging to her back with an expression of restrained panic, she gave me the signal. They were ready to go.

I waved them off, and in a burst of wind and snarling dragons, the first group departed. Then it was just Felix, Kiran, and I left standing there, staring up at the sky.

"She'll be fine, Jae." Felix punched me in the arm. He probably thought I was worried about her. "She's got more grit than any male dragonrider I've ever heard of. If anyone can handle this, it's her."

"I know." I turned away. Watching the silhouette of her great, black dragon sailing away across the night sky was too much. "But it's more than that. Destiny is with her. She cannot fail."

"Neither can we," Kiran said suddenly. He was standing next to me, holding his bow and wearing an especially resolved expression. "Not with you on our side, lapiloque."

I couldn't resist a grateful smile. It was nice to hear someone have complete faith in me. I nodded towards Felix and his dragon, Nova. "Time to saddle up. You'll like her better. She flies slower."

"It isn't the speed. Our shrikes fly much faster," Kiran scoffed, all the while keeping a wary eye on Mavrik. "It is the fire."

Felix studied our Gray elf companion as he prepared to mount up. "You're not gonna puke, are you?"

"Relax. He's fine. And a much better shot than either of us, thankfully." I tried to sound confident. "Ready for this?"

Felix laughed. "No. Of course not. Who the heck would be? We're about to storm the king's castle, steal his most prized possession, and potentially murder him if he tries to stop us. Not exactly something I have any experience with."

I offered a hand out to him. "No. But it will be amazing—especially if we succeed."

He seized my palm and shook it, "Definitely. And unexpected, too. Your specialty."

"It's been an honor flying with you," I squeezed his hand firmly.

Felix made a face. "Don't say that. It sounds like goodbye, which makes me think we are definitely about to die."

"Not goodbye," I laughed. "But definitely good luck."

"Lucky." He reared back to give me one more solid punch in the arm. "That's practically my middle name, you know."

THE ROYAL CITY OF HALFAX ROSE UP FROM THE DARKNESS BEFORE US, A POOL of light against the dark landscape. Through the visor of my helmet, I saw the sun rising on the horizon, turning the ocean into a rippling pane of blood-red glass. I tried not to look at the prison camp that was throwing plumes of foul, black smoke high into the air, but my eyes were drawn to it.

I curled my lip in a snarl. Beneath me, Mavrik did the same. There was our first target. I had come to finally end my brother's war, and all the disgusting madness that went along with it.

"Get in close. We'll do one pass, focusing on the soldiers guarding the ramparts," I murmured, knowing that Mavrik would hear my thoughts even if he couldn't hear my words. "Let Nova know what we're up to. Let's make this quick."

Mavrik made a series of chirps and growls, and together our dragons moved as one, flying in perfect sync. Mavrik and Nova leaned into a spiraling dive, dipping down to begin a close-in assault of the prison camp. I leaned into Mavrik's speed, feeling his heart beating in harmony with mine. We were one being in that moment. Deadly, powerful, and as fast as a tongue of blue lightning in the night.

Flying two abreast, Mavrik and Nova stormed the prison camp walls with a cacophony of roars and a shower of burning venom. Their flames lit up the dark, focused on the prison camp walls and the guards keeping watch there. I saw our enemy scramble. Some managed to fire a few arrows at us, but not a single one hit its mark. As quickly as we'd come, we disappeared, leaving behind an inferno that was sure to keep our enemy busy.

More importantly, it was going to draw Hovrid's eye.

We touched down less than a mile outside the prison camp, taking refuge in the rolling hills that shielded us from plain view. Felix and I dismounted quickly and left Kiran clinging to Nova's back like a scared baby monkey. He wasn't wild about the fire.

It was eerie to be back here. Felix and I had come here once before under similar circumstances when we were just fledglings. This time, however, we weren't here to deal with a mere Lord General.

I rubbed Mavrik's snout as I fed him my thoughts, careful to make sure he would wait for my signal. "Don't try to save me if things start to look bad," I told him as I scratched behind his scaly ears. "The last thing I want is for you and Nova to be caught the fray. Just stick to the plan. Wait for my signal."

His bright, yellow eyes focused on me, glittering with intelligence and concern. I could feel his thoughts and moods flowing through me. Images of myself, or rather, a much smaller, pitiful-looking version of myself from a few years ago, flashed through my mind. Regardless of what the dragonriders' academy or Paligno had made me, in his eyes, I was still that fragile, little kid. I was still his—and it was his duty to protect me.

He growled deeply and pushed his nose against my chest.

"I know, and you're right. It's dangerous." I gazed past him at the flames from the prison camp. They had the whole skyline glowing red. "But after this, we're both due a retirement, I think."

"We all will be," Felix agreed as he gave my arm a punch. "So let's just get this over with, shall we?"

I nodded. From my saddlebag, I pulled out two big, long, black cloaks—one for Felix and one for me. They were long and baggy enough to cover our armor. Well, Felix's anyway. I took off everything but my vambraces, the belt holing my scimitar, and greaves. I needed to be able to move freely and couldn't afford to be weighted down.

Leaving my dragonrider helmet on the grass, I donned the cloak and pulled the hood over my head. Once we were ready, Kiran gave us a Gray elf salute and we started for the city. Behind me, I heard the thunderous pulse of dragon wingbeats and felt the wind as Mavrik and Nova took off again. I couldn't bring myself to look back and watch them leave.

Side-by-side, Felix and I walked up to the grand main gate that led into the prison camp. The complex boiled with chaos as soldiers tried to douse the flames. Dragonriders were coming from the royal city, only a few miles away. I could sense them and their mounts, but something about them was ... off. It wasn't Paligno's curse. Or if it was, I'd never experienced it this way before.

I knew better than to let my guard down or to hesitate. The time had come. No more hiding. No more shame. It was time to become what I had been born to be.

Next to me, I saw the flames dancing in Felix's eyes as he looked at me, waiting for my cue. I gave him one second's worth of a smirk.

Then I let myself go.

Something rose up from deep inside me, tearing past every barrier like a tidal wave. It was primal rage—Paligno's rage. I couldn't control it and I didn't try to. Heat swelled inside my body, sizzling through my veins and stretching out to every fiber of my being.

My mind cleared. My doubts, fears, and inhibitions vanished. Every flicker of life—from soldiers, slaves, and everyone in between—twinkled before my sight like an ocean of stars. I could feel the pulse of their energy, the thrumming heat of their life force.

I sensed the soldiers gathering on the other side of the prison gates, preparing to rush us as soon as they were opened. They scrambled to douse the flames on the ramparts above so archers could get in position.

I stretched out a hand, calling forth a burst of power that pulsed through the earth under my feet. The ground began to shake. Next to me, Felix stumbled to keep his footing. His hand was on his sword hilt and his face was pale.

The golem shook itself free of the ground, as though it had been buried there since the dawn of time. An entity made of rock and root, clumped with soil, arose at my command and towered before us. It swung its arms wildly, pounding down the prison gates and bellowing with fury as it was met with a volley of arrows.

I sent the golem ahead to stir things up. It was like throwing a rock into a hornet's nest. With the prison gates now standing wide open, soldiers and Gray elf slaves alike came pouring out. The slaves ran right past us, as though we were invisible. Some of the soldiers did, too. But others recognized that we were the source of the commotion.

It was time for another golem.

I raised a second golem much like the first and sent him lumbering into the compound to pound anything too slow to outrun him. With my two monstrosities keeping most of the soldiers distracted, the few that came rushing out were all we had to deal with for the moment. They encircled us, their swords and bows drawn.

Next to me, Felix had drawn his sword and was squared up for a fight. He bared his teeth like an animal, his nose wrinkled in a snarl as he shouted, daring one of them to make a move.

I moved before anyone else did.

With a flex of my hand, the wooden shafts of their arrows and the staves of their bows came to life. They sprouted new limbs and began growing—attacking the men holding them by entangling them in branches and vines that grew bigger each second. The soldiers screamed and some of them began to flee, however, others weren't so easily intimidated.

One of the soldiers lunged at Felix and the two crossed blades. Out of the corner of my eye, I spotted two more gathering the courage to rush me. I drew the scimitar from my belt and waved them in.

The soldiers came in waves. As soon as I had beaten one down, there were three more to take his place. Back-to-back with Felix, I knew we were outnumbered and running out of time.

Then I heard it—the cry of a dragon over the roar of combat. The cavalry had arrived.

Only, it wasn't our cavalry.

Hovrid's reinforcements were upon us, bathing the ground around us in flame so we couldn't retreat. They burned up several of their own soldiers in the process, but I got the feeling they weren't too worried with friendly casualties.

In fact, I couldn't feel anything from them at all. Not a pulse of energy, not a light of a soul. These dragonriders, and the beasts they rode, gave off no suggestion that they were living beings.

Ten of them landed, encircling us on the other side of their fire barrier. Beside me, Felix panted and growled as he eyed them. Suddenly, his expression became confused, then surprised. Then horrified.

"T-this can't be. These riders," he whispered. "I know them. They were supposed to have died at Barrowton."

"Drop your sword," I said.

"Are you insane?"

"Do it," I repeated and let my own scimitar clatter to the ground. I raised my hands in surrender.

Reluctantly, Felix followed suit.

The dragonriders came through the flames one-by-one, their helmets covering their faces. None of them said a word. They kicked our weapons out of reach and began to search us, taking away every other instrument we might use to fight back. Even without a blade, it took two of them to bring Felix down as they began shackling our hands.

I didn't resist. So far, everything was still going according to plan.

16

CHAPTER SIXTEEN

Alarm bells tolled in every tower of the royal city. Halfax buzzed with activity, as the dragonriders who caught us outside the prison camp forced us through the streets at sword point. Citizens poured out of their shops and homes, filling every avenue and clambering to see us. They took one look at me, the half-blooded traitor who laid siege to their beloved prison camp, and I could feel their hatred and anger building. It was like a disease, a madness that spread through them. They fed off one another, becoming a mob that the soldiers and city guards could hardly keep restrained.

They spat on me. They cursed at me. They slandered my parents, accused me of heinous things, and dared me to show them some of my pagan power.

"Why don't you free yourself, if you're some kind of great sorcerer?" One man broke free of the guards and got right in my face, so close I could see the pores on his nose.

"Hah! I've killed and burned hundreds of filthy halfbreeds just like him. He's nothing special," a soldier sneered.

Someone threw something at me—a shoe it turned out. That began a shower of everything from pots and pans, rotten food, and ... worse things, raining down on Felix and me from every side.

"Why did you come here? Did you really think you could defeat the power of the Maldobarian Army?" Another soldier laughed at my back.

"No." I looked back at him. "I came to save you."

His expression twitched. I saw fear and confusion for the briefest second. And then he laughed again and gave me a violent shove that made me stumble. I fell face down in the middle of the street. With my hands shackled, I couldn't catch myself to break the fall.

My head cracked off the stone surface of the street. For a minute or two, I was delirious. I could hear Felix shouting, calling my name. He was fighting them again.

One of the dragonriders grabbed me by the hair and dragged me back to my feet. He forced me to start walking again. My vision was still swimming from the fall. I caught glimpses of Felix as he kicked, fought, and wrenched against his chains.

My head had finally cleared when they brought us into the courtyard where I had sworn my oath to become an official dragonrider. Memories of that day snapped at my heels, mocking me for my ignorance, as I climbed the steps into the grand front foyer of the castle.

The doors were standing wide-open to receive us. The wave of raw power that seeped out through them hit me like a boulder to the forehead, which didn't exactly feel great considering what I'd been through. For a few seconds, I was dazed again and I staggered. I knew that power came from the god stone. It really was here, hidden somewhere behind these walls. And the closer I got, the stronger the pull of its presence on my soul became.

"Remember what I said. You mustn't touch it. Don't even look at it." I murmured to Felix, as we were taken down a long, cavernous hall into an even larger room, with ceilings so high you could barely make out the details of the sky that was painted there. Any other time, I would have been awed at the beauty of this place.

Before us, on a raised platform of alabaster, was a throne made in the shape of three dragons. Two made up the seat, with their heads fashioned into armrests and their clawed feet as the legs. The last had been carved into the back of the chair, rising up with wings spread and its head looking straight down at us. The light from the burning golden braziers made the rubies set into its eyes seem to flicker with life. There was a large, jagged black crystal set into the center of its head that shimmered like obsidian glass.

Seated in that grand chair, his face still covered by an intricate mask, was the King of Maldobar. He was slumped to the side, as though this whole ordeal bored him. The fingers on one of his gloved hands rolled as he drummed his fingers impatiently.

On either side of his throne stood ten of his elite guards. All of them were dressed in black, wearing their trademark white masks, and were armed to the teeth. I saw swords, scimitars, bows, spears, and all manner of weaponry strapped to them. One was even carrying a belt loaded with round canisters made of clay. I had a bad feeling about those.

Felix and I were brought forward and forced to our knees, with swords held to the backs of our necks in case we made a wrong move. Behind us were the ten dragonriders who's captured us at the prison camp, although I still couldn't sense even a hint of life from any of them. They stood between us and the only exit.

Thirty-one to two. Exquisitely bad odds, even for me. So much for being lucky.

I imagined that right about then, anyone would wonder how this was possibly a part of the plan. Hovrid could just have us killed without letting us say a word. But I was counting on something—that his pride wouldn't let him end this so quickly. He had an ego to feed.

"So, these are the traitors who have stepped forward to challenge my rule," Hovrid's voice dripped with sarcasm and amusement. He pointed to me. "That one, I want to see his face."

The dragonrider looming behind me grabbed a fistful of my hair and jerked my head up so that I was forced to meet Hovrid's seething glare.

The moment he was able to see my face clearly, Hovrid sprang out of his chair with surprising agility. He prowled towards me, dragging the length of his kingly robes behind him. He grabbed my chin and forced me to look up into his eyes. There, I could see something I hadn't expected:

Fear.

"You—you—*you!*" He hissed in a fit of rage. "Tell me your name, swine!"

"Jaevid Farrow."

Hovrid snatched the sword away from the dragonrider standing nearby and beat Felix over the face with it. It made an awful sound. I cringed and looked away.

"Care to try again?" Hovrid leaned down closer to my face. I could hear his furious breaths hissing through the holes in his mask.

"Jaevid," I snarled. "Jaevid Broadfeather."

I saw him hesitate. I wondered if he actually remembered my father's name. Then, slowly, Hovrid began to pace around me. I felt his gaze all over me, sizing me up from every angle. I heard blood dripping onto the marble floor next to me. Felix was hurt, but I couldn't see how badly. I didn't dare look at him; I was afraid I might do something reckless if I did. I couldn't lose it, not now. Not when we were this close.

"Why did you come here?" Hovrid demanded.

"To surrend—" Felix began to answer.

Hovrid hit him again, even harder than before.

"Your friend isn't very intelligent, is he? Humans seldom are, I've found. Don't think for a moment I don't know who and what you are. You may not look like her, but you are the son of that foul witch, Alowin. You are the chosen of Paligno. The stonespeaker. The one they call lapiloque. Why else would you be here? Why else would you be willing to risk your own life, however vain and pathetic a gesture it may be. Dying for these wretches? Honestly. They're like rats. Worse than rats, really, for even animals have a base sense of what's going on around them."

Hovrid kept pacing around me, his steps smooth and calculated. He spun the sword over his hand with expert ease, twirling it over and over again. I could see Felix's blood on the hilt.

"But then again, Paligno is the source of all life. And so you are duty bound to care about these pitiful creatures, too." He pointed an amused smirk at Felix. "You must know I have no intention of surrendering the stone. It is *mine*. So why would you come here? Or is this fool the only one who was willing to follow you on this futile crusade to save your mother's people?"

"They're your people, too," I reminded him. "You may have everyone else fooled, but you cannot hide from me. I see what others can't. With or without the mask, I know exactly who you are."

"Oh? And who is that?"

I clenched my fists, flexing against the heavy shackles on my wrists. "By name, Hovrid. By blood, my brother."

He stopped. Standing before me, I saw him sizing me up from behind that gilded mask. Slowly, he brought up a hand and took it off.

I HEARD FELIX SUCK IN A SHARP BREATH.

I tried not to do the same.

It was heinous, what he had done to his face. It was gnarled, skeletal, and warped like a wax-carving that had been held close to an open flame. It didn't look like he should even be alive. I fought not to gag.

"A strange thing, shrike venom. At first, I feared I hadn't diluted it enough. I thought I might die. So much pain ... I even prayed for death, before it was over," Hovrid mused as he dropped the mask on the floor between us. "But it was the necessary price for anonymity. You know, it was that stupid human boy who helped me do it. I believe you call him Father, don't you?"

I bit back a curse.

"Now you must tell me, Jaevid Broadfeather," he stepped in closer and put the point of his sword against my throat again. "Tell me why you came here, if only to satisfy my own curiosity. I should like to know before I cut off your head and use it as my footstool."

I reached into my belt and took out a seed—one about the size of a pumpkin seed. I'd been carrying it around for quite some time now, waiting for the right time to use it.

Now, while I stood at the epicenter of our enemy's stronghold, was that time.

I held it out to him in my open palm. "I came to give you this."

Hovrid laughed like a maniac and plucked it out of my hand. "Is this some sort of offering? Something you hope to bargain with?"

I didn't answer. I was waiting. Every muscle in my body was tense.

"You're every bit as stupid as your father before you," he hissed and crushed the seed in his fist.

The whole room burst into chaos.

Out of that tiny seed exploded a monstrous boar, who was every bit as enraged as he had been on the battlefield in Barrowton when I'd captured him. It broke free of my magical prison and sent Hovrid flying across the room before charging headlong for the elite guards. They drew their weapons and rose to attack the beast. Behind me, the dragonriders immediately rushed in to join the fray.

Arrows zipped through the air. Men shouted. The enormous boar bellowed with fury, using tusks, size, and speed to tear through Hovrid's ranks. The guard holding those strange clay spheres threw one against the floor. It smashed, and fire burst into the air along with an acrid smell I knew all too well—dragon venom.

"Felix," I shouted and leapt to my feet. "Now!"

He was already moving. He jumped up, sweeping his arms underneath him to get his shackles in the front. Then he took off running for the body of an elite guard that had already been mauled by the boar. He pried the sword out of the corpse's hand and reared back.

I dropped to my knees and held my arms out behind me, my wrists as far apart as the chain allowed. One stroke with the sword severed the chain.

I was free.

"Go!" Felix yelled over the noise. It looked like his nose was broken. Blood was pouring down the front of his shirt.

I hesitated, not wanting to leave him here in this mess.

"Idiot, I said go!" He pointed the sword across the room. "He's getting away!"

I spotted Hovrid and one of his elite guards fleeing. They made straight for a hidden doorway tucked into the corner of the throne room and vanished behind it.

I sprinted after them, seized the door, and flung it wide open. Beyond it, I could see only a few feet down a narrow corridor that led into utter darkness.

I had no weapon. I had no idea where I was going or what new terror might be waiting for me down that dark passage. I was outnumbered, and there was no telling what traps Hovrid had set for me. Once again, my odds were beyond terrible.

So naturally, I plunged straight into the gloom without looking back.

17

CHAPTER SEVENTEEN

The corridor ahead of me was so small that I had to stoop at an awkward angle as I ran. I heard nothing except my own shuffling footsteps and noisy, panting breaths. I felt like a rat running through a tiny maze, the walls shrinking around me with each step.

Then, suddenly, the tunnel opened into a small room. I made a fist and squeezed it as tight as I could. I brought it to my lips and breathed into my hand. Green light bloomed through my fingers. As I opened my palm, an orb of light formed and hovered above my hand, shining brilliantly against the darkness.

The air was colder here. Immediately before me was a staircase leading straight down into pitch darkness. Looking at it made my stomach swirl with anxiety.

But I could hear footsteps and voices echoing up the stairs, from within the catacombs beneath the castle. Who knew how far those passages went? Or where they went?

I swallowed. Step-by-step, I descended the staircase. I cursed myself for not thinking to grab some sort of weapon before charging after Hovrid. Stupid, stupid, stupid.

"*You are my weapon*," Paligno's voice roared through my mind, startling me. It made me trip over my own feet and nearly fall face-first down the stairs. Some weapon I was.

"You've made a huge mistake," I muttered back under my breath. "You chose wrong. I'm not the right person for this task. I don't even know what I'm doing down here. Why didn't you pick someone braver, like Beckah? Or stronger, like

Jace? I can barely beat my best friend in a sword fight and you expect me to go head-to-head with Hovrid and win?"

"*No*," came the god's bellowing reply.

It was so loud it made me cover my ears—which didn't help. It's hard to block out something coming from inside your own head.

"*I expect you to have faith; faith that cannot be broken. Many candidates were considered, but you alone were found worthy. I am Paligno, and I do not make mistakes.*"

I curled my hands into fists. More than anything, I wanted to believe that.

The shining orb hovered next to me at my bidding, offering guiding light as I reached the bottom of the staircase. Before me was another long hall. I passed by open archways and tunnels on every side. My fingers twitched. I was sweating and nervous, but focused on keeping my pulse calm and steady.

My focus was breaking. The orb's light started to wane. But even when I could hardly see my hand in front of my face, I began to sense things around me with much more clarity. There wasn't anything visual to distract me, so I had to trust my ears and powers to discern where to go. It was bizarre. The further I went, the more aware I became of just how far underground these tunnels were. I sensed the weight of the earth pressing down from above. It thrummed with energy from the surface world like vibrations through a tuning fork.

I felt Hovrid's presence, along with that of the god stone. The stone, however, sent raw, unfettered power snapping through the air like tongues of lightning. Every step I took brought me closer, until I could practically feel the heat on my face as though I were walking towards an open furnace. But instead of wincing and turning away, I was drawn to it like a moth to a flame.

And then I saw it—light coming from one of the passages to my left. I headed straight for it. The intensity of the god stone's presence grew until I was pouring a cold sweat. I felt flushed and energized. That was it—the reason my senses were so enhanced. Its presence strengthened me, made me sharper.

My foot crossed through the doorway to the chamber. I glanced around, and a second later, a searing pain shot through me. I felt a ripping jerk as someone yanked a blade out of my back, right at my shoulder.

I crumpled to my knees. Pain made my vision go spotty and I could barely breathe. Someone had attacked me—someone whose life-energy I couldn't sense. They might as well have been invisible.

The elite guard who had followed Hovrid was on me in an explosion of speed and strength that reminded me of Jace. The light glinted off of the dagger he'd stabbed me with. It was as long as my forearm and dripping with my blood. Through the holes in his white mask, I could see his eyes flicker.

He lunged again, poised for a killing blow.

I spun and swept his legs out from under him. He hit the ground hard, and the impact sent his dagger skidding across the floor. I pinned him down and planted a hand on the wooden mask that covered his face. I pushed my power into it, awakening the dormant fibers of the wood. They sprang to life. Roots burst from it, wrapping around his head and spreading over his body.

The guardsman howled in fury and tried ripping the roots away, but they grew back as quickly as he tore them away. That was bound to keep him occupied for a bit, I hoped.

I staggered to my feet and scrambled to seize the dagger. It had pierced me through, and warm blood oozed from the open wound. It hurt to move my arm at all.

I looked for Hovrid. The air was tinged with a metallic, sour smell that made me want to retch. The chamber before me wasn't very big. It was like a vault of stone with a low ceiling and no other passages in or out—a secure place. The perfect place to hide something precious.

Every flat surface in the room was covered in rust-colored ink. Strange writing in a language I didn't recognize was scrawled in patterns that swirled from floor to ceiling and back again. It was like a strange, disheveled web.

And resting in the very center of it, on an intricate gold stand surrounded by small braziers, was the god stone.

It had been placed in some sort of silver bowl. From where I was standing, I could see that the bowl was filled with a liquid. I was standing too far from it to see exactly what it was. That is, until Hovrid stepped forward from the shadows and dipped his hand into it. It was thick and an unsettling shade of red.

Blood.

HOVRID DREW HIS HAND OUT OF THE BLOOD-FILLED BASIN WHERE HE WAS letting the god stone soak. He began licking the blood from his fingertips.

"For the longest time, I tried to appease Paligno's curse with my own sacrifices. I thought I might win its approval and cooperation. But coincidently, I stumbled across an interesting fact that made all that fuss completely unnecessary. You see, when a divine artifact touches blood, the blood becomes infused with the power of that artifact. Partaking of that blood grants the drinker that same power, albeit temporarily. So more must be consumed. More, and more, and more. It becomes a need, an addiction. In ancient times they called it sanguimancy—blood magic."

"That's sick," I snarled at him.

"Indeed. The rest of the world deems this practice wicked, as well. It was banned from ever being used, stricken from all historical records in the hopes it would never be discovered again. But there is a legend older still about the one who discovered this art. One not unlike you. A god's mortal pet. The one they called God Bane. Legend has it he discovered this precious procedure and sought to use it to destroy the very god who'd enslaved him." Hovrid smiled as he wiped his chin of a few droplets and then slurped them into his skeletal mouth. "After a while, it becomes delicious. I've found that using the blood of the innocent yields more potent results. I wonder what it could do with your blood."

I glanced at my wounded shoulder. Then I raised the dagger, sinking into a defensive stance.

"Fortunately for me, you don't have to be alive in order for me to test it." He surged towards me suddenly, a hand outstretched. From it came a burst of light, an explosion of magical energy that overwhelmed my senses and sent me flying across the room.

I hit the wall on the other side. My head bounced off the stone, and once again I was seeing stars.

"Did you honestly believe you were the only one in this world who could do miraculous things with divine power?" Hovrid sneered. "Don't be so naïve. The stone is mine now. It answers to me alone. That Paligno sent a filthy little half-breed to do his bidding it utterly pathetic ... futile ... Insulting!"

He zapped me again, and this time it felt like my skin was on fire. I flailed my arms to get away. My hands groped for anything to cling to while my soul felt like it was being stretched outside of my body. I couldn't get my breath long enough to even scream.

The burning stopped as suddenly as it had begun. I was left lying on my back, staring up at the stone ceiling while my ears rang. I was in shock. I couldn't move.

"Take his weapon," Hovrid commanded. "And cut his throat."

I heard footsteps coming closer. It had to be that elite guard. When he leaned down over me, I realized his mask was gone. I could see his face.

I knew him.

"L-Lyon?" I rasped.

His eyes were vacant and dark. His complexion was ashen. When he touched my hand to pry his dagger out of my fist, his skin was as cold as ice.

No matter how I searched, I couldn't sense anything living about him. No spirit. No pulse.

"You can only heal the living, and not even yourself. It's almost cruel, isn't it? For Paligno to cripple you so?" Hovrid's voice was filled with pleasure as he read the horror on my face. "But I can raise the dead, and they make such obedient soldiers. So do the living, as it turns out. One drop of cursed blood and their minds become as useless as mud."

It wasn't him. It couldn't be. The Lyon I knew was dead. I had watched him die with my own eyes. His body had been burned on a funeral pyre overseen by his entire family ... hadn't it?

Suddenly, I was on my feet again. I grabbed Lyon's reanimated corpse, flung him across the room and turned on Hovrid.

He shrank before me. I saw panic in his eyes. But more importantly, I saw myself—my reflection. My eyes burned like green fire. My teeth flashed like fangs. From my head grew two white horns like those of a stag.

Hovrid flung his power at me again, screeching with fury.

I raised a hand, forcing outward with my will. When the two collided, it turned his wicked magic to nothing but mist.

"*You have no idea what divine power is,*" I roared in Paligno's voice, a chorus of whispers from the melded souls of my predecessors.

Hovrid staggered backward, tripping over the stand and bowl where the god stone was placed. They clattered to the floor, sending blood spraying everywhere and the stone rolling away into a corner. He began screaming again, this time in the elven language. He called me every vulgar name he could think of. He cursed Paligno and all the gods.

When his back touched the opposite wall, Hovrid realized he had no more room to run. He kept looking behind me, as though he expected someone to come in and save him. Maybe he was hoping some of his undead dragonriders or his prized elite guard would find us just in time.

This time, he was the unlucky one.

I seized him by the throat and held him off the ground. He felt so fragile in my hand. With Paligno's power coursing through my body, I could have crushed him. I wanted to. I was supposed to.

"Pathetic! You want to kill me—you've been ordered to—and still you hesitate!" Hovrid choked as he clawed at my arm desperately. "Sentiment. Weakness. Just like your coward father!"

I bared my teeth. A growl ripped from my chest that sounded as monstrous as I felt.

A second too late, I saw the knife. He'd pulled it out of his robes. It was a wicked-looking knife made of white wood—a greevwood knife made by the Gray elves.

He plunged it straight at my heart.

18

CHAPTER EIGHTEEN

I should have died. That blade was made of the sharpest material in the entire world. It was supposed to be indestructible. A blade that never dulled, that could split iron like butter.

But the instant it touched my skin, the knife shattered into a million pieces, leaving Hovrid holding nothing but an empty hilt.

"*You swore upon my stone that no member of his household would be harmed by your hand. I hold you to your oath,*" Paligno's voice thundered around us. It shook the foundations of the castle. The earth quaked, making the stones of the room chatter like teeth.

A deep fissure split open beneath my feet, like the earth's gaping maw. Hovrid was dangling over it, suspended only by my hand.

"*Deliver him to me,*" Paligno commanded.

The fissure was growing wider by the second, devouring the entire room. Lyon's corpse was swallowed first. He didn't even scream. The dead can't beg for a life they don't have.

"No," Hovrid was pleading over the roaring of the shifting earth. "Don't do this, please."

I hesitated.

Questions and doubts blurred through my mind. Was this even his fault? He'd only looked at the stone and been driven mad by it. Could he be blamed for every terrible thing he'd done because of that one mistake? What right did I have to be his executioner?

I looked into what was left of Hovrid's face and saw what I'd been dreading. I saw my brother. I saw someone my mother had loved, a child she'd carried and raised. I saw how, in another life, we could have been close. We could have been friends rather than enemies.

But that wasn't this life.

And this wasn't my choice to make.

"I'm sorry," I said.

And I let him fall.

The fissure opened wider, a yawning mouth of the earth, hungry to feed. Far below, I saw a pinpoint of boiling red light. Then the ground began to cave in under my feet. The god stone rolled towards the abyss, teetering on the edge. I dove after it, seizing it in my bare hands. Then I ran—even thought I knew I couldn't possibly make it. The ground was falling away beneath me. I was too late. The pit was going to swallow the stone and me.

But it didn't.

One step became two, then three, then four. I couldn't fathom how I was making it to the exit, even as the earth crumbled around me. I glanced down and saw that beneath the places where my feet fell, fragments of rock and soil gathered like hovering stepping stones. They created a floating pathway.

This was new. None of the whispers had ever told me about anything like this.

Tucked away into the folds of my cloak, the god stone thrummed with energy and power. Just touching it made me feel like my bones were rattling. I wondered if I was able to draw more power from the stone when I was touching it. I stretched out a hand and decided to test it.

Instantly, a curved, hovering staircase materialized out of the debris, bringing me up out of the depths to safe ground. But the castle was collapsing, splitting at the foundations. Soon, it would be completely destroyed.

Unless I did something to stop it.

I willed the rocks to move around me. I brought forth more and more of them, gathering them around the weak points at the foundation and drawing them in tightly to hold the castle together. Then I willed thick and mighty roots to weave around them like a subterranean net.

My pulse raced. I was running, focused on the path ahead, but my mind was ablaze with power I'd never known. It was a thrill unlike any other. I didn't realize that I was pushing things too far.

I wasn't leaving without Felix. Even if I had to haul his dead body out of here over my shoulder, I wasn't going anywhere without him.

But when I found him standing, spattered with gore, amidst the carnage and smoldering pools of dragon venom in the throne room, I realized I might be the one who needed to be carried.

My head swam and my arms started to feel heavy. Something wasn't right; I was losing a *lot* of blood. It made my focus slip and I knew I wasn't synced with

Paligno anymore. At least, not like I was before. The horns were gone when I touched the side of my head. I couldn't feel fangs in my mouth anymore, either.

I caught a glimpse of Felix as my knees began to weaken. He looked awful, but he was alive. Furious—but alive.

"You," he snapped and pointed the business end of his sword at my face as soon as he saw me. "You said it would only be a few guards. You said we'd fight them together. But more importantly, you failed to mention that stupid pig has a hide four inches thick!"

I glanced hazily at the beast's corpse lying before him. There were arrows sticking out of nearly every inch of it. It looked like a pincushion, and it wasn't moving. But he still rammed his blade into the boar's neck one more time. I got the impression that was just for spite.

"I was nearly trampled to death," he yelled, although he seemed satisfied now that the animal most definitely was dead. "Killed by an overgrown pig!"

For all the noise he was making, it didn't seem like he was hurt any worse than when I'd left him. The most serious wound I saw was a deep gash across one of his palms that was bleeding everywhere. That was a relief.

"H-how did you beat so many of them?" I stammered in disbelief.

"I'm bloody Felix Farrow, that's how," he fumed and thumped his breastplate.

"We need to hurry. Kiran is waiting for our—"

The castle shuddered dangerously.

There was another low, droning sound that echoed off the cavernous ceilings. It sounded like a muffled roar.

Felix and I looked at one another.

"Please tell me that was you," he murmured.

I shook my head slowly. This wasn't anything Paligno was doing. I would have been able to sense that. And as far as I could tell, my mending of the castle's foundations was holding fast. No—this was something else.

I couldn't sense them, but I knew that sound all too well. There were more dragonriders mobilizing, no doubt heading straight for us.

"You got it, right?" Felix was looking up, his eyes tracking the sounds of angry dragon coming from outside.

I pressed a hand against the round lump tucked away under my cloak. I had to keep the stone hidden. No one could see it—not even by accident. Just one glimpse would plant a seed that could grow into madness the same way it had in Hovrid's mind. I was the only one who could look at it or touch it without risking those effects.

"Good. Give them the signal. It's time to go." Felix seized my arm and began dragging me behind him. Together, we ran out of the throne room through a side door and into the castle halls.

The entire royal castle was in shambles. The alarm was raised that someone had broken through the King of Maldobar's private guard and murdered him. Soldiers were storming every hall, searching for us. Servants ran around in a frenzy, terrified of the armed men pouring inside. It took everything we had to stay one step ahead of them.

I knew the courtyard was bound to be a veritable hornet's nest of people waiting to kill us, but our main concern was the dragonriders. Losing them wasn't going to be easy.

In fact, I seriously doubted we could.

As we darted through servant's passages and hallways, hiding and dodging soldiers at every turn, I sent out my signal to Mavrik. It was time to move. We'd be waiting at the top of the tallest tower for them.

At least, that was the plan. I had to trust Felix's judgment now. Of the two of us, he was the only one who'd actually been here before. The perks of being a high noble.

There were just three little problems with our plan.

One: based on what I could sense mustering outside the castle, there were a lot more dragonriders waiting for us than I had anticipated.

Two: Hovrid had built himself a literal army of reanimated dragonriders using that foul blood magic that were all immune to my abilities. I couldn't communicate with any of their mounts like I'd intended, so I had no way to slow them down.

And three—which was actually something I hadn't even considered would be a problem—I was hurt, badly. And it was taking every ounce of my strength and concentration to keep myself moving.

It was worse than I'd initially thought. I couldn't see the wound because of my clothing, but I definitely felt it. I was also getting extremely lightheaded from blood loss. I didn't know how much time I had before my body gave out, but I had to hang on. None of this was going to matter if I died before we got to Luntharda.

Felix kicked in the door to the staircase leading up to the castle's tallest tower. By now we were definitely being followed, thanks in part to my leaving a very obvious trail of blood behind. I gawked at the staircase. It made me nauseous just looking at it.

I wasn't going to make it.

"Come on." Felix didn't give me the option to turn back. He started running up the steps.

I tried to keep up.

In my mind, I reached out to Mavrik. I told him I was hurt. I didn't know if I was going to have the strength to catch the saddle when I jumped. He filled my mind with worried, urgent hues of orange and yellow. They were coming as fast as they could.

My body began to give out halfway up the stairs. My knees buckled under me and I hit the wall. Everything was spinning. I fell backward, back towards all the steps we'd already climbed.

Suddenly, Felix caught me by the front of my shirt. He yanked me forward and draped one of my arms over his shoulder so he could basically drag me up the rest of the way.

"Hovrid did this to you?" he gasped between panting breaths. He had to lean over and wheeze for a minute when finally we reached the top of the stairs. Before us, a small door led out onto the turret.

I didn't answer. There were some things better left unsaid.

The wind was fierce so high up in the air. We looked down at the staggering drop and the castle grounds below. Dragons were circling, scouring the perimeter for us. They didn't know where we were and so far, they hadn't spotted us.

Not yet, anyway.

Felix squinted into the sunlight. "I don't see them. I don't understand, why can't you just get their mounts to rebel? Wasn't that the plan?"

"Hovrid did something to them, something I'd rather not go into right now. They can't hear me. They won't do anything I say."

Then I heard Mavrik's thundering cry. Not literally, of course. I heard him in my mind. He was close.

"We have to jump." I pushed away from Felix and staggered to the edge of the turret.

He tried to stop me as I climbed over the edge. "Are you insane? They aren't here. I don't see them anywhere."

There wasn't time to explain. Mavrik was insisting. His thoughts overwhelmed my own, telling me to jump *right now.*

I grabbed Felix and dragged him over the edge of the turret with me. I flung us both out into the open air.

He cursed me all the way down.

At least, until we both smacked into our dragon saddles.

Felix hit Nova spot on, catching his saddle at just the right angle.

Mavrik, on the other hand, barely snagged me. I hit his back hard and rolled off, frantically trying to get a good hold of the saddle as I felt myself beginning to fall again.

Then someone caught me. Someone strong.

I looked up to see Kiran sitting on Mavrik's back, gripping my arm. With his help, I was able to get back up into the saddle.

I didn't know how he'd gotten over to Mavrik's saddle, or how the dragons had ever convinced him to do it in the first place—since they couldn't talk to him the way they were able to talk to me. I wasn't all too worried about it right then. The dragonriders gathering below had seen us now. They gave chase, taking off by the dozens. Soon there were so many I lost count.

This wasn't good.

Prax, Beckah, and the rest of our friends were waiting for us at Solhelm. They were prepared for a fight, but not for one on this scale. We were vastly outnumbered, with only a few hours at most until we arrived. Worst of all, I had no way to warn them.

We were going to need help—and lots of it. So I closed my eyes. I gathered what I could of my scrambled, frantic thoughts, and sent out a desperate request that rippled across the kingdom.

I just hoped they'd be willing to assist.

I WASN'T DOING SO GREAT, AND THAT'S PUTTING IT LIGHTLY. I'D ALREADY LOST a lot of blood. My body felt weak and sluggish, and I could barely keep my head up. I tried my best not to move any more than necessary; to conserve what was left of my strength.

Felix used the dragonrider's code of hand signals to communicate to me. While we were in flight, it was the only way to talk because of the noise from the wind.

Are you sure about this? He signed.

No, of course I wasn't sure. I was doing my best not to completely freak out. But in the limited time we had before we reached Felix's estate at Solhelm, I'd come up with a frantic, last-minute, more reckless than usual, Plan B. Now I just had to pray it would work and that my request might be granted.

You know what this will mean, Felix continued to gesture. *No turning back. No matter what happens, we can't stop.*

I didn't reply. I knew he was right. This was our one and only shot. Our only advantage now was a decent head start. If we hesitated, if we stuck around even one minute too late, we might not make it to Luntharda at all.

I tried not to look back because every time I did, it seemed like the dragonriders chasing us were getting closer ... probably because they were. Nova couldn't keep pace with Mavrik, and even he wasn't making spectacular time while weighed down with two passengers. Even so, we pushed hard and managed to keep our lead up until I spotted Solhelm on the horizon.

Then I heard a dragon's roar that sounded like it was right behind us. I felt the heat from a blast of burning dragon venom.

They were close—really close.

I had about a second to loop an arm around Kiran so he didn't fall off before Mavrik whipped into an evasive dive. We whirled toward the ground, Nova following right behind us.

I struggled to suppress my panic as I clung to Mavrik's back. I trusted in his speed to save us. He shot through the air, weaving and rolling through erratic patterns to try to lose the dragonriders who were right on our tail.

I couldn't see Nova and Felix anymore. Kiran was hanging on for dear life. Every time I got a clear look at what was around us, I saw more dragonriders than before coming straight for us. They seemed to come from every side.

Then, straight ahead, there it was—Felix's family estate.

"You can do it," I urged Mavrik with every ounce of my concentration. "We can make it."

Suddenly, there they were. The dragonriders of Emerald Flight were rising up from where they'd been lying in wait behind Felix's family home. Beckah and Icarus lead the surprise attack, headed straight for us.

Mavrik tucked into another whirling dive as the dragonriders of Emerald Flight clashed in combat with our pursuers. Immediately, the sky erupted into fiery chaos. Everywhere we turned, there were plumes of burning dragon venom. Dragons locked into aerial combat like eagles, clawing and snapping as they fell. It was a deadly game of chicken to see who would pull away first before they hit the ground.

I caught brief glimpses of my friends through the fray. Icarus was the only king drake, and the biggest dragon by far, so I found him easily. His size wasn't exactly an advantage for him, though. Since he was obviously the leader, it made him and his rider primary targets.

Beckah was like an avenging angel, wielding her bow while standing up in the stirrups of her saddle. The golden wings painted on her black flashed like fire in the sunlight. At her back, her father rode tandem and fired his bow with that same deadly accuracy.

Injured or not, I wanted to join the fight, to stand with the people I loved till my last breath. I could taste the flavor of bloodlust on my tongue. Judging by the way he was gripping his bow, Kiran wanted the same thing.

We were still outnumbered by a lot. They couldn't hold our enemy off for long. We were overwhelmed and flying for our lives.

Mavrik zipped through the sky— rolling, diving, climbing, and falling. My strength was nearly spent, and I was losing my grip on his saddle. Kiran had to put his arms around me to keep me from falling off. I was cold. My sight was growing dim and I couldn't comprehend anything going on around me.

Then I heard a chorus of roars louder than all the rage of combat. The sound cleared my head for an instant. Over my shoulder, I saw them, flying in from the cliffs, the sea wind under their wings. All the wild dragons of Maldobar had heard my request.

The cavalry had arrived. The odds were evened now, and the battle raged on with fire and steel, scales and claws, over Solhelm. People in the town below were running for cover as stray bursts of dragon flame scorched the rooftops.

Felix appeared next to me, frantically signaling that this was our chance. It was time to go, he was right.

But that meant leaving our friends behind to their fate—to victory or death.

My insides churned at the idea of turning my back on them now. I was faltering. There had to be something more I could do.

Felix made his dragon veer dangerously close to us. Mavrik had to swerve to avoid colliding with her. It got my attention and I saw him signaling.

We don't stop. We don't turn back. If we mess this up, then everything they've done will be for nothing.

I clutched the round lump in my robes where the god stone was hidden "Go," I told Mavrik, before I could think about it anymore. "Go now! And whatever I say, do not turn back!"

He aimed away from the battle and started for the north—for Luntharda.

I couldn't let it go that easily, though. Not when half my heart was in the thick of that battle. I reached back with my mind, scouring the thoughts of every dragon on that battlefield that would still let me in—the mounts of my friends. I searched until I found Icarus.

He was fighting hard. I felt his intensity, his rage—and that he was hurt. One of his wings had been wounded. It was slowing him down, making him vulnerable, and Beckah was being pressured that much more because of it.

I saw her and her father through Icarus's eyes, like peering through a looking glass. Sile was nearly out of arrows. Beckah had torn her helmet off. Her dark hair was wild about her face. Her expression revealed a level of intensity I'd never seen from her before. Over and over, she drew arrows from her quiver, firing them into the battle, hitting marks as effortlessly as she breathed.

I saw it coming only a fraction of a second before it happened.

One of Hovrid's riders swooped in from behind. Icarus's injury prevented him from rolling fast enough to evade the attack. The enemy dragon's wings flared, its hind legs outstretched.

Beckah's expression suddenly went blank. In an instant, those powerful, crushing claws ripped her from her saddle. Her father reached for her. Their fingers brushed.

Icarus and I cried out in unison.

But it was too late.

I commanded Mavrik to turn around. I screamed at him. I didn't believe it. There had to be some chance I was wrong, that she was still alive, and that I could still save her.

Mavrik knew otherwise. His thoughts were melded with mine. He'd seen everything I had—felt what I had felt. So he refused to turn around.

And little-by-little, the sounds of battle faded behind us.

PART THREE: FELIX

19

CHAPTER NINETEEN

Something had happened. Something bad. I'd heard Jae make a lot of strange sounds and do a lot of bizarre things before, but never anything like that. Now he was just slumped over in his saddle, with our weird, little, Gray elf sidekick struggling to keep him upright. I couldn't see his face to tell if he was even conscious. It gave me a bad feeling. All I could think about was landing as soon as possible.

We couldn't stop, though. Not until we reached the edge of Luntharda's towering jungle on the northern border. By now, there were bound to be orders sent out by frantic messengers to every corner of the kingdom. We'd just given every soldier and dragonrider in Maldobar the perfect reason to grant Hovrid's final wish to launch an all-out attack on Luntharda and the wipe Gray elves off the map once and for all.

Forces would be mustering now to take up the pursuit, to capture or kill us at any cost. And according to Jae, we would be essentially be leading them to the one place in the jungle that his people had left to hide. So, a lot was riding on this.

On, Jae, rather. A lot was riding on him.

I just hoped he was still up to the task.

When we touched down in the wreckage of Barrowton, I sprang out of my saddle and ripped off my helmet. I sprinted to Mavrik's side as the blue drake flattened himself against the ground. That's when I got my first look at Jaevid.

His face was ashen, with eyes wide and fixed. His shirt and cloak were drenched with blood coming from the wound on his shoulder. I called his name, but he didn't even look at me. Behind him, Kiran fumbled with the straps to get them out of the saddle. When the last buckle was undone, Jae keeled over sideways and started to fall.

I threw myself in the way, arms out to catch him before he hit the ground. My back creaked in protest. For a tall, lanky guy, Jae wasn't light.

"Grab the gear." I started to give out orders. "Empty the saddle bags, all of them. We have to take cover as soon as possible. We can't move until nightfall."

Suddenly, Jae started to revive.

He swung at me, catching me with a fist on my chin. He pushed away and scrambled to his feet. It was like he didn't know us. His eyes looked wildly between Kiran and me as he staggered back.

"Jaevid, just calm down." I raised my hands, hoping he'd snap out of it. "You're hurt. You've lost a lot of blood. We need to take a look at—"

He threw up.

Kiran flashed me a worried glance. Together, we rushed to catch him again as Jae dropped to his knees and started screaming. He yelled like a maniac and hammered against the ground with his fists until his knuckles were banged up and bleeding, too.

It took both of us to restrain him. With Kiran pinning his arms down with a bear hug from the front, I got him in a headlock with a hand over his mouth. Together, we forced him to be still.

"Calm down, you idiot," I repeated. "You keep that up and anyone who might be on patrol around here will be heading straight for us."

His chest heaved with deep, fast breaths. Tears were streaming down his face. I didn't understand any of this. He'd seemed just fine when we left the castle.

I looked to Kiran for an explanation. Maybe he'd seen something I hadn't. "What's going on?"

He shook his head slowly.

Great. So neither of us had a clue.

"Well, we can't stay out here in the open like this." I tried to come up with a way to restrain him—something involving tying him up like a mental patient. Then, out of nowhere, Jaevid went limp again. He stopped struggling and his whole body went slack in our hold.

I thought it might be a trick, but when Kiran loosened his hold, Jae didn't lash out at us. He just laid there, limp as a dead fish, as we slowly let him go.

"Something's not right. You know better than any of us what's going on with him and that forest god, right? So what would set him off like this?"

Kiran's brow furrowed and his mouth mashed together into an uncomfortable, crooked line. He was looking Jae over, thinking. At last, he met my gaze and answered, "Death."

It took a second or two for that to sink in. It took even longer for me to make sense of it. Meanwhile, Kiran and I worked together to get everything prepared for nightfall. I carried Jae into the burned-out, skeletal remains of a building in Barrowton's former city square. It offered some cover from aerial scouts who would soon be launched to search for us.

Kiran unloaded all our gear and supplies, stacking them in a corner and bringing me all the medical tools he could find while I ripped open Jae's blood-soaked shirt and started treating his injury. It was a deep puncture through the middle of his shoulder. It was going to keep him from being much use in combat. Actually, it was a miracle he'd made it this far. He had a lot more grit than I'd ever given him credit for.

"Is he dead?" Kiran appeared over my shoulder, leaning in to watch while I put the final stitches in place.

"No. You think I'd bother to stitch up a corpse?"

He made a 'pfft' sound and walked around to sit across from me, huddling underneath a coarse blanket he'd swiped from Jae's saddle bag. We couldn't light a fire, even though the evening air was chilly. After I got Jae's shoulder bandaged up and wrapped in a few layers of gauze, I took the blanket from my bag and wrapped him up in it. Then I sat back to think.

Outside, our dragons were hunkering down in whatever cover they could find—lying in wait for further orders. Orders that I wasn't sure I could give. If Jae was out of commission, that meant completing this mission had just become my responsibility. Only, I had no idea where to go or what to do when I got there.

"You know," I started to talk because the silence was crushing me. "Hovrid actually came to me right before this. He asked me to be his new Lord General."

Kiran canted his head to the side. Duh. He didn't know what a Lord General was.

"Basically, the leader of all dragonriders. His number one in command," I explained.

Kiran made an O-shape with his mouth.

"I refused. I mean, not that it wasn't tempting. But something about him ... I don't know, I guess it was my intuition that he was after more than just a new Lord General. He wanted me—someone Jae trusted—to turn on him. And then when I actually saw what he was underneath that mask? Gods and Fates, I can't believe I ever doubted Jae for a second."

"If it had been easy to believe, then Hovrid wouldn't have gotten away with it for so long," Kiran replied quietly.

He was a weird guy. Short, you know, because of the whole elf thing. He never said much, or at least never more than was absolutely necessary. And his long, silver hair, multi-hued eyes, pointed ears, and colorful silk clothes were odd, too.

But I was starting to see why Jaevid liked him.

"Why'd you come with him?" I asked.

He glanced up at me then quickly looked away. "There was ... someone I was hoping to see."

"A girl?" I guessed.

He didn't answer. But I knew I was right. His mouth scrunched uncomfortably and his brow creased with worry.

"Someone from the prison camp? Or the ghetto in Halfax?" After all, it had to be another Gray elf, right?

He shook his head slowly. He had that faraway look on his face. "No," he answered softly.

"Well, I'm sure she's fine wherever she is." I tried to offer him a little hope, since that was in short supply at the moment. "And when all this is over, you can go find her and tell her you helped save the world."

Kiran swallowed hard. "I hope so."

"We can't stay here much longer." Kiran shifted his weight from one foot to the other, peering up at the starry night sky through the charred rafters of our hiding place.

Technically speaking, we should have been long gone by now. We should have sent our dragons off as a diversion while we slipped through the border into Luntharda undetected. But Jae was in bad shape. I didn't know exactly how bad off he was; I'm not any sort of doctor. Although, I could guess that the pale color to his skin, the dark circles under his eyes, and the frantic, shallow way he was breathing weren't good signs.

"I don't see how we can move him like this," I muttered back.

Kiran puffed a frustrated sigh through his nostrils. "I'm going to get a better look. If there aren't any scouts or patrols in sight, we will have to take the risk. The princess is waiting for us."

He didn't hang around for my opinion on the matter. He scurried away across the debris-strewn city like a silver-haired squirrel, leaving me to sit by Jaevid's unconscious body.

Only, he wasn't unconscious anymore.

"H-how late is it?" His voice sounded dry and hoarse. Thanks to the faint, sterling light from the sky, I could see his eyes were open. Even so, he still looked dead. His expression was vacant and his gaze was fixed straight ahead as he lay on his back, not moving.

"Not very. An hour past dark. We're behind, but not by much."

He blinked slowly. "I'm going on alone."

"Like hell you are."

Jae didn't argue. He didn't look at me or make any sound at all. It wasn't normal, even for him.

I turned away because I wasn't sure how to start or what to say. I had to ask him. Someone needed to, and that someone had to be me because I was his best friend.

"It was Beckah, wasn't it?"

When he didn't answer, I dared to glance down at him again over my shoulder. He hadn't moved. He was still just lying there, staring up at the sky.

The light glinted off something wet sliding down his cheek.

"I failed her," he whispered.

"No you didn't."

He looked back at me, then. His jaw tensed and I saw something crazed cross his face, a primal anger he didn't have the ability or strength to express. It was the look of a broken man. "I promised her, Felix. I promised her I would protect her! And I couldn't do anything to stop—"

"She knew the risks," I shouted as loudly as I dared. "We all did. And we understood what was most important. The only thing that matters right now is getting you and that stone into the jungle so we can put an end to all this. If that means a few of us have to die to get it done, so be it. That's the gamble we all took. And if Beckah were here, she'd be telling you the same thing. This is war, Jaevid. People die—and sometimes it's the people we love."

We stared at each other in silence. I could tell I'd made him even angrier. His face got a little bit of color back—just enough to let me know he still had enough blood in his veins to keep him going.

"Look, I'm not saying you shouldn't be upset. I'm not saying you shouldn't grieve. But don't go off blaming yourself for something that wasn't your fault. I made that mistake already when I thought I'd lost you. I know where that path ends. Trust me, that isn't where you want to be."

Slowly, Jae turned his face away to stare back up at the sky. He blinked owlishly and never said a word, even after Kiran came back. Kiran was out of breath and frazzled, his eyes darted everywhere like a nervous cat.

"I saw them. A scouting party of four dragonriders coming from the east," he whispered. "They're headed straight for us."

"They must be coming from Northwatch."

Kiran bobbed his head eagerly, and then gestured to Jae. "Our time is up. We must move now. Can he walk?"

"I'm not sure. Maybe. But walking might not get us there in time." I glanced at all our piled up gear. Saddlebags stocked with food, medical supplies, and survival gear. All were things I'd been trained to believe I needed in order to survive in Luntharda, and we weren't going to be able to take any of it with us. "You're sure that princess of yours is going to be there?"

"Yes," he answered sharply.

That was good enough for me. "Gather only the weaponry. The rest we'll have to leave behind."

Kiran bounded off again, rummaging through all the bags and laying out our spread of deadly tools. Meanwhile, I hauled Jae to his feet. He was catatonic, staring around aimlessly with a dead look in his eyes. It was starting to freak me out.

I smacked him across the face. "Snap out of it, hero. You've got to get the dragons to draw off the scouts so we can get out of here without being burned to a crisp. You hear me?"

He blinked a few times and finally nodded.

It only took a moment or two before I heard the deep percussion of wing beats. I saw the starlight glint off our dragons' scales as they sailed upward, spitting plumes of flame that would be visible for miles. A few minutes after they wheeled away and disappeared, four more dragons zipped past, flying low and fast in hot pursuit.

The clock was officially ticking.

After I packed what weaponry I could into every nook and cranny of my armor, I gave Kiran the go-ahead to take the lead. He was gonna have to get us out of the city and all the way to the border of Luntharda, because I was on watch to make sure Jaevid didn't pass out again or die before we got there.

I approached him carefully, holding out his elf-human hybrid scimitar with the stag head engraved on the pommel. "I need to know you're still in there, Jae. I need to know you can finish this."

His eyes were clearer when he met my gaze. "Yes, I can."

"Good." I pushed the hilt of the blade into his hands. "Now do whatever magical thing it is you do and let that princess know we are coming for her."

20

CHAPTER TWENTY

Kiran ran point, his bow at the ready as he scaled mounds of debris and kept his eyes on the horizon. He found a manageable path for us out of the city, and I had to give him credit—he didn't even stop to consider all the decayed corpses of his kinsmen lying everywhere from the battle. Granted, there were a lot of human remains, too. But if seeing the carnage filled him with any kind of resentment for us or made him second-guess his decision to join our cause, it never showed. He was steady as a rock, focused, running ahead of us without making a sound.

Once we left the city ruins, I got nervous. We were out in the open, plainly visible to anyone who might fly over. There was nowhere to run and nowhere to hide. We were completely on our own, trekking to the border of Luntharda as fast as we could, which wasn't nearly fast enough.

Jae was weak. He leaned heavily against me, stumbling now and again so that I was forced to catch him to keep him upright. That's when I realized ... he wasn't going to make it, at least not at this rate. We were still miles from the border. I couldn't even see the jungle yet.

Suddenly, Jae stopped. He pushed away from me and whirled around, his eyes going wide as saucers as he looked to the sky. In the distance, I heard the low rumble, like thunder from an approaching storm front.

"It's the dragonriders from Northwatch," Jae said. "They're coming this way."

"How long?"

"Five minutes at the most." He blinked slowly.

"Can you hold them off? Get their mounts to turn around?"

He shook his head slowly. "It's the same as before. Hovrid has done something to them. They won't listen to me."

Then his body shuddered, and when he gazed up at the sky again, I saw his irises light up like two green moons. He was using his powers—brewing up another miracle to try and save us.

I knew I should've stopped him. He wasn't up to this. He could barely walk, how could anyone expect him to—

The ground started to rumble beneath us. Jae snarled, baring teeth with incisors pointed like a wolf's fangs. He made a primal, roaring sound and stretched out his hands. Jae made a ripping gesture in the air, as though pulling apart invisible dough with his fingers.

Before us, the ground shuddered open like a cracked piece of pottery. Kiran and I stumbled back to get out of the way, and not a moment too soon. Out of the fissure crawled a creature out of someone's worst nightmare, with eyes glowing like two pits of bottomless, green fire. It looked like an enormous dragon made of roots and earth, held together by raw magic, easily twice the size of any king drake. Horns of twisted roots, scales of shale, claws of crystals, and a hide spotted in moss and plant life. It shook itself free of the ground, as though it had been imprisoned there for an eternity, and let out an earth-shaking screech.

I couldn't keep my mouth closed or take my eyes off it. The dragon spread its huge wings. Each beat was like a mighty clap of thunder. I had to shield my face, as the force of it taking off blew debris everywhere. Once the monster was airborne, we watched in total silence as it soared towards our approaching attackers—ready to intercept them.

"What the heck is that thing?" I heard myself ask.

"Another distraction," Jae replied hoarsely. "But it won't last long. We need to hurry. I've asked Mavrik and Nova to hold them off as long as possible."

I saw him start to wobble. He staggered, and I rushed forward to catch him under the arm before he could collapse.

"I called out to the jungle. Araxie and Jace ... t-they're ... w-we have to ..." Jae tried to speak, but his voice was lost as he took in deep, ragged breaths. His head lolled against me, and I could see that his skin was more ashen than before. Casting that magic, drawing from that power, was costing him too much.

"We can't let him do that again." I growled at Kiran. "He's killing himself a little more every time he does."

Kiran nodded in agreement. "Let's move."

We took off as fast as we could across the rolling prairie. Kiran stayed right beside me, watching our backs with his bow at the ready and his eyes on the sky. Behind us, I could hear the sounds of aerial combat. Dragons snarled and bellowed. The night lit up with plumes of dragon flame erupting into the darkness.

Jae was right. His earth-dragon didn't last long. It made for an amazing spectacle, but it didn't hold up well against fire. Once it caught a few good blasts of burning dragon venom, it only had minutes left before it came crashing back to the earth to smolder and crackle in a giant heap.

Then they were on us. With a skull-rattling boom, a dragonrider touched down right before us. His sword was drawn. His mount's scales glittered in the starlight like black diamonds. I saw the dragon's plated chest heave and its head recoil as it took in a mighty, venom-spraying breath.

She came out of nowhere—my girl. Nova blitzed down out of the sky and smacked right into them at full speed, legs outstretched and jaws open wide. The impact threw the rider from his saddle and he hit the ground with a nasty-sounding crunch. The two dragons rolled across the ground like two brawling cats, snarling and hissing. My girl was bigger, stronger, but her opponent hadn't come to the fight alone.

Three more dragonriders dove in at her at once, overwhelming her and burying her under a heap of scales, claws, and teeth.

I yelled for her. I heard her screeching, screaming in panic.

A sudden explosion of flame sent her attackers retreating back. Mavrik landed beside her, his teeth bared and his black spines bristling as he took up a protective stance between them—daring one of the other dragons to make a move. It gave Nova a chance to recover. She shook herself off and joined him in squaring off with their enemies.

I never saw what happened next. We descended the hill on the other side of the fight and kept going. I couldn't stop, or look back to see if she was all right, I just had to trust that she would be.

It was a race against time, and we were definitely losing. I saw the shadows of the other dragonriders against the gentle light of the stars as they made low, zooming passes over us.

They were coming, growing closer by the second. They were just looking for the perfect place to rally and corner us.

I didn't stop to look at them. I kept pressing forward, running as fast as possible while basically dragging Jae's unconscious body along. Kiran was shouting in elven, firing arrows at the dragonriders who swopped in close to us.

Suddenly, ten of them landed in front of us. We came skidding to a halt, staring into the swords, teeth, and flame of an enemy that outnumbered us. Then a dozen more landed behind us. Kiran took a protective step in towards Jae, his bowstring taut with three arrows ready to fire. The dragonriders moved as one, enclosing us in a circle.

Because I was one of them, I knew that next came the inferno. They'd bathe us in an onslaught of venom that wouldn't even leave bones behind.

"Well? You gonna just sit there and chat about it or are you gonna do something, ladies?" I shouted at them. With my free arm, I drew my sword. No way in hell was I going down empty-handed. I clenched my jaw, squared my stance, and waited for the axe to drop.

It came out of nowhere.

A hailstorm of arrows from the sky rained down all around us, hitting the ground only feet away from Jae, Kiran, and I. But not a single one struck us. They sent our enemies scurrying for cover, however. Three dragons bellowed in pain, one dropping immediately after taking a well-aimed arrow to the back of the skull.

Next to me, Kiran started cheering. He raised his bow in the air, and I looked up to see why. A small group of Gray elves on shrikes went streaking past us, quicker than shooting stars, chasing down the dragonriders and locking them in combat. Well, all save for two.

Two shrikes landed before us. They moved so fast it was like they'd materialized out of thin air. Their scales shimmered like mirrors, reflecting the starry sky. Their bony jaws snapped and their eyes gleamed, eyeing us down. Each was carrying a rider wearing a long battle headdress fitted with white horns.

One I knew right away. I'd seen her before, although not up close. She had to be the Gray elf princess I'd heard so much about. She pulled back the mask on her headdress, letting her long, white hair spill freely down her shoulders. Her eyes reminded me of a wolf's—unpredictable, wild, and secretive.

The other rider removed his mask.

My mouth fell open.

"Don't just stand there like an idiot, Farrow," Jace Rordin was yelling at me over the noise of combat, outfitted from head-to-toe in full Gray elf battle-dress. "Get on!"

"You have got to be kidding me."

With Kiran giving me cover, firing arrows at any dragonrider who came too close, I dragged Jaevid the last few feet and flung him over the princess's saddle. The shrikes weren't large, not nearly as big as a dragon, and I wasn't even sure they could take the weight of two riders. But it's not like we had any time to test it out.

Once Jaevid was secure, the princess took off without us. I climbed onto the back of Jace's shrike. The creature tensed, moving like a feline and preparing for takeoff. Kiran backed up a few feet and gave me a smirk and a dragonrider's salute.

"Wait!" I shouted. "What about him?"

"No room," Jace yelled back.

We took off, streaking away from the ground and leaving our Gray elf companion standing there, watching us with a knowing grin on his lips. What I would have given right then to have some of those powers—to tell Nova or Mavrik to look after him.

But I'm not the one who works miracles.

"Hold him down," the Gray elf princess spoke sternly. She scooped up a glob of something green, pasty, and smelly onto her fingertips.

By the dim light of a small oil lamp, Jace and I struggled to hold Jaevid still while she forced his mouth open and fed him more and more of the stuff. It must have tasted bad because Jae fought us hard, but when she finished, he was already looking better. His color wasn't so corpse-like and he was breathing more steadily.

Jace and I stood back, giving the princess some space while she tucked a blanket around him snuggly. All around us, Gray elf warriors rushed to and fro, mustering their arms in preparation for the coming attack. Their makeshift compound was pathetically tiny. They had maybe three hundred fighters, not counting the ones who were obviously children that normally would have been way too young to fight.

We were only a mile inside the jungle, if that. They didn't expect their aerial force to hold long. More dragonriders and legions of ground infantry would be headed straight for this jungle, ready to raze it to the ground.

"Is this really all the soldiers they have?" I murmured to Jace, who was looking more concerned than I'd ever seen him. Not good.

"Yes," he replied.

It wasn't nearly enough, which I guess he knew. "Then we can't stay here for long."

"The temple is two days away, on foot. Longer, if Jae can't walk there himself." He growled quietly.

"Why not take the shrikes?"

"It's too dangerous, the altar is calling to the stone. The closer you get with it, the stronger the pull. We already had to evacuate the village. The shrikes will go mad if we try to take them anywhere near it."

"Jace, we don't have two days." I stepped in his way so he had to look at me instead of Jaevid and the princess. "There has to be another way."

"T-there is." Jaevid interrupted us. He sounded so weak I almost didn't recognize his voice. "I made a way."

"What are you talking about?" The princess looked as puzzled as the rest of us.

Slowly, weakly, Jae pushed the blanket off himself and unbuckled the vambrace on his left arm. When he rolled his sleeve up, I could see he was wearing a bandage. He winced as he tore it away and showed us his arm.

The Gray elf princess gasped sharply. Her eyes went as wide as two moons.

There was a mark on Jae's arm—a black tattoo with a strange, swirling design. The skin around it was inflamed. It must have hurt badly, because Jae couldn't stand to wrap it back up himself. The princess had to help him with it. While she did, I could see tears pooling in the corners of her eyes.

"Why would you do such a thing?" she scolded him in a soft whisper. "You cannot trust those spirits."

"I didn't have a choice," Jae was smiling that stupid, self-sacrificing smile that made me want to punch him in the neck. "I had to be sure we made it."

"What is that? What's going on? What exactly did you do?" I demanded.

"He's made a pact with the foundling spirits," the princess explained. "They're the direct descendants of Paligno, his firstborns. They have no loyalty or love for humanity—or my people, for that matter. Whatever bargain Jaevid has struck with them no doubt came at a terrible price."

I glared down at my sneaky, scheming, moron of a best friend. "Is that true?"

"Felix, I had to. Surely you can see that now. Without their help, we don't stand a chance."

I cursed and turned away. "What was the price, then?"

He didn't answer.

"Was it your life?"

When Jaevid still didn't reply, I had to take a walk to keep from losing my temper. I didn't make it far, though. There was a commotion in the camp; Gray elves ran past me, hurrying toward the sound of calling voices coming from the jungle border.

Over the white-haired heads of strangers, I saw a man standing head and shoulders above everyone else. He was dressed in dragonrider's armor and bled from an open gash on his brow. I saw him looking—searching through the crowd —until our eyes met.

"My son!" Prax started shoving through the Gray elves thronging around him as though he were some sort of deity.

He embraced me. In fact, he nearly choked the life out of me. His breathing sounded ragged, like he was trying to hold it together. Before I could get a word out, he grabbed the back of my head and kissed my forehead. "I saw your dragon. Gods, I feared the worst."

"My dragon?" I wasn't sure what he meant.

The look on his face, the dimness in his eyes, made my chest suddenly feel constricted. I couldn't breathe.

"No. Not Nova. I just saw her. She was fighting. She was with Mavrik. They were going strong."

Prax bowed his head. "I'm sorry, boy."

21

CHAPTER TWENTY-ONE

My dragon was dead.
My girl. My Nova. Before I could even fully process that information, things began happening all around me that kept me from being able to let it sink in. Our comrades in Emerald Flight had arrived just in time. They were helping the Gray elves hold the line and keep the dragonriders at bay. But according to my father, that wasn't going to last long. So the Gray elves began to muster, to rally and prepare for the inevitable.

Hovrid's forces were moving. Northwatch had emptied and was headed straight for us. Eastwatch, too. Every minute that passed brought them closer and made our chances of success that much slimmer.

Prax had left our friends behind, locked in combat, to find me. I guess he knew I wasn't going to leave Jae's side. He explained the situation to the rest of us while the Gray elf princess stitched up the open wound on his forehead.

"We need to get going." Prax winced as the princess finished her stitching. "Once they hit the border, they're going to come in like an unending flood. They won't stop until there's nothing left. What they can't kill with blades and arrows they'll drench in dragon venom. It's going to be a massacre."

"We are prepared to do what we must to see the stone safely returned." The princess didn't look the least bit concerned. She flashed Jace a meaningful glance as she stood and picked up her war headdress.

"That's very noble, but I think you're missing the point." Prax countered. "Say you make it to that temple. Say you even manage to put the stone back where it belongs. What's going to keep the forces from Maldobar from running you into the ground and taking it right back? I think we both know they've got you pinned into a corner. If these are the only fighters you've got left, then the war is as good as over already. We may have the stone now, but we can't keep it. They're going to take it back and there's nothing we can do to stop them."

There was a tense silence. I had my suspicions that the princess, Jace, and probably everyone gathered here to make a final stand was relying on one thing—one person—to make sure that didn't happen.

And that person was Jaevid.

None of us, however, seemed willing to say that out loud. We didn't know what he could do, or if he could do anything to keep history from repeating itself. He was trusting in that deity, and we were trusting in him.

"It's time," Jaevid appeared behind us like a phantom, dressed in his long, black cloak and resting his hand on the pommel of his scimitar. He was standing on his own, which was a vast improvement from before the princess had rammed that salve down his throat.

"Time for what?" Prax glanced around at the rest of our group for an explanation.

Jaevid pulled the cowl of his cloak down low over his head. "Our escorts have arrived."

While the Gray elf forces continued to assemble and prepare for the proverbial meat grinder that was headed their way, Prax, Jace, the Gray elf princess, and I followed Jaevid away from the camp. We went deeper into the jungle. Gradually, the sounds of the camp faded behind us. The air grew hotter, thicker and heavier with moisture. There was no light except from a single torch the princess was carrying. I'd heard Jace call her Araxie a few times. They must have had something going on, because he seldom left her side.

We stopped when Jae did. He ordered us to douse the light. Darkness swallowed us, and I couldn't keep myself from gripping the hilt of my sword. Alien sounds echoed everywhere. The calls of birds were like eerie laughter. Leaves rustled. Twigs snapped. My pulse was pounding in my eardrums.

Right in front of me, Jaevid stood perfectly still. I could barely see him through the gloom, because his eyes were glowing again—bright green like emerald fires.

I stepped in closer to him, letting my shoulder bump his on purpose. "I'm sorry, you know, for what I said before … about Beckah."

He didn't look at me, but I could see the corner of his mouth twitch in a smile. "There's nothing to forgive, Felix. You were right."

Somehow, that didn't make me feel any better. "Doesn't happen often, does it? Me being right?"

"There's a first time for everything, I suppose."

That made me laugh. It gave me hope. Even with those glowing eyes, the real Jae—my friend, my brother—was still in there somewhere. "As fun as it is, guessing what the heck you're doing and how you plan to pull this off, I'd sure love to know what's going on here. What are we waiting on?"

He let out a sigh, as though he were steadying himself. "When I made a deal with the foundling spirits, they promised to give us their protection and help to reach the temple."

"You heard what Prax was saying to us, didn't you?"

Jaevid nodded. His expression had gone solemn and steely.

"He has a point, Jae. All of this could be for nothing if the armies of Maldobar reach that temple. They could slaughter every last one of us and take the stone back. Then there'll be nothing to stop the curse."

"Nothing except you," he said.

"Me? What can I do? I hate to be the bearer of bad news here, but I'm not the one with magical powers."

"Magic isn't what started this war, Felix. And magic isn't going to be what ends it, either," he explained, so calmly that he might as well have been discussing our dinner options. "You have something I'll never have, something that you said would take me a lot further in life than sword fighting or air combat techniques ever could. Something that has saved men's lives and reputations countless times."

"Jae—" I knew where he was going with this.

"Charm," he interrupted.

"I was talking about girls," I clarified. It was embarrassing that he even remembered that, but he was taking it way out of context. "I seriously doubt a bunch of blood-hungry dragonriders and infantrymen are going to stop and listen to me try to schmooze them."

He turned to face me. The colored bands of his eyes were still glowing brightly, making me wonder who I was actually talking to—him or that Gray elf god. "Hovrid is dead. The throne of Maldobar is empty. In truth, it has been empty for a long time. And once I put the stone back, Paligno's curse is going to break. I have his assurance of that. The people who were deceived and enchanted into following his orders are going to have their eyes opened. They're going to see what's really been happening. They're going to be confused, angry, and filled with shame for what they've done. They are going to need a new king, someone to guide them toward a peaceful future. There is only one person worthy and capable of making sure that happens. And that person is you, Felix."

I swallowed. "But I'm not even a legitimate noble. I'm a bastard child. The duke wasn't my real father."

"It doesn't matter. You're all Maldobar has and everything it needs. You're the natural selection, being the heir of the next most powerful noble family in the kingdom. But you're also the best selection, because you know there can be peace between Maldobar and Luntharda. You have a way with people. They listen to you, even if they don't know you. You're going to need that charm of yours."

"I don't know how to be a king," I protested weakly. It sounded like a pathetic excuse, even to me. The idea of a crown—any crown—being placed on my head was horrifying to me.

Jaevid gave me a reassuring punch in the arm. "I'm sure you'll figure it out. Just promise me you will do everything you can to make sure the peace is lasting."

I told him I would, although I had no idea how I was going to keep that promise. I was too caught up in the way he was talking, the way he phrased things. It wasn't like him. It wasn't normal.

It almost sounded like a goodbye.

I WAS TRYING TO WRAP MY MIND AROUND THE IDEA OF BEING THE KING OF anything. How was I going to tell Julianna? What was she going to say? What if I died, too? Did that mean my mother would be the next queen? Gods and Fates, I hoped not. She might've been worse than Hovrid.

All of a sudden, Jae reached out his hand into the dark, empty air before us, almost as though he were inviting a dog to sniff it. Only it wasn't a dog.

A large, strange-looking creature appeared before him. It materialized out of nowhere, silently taking form and looming over us with an unsettling sense of intelligence winking in its eyes. With tall, black ears, a tapered snout, and a slender body, it looked a great deal like a fox. Granted, an enormous fox. But its jet-black fur was mottled with feathers. It had long tail feathers that dragged over the ground, and there were faint silver, swirling markings all over its body that were only visible when it moved. Two black wings were folded at its sides, and when it looked at me, I got a falling sensation in the pit of my stomach.

More creatures appeared. They were smaller, about the size of horses, and while they definitely had vulpine faces and ears, their bodies were a mutant mixture of bird and fox. Their feathers came in a variety of vibrant colors and their glowing eyes seemed to peer straight through me. One with bright green, blue, and yellow feathers hedged towards me with its head down, ears back, and snout twitching vigorously.

"They're going to help us get to the temple," Jae explained. He was already sitting on the back of one, holding onto fistfuls of its scruff for balance. "Don't be afraid."

"How do we know they won't turn on us?" Araxie glared suspiciously at the one that had apparently chosen her as its passenger.

"*We are not bound to the stone,*" the big, black fox-monster's voice hissed through the air as though it were insulted. It was so loud I had to cover my ears. "*We came before it.*"

Araxie winced, but she didn't falter. She had a lot of nerve. She eyed her mount skeptically, and then finally conceded with a frustrated snort.

The rest of us mounted up, trying to balance on the backs of the twitchy, anxious creatures that yipped and chirped to one another like they were complaining or telling jokes about us that we couldn't understand.

I grabbed a meaningful fistful of my mount's scruff. He could badmouth me all he wanted to his buddies, but I wasn't about to let him drop me. It was a good idea, too, because the way they maneuvered through the jungle wasn't anything like a dragon flew. It didn't even compare to a shrike, really. They flew like a flock of owls, completely silent except for the eerie yipping sounds they made to one another. They leapt from branch to branch, using their wings to flutter and soar between the gaps.

Okay, I sort of liked it. It was smooth, fast, and graceful. I could feel the power emanating from the creature—a being that was probably older than all the mortal kingdoms in the world. Its strange, feathery pelt was as soft as silk between my fingers.

The jungle awoke with the rising of dawn, but we didn't stop to marvel at it. We raced through a living labyrinth of green, riding hard all day without stopping. We passed twisting rivers, hidden cliffs, waterfalls, lagoons, canyons, flowers as big as carriages, and groves of trees covered in weird-looking spiky fruit. Everything was more wildly beautiful than I'd ever imagined. Being a dragonrider, I'd always imagined this place would be dark, swampy, and filled with terrors with jagged teeth. That couldn't have been further from the truth.

The road appeared out of nowhere. It was a path made of mismatched, pearlescent white stones. They began sparsely, but the nearer we got to the temple grounds, the more they came together to form an overgrown avenue. We burst through a line of trees that had been planted close together to form a sort of fence. And there it was—the temple. We'd reached it in what seemed like mere hours. It should have been impossible. But then again, I'd witnessed a lot of unbelievable things lately.

The foundling spirits landed before it. They huddled close together, their feathers bristling and their eyes glinting with anxiousness. I remembered what Jace had told me about being near this place. The closer we got with the god stone, the more intense the madness would be amongst the animals. Maybe the foundlings weren't affected by it, but it definitely seemed like they could sense it. It had them on edge.

I could sympathize. I felt it now, for the first time. It was like a weight on my chest, or an intense, thick heat that made it difficult to breathe. I glanced at Jaevid. He was already looking at me. When our eyes met, he nodded across the empty, crumbling courtyard, away from the temple, to an enormous pit.

"Let's get this done." I climbed down from the fox spirit's back.

Jae did the same.

Together, we started for the pit. Out of the corner of my eye, I saw him holding onto that roundish lump under his robes—the god stone. It was almost over, I kept telling myself over and over. We were here. We had time.

And then, all of a sudden, we didn't.

They came from every side, bursting through the trees. Wood splinters showered everywhere. It was an onslaught of shrikes from the air, giant elk-looking beasts and boars charging at us across the ground, along with all manner of jungle monsters I'd never heard of. Some were as big as bears and resembled tusked, stony-skinned gorillas. Others were giant lizards with color-changing scales, long, whipping tails, and snapping, toothy jaws.

We were outnumbered, surrounded, and at a serious disadvantage. I saw Jae's expression twist into a look of rage. His eyes gleamed brighter. His teeth became pointed and he ripped his scimitar from its sheath. I rushed to stand back-to-back with him, with my sword already drawn.

"Never a dull moment with you, eh?" I smirked as one of the lizards lunged at me. I drove my sword through its neck with one swing.

"I aim to please," Jae snarled back. He was squaring off with a shrike. It struck first and he reared back, bashing it over the head with the blunt end of his scimitar. Once it was down, a flourish of his hand summoned vines that burst from the ground, wrapped around it, and held it down while he sliced through its chest.

One of those giant, scaly gorilla beasts charged straight for us, bellowing and swinging its fists.

"Head's up," I yelled, as I ducked into an evasive roll.

Jae did the same, skidding off to the opposite side. We came up at the same time, our blades moving in unison, and took out the beast's stumpy hind legs as it barreled past us.

The monster went down with a boom. Immediately, Jae brought his hand up in a sharp gesture, summoning more vines from the ground. They burst straight through the ugly beast.

"Got any more of those rock dragons up your sleeve?" I asked, as I ran back to get in formation beside him. "We can't keep this up forever."

The foundling spirits were helping. To their credit, they were keeping the biggest and baddest of the monsters away from us. If not for them, we would have been completely overrun.

Even so, if Jace was right, the entire jungle was focused squarely on us right now. We were standing in the eye of the storm, and eventually that Gray elf princess was going to run out of arrows.

We were only yards away from the edge of the pit. I could see Jae's eyes focus there with intent. That was our destination. I just had to get him there.

"Go! I've got your back!" I shouted over the roar of battle.

"We all do," Araxie chimed in. She darted past me and planted a well-aimed arrow right between the eyes of another lizard.

Jaevid didn't question us. He took off, and I ran after him. He deflected the creatures attacking from the front, and I did my best to fend off the ones that were chasing us toward the pit. When we got to the edge and I caught a glimpse at the spiraling staircase that went round and round the edge of it, I yelled a curse. It would take us forever to get to the bottom.

If we went down like normal, completely sane people, that is.

Jaevid grabbed me and jumped out into the open air. I didn't have time to react or brace myself. I couldn't even scream, because as soon as I got a good breath, we were caught out of midair. One of the foundling spirits had swooped in out of nowhere, caught him by the back of his clothes, and was carrying us down into the deep darkness.

We went down ... down ... down—until I was sure we had to be getting close to the bottom.

My feet hit first. Jae let go of me then and I lost my balance, landing on my rear at the bottom of the pit. Overhead, the opening was so far away it looked like a small circle of light the size of a full moon. I heard sounds of commotion echoing from above, the occasional shriek and cry of the jungle animals, and the shouts of our friends.

A hand appeared in my face. "We don't have much time," Jae said, as he hauled me up to my feet again.

With a flourish of his wrist, Jae brewed up a bit more of his magic to light the way. Before, I'd seen him use an orb of light that hovered over his palm. This time, however, he summoned some sort of creeping plant that grew in long tendrils along the floor and then climbed the walls. It had tiny blooms on it and when they opened, they glowed with a soft light that reminded me of stars. Those shining flowers led the way to a gaping tunnel.

I shivered. Something about it gave me a creepy feeling. It was almost as though I'd been here before, somehow—although I knew I definitely hadn't.

The foundling spirit started following us. It wasn't until I got a better look at it by the light of Jae's magic, glowing flowers that I realized it was the same spirit I'd ridden here.

"She feels bad about Nova," Jae said quietly.

I glanced at the spirit again, watching it creep along behind me on four birdlike legs. It looked like some sort of fox-griffin, although instead of being mixed with an eagle it was mixed with a parrot. Unique, pretty, but totally weird.

"So it's a she?"

Jae dipped his head. "Her name is Pasci."

"Pasci, huh?" I eyed the foundling spirit, watching the way she was sniffing at me with her long snout twitching and her tall ears perked up at the sound of my voice. "Well, tell her I'm not exactly emotionally available for another relationship yet. I only just lost Nova."

"If it's any consolation, she didn't suffer."

I stared at the back of my best friend's head. I felt the urge to hit him for talking about that right now. Of course, it was a little comforting to know that. I just ... wasn't ready to feel anything about it yet.

Just like I wasn't ready for us to reach the end of that tunnel, either. Because a better part of me, a smarter part, knew something bad was going to happen there. You didn't find anything happy in a damp, dark cave like this. This place had a powerful silence that made my skin prickle.

In the center of a round, empty chamber, I saw the same altar made of a single slab of milky, white stone that I'd seen in my dream. I saw the bones laid out on it, and my heart started to pound against my ribs. The heat of the curse was so alive in the air I could feel it like the crackling heat off a furnace.

Jaevid was strangely calm. He walked toward the altar, brushing back the cowl of his cloak. His hand went to that round, stone-shaped lump under his robes. I could hear him muttering, whispering under his breath as though he were talking to someone. Then he stopped, turned, and gazed back at me.

I could see it from a mile away—the look he gave me whenever he was about to do something reckless, stupid, and potentially life-threatening.

His hand moved and he took out the stone. Out of pure reflex, I turned away and shielded my eyes. He'd told me not to look at it—not even for a second. I cringed and braced myself, waiting for something to happen.

I heard a horrible cracking sound.

Someone screamed.

Jace and Araxie were running toward me through the tunnel. Araxie was shouting in protest, her face pale with horror.

I dared to look back at Jae, just in time to see him rear back and smash the stone against the edge of the altar.

Crack!

Araxie was still screaming for him to stop, with Jace struggling to hold her back.

Crack!

Next to me, my foundling spirit friend, Pasci, was shrieking and yelping, spinning in circles. She began to cower with her ears pinned back and her hide shivering.

Crack!

The god stone shattered into a million tiny pieces.

"What have you done?" Araxie was hysterical. Jace fought to keep her at bay.

Pasci howled. Somewhere beyond the cave, I heard a mismatched chorus of similar panicked sounds coming from the other foundling spirits.

Jaevid collapsed to the floor, barely catching himself against the edge of the altar. I dropped my sword and ran to him. The pieces of the god stone crunched under my boots as I grabbed his shoulders and tried to hold him up. He was limp. When he looked up at me, I could see that he'd lost all the color in his face.

"No. No, Jaevid. Not here. Not like this," I smacked his cheek to try and revive him.

His head lolled to rest against me. "It's okay, Felix. It's done. It's over now."

"What are you talking about? Nothing's done. You just broke the stone, you moron!"

"No. Look." He raised a hand and pointed shakily to the altar.

The bones were melting away. The white skeleton of that animal was slowly dissolving into a fine, white mist that shimmered in the light as it faded away.

"It's going to be okay now," Jae rasped. He reached into his vambrace and pulled out a dirty, rumpled piece of cloth. It was a handkerchief with two dragons stitched on it. He handed it to me. Then he grabbed the pendant around his neck—the one he always wore—and with a swift jerk broke the resin string. He laid it carefully in my hand, too.

"I'll be wanting these back. You'll keep them for me, won't you?" He asked with a strange, distant smile. All the while, his skin was turning whiter by the second. Only, it wasn't just his skin. His clothes were beginning to turn white, too.

"Jaevid, what's happening?"

"There has to be a stone. Paligno's essence has to walk the earth to keep the balance and to keep things living and growing. His mortal body perished here, but his essence was contained within the god stone. Now ... it will be contained within me. There will be no more lapiloques, and no more god stone. From now on, it will only be me."

Araxie had gone silent. She stood next to Jace, tears streaming down her face and smearing the war paint under her eyes. Next to her, Jace was scowling. His brow was furrowed and his mouth was open, but he didn't say anything.

"This isn't goodbye." Jae closed my hand around his belongings.

I bit down hard. "It better not be."

He tried to stand. I had to basically carry him to get him up on the altar. He sat there a moment, looking at his own hands as though amazed. Second by second, they were turning the same milky hue as the stone he was sitting on. Shaking his head, he muttered under his breath as he turned and shakily lay down on his back.

His eyes traveled slowly around the cave before finally staring back at me. "It's so quiet now. I wish you could hear it the way I can."

"Way overdue, isn't it?"

"You have no idea. I'm so tired, Felix,"

I took his hand and gripped it fiercely. "Rest, then. I'll be here when you wake up, ready to do something else amazing and dangerous."

He squeezed my hand back. His legs had turned to solid, white stone. "Take care of yourself, brother. Watch over our friends—our family. And please ... tell Mavrik this wasn't his fault. Tell him to have a good life. Tell him I said 'thank you.'"

"I'm sure he'd rather hear all that from you," I replied.

"I had to shut him out of my mind. Otherwise ... he'd try to come here and find me. I couldn't let him take that risk. I couldn't lose him, too."

"Fine," I agreed as I clenched my teeth. "But only if you tell Beckah hello for me."

Jaevid smiled weakly. He let go of my hand just as his fingertips started turning to stone. I watched him grow stiff. I watched his eyes glaze and become fixed. His chest rose and fell slowly, one last time.

"*When you need me, I will return.*" His voice didn't come from his lips. His body had already turned into solid stone. Instead, the sound came from everywhere. From the air around us, from inside my own mind.

In an instant, Paligno's curse broke over us. I could feel it—the sudden rush of freedom, of relief, of cool serenity. Peace that surpassed anything I'd ever felt flooded that place. It filled every corner of my soul and brought tears to my eyes.

It was finished.

We were free.

22

CHAPTER TWENTY-TWO

I stood nearby, watching as the Gray elf princess pressed her lips to the cold, stone surface of Jaevid's forehead. Between her broken sobs, I heard her speak to him in her native language, brushing her fingers over his face. Jace lingered next to me, still solemn and silent. His forehead was creased with concern and his arms were folded over his chest as he gazed down at all that remained of his student, my friend, and our last hope.

The curse was broken. The stone had been officially taken out of play. But that didn't mean the war was over. Jaevid had left the last task in my hands. He'd seemed so sure that I was capable of it. I told myself that I could trust him; I'd always been able to trust him. He wasn't a liar, and even if I screwed everything up, he would be back. This wasn't goodbye.

It still hurt, though.

Araxie was still trying to pull herself together as we walked back through the tunnel. Jace was holding her hand, which definitely betrayed that they were together. She'd just let her head fall onto his shoulder, leaning against him some as we left the tomb in silence ... when the earth began to shudder violently under our feet.

Jace and I exchanged an alarmed glance. Time to go.

We sprinted for the exit, dodging falling rocks shaken free from the tunnel's ceiling. Suddenly, what looked like giant roots burst through the walls of the tunnel. One whooshed right past me, narrowly missing the end of my nose. We dodged them, ducked down, and wove our way out to the pit where a lifetime's worth of steps stood between the surface and us.

Not good.

Something huge erupted from the ground beneath our feet, catching all three of us entirely off guard. I heard Araxie shriek and Jace yell. We were tossed with incredible force through the air like ragdolls. I tried to grab onto something, anything, but I was tumbling end over end.

A pair of big, strong talons closed around my arms, catching me under the shoulders. In the blink of an eye, Pasci had me. She yipped triumphantly and zipped through the air with me dangling under her. She sped out of the pit and into the open sky, just in time as an enormous tree exploded out of the pit behind us.

I saw Jace and Araxie running toward me, covered in dirt with equally panicked expressions on their faces as the tree grew bigger and bigger, dwarfing all the others in the jungle—which were already giant by anyone's standards. But this one was a behemoth.

It swelled, sprouting more limbs, breaking through the canopy and unfurling leaves the size of houses. The trunk completely covered the pit, as well as most of the courtyard around it. The roots fanned out, snaking across the ground to wrap around the various structures on the temple grounds. Nothing was crushed, or destroyed, but the tree's roots seemed to wrap it all in a protective embrace.

And as abruptly as it had begun, everything became still again.

Jace, Araxie, and I stood gaping up at the tree. No one said a word. The trunk had to be at least two hundred feet in diameter. It towered over the jungle, disappearing above the canopy and out of sight.

"That's one way to make sure no one goes down there, I suppose." Jace muttered.

I scowled. "But ... how is he supposed to come back with that thing in the way?"

I expected Araxie to offer some expert opinion. Being the resident Gray elf royal, she might have had a better idea than the rest of us. She was a little distracted, though.

While Jace and I were staring up at the tree, scratching our heads, she whirled around and drew back her bow, hissing a few angry words in her native language.

Too late, I realized we were completely surrounded.

The Maldobarian infantry had us pinned on every side. They stood all around the perimeter of the temple grounds, swords drawn and shields raised. The worst part was ... they had my father. Prax had been forced to his knees with the sharp edge of a blade held to his throat.

The pressure in the air was palpable. The soldiers seemed rattled and anxious. I spotted more than one pair of wide, frightened eyes fixed upon the tree that had just spontaneously popped out of the ground. Not something you saw everyday in Maldobar. No doubt these guys had already fought through all manner of jungle hell to get here in the first place. Looking through their ranks to take a quick inventory, I saw a few Gray elf hostages who must have made it much easier to find us—in fact, there was one Gray elf warrior in particular that I happened to know.

When he saw me staring at him, Kiran gave an annoyed eye roll and shrug. Typical. Even with a dagger at his back and his hands in shackles, he still had an attitude.

"Drop your weapons immediately!" A soldier with a general's insignia stitched in gold onto the breast and shoulders of his uniform stepped forward. He sounded confident, but I saw fear written all over his face. "Where is the traitor? The one called Jaevid Broadfeather? Produce him at once!"

"Sorry. Can't do that," I called back, keeping my sword drawn and firmly in hand. He could have it when he pried it from my cold, dead fingers.

"Soldier, I strongly suggest you take inventory of your army here. We have you outnumbered and surrounded. You cannot escape. You cannot win this," the general threatened. "You're guilty of high treason, and murder as well. But if you give up peacefully, I'll see that you are treated well on your way back to answer for your crimes."

"Jaevid Broadfeather is dead."

You could have heard an ant sneeze.

Kiran's face went completely pale.

"He sacrificed himself to put the stone out of our reach—yours and mine. No one else can have it now. It's gone for good," I continued. "He did it to break the curse that has been spreading across our lands, making the animals turn on us. He did it to break the hold our real enemy had on you. He gave up everything so that we could live. He set us free."

A few of the soldiers were lowering their weapons. They were listening to me, so I kept talking. Charm? Pfft. This was downright insanity. All I had to go on was Jae's confidence that I could do this, and his warning that the people of Maldobar would be in a vulnerable state now that Hovrid's hold on them was broken.

"I know you can feel it, just as I can—the peace that's here now. Think about it. Do you even remember coming here?"

They glanced at one another, looking bewildered and rubbing their eyes like they were waking up from a dream.

"I know you must be confused. You must feel lost, like you've just come out of a nightmare," I said, and more and more of the soldiers began lowering their arms. The one holding a blade to my father's neck let him go, and Prax immediately got to his feet.

"Over two decades of war and bloodshed have brought us here. We've all done things—terrible things that we'll have to live with. No one is blameless because every single one of us was deceived by a man we believed we could trust;

a man who called himself our king. I'm asking you to see him for what he truly was—a liar and a murderer."

The general narrowed his eyes at me dangerously. "Who are you to levy such an accusation?"

"I am Duke Felix Farrow, high noble and the only rightful heir to the throne of Maldobar," I declared. "And it is by that authority that I command you to stand down, lower your weapons, and release your captives."

"WHAT HAPPENS NOW?" PRINCESS ARAXIE WAS SITTING ACROSS FROM ME, THE light of the small fire pit between us making her eyes shimmer like opals.

Sitting beside her, King Erandur still looked haunted by the news that both Jaevid and the god stone were gone. His eyes were wide and fixed on the crackling flames, as though he were lost in his own mind.

"We start over." I sighed, rubbing my fingers around the things in my pocket —Jaevid's things. "He said he's coming back. And I, for one, believe him. So all we can do now is wipe the slate clean and rebuild. Neither of our kingdoms are in a good state, as it stands."

That was putting it lightly—*extremely* lightly. But I knew everyone sitting around that fire pit was acutely aware of how tense things were outside. Jace, Kiran, Araxie, and I were resting inside the treetop hut reserved for the king and his guests. But outside, it was a different story. The remains of the Gray elf forces were housing the riders and infantry from Northwatch who had come here to kill them. Evil imposter king aside, there was a lot of bad blood in the air. A lot of distrust. A lot of anger. Tensions were high and it wouldn't take much to fan the flames. I'd dispatched my father to keep an eye on thing, walk the grounds, and make sure no one put a toe out of line at least for the rest of the night.

We all deserved at least one quiet night.

"Perhaps, then, what we need is a gesture of good faith." Erandur spoke up suddenly.

Araxie looked stunned, like she hadn't expected her father to be so accommodating.

"Your man Jace wishes to stay here in my kingdom. He's already expressed that desire to me, and I have granted it. If you were to appoint him as an ambassador, I could make him an official member of my court. He would become a presence here representing your efforts to work toward peace," the king continued.

I nodded. "A good idea."

"We should send an ambassador of our own to Maldobar, as well," Araxie suggested.

"Kiran," I said suddenly.

He looked at me out of the corner of his weird, color changing eyes.

"If he's an acceptable candidate to you, that is. I've gotten to know him well enough to trust him. Jaevid had a lot of faith in him, too. He speaks our language and has firsthand knowledge of our customs. I think he'd be a good fit."

Araxie was rubbing her chin thoughtfully. She looked at Kiran hard—studied him from head to toe like she was searching him for some hidden flaw. It even made me a little nervous. She definitely had a steely way about her, like a she-wolf who wasn't going to tolerate any members of her pack embarrassing her.

"True. But he is young and impulsive. It took him two years to pass his trials and become a scout. Are you up to this task?" she asked him outright.

Kiran straightened. His expression was determined. "I can do it."

"Then you will have your chance. Serve your kingdom well, young warrior," Erandur decreed and put a hand on Kiran's shoulder. It made the young Gray elf blush.

We ate a meal of grilled meat and dried fruit in silence. Not that there wasn't anything to talk about. But if any of the others felt the way I did, then they were too overwhelmed by the task before us to even try talking about it. Right about now, the small company of riders I'd sent back to Northwatch would be arriving bearing the news that the war was over ... and that Maldobar had a new king. It wouldn't take long for that news to spread. Maybe there would be riots. Maybe they'd burn the royal castle to the ground in rebellion.

But then again, maybe not.

Regardless, there wasn't a single thing I could do about it from here. And honestly, I wasn't worried about riots and castle burnings. I was worried about the only thing that mattered: what was Julianna doing right this second?

After dinner, Erandur and Araxie retired to their private quarters. Jace tagged along at the princess's heels like a faithful guard dog. As much as I would have liked to give him a hard time about that, I had a shadow on my heels as well.

Kiran followed me as I wandered out of the hut onto a balcony overlooking the jungle. I leaned against the railing and let the cool night air blow over me. The lights from other tree huts shone like floating orbs all around us. There were fragrant, floral smells on the wind and the musical calls of birds echoing in the night. It was strange, but beautiful. Once again, this place wasn't anything at all like I'd thought it would be.

Far below, I could hear the commotion of the camp. I wanted to be down there, amongst the other riders, drinking ale and having a good awkward laugh with our new pointy-eared friends. But here I was, having responsibilities. Geez, when had that happened?

"You seem troubled." Kiran came to stand next to me.

I rubbed the back of my neck. "You would be, too, if you had the eyes of two kingdoms looking to you to fix two decades worth of damage."

He gave me a challenging smirk. "Do you think you can peacefully unite our kingdoms?"

"I don't know," I admitted. "But I think I can try. You think you can convince your kinsmen who were sent to prison camps to die that they can trust me?"

His sarcastic expression started to fade.

I patted him on the back. "Relax. We've both got our work cut out for us. So we'll just have to take it one miracle at a time. But I'll make a deal with you, Kiran. I need someone working for me I know I can trust. So you stay with me, watch my back, and help me make sure this peace lasts, and I promise that together we will do whatever we can to make this right for your people."

I held a hand out to him.

Kiran drew back for a moment, as though he were unsure of the gesture. He studied me, my hand, and finally reached out to grasp it firmly. "A deal."

"You mean 'deal' right?"

"Yes. A deal."

"No, no. You just say 'deal' and then we shake."

He narrowed his eyes suspiciously.

I laughed and shook on it. "Don't worry about it. It's a deal."

23

CHAPTER TWENTY-THREE

It wasn't at all what I expected. Not just any tackmaster lived here. Ulric Broadfeather was held in the highest esteem by Blybrig Academy as the very best money could buy. He should have been able to afford a much nicer place. But as Sile, Roland, and I rode up to the front drive on horseback, I got the feeling we weren't going to be welcomed in with open arms.

The house looked nearly abandoned and the message painted on the front door read "TRESSPASSERS BEWARE." The gardens were overgrown and wild looking. The roof was in bad need of repair and the front door was sagging on the hinges. If not for the smoke rising from the chimney, I would have just assumed it had been left to rot.

After months of searching, I'd finally managed track Ulric down. Not that he was in hiding, per say, but every time anyone mentioned his name there was an awkward pause and sudden reluctance for anyone to say anything about him. His crime was common knowledge now. And so was his insanity. Both had probably driven him out of business. No one wanted anything to do with him now.

I looked to Sile to make the first move. This whole errand had been his idea. It was some kind of personal vendetta, I figured. Roland and I were just here to bear witness in case things got ugly. Roland had even suggested to me that he wasn't sure if Ulric would even agree to see Sile at all.

The woman who answered the door was as thin as a broomstick. Her hair was frayed and her apron was stained and tattered. She cracked the door just wide enough to peek at all of us. When she saw Sile, she went pale and I thought she might faint.

"No! Go away! He doesn't want any visitors!" She screamed and tried to slam the door.

Sile jammed the toe of his boot into the doorway before she could close it. "Let me in, Serah," he growled deeply. "I'm standing here with your son and the King of Maldobar. I suggest you don't turn us away."

Slowly, the trembling woman moved away from the door. But when Sile pushed the door open, she darted away into the dark, disheveled parlor like a frightened mouse. Roland and I followed him inside.

Hiding in the dark corners of the house, I spotted the pale, frightened faces of two young girls cowering behind the woman. These must have been the twin sisters I'd heard Jaevid mention once or twice. They were as gaunt and wild-looking as their mother.

There was an odd, musty smell like sour laundry. I wasn't sure what to make of it until we found Ulric. He was sitting on the dirt floor of the cellar, wrapped up in old blankets that reeked like they hadn't been washed for months. The mattress on the floor was in the same state, and there was a waste bucket that was nearly full to the top of ... some pretty nasty stuff.

I'd seen Jaevid's father before, once or twice, at the academy. But the man we found crouched on his knees, scratching at the walls with his fingernails hardly looked like anything more than a haggard shell of a human being. His beard was long and as filthy as the rest of him. His eyes were bloodshot and glazed. He looked thin and fragile, as though he were slowly wasting away to nothing but bones and skin. He didn't even look up when we came down the steps.

"Ulric," Sile said as he ventured closer.

But if Ulric was even aware of our presence, he never let on. He was scrambling around on his knees, muttering under his breath. He kept repeating something over and over, although I couldn't quite make out what it was.

"Ulric, I came here to tell you something." Sile touched him on the shoulder.

Instantly, Ulric bounded to his feet with alarming speed and started screeching at the top of his lungs, "Soon! It's coming! I know it! I can see it. I can smell it in the air."

Next to me, I saw Roland's jaw tense and he looked away.

Ulric was pacing back and forth and rubbing his hands together. That's when I noticed the marks he'd been making—there were hundreds of them covering every square inch of the stone walls of the cellar from floor to ceiling. They looked like symbols in some language I didn't recognize, but they looked far too precise to be nothing at all.

Suddenly, Sile caught him by the arm and forced him to stop, all but pinning him up against the wall. "Listen to me now. I came to tell you your son is dead. Do you understand me? Jaevid, your son, paid for your crime with his blood."

Ulric was shaking like a leaf. He looked at Sile, Roland, then at me. "Son? What son? I have no son."

Sile's eyes flickered dangerously. "I have kept my word and it's cost me much more than I can say our friendship has been worth. We are finished now. Roland is taking those women from here. You can die here in this hole, if you choose, but you won't take anyone else with you."

"Finished ... finished." Ulric was whispering again.

With a curse under his breath, Sile let him go and nodded to Roland. It was time to go. Whoever this person was, the god stone had addled his brain until there wasn't much left.

Sile and Roland started for the stairs. As I turned to follow, I heard Ulric scramble back over to the wall and begin etching and scratching with his nails again. He was still muttering, laughing, and taking in frantic crackling breaths.

"Nothing is finished. It's coming soon. I can see it. I can feel it. The legacy of the God Bane ... the *harbinger* comes!"

"MASTER—ER—I MEAN YOUR MAJESTY! IT'S NEARLY TIME, YOU SHOULD BE inside getting ready!" Miss Harriet came hurdling across the yard with all her skirts in her arms. Her puffy face was flushed and her hair was flying everywhere. She looked like she'd just weathered a hurricane.

Behind her was my new bride, following along and covering her mouth to hide her smirk. Julianna waited until Miss Harriet finished giving me grief over my appearance before she hurried away to make sure all my attire for the coronation was still in order—though she'd only just left it. We were preparing to leave my estate and head to the royal city of Halfax. Rumor had it there was a golden crown on a red, velvet pillow waiting there with my name on it.

Everyone was waiting for us to arrive. Supposedly, the whole city was in an uproar, ready to welcome their new king and queen. Prax had sent me several letters describing how the entire castle had been redecorated. It was as though the people of Maldobar were desperate to purge every trace of Hovrid from their land.

"Harriet's dreadfully proud of you." Julianna said, giving me a coy smile as she wandered over to drape her arms around my neck. "As am I, Your Majesty."

"Hm. You know, it's significantly less annoying when you call me that for some reason." I grinned and looped an arm around her waist to reel her in closer.

She giggled and blushed.

I enjoyed kissing her now even more than before. Something about her having my last name made her taste even sweeter. It didn't take long for her gaze to wander away from me, though, and over to the three statues that loomed before us.

One was older than the rest. It was the one I'd commissioned in Jaevid's honor. On his right side was a much newer one that had only been put in place a week or so before. It was carved into the shape of a young woman with long, braided hair, wearing the armor of a dragonrider and standing proudly with a bow in one hand and a sword in the other. It seemed only fitting to put her there, at his side. I was sure that was what she would have wanted.

Next to her was one last structure, a large granite box with a single dragon scale set into the top. That was where I had ordered Nova's ashes to be placed. It just felt right to keep her with me, here, on the same cliffs and breathing the same air as her wild kin.

"I know Jae would be very proud of you too, Felix." Julianna added in a quiet, cautious voice, afraid of upsetting me.

I smiled. "Maybe so."

"You've already seen to it that all captives of war on both sides be freed, including the Gray elf slaves. So many families will be reunited." She was smiling, too. "Yes. I believe that would make him extremely happy."

"Tearing down all the Gray elf ghettos has made a lot of other people unhappy, however," I sighed at the thought. There was a lot to fix, a lot that had to be changed if we were ever going to move forward and heal. Jaevid had sacrificed everything for this chance, though. I wasn't about to waste it.

"People are always afraid of change." Julianna had a contemplative glint in her eyes as she stared at Jae's statue. "But that doesn't necessarily mean change is bad. Change is necessary, even if it frightens us. Without it, we would never grow."

"Maybe you should just give my coronation speech instead. You're better with words than I am."

She swatted playfully at the back of my head. "Felix Farrow, don't you dare try pushing your responsibilities off on m—"

I stole another kiss before she could finish, making her blush and pout.

For a long time, we stood together in the gardens of my family estate. We stared at the statues of Jaevid and Beckah, standing side-by-side against the backdrop of a gray sky. The winds picked up, and in the distance I could see the waves frothing and capping. There was a storm brewing, unusual for this time of year.

"What do you suppose he meant?" Julianna was whispering again.

"About what?"

"About returning to us when we need him." She turned to look at me with worry in her eyes.

I didn't want to tell her that I was concerned, too. After that encounter with Ulric ... I was still rattled and trying to assure myself that you couldn't put any faith in the ravings of a madman. Still, something about it sat wrong in my mind. And when I thought about Jaevid's parting words, I was even more nervous. I still had absolutely no idea what he'd been talking about. I was restless at the thought that there might something else—something worse—coming our way.

"Whatever he meant, there's nothing we can do about it right now except continue to do everything we can to rebuild," I replied. Reaching over, I took her hand in mine and held it firmly. "And as for Jaevid ... I've decided to believe in him the way believed in me. He thought I could rule Maldobar and change things for the better. I think we haven't seen the last of him. I think that if anything threatens this kingdom again, Jaevid is going to have something to say about it."

Julianna gave my hand a little squeeze. It hurt. I'd accidentally cut open one of my palms on that jagged black crystal that was set in the royal throne while battling that stupid pig. It still hurt, even if it was hardly more than a gnarled pink scar now. The soreness hadn't gone away.

I could see a difference in the way Julianna regarded Jae's statue, as though he baffled her. "It's nearly impossible to believe what he could do. A timid, gentle, halfbreed boy from the Gray elf ghetto?"

Something caught my eye, a glimmer on the horizon reflecting the light from a break in the clouds. The shimmer of dragon scales. I couldn't be sure from so far away, but I thought I recognized the familiar silhouette of a certain blue dragon—now free of his saddle—sailing proudly on the stormy winds.

"No, not impossible," I corrected her. "But definitely unexpected."

WANT MORE DRAGONRIDERS?

Continue the adventure with the
#1 international bestselling and
award-winning series,
THE DRAGONRIDER LEGACY:

SAVAGE

HARBINGER

LEGEND

Available in ebook, paperback, and audiobook from Amazon.com

ABOUT THE AUTHOR

Nicole Conway is a graduate of Auburn University with a lifelong passion for writing teen and children's literature. With over 100,000 books sold in her DRAGONRIDER CHRONICLES series, Nicole has been ranked one of Amazon's Top 100 Teen Authors. A coffee and Netflix addict, she also enjoys spending time with her family, rock climbing, and traveling.

Nicole is represented by Frances Black of Literary Counsel.

Made in the USA
Las Vegas, NV
14 May 2023